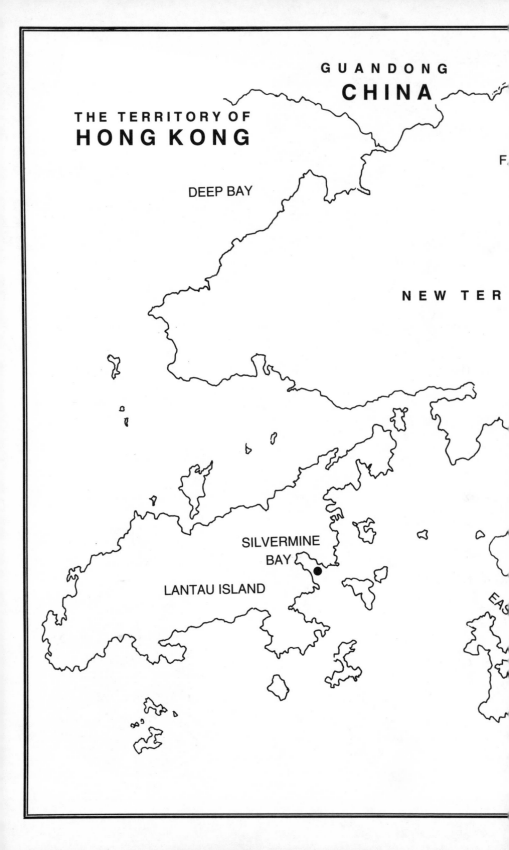

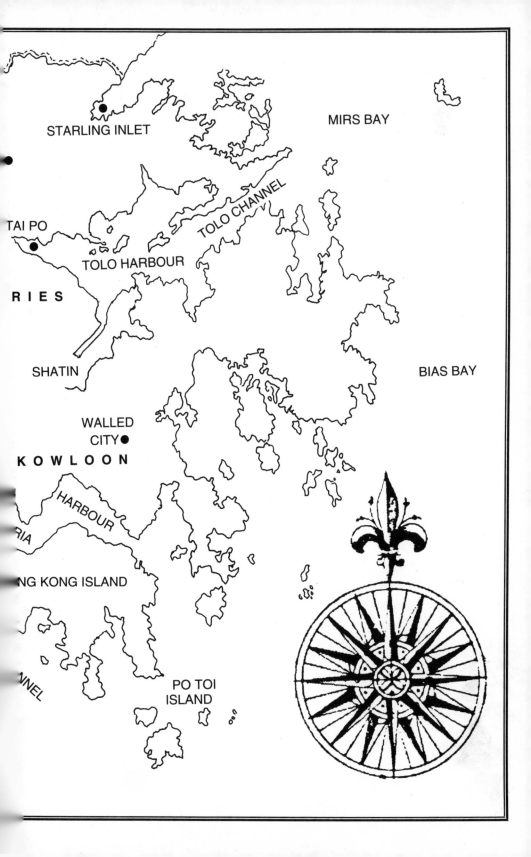

THE SECOND SUNRISE

ALSO BY GEOFF PIKE

FICTION

Henry Golightly
Golightly Adrift
Golightly Outback

•

NON-FICTION

The Power of Ch'i
Youth and Beauty Secrets of the Orient
The Power Is You

THE
SECOND
SUNRISE

GEOFF
PIKE

RANDOM HOUSE
AUSTRALIA

Random House Australia Pty Ltd
20 Alfred Street, Milsons Point, NSW 2061

Sydney   New York   Toronto
London   Auckland
and agencies throughout the world

First published 1993

National Library of Australia
Cataloguing-in-Publication Data
Pike, Geoff, 1929-   .
The Second Sunrise.

ISBN 0 09 182703 5.

I. Title

A823.3

Designed by Trevor Hood, Anaconda Graphic Design
Typeset by Midland Typesetters, Victoria
Printed by Australian Print Group, Victoria
Production by Vantage Graphics, Sydney

Contents

*Certainly there is no kingdom in the world
    so vast as this,
that enjoys the like adventure.
Nevertheless what I am now going to relate
    will indeed
seem to be yet more incredible,
and, indeed, I should hardly have believed
    it myself,
had I not seen it with my own eyes.*

**The New History of China 1688
Gabriel Magailans, Missionary Apostolick**

*Love is a luxury few can afford.
Lust is a currency in all languages
and in all places. I will teach you
to spend it wisely.*

Ah Gum, the Golden One

The Second Sunrise is for my wife
Phyllis Madelaine, who taught me
patience, tolerance and discipline

• IMAGE FOR SUNRISE •

Acknowledgements

I have found that when you decide to sit down and write a book, most of the people you value are very kind about it. They seem to look upon the telling of a story as a worthwhile thing. I'm glad they do because without them this is one book that would never have been finished.

With relief and gratitude now that it's done, I thank my wife, who knows so much about the story and kept a patient and critical eye on it throughout; Bryce Courtenay, my friend for nearly forty years, for his unconditional encouragement; Doctor B.M. Kotewall, MBE, OBE, who allowed her expert knowledge of Hong Kong and China to bend a little for the sake of the story-teller; Arthur Hacker, MBE, who opened up his remarkable archives without hesitation one hot afternoon in Discovery Bay; Benno Gross for being the first to show me the real Hong Kong so many years ago, and his wife Kit Yu for her excellent calligraphy; Dr. Elizabeth Sin of Hong Kong University's Department of History for her advice; Des Inglis who remembers the last pirate raid so well; Bryan Leving and Tony Morias who are the kind of people who make Hong Kong what it is.

I also thank G.R.G. Worcester, formerly River Inspector, Chinese Maritime Customs, for his great knowledge of sail and sweep in China; Colonel Valentine Rodolphe Burkhardt for his works of Chinese creeds and customs; Grand Master Shakespeare Chan for showing me the power of Ch'i and Doctor Kour Fong Chong for the generous sharing of his great knowledge of Chinese herbs. I thank Angela Panich for endless typing without complaint; Jean Bedford for her skill and patience as editor; Ted Blackall for putting his formidable energy and talents into designing the dust jacket; and Suzanne Delmont, whose faith in *The Second Sunrise* turned an idea into a book.

Author's Note

The Second Sunrise is entirely a work of fiction, and all characters, dialogues and events are purely fictitious. I have observed a great deal in my twenty-five years of travelling and living in Asia—but I still extend my apologies to those old China hands and permanent residents of Hong Kong who will no doubt find things with which they don't agree.

The melding of Chinese medicine, Taoist and Buddist religion and authentic martial arts is a timeless treasure of Chinese heritage. Once a way of life, this ancient tradition, its origins cloaked by myth and legend, is sometimes confused with fantasy, quackery and the playing of tricks. Nothing could be further from the truth, which is why its credibility in the western world grows as we approach the twenty-first century.

Lastly, the phenomenon of the black Tao is all too familiar to those dark minds on any continent that believe only in the havoc of evil. From African witch-doctor to voodoo priest, from witches' coven to the bone-pointing ceremonies of Aboriginal Australia— those who seek to possess the private universe of another's soul are the mind-poisoners. They have always been with us, they are with us still.

Geoff Pike

WRITERS' BLOC

THE READER IS ALWAYS RIGHT

Prologue

THE EARLY China trade attracted a special breed of men: adventurous, enterprising, unable to conform. They came mainly from the merchant fleets of Europe: British, Portuguese, French, German, Dutch and American, to compete with those from India, Persia, Arabia and the Orient, to do business with the Middle Kingdom. A century before Columbus reached America, China had been sending its sea-going junks across the oceans of the world, their holds filled with silks and silver bullion, lotus root, rare herbs, water chestnut, jade and mountain furs—the ambassadorial gifts of emperors. They returned with ivory, spices, aphrodisiacs . . . and chests of opium.

With the Opium War of 1842 the Manchu Emperor Chienlung reluctantly opened China's trade ports to foreign ships. Many grew rich and powerful, sailing their fast-raked schooners into the silk-growing Pearl River delta or up the southern coast to Shanghai and on into the lower Yangtze valley from the trade centres of Nanking, Hankow and Foochow. The boldest of them infiltrated the riverine networks to Chungking and as far inland as the Ya River. But the real fortunes, the greatest success, belonged to those who crossed the South China Sea to the opium ports of India, Java and Formosa.

The greatest risks were run on the oceans between the mainland and Formosa, the Philippine Islands, Korea and Japan. Piracy was the price of doing business and as predictable as the weather— to be prepared for, avoided or taken head on. Fortunes were made and lost in a single run, life and limb gambled with the weighing of anchor. For those men who survived the gauntlet, whose ships were fast enough to outsail the pirate fleets, strong enough to defeat the captured Manchu war junks manned by crews little better than wild beasts and to ride out the perennial typhoons, rewards were greater and swifter than anywhere else on earth.

Part of this reward, often prized by such men, was the exquisite woman of China, exotic in her difference, mysterious in her culture, aloof by her nature, beautiful to the western eye that seeks the extraordinary. As a rule she was unreachable, perceiving the foreign devil as an ugly, unwashed ape to be avoided even by the eye. The exceptions, whatever the circumstance, were rare. But whenever and wherever they flourished, they created a force of their own.

Like all else in the trade she had her price and it was high. For a woman of China to be seen with a 'gwai-lo', a foreign devil, was to earn the horrified rejection of her family and the violent scorn and hatred of her kind. To be known or suspected of lying with the barbarian was to be damned and the offspring were cursed as jarp-jung, the mongrel breed, belonging to no one and welcome nowhere—a terrible sentence upon the innocent but not so hard to believe of a race to whom a girl child was of far less value than the family buffalo, or a fattened pig, to be strangled at birth or buried with the placenta and left to rats and dogs.

This was a time and place when a life was frequently taken for the price of a bowl of rice; beheading and unspeakable torture were the way of everyday punishment and justice was the whim of the mandarin. This unbending contempt for the mixed blood of east and west, and the dangers it created, did not prevent them from mingling. The Eurasian identity was forged in the face of bitter racial bigotry that easily flared to hatred, a blind indifference from both sides that quickly became injustice and cruelty. Perhaps that is why it also bred a fierce pride and a special kind of courage, an unbeatable determination for survival, for recognition, for success and for power. Eurasians were to play a leading role in the establishment and development of the colonial outpost that would be called Hong Kong, in industry, commerce and administration from those ferocious, adventurous times to the present day. They would contribute greatly to the British Crown Colony's place among the world's most influential manufacturing centres.

It is certainly why, once established, Eurasian society closed its ranks as tightly as the Jews of Israel. The great families who came to power from the conflicts of the early trading days inherited the acumen and intelligence of both the European and the Oriental, creating a world in which only they could live, a culture only they could understand: the world and the culture of the individual forced to stand alone.

PART I

Cloud Chaser

A journey of ten thousand miles begins
with one step.

MASTER TO-TZE

· IMAGE FOR JOURNEY ·

Cornwall, 1910

THE DAY he killed the gypsy boy, Ben Deverill came over the cliff hill path whistling a tune. Worn through the salt-stunted bracken by sheep, the path went nowhere in particular except away from the village to follow the sea. In the bare patches scoured by wind, mounds of freshly turned earth showed where the rabbits were and the smaller, finely dug hills of moles.

A shuddering squeal, thin and alone as a penny whistle, sent the dog bolting and Ben called it back. Another snare. The fine silver loop of piano wire was carefully concealed and staked at the burrow and closed tighter with every jerk. Following the squeals he came upon the rabbit, its tawny coat thickly matted with blood, and silenced it with the knife-like blow the gypsies called a rabbit punch.

The gypsies had set snares for a mile around their camp along with their strings of mole traps. He had seen them roll their caravans off the road and into a stand of willows just outside the village, to cut clothes props and make pegs to peddle in the market. When he came upon them, Ben opened the chicken-wire cages and let the moles go, collecting the snares and throwing them into the sea tied to a stone.

The rabbit had chewed part of its leg away to get at the wire that had closed slowly and relentlessly to the bone. He walked back to the pathway with the lifeless carcass dangling from his hand by its back legs, flopping like a broken doll. The dog ran behind, sniffing the dark spots of its blood trail on the dry bracken.

Ben Deverill spent a lot of his time on the cliff hill path, alone except for the dog that always followed him. This May morning he had looked through the black iron railings across the asphalt playground to the school, old and grey as a tombstone. The bell had stopped ringing and the voices of the children sang the morning hymn behind its tight-shut oaken doors.

He'd been late too often; his knuckles were still grooved from the ruler's edge, and a gouge that wouldn't heal from Zek Trevallien's broken front tooth: 'Half-breed. Half-breed. Your father's a drunk.'

Zek's lip had split like a grape before he could say it again and Ben hadn't been to school since.

It was things like this, and the fact that Zek was almost twice his size, that gave Ben Deverill a bad name among the village mothers. Any ordinary child of his age would have turned and run or had the decency to cry. But Ben Deverill was no ordinary child, everybody knew that.

He was of mixed blood, a 'quadroon' the headmaster had called him as, purple-faced, he had delivered another cluster of strokes across the boy's familiar backside.

'This'—whack—'might'—whack—'teach'—whack—'you'—whack—'not to'—whack—'fight'—whack.

Six of the best laid on with relish by Gaffer Trump was usually enough to keep most kids out of trouble for a while, but not Ben Deverill.

He stayed away from school for a day or two and then came back for more. It was the same look in his eyes, or as his ruler-wielding teacher, Polly Whitmill, often said, the lack of one, that got him in and out of fights. His mother had been a Eurasian of great beauty and exotic background. Somewhere in her wild blood there had been the fierceness of the Afghan hill tribe and the pride of the Persian. His hair was a carroty shock of uncombed ginger. It was his eyes that were most peculiar. They were the blue-grey of the unripe damsons he picked from the hedgerows along with blackberries and hazelnuts. For those few who saw him laugh they were peaceful and summery, in anger they flashed like splinters of uncut opal. Their upper lids sloped to meet thick, finely drawn eyebrows, making them seem slightly closed, which they quite often were from wine-coloured bruises. Whatever their mood or colour, what most people of the village saw in them was challenge or contempt. So the round-eyed, blue and brown-eyed kids had named him 'Half-breed'. Zek Trevallien would be the last.

The cliff hill path was the short cut home to the Deverill boatyard, so far out of the village that it was hardly used except by the gypsies and occasional lovers. It had been all Frenchy Deverill could afford when he came back from China with his five-year-old son. That had been seven years ago and the two of them had put it back together with their bare hands and the broad of their backs.

Frenchy had borrowed the money from the bank in Truro to lay down the keel of his first smack. He bought only the best elm, white Norwegian spruce and good English oak, digging his saw pit eight feet deep on the side of the hill and carting everything he needed from the village over the cliff hill path. It had made them more like friends than father and son. So if the boy spent more time in the saw pit than he did at school and had learned the hard lessons of the street fight before his time, Frenchy thought it would be better for him in the long run.

There was schooling enough in the building of boats and later, in the sail loft where they slept, there were all the lessons a boatbuilder and a sailor would ever need. Frenchy's father and grandfather had built boats on the storm-lashed island of Brittany. He had learned from them when he was Ben's age and, but for the Boxer Rebellion that had burned him to the ground, he'd done well.

It was a blustering bully of a day. The kind that snatched Ben's breath away and flung it out to sea. Clean, white puffs of cumulus cloud sailed in swift, shifting patches in a sky so blue it made him blink.

Clouds were the most beautiful things in the world, Frenchy said, and the only things worth chasing: 'Chase a cloud and you never know where it will lead you.' Ben stopped to watch as the shadows they made swept up and down the flowering slopes where the winds teased the bracken and went buffeting off over Bodmin Moor.

Far below, the waves rolled in from France, breaking bright as glass over the rocks. He breathed it in. Let it slap his cheeks, tug at his hair and roar in his ears: the sound and smell of the sea. The smell of kelp churned from the sea bottom, shellfish and the breath of seals barking from the rockpools. All the winds of the world met Ben up here on the cliff hill pathway as his playmates, lashing the clumps of coltsfoot daisy around his legs and sending the dandelion seeds flying. He was never lonely up here. Days like this he believed he could smell the flower fields of the Scilly Isles.

Far out, off Land's End, the full-blown canvas of a fully rigged sailing ship heeled tall and steady as a thunderhead, on its way to Africa, India or the China seas. Days like this, Ben Deverill knew, belonged to the sea.

He didn't see the gypsy boy until he spoke.

'That be my rabbit, little 'un. And them be my snares you been chuckin' in the sea.'

He was a young man of perhaps seventeen, the skin of his neck and arms burned brown as a cobnut. The wind flapped his moleskin trousers, tied below the knees with string, as he stood boots planted wide apart and his short, thick arms held loose and ready.

He reached out a hand. 'Give it here.'

Ben was seldom startled but the gypsy had surprised him. He must have come from across the moor, the wind-song stronger than the swish of his boots through the bracken. The dog had barked but Ben had thought it was chasing rabbits again. He hesitated.

The gypsy's tone was unchanged, his hand still outstretched. 'Give it here, half-breed.'

With a wide swing that turned him right around, Ben flung the rabbit out over the cliff edge and was facing the gypsy before he could see how far out to sea it went.

The gypsy boy rushed forward to stop him and Ben used the momentum of his turn to swing a powerful punch that hit the side of his face like a plank. Knocked sideways by the blow the gypsy took two more wide, unsteady strides and disappeared over the edge. Ben heard a reedy cry, like the wind in a bamboo flute, as death flew into his wide-spread arms.

The inside of Deverills' boatshed had once been filled with freshly-sawn timber—green elm stacked beside the steaming press, slung by gantlines from the high beams and stored in every corner; squared slabs of red and black oak for stem and stern posts brought in by boat from Plymouth and enough in the racks to lay a dozen keels. There had been drums of red lead, tallow and paint, linseed oil and turpentine. Outside, facing the sea over the granite breakwater and through the narrow inlet of the cove, more oak had been laid out to cure in the weather.

Two fifty-foot smacks had left the launching run in the first year and Frenchy had bought the new Ford AA truck that stood proudly in the yard covered by an old sail. Things had looked bright in that first year.

There was nothing now. Most of the lumber had been sold. There was no fire under the boiler, the tar in it was old and cracked. From the sheerlegs that squatted over the saw pit the pulley chains hung rusting for want of use; the purchase block had all but seized up. No fresh sawdust covered the ground around its edge and the yardmen's voices no longer gauged the weather and joked about their wives or yarned of the sea and seamen. The keel and ribs of a smack sat on the launching run, unfinished for so long it was now unnoticed.

Frenchy Deverill was still a physically powerful man. He was a man of great pride and enormous strength, a huge man whose shoulders drooped, who held his head forward, as if aware of his height. He was working on a lugsail, spread out on the stony ground where there was room enough beside the shed. He had anchored the edges with round stones from the beach, his thick-fingered hands working strongly and perfectly, stitching a hemp bolt-rope into the foot of the sail. Push in, pull through, draw tight. Push in, pull through, draw tight—the steel butt of the worn leather palm he wore forced the big, curved needle into the lay of tarred rope and through the stiff canvas as though it were a linen tablecloth. Push in, cross over, draw tight.

This was all his life had come to but he was thankful for it. The mechanical precision had the same therapeutic, dulling effect as the stitching of mailbags or the picking of oakum in a prison yard, the weaving of baskets in the day ward of a lunatic asylum. It was a way to survive.

Frenchy had learned to live with the tightrope balance of depression. The terrible, gut fear of madness had never been far away since he had left Shanghai. Some days closing in, some days blown away, as changeable as the wild Cornish weather. But now it hardly ever left him. Jean Paul Deverill had become a solitary man and he had raised a solitary son.

Inside his head he fought a battle which he knew he was slowly losing, thinking of the boy and of the boy's mother. Hoping that the rum could blot out the sight and sound of that one half hour in Shanghai, when they had broken down the door of his house on the Bund, slitting the throats of his servants on their way up the stairs. The Chinese rebels had raped her repeatedly, to the tune of their excited chatter and the howls of their pleasure. Raped her and raped her until her screams had become the low moaning of his name, pleading for his help.

While they looted the house, smashing everything they could not carry, destroying the collection of a lifetime, he lay half conscious, the stab wound in his side taking hold like a slow fire. They had stepped over him carrying the coramandel screen he had bought her on a trip from Peking, cursing their way back down the stairs and into the chaos of the street. When he had reached her, she was mercifully dead.

He had told himself a thousand times that it was not his fault. He had fought them as hard as he could when the Luger was empty, seen four of them fall before he went for them with his hands and feet. But Boxers got their name from fighting skills learned in the ranks of the tongs. They were the I Ho Ch'uan— the Fists of Righteousness and Harmony. Theirs were ancient arts, meant for self-defence in temples and mountain monasteries, now used in the training for the wholesale, bare-handed murder by secret societies. Even so, they had found him hard to stop until the knife came from behind. The foot that stamped down on his neck was bare and filthy, hard as horn. It forced him to watch while he prayed the baby hastily hidden in a cupboard would not cry out.

Frenchy Deverill had hoped that distance and time would bury the sight and sound of that half hour, perhaps wipe them from his mind forever. It hadn't happened that way. Only smuggled, extra-proof navy rum chased the memories for a time . . . and when he made connection with certain homeward bounders off the China run, the drug that had made and lost his fortunes.

He had thought the nightmare had faded, with the rebuilding of the shed and seeing the broad, tubby hull of his first fishing smack take shape on the launching run; in the teaching of the boy to work the steamer and hang on the end of a cross-cut saw, knee deep in sweet-smelling sawdust. At first, his return to the business he loved with a passion, the building of fine boats in the way of the Breton mariner, had been enough—showing his son how to trim planks with a well balanced adze as cleanly as whittling a stick with a jack knife—watching the boy's muscles forming long before their time while he listened, silent and lost in stories of the China trade.

But it hadn't been enough and the rum had come more and more to hand, kept inside a coil of rope in the shed, always in reach. He had fought with the yardsmen demanding more than they were paid for, until one by one they had left and none had come to replace them. No one would work for the wild-eyed Breton with his talk of China and the strange half-caste boy he worked like a man.

Only at night in the loft, under festoons of rope and cordage, bolts of canvas, rigging and sail tackle, did he find some sort of peace when the boy was asleep. Every few months, when there was money enough, he would drive the Ford tabletop all the way to Plymouth, telling the boy he was going to buy lumber to finish the smack. When he returned he was drunk, there was no lumber and the smack remained unfinished, its keel gathering barnacles with each new tide.

Frenchy did not look up when he heard the boy climb the fence behind the shed where the bracken sloped down straight off the moor. He had not been to school again. It did not worry Frenchy. His own schooling had been at the oar of a whaling gig in lively weather and in the sail locker of a four-master. It hadn't kept him from making his way. He had watched the boy build his arms and shoulders from long hours in the saw pit and his legs from chasing clouds and brown hares over the hills, and he learned well one of the oldest and noblest crafts a man can master. No tight-arsed teacher could give him better.

When Ben had finished talking and stood, catching his breath, his heart hammering from the mile he had run, Frenchy knotted and cut off the stitch. Reaching for the ball of sailmaker's twine and the lump of beeswax he showed no sign of alarm.

'Was there anyone else up there?'

Ben let his chest heave a couple of times before he answered. 'I don't know. There was no time to look around. It happened fast.'

He watched in silence as his father's thick fingers drew the twine through the wax and threaded it easily through the eye of the needle.

'I hit him hard. Behind the ear,' Ben said haltingly. 'He went over . . . so fast.'

'Did you see him hit the rocks?'

'It's high tide. Heavy seas. There was nothing.'

For the first time Frenchy looked up to see the fear in his son's eyes. Setting aside the palm and needle he stood and put a hand on Ben's shoulder.

'It was an accident. It could have been you over the edge. Think of that.'

Leading the way into the shed he reached into the rope coil and uncorked the greasy rum bottle. Pouring a stiff tot into an enamel mug, he handed it to Ben without another word and raised the bottle to his lips.

The young gypsy's body washed up in Careening Cove, half a mile from the shed. There was no knowing if others had been watching when he went off the cliff, but the chance was not worth taking.

When the gypsies and three constables came surging down the cliff hill path, Frenchy was sitting with the head of a jibsail across his knees as he sewed in a cringle. He didn't look up when they asked to see the boy, just said he'd gone to China and kept on stitching. Push in, pull through, draw tight. They scoured the shed but not the rafters of the loft where Ben looked down on them between the bolts of canvas.

The Ford reached Plymouth Docks early the next day. There had been fog on the moor and they had passed the gypsy camp without even seeing their fires. As they drove Frenchy told Ben about his old friend Nathaniel Barcoo, Captain of the *Moshula*, the great sailing ship that would leave with the morning tide. He spoke of others in Shanghai who would help him when he got there. Ben sat silently beside his father as they stopped at the wharf gate, the police constable at the door of his official box, a steaming mug of tea in his hand, behind him the sizzle of frying kippers. The Deverill truck was a familiar sight on the wharves when a China boat was in. He waved them on with the mug. They drove slowly past the wharf sheds, scattering the pigeons pecking spilled grain from the crane lines.

The rust-streaked hull of the *Moshula* grew out of the cold Devon mist as an iron wall, bigger than anything Ben had ever seen man-made. Her four towering masts soared above the shed roofs, their trucks lost in the dawn drizzle. The miniatures of men moved along the yardarms casting off gaskets, checking running gear and making ready for sea, black as beetles in their oilskins. Ahead of her, its funnel poking up among the iron bollards, a steam tug belched black smoke and a gush of sparks as it blew its boilers ready to take her tow line.

Frenchy told Ben to wait in the truck while he mounted the gangway to talk with the watchman. The two of them moved from the pale light of the companion lamps and disappeared midships. Ben watched the sparks swirling from the tug's funnel, reaching up into the mass of shrouds and halyards. The thought of climbing them chilled him to the bone. The watchman appeared at the top of the gangway, beckoning him aboard.

It had not been hard to find the son of Frenchy Deverill a berth aboard an outward bounder. The captain of the *Moshula* had sailed as mate for Deverill Shipping a dozen years before. He shook his head at the passage money Frenchy offered.

'There's no need for that, Jean-Paul, the lad will earn his keep on this run.'

Captain Barcoo, it seemed to Ben, had been built to fit the vastness of his ship, looking down from a great height, with eyes that seemed to reach inside. For fully ten seconds they stared at each other, the brass clock on the bulkhead ticking them away. When the captain stretched out his hand it took Ben's in a grip that was warm and strong. The hint of a smile jerked briefly at a corner of his mouth.

'Welcome aboard the *Moshula*. I hope you'll be half the man at sea that your father was.' He turned back to Frenchy.

'Don't worry about him. He is a Deverill.' He shook Frenchy's hand again, short and hard.

'I'm due on deck. Take the lad forrad and give him to the bosun. You'll want to say goodbye.'

When the door had closed Frenchy said, 'Unbutton your shirt, I've something for you.' As he spoke, he opened his jacket and took a canvas money-belt from around his waist. It was made from American sailcloth, the kind used in tropical seas, light and strong.

'Put it on and keep it on. There's enough to get you started. The captain will steer you on the right course when you reach Shanghai.'

There was something else, heavy and wrapped in burlap. 'You'll be needing these. They belonged to my father.' Frenchy watched as Ben unwrapped a set of steel marlin spikes and a Swedish Greenriver knife set in a broad leather sheath.

'The tools of the sailor's trade— wear them with pride.' He lowered his voice. 'You are a boy among men now, Ben. Sleep with them under your pillow.'

Picking up his kitbag, the money-belt unfamiliar against his skin, Ben followed his father along the flying bridge towards the fo'c's'le. Below them men were standing by the moorings and at the fo'c's'le head the steel towing hawser was being taken aboard the tug.

The captain's cabin had smelt of metal polish, waxed oak and pipe tobacco. The stink that met them at the fo'c's'le was the stench of an abattoir. Frenchy found the bosun, a red-haired Scotsman who looked at them with narrowed eyes and said his name was Gorbals. He was coiling a new heaving line with smooth hand-over-hand movements.

It took a hard man to control the deck crew of a square-rigger as big as *Moshula* and Gorbals looked as though he enjoyed it. The woolly red curls that crowned his head also covered his jaw and chest. They spread in a coarse fuzz along his thick forearms, almost hiding a gallery of tattoos, and ended on his knuckles. His belly flowed over a broad leather belt and the outer corner of one eye was distorted by an old scar. Frenchy stood back, letting Ben step forward.

'This is my son. He's to sail as unpaid deck boy.'

The bosun continued measuring the loops of tarred hemp. His eyes fixed on Ben showed a faint amusement. 'Is he now? And who says he is?'

'Captain Barcoo,' Frenchy said quietly. 'He's an old shipmate.' He took a pace forward and offered his hand. 'The name's Deverill, Frenchy Deverill.' Gorbals ignored the hand and laid the neatly coiled line aside.

He looked Ben over swiftly and showed broken teeth in a sly grin. 'He's a fair lump of a laddie. Have you been to sea before this, Jimmy?'

Ben shook his head. 'Only on smacks along the coast. My name's Ben.'

The scar reached to the Scotsman's top lip, twisting into a grin before it closed over his snaggle teeth. 'Smacks is it? Well, the *Moshula*'s no wee tub of a fishing smack and your name is Jimmy.' He spoke to Frenchy without taking his eyes off Ben. 'Is he up to it, Mister? The *Moshula*'s iron from truck to keel.'

Frenchy answered shortly. 'He is.'

Gorbals grinned again. 'Well Jimmy, there'll be salt water behind your foreskin before I've done with you.' He showed his teeth again in the snatch of a grin. 'Go forward to the fore peak. You'll find a bunk outside the chain locker.' Hooking his arm through the coiled line he pushed past them and into the fo'c's'le. 'It's used for stowaways and hard cases. It'll do to get your head down.'

Before Frenchy left the ship he held Ben roughly. 'Chase the clouds, Ben,' he said for only the two of them to hear. 'Chase the clouds wherever they take you. But stay away from the opium. Opium is bad joss.'

When the *Moshula* had sailed, Frenchy lay down alone in the sail loft surrounded by the comforting clutter of ship chandlery and the smells peculiar to his trade. Carefully twirling the shiny black bead of opium in the flame of a candle, he waited until the thread of blue smoke crawled steadily upward. Careful as an alchemist creating a droplet of gold, he transferred it to the thimble-sized bowl of the long, pig-bone pipe and lay back.

Nate Barcoo had said this would be the last, handing him the heavy plug of black sticky dope the size of a cricket ball as he had every six months for almost five years. The amazing thing was, the addiction didn't show on Frenchy Deverill's face the way it did on the Chinamen. There was a slight yellowing of the skin and some gradual loss of weight but nothing like the Chinamen, with their skin drawn tight as a drum over the bones till they shone like old ivory.

It was in Frenchy's eyes where it showed. But even then only if you knew him well; Nate had known him before, when his eyes were so full of life and daring that they roused those around him. It had taken time for the fire to go out in his old friend's eyes. The intense blackness that once burned bright with the love of life was turning to the dull grey of cooling ash.

Bad Joss

THE FARMER, Yip Man, poured himself another cup of hot rice wine. His hand shook as though he, too, felt the pain endured behind the door so close behind him. But he had heard his wife's commotion many times before and to him her shrieks of agony might just as well have been the squeals of a pig advanced upon with a knife.

He supposed it was to be expected from a woman giving birth, although he wondered why such fuss was necessary on this, her tenth time. His hand shook, not with sympathy, but with the anticipation of another fine son and he placed the cup of wine reverently before the shrine of his ancestors.

This was the tiny room where their spirits dwelled. Their faded faces watching him unsmiling from an assortment of wood and metal frames. The sparks of freshly-lit joss clustered beside the wine, its thick ropes of smoke rising undisturbed to beseech the rows of ancestral tablets displayed on the upper shelves—small slips of wood bearing the names of the dead and the reign in which they had lived. The tiny altar was crammed with fresh fruit and flowers and in a brass urn beneath them the thick ash of burnt paper offerings was still hot.

When the screaming changed suddenly to a choking moan and the first feeble cry of his son reached him, Yip Man fell to his knees and kow-towed deeply three times with three large and expensive sticks of burning incense between his clasped hands. Only when seconds later a long wail of despair rose from behind the door and it opened to the wizened face of the midwife, did he know that his offerings were not enough. This was bad rice.

It told him that all gods had turned away from him and allowed the beggar spirits to snatch away his son. There would be no new boy-child to join the others, to add filial strength to the comfort of his father's old age and to care for his soul in the afterworld. He had been cursed with a female.

Yip Man left the small square farmhouse in its shelter of dark box pines and waded deep into the field of foxtail millet he was ready to harvest. His heart was bitter but he dared not show it. In the middle of the field he stopped, the silvery tide shifting gently around him in the late afternoon breezes. Why had the gods betrayed him? Had he not burned offerings every day without fail for these many months, to Kuan Yin, the Buddhist goddess of mercy? Where had he caused her displeasure?

He was a cautious man. He had appeased the Eight Immortals at the Taoist temple and all their attendant protectors. Burned gold and silver paper at the shrine of the earth god and pinned his prayers on the sacred banyan in the village to please the tree spirits. There was nothing to say a man should not travel all roads to heaven and call upon all gods when a son was to be born.

His gall rose bitter as snake bile. What would they say at the village where he went to play checkers? He had indeed lost face. He was a mournful man and also a greedy one. His farm had prospered when compared with others of the district but always he complained of poor rice to the gods of prosperity. He had never forgotten the long years of breaking ground, sleeping in the fields with his hoe as a pillow so that it would not be stolen from beneath him, and he took no chances.

Across the field he could see his eldest son riding the leading buffalo slowly to the pond for washing, the others following. He would soon be married and already there were plans to build another house to make room for grandchildren. But this did not comfort Yip Man. A girl-child made a poor man poorer. Daughters were an affliction, taking up sleeping space, sharing precious food, until the cost of a dowry sent them off to give fine sons to another clan.

His other sons would be herding the goats from the hillside, driving the ducks from the paddies and swilling the pigs. His wife had borne him seven sons and five had lived. There had been two girl children in the first hard years when there was nothing but unbroken ground and the pains of hunger. One had died within a week and he had carried it himself the many miles to the baby tower outside a northern city.

It was unlucky to bury a child under the age of three for it had no soul, and custom denied the right of a tomb for fear of death striking another member of the family. Yip Man did not throw it into the muddy waters of the Pearl, or leave it to the dogs or the fox spirits as others might.

The baby tower was built of stone to receive the dead bodies of infants and was a place to leave unwanted children. It was a terrible place where wild dogs scampered at his approach and carrion eaters beat their ragged wings along its ramparts. Yip Man thought himself compassionate and had paused at a wayside shrine to burn the traditional effigy of a girl-child riding upon the back of a white crane. When his baby sons had died, he had burned the effigy of a boy-child seated on the back of a lion to send them safely on their passage to oblivion.

This was the custom of the boat people but Yip Man's faith was wide-ranging; worship knew no boundaries when fortune was at stake and the whim of the gods was as fickle as March wind. When each of his sons had been born he had dressed them as girls in their infancy and each wore a jade or silver anklet to deceive the evil spirits into thinking that they were female and not worth claiming.

He gave them names such as Ah Gow, the dog, and silver dog collars to wear so that they would be passed over as something unworthy of attention. Yip Man knew how careful a man with young sons must be with the hungry ghosts roaming the skies ready to snatch them away. He had entrusted each to Chang Hsien, whose portrait, bow in hand, hung where they slept, his heavenly arrow ready to shoot down the spirit of purgatory who seeks to devour the young and innocent.

He turned and walked slowly back along the swathe he had cut through the millet. The house was silent now and he knew the midwife would be awaiting his instructions. He remembered the second daughter, whom they had kept to act as unpaid nurse to his sons and to help keep the house and cook the food. Then one day a party of soldiers sent by the local Manchu warlord to gather taxes, rode across his fields with banners streaming. Yip Man had nothing to pay them and little to offer in the way of food.

They had ordered him to catch the doves in his barn and to cook them with the remainder of his winter rice and bring them to their camp on the river bank. They had taken his daughter, and, as his wife prepared the doves, they could hear the girl's screams, like the cry of a curlew on the wind. She had died a week later.

Behind the house he watched the washing of his three buffalo and the last of the sun warming the backs of his many ducks as they flowed across the narrow terraces of young rice.

Yip Man the farmer tried to lift his heart. Girl children were very marketable now. Perhaps she would be beautiful. Her mother was from Soochow, where women were strong and shone with the lustre of pearls. She might marry a rich man, to merge with his clan and pay a handsome bride price. If she did not grow up to be beautiful she might find work at the mulberry farm, raising silkworms, or even become a spinner.

He felt his depression lifting. Yes, of course. If her hands were small enough and her fingers light as butterfly wings they might take her at the silk weaving factory for a good price. If her hands were too large and clumsy she could be sent to the Yangtze valley to pick tea, oranges and peaches, or apricots and jube jube. Or downriver to Canton, Macau or Hong Kong to be sold as mooi-jai, child slave to the household of a rich Chinese or Parsee, even a foreign devil.

The contented sound of his pigs at the trough and the sight of his sturdy sons going about their work reassured him. He felt better. Yes he would feed her and use her until she was old enough to be taken to the silk factory. If he fed her well and she was comely she would bring a good price. Yip Man returned to the house to light more joss. The goddess Kuan Yin must not read his true heart. He was a good and grateful man. He would call the child Li X'ia, the name of great beauty. He would not drown her as his neighbours would.

Slowly he lifted his arms, his eyes squeezed tight against the tears as he moaned to the heavens.

'Bad rice . . .' He howled long and loudly. 'I have only bad rice.'

Moshula

THE SAILING vessel *Moshula* out of Plymouth sailed up the China coast from Keelung in Formosa, through the straits, up past Foochow and Pagoda Anchorage, through the narrows at Chusan and Ningpo to Soochow Creek in Shanghai.

It had taken ninety days to reach Shanghai, ten of them spent rounding the Cape of Good Hope driven by the Roaring Forties. Ben Deverill had never been happier to see a journey's end. The Scots bosun had set out to prove him worthless from the moment Frenchy had turned his back. The stench that had met them at the fo'c's'le head was the result of uncleaned latrines after a month in port and a drunken crew. Ben's first job was to clean them out.

The *Moshula*, he had soon learned, was the biggest square-rigger afloat in 1910. It was in the plough-steel shrouds and tarred hemp rigging of her four towering masts that Ben had left whatever boyhood he had in him behind forever. Gorbals had wasted no time testing the deckboy whom he saw as a friend of the captain, a special case. There would be no special cases in *Moshula*'s fo'c's'le while he was bosun. His job was to make a seaman of the boy.

They had been still in the Sound, less than twenty minutes out with all sails set, the day still breaking cold and bleak when Ben was sent aloft to 'know the masthead'. First, up the steel-braced rigging to the mainmast yardarm, trussed to the mainmast with an iron axle and preventer chain.

'Out. Out to the end.' Gorbals' voice had reached him thinly on the teeth of the wind.

At first Ben had frozen, clinging to the ratlines, afraid to venture out along the yardarm. The wind had clawed at him, reminding him of the moors and the gypsy cartwheeling down to black rocks, and why he was there. It made him move. With his feet firmly on the footrope, fear had turned into a defiant determination, as it often did with young Ben Deverill.

The place Ben had been given to sleep was by way of being a ship's brig—a steel lockup that was part of the forepeak where the great anchor chains were stowed when *Moshula* was at sea. Iron cuffs and leg-irons were secured to ring bolts in the bulkhead. When he lay down the crash of the bow wave exploded inches from his head. The Scottish bosun gave him little time for rest but when he sat down in this dark and narrow space, balanced on the wooden shelf that was to be his bed, Ben could think only of the snug security of the sail loft above Deverills' shed.

The lizard light was well astern when the great ship entered the tumultuous seas of the Bay of Biscay, plunging like a runaway horse through the white-crested hollows of Phom Ushant, her massive spread of canvas lifting her bows high then driving them deep into the troughs with the boom of cannon fire.

In the close, airless stink of his bunk space with only a hurricane lamp to give him light, Ben endured the lone purgatory of seasickness, a misery unimagined on his few short trips along the coasts of Devon and Cornwall.

When he slept, exhausted, Ben saw again the loom and sweep of Wolf Rock Light from the deck of the *Guillemot*, bright as a blade sweeping the channel approaches into Porth Harbour. The *Guillemot* had been Frenchy's first smack, built for a blustery Porth fisherman who had named her after the wild seabird of the Channel Isles, and her maiden voyage had been Ben's first time at sea. Still smelling of new rope, fresh paint and varnish, the brown canvas of her lugsail was stiff with size, yet to be blown out and cured by wind and salt spray.

Ben had grown almost a year with the building of the *Guillemot*, watching her take shape on the slips from the adzing of her stout oaken keel to the stretching of her rigging. He remembered how at night the Channel rain had slanted through the glare of her sidelights. How the phosphorus tumbled like emerald fire ahead of her blunt bows. He had cried when they returned by train with nothing to show but a slip of paper that Frenchy said would help them build another one.

Ben had sworn there and then that one day he would build a boat of his own and that when he did, no one and nothing on earth would take it from him. The dream had wrapped him like a cocoon.

When Gorbals had seen him reach the tackle at the tip of the starboard yard, he brought him in and sent him up and up past the crosstrees to the topgallant mast and on to the royal skysail yard 178 feet from the surge of the waves. The thin steel spar was hoisted and lowered on a greased mast track. Its thick axle grease had smothered him as he climbed the narrow topmast rigging. Up there the movement of the ship was magnified a hundred times, swooping him through an icy sky. There remained only two metres of bare pole to the mainmast truck.

By now all fear had left Ben, replaced by a wild exhilaration. Far below, the familiar, grey sweep of the English Channel, flogged white by the winds, had spread around him, its horizons still lost in mist. But those winds that threatened to tear him from his perch high above the world were the same winds he'd met so often on the cliff road. They gave him strength.

Through the loud hailer Gorbals' voice had drifted up. 'Come doooown. Come doooown now.'

'Know the masthead' the Scots bastard had said. Well, there it was, a flat cap of painted wood no bigger than a cowpat, two metres above his head and as far into the wild heavens as a man can go without wings. Normally reached by a bosun's chair, there was no rigging to climb this last span of the topgallant.

Ben never knew where the strength and courage had come from, but suddenly it was there. He had shinned the slippery wood to touch the truck, shouting into the howling winds, every nerve and sinew burning like fire with the effort and his thigh muscles threatening to cramp. But his hand had reached its lip in spite of the grease and hung on long enough for those below to see how Ben Deverill took his first test.

It hadn't satisfied the bosun but it satisfied Ben and it satisfied the crew. After that there wasn't much that Gorbals could do to break him, but he never stopped trying.

Ben knew all the ways of intimidation. From Gaffer Trump to Zek Trevallien and a hundred like them, he had infuriated bullies by standing his ground since he was six years old. He had done more than that, when pushed too far. The bosun was a Glaswegian; bred in the Gorbals, he was named after a dockside slum to rival any in Liverpool, Cardiff or Swansea where the hardest men afloat were raised on violence.

The blooding of a deckboy was a tradition at sea and Ben went through it without complaint. Sent out onto the prancing bowsprit to be plunged into the sea, he thanked Frenchy for giving him his sea-legs at the age of eight, taking him on crossings to Porth Bay in the huge Atlantic seas that batter the murderous Cornish coastline. Gorbals quickly learned that the sea held no fears for the son of Frenchy Deverill, nor any hardship of shipboard life.

When sent aloft on some piddling pretence Ben stayed longer

and climbed higher than he was told to, until he knew every halyard and jackstay and every inch of the massive crosstrees as well as he once knew the branches of old elms on the edge of Bodmin Moor.

If the bosun set him a task that would tax the strength of a full-grown man beyond normal endurance he conquered it if it took all day and night. Blisters and rope-burns soon became calluses, fear became courage and stamina was forged from exhaustion aboard the iron ship *Moshula*. The deckboy shrank from nothing and spoke no word of grievance.

The Scotsman's frustration was enjoyed by the fo'c's'le crew. Gorbals was an unjust man who used his authority badly and it pleased them to see a boy get the better of him. Young Ben Deverill, it was decided, was made from heart of oak and they lost no chance to encourage him, until their approval had infuriated the Scot and driven him too far.

It was well known Gorbals kept a supply of rum hidden in the clutter of the bosun's locker. Like every British merchantman the *Moshula* was a dry ship, where rum was only taken on captain's orders, but the reek of it was often on the Scotsman's breath.

Ben smelt it strongly one night. Asleep in his coffin-sized bunk beside the chain-locker, it took him back to the boatshed and from a half-dream he saw his father reaching into the rope coil, heard the squeak of the cork in the neck of the bottle.

The tradition of the golden rivet was said to have started in the shipyards of Birkenhead, the Tyne and the Humber, where a young apprentice was fair game for the seasoned riveter or boiler-maker, the chippy or the rigger. It had been carried on aboard the ships of the British merchant navy and no deck or cabin boy was safe from the threat of sodomy.

First had come the rum fumes close in the dark and then as Ben became fully awake, the sound of heavy, rattling breath. A hard hand that tasted of paraffin clamped down over his mouth, the powerful odour of sweat as his smothering weight invaded the narrow space.

'Make a sound and I'll crack your neck.'

The warning burned against Ben's ear on the heat of Gorbals' foul breath. He felt the thick forearm jammed into the nape of his neck and the hand that covered his mouth hauled back on it to prove the point. Ben knew better than to struggle against such a headlock.

Instead he went limp, allowing the man's full weight to stifle

him. He was amazed by his own calm. As though this scene had
been rehearsed, his hand crept up to find the hard, salt-cured
leather beneath his pillow, fingers seeking the cold steel of a marlin
spike, easing it from its greased sheath. His lack of fight deceived
Gorbals and he sensed consent, arching his loins to pull away
the coarse blanket that covered Ben's naked body.

'You'n' me got a little settlin' t'do. We don't want no trouble
now, do we?' His voice wheedled. 'We can make things real easy
on this trip.'

Ben's fingers closed carefully around the hempen seizing that
formed the grip of the spike. Nine inches of smooth, tempered
steel slid from its sheath, tapered to needle sharpness, hard as
tungsten, to open the lay of wire rope.

His breath rasped against the hand that covered half his face
as the crushing weight settled on him and the bosun heaved a
harsh sigh. Ben felt the hot belly pressed against him, the stink
of rum and stale tobacco overpowering, felt the rigid stiffness
probing his flesh as he swung the spike downward and back,
driving it deep into the Scotsman's trembling thigh.

The gasp of pain that came from Gorbals was almost soundless
in its surprise—a rush of foetid air that belched from him as Ben
heaved upward and rolled away to disappear into the dark.

An oil lamp burned from a stanchion in the fo'c's'le, its wick
turned low. The snores that came from the rows of hammocks
were undisturbed, blending with the creak and grind of the
bulkheads, the hiss of passing sea, as Ben moved swiftly through
to gulp the night air.

He spent the hours till dawn beneath the stars, letting the night's
dew and tossing spray cleanse his skin, the boom of wind on
canvas sooth his senses. When he returned to the fo'c's'le head
and his bunk space only the patch of drying blood proved it had
not been a bad dream.

Nothing more was said. The bosun's limp was explained away
and Ben was left alone. The crew put it down to the fact that
Moshula had entered the South China Sea and the voyage end
was only days away.

They sailed through the Yangtze entrance into the Woosung
River, passing the sluggish mudflats where the tide flooded the
brown fields, studded with fish traps, and the Shanghai waterfront
showed through a light morning mist. As the ship crossed the
North Channel there were the grand houses of the Bund, European
villas with smart white facades and elegant balconies awash with

pale sunshine. Their lawned and tree-lined gardens stretching to the quay looked as neat as a plush Parisian suburb.

Now as the great ship, her furled sails towering above the stunted masts of countless junks, was slowly towed to her anchorage off Soochow Creek, Ben breathed in the Shanghai waterfront, the sounds and smells returning from a past he had forgotten: the endless babble of voices, the smell of garlic, ginger and expensive perfume, unique to the Shanghai Bund.

All around him the river was alive with water transport of every kind, chugging, sailing or riding its moorings; trawlers, junks, sampans, bamboo rafts, floating reed stacks, night-soil boats to ocean liners; British, French, American and Japanese gunboats, customs and excise launches, maritime police cutters and foreign ships of every flag and rig. Along the foreshores clung the thickets of masts and rigging that were the home of the water people.

Captain Barcoo was the only man aboard *Moshula* who knew Ben Deverill would not be with them when she was loaded and ready for the return voyage. He had not interfered with the goings on in the fo'c's'le, although he knew of the Scottish bosun's zeal. Frenchy wouldn't have expected it and, from what he'd seen of him, neither would the boy. Which was why he turned his back when Ben took the Scotsman on. It was a tradition of seamen to settle scores in port. He wouldn't tolerate trouble at sea when every man was needed sound in wind and limb but now he went to his cabin and watched from the port overlooking the foredeck.

Nate Barcoo had known when he handed the heavy, fist-sized ball of raw opium to Frenchy Deverill that it was the last time they would meet. He had tried many times to break into the melancholy world that was closing in on his old friend but he was unreachable. Instead, Frenchy had entrusted him with his sinister secret and now he had entrusted him with his only son, the one thing of value he had left.

China was no place for the faint-hearted but no one could accuse his boy of that. Ben had inherited his father's guts and vision and Nate could only hope he had not inherited his bad joss, as he watched the bosun stripping off his shirt.

The fight took place on the cargo hatch as was the rule, surrounded by the deck crew and a second with a bucket of salt water for each man. They had all heard the remark that Gorbals had made as they made ready to go ashore: 'You should feel right at home here, Jimmy. Isn't this where you started out?'

Ben ignored the remark as he soaped himself with the others

on the well deck. *Moshula* was tied up, her hatches open and the grave-like stink of kaolin, the fine, white china clay from Devon and Cornwall, hung in the burning air as coolies began swarming aboard to empty them. The bosun's heavy gut shook with his laughter and from the corner of his eye Ben weighed it up as his weak spot—a boozer's belly.

'He's got a prick on him like the lower boom of a Thames barge.' Gorbals tried again to provoke the boy he'd been unable to break, the wound in his left leg still throbbing and unhealed. 'Don't go sticking it in these Shanghai whores like your daddy did. One half-breed bastard is enough.'

Ben felt the familiar quickening of his heart, the hot rush of adrenalin spreading from the centre of his being to flood his limbs, the tingling in hands and feet, the burning second that decided fight or flight. Since the incident in the forepeak, he had stayed clear of Gorbals and it had seemed to suit the bosun. He harboured no great horror at what had happened. This was life at sea and it would not damage him. But a loathing for injustice closed upon him now, a fierce defence of his pride and the dignity of his name.

He set down the bucket and shook salt water from his hair, pulling on his pants of thin duck cloth. 'You'n' me got a little settlin t' do. Remember?' He used the tone that only he and Gorbals could recognise, his bare feet spread solidly on the sun-warmed wood of *Moshula*'s deck.

It was a good ten minutes before the captain sent forward to stop it. By then it was clear to everyone that the boy would never give in, that the Scotsman would have to kill him to stop him. Ben fought with his heart as well as his fists. The difference in weight and brute strength meant nothing to him and he matched it with speed and courage, blow for blow. A good twenty kilos heavier and of much bigger girth, Gorbals had welcomed the challenge. Certain of panning the boy out in front of the crew he had not been ready for the agility and pace that Ben set, or the power of the punches that worked on his solar plexus. Within minutes he was wind-blown and still trying to land a blow on the figure that danced around him. No one was left in doubt that the boy who had joined the *Moshula* in Plymouth would step ashore a man in Shanghai.

When neither man could lift an arm, but neither would stay down the captain sent his first mate forward to break it up. 'Send the lad to my cabin when he's cleaned up,' he said. 'And tell the bosun I'll have no more of it.'

Half an hour later Ben stood before him. The captain was seated in the spoke-backed oaken chair, applying a match to his pipe of meerschaum clay. When it was going well he looked Ben over, from his roughly bandaged hands to the cuts and bruises on his face.

'Your father used to settle his accounts in the same way,' he said, the same slight grudge of a smile pulling at his mouth. Opening the drawer of his chart table he took out a square flat package wrapped in waxed paper and tied with sailmakers' twine. He handed it to Ben. 'He asked me to give you this as soon as we dropped anchor in Shanghai.'

Ben took the package. His name had been carefully printed on both sides with Frenchy's bold strokes and it had been sealed with a blob of melted beeswax.

The captain rose and moved to the small writing desk of polished oak slung by brass gimbals from the bulkhead. From the shelf above it, secured into fitted slots against the movement of the ship, he took a bell-shaped decanter and two glasses.

'He asked that you open it in my presence,' he said, removing the smooth glass stopper and pouring a stiff two fingers of rum into each glass. 'You'll sit and take a tot first?' It was more like an order than an offer.

The captain resumed his seat heavily, sliding a second chair towards Ben with his foot, nodding to its green leather seat. He seemed in no hurry to see the package opened or Ben's departure and placed the lead crystal decanter between them.

It was a classic ship's Cape Horner, designed to stand safely when the decks are shipping green and the spars are under water. He twisted its long slender neck on its flat base until the silver plaque slung around it on a fine chain faced Ben.

'It's the only thing I ever stole from your father. It's yours now.' He let go a short bark of laughter at Ben's look of surprise.

'The name lad, read the name.'

Engraved in flowing copperplate on the ornate silver plaque was the name 'Deverill' and beneath it, 'Windsong'.

'One of his finest vessels. I was privileged to be her master for two years. This was a souvenir.' He refilled the glasses, pushing the decanter across the polished oak. 'Take it, and may it bring you luck.' Then, reaching beneath his bunk for an iron cashbox, Captain Barcoo counted out ten one-pound notes.

'You earned it, the Scotsman saw to that.' He grinned as he shuffled the notes into order and pushed them across the deck.

'Ninety days at Ordinary Seaman's rates. Don't change money with anyone but Aggie Gates. She's an old friend of your father's and mine too. Take this chit to her. You can trust her with your life.'

He handed Ben a folded slip of paper, a crude map drawn on it and addressed to Aggie Gates, The Flying Angel Mission to Seamen, Garden Bridge, Broadway East. He tossed back his rum and banged the empty glass down. 'Open the packet now.'

When the seal was broken and waxed paper spread across the desk flap it contained a pile of folded charts tied with sail twine and a letter. Ben unfolded the paper and read slowly.

'Well lad?' The captain's voice was tinged with impatience.

Ben finished reading then looked up. 'These are his charts of the China coast and the riverine tributaries.'

There was a long pause. 'What else?'

'He says that by the time I read this he will be dead,' Ben said thickly.

Captain Barcoo sat silently twisting the cut glass tumbler. Light from the porthole struck through it, scattering chips of colour onto the desktop. 'You know why, don't you Ben?' he said quietly. 'He never forgave himself for your mother's death.'

Ben searched for a reply but none came.

'You were the last and only thing he cared about. The only thing left in his life. He only lived because you needed him. Many times he told me so.'

Ben sat, still staring at the big free-flowing words scrawled in blue ink. They were full of life. Not the feeble scribble of a dying man.

'He was strong,' he said at last. 'He could have shipped out with me. We could have started again. Together.'

'I've never known a man fight harder or cleaner to get where he was going than Frenchy Deverill,' Nate Barcoo continued in the same low voice. 'He lost it all, Ben. His life was all used up.'

When Ben looked up there was no mistiness in his eyes, they were bright with a kind of anger. 'What happened to my mother? He never told me. I want to know.'

Nate poured another stiff tot for himself. 'They killed her. When she died, he died with her. It's as simple as that.' He sipped the rum and studied the prisms of the glass.

Ben's voice was a whisper and his head was bowed as he spoke. 'He could have come with us. You could have brought him too,' he accused.

'It was too late for him, Ben. Believe me.'

'You knew he was going to die. You could have stopped him. He'd have listened to you.' Ben protested huskily.

Nate paused. 'I didn't know, but I'm not surprised. It was opium. Your father was an addict. I'd been supplying him since he left Shanghai.'

Ben Deverill folded the letter into the envelope. 'Then you killed him.'

'No, Ben. Frenchy killed himself. I just made the doing of it easier. He'd have gone a worse way if he hadn't had the drug to drive away the demons.' He paused, looking straight into Ben's eyes. 'I was his friend for twenty years. It was better coming from me. Try to remember that.'

Reaching out he laid a hand on Ben's shoulder. 'Believe me lad, your father's life was over long ago. He'd have done it then, if he hadn't had you to care about.' He raised his big hands. 'When he lost you there was nothing . . .'

Ben stood up, folding the charts. His voice had cleared. 'Did my father trade in opium?'

Nate emptied the last of the rum into his glass. 'There was no other way, Ben. We all did.'

Ben was wrapping the decanter in a clean shirt and stowing it with the charts in his sea-bag. 'I'll find another way,' he said, holding out his hand to Nate Barcoo. 'You were my father's friend. I owe you thanks for that.'

The sea captain took it warmly. 'Good luck, young Ben. Remember, trust no one but Aggie Gates, she will set your course.'

Nate was reluctant to free his hand as Ben shouldered his bag. 'Shanghai is a wily old whore and she has many sisters. Don't fall into her arms too easily.'

Shanghai

THE WAY things sat for a man in the place they were calling the Paris of the Orient, or the whore of the Orient depending on who said it, was a lot to do with who he was, where he came from and where he thought he was going. For the sailormen drinking free tea and singing hymns in Aggie Gate's mission it was entirely different to what it was for the nobs in English Town or French Town, or any other quarter set aside for the Dutch or the German or the Portuguese.

All a sailor saw of those places was from a distance across the river or when he had call to go to the Consulate or the shipping office in the hope of a letter, where he was almost always met with a shake of the head. So the nobs stayed where they were in their fancy clubs, like the Race Club with its indoor swimming pool, and in the grand houses on the Bund or the pleasant residences of Bubbling Well Road, while the seafaring man who kept them rich stayed where he was in Aggie's Dry-Dock or in the boarding houses strung along the other side of the river north of Garden Bridge.

But to anyone who lived there Shanghai was the most exciting city on earth. The city centre and residential areas of the west side and the docks, shipyards and industrial quarter of Pudong in the east were split by the Whangpoo River, the gut and artery of the city. Along the Whangpoo the big cargo junks from all over China crept under huge mud-brown sails, past the busy lighters and launches of Jardine & Matheson or Butterfield & Swire, headed for the jute and cotton mills, sugar refineries and breweries of Pudong.

Immediately behind the northern stretch of the waterfront the streets ran in a vast grid: Nanking Road, Jiujiang Road, Hankow Road and Fuzhou Road. In this maze of streets everything in the world was bought and sold. Each street was famous for its wares and for the craftsmen and traders lining its alleys and lanes. In the bookshops of Fuzhou Road you could buy anything from the latest European classics to ancient scrolls of Chinese mythology; in the stationery shops everything from a Parker pen to a soapstone chop—the seal carved in the image of a dragon or a lion—with its pot of vermilion sealing wax. In lower Fuzhou you found the medicine shops of the herbalists, ivory and jade carvers, gold and silversmiths.

Fujian Road was lined with secondhand clothes shops, silk merchants and antique dealers. For ladies' shoes you went to Zhejiang Road and for the best mens' tailoring there was the Avenue Joffre; for jewellery direct from the salons of Europe, the Avenue Foch.

Rickshaws jogged beside sedan chairs and bicycles, the pavements were crammed with life, the white linen suits and fashionable frocks of the Europeans and the sweat-slicked backs of coolies straining under their bamboo carrying poles.

Ben breathed it all in as he jogged along on the hard seat of a rickshaw.

Aggie Gates was known by some as Aggie the Angel. To the hard cases she was just 'Tugboat'. They gave her these names because she was always busy picking up seamen in need of help and towing them back to the mission whether they liked it or not. To the seamen who crossed her bow Aggie had a beam on her like a Thames barge, arms like a deck winch, and the strength of an eight-inch bowline when she was going about the work of the Lord.

The place she ran like a master-at-arms was in the basement of the Flying Angel Mission to Seamen where a bed was ninepence a night. If you didn't have ninepence, or had better things to do with it, you could go through the trapdoor in the floor and down the ladder to Aggie's Dry-Dock where the beds were free. They called it that because of the big Tibetan tea urn that squatted in the corner, polished bright as an engine-room boiler and brewing a head of steam like one, always full of ching cha, the common green tea of China. That was all you got to drink at Aggie's and any man caught with anything stronger on his breath was out among the heathen with no way back.

Another thing about Aggie was her glass eye. She had lost her right one along with a husband and everything else she owned, in the Rebellion. It gave you an idea of the hard times she must have gone through to see that the one she had replaced it with was a different colour to the good one. It was the same bright green as a birdcage aggie—the glass marble kids bowl along the gutter—and by the scratches on it, her glass eye had been used like one. Rumour was, she'd knocked it out of a Swedish whaler who changed the words of a hymn to suit his sense of humour and he'd never come back for it.

One green and one red, they used to say behind her back. Sometimes she'd slip it out and drop it into a glass of tea to clean it. Another yarn told of the unsuspecting sailor who swallowed it accidentally and put it back next day. So in her own way Aggie Gates was a legend on the Shanghai waterfront.

The Flying Angel was a big run-down place just across the water from the British Consulate. The people who ran it knew she could do more with undesirables than they could, so they let Aggie have the basement and she opened up in opposition to the doss-houses strung along the river.

The doss-houses were always full of 'beachies'—sailors out of work. They were deserters from half a dozen navies, kicked ashore off Yankee down-easters because they were too much trouble; those who had jumped ship from some half-starved British merchantman; even Russian whalers who had poked too far into the China seas.

The boarding-house owners, mostly hard cases themselves, took them in, fed and bunked them and found them a berth. For every man they placed aboard a homeward bounder, they collected the first month's pay for their trouble. Crew for a coastal packet, a gunboat or a river trader got them the same, so competition along the Whangpoo riverfront was fierce.

Tugboat Aggie was well ahead of the boarding houses. They knew that the men she had, slipped and waiting in the dry-dock, were serious about shipping out or they wouldn't be there drinking coolie tea and praising the Lord. The others had their beer bars and skittle alleys, spending what they had on the flower-girl sampans or in the gambling dens off Nanking Road.

As soon as a vessel dropped anchor in the stream or tied up at Soochow Creek to unload, Aggie would take a sampan under the stern and fetch off any man looking for a spell ashore, whatever his reasons. Before the congee stalls had their fires going next morning and with the cockerels still crowing from the poop decks of junks up and down the river, Aggie would be up the gangplank with a string of replacements fresh out of dry-dock and anxious to put to sea.

The consulates and shipping agents looked the other way, while the captains were glad to be rid of malcontents and refitted with men rested and willing to work who had already been shown the stern face of God. Every penny Aggie collected went to help the poor, and you didn't have to step far outside the mission to find them.

When Ben Deverill tossed his kit through the trapdoor and climbed down the ladder after it, the voices slowed like a wave troughing, then rose and rolled on over him. Through the fog of smoke and noise he steered his way over to the short, stout woman stirring huge copper pots on a coal range that roared like a stokehold furnace.

When she heard the name Frenchy Deverill, Aggie Gates pushed a strand of faded hair from her brow, hung up her ladle, wiped her face and hands with a sweatrag and folded him tenderly in her leg-of-mutton arms. Frenchy Deverill had crewed all his boats through Aggie Gates it seemed, and so had his skippers. Her good brown eye glistened at the news of his death, while the other continued to glare cold and glazed as a dead cod's.

Aggie Gates and Ben Deverill talked through that evening and well into the night. The weather was sultry, the heat and steam from the stove springing a fine sweat on Aggie's hard-working brow. After supper, they walked down to the river. The stretch of land behind the old place had its own sampan jetty, a rickety arrangement, much of it made with bamboo as thick as a man's leg. This strip of land was another thing that had benefited from Aggie's endless energy and care.

She had turned it into a kitchen garden. An orchard really, growing lychees, mandarins, oranges and pears, several kinds of plum and a magnificent cherry. In springtime the scents from 'Angel's Garden' as she liked to call it, could be breathed from a half mile up or down river and the shock of unexpected colour from its blossoms was a well-known landmark to river craft. Closer to the water was a carefully tended vegetable garden, its wide variety of local produce flourishing weedless and healthy.

The strong smell of nightsoil, so much a part of Shanghai after dark, hung heavily with the river mist and the smells of street cooking and drying fish. As they walked to the jetty Aggie told him with motherly pride how, when she had first come, this patch was choked with wild barley grass and hawthorn. Now it fed the mission and kept idle hands busy, as each sinner she towed in had to work a watch or two in Angel's Garden.

They sat in the seat she had had the men build for her so that she could watch the river. It was where she spent her rare moments of relaxation. A great, golden moon, slung like a gong over the river, was throwing a path across the water, mingling with the yellow glitter from the lighted windows of the Consulate, as Aggie told Ben all he wanted to know about his father's days in Shanghai.

It took him longer to ask about his mother and when he did, he wondered if she could hear the painful beating of his heart. She gazed out at the burning flares of fishing sampans for a long time before she answered.

'She was more than just a beautiful woman. But to the Chinese she was ugly. A thing of ridicule.' Aggie smiled at Ben's reaction.

'You will learn that all things that are not pure Chinese are looked upon this way. A woman of mixed blood is of no value, but when she becomes the woman of a barbarian she is worse than worthless. Your mother had Chinese blood but somewhere in her background were the round eyes of the Parsee and the fine nose of the Afghan. This mixture gave her the golden skin and proud bearing of the hill tribes and the noble grace of a Persian princess. None of these things were Chinese.' Aggie paused, but when Ben had no questions she continued.

'They learned to know her pride and her courage though. When your father first brought her here, they threw rotten eggs and fruit. She just picked them up and threw them back.' Aggie was silent again for a moment. The scented smoke of joss drifted from the deck shrine of a passing junk, its shadowy bulk so close its bow wave rocked and bumped the sampan she used as a ferry.

'Your father was a very wild man until he brought her back from Bandar Rig. She was his salvation, she calmed him. Not tamed him, calmed him. It is a big difference.' Aggie's voice was softened, suddenly tender. 'She used to come here, to ask if she could help when he was away. She was so alone, you see. So terribly alone.'

Her voice suddenly regained its customary strength, and she blew her nose loudly into the sweatrag. 'What can I do to help you, young Deverill? What are your plans?'

Ben's answer was steady and certain. 'I want to work the rivers. I want to know every craft and its build and its purpose, every port and its produce, every cargo and its price.' He went on without hesitation. 'My father gave me his navigational charts. I have studied them since I could read. I want to know the China trade. I will rebuild the Deverill Company.'

Aggie had been watching him as he spoke. She could see the Frenchy Deverill she had known so long ago. It was the same spirit. The same determined man.

'That is exactly what you will do and I will help you.' She rose, a little stiffly. 'But now I must get some rest. There will be porridge to put on in an hour or two.'

A cloud had dimmed the moon as again Ben felt she must be aware of his thudding heart. Trying to keep his voice steady, he asked: 'What happened to her?'

He couldn't see her face as, after a pause, she said. 'Your mother was greatly loved, in a way that most women can only dream of. She was brave and proud and fine. She brought your father peace and now they have both found peace of their own. It is all you need to know. If God is just, they are together.'

When the cloud had passed, Aggie Gates had disappeared into the shadows of her fruit trees. He stayed, watching the silhouettes of boats slipping almost silently across the moon path. Never quite silent—always from somewhere over the water came the shuffle of mahjongg tiles, sudden raised voices, the bark of a dog. Along the Bund carriage lamps twinkled in endless parade and he could see the lights of Jardine & Matheson and Sassoon House. Across the bridge the towering shadow of Broadway Mansions, where his father had once had his offices, filled him with an impatience to be started that he could hardly bear.

Trinidad

As good as her word Aggie found Ben a berth by noon next day. With the sun well up, just above the jumble of junk masts, the ringing of voices had woken him on the bench where he had fallen asleep. At first he thought he was back at the village school—there was the same muffled rise and fall of a hymn. 'Oh hear us when we cry to thee. For those in peril on the sea.' But these were the voices of men, deep and rasping and strangled falsetto, with one unmistakable contralto leading the way, rich and fruity as a bassoon.

After breakfast he and Aggie made their way across the jam of rickshaws, handcarts, ox-wagons and throngs of people up Tengdong Road and along Szechuan, criss-crossed by hurrying coolies balancing their loads on springy bamboo poles or shouldering weights meant for donkeys. At the western end of the Soochow wharves, junks and river boats of every size and description loaded and unloaded their cargos, manhandled between the holds and the godowns by nothing but manpower.

To Ben it had a tangible, infectious vibrance. The energy of it seemed part of the air he breathed. He felt himself thrill to the sheer power of it—physical effort strained to its limits, a vast machine lubricated by sweat, driven by muscle and sinew. How easily he would become part of it, flow with it, use its unlimited strength. Tap the force and endurance of survival.

The large junk Aggie led him to rode high in the water, its hatches open and holds almost empty, a cargo of sacked grain stacked on the wharf. Coir mooring ropes, looped loosely over the granite bollards, creaked in the wake of passing craft; its gangplanks bounced under the weight of barefoot coolies hefting the last sacks ashore. Eighty-five feet, Ben guessed, from stem to stern. A whaleback, turret-built hull with a high-swept transom, the crude redwood rudder between two red-painted knees rode well above the drifting flotsam of the Creek.

At a glance Ben could see that the workmanship was crude though sturdy. No time had been wasted in superficial finish but its heavy, roughly-hewn timbers had been shaped and fitted to a timeless plan that made its clumsy hull seem indestructible. In contrast to its rugged crafting, the trader was richly decorated in bright painted detail. The blunt bows carried the vivid image of a crouching tiger, claws unsheathed and ready to spring upon all those who crossed its path.

Bolted to the deck of its forepeak was a brightly polished brass cannon. On its stern the 'pa-kua', or eight diagrams, representing all the elements of heaven and earth, surrounded the symbols of Yin and Yang, paying homage to the gods of thunder and lightning. Its side panels displayed splendidly painted scenes of sages and emperors, scholars and healers, surrounding the sea-goddess of the vessel's home province of Chekiang, bedecked in plum blossom signifying beauty and squirrels eating grapes for long life and endurance. She was, Aggie pointed out, a Hangchow trader, one of China's most colourful and legendary river craft, and she reminded Ben of the vividly painted caravans of wandering gypsies. On her bows and stern, deep-carved and gilded, was the name *Trinidad*.

Her owner and captain was a Macanese, the Portuguese-Chinese mix considered inferior to even the contemptible foreign devil. Such a man had to be strong enough to live with the challenge, to ride the derision that was part of his life.

Carlos da Silva looked as though it was no difficulty for him. He was tall and gaunt, the muscles of his bare arms were long and lean as an athlete's, his forearms and the backs of his hands corded with the veins of hard work. Dressed in loose-fitting pantaloons of the kind worn by coolies, that left his brown shins bare, he wore the faded, threadbare jacket of an officer in the Portuguese navy over a brocade waistcoat open to a mat of dark hair that stretched from his throat to his belt buckle. The black hair on his head was uncut, hanging in oiled ringlets over heavy gold earrings and tied back from his forehead by a strip of red cloth. On top of this he wore a wide-brimmed straw hat, more suited to the veranda of a gentleman's club than the deck of a trading junk. His large feet were comfortably encased in hand-made sandals of woven reed, rope-soled. His thick moustache was neatly trimmed and between strong teeth he held the stub of a manila cheroot. The steady black eyes set close to his large, hooked nose danced with devilment and every inch of his skin seemed to have been stained with walnut juice.

Over his shoulder was slung a magnificent telescope, its leather casing polished to the oxblood brown of a cavalry boot, its brass fittings shining like new gold. The butt of a heavy revolver stuck out from a wide leather belt and the long sheath of a stiletto hung beside it. Captain Carlos da Silva looked half tea planter and half buccaneer. Embracing Tugboat Aggie, he swung her like a girl.

'What have you brought me this time? I asked for a first mate. A man to run the Hangchow Bore. A sailor with iron in his belly. I ask for a rooster, you bring me a pullet.'

The Macanese captain whacked her vast behind, but his wrist was swiftly grabbed by her short, strong fingers. 'Behave yourself, Captain. This young man is here to work.'

Carlos grinned with delight. 'I hope so, mother. The last one you sent me drowned in the Battle of the Waters. He was no sailor.'

Aggie stepped back and beamed. 'This one is the son of Frenchy Deverill,' she said.

Da Silva's grin grew instantly brighter. He held her at arm's length. 'Frenchy? He is here, in Shanghai? He is back?'

She shook her head. 'No. It grieves me to tell you he is dead. This is his son, Ben.'

The wide smile quickly faded. He stared, one to the other, and sank down on the hatch combing. At last he said, 'He should have stayed with us. I told him. He should have come with us to Macau.'

Aggie's voice consoled him. 'Ben sailed here, before the mast in *Moshula*.'

The smile returned quickly, the brief shadow that had shown

in Carlos da Silva's eyes was just as suddenly gone. 'Of course. The tallest ship in any sea. What else would Frenchy Deverill's son arrive on?'

Aggie put an arm round Ben's shoulders. 'Remember he is mixed blood, like you. You two should do well together.'

The junk captain took a fresh cheroot from his shirt pocket and offered it to Ben, who took it gingerly. It was the twisted black and green of a dried cat turd and when he sniffed it as he had seen his father do, the aroma seemed to Ben to confirm its appearance.

'Rolled on the thigh of a Filipina in the hills of Zamboanga,' said the captain, holding out a lighted taper to Ben's cigar. 'They call me Indie, because I spent my tender years in the Caribbean trade. Twenty years on the China rivers.' He held out his hand and Ben shook it.

'If you are half the man your father was, Mr Deverill, you are welcome aboard the *Trinidad*.' He noticed Ben's eyes on the handsome telescope and stroked it fondly.

'Lesson number one. If you value something, keep it next to your skin. These Chinamen can steal the gold from your teeth while you are sleeping and you will not open an eye.'

There was no fee for Aggie's services and she assured Ben of a bed, a meal and a prayer whenever he needed it. 'This man is the best foreign junk skipper on the China coast. He is a good man and you can trust him as your father did. Sometimes he is foolish. If he gets you into trouble, you know where to find me.'

Ben choked on the raw tobacco leaf, watching the gangplank bow under Aggie's weight as she strode ashore.

'Remember your prayers, Ben Deverill. This is a place of many gods. Do not confuse them.'

When she had disappeared into the crowd, da Silva blew smoke and turned to Ben. 'This is a Hangchow trader. The only one on the coast owned by a foreign devil.' He tapped his chest. 'I am that devil and I don't let them forget it.'

He took Ben forward to where the brass cannon shone like gold in the strong sun.

'Is there need for this?' asked Ben, admiring its antiquity.

Indie's teeth gleamed as he answered. 'A junk without arms would not last a single voyage.' He grinned, patting the burnished barrel. 'This one is for show. Does she not look grand?'

'Indeed, she looks fit for a royal salute,' said Ben. 'But what other arms do you carry?'

'You will see soon enough,' the Macanese replied, moving on.

He pointed to where deckhands were battening down the hatch under the eye of a thin, stern Chinese, drawing the canvas covers tight and hammering home the wedges. 'These are my schroffs, my deckhands. The skinny one is the laodah, the same rank as bosun. His name is Yum Sup—it means cunning one. You can trust him as much as you can trust any Chinaman, which is about as far as you can spit to windward.' Indie demonstrated by spitting expertly over the side. 'To the rest of them we are dog-shit, you and me. Together we must show them what dog-shit can do.'

His grin was suddenly gone and the lightness left his voice. 'I need a mate to guard my back. To stand watch when I sleep. To work as I work and play as I play. I pay well and you get a small commission on the cargoes we carry. What you don't know I will teach you.' He held out his hand.

'One voyage and we shall see. The China trade has no place for small men. You are not small. Do you agree?'

Ben took it gladly. 'You will have the best of me.'

'We will celebrate,' the captain said and swung below with the agility of a monkey, reappearing a moment later with two steaming mugs. 'This will help to keep you alive,' he said, handing one to Ben. 'What you English call Nelson's blood.' He raised his mug in a silent toast and took a deep draught. When Ben raised his own it brought tears to his eyes.

'It is called Dragon's Breath out here. Rum and cocoa with a pinch of saltpetre—your father's favourite brew.'

Every mile of Ben's first trip abroad the Hangchow trader left him spellbound. It was a voyage of magic that he would talk about for the rest of his life. He had thought that rounding the Cape in *Moshula* had prepared him for any tricks the ocean could play. They were nothing to the running of the Hangchow Bore aboard Indie da Silva's trading junk *Trinidad*. Indie had chosen the grand old city of Hangchow as his main trading centre and home port. Reaching it meant navigating the most treacherous body of water in the whole of China's intricate river system. To the Chinese who preferred to avoid it, the Hangchow Bore was known as 'The Great Battle of The Waters'.

One of the principal waterways of the south-eastern provinces, the Ch'ien T'ang River estuary was among the most turbulent and dangerous tidal upheavals on earth. Captain da Silva told Ben nothing of the excitement that lay ahead. He had run the Bore countless times and knew all its surprises. The way his junk was handled in this stretch of water would tell him all he needed to know about his new first mate. There was no better way to prove if he was right in his judgement of Frenchy Deverill's son.

The trader sailed steadily up the coast under her big mustard yellow sails. Ben spent much of his time on deck with Yum Sup, whose responsibility was that of sailing master, supercargo and compradore in one. Although surly and demanding of his three-man crew of waterfront schroffs, the laodah was eager to please the strange gwai-lo who had joined the ship in Shanghai. His command of the English language was limited to the fewest of essential words but with Ben's eagerness to learn the Chinese dialects they soon established an efficient working communication.

The laodah was a Hoklo, one of the water gypsies and primitive fishermen of the southern coast. Born to the sea, he was an excellent sailor and quickly taught Ben the unique and cumbersome sail and rigging system of the junk. Compared to the great sails of *Moshula* it was more like sailing a toy boat on a lake. The junk's balanced-lug rig was not unlike that of a Cornish fishing smack and it soon became second nature to Ben.

They sailed well into the coast, hugging the muddy yellow water of the shelf instead of staying wide of the rocky shore and in the emerald green of the deep. Indie raised his telescope to study every sail that showed itself on the horizon. On several occasions he rapped an order to Yum Sup and the canvas covers were quickly pulled from three machine guns. A Lewis gun was mounted in the wheelhouse and two heavy Maxims were concealed by gunports below deck.

'Pirates,' Indie said. 'The first thing to get used to. They're everywhere.' He closed the telescope. 'The shit-eaters don't show themselves until they're upon you. They don't like to run in too close, prefer deep water and room to manoeuvre.'

Back in the wheelhouse, he slapped the dull metal of the well-oiled Lewis gun. 'And they don't like to come up against this,' he grinned. 'Most of them are slow, stupid, badly armed and they lack guts.' He patted the flat magazine pan.

'You asked about weapons. A burst from this and they usually sheer off and look for easier pickings.'

'And if they don't?' Ben asked the question out of genuine interest. Indie looked at him keenly before he answered.

'You kill them before they kill you.' He pulled the cover back over the light machine gun. 'Make no mistake, Mr Deverill. If you let them get close enough, they'll gut you like a herring.' He beckoned Ben aft and hoisted a deck-flap in the stern. 'There are also these when they are needed.' A pair of well-cleaned diesel engines sat side by side.

'Compliments of the Greater Shanghai Motorbus Company.' He grinned with pride. 'German engineering. They give me the edge on every junk on the coast.'

They were sailing so close to the shoreline that Ben thought he could smell the thyme growing wild on the steep hillsides where herds of goats cropped among the rocks. It reminded him for a second of the cliffs and moors of Cornwall and the smell of the Channel on a fine day—except for the spell of the unknown.

The beauty of China seen from the sea filled Ben with a joy he could not explain and when the trader entered the mouth of the Ch'ien T'ang, its cabbage-green waters whipped up by a clean wind, he felt like singing for pure joy. Hundreds of junks ploughed their way through the brisk chop under earth-coloured sails, from deep, blood red, burnt umber and raw ochre to the bright, mustard yellow of the *Trinidad*.

They criss-crossed the hundred-kilometre-wide entrance on slow, patient tacks. Standing out against the long, wide blow of the estuary, the green hummocks and grey towering mountains loomed under a bright, cloud-strewn sky, the sun coming and going in a kaleidoscope of colours. Indie must have sensed Ben's feelings, perhaps remembering his own first approach to this gateway to the great riverine world of China.

'China, Mr Deverill. You'll never meet a whore quite like her. She'll seduce you with her beauty—then slit your throat while you're dreaming.' His voice carried cheerfully through the open window of the wheelhouse. 'Have them stand by to ease off the mainsail.'

Ben turned his attention to the complex sheeting system of the huge, lug mainsail stretched on its rows of double bamboo battens.

'It's not as complicated as it looks,' Indie called. 'Most reliable sail design in the world when you've got a long way to go.' He came from the wheelhouse to lend a hand slacking the main-sheets.

'Bamboo slats keep the sail flat in any wind, easy to reef, you can get it up or down in ten seconds flat. The battens take the strain off the sailcloth so you can use cheap canvas, you can use them to go aloft so you don't need ratlines and most important, you can get her shot full of holes, she's easy to mend and she'll still draw a fair wind, sound as a bell.'

He pointed out red and brown patches sewn into the gay yellow canvas. 'Gingall,' he shouted over the wind. 'Chinese blunderbuss— seven feet long. It takes two men to fire it. Full of nuts and bolts and they've got old breech-loading cannon captured from Manila galleons a hundred years ago.' Indie flicked the butt of his cheroot over the side. 'We have nothing to fear from such antiques.'

As hours passed and the *Trinidad* sailed strongly upriver on the turning tide, water transport grew scarcer until it seemed she was the only vessel left afloat. Ben noticed the wide spread of the river had narrowed to a distance of some eight kilometres across and that along the bank they followed, a colossal sea wall of giant hardwood pilings and massive blocks of stone had been built. Every thousand metres or so great elliptical buttresses stood out into the flow of the river. It was behind and between these ramparts that the river craft had taken shelter.

'Is there a storm coming?' shouted Ben from the foredeck.

'You could say that,' Indie yelled back from his place at the helm. 'Just about the biggest storm you've seen yet.'

Ben scanned the flawless blue, clear as any Cornish summer. 'But there's hardly a cloud in the sky.'

'It's coming, though. We've got around seven minutes to get tied up.' The engines started and every timber of the trader vibrated to their even throb.

Indie steered into the sea wall and found her a berth among the line-up of similarly built junks between the parapets and securely made fast to trees lining the top of the sea wall. The sails clattered down in a rush and were quickly secured. Indie obviously delighted in Ben's bewilderment but refused to enlighten him. Instead he scaled one of the wooden ladders built into the sea wall and stood on the highest point of the nearest buttress. Extending the telescope he levelled it towards the distant mouth of the river.

'Up here, Mr Deverill,' he called, after a moment. 'Something you'll see nowhere else in this world. Hurry now.'

Yum Sup and his schroffs squatted on the forrad hatchway, unconcerned by what was coming. They grinned and chattered quietly as Ben clambered up the ladder.

'There. Between the headlands. It's on its way.' Indie handed Ben the telescope as he spoke.

Between the points that marked the mouth of the river the glass showed a long, rolling streak of broken water, electric white in the sharp light, rising and falling as it gathered strength and swept into the estuary. As he watched, it grew higher and higher, rushing into the narrowing river, gathering speed and height as it roared towards them.

'God save us,' breathed Ben. 'What in hell's name is this?'

'Listen.' The Macanese skipper was enjoying himself. 'You can hear her shout a warning.'

A tremendous roaring came from the racing wall of water.

'What is it?' shouted Ben, unable to lower the glass from his eye. 'By God, it'll flatten us.'

'You're looking at the Hangchow Bore, my friend,' Indie called back over the increasing rumble that shook the sea wall like the first stirrings of a volcano. 'The ocean tides collect off the mouth of the river and come down it in a tidal wave.' He laughed aloud at the look of alarm on Ben's face.

'Don't worry, Mister. This dyke was built in the tenth century and it hasn't been breached yet. Three minutes and she'll be passing us like 10,000 dragons. The Chinese believe that if you look hard enough you'll see the ghost of Wu Tzu-hsu, patron saint of the riverfolk, leading a troop of wild white horses on its crest.'

He took the glass and climbed smartly back down the ladder. 'Let's get aboard and ready to cast off when she's past.'

Towering geysers shot more than 100 metres into the air with the sound of a cannonade, as the monumental escarpment of seawater smashed into the line of breakwaters on its mad course between the wide river banks. Minutes later it burst over the rampart they had sheltered behind and swooped past them with the deafening thunder of a breached dam.

As it passed, the crews of the moored junks added to the monstrous sound with the beating of gongs and drums and the exploding of firecrackers, yelling at the top of their voices to send the demon-dispelling Wu and his herd of mad steeds stampeding on their way, to spend themselves at the river's-end town of Zahkow, more than 300 kilometres downstream.

'As soon as she's gone through,' shouted Indie, 'the speed of the current will slow from twenty knots. The boats that get adrift first catch the tail end and get a free ride all the way to Hangchow. That's where the engines come in.'

Yum Sup was already standing by to cast off, a hatchet poised over the tight-stretched mooring rope.

'She'll never handle in that mill race,' said Ben, still thrilled by the energy of the Bore.

'She doesn't have to,' roared Indie, raising his hand as though to start a regatta. 'Let the rest of them wait till it slows. Meantime we'll be unloading on the wharf with an evening of entertainment ahead of us.'

Gauging the mud-yellow swirl and eddies midstream he brought his hand down and Yum Sup chopped through the mooring line with a single blow. It parted with the sound of a rifle shot and the trader was whirled away from the wall and into the current.

'The fun's just beginning, Mr Deverill. I'll wager you've never set sail like this before.'

The Hangchow trader, all eighty-five feet and 100 tonnes of her, flew downstream on the tail of the Bore, spinning in giddy circles. Ben clung to the mast while Indie da Silva gave a series of wild rebel yells.

'I've done this a thousand times and it never fails to make me horny,' he bawled.

'She's out of control,' shouted Ben, unable to believe what was happening.

'There's nothing to hit,' Indie yelled back. 'No other boat will leave the shelf for half an hour. We've got the river to ourselves.' He roared with laughter. 'Remember, Mr Deverill. We're mad.'

As they shot past the rows of moored junks, their Chinese crews banged gongs, beat drums and shouted even louder for the foreign devils who clung to the flying tails of Wu Tzu-hsu's wild herd of horses. Gradually the maelstrom of undertow began to slacken and the junk's progress eased off.

'Now, Mister. Let's see what you've learned about this tub and her rig.' Indie stepped away from the helm. 'Get her on an even keel and under sail.'

Ben took command and, with Yum Sup and the schroffs bending their backs, soon had the trader sailing smoothly, helped on her way by the slow rev of her engines. But the exhilaration of running the Battle of the Waters stayed with him long after it was over.

By the time they approached the docks of Hangchow the current had slowed and the *Trinidad* tied up in an orderly fashion. Captain da Silva was more than satisfied with his new first mate's display of seamanship. There had been no sign of panic, only the shared excitement of a rare and unique experience. When the time had come for calm and capability Ben had quickly taken the situation in hand.

Now that they were safely docked and the laodah already had the hatches uncovered, Ben turned to the Macanese skipper. 'Does the Hangchow Bore run on every high tide?' he asked, still intrigued by their remarkable journey.

Indie nodded as he lit a fresh cheroot. 'Every tide. That one was as small as it gets. It's spring and autumn, when the highest tides of the year gather, that you should see.'

'Does it only happen here?'

'No. There's the Demons of Tungchow and the Thunder of Lungchow but they're ripples compared to the Hangchow Bore of the eighth and ninth moons.'

'Why this river? Why did you choose it?'

'Because no one likes to take it on. Foreign ships cannot run the Bore and if they could, Hangchow Bay is too shallow for ocean-going vessels. Most of the trade is routed through Shanghai by the Grand Canal. Tapestries, cotton textiles, silk fabrics, porcelain, antiquities. It's rich pickings for those that get in and out of here in one piece. Cargoes to Hangchow can bring double the price. I'm the last to take shelter and the first to cast off, so I make the trip in half the time.'

He drew on his cigar with deep satisfaction. 'I'm the only dogshit foreign devil to run the Bore and I run it better than the Chinamen. It's my territory.' Indie lifted his planter's hat, removed the headcloth and wiped his face and neck. 'Now, Mr Deverill. You've earned a little relaxation and perhaps a little real excitement. If you'll follow me . . .'

The streets leading from the docks were wide and lined with public gardens. Magnificent temples, memorial halls, shrines and monasteries, half hidden by giant fig and banyan trees, stood like sentinels wherever Ben looked.

'Marco Polo called this the most beautiful city in the world,' said Indie da Silva as they drew away from the sounds of the waterfront. 'That's why it's surrounded by twelve miles of massive stone walls.' He placed a fatherly hand on Ben's shoulder. 'Or perhaps it's because it also has the world's most beautiful women. Some say Soochow, but I say right here.'

The place they entered was a block or two back from the wharves, a lovely old building under a sweeping, winged roof of bright scarlet tiles. Its doors and windows were painted the same cherry red and its walls had been lime-washed a blushing pink. The path leading to its entrance was flanked by beds of orange and yellow marigolds. Inside, the shutters closed out the last of the day and a huge dragon lantern of carved rosewood and painted glass, hung with silk tassels, lit the large reception room with a soft, exotic glow.

'Welcome to the House of Happy Hours,' said Indie, lifting a small silver bell from a polished, inlaid table and ringing it as discreetly as a lady ringing for tea.

Almost immediately the small figure of a woman appeared from behind a beaded curtain. With the tiny, mincing steps of a clockwork toy, she advanced upon Indie, bowing and smiling an obvious welcome. The neck of her black cheong-sam was exceptionally high, denoting a lady of quality and giving her the carriage of a Victorian spinster. Her white hair was drawn back into a bun and held with a high fan-shaped comb of pearl-shell. Her strange, shuffling steps drew Ben's attention to her feet. They were little distorted stumps bound in white linen and encased in beautifully embroidered silken slippers. As he stared, Ben realised that they had been bent double, the deformed result mounted proudly on thick padded soles.

'Meet Madam Zhu,' said Indie, removing his hat with a flourish and presenting Ben. 'You can call her Fanny. Fanny Zhu is the world's most exquisite Madam, a lady of taste and discretion . . .' A brightly flowered fan spread as if by magic in Fanny's tiny hand and she hid her face behind it.

Before he could finish his introduction, squeals of delight came from behind the bead curtain as it parted to admit half a dozen girls of different nationalities. They ranged themselves before Indie and Ben, bowing and giggling behind their delicate hands.

'Some of Fanny's girls,' said Indie, introducing Ben, who could think of nothing to do but bow.

'Later you will make their acquaintance but first we must bathe and dress.' He again lifted his hat to Madam Zhu and the girls ushered them both to the staircase.

'Don't worry,' said Indie, delighted by Ben's confusion. 'I have a room here. Everything we need is here.'

The room they entered was large and lofty, furnished with a solid-looking bed and a large cupboard. The shutters had been opened and the windows thrown wide onto a small balcony. From it Ben looked out across the city of Hangchow. Everywhere in the pale purple twilight the roofs of temples gleamed in shades of red, gold and jade green.

From the adjoining bathroom he heard the splash of water and

Indie da Silva's lusty voice raised in song. Ben drew a deep breath; the pungent smells of the streets mingled with the scent of gardens. The excitement of the day and the strange beauty of the place swept through him like a drug.

Indie came from the bathroom ten minutes later wrapped in a gown of silk embroidered with dragons. Throwing open the tall cupboard and opening drawers he threw fresh clothing onto the bed. 'Welcome, Mr Deverill, to the finest little whore-house in China.' Turning for Ben's response he found his new first mate spreadeagled on the bed, soundly asleep.

In the two years Ben sailed the inland waterways and the coast of China aboard the *Trinidad* he learned a great deal about the China trade, about China and about the Chinese people. For a start, he learned to speak fair Mandarin and fluent Cantonese. It came easier to him than most, as though somewhere in his infancy he had already made a start. He also made it his business to learn everything he could of Chinese myth and legend. In a land where life was lived by the intricate superstitions of the Chinese calendar, to laugh at fantasy was to spit in the face of faith.

It was easy to see why Frenchy Deverill had spent his life here, why it had won the hearts and souls of so many like him. The inland waterways of China wound their way into its heart through a grand network of broad rivers, narrow tributaries, creeks and canals both swift and slow, flowing through towering gorges and white-water rapids, threading across navigation charts like fine embroidery.

There was no city or village of note that could not be reached by water. By sail or sweep, the thirty or more types of provincial trading boats plied the coast from Hong Kong to Antung. They took the Grand Canal from Ningpo over 1500 kilometres to Peking, the Yangtze from Shanghai to Chungking; followed the swift currents of the Pearl to Wuchow, or the Yellow River through the Ordos Desert.

For a boatbuilder and a man of the sea it was a time and place of endless challenge and fascination, every port of call a new experience, the clamour of life seen by only the most adventurous of western eyes. The very sight and smell of it nourished Ben. Impatience filled him, fed his muscles, hardened his bones and put iron in his resolve. There was nothing he could not do.

With his father's charts to guide him, he had mastered navigation of the rivers and the coast under the experienced eye of da Silva and had studied the makes and methods of every provincial riverboat that came their way. He knew the historical background, the authentic building techniques, of sea-going junks, riverine junks, fishing junks and the flat-bottomed plank-boats used to cross the lakes and shoot the rapids of the mighty Yangtze Kiang. They fascinated him. The art of Chinese shipbuilding was lost in time yet the designs had remained almost unchanged.

Whenever he could, Ben had visited the boatyards south of the Yangtze, nestled in the well-protected harbours of Kwangtung, Fukien, Chekiang and Kiangsu. There he saw at first hand the methods and materials of the Chinese boatbuilder, tools and rule-of-thumb craftsmanship untouched by the passing of time. He got to know their crude techniques of seamanship handed down since the first sea-going junks crossed the oceans of the world centuries before Marco Polo. Yet these were the skills that created the first watertight compartments, the first rudder steering and developed canal locks, hundreds of years before they were seen in the west.

Although the sailing craft of Europe had long overtaken them, the 'lumbering junks' remained unaffected, reflecting in their fashion the infinite patience and durability, the immeasurable staying-power of the Chinese way. Ben learned that nowhere else were sailors worked so hard on such poor fare or faced with so many dangers for such little pay. And yet, he told himself, these were the vessels and the men that carried on the richest and furthest-flung trading empire on earth.

There was more than fascination behind Ben's enthusiasm. He intended to build boats of his own and these were to be his competitors. By the time he parted company with da Silva and said goodbye to Yum Sup he had a working knowledge of twenty-seven different types of river craft and knew every river, lake and estuary for 5000 kilometres. He had visited every important trading port from Hong Kong to Peking. As da Silva's home port, he had come to know the ancient and splendid city of Hangchow better than any other.

The two years had gone so quickly, it seemed, Ben almost resented their passing. It made him even more greedy for life, more impatient for his father's place in Broadway Mansions on the Shanghai waterfront and a house on the Bund. He understood perfectly what it was that had driven Frenchy to the risk and adventure that had shaped his fate and it made him want it all the more. Every day was charged with excitement and event. Nothing really stopped or stood still. Everything was a promise of the future for those strong enough to claim their share.

He had been right about the power of human survival. It became a greed for life itself and in the Chinese way since the dawn of civilisation, the pursuit of wealth and prosperity became as much hunger and thirst to the blind beggar or the peasant farmer, as for the merchant and the mandarin. Ben understood this perfectly: life was a battle of wits, a matching of skill and cunning, an unending contest of strength and endurance, faith and willpower. It was a language he already knew by heart.

Ben could also see how easy it must have been to deal in opium. He had made it his business to find out as much as he could about the drug that had killed his father, even visiting the poppy fields of Kweichow, to watch the coolies bleeding the capsules of the creamy sap, to be scraped off with slivers of bamboo the next morning. He had seen it dried by the sun into hardened cakes of chestnut brown and treacle black, the size of cannonballs, stacked into chests for shipment to those rich enough to pay its weight in solid silver.

Its history fascinated him, stretching back to the end of the first century when it was known to China's barefoot doctors and court physicians as a healing plant, given to infants and the elderly to promote sound sleep. A hundred years later the narcotic value was discovered and to the shocked and offended Confucian mind the door to China's greatest disaster had opened wide.

China had found her vast tracts of rich, light soil perfect for cultivating the purple, pink, red and white poppy. But it could never grow enough and when trade resumed, opium from Turkey, India and Java was the most valuable cargo a ship could carry. Throughout the seventeenth century the Portuguese had built the opium trade into the richest of imports. The British, always blamed for its introduction, had not become involved for another 150 years, when Clive of India took Bengal and the East India Company controlled the poppy fields.

By the time Frenchy Deverill had set foot in China the Opium Wars had been fought and, although outlawed by the Ming emperor, opium was still the most precious of all cargoes. Along with every other trader, Frenchy had filled his holds with chests of the rich brown cakes. It could still be done and Ben saw it all about him. There was hardly a trading junk afloat that wasn't carrying opium in some quantity. It made him determined that whatever the future

held for the Deverill Cloud Line it would not be built on the drug
that had killed the only person he had ever loved.

With the money he was paid by da Silva and the contents of
the money belt, Ben had saved enough to begin. There had been
nothing that Indie could do to persuade him to spend it on the
women in the House of Happy Hours, or those that came down
to the jetties, or aboard the flowerboats or in the waterfront bars
of a hundred ports. The problem of Ben Deverill's virginity remained
a mystery to Captain Indie da Silva and one that even his strongest
persuasions could not shift.

'When I'm ready, Indie.' Ben would say. 'And when I am, I'd
prefer not to buy it like a sack of rice.'

PART · II

China Cloud

They shrink from the madness of the
barbarian as they fear wraiths of the dead
and the spirits of evil.
When one such walks among them,
it is as though he did bring back the pox.
And they will shun him as a verminous rat.

FRIAR ANTONIO ASSAD
The monastry of St Thomas Aquinas
Dominica, Macau 1706

• IMAGE FOR CHINA CLOUD •

The Fox Fairy

A GREY fox moves silently through the field of winter barley. Bright moonlight silvers its back, the long sweep of its brush held straight and low as it follows the contours of the earth, fluid as a shadow. Up the bank of the irrigation ditch, it leaps it in a single, graceful bound, runs swiftly through the narrow rice terraces and over the low ironstone wall of the kitchen garden. Only brief ripples in the shallow water of the paddy show its passing. Loping over a wooden plough still harnessed by its trace chains to the buffalo yoke, it reaches the dense shadow of box pines that screen the farmhouse from unfriendly winds.

In the safety of darkness it pauses, slender snout delicately feeling the air for danger, one neat forepaw lifted in readiness for flight. The place is asleep. Confidently, it trots around the house. Through a fence of split bamboo, leaning with age, moonlight throws a pattern across the resting flanks of buffalo and the pale bellies of sleeping pigs.

In her cot by the back door Li X'ia is awake a second before the sudden, short bustle of feathers and strangled quack of fear as the fox's jaws close over the neck of a duck. A brief chorus of quacks is joined by the honk of disturbed geese and the barking of dogs. Li rolls from her cot in the kitchen and opens the door in time to see the silver back, unhindered by the flailing wings of the duck, leaping the rice terraces to disappear into the barley field. It is over in seconds and the noise settles to an uneasy rustling and then silence.

She waits to hear voices from the room where her brothers are but she knows they sleep like oxen and no lamp is lit in her father's room above. She closes the door and crawls beneath the thick quilt. Already the sky is pearly in the east. Soon she must light the fires and prepare the early meal.

Two hours later, his belly warmed with thick porridge of mixed grains flavoured with pork, Yip Man stands looking at the scattered feathers, splashed with blood. It could not be said that he was more superstitious than his neighbours, or more cowardly when faced with the supernatural. He was a bad loser at checkers and not known to be light-hearted, but he had no greater fear of evil spirits than any other man, or so it seemed.

In truth Yip Man's heart was filled with terror. Like everyone else, he followed closely the dictates of the twelve moons and the intricacies of the Chinese calendar but since the birth of the girl there had been no more sons and for three of the past eight seasons his crops had been poor. Livestock had grown thin and some had died; the well was low and drought had almost emptied his ponds. The fact that this was also the fortune of all farmers in the district of Tailiang, Shunde and much of the southern countryside did not ease the feeling that the gods had truly turned against him.

And now they had sent the fox fairy. Everyone knew the fox had magic powers and communicated with the dead. Did it not prefer to dwell in cemeteries, where digging was easy and it could share the ancient sepulchres with the bones of those whose troubled souls still lingered? Could not a fox transform itself in the twinkling of an eye into a beautiful woman or into an elf of the forest?

This was the fourth time in a month the fox fairy had visited the house of Yip Man and each time only Li X'ia had been awakened and drawn to the door. Was she beckoned to follow? Had she been chosen? Could it be that she was a fox fairy herself? That her presence in his house had brought ill fortune? He had never looked closely at her, preferring to leave her to the care of her mother. As was the custom, she slept apart and ate separately from the rest of the family and as he had heard no complaints about her work he had assumed she presented no problems.

Now, as he entered the room of his ancestors with the day's offering and lit the joss, he prayed to them to forgive him for his blindness. Was she not exceptionally fair? Taller than the girls of the village, were not her feet and hands longer and more slender, her eyes rounder? He burned many prayers in the brass urn, watching the strips of red paper and their carefully drawn characters curl and flare, tiny petals of ash rising with the smoke. She was almost eight years old. The time had come. He would take her from his house today.

Macau

WHEN THE trader *Trinidad* arrived in Macau at the beginning of the summer of 1913, Ben was not quite eighteen. With the deck cargo of live pigs and a hold full of dried mushrooms and chinaware unloaded, he announced his intention to start building a boat of his own. The first of his trading fleet. Indie da Silva laughed long and loud.

'You'll never do it alone. Stay with me and you'll have enough to buy a trader in a few years and you'll learn all you need to know.'

'I don't have the time,' answered Ben, trussing his sea-bag. 'And I've already learned all I need to know.'

Indie's smile slipped away for a second but soon returned. 'You are truly the son of Frenchy Deverill, so, I believe you. But do not be careless. What you say you will do, no white man has tried. Do not expect help—they will try anything to stop you.'

When he himself had tried everything to change Ben's mind Indie paid him off with a generous bonus and quiet words of advice. 'Macau is not the peaceful rivers of the Canton Delta or the civilised shores of Hangchow. Here they will slit your throat for a bowl of rice and eat it over your corpse. Remember that.' He removed his cheroot to spit. 'You'll never do it alone. They won't let you. But my joss goes with you as I know you must try.'

He went below and fetched the powerful German telescope from his cabin. 'I never did trust a painted tiger to watch out for trouble.' He tossed it to Ben. 'Keep your eye on them with this.'

Together they found a room above a coffin-maker's shop. It was cheap rent and no one would bother him there, Indie assured him. 'Two things the Chinaman is afraid of—lunatics and ghosts. They think you're a little of both. Living here will make them sure of it.'

As Ben threw off the Hangchow trader's lines and stood watching as it left the wharf for the return trip to Hangchow, Indie called through his cupped hands. 'You're as mad as your father. I hope you're half as smart and twice as lucky.'

They waved their arms until the trader was lost in the tangle of masts and rigging.

Macau was like no place Ben had seen on any journey through the rivers of China. It did not have the splendid temples and palaces of Hangchow or Peking, the bustle and power of Shanghai or Hong Kong, or the slow, bucolic beauty of the river ports.

Macau was like an exciting woman who, deserted by her lover, cast out by family and rejected by friends, had turned thoroughly bad. Her life was one of sex, gambling, eating, drinking and the smoking of opium.

A meandering maze of narrow cobbled streets and alleys, lined with opium dens, fan-tan parlours, joss houses and brothels that never closed, her people were a clamorous, violent mixture of Chinese, Portuguese, Macanese, Indian, a sprinkling of Arabs and the natives of the Cameroons. Among these, connected like the backbone of a snake, a murderous fraternity of Europeans vied with the triad-protected Chinese taipans for control of the vice dens.

There was a faded beauty in the old houses lining the inner harbour. The pale pinks, blues and yellows of the Mediterranean were set against the curling grey tiles of Chinese rooftops. Taoist and Buddhist temples stood side by side with the Dominican church and the Christian monastery and the East India Company's buildings still looked out over the Praia Grande along the boulevarde from the governor's palace.

On its promontory at the mouth of the Pearl and West rivers, the city lay hemmed in and overshadowed by the green escarpments of China, surrounded by the battlements of old forts, still watched over by ancient cannon. Below the old Guia lighthouse, grand houses, domains of the first Portuguese taipans, slowly decayed in their walled gardens.

With the growth of Hong Kong, Macau's industry was reduced to fishing, boatbuilding, the making of firecrackers, wine and incense sticks, its life centered along the thriving waterfront of the inner harbour: behind the doors of the whore-houses and peepshows, at the gambling tables or lottery stalls, in the chophouses and on the opium divans; in the restless press of people, bent on profit or pleasure; among the pungent smells of salt fish, chilli and opium smoke; where half naked coolies, road-dusty farmers and ragged fishermen rubbed shoulders with fugitives, thugs and seafarers and where the rich of Hong Kong came to find the true taste of decadence.

From his cheap bed above the coffin-maker's, Ben set about finding the boatyards, discovering quickly that Macau was no different to the rest of China when it came to cooperating with a foreigner. They thought him a fool, to be lied to, cheated and easily parted from his money. He soon realised that Indie da Silva was right—whatever he did in Macau, however he might make his beginning, he would have to do it alone and against great odds.

Seeking out the shipbreakers' yards and salvage pens, visiting the boatbuilders and shipwrights, he did not find what he was looking for, discovering it by accident as he walked the breakwater of the typhoon shelter. It was the hull of a lorcha and he had chosen it above all the other half-submerged wrecks he had been shown by cunning-eyed owners. Its design came from the Portuguese, the very first barbarians to trade with China. Built to pursue and out-manoeuvre the pirate fleets that infested the China Sea and had once laid siege to Canton, it remained the fastest vessel seen in Chinese waters since the fifteenth century.

The hull, more schooner than junk, retained the high Chinese stern and reliable rudder system, with sail and rigging that owed something to the west and the Far East and was styled after the sleek opium clippers that crossed oceans faster than any vessel afloat.

Its owner, too far gone from opium to maintain it, accepted Ben's offer willingly. Only a gwai-lo would be mad enough to pay good money for such a wreck. He led his large family, herding a procession of dogs, several pigs, ducks and chickens, onto the breakwater without a backward glance.

When Ben saw the true condition of his first command his heart sank. It had been moored for so long in a corner of the typhoon shelter that when he dived beneath the waterline he found it crusted with barnacles and thickly bearded with weed, but as far as he could see its timbers were sound.

Bailing out the bilges he found yawning gaps in its planking had been stuffed with rotting fish-net mixed with oakum and tung oil, kept in place with flattened tin nailed on the inside.

Sails and rigging had rotted from disuse and the unpainted timber seemed petrified by time and weather, hard and grey as stone. He found rot in the decking and several of the cross beams and one of its mainframes needed replacing. It would cost more and take longer than he had hoped.

Again, Indie's words came back to him: 'You'll never do it alone.

They won't let you.' He took them as a challenge and towed the hulk out of the crowded shelter by hired sampan.

Beaching the hull on a deserted end of the flats where only fishermen moored, he set about the task of restoring the lorcha he had already named *China Cloud*. Working between the tides, he began by smoking out rats from the bilges and the swarms of roaches that clung to the bulkheads in shoals of shiny brown blisters. Next, he set about careening the lorcha's bottom, burning off the years of growth. The sound of his scraper and caulking mallet, the ringing of his axe, became a familiar sound to the Tanka and Hoklo boat people who shared the mudflats.

Whenever the tide was out, day or night, the mad gwai-lo worked on alone, scorched by the sun or lit by the flames of tar and hemp torches or the glow of fire beneath the drum of pitch that he kept burning. No one spoke to him. The water people sculled past when the tide was in, staring from beneath their wide, bell-shaped hats, certain he was possessed by evil spirits. This strange foreign giant was best avoided like a carrier of the plague, and there were those who said he was a baby-eater.

One old woman was not afraid, her skinny arms still able to scull the yuloh, the heavy steering oar mounted on a wooden pin and operated by a rope lanyard. She came out to him every day, toothless and grinning, offering her wares, cackling as she charged him three times the price for eggs, fruit and vegetables.

At low tide the stern of the lorcha sat four metres above the mud. He reached it by unrolling a rope ladder and pulling it up after him. At high tide he fished and lowered his hand-made crab pots. The hull of the lorcha became an island from where he watched the activity around him, but took no part in it.

Each day the old woman sculled past on her way out to the anchored junks to sell her produce, flat brown feet that had never known shoes solidly planted on the raised stern, working the long sculling sweep with strength and skill.

She soon became the only one in Ben's world outside his own thoughts. He did not mind that she charged him more than she asked of the water people. A little squeeze was to be expected. He hauled up his purchases in a basket on the end of a heaving line and sent back the money. When she brought him half a dozen scrawny chickens and a ferocious cockerel he housed them in the hen coop on the stern.

'Now you will have eggs of your own, young lord, and a fine bird to wake you at sunrise.' She crowed as she rowed away.

Their relationship grew. She never passed *China Cloud* without lifting a hand from the yuloh long enough to wave and shout a greeting. The old woman was a Hakka, a farm woman, but she spoke a rough Cantonese and they understood each other well. She was too old, Ben guessed, to be afraid of him. He began to look for her, to miss her if a day went by without her voice, raucous as a crow across the water. A time came when his affection grew beyond all measure.

She came as always, the strong push-pull of the sweep bringing her loaded sampan out from the sea wall, steering towards him and calling loudly. 'Jo sun, lord.' She yelled a cheery 'good morning' as the bows of her sampan bumped the hull of *China Cloud*, grinning up at him from under the black cotton frill of her hat.

'Jo sun, Ah Paw.' He called back, using the respectful term for old woman.

'I have brought you a great thing.' She chuckled, reaching into a basket. 'How much will you pay?' She lifted a red-coloured puppy and held it up, wriggling, for him to see.

'This is a fine dog, lord. Its mother comes from the farm, not the street. It will guard your fine ship and keep you company. How much will you pay?'

Ben threw down the ladder to fetch the dog, holding it in his big hands while it twisted and licked, its heart tripping wildly against his palm. 'Name your price, Ah Paw. I will pay whatever you ask.'

Months of endless toil tested Ben's body and mind as never before. To ease the strain of isolation he swam each day and ran for miles along the sea wall. Aboard the hulk, he manhandled timbers that were the work of three men, tackling it alone, studying the task and thinking it out before using his strength and rigging counterweights, one against the other.

The countless hours of scraping and sanding, sawing and hammering on a lean diet of boiled water, fresh seafood and the old woman's fruit and vegetables, had shaved every scrap of fat from his body and the muscles of his chest, arms and stomach were carved cleanly under his sunburned skin. There seemed no reason to shave and he had allowed his hair and beard to grow. A band of cloth wound around his head kept it from his eyes and a scrap of twine tied it back from his shoulders. He began to enjoy the image expected of a madman, plaiting his beard with strips of coloured cloth and singing loudly as he rowed ashore at high water or plodded through the mud when the tide was out. For his visits to the waterfront he wore nothing but the cotton canvas trousers of a Tanka fisherman; his upper body, bare of clothes, shone like oiled leather.

To go unprotected in the sun was further proof of his derangement to those who saw him running the sea wall to return an hour later sweating and blowing like a stallion. The Chinese believed that well-being was found in quietude, comfort, good food and drink and the company of others. They saw this as the final proof of his insanity, and as if it was not enough, a mongrel dog now accompanied the lone barbarian, running at his heels, to be fed and fondled like a child.

Ben did not realise he had grown over 183 cm tall since leaving Plymouth aboard the *Moshula*. He did not know or care that his eighteenth birthday had come and gone. Neither could he gauge the physical strength and power of will his voluntary exile had given him.

The red dog grew quickly, filling his every moment with its presence. He named it Sinbad, spoke to it as he would a human companion and it slept at his feet. When it ran with him along the seawall, he thought of the brown hares on Bodmin Moor and the brown dog that had raced with him among the molehills. Sinbad brought a kind of happiness, but also showed him the true depth of his loneliness.

Energy was his other companion. Boundless. Bubbling in him like a spring that only continual back-breaking work could quench. The Christmas of 1913 came and went without a change in his days and nights. He was not aware of it.

Late one night, he was caulking the deck seams by the light of a flare and thinking of sleep when the dark shape of a sampan rocked its way across the black water from the shifting lights of the typhoon shelter. With it came the sound of a sweet voice singing. As it came closer, the soft glow of an oil lamp showed beneath its arched canopy.

A young Chinese woman dressed in bright yellow silks sat among cushions combing her hair. Her high, discordant notes made no musical sense to his ear, but he found them strangely enticing. Above the song he recognised the lusty croaking of the old Hakka woman.

Ben looked down at her, resting on the oar.

'It is the thirtieth day of the twelfth moon, lord. The time of the New Year. It is bad joss to be alone.'

She tied up to *China Cloud*'s boatrope and spread her arms wide, laughing up at him. Huge bunches of pink blossom were tied to the stem post of the sampan and a fruit-laden kumquat tree stood in a pot in its bows.

'I bring you a flower girl. She is one who is not afraid of gwai-los. I have told her you are not crazy. How much will you pay?'

'You are most kind, Ah Paw, but I am afraid I cannot accept such a great honour.'

The old woman was dressed in her best 'tzow', the loose trousers and smock of black cotton. Around her forehead she wore a ring of pale green jade stitched to a black velvet headband. Jade bracelets clicked on her skinny wrists. She was dressed for the celebration of Sun Leen, the Chinese New Year, but he saw that her feet were still bare.

She stared up him, open-mouthed. 'But young lord, this girl is almost a virgin,' she protested. 'She is white as milk and well-fed. How can you refuse?'

The girl had stopped combing her waist-long hair and the white oval of her face smiled up at him. Ben felt a familiar ache rising in the pit of his stomach but forced it from his mind.

'Forgive me, Ah Paw, but I must.'

She shook her head sadly and sighed, her words became subdued. 'Is there something wrong with the great lord?' Shielding her mouth as though offering up a great secret, she said, 'her name is Three Times Mei Mei. She is most skilled. If the lord is tired,' she suggested, 'this girl has many ways to awaken the tiger.'

Ben laughed and shook his head at the deadly earnestness of her offer.

'Tell her she honours me greatly but the twelfth moon is not on my calendar. I do not celebrate Sun Leen.'

The old woman waved her arms about in great bewilderment. 'Now that I have brought her across the water you must give her lucky money or she will lose much face. I too will be disgraced.'

The girl in the sampan had said nothing, her powdered face expressionless as she listened to the exchange. Now she spoke quietly to the old woman, her musical voice reaching Ben on the perfumed waft of sandalwood incense. He could not deny it stirred him.

'She is sad that she does not please you. She says you can find her at the Place of Red Lanterns if you wish to see her more closely.'

'Tell her I shall remember it,' said Ben, putting money in the basket and lowering it down. 'I am sorry I have no red packet to hold this lucky money, but may it bring her good fortune. You also, Ah Paw.'

She took the money and dropped something in the basket to replace it. 'I send you a piece of the cypress tree. You must burn it to keep your ship safe from evil spirits.' She waved to him. 'Kung hai fat choi.'

Her good wishes for a happy New Year drifted back as she pushed off with the yuloh and sent the sampan bobbing across the oil-black water to the dancing lights of the typhoon shelter.

Long after they had gone, Ben stayed on deck. Unable to think of sleep he watched the fat moon, ripe as a fruit, listening to the rattle of fire crackers, the beating of drums and cymbals as the lion and the dragon pranced through the streets of Macau.

He burned the cypress sprig but its smoke could not hide the hint of incense. Just as the noise riding out from the sea wall could not rid his mind of the girl's voice. The question would not leave him. Why had he refused her? Why had he always refused, as though this was forbidden to him? Why? When he wanted nothing more in life at that moment than to go after her. To bring her back. Was he afraid?

There had been too many things in Ben Deverill's young life to think for long of his need. At times his body ached to the core but his mind could not come to terms with it. To lie with a woman seemed like a precious dream to him, as remote as his goal of great fortune—something altogether sacred, the most treasured gift he would ever give or receive. To reach for it too soon could see it lost forever. The thought of offering it filled him with a kind of fear. It would come, just as fortune would come. He was certain of it. It was a thing that drove him but it belonged to the future.

Ben walked the deck of *China Cloud*, the loneliness in him greater than he had ever known it before, unable to drive the sight and sound of the flower girl from his head. All around him the waters of the harbour exploded with the reflection of fireworks as the celebrations grew towards the new lunar year. The sounds of feasting and drinking increased and he could see the crowds thronging the waterfront, clustered around open cooking fires. The smells of roasting pig reached him with the night air.

The solitude Ben felt among these great festivities became too great to bear and he went to the grog locker to find it almost dry. Draining the last of his rum, he flung the bottle far across the water.

The sound and the scent and the thought of her filled the night. It was not the noise and the people he craved; Ben Deverill's desolation was far, far deeper than that. It had depths that even he could not fathom, dimensions that only the small figure of the flower girl in her pajamas of canary yellow silk could reach.

He was drawn to the rail of *China Cloud* and stood for endless moments watching the lights of the sampans behind the breakwater, the flicker of flares floating bright as stars on inky water. The Place of Red Lanterns stood out clearly, a short necklace of ruby-red sparks glowing in the shadow of the sea wall. As though his hands were guided by another's they began to haul upon the line that tethered *China Cloud's* small dinghy.

When it was alongside he bundled the wooden rungs of the rope ladder to the rail and sent it clattering down. He knew very well the risk he was taking by leaving the lorcha unguarded but the heat from within was suddenly so great that his breath came hard, sweat ran unchecked down his face, his belly was tight and the sensation in his groin was close to pain. He felt himself consumed with excitement at the decision he had made.

Rowing strongly for the typhoon shelter, Ben rested on his oars just outside its entrance. Perhaps a hundred deep-sea junks were packed around its perimeter, so closely they formed a jetty of their own. The rest were cargo and fishing boats, roped together in blocks like floating islands. Every deck was brightly lit with oil flares and strings of paper lanterns and the scramble of mahjongg tiles came from below decks. Rigging and deckhouses were hung with branches of pink and white blossom, green swathes of cypress and potted mandarin trees lined the decks. From aloft hung long braids of firecrackers waiting to be lit. Between them shuttled passenger sampans and others playing music and serving seafood from sizzling woks, sending the smell of spices and garlic across the water.

For one moment he nearly turned the dinghy around. The cold resolve that had doused these feelings so many times before almost won. He cursed himself for not keeping her there when he had the chance, when only the old woman would know. He could have had her then, in the familiar privacy of *China Cloud.* How would he find her now? His arms began pulling on the oars again, manoeuvring through the mass of decorated boats, his eyes fixed on the Place of Red Lanterns.

The flower-girl boats were set apart, allowing a stretch of clear water for visitors to inspect them at their leisure. Those already entertaining customers had rolled down their canvas covers and rocked in darkness but for the red lantern hung from the bow or mounted on a stubby mast. Those still open for business blazed with strings of red paper lanterns, gay as Christmas trees, the black-clad amahs crouching in the prows like spiders ready to pounce. Their coarse Cantonese voices rose as Ben rowed slowly past, loudly calling out the beauty and celestial aptitude of the girl inside.

He saw no sign of yellow silk pajamas. There were perhaps thirty flowerboats but although each girl that looked out at him could have been the one, they showed no sign. Nor could he find the old Hakka woman. Off somewhere, he thought, peddling Three Times Mei Mei among the junk crews. Or was the girl behind one of the other closed canopies, under some grunting coolie?

The anticipation he had allowed to build up would not let him turn back now. A zealous amah reached out with her boathook and captured the bow of the dinghy, pulling him in with urgent whisperings, assurances that heaven awaited him for the smallest consideration.

'You makee jigajig then you give lucky money all same Chinee New Year.'

She clawed at the gunwale of the dinghy, securing it to the flowerboat with expert boat work. Ben stood up, uncertain of his actions. He felt his hand gripped with surprising strength, a dry rough claw that took advantage of his hesitation to haul him aboard, the sampan rocking wildly beneath his weight.

'This girl name Ling Ling. Very special. Come Shanghai, know plenty trick. Makee plum blossom jigajig. Very special price for you.'

Ben allowed himself to be pushed beneath the canopy, striking his head on the iron hoop of its arch as he stooped to enter. Behind him the canvas dropped with alarming suddenness and he found himself looking into the white powdered face of Ling Ling the Shanghai flower girl. The eyes that returned his stare were like wet chips of anthracite. In a flour-white face, scarlet lips were perfect as a painted heart. With the entrance sealed, the tiny world of the flower girl enclosed him. The noise outside dimmed, incense smouldered discreetly and buds of flame from a row of squat, rose-scented candles burned behind her.

She said nothing. Her eyes did not blink, her lips did not smile. Instead she turned to blow out all the candles but one. Leaving the perfumed smoke to rise in the dark she lay down among the cushions and waited, a silk gown the same crimson as her mouth fastened around her.

Indie's words came back to him: 'Flower girls are not like Sin Alley whores. You have to go slow. Some of them don't kiss.' He had laughed. 'And they probably haven't seen men of our size. We are not like Chinamen.' He had held up his little finger and wiggled it.

The desire Ben felt for the girl in the yellow silk was replaced by doubt, he could feel it slipping away. It was her voice that had captivated him and the tinkling of her music; the way the radiance of the glittering harbour had surrounded her like a cloak.

This girl before him lay silent and inert, even her breathing seemed subdued. Without speaking her small white hand fluttered like a pale moth to the silken belt that held her gown. It parted to show the naked whiteness of her body, the smooth down of black hair at her crotch, neat as a brush stroke. Her breasts were half-formed, the nipples small and childlike.

Ben felt the urgency return, felt himself stirring, rising to aching hardness. The reckless need that had gripped him aboard *China Cloud* returned in a rush. His groin straining for relief, he dropped to his knees astride her; the Tanka trousers slipped from him and his manhood sprang free. He tore the shirt from his shoulders and fell upon her. Forcing her legs apart with his knee he felt for her blindly, angrily, as he pushed into her, exploding instantly in a series of shocks that shook his frame and spun his senses out of all control.

His mind whirled with each excruciating spasm and he heard himself cry out, again and again, until utterly spent he fell upon her with all his weight. She had made no sound. No movement. Now as he lifted his head from her hair to look at her, searching for words to express feelings he could not define, the heart-shaped mouth he leaned to kiss drew back. Gathering saliva, Ling Ling spat fully and directly into Ben's face.

Chinese New Year in Macau created separate groups of revellers. The waterfront rang with German marching songs, Chinese opera, the wheeze of the missionary organ and the singing of hymns. There were drinking contests among the Portuguese and French, war chants among the Africans, loud music and dancing bears among the Indians. Knife-fights, wrestling matches and bare-knuckle contests were part of every evening's gambling. The festival brought out jugglers, touts, cut-throats, acrobats, every other form of street entertainer and the usual abundance of beggars and pickpockets.

When Ben entered the bar and ordered rum he was not aware that he had been followed from the Place of Red Lanterns. The man was a mulatto, deep-chested, with the short, thick arms of a professional dock fighter. His scarred face showed no great hostility as he spoke.

'They say you are strong like three men.' He thumbed his chest. 'Jo Maltese is strong as six.' He tapped the side of his head and rolled his eyes.

'They say you are also crazy. They are afraid of you.' He stepped back. 'Jo Maltese is not afraid. He is also crazy.' He performed a strange little dance in front of Ben, ducking and weaving, light as a girl on his feet, while those around them laughed and quickly made room.

Ben found in himself an unexpected calm, accompanied by a kind of relief, even gratitude. The humiliation of the flowerboat had so confused him that he welcomed this distraction. The feelings he had smothered for so long with the need to work and not to think came together in him with a rush. They fused with resentment at the way he had been treated by those he tried to live amongst and now this greatest of insults was all he could bear. His blood ran fiery hot.

Ben Deverill smiled at the man who had taken his mind off the Place of Red Lanterns and offered him the opportunity to express the way he felt, to unleash this anger that threatened to explode within him. Emptying his pockets of money, holding up a fistful of notes, Ben hammered the bar for quiet.

'I back myself against this challenge. Who will hold bets?' An old Portuguese sitting over his wine bottle held up a hand. He had seen many nights like this. 'I will hold bets,' he said and the crowd closed in on him.

The contest between the mad gwai-lo and the mulatto took place beside the sea wall across the boulevarde opposite the bar. There was no waiting. The mulatto charged in like a fresh bull in the arena, head down, his damaging arms driving like pistons.

When Ben stepped nimbly to the side and slammed a fist into the side of his jaw with the wide, swinging force of a sledgehammer, Jo Maltese grunted, shook his head and blinked with amazement. Spitting blood, probing loosened teeth with his tongue, he backed off and invited Ben's attack. It came in a barrage of perfectly placed punches that jolted the mulatto's hard torso, rocking him on his powerful legs.

Ben found himself almost feeling sorry for the blind courage that absorbed this punishment, transferring his frustration with every ripping, whiplash blow. The feeling did not last. In another hurtling rush Ben found himself lifted bodily as steel-muscled arms locked around his ribcage, closing like a hoop of iron.

The sudden clap of Ben's palms against his ears exploded inside the mulatto's head, breaking his grip. In that second Ben unlimbered another roundhouse from his right hand that spun the mulatto sideways. It was followed by a left that came up from the ground to send Jo Maltese backwards over the sea wall and into the black ooze of the mud flat. The betting frenzy mounted when Ben leapt after him and the battle continued among the fishheads and offal discarded by the Hoklo sampans.

Among the bellowing crowd thronging the sea wall Ironhead Chang the Fierce cursed himself for paying the mulatto good money to fight the gwai-lo. Another roar went up, as Ben, with the mulatto in a headlock, ran him hard into the barnacled side of a junk. Jo Maltese dropped onto his hands and knees then sank to the mud. Twenty minutes later Ben collected his winnings and returned to the bar with Jo Maltese and they drank together till dawn.

Chang-wa turned his back and pushed a way through the cheering mob, crossing the boulevarde into the crowded streets. It had not been a total waste. He had seen the best of the gwai-lo. It did not impress him. To a temple boxer such as Chang the Fierce this foreign devil was a plaything.

Ben knew his progress was being carefully watched by the Chinaman named Chang-wa. As overseer and part owner of the Ho Sung boatyard, he and Ben had faced each other over the price of timber many times and in spite of the hours of haggling Chang had always squeezed him in the end.

'The gwai-lo is a fool,' the yard boss had boasted. 'I sell him wood at a great price. Soon he will leave and I will take back the wood to sell again.'

It had become a contest. Chang-wa was from the province of Shantung. His hairless head was set upon his shoulders as rigidly as a boulder and it was said he could break a sculling oar over it as easily as snapping a toothpick. His reputation as a ruthless fighter had earned him the name of Ironhead Chang the Fierce. Born among boats, he was a master craftsman and a renowned boxer, both necessary qualifications to run a Macau boatyard.

Chang frowned in disbelief when weeks later, he heard that the lorcha hull was almost completed. A true gambler with face to save, he bet heavily that the gwai-lo would never last to see the wreck restored, rigged and ready for sea.

The twenty-third day of the Third Moon was the birthday of the Queen of Heaven. Every craft afloat in Macau Bay had been dressed with flags and banners, elaborately decorated with flowers of paper and silk, gods of the sea and mythical effigies. The rising phoenix, dragons, lions and unicorns entwined with serpents were raised high in the bows of every junk in the harbour, the pennants of the Tanka clans streaming from the mastheads.

Hundreds of passenger sampans shuttled between the larger vessels, taking the boat people ashore laden with offerings to the goddess T'ien Hau, the patron saint of seamen. They carried roasted pigs, pyramids of rice cakes, baskets of fruits and garlands of flowers. Under their arms the women and children had bundles of joss and scented red and gold candles.

Thousands trooped ashore and thronged the narrow path that led up the hillside to a small temple, so old and weathered that it blended into the headland as though carved from the rock. Above it the pall of smoke from burning prayers smudged the sky.

'Jo sun.' A voice called up from under the stern and Ben felt the bump of a boat against the hull. Going to the rail he looked down upon the shining brown skull of Chang-wa.

'Jo sun,' Chang repeated, with a strange rearrangement of his features that resembled a smile.

'Good morning,' Ben replied with the same civility.

Beside Chang stood a strange little being partly hidden by a brightly coloured sunshade. A monkey sat on one narrow shoulder wearing a red flowerpot hat and over the other the little man carried a large wooden box slung by a twist of cotton rope. Ironhead Chang held up a large green apple.

'I bring the fruit of peace and harmony. And a wise man to bless your vessel on the birthday of the Queen of Heaven.'

Hiding his surprise, Ben let down the ladder, taking the apple thrust into his hand as they climbed onto the deck.

'This man is the teller of fortunes,' Chang said solemnly, when the little man had clambered safely aboard with his box. 'The seer of all things. He makes great and powerful magic.' Bright as a parrot the little man faced Ben and bowed.

'He is a feng shui seen sarn,' growled Chang-wa. 'A professor of wind and water. He will advise you well.'

As though the words were a cue, the seer of all things spread his arms and turned in a circle, presenting himself for inspection. His hand rose with a flutter to pluck from the air what looked to Ben like a length of pea-green ribbon, writhing and contorting itself to become a long thin snake, entwining his fragile wrist and coiling in the palm of his hand as he lifted it ceremoniously to his chin.

'Bamboo snake,' murmured Chang. 'Very bad. Kill tiger, this snake.'

Raising its tiny pointed head, the snake entered one wizened nostril and began to disappear smoothly, unhurriedly, up the little man's nose. It then began to reappear from the other nostril and follow its own tail until it had disappeared altogether.

'Number one magic,' muttered Chang as the snake's tail slipped completely away.

The expression on the face of the soothsayer was unmoved and his hand remained steady, palm up beneath his chin. Ben stared in disbelief as the head of the snake popped from between the man's closed lips and began slowly emerging, inch by inch, from his mouth and back into his hand.

'Waauugghh,' murmured Chang, in the way of all Chinese when greatly impressed. 'You see how great are his powers.' His tone became businesslike. 'Now he will tell you of the future.'

The lid of the box was lifted and the deadly bamboo snake popped inside. In its place, the maker of great and powerful magic withdrew a tiny, yellow-breasted bird. It perched on his finger, cocking the yellow seeds of its eyes as the little man lowered himself to squat on the deck. With the other hand he offered Ben a hollow bamboo cup filled with wooden sticks about twenty centimetres long.

'Throw them,' said Chang. 'Your true fortune will be revealed.'

Ben had seen fortunes told on many Chinese streets. He shook the cup vigorously and spilled the sticks in a jumble on the deck. The little bird fluttered down, pecking among them then taking one in its beak. The fortune-teller reached for it and read the characters burned into its length, reciting his findings in a dialect Ben did not recognise. Ironhead Chang listened intently with a slow nodding of his head.

'Number one fortune-teller say you must leave Macau,' he announced dramatically. 'He say your feng shui no good here. This lorcha never sail away. He say you die and lorcha burn. You must leave this place, chop, chop.' He waved his hand in the general direction of the Praia.

'Go Hong Kong. More better for you.'

Ben thanked them both with all the expected politeness but made no comment on the advice of the professor of wind and water.

As the feng shui man, complete with box, monkey and parasol, climbed back over the rail, Chang-wa stooped and picked up one of the heavy clay ballast tiles stacked on the deck. Ben had taken them by night from a derelict godown and carried them two at a time back to the dinghy. He guessed their weight at twenty pounds each. With a slight bow Chang tossed the tile spiralling high in the air and allowed it to shatter into a dozen pieces on the point of his head.

With another short bow to show that the scalp had survived without a scratch, Ironhead Chang the Fierce followed the feng shui man over the side with a last word of advice: 'More better you listen number one fortune-teller.'

Ben watched him reach the sampan before calling down, just loudly enough for Chang to hear, 'Chang-wa. Again I thank you for bringing such a great and powerful feng shui man to my miserable craft. I am not worthy of his powers.'

Chang stopped with his face upturned, nodding at the wisdom of the gwai-lo's words.

'But I cannot leave this place until my work is finished.' Ben continued. 'I must go beneath my own sail. I will kill the man who tries to stop me. This is my true fortune.'

He held up the green apple. 'This should not surprise you. Is it not well known that you cannot frighten those already mad or harm those who are ghosts? They have nothing to fear.'

Taking a bite from the apple he threw it far across the water and began hoisting the ladder.

The day after Chang-wa's visit Ben awoke to find Sinbad's body hung from the stern of *China Cloud*, his belly ripped and gut trailing in the mud. The grief that swept over him at the discovery quickly fused into fury. Without thinking he reached for the heaving line that tied his dinghy to the rail and hauled it in. To get ashore. To go to the Ho Sung yard and find Chang-wa. Nothing else mattered to him. The heaving line yielded too easily. There was hardly any weight.

He looked over the side to find it held the saturated corpse of the old Hakka woman in place of the dinghy. Ben's cry of rage echoed across the water and turned the heads of the Hoklos bent over their nets. Even on shore people stopped to listen. But soon they returned to what they were doing. It was only the howling of the mad gwai-lo. Nothing he did surprised them.

The warning was clear. The stealth that had allowed the dog to be taken from aboard *China Cloud* said enough about the danger he was in, the weakness of his security. To Chang-wa, the life of the old woman would have meant no more than the life of the dog. For the first time since coming to China Ben felt the cold stone of hatred weigh heavy in his gut, knew what it meant to want to kill and to know that he could.

There was no doubt what this further warning meant. If he did not leave, he must be alert day and night. If he left the lorcha unprotected he would return to a burned-out shell. It was clear that Chang-wa wanted him to come ashore, to seek him out. It was something Ben could not do. Great as his hatred was he could not risk losing *China Cloud* now.

Every inch of her had been painted, oiled or varnished, her decks scoured white. He had chosen the Chinese colours of protection and prosperity; her hull was a rich plum red that shone like copper in the sun. The deckhouse and handrails gleamed white, the stem and stern posts were picked out in brilliant yellow, the gunwales trimmed in scarlet. The lorcha was ready for sea but she could not move without sails and rigging.

In the six months since Ben had begun work on *China Cloud* he had been forced to search hard for everything he needed. Every pot of paint, every bag of rice, every catty of tea had cost him dearly. Most of those he went to turned their backs or threatened him with the choppers and antique firearms they kept to protect themselves from thieves. Only the bravest did furtive business with him against the wishes of Ironhead Chang.

The last of his rice was almost gone and his tank of fresh water was low. Only by going ashore could he survive for long and he knew this was what Chang-wa was waiting for. As he sat contemplating his dilemma, the boom of a cannon echoed across the Praia. It brought Ben from the wheelhouse in a single leap, the German telescope quickly to his eye. A bright yellow sail showed between the headlands, standing out from the others. Ben shouted with disbelief. There was no mistaking the sail of Indie da Silva's Hangchow trader.

He watched its slow tacking into the mouth of the harbour. As it drew closer Ben could see the glint of the brass cannon as Yum Sup and the schroffs made ready to drop her sails. The clank of the anchor chain rattled over the water as Indie came on deck to wave his arms. The bamboo battens clattered down and hauling gear squealed in the blocks as the sampan was lowered. Indie da Silva's voice carried across to him.

'Ahoy. Mr Deverill. I don't know how you got this far without your throat cut but you're a welcome sight to see. She's a fine-looking ship.'

'How did you find me?' Ben called back.

'Every junkman from here to Hong Kong is talking of the mad ghost who used his evil forces to build a lorcha and paint it with his own blood. How could I miss you?'

Yum Sup rowed him across in the *Trinidad's* sampan and Indie scaled the ladder and jumped onto *China Cloud's* deck, throwing his long arms around Ben, hugging him close.

'Frenchy couldn't have done better, by the look of her.' He held Ben at arm's length and eyed him up and down. 'I expected to find you crab bait by now or run off to the Place of Red Lanterns and living off a whore.'

The joy of seeing his old friend filled Ben's eyes with unexpected tears. Only as they embraced did he realise how much he had missed the reckless Macanese.

'There's been no time for that. But I've thought about it.' He laughed, holding on to the strong grip of his friend's wide brown hand.

'That's a matter we'll have to do something about, before another sun rises,' said Indie, studying him seriously. 'Your father would expect me to look after you and to see you living like a Trappist monk would not make him happy. It is not natural. But first: show me this vessel of yours.'

'The way I've restored her she'll trade for another fifty years,' said Ben, proudly running a hand along the solid handrails of Sumatran teak.

He led his friend over every inch of the lorcha, pointing out the new beechwood decking—every plank had been pegged with dowels of willow and sealed with tar, he explained with genuine pride. Where nailing spikes had been used he had forged his own from worn-out horseshoes shipped as ballast aboard English merchantmen, so well tempered on the flint cobbles of London and Edinburgh that they made the hardest of steel.

He left the master's cabin till last, showing off the beautifully finished ceiling where a skin of fine walnut panelling shone the deep gold of tobacco leaf. Half the space was filled with a gigantic bed, large enough to accommodate six people side by side. A deep camphorwood combing prevented its occupants from being tossed out even in the wildest typhoon. The great fixture was secured with posts of mahogany bolted from deck to deckhead.

Indie stared at it, whistling softly. 'This was never built for the lonely musings of a monk.'

He clapped Ben on the back. 'And I say she is ready for launching this very night. I shall fill this monument with flower girls. You say you will not pay for love. Then I shall buy it for you.'

'Forgive me, Indie old friend.' Ben laughed. 'But there is something I need much more at this time than love.'

Indie pondered the seriousness of Ben's tone, producing two cheroots and lighting them. 'I know of few things more important than love.' He frowned, drawing in the smoke. 'Perhaps you should tell me.'

Ben told him of Ironhead Chang's warning and the need for sails. He told him of Sinbad and the old woman. Indie listened carefully. When Ben had finished, he said, 'I know of this Chang-wa. He is truly dangerous, a temple boxer. Chinamen like him are not easy to defeat. It is better that you leave him alone.' He blew on the end of his cigar thoughtfully.

'Tomorrow Yum Sup will go ashore to barter for your sails. They will be made quickly and cheaply for a Chinese laodah.' His smile returned and he put an arm around Ben's shoulders.

'While he and his schroffs are rigging your *China Cloud*, you and I will enjoy the delights of Red Lantern Street.'

Back on deck he looked around him. 'It seems I arrived just in time,' he said. 'Let me show you what I have brought you.'

The stack of provisions the schroffs had hoisted aboard were brought forward. There were sacks of rice, onions and sweet potato, cases of dry goods and canned food, bottles of cooking oil, bags of salt and sugar. Two more cases of wine and six of ale. Everything to stock a galley.

When all this was set aside one long wooden crate remained unopened, so heavy it had to be dragged like a coffin. Indie straddled it and with the blade of his knife cut the lashings and pried open the lid. From it he withdrew a beautiful old Thomas Godfrey sextant, a flare pistol and a copper masthead light.

'All from Honest Wong's Sincere Pawnshop in Shanghai.' He grinned, handing each of them to Ben for inspection.

'And this,' he added. 'I've adjusted it to shoot out a shark's eye at a cable's length.'

Ben took the heavy revolver uncertainly.

'A Colt breech-loading pistol . . . it'll blow a hole through a buffalo. Something a fist can't do. Take it. Believe me you will need it.'

Stooping again over the crate, Indie stripped back a covering of greasy burlap. 'And here, Mr Deverill, is its big sister.'

He lifted a Lewis light machine gun onto the deck, complete with mounting legs, spare magazine and cleaning kit, kneeling to wipe it over with a clump of oily cotton waste.

'Keep her cleaned, oiled and loaded always. Don't think twice about using her or they'll have your gizzard on the deck while you're making up your mind.'

Ben spoke for the first time: 'How can I thank you?' He took Indie's hand. 'I will repay you for all of this. You must give me an inventory. From my first cargo I'll repay every penny.'

Indie appeared not to hear as he stacked three watertight cases of ammunition beside the gun, tearing back the waxed paper to expose the new brass of cartridges.

'Keep it always out of sight. A pirate will sail through hell and out the other side to fondle a weapon like this.' Lovingly, he wiped protective grease from the walnut stock. 'It is worth fifty antique blunderbusses, ten knee cannons and will stop a hundred blades.'

Within two days the sails were finished. Yum Sup had bargained well. They were a fine example of Chinese sail-making, the stiff new canvas a dark moss green against the long battens of pale yellow bamboo and new white ropework. Ben watched the schroffs carry them across the flats at low tide together with coils of new wire and cordage for the rigging. He had refused to go ashore until *China Cloud* was fully rigged, her sails hoisted and tested. A week later she was ready for sea.

If he refused to celebrate ashore, Indie insisted, Ben's monumental achievement must at least be commemorated with the traditional junk-warming ritual. From his lockers aboard the trader he supplied a red silk banner to stretch across the well deck, reading, in Chinese characters, 'Peace and tranquillity on sea and land'. Compliments, he said, of the Hong Kong and Shanghai Lightermans' Guild. Yum Sup and the schroffs set about protecting the ship against demons: a bunch of evergreen was hoisted on the jackstaff to wish the ship long life. Above the door of Ben's cabin they fixed a talisman of red silk ribbons surrounding a pummelo leaf, symbol of the ritual bath taken by a bride on her wedding night.

This, Indie explained solemnly, was to assure the captain a large and prosperous clan and a long and active sex life. A piece of fat pork, symbolic of many fine feasts and a spike of cactus to keep unwelcome strangers from the threshold were hung in the galley.

A feast was prepared by a fat and elderly schroff Yum Sup had recruited as cook. The man was a Hainanese who chuckled with pleasure as he bellied about over the clay stove. Yum Sup introduced him by pretending to bang two invisible rocks smartly together.

'His name is Ah Poo. Him no balls. No give trouble when you bring sing-song girl on board.' He grinned.

Indie roared with merriment at the look on Ben's face. He repeated the rock-slamming action. 'That's how they do it. Bang. The old boy's a eunuch. They say if it's done just right, it numbs the cods. Just long enough to . . .' he made a swift slicing motion with the blade of his stiletto. 'Then they wrap the wound with brown paper soaked in herbs and vinegar and it's all over.' He sat back and spread his hands as though it were the simplest operation in the world.

After an excellent dinner of chicken soup followed by braised shrimp and mushrooms, then Ah Poo's specialty of abalone and Macau mudcrab stir-fried with ginger and garlic in a rich blackbean sauce, Indie opened a fourth bottle from the case of Portuguese wine, and proposed a toast to *China Cloud* and her young captain. They also drank a toast to Frenchy Deverill and the China trade, past, present and future.

Yum Sup appeared the next morning with a wild-looking old man he said was a Taoist priest.

'Cannot makee sail without gods. No makee trade without protection from bad spirit.'

The laodah was so agitated that Ben agreed these important things should be put to rights. The priest roamed *China Cloud* from stem to stern waving a large incense burner that belched thick smoke into holds and cabins. On the bows were fixed two strips of green cloth bearing mystical inscriptions to ward off sickness.

Joss was lit, fresh fruit, Chinese wine and rice cakes were set before it and paper prayers burned to assure the blessing of the goddess. Bowing his satisfaction, Yum Sup saw the priest safely over the side and into his sampan, pronouncing *China Cloud* 'Ready to makee trade'.

Indie da Silva took Ben's hand. 'A proud moment, Mr Deverill. No doubt you'll do a lot more to be proud of before you're done.' He looked up at the Cloud Line house flag. 'But this is a day you'll never forget.'

But even Yum Sup had not reckoned with the anger of Ironhead Chang the Fierce. To lose money in a wager was one thing, to lose face was another. When it was reported to him that the lorcha of the mad gwai-lo was making ready for sea he despatched a band of waterfront idlers with pitch flares to burn it to the waterline.

A short burst from the Lewis gun sent them scampering back to the sea wall, leaving their flares spluttering harmlessly in the mud. But it had told Chang-wa and everyone on the Macau waterfront that the lorcha carried a machine gun.

The next day, on the early tide, *China Cloud* raised her main sail and caught the wind of the Praia Grande. On the sea wall firecrackers exploded in celebration as Ben Deverill and his first command cut through the water away from Macau and headed for the Ch'ien T'ang River and the Hangchow Bore.

'They happy to see you go,' grinned the laodah. 'They say you makee plenty trouble.'

Indie had advised against running the Bore on his maiden voyage but Ben was adamant. 'If you can do it in the *Trinidad*, I can do it faster in *China Cloud*.' He grinned at his old friend. 'Or are you afraid of the competition?'

Indie had relented, but insisted that Yum Sup go along as his laodah.

'Just to make sure you make Hangchow.' He laughed, slapping Ben on the back and shoving a cheroot into his mouth.

'God go with you, Ben Deverill, because the devil's bound to.'

China Cloud had covered less than a hundred miles along the coast when Yum Sup pointed dead ahead to where two fishing junks appeared to be hove to. From his place at the helm he called to Ben who was still testing the efficiency of the lorcha's sails and rigging, looking up at the broad expanse of sail responding to the wind.

'No likee this junk. Better we stay clear. No trust Chinee fisherman.'

The lorcha was sailing perfectly, her sharp bow slicing the water, heeling in the brisk north-easter to a perfect balance, running with the speed and grace of a Grand Banks schooner. Ben opened the telescope and levelled it at the two heavy junk hulls squatting ahead with their sails lowered. He recognised them as trawlers and guessed they were drifting their nets.

'They look like Amoy fishing junks to me,' he called back to Yum Sup.

The laodah shook his head violently. 'Amoy junk no fish close together. Nets on deck, not in sea.'

Ben studied them again. Yum Sup was right. The long bamboo poles that spread wide to tow the net had not been swung out.

'Well,' said Ben, lowering the glass, his eyes still fixed ahead. 'They're probably handlining.'

Yum Sup shook his head even harder. 'All fishing boat in China sea can be pirate or smuggler,' he persisted. 'More better we ready.' He pulled the cover from the Lewis gun. 'They like takee this one.'

As he spoke the crack of a cannon carried across the distance between them. A puff of black smoke trailed away from the deck of one junk and a plume of spray lifted high in the water ahead of them. A second cannon discharged from the deck of the other and a thin whistling caused Yum Sup to crouch behind the helm and the schroffs to dive for cover.

A volley of plucking sounds close to his ear made Ben duck just as quickly. A pattern of holes had ripped through the cotton twill of the mainsail. The crew of three schroffs Yum Sup had recruited remained hidden behind the hatch combings and the cook stuck his head from the galley.

'Go about and tell your men to arm themselves,' Ben shouted.

The double crash of cannon rocketed again across the distance as the sails on both junks swiftly climbed their masts. More holes opened up in the fore and main sails of *China Cloud* as Ben leapt into the deck house.

The wheelhouse windows of *China Cloud* were fitted to slide apart to give the Lewis gunner a broad field of fire. The lorcha had responded smoothly and quickly to the helm and was well out of range as Ben fitted the circular pan of the magazine over the breaching mechanism and slammed it into position.

'Take her back on course and steer straight between them.'

Yum Sup muttered curses but put the helm over and gave his schroffs the order to come about. Ben's next command was barked above the booming of the mainsail. 'Now steer in close-hauled and let's see how she makes way.'

China Cloud's three big balance-lug sails thrashed as they luffed, then swung on their yards to fill again, the bamboo ribbing creaking loudly as the sheets strained in their system of purchase blocks and pulleys. More cannon shot fell wide and musket balls whizzed harmlessly by as she closed with the junks.

'If this is what they want,' Ben muttered to himself, as he adjusted the sights, 'then this is what they'll get.'

The hammering of the Lewis gun swept the decks of the pirate junks, splintering taffrails and deck housing. Four men fell and the rest lay low as the lorcha flew between them, raking one, then the other, leaving them rolling sluggishly in her wake. Yum Sup and his schroffs yelled their delight at *China Cloud's* speed as she showed the pirate junks a clean stern and a wide wake.

A day later, off Swatow, the sky took on the angry look of sawn steel as thunderheads darkened overhead. The sea had turned from the olive green and muddy yellow of the coastal shelf to sooty black within minutes. The squall came down upon *China Cloud* so fast there was no chance to make for shelter. It blasted its way in a curtain of rain that cut off all visibility in under a moment, so fierce and sudden that the lorcha, designed to handle the wildest of seas, heeled wildly and ran before it with its leeward gunwales awash.

There was no need for Ben to give the order to strike all sail. Yum Sup had yelled to his schroffs as the dark veil of wind and rain raced towards them and the sails had clattered to the deck in seconds.

Ben watched with satisfaction from the spray-lashed windows of the wheelhouse as the laodah supervised the efficient securing of the gear lengthwise along the deck, trussed into the hatch combing. The schroffs were good seamen, nimbly going about their tasks barefoot and able, reefing and lashing the gear to ring bolts set in the deck with reassuring ease, keeping a footing against the pitch and roll as Ben headed *China Cloud* into the thrust of the wind.

He had not interfered with Yum Sup's choice of men although he had seen first hand the dives and dens he recruited them from. He guessed they had sailed with opium runners, which put them a cut above the kind of waterfront dross most junks were manned by. Opium clippers were commanded by expert European master mariners, many of them captains and officers who had had long and distinguished careers with the navies and merchant fleets of Europe. They chose their crews carefully, trained them well and treated them fairly. A man with papers to prove he had served in the opium trade was assured of a berth before any other and the laodah had assured Ben these men were qualified schroffs.

No sailor anywhere was better suited to handling a ship of Chinese rig in any weather than these. Scantily-clad, with their shaven pates and greasy pigtails, they were accustomed to riding out the full force of a typhoon under bare poles, battened down and tossing like a cork for hours, days and sometimes weeks on end.

Ben did not expect the gale to last but as the wind strengthened and they were cut off from any sight of land, he was not so confident. Yum Sup appeared at the wheelhouse door, braced against the swooping pitch of the lorcha's stern and the powerful tug of the wind.

'More better we put out sea anchor and run with storm,' he yelled, over the shriek of wind in the rigging. 'Then batten down and go below play mahjongg,' he added, grinning widely.

Ben knew this was the common practice aboard the Hangchow trader in such weather and that the laodah's reading of the weather was superior to his. He nodded his agreement and Yum Sup swung forrad to the chain locker to break out the gear. The sea-anchor was a big canvas cone made from an old sail. Let out over the stern on a long line, it quickly filled, acting as a drag to keep the lorcha's head into the wind. *China Cloud* rode the mountainous waves like a roller coaster for half a day before the squall showed signs of abating. From his chart table in the wheelhouse, the helm lashed amidships, Ben kept a sharp lookout for signs of any other craft looming suddenly from the silver curtain of torrential rains. More than once he wondered how his repairs were holding up. The lorcha's hull had been almost entirely refitted but there had been no way to test her true strength until now.

As suddenly as the blow had come up it cleared away. A brassy sun shone through and cloud melted to leave patches of violent blue reflected by the sea. Whitecaps rode the waves, glittering and brilliant. The fresh smell of rain-soaked earth came off the land, filling the wheelhouse when Ben slid open the windows and latched back the door.

The forrad hatch to the crew's quarters opened and Yum Sup appeared followed by the crewmen, as Ah Poo came up from the pantry with a mug of strong black tea. The sails reset and back on course, Ben decided to check the main cargo hold for damage while the schroffs got busy patching the ripped canvas. Opening the hatch himself, he descended the ladder with a lighted lantern.

The hold smelled strongly of hessian bales, pine boxwood and the dry goods he was carrying, mixed with still-fresh tar and tung oil. An inspection of the ship's planks showed no sign of leaks but the cargo appeared to have shifted.

Lifting the lantern high he found a chest had broken open.

The smell that came from it made him pause and look closer. It was a smell that was unmistakable: the densely aromatic whiff of raw opium. Pulling away the remaining boards of the broken chest, he uncovered the tightly packed mass of reddish brown balls known as Benares patnas.

An investigation of the remaining chests showed that it was the only one. Under Ben's orders, Yum Sup lined up the three schroffs on the well deck. One by one Ben went to each of them and peered unflinchingly into his eyes. Not one of them found it possible to hold his stare but all three denied any knowledge of the opium.

The laodah harangued them in turn with every imaginable threat but they steadfastly denied having anything to do with the smuggled crate. Ben ordered Yum Sup to make it clear that none would be paid until the smuggler was exposed and that all three would be handed over to the police in Ningpo.

Sullenly they went about their work, with the laodah promising Ben that he would deliver the culprit before a day had passed. The next morning at the start of the dogwatch, while it was still pitch dark and blowing fresh, he reported that one of the men had disappeared overnight with an inflated goatskin, preferring to take his chances, the laodah scoffed, than face maritime customs and river police, known for their brutality when questioning a suspect.

Ben knew that Chinese seamen often carried inflatable goatskins known as the Huang Ho raft, preferring them to the kapok life jackets supplied on most Hong Kong registered vessels. He had also heard of the methods of interrogation used by the riverine cargo inspectors and saw no reason to doubt the laodah's report.

Entering it in the ship's log along with details of the storm he considered the episode closed but he knew he would need to check every crate, bale or drum he might carry in the future.

The man who had disappeared was the eldest of the schroffs, one who had sat apart when off watch, content to smoke his water pipe filled with rank cord tobacco. He had not looked like a smuggler of opium to Ben, or a man who would attempt to swim miles to shore in a heavy ground swell that still tossed and rolled the lorcha like an empty drum. It worried him more than he wished to admit. So did Yum Sup's expressionless face as he reported the incident.

The first metallic crack of dawn seamed the dark horizon to the east. On his port beam the lights of Ningpo glowed faintly, channel markers pricked the blackness far ahead and somewhere inshore a bell-buoy clanged like a funeral chime.

Ben handed the wheel to Yum Sup and went below. He stood for a moment, his hands gripping the shrouds, gazing out to where the land-mass slowly etched itself against the sky, the stars circled by misty rings, their flint sharpness gone. Somehow, he knew it would be pointless to put about in search of the old schroff and his inflated goatskin—so did Yum Sup, he was sure of that too. As Ben left the windy deck for the paraffin warmth of his cabin, the ruby and emerald navigation lights of a tramp steamer blinked on *China Cloud's* beam. Perhaps, he told himself, they had picked the old man up.

PART · III

Li X'ia

She who accepts the comb
will wear the black tzow of her sisters.
She will know only them
and her bowl will never be empty.
She who breaks the oath
will wear only the rags of a beggar.
She will know no one
and she will have no bowl.

THE OATH OF SAU HAI
Women Without Men

• IMAGE FOR LOVE •

The Cloud Line
Macau, 1924

FROM HIS office overlooking the Deverill boatyard, Ben could look down and see every corner of its workings. The sight of the magnificent vessel on the main slipway filled him with an immense pride. It represented all his dreams, all that he had ever wanted or loved. The perfect ship.

Almost fifteen years had passed since he first stepped ashore in Shanghai and at the age of twenty-nine Ben Deverill was a success. Since the launching of *China Cloud*, he had perfected the Chinese skill of buying and selling goods. While those European traders who operated their own vessels were almost entirely involved with the carrying of opium, Ben had looked to China's other richest trade-goods—silk, ivory, jadeite and fine porcelain, antiques, carpets, embroidered tapestries—the treasures of early Chinese culture that dated back thousands of years and which the salons of Paris and London, Rome and Berlin paid for handsomely.

He had made it his business to discover their sources and to study their origins and the various levels of value that distinguished them from each other.

In the early years he had explored the close reaches of the Canton Delta and soon discovered the silk-growing mulberry farms and spinning factories of the Shunde and Tailing districts. Buying the raw material, full cargoes of spun silk cones direct from the farms, his own lorchas now shipped them to the silk-crafting centres of Foochow, Shantung and Soochow where they were exquisitely woven and embroidered into the seductive products so sought after in fashionable continental salons. He also traded in certain rare herbs with life-preserving qualities, such as ginseng, aphrodisiacs and aromatic teas—all the popular fads and artifacts that graced the nobler homes of England from Bristol to Brighton. He was among the first to take advantage of the growing textile business of Canton.

In addition to the prosperous Deverill Company, he had established the Cloud Line. The Deverill yard had built seven lorchas, half of them designed specifically for the shallow-draught riverine trade and half for the heavier coastal and deep sea runs. With the help of Aggie Gates he had crewed them well and Ben had found experienced officers to command them.

All Cloud Line vessels were armed with modern weapons and had soon become known for their speed and efficiency in dealing with the cumbersome pirate junks foolish enough to approach them. This, coupled with the well-known fact that Ben Deverill's lorchas did not carry opium, but did carry heavy firepower, had kept them free from the hazards of piracy.

The mad gwai-lo who had risen from the mudflats of Macau had become known as Dai Fo Lo—the closest a Cantonese could come to his name, and his ships were given a wide berth. The jadeite ore he bought straight from the mining centres of south-eastern China was of no interest to them nor were the carved artifacts of ivory or the hand-painted chinaware, nor the bolts of silk or cheap cotton that filled his holds, when compared to the easily transported chests of opium balls. He had established trading contracts with several of Europe's leading dealers who took all that he could supply at prices that yielded an immense profit.

To do this he had sought out Captain Nathanial Barcoo, who had left the sea and was enduring a modest retirement in the London suburb of Battersea. The unexpected opportunity had given Nate a new reason for living. At a time when he had resigned himself to the prospect of building ships in empty rum bottles, he gave every ounce of his keen intelligence and formidable energy to the promotion and sale of Deverill trade goods. It had also opened up to him a level of society that he would otherwise never had known and he saw to it that the name of Deverill became the only one worth considering among the richest buyers and most prominent dealers in Europe. Above all else it had given him the opportunity to exorcise some of the guilt he felt over Frenchy Deverill's death and to play a useful part in the ambitious undertakings of his old friend's remarkable son.

Still a very active man with a lifetime in mercantile commerce, Nate had been overjoyed at the prospect of acting as Deverill's Limehouse-based agent. Both the fascination of the challenge and the generous commission he received had given him a renewed purpose in life and Ben Deverill's interests received the full benefit of his expert attention.

In no time Nate Barcoo had reinforced insurance and customs connections made over a long career at sea, selecting only the most reliable and efficient shipping lines engaged in the China trade, with many of the windjammer skippers well known to him, organising warehouse storage and a freight delivery service as efficiently as he had once supervised the manifests of *Windsong* and *Moshula*.

After the first three shipments, the last of them brought from Shanghai by his old command the *Moshula* on her final run, he had established a London office with the necessary tally clerks and runners plus the appointment of representative agents in the main trading cities of Europe. These activities too benefited from Nate Barcoo's skill in the choosing and commanding of personnel. The success of the Deverill trading company and its astonishing growth was largely due to the dependability and integrity of its London office.

Ben reached for the beautiful ship's decanter Nate had passed on to him on his first day in Shanghai and poured himself a stiff measure of rum. He thought fondly of those early days when Tugboat Aggie Gates had delivered him as a boy not yet sixteen aboard Indie da Silva's Hangchow trader.

He drank slowly and with quiet pleasure as he contemplated his plans. A year or two at the outside and the first stage of his goal would be complete—a sizeable fleet of riverine and coastal craft designed to travel faster and carry more than his fastest and biggest competition. Orders for Cloud Class trading clippers lined up for the next five years and beyond that would enable him to take over the Ho Sung yard.

From the slips below the voice of Captain Indie da Silva cursed loudly as he inspected the final touches being put to the beautiful clipper Ben had named *Cloud Chaser*. It had not been hard to persuade the Macanese to join him. Indie had run the Hangchow Bore for fifteen years and been at sea since childhood. Although Ben guessed he was well over fifty years old, a vintage Indie refused to discuss, Captain da Silva had the strength and boundless vigour of a much younger man.

At first he said no to joining Ben as shipping supervisor and partner. Then, when he saw the neat little villa close to the yard, with a view of the bay, a shaded garden and enough servants to let him live like a maharajah, Indie said he'd think it over. Reluctantly, he admitted that he had spent and gambled most of what he had made in the river trade. The profit share Ben offered him was too generous to turn down. It was time, he decided, after a respectable degree of persuasion, for a spell ashore. The *Trinidad* joined the Deverill fleet and Indie da Silva bought himself a wardrobe of fancy shore clothes.

Ben's attempts to buy out the Ho Sung yard were resisted as a matter of face. Chang-wa had never forgotten Dai Fo Lo, the gwai-lo. Although the price offered was far greater than its true worth, to admit that the gwai-lo who had once only commanded the laughter of children on the waterfront had beaten him was more than Chang-wa could allow. He had refused to discuss the subject of selling out to Deverill's and made it clear that he would find a way to close them down. It was the threat of a Chinese strongman who had sworn retribution and Ben did not take it lightly. It was a warning, given with all the menace and patience of a curse. He had put Yum Sup in charge of the yard under Indie da Silva's eagle eye and left for Hong Kong to open up Deverill's office in Queens Road Central, knowing that a day would come when he would have to face Chang the Fierce.

All had gone well over the next few years, and, now as he looked down at *Cloud Chaser* he could not have asked for more. She was the ultimate sailing vessel, magnificent even alongside the fast-raked opium schooners, the élite of the China trade, their owners sparing nothing in materials, workmanship and fittings. Ben had followed their example, importing what he couldn't buy and making with his own hands those features exclusive to a Cloud Line clipper.

Cloud Chaser boasted the best of the opium schooner, the best of the lorcha and all that he had learned of Chinese boat building. The splendid vessel was in the final stages of rigging and painting. He looked down to where coolies, with big chunks of pumice stone wrapped in sailcloth, scoured her decks.

Riggers swabbed the shrouds and ratlines with a mixture of white lead and tallow, coating the seizings with fresh layers of tar. Painters had picked out the topmasts in the same glossy black. Gleaming yellow masts and the rows of white gunports contrasted with the sleek length of her hull, black and polished as ebony. An artisan hung over the sweeping counter stern picking out the deep carved name in gold leaf—CLOUD CHASER. MACAU.

Ben was well aware that many in the trade were abandoning sail for steam, but for infiltrating the rivers and plying the China coast, sail could never be replaced and fine craft like the Cloud Class would always be in demand. The Ho Sung yard had finally sold out to him, Chang-wa's partners overriding his fierce protests.

The first thing Ben had done was to fire the yard boss and Chang had left swearing to take bitter revenge. The bad blood between them was widely known in Macau and Indie had doubled the security of the yard with a squad of armed sikhs. But the taipan of the Deverill Company was ready for the second stage of his plan—the move to Hong Kong and his place in colonial society.

The compradore he had established there had done well and although Ben knew the man was taking his squeeze, the Causeway Bay godowns were full and the trade goods were well purchased. Only one thing seemed to evade Ben in the steady fulfillment of his goals. Since the incident with Ling Ling the flower girl he had tried hard to forget about his need of a woman.

Now the time had come. As surely and as clearly as a storm leaves windswept sky Ben knew he must find himself a mate to give him a son, exactly as Frenchy had done. With a son beside him it was only time that could keep him from Shanghai—the fine house on the Bund and his place in Broadway Mansions towering over Soochow Creek. Once there nothing would take it from him . . . nothing could drive him away.

He raised his glass to the memory of Frenchy Deverill and contemplated the hardest task of all among these resolves. The finding of the mother of his child. He had no idea where to begin and found that of all his grand endeavours it bedevilled him the most.

Ten Willows

L I X'IA had never seen a foreign devil before, or anything like the strange and beautiful ship he came in. Its masts were taller and its hull sleeker than the fat cow shapes of the junks and river sampans that usually tied up at the wharf. From her place in the silkworm shed, its mat sides rolled up for the summer weather, she could see him clearly as he stepped with the laodah to the foot of the gangway.

The owner of the silk-weaving factory was already waiting. Although the great house was only a short walk from the river's edge he had come in his sedan chair and stayed in the shade of its embroidered canopy. He was a mandarin of high station and seldom spoke to those who came to load his silk. He watched as his compradore and foreman met with Ben and Yum Sup and the bargaining began.

Li X'ia marvelled at the colour of the gwai-lo's hair, how it gleamed like new bronze in the midday sun, curling low on his neck. His bare arms and shoulders were strong and wide beside those around him. When he turned his head she could see that the same coppery curls covered his cheeks and chin. It made her gasp. Li had never seen such hair on the face of a man.

'Why do you stare at this barbarian? Is he not an abomination to eyes such as ours?'

The voice of Ah Chai, the overseer, was close beside her and Li X'ia started in surprise. Ah Chai was the name given to Elder Sister but it often seemed to Li that she did not always behave like a sister. Her tongue was keen and cruel as a naked blade and although there were times when she seemed kind, even with the sweetness of lotus honey, she would quickly change like a cloud crossing the sun. Ah Chai turned on the other girls and stopped their giggling with the sharpness of her voice.

'Do you think, little fools, you will become true sisters of Sau Hai if you gawp like fish at this lumbering ape? You offend me and you offend your ancestors. You will never work at the looms if you behave like clucking hens in search of a rooster.'

Ah Chai's voice lowered and was gentler as she smiled at Li X'ia. 'Six years you have been with us. Soon you will be ready to join the sisterhood.' Her hand lifted hesitantly, then briefly touched Li's hair. 'You are not like the others. I have watched you grow. You are known as the Silent One. You work hard and do not complain. Soon you will be ready for the looms.'

Her smile was gone as she looked towards the group on the jetty. 'Is not the barbarian hideous?' she sneered. 'He is like all men, an abomination to all things gentle and beautiful. It is better to close your eyes to them. Barbarians are evil-smelling as the wild goat, hair grows upon him almost as thickly. He is a creature of foul habit.'

She flapped a hand before her nose and pulled an unpleasant face. 'Many of them do not wash and they blow snot into a piece of cloth to keep it in their pocket. I have seen them do this with my own eyes.'

Her hand closed with one firm squeeze of Li's upper arm then slid lightly down to take her hand. She spread the fingers gently and stroked the palm. 'These fingers should not be red as steamed shrimp from the boilers. This palm should not be rough from tending trees on the hillside. These hands are butterfly hands.'

Li X'ia ate her rice and fish alone when work was finished for the day. While the others chattered she stole glances at the barbarian's magnificent ship. The hatches were closed and the crew squatted around the cooking stove on the stern and played cards. Ah Chai ate her meals with the compradore in the special room attached to the large kitchen, so Li was free to look as much as she wished.

Until coming to Ten Willows she had never set eyes on a river craft of any kind and she had thought them grand when first she saw the heavy hulls of trading junks ploughing up and down the river as slowly as oxen, the sun lighting their great wings of sail, rich brown as newly turned earth, or the deep magenta of an abbot's robes. She had soon found that the men who sailed them were crude and oafish as herdboys or the wood carriers who scoured the hills to feed the boilers, plodding like donkeys, bent beneath their loads.

She had heard the junkmen talk of this gwai-lo and his many lorchas, faster than any other, swifter than the clouds they were named after when driven by the wind. They said he was mad and dangerous as a stray dog in search of food and that aboard this, his finest ship, he kept weapons of great destruction. This was why the lord of the great house had chosen him to carry the silk. Not only was his ship faster and able to carry greater loads, but it also protected its cargo from pirates. All those along the river who shipped raw silk to the northern cities knew of this.

As she watched, the laodah cuffed a crewman, sending him scurrying to slacken the lines that tied the tall ship to the factory wharf as the rising tide put strain on them. The sun had almost set and its last light glinted on the gilt dragons carved on the broad stern and shone warmly on oiled wood. She looked for the one the junk crews called Dai Fo Lo, or 'Lionhead who flies with the Clouds', but he was not there. Brasswork gleamed, turning red as flame, the topmasts and rigging white as pipeclay against the evening sky. The ship was the most wonderful thing Li had ever seen. The next day, it was gone.

She did not sleep well. It was a windy night and the mat shed she shared with the other uninitiated girls creaked and flapped against its bamboo frame. What sleep she found was filled with visions of the barbarian at the wheel of his vessel, sailing the stormy clouds. It was still dark when Li X'ia heard the wood gatherers lighting the fires under the boilers. Each morning she had been woken as they cursed the blackness of their lives. The big iron boilers where the cocoons were scalded to kill the moth were close by the sleeping quarters and the foul language they used was intended to be heard.

Their taunts were always the same. About the sisters of Sau Hai, the eternal virgins who, they whispered, would never know the weight of a good man. Those who were afraid of the jade stem. Inviting them to meet among the mulberry trees, to open the jade gate before it closed forever. This would cause much laughter among the wood gatherers as they whispered their names close to the shed, promising great pleasure to the one who chose them.

At first Li did not understand. There had been no servants on her father's farm and few visitors. The days had been long and hard with little time for chatter and gossip. She knew nothing of the world when she was sold to the silk factory and had never heard of the sisterhood of Sau Hai. The older girls had told her. Some of them giggled behind their hands. Others, less foolish, spoke of it in whispers and there was fear or wonder in their eyes.

Once they reached the age of fourteen, the girls had explained, a wooden comb and a small mirror would be found on the bed space beside the wooden block of the pillow. It gave the occupant of the bed two choices: to toss the comb and the mirror aside with the words 'These things do not belong to me. I wear my hair in a pigtail,' or to take the comb and the mirror to Elder Sister, and say, 'Ah Chai. These things have been given to me. I no longer wish to wear the pigtail.' The girl who made this choice would then be initiated into the sisterhood of Sau Hai and from that moment take the oath to remain celibate and forever separate from men. Her pigtail would be wound into a tight bun at the nape of her neck and she would wear only the black tzow of the Sau Hai, a uniform of high-necked tunic and wide-legged trousers. Once she wore the comb she would depend on Elder Sister for all her needs, forever proof that she had taken the sacred oath of sisterhood.

To deny the comb meant there would be no promotion to the loom or the weaving shed. No sleeping in the comfortable hut of the sisters. None of the privileges and protection they enjoyed. She would be cast aside to remain on the hillsides tending the silkworm and killing the moths until she was old and sick. If she was not owned by the factory, Ah Chai would send her away. If she stayed her life would not be a pleasant one. No girl had ever denied the comb since Li X'ia had joined the factory.

The privileges of the weaving shed were great. The sisters took care of each other and even those bonded to the mandarin were paid a small wage when they became productive at the looms. The work was interesting compared to gathering cocoons and once the skill of 'finding the thread' was achieved it was also pleasant. The silkworm wound the cocoon into a ball so tight that only the sharpest eyes and nimblest fingers could be trusted to find its end, fine as a spider's web, and wind it onto the spindle without breaking. Then came the bleaching, threading and twisting into two, three or four ply before spinning the silk onto spools for shipment to the dyers and embroiderers in Soochow, the great rail centre on the Grand Canal, and Swatow, the place of foreign trade on the Han River.

When Li returned from the hillside the day after the barbarian's ship had sailed away, the wooden comb and small round mirror lay neatly arranged beside her head-rest. After the evening rice and vegetables had been eaten she picked them up and looked around at the girls who had become her friends.

'What choice will you make, Li X'ia?' one of them asked in the hush. Li shrugged.

'What choice is there? I will become Sau Hai.'

A younger one spoke, her voice a whisper, 'It means you will never marry. Never bear children of your own.'

Another girl said, 'You will never wear pretty things. Your hair will never blow free in the wind.' She giggled behind her hand. 'Nor will you ever know the pleasure of the jade stem.'

'They will never let you go.' said another. 'You will die the death of a pig if you break the oath.'

When Li had left the shed they looked at each other in silence. Some with envy. Some with fear.

The quarters of Ah Chai were quite splendid after the bare earthen floor of the mat shed. Li had left her wooden kegs at the door and she stood with her bare feet upon a carpet for the first time. A red-painted shrine to Kuan Yin, lit by candles, hung above the door behind her and the scent of burning sandalwood filled the small room.

'These things have been given to me. I no longer wish to wear the pigtail.'

Li X'ia spoke as strongly as she could but she trembled inside. She did not know why. Beside the scarlet bed curtain Ah Chai sat at a round table, upon a painted stool of glazed porcelain. She had reseated herself after answering Li's knock, now she indicated a matching stool on the other side of the table.

'Sit down, Little Sister.' She studied Li for a long moment without speaking, her eyes almost closed. At last she spoke. 'You understand the meaning of Sau Hai? You know what is required of you?'

Li nodded. 'I think so, Elder Sister.'

Ah Chai waited again. 'And you have made your choice?'

'I think so, Elder Sister.' Li laid the comb and the mirror on the table.

'It is not enough to think,' Ah Chai said softly. 'You must be sure.' She rose and came around the table. 'I too must be sure you are worthy of the sisterhood.' Passing her hand gently over the top of Li's head she lifted the heavy plaited pigtail. 'If you accept the comb and the mirror you will no longer have need of this.'

She began undoing the plaits with strong, deft, fingers. 'Your hair is dry as summer grass, mui mui. I will oil it for you.' She used the endearment for a beloved little sister, reaching for a small bottle and shaking drops of perfumed oil into her palms, rubbing them briskly together, the jade bracelets on her wrists clinking sharply. Shaken loose, Li's hair cloaked her shoulders and hung down her back in a glossy cape.

Ah Chai's strong hands smoothed it, wound and twisted its thickness into a rope, running it through her scented fingers again and again, coiling it skilfully at the back of Li's head and fixing it in place with the comb. She handed Li the tiny mirror.

'Look closely, Li X'ia. If you are to become Sau Hai only a woman's eyes may gaze into yours. You must be sure.' Her hands rested lightly on Li's shoulders, 'and so must I.'

Almost without movement her fingers began to knead and press and stroke the shoulders.

'Only a woman's hands may comfort you.'

The fingers slid to the exposed nape of Li X'ia's slender neck, the balls of her thumbs expertly feeling for the vertebrae, applying gentle pressure. Li felt her tension melt. It was the first time in her life that hands had touched her with such tenderness.

'Only a woman may care for you.' Ah Chai's voice was low and close to her ear as the comforting movement grew slightly stronger, bolder. Li's head learned forward, exquisitely relaxed, exposing the full length of her neck to Ah Chai's hands, the protected skin beneath her hair white and soft as an infant's. So deep was the sense of relaxation Li felt engulfing her that she hardly noticed Ah Chai's hands slide forward to caress her throat, hardly heard the words now whispered into her ear. Only the warmth of Ah Chai's breath told her how close she was. Lips touched her ear, lightly as moth's wings.

'Do not be afraid. I will teach you.'

Only when she felt the comforting warmth of Ah Chai's hands move smoothly from her throat into the loose-fitting tunic to find her breasts, were her senses fully awakened. So sudden and sure was the movement that Li felt her nipples rise and stiffen as they slipped between Ah Chai's warm oiled fingers, the strong palms cupping the fullness of her bosom. The fluttering in the pit of her belly that she had thought of as fear, suddenly flared. Blood rushed to her face and her cheeks burned hot. It was as though she were under a spell.

'Only a woman may give you the pleasures of the flower drum.'

Li felt Ah Chai's parted lips suddenly pressed to her neck, the moist tip of her tongue. Part of her wanted it to continue and as though she knew, Ah Chai's thumbs grazed simultaneously over the points of her breasts. The shock of it was electric, acting as a trigger to Li's whirling emotions. Her head connected sharply with Ah Chai's mouth as she shot to her feet, overturning the table, smashing the mirror. Ah Chai's curses flew in a string of abuse. Clutching her bleeding lip with one hand, the other struck out as Li tried to reach the door. Flinging it open, Li X'ia ran from the hut to where the lamplight showed through the cracks of the mat shed.

It was almost a month before Li saw the barbarian's ship again. Through the weave of the pig basket she could see the white tops of its masts gliding above the abundant willows that gave the village its name. Its scarlet and yellow pennant streamed above its snow-white sails. She tried to move her head to follow its progress but the pig basket held her too tightly and her muscles had grown stiff throughout the night.

Since the time in Ah Chai's quarters life for Li had been a succession of cruel injustices and great misery. The supervisor had left her alone for a week and then approached her again. She regretted the incident, she said. She had been too hasty, too eager to please her little sister and had not meant to frighten her.

But Li had had time to think. She did not understand the emotions that had gripped her. She only knew that they were not natural. That they were wrong in the eyes of the gods. She had been allowed to share little of her father's deep religion but on the few occasions that she had knelt with him and her mother and brothers before the stern faces of those she was told were her ancestors, she had been deeply afraid of offending them.

Her mother had told her nothing of men but she had heard enough talk among her brothers and among the wood gatherers and herdboys to know that what had happened was wrong and that only evil spirits could have led her on such a path.

When she tried to explain her fears, Ah Chai had smiled with understanding, spoken encouragingly and tried to take her hand. When Li stepped back from her touch, the smile had vanished and the flat mask of anger had replaced it. She must accept the comb and she must take her place with her sisters. If she did not, her hands would grow red as the comb of a cockerel and her bones become stiff from the steam of the boilers and the frosts of the hillside.

On the day the sisters went to fetch her from the mat shed Li X'ia was not in her cot. She had not been there when the wood gatherers lit the boilers, the others said. In the night Li had run the five miles to her father's farm and thrown herself at his feet. He had beaten her for her ingratitude and for causing him to lose face at the house of the mandarin and in the village of Ten Willows. Then he had taken her back to the supervisor, insisting that she be punished for her disobedience and presenting six live chickens and small money in a red packet. Ah Chai had smiled tolerantly and promised that it would not happen again. Li X'ia would be suitably punished.

Li had been made to work at the boilers, without the diversions of the hillside. She was tethered like a goat to an iron stake in the ground to show she could not be trusted. She wore only a smock cut from a corn sack. Her hair had been roughly chopped off and around her neck a dead chicken was hung. Its stink kept the others well away from her and she was forced to sleep in the open with the animals. It made great sport for the wood gatherers.

When it was over and Li stood before Ah Chai, scrubbed raw with brooms and wearing a new tunic and trousers, the overseer's manner was again honey-sweet. 'This terrible thing is done now. You have had time to think about your decision.' She poured the bitter tea of Swatow from the pewter teapot and handed a thimble-sized cup to Li.

'It is the rule of the great house to punish those who break their bond. I could do nothing to help you.'

The effect of the punishment had been to dull Li's senses to everything around her. She had learned to look only at the sky and the ground, the clusters of cocoons and the flames under the boilers as she killed 10,000 times 10,000 moths. Her mind had hardened but her heart knew that she had done no wrong. The wooden comb of Sau Hai and a new mirror were placed on the round table exactly as before.

'Have you reconsidered?' The smile was bright on Ah Chai's face. 'Surely nothing can be so bad as that which you have suffered,' she crooned, slowly offering her hand. 'Come, mui mui. Nothing can be so bad.'

Tears gleamed in Li X'ia's eyes, escaped down her cheeks. She made no attempt to stop them except to close her eyes tightly and bow her head.

'I cannot,' was all she said. And the sun on Ah Chai's face quickly went behind the cloud.

Ah Chai thought very carefully on what to do about the Silent One. She saw nothing but good in the sisterhood of which she was proud to be an elder. Her strict adherence to the code was one of the reasons they had made her supervisor. Those at the great house wanted none of the village pregnancies and misguided relationships that plagued so many other businesses and were often the ruin of many a poor family. The 'larn jai', the 'louts' who laboured in the fields or stole from the market had no more sense of conduct when it came to rutting than the animals they worked among and many of the girls knew little better.

As in the houses with many female servants, the disciplines created by the oath of Sau Hai were held as a respectable alternative to chaos. Without them the cook would be pregnant to the gardener, the kitchen maid to the houseboy and in the case of her own domain, half of the factory staff would be lost to her with broken cherries and bastard children.

It took many years to train good silk weavers and they were too valuable to replace easily. So, the sisterhood protected and cared for its own as surely as the nuns in a convent. When it came to desires not easily contemplated without a male there were skilful methods of satisfying them without harm or offence. It was why Ah Chai accepted the responsibility of assessing a novice's understanding before the ritual step was taken. What she did not fully admit was that this aspect of her power had become a fascination, beyond her contol.

To some it was of no importance, as such thoughts seldom if ever raised themselves and the prospect of total celibacy was not seen as a challenge or a sacrifice. To others it was a welcome alternative to the clumsy and often brutal attentions of village men. There were some who embraced it fully, establishing strong and lasting relationships. Occasionally, there was one such as Li X'ia who thought more deeply and whose passions were stronger than she knew. Such a one was a disturbance to stability and, an even greater danger, a threat to Ah Chai's position and authority.

She did not particularly like what she had decided to do but she comforted herself that she had been both patient and forgiving. It was quite clear that Li X'ia had no intention of changing her mind. This girl had excited her and she had moved too quickly. For this Ah Chai took some responsibility. But if she took no further action the others would see Li X'ia's victory as an alternative to Sau Hai and this would quickly weaken her influence.

She reminded herself that before the great house accepted a girl child, the parents were told of the Sau Hai code upon which the spinning sheds were run and that they could buy back the child before the age of sixteen if a suitable husband had been found or family fortunes had changed for the better. It was not her fault if Li's father had chosen not to tell her of the arrangement, and had no intention of reclaiming her. She would make an example. It was her duty.

The boy she had chosen was from the far north. He had come to Ten Willows aboard an Antung trader, one of the big, barge-like junks that seldom ventured as far south as the Pearl River. The junk was far from home, its holds packed with gnull-see, the cattle dung fertiliser used on the riverside farms to fortify the nightsoil. Such a shit-scow as this could be smelled long before it reached a river bend and when tied up it stayed well away from other craft to avoid being stoned.

This one was moored a quarter mile from the silk factory jetty, almost hidden by an arch of willows in a rush-choked backwater. The boy stank as evilly as the barge he worked on when Ah Chai had approached him. He had put down his wooden buckets and watched her coming down the tow path. The money she offered was little enough but more than the boy had ever held in his hand before and he snatched it greedily. He knew of little but hardship and filth but his slow brain comprehended well enough what was expected of him in exchange.

Ah Chai had told him exactly where to find Li X'ia and what he was to do to her. The teeth had been knocked from the front of the boy's mouth and he had shoved his tongue through the gap in an obscene show of relish. He would go at night. The girl, Ah Chai explained slowly, would be tied like a goat. She could not escape. When her screams brought others from the mat shed, he would claim she had consented, that she was willing. Then he would run back to the tunnel of trees and the shit-scow where no one would follow. She, Ah Chai, would see to it.

The plan had worked well. No one questioned the details of what had taken place or the justice of Ah Chai's verdict. The boy from Antung had been very convincing in his lies before running away and the junk had sailed the next morning as she had been told it would. It had not been difficult to stir the feelings of the Sau Hai sisters—while there was one among them to condemn, they were safe. It was a chance to show Elder Sister their loyalty and even those who had been a friend to Li were soon caught up in righteous frenzy. She had broken the code.

Ben was below entering figures into the cargo log when he heard the noise. It ebbed and flowed like a tide beneath the voices of his men preparing to take aboard the silk. It became louder and more excited as he closed the book with a sigh. Another fight among his crew and the junkmen. He went on deck to stop the trouble but found his deckhands lining the handrails and in the rigging. They were watching a group of women dressed in black, their hair tied severely back in the style of the household servant. He had seen their kind before but never in a large group of twenty or more. It made them a sinister and formidable sight.

From a distance they seemed to be all alike but as they drew closer to the edge of the river he could see some were very young and others older. Between them they were half dragging, half rolling something towards the river's edge just astern of *Cloud Chaser*. He saw that it was a common pig basket, seen on every farm and in every marketplace, woven of willow twigs, made to restrain the struggles of a doomed sow. Yum Sup watched from the stern rail.

'Who are they? What are they doing?'

The laodah turned at the sound of Ben's voice. He was grinning happily. 'They are Sau Hai. Women without men.' He laughed, turning back, not wanting to miss the eerie spectacle. 'In the basket is one of their kind who has disgraced them.'

Ben was beside him, his wide brown hands gripping the rail. Yum Sup hauled himself up into the mizzen ratlines to get a better view.

'If she has broken the code of Sau Hai, they will drown her. She is no longer Little Sister. She is hah dung gai—low class whore.'

Ben watched fascinated as the grotesque bundle was hauled down the muddy river bank, almost under the swoop of *Cloud Chaser*'s stern. He was aware of a sustained and terrified wailing, almost smothered by the hissing and nattering of the black-clad women.

The bundle was rolled down the last stretch of river bank and into the shallows and the wail became a shrill squeal of despair. His loud shouts had no effect as the thing was jostled further into the waters. The women slipped and slid after it. The clinging yellow mud increased their yells and mocking laughter. The basket pushed and kicked, to sink, pale as a corpse, into deep water. The pitiful cries were stopped by a welter of dirty bubbles.

Ben's dive from *Cloud Chaser*'s stern brought crows of delight from his crew. He entered the water cleanly and surfaced only yards from where the basket had submerged. There was sudden silence as with one quick breath he again disappeared, swimming strongly down the slope of the bank, sheering steeply into the green depths. Following the mud trail left by the weighted basket bumping its way to the bottom, he saw the awful coffin, already rolling in the current, a chain of bubbles belching from inside. His knife ripped at the straw binding; loosened by the water, the tough twig casing came away.

A howl of fury greeted him as he surfaced with Li in his arms, to be quickly joined by the cheers of his crew. They had produced drum and cymbals to add to the spectacle, and someone had lit a string of firecrackers. The Sau Hai had waded into the water up to their knees as he dragged the girl to the shallows, falling upon him like crows on a carcass when he tried to rise and lift her clear. Some clawed at him while others tried to push and pull Li's unconscious body back into the swift current. Only when Ben made wide sweeps with the knife was he able to drag her clear, shouting for Yum Sup to bring help.

The big joke over and still grinning with the fun of it, *Cloud*

Chaser's crew herded the Sau Hai sisters back up the river bank and into their factory compound, while Ben drained the river water from the girl's lungs. From the window space of her quarters Ah Chai watched, calling down the curses of all gods upon the foreign devil and all his heirs and ancestors.

Ben was amazed at how little he had to pay for a sixteen-year-old girl. The owner of the silk factory and his compradore showed very little interest in the fate of Li X'ia. They were more concerned with the time that was being lost in the weaving sheds.

Ben pointed out that to drown the girl was a waste. She was worth good money. He apologised to the mandarin and offered the leather and brass-bound telescope as a gift of respect. The compradore relayed his apologies and presented the telescope and it was accepted, along with a tael of silver. Li X'ia's papers were brought from the house and she was legally his.

The Fish

I T WAS three days before they reached Macau and tied up at the commercial jetty. Ben had left the girl down in the small after cabin he kept for occasional passengers. She stayed shivering with fear when he brought her hot food, unable to even reach out for it. He had left it on the floor and withdrawn, locking the door, afraid she would run for the rail if she were loose. After a while he sent Ah Poo down with a bucket of hot water and a dry blanket but she had refused them and he had left shaking his head. Ben was thankful when, at last, she was brought safely into the house.

Ah Ho, the senior amah, looked Li X'ia up and down with open disgust. Foul yellow mud still clung to her and matted her hair.

'She would let no one on board wash her.' said Ben. 'Not even Ah Poo.'

Before the amah could speak, Li raised her head and saw the flat featureless face, the hair drawn severely back into a tight bun, the black tunic and trousers of Sau Hai.

She shrank away in terror and crouched in a corner, the fear in her eyes centred on Ah Ho. Nothing Ben could do or say would shift her. Only the old kitchen amah, the one they called the Fish, could get close to her. She was very old, good only for peeling vegetables and sweeping the yard, but the hardship of a long and difficult life had not taken the kindness from her face or the trace of sympathy from her voice. She squatted beside Li, pushing the muddy hair from her face.

'Let the old woman take care of her,' Ben ordered. 'She has been through bad times.' He signalled the Fish to get up.

'Get her clean and let her rest. Then find something for her to do.'

Ah Ho's eyes showed no expression as she spoke. 'Is she to stay in this house, master?'

'Yes. I have paid for her. She will be mooi-jai here.'

Ah Ho paused, her eyes avoiding his, then turned to the Fish crouching beside the terrified girl. 'Set her to work in the scullery,' she hissed, unable to hide her disapproval. 'She is your responsibility.'

As Li X'ia was led away, Ben wondered if he had been a fool to interfere. He knew that life was cheap in China, especially the life of an unwanted female. Well, she was not seriously hurt and the strength that had returned when he tried to examine her for injury had surprised him. He shrugged. It was done. Ben Deverill now owned a girl slave.

The old woman was patient and kind. She left Li to bathe in the scullery, an annexe off the kitchen filled with brass and clay pots, earthen crocks, pots and jars. The walls were hung with ladles, knives and choppers and from the ceiling dried meat, fish and herbs surrounded a half-eaten side of pork. A huge stone sink dominated the crammed space and it was here, with pans of hot water from the kitchen stove and at the iron pump, that Li had cleaned herself. Cotton nightclothes and the fresh white tunic and black trousers of a mooi-jai had been left on the stretcher. She had slept for fifteen hours.

For the first week Li was confined to the little space the Fish had made for her in the store-room. A cot of jute cloth stretched across a wooden frame had been placed beside the one the old woman slept in. Both were surrounded by sacks of rice, jars of wine and cooking oil, pickles, dry goods, and produce from the market. The smell of it was comforting to Li, reminding her of her place on her father's farm, and its semi-darkness was cool and somehow safe. The old woman let her stay there and brought her food until she was well enough to work.

For several weeks Li X'ia saw nothing of the gwai-lo master. He had saved her life, yet showed no further interest in her. He was away at sea, the old woman said when she asked, or at the boatyard where he built his ships. She also saw very little of Ah Ho, the house amah, or any of the other servants. The scullery and storeroom were the domain of the Fish. The others had their own work to do and their own quarters; for them to enter the scullery was not necessary.

Li told the Fish what had happened to her at the hands of Ah Chai and the Sau Hai at Ten Willows, and the reasons for her fear of Ah Ho. The Fish chuckled reassuringly. 'Have no fear of her in that way. She is too busy squeezing this household and playing mahjongg to bother with you. You are safe here with me.' She cackled again. 'That one wears the comb of Sau Hai but she is more interested in the gardener than the little sisters. Things are different here in Macau.'

Through the open door of the scullery Li could see the tiled rooftops of the city and beyond them the misty green mountains of China. Each morning a cheerful Hakka woman, full of gossip, came to the door with a cartload of fresh produce: plump wongbok cabbage, bunches of long white radish, dark green clusters of buk choy, the Chinese spinach, choy sum, onions and a succulent choice of fresh fruits. Li was perfectly content to chop and peel and dice and shred, taking her meals with the Fish on an upturned box in a corner of the scullery or outside on the doorstep with chickens pecking around their feet.

Twice each week there was fresh fish to buy from the Hoklo fishermen on the waterfront. This was a task especially left to the Fish by Ah Ho who considered herself above the business of haggling with fishermen.

'You may come with me today. You are strong now and will be much faster than these old bones. I will show you how to choose fish and how to bargain with fishermen.'

The abundant food, the company of the kind old woman and the sanctuary of the store-room had combined to restore Li's health. The thick black hair the Sau Hai had hacked off was quickly growing, her skin was clear and her eyes were diamond bright. Li had never felt so well in her life. The Macau waterfront surrounded her with wonder. The Fish showed her the markets where everything was sold from songbirds to sausages, sunshades to live monkeys, where fortune-tellers did business beside tinsmiths, snake charmers, acrobats and performing bears. Eating houses and teashops thrived beside coffin makers and calligraphers. In the kite-maker's shop she was presented with a bright yellow butterfly kite. The kite-maker also sold joss sticks, paper money for burning as gifts for the dead and demon-dispelling prayers painted on strips of red paper. The Fish bought all such things from his shop, so a paper kite was no sacrifice for good business.

But it was the wide, cobbled boulevarde with its granite sea wall, noisy with rickshaws and sedan chairs, donkey and ox carts, motor cars and lorries that fascinated Li X'ia. Past them, on the wide waters of the Praia Grande, sampans surrounded the anchored ships like ants feeding off cicadas. It was here that the Hoklo and Tanka fishermen beached their boats on the mudflat at low tide and sold their catch fresh from the wide mouth of the Pearl River.

The Fish was well known to all she spoke to, and when she told them Li was the mooi-jai to the house of the lion-headed gwai-lo, the chaser of clouds, they were filled with sympathy. Had he not once defied Chang the Fierce and built a ship single-handed right here on the mudflats? The same mad giant who had left Jo Maltese the mulatto half dead among the fishheads. They remembered him well. He was known to eat the flesh of babies. Li told them they were wrong about her master. He had saved her life, given his magic eye and a tael of silver to save her. He treated her well.

'He is no ordinary gwai-lo,' she protested. But nothing she could say would change the minds of the water people. To them Ben Deverill was still a baby eater.

Villa Formosa

IN THE year of 1925 Ben spent much of his time on Hong Kong island, leaving the Macau yard and its business to Indie da Silva.

The colony was crippled by an engineers' and seamens' strike that tied up normal foreign shipping and left Deverill's to continue trading under the Cloud Line's Macau registry. They had fifteen lorchas doing business in China waters, mainly in the silk and jade trade, with the others on the Grand Canal carrying porcelain and artifacts from Peking to the Shanghai godowns. The Deverill house flag had become a common sight coming and going from Macau's commercial jetty or tied up in Hong Kong's Causeway Bay.

The trouble had begun in Shanghai's international settlement when British police had opened fire on anti-foreign demonstrations. It had swiftly spread to Hong Kong where Communist and Kuomintang agitators cooperated with the secret societies to boycott British goods. The Cloud Line took full advantage of the forced trade embargo and the Deverill Company flourished because of it.

Ben was building a house on a large section of land on Hong Kong Island. It faced the South China Sea at the place they had named Repulse Bay, far enough out of the fast-growing business centre and first choice of any who could afford to live there. Villa Formosa was to be a mansion, grand even by the standards of the few wealthy merchants who had made their selection in the hills around the bay, surrounded by verdant cow pasture and the acres of their walled gardens.

The wide portals of its entrance, balustraded balconies and high, shuttered windows were styled after the homes of the Macau Portuguese. The richly ornate roof of rice-green tiles trimmed with gold swept in gently curving eaves and winged corners that were classically Chinese. Ben had shipped much of the material himself; the porcelain tiles had come from Peking, ornamental stone and rare timbers from Chinchow and Tunghwa.

The holds of *Cloud Chaser* had carried fine antiques, rosewood and blackbean furniture, and silken tapestries from Hangchow. Only the finest craftsmen worked on the site of Villa Formosa and he was there every day to check on its progress.

The gardens were planted by landscape artists he brought from Canton to lay out rare trees and shrubs—shore juniper, dawn redwood, cherry plum and red silk cotton trees and an orchard of persimmon, kumquat and prince of orange.

As he watched the house rise, Ben thought often of Frenchy and wondered where they had buried him. In the little churchyard lined with yew trees within the sound of hymnals and amens? Or in a pauper's grave in the unkempt plot set aside for gypsies and vagabonds?

Success had given Ben position and was well on the way to giving him greater power. He had been welcomed into the Royal Hong Kong Yacht Club where his Cloud Class vessels were officially recognised and he had been asked to become the club commodore. He was a member of the exclusive Hong Kong Club and the Kowloon Cricket Club. He owned horses at Happy Valley and was on every worthwhile guest list in the colony. It wasn't enough. There was no one to share it with.

It had not been possible for him to allow Li X'ia to pass unnoticed when he stayed at the house in Macau. In six months the girl in the pig basket had blossomed into a beautiful young woman, radiant with health. Her face shone from within as though what had happened to her had given her strength and vision beyond others of her class. Although he had little contact with her, it was impossible to ignore the strong lines of her body, the capable, graceful way she carried herself when she passed the window of his study to work in the garden. Ah Ho did not allow her beyond the kitchen within the house and he noticed the amah's attitude towards the mooi-jai had not softened with the passing months. Outside her scullery work Li was given only hard and demeaning jobs to do, kept at them from dawn to dark. The girl seemed to take it all without complaint and he had often heard her humming to herself as she struggled with the larp sarp bins, the accumulated rubbish of the house.

Ben's hatred of opium and the people who traded in it had always kept him well away from the elaborate establishments that were Macau's main attraction for the rich Chinese from Hong Kong and the mainland. The tiny enclave's lawless reputation, its gambling dens and brothels, catered to every taste, from the exquisite to the abominable. The sickly haze of opium smoke hung behind almost every door that had pleasure and enjoyment to sell, from the richest of casinos and bordellos in the fashionable quarter to the most squalid of opium divans, fan-tan parlours and whore-houses along the waterfront.

As the memory of Ling Ling the Shanghainese flower girl faded, sex, like the company of true friends, was something Ben had learned to do without. The slums of the dock area and the fringes of the city were always a reminder of the unchecked ravages of syphilis. The blind, the disfigured and the insane peopled them like a leper colony. He had seen sailors in Shanghai rotting with shankers and the horrific buboes that could be the price of a moment's abandon. It was a risk he was not prepared to take.

Although he often accompanied Indie to the finer clubs and restaurants, gorgeously decorated and luxurious palaces of pleasure, Ben had resisted all attempts to find him a woman. Indie da Silva looked upon those things quite differently and was an honoured guest in such places. He was a spender, a gambler and a giver of generous gifts to the women he took to bed. His suspicion that Ben was still a virgin filled him with genuine concern. He had begun to fear the worst. Impotence was looked upon in China, or anywhere else so far as Carlos da Silva was concerned, as the ultimate horror, and one of the few things to be truly feared above all others.

Tall, stately mandarin beauties, dark-skinned creatures from the Malay States, India, the Celebes, the Philippines, Siam and Burma, even a half-wild Dyak from the jungles of Borneo were laid at Ben Deverill's feet, set upon his lap, sometimes sent to his door and on occasions found waiting in his bed.

The fact that they were all sent away wined and dined but otherwise intact, threatened da Silva's sanity. Had he not tried everything to make the son of Frenchy Deverill happy? Eventually, with a sad shake of his head and a short prayer for his partner's manhood, he had accepted the situation as hopeless and given up.

Ben had not expended time or thought to the emptiness that he had lived with for so long. There had been too much to be done and he did not feel the loneliness for long. The excitement of where he was going and what he was doing had been enough. But now, with so much accomplished, the ache had come to stay and there was nothing to replace it. He was almost thirty and knew the time had come.

It was not an easy thing to do. The European women he sometimes met at the clubs in Hong Kong viewed him either with extreme caution or made themselves too readily available. The young colony was breeding very definite social strata and although his success and financial standing gave him entry, Ben Deverill did not quite fit.

His reputation as the renegade of doubtful heritage who had carved his start single-handed on the mudflats of Macau gave him colour but not status in the eyes of the Hong Kong establishment. He was seen as a waterfront brawler who had gone native with a knife-fighting Macanese and it was whispered that together they had scoured the fleshpots of China.

There was no place for him among the ranks of the Eurasian families that were beginning to expand from mainland business centres like Shanghai and Harbin, or those already established as pillars of the merchant community. Their ranks were closed to all but their own people and a soldier of fortune like Ben Deverill was welcome to do business but that was all.

One sultry night at the height of summer, it was too hot to sleep. Reading was made difficult by the shrilling of crickets, a cloud of moths circling the gas lamp and the endless clatter, shuffle and bang of mahjongg tiles from the gardeners' gatehouse. It made him think of the Place of Red Lanterns and the candle-lit sampan. At times like this the thoughts returned—even the humiliation he had felt could not bury the sight of her nakedness beneath him or the taste and feel of her skin. He reached for the ship's decanter to find it was almost empty and when he went to the lacquered cabinet where he kept his grog, there was no rum. Cursing Ah Ho for her negligence he padded barefoot through the house to fetch a bottle from the store-room.

Approaching the scullery doorway, he stopped, stunned by what he saw. Standing in a wooden washtub by the big stone sink, lit by a single candle flame, stood the girl from Ten Willows. The soft glow of the steady flame traced the contours of her naked body. She had her back to him and the straight, supple line of her spine made a slight shadow leading to sleek flanks, legs that were exceptionally long and slender for a Chinese peasant girl. As she worked the pump handle to fill the water pitcher, he could see well-formed muscles working beneath the smooth, dusky skin. Her hair clung to her strong shoulders as she tipped cooling water slowly over her head, the shock of it causing her to rise on her toes, stretching and arching her body to receive its touch. Her head thrown back, her eyes closed tight, she turned slowly in the tub, on her toes like a ballerina.

Ben watched breathlessly as the water cascaded down her hair, her face, her neck and shoulders to trace the intimate curves and crevices of her body. Her lips parted in a gasp of pleasure as it flowed over her hot skin. Over her breasts, their plum-dark nipples tight and awake, down the slight swell of her belly to the small tuft of pubic hair and on down her parted thighs. He heard her sigh. Little more than a breath. So ecstatic, so exquisitely yielding that it sent a wave of pure longing through Ben's tense body.

Scarcely breathing in case she should hear him, he had not moved or made a sound but her eyes flicked suddenly open. The sigh became a sharp cry of alarm. She stood staring, still as a bird before a snake, her mouth still formed by her exclamation of fear.

He knew the light from the candle flame could not have defined more than his outline and he stood very still, afraid she would scream if he spoke. It seemed to Ben they stood like this for an eternity. Only one thought broke the grip of the moment: *She is yours. You own her. You can do what you like with her.*

When Li X'ia became Ben Deverill's concubine, it brought many changes into her life. It brought comfort and security beyond her imagination. Although it would take time and events for her to fully realise it, it also brought power. These things would inevitably also bring hatred and tragedy but for those first remarkable months they gave her nothing but undreamed-of happiness.

Until then, contentment to Li had been her view of the mountains beyond the rooftops of the Ma Cho temple and the great bishop's palace from the store-room window, or the longed-for walks to the waterfront. When the Fish had come to her to carefully explain the master's decision, the old woman was filled with pride. It was every mooi-jai's dream to be chosen as concubine. It was the greatest of honours. The most golden of all opportunities. If she pleased the master there would be no end to her good fortune and favours would fall around her like ripe peaches in summer.

To Li it was neither joy nor fear at first. Ben had chosen not to speak to her himself, afraid that his Cantonese would not communicate his feelings and intentions. He told the old woman of his decision as though he were employing a new gardener.

'Speak to her,' he said, trying to keep his tone as businesslike as a Chinese master might. 'Tell her she is not forced to come but she need not be afraid. She trusts you. Tell her I will treat her well and that you may take care of her.'

She immediately bowed her way out of his study. Although Ben prided himself on his understanding of the Chinese mentality, especially of those who worked for him, and always heeded the finely-balanced principles of face, he could not have guessed the true thoughts of the Fish or the trouble he would cause by this instruction.

He had left the fleeting episode in the scullery with his senses aflame and lain for the remainder of the night in a state of raw sexual excitement he had never believed possible. Everything he had aimed for and achieved seemed nothing compared with the desires that now grasped and held him. By the time approaching dawn cooled his sweat and the daylight showed through the windows, he had thought it out. He weighed the problems and complications against the promise of incredible joys, all his thinking guided by one repeated, scarcely believable fact: Li X'ia belonged to him. He owned her.

The Fish hurried through the house to the scullery and found Li pulling weeds from the small vegetable plot in the kitchen garden. Squatting down on the step the old woman called to her in a low voice. 'I am to tell you the young lord has chosen you for his bed,' she whispered. 'The gods have smiled on you.'

She did not confide her true feelings, or frighten Li with her own thoughts of sharing the bed of a barbarian. To her Ben was a baby-eater just as the fisherfolk of the waterfront said he was. She had listened to the many stories of his madness and his violence—the gwai-lo master was a legend in Macau. Many strange things were said of his past and she believed them all. Since childhood she had been warned of such madness and the terrible fury of these foreign devils, unpredictable as a summer storm, loud as the thunder of angry gods. Although she had not seen this fury with her own eyes she was sure it was not far away. He was from another world, as remote to her as the moon. But she would not share these thoughts with Li—the farm girl was young and pleasing to look upon, she might calm him.

She watched the small frown on Li X'ia's face. 'You are a fool if you do not go to him. You will be mistress of this fine house.' She chuckled wickedly. 'Mistress of Ah Ho . . . and I will be by your side.'

The Fish was afraid of the heavily-built amah from Fukien. Aware of the power she claimed for herself in this house with no one to stop her. It was not the strong arm that made the Fish avoid the eyes of Ah Ho, it was the heart of her that she feared—the heart of an elder sister of Sau Hai, hardened by a lifetime of service and sharpened by the ways of survival.

It took all the old woman's courage as she came from the scullery, hesitating in the doorway that led to the yard. Ah Ho sat with tea at her elbow and a sheet of lottery numbers spread before her.

'Aaayyaaahhh! Am I never to be smiled upon by fortune? Must

I die a turtle for others to step upon.' The amah screwed the sheet into a tight ball. The Fish almost retreated, this was not a good time. At that second, Ah Ho saw her and her voice rose a pitch.

'Why do you stand staring, old dog bones? Have you no work?'

'I . . . I come to warn you.' The Fish was startled by the dryness of her own voice. 'No longer can you spit in the food of the mooi-jai. She is chosen by the master. Soon to become mistress of this house.' With this said, she turned to go. The amah's eyes followed her increduously.

'Who spreads such lies?' she asked in a coarse whisper.

'It is the truth, Ah Ho,' the Fish persisted, stopping short. 'Last night he came for her, here in this kitchen. I am to prepare a bath . . . I am to be her hand-servant.'

'You are mistaken, old fool. Already you are seeing ghosts.' Ah Ho flung the ball of paper at the old woman as she scuttled off. 'The old one is mad,' she told herself, 'Dry as grave dust with only the spirits to talk to. Her head is as empty as a melon gourd.'

Only when Ah Ho had brought him the strong Arab coffee he had taught her to make and he told her of his decision, did the full force of such treachery strike the amah. She had feared that this would happen, had seen with her own eyes how the farm girl had opened like a flower before him. The presence of a mooi-jai fresh from the country was the dread of every Sau Hai amah, especially in the house of an unmarried master.

A favoured concubine soon became the mistress of a house if she were clever enough and this one must be clever. Had she, Ah Ho, not been deceived, believing the girl to be safely hidden from the master's eyes among the buckets and brooms and chickens' entrails when all the time she must have been coming to his bed at night?

And the old dog bones. She too had planned and schemed behind her back. It was all a plot against her. Why else would the master inform the old one of his intention instead of telling her, the senior amah of this household? Had she not served him faithfully for five long years? Her face was forever lost in this house, to be commanded by one beneath her, good only for shelling peas. Ah Ho's heart set there and then with grim determination. She called down the curse of all the gods upon them both, praying that the pig-girl would displease the master and be sent away. So that things could stay as they had always been. If this did not happen she would wait, but she would find a way.

When Li X'ia was brought by the Fish to Ben's quarters where the steaming bath stood ready to receive her, she was relieved to find that he was not there. At first, the sight of the huge white tub standing on four iron feet like the claws of a dragon, made her hold back. She had never seen such a thing or lain down in hot water. Was she to be drowned, or boiled alive? Such things might be possible in the house of a gwai-lo.

'Come mistress. Take off your clothes and get in. There is nothing to fear.' The Fish encouraged her kindly. 'I have seen many like this in my day. It is the way they do things.'

Once submerged in its comforting warmth, Li overcame her doubts and sniffed the perfumed soap, the hot water soft as silk against her skin and scented with oils. She stayed so long in the bathtub that the water began to grow cold.

'Come out Li X'ia. You must be ready for the young lord when he returns.' She chuckled. 'I must make you beautiful for him. He is impatient for you. I have seen this in his eyes.'

'What must I do to please him?' asked Li with concern.

'Do whatever he asks of you. Do not be afraid. It is not difficult.'

When Li came from the bath and dried her body it glowed with health. The old woman clucked her tongue with approval.

'Ayeeah! He will devour you like ripe summer fruit,' she said. 'But you must tell me,' she lowered her voice. 'Have you been taken by other men?'

Li frowned, remembering Ten Willows. There had been the junk boy who had tried to force her. 'I do not think so.'

'He will not want second-hand goods.' Her words dropped to a whisper. 'I will give you a small bladder of chicken's blood if your cherry has been taken. He will not know the difference.'

She handed Li a silk robe, the palest colour of lilac. 'This is yours now. A gift from the master. There are many more but first we must brush your hair and dress it with sweet-smelling flowers.'

Later, Li gazed upon the vast four-poster bed in the master's bedroom with awe and amazement. On it stood a pile of boxes and coloured paper packages.

'These are for you,' said the Fish grandly. 'You may open them and see what the gods have showered upon you.'

There were silks, bright with flowers and birds, a silver-backed mirror, hairbrush and comb. There were soft slippers and more beautiful robes and smaller things delicate as a spider's web. These, the Fish told her gleefully, were to be worn only in the bedroom. There was a glittering ball of crystal which sprayed a fine mist of fragrance. Most wonderful of all was a musical box—a tiny ballerina, turning slowly on her toes to tinkling music.

Ben had been in China long enough to understand the barrier that stood between Li X'ia's race and culture and his own. He knew also the odds against breaking it down without damage. If he were too hasty, too impatient, it would always remain. If he tried to close the gulf too clumsily it might never be crossed. He had learned enough from the compradore at Ten Willows to imagine the life she must have led. Things were very different for her now and he intended to dedicate himself to her happiness with the same determination he put into everything he did. There was no way of knowing how she would feel. He doubted that she had ever been touched or held or admired in any way other than violently. He doubted if she had known a kiss, a thing unknown in her level of Chinese society. The memory of Ling Ling the flower girl returned when he contemplated such things. He would have to tread carefully if he was to win her confidence and not frighten her from his reach forever.

For almost a week he left Li untouched except to take her hand in his. To him it was like taming a wild bird or gaining the trust and confidence of a wounded creature. He knew that the past months for her had passed reasonably free of fear or anxiety, it was why he had given her exclusively into the care of the old woman. But it was not long enough to blot out the horror of her ordeal in the pig basket or whatever other cruelties and indignities she may have suffered at Ten Willows.

For three nights he listened to her gentle breathing beside him, measured only by the beat of his own pulse, somehow finding sleep himself without revealing what he expected of her. When he reached out to touch her, no matter how tenderly, he felt her body tense under his fingers. If he persisted a violent trembling gripped her. It was the trembling of fear, not of passion, and it told him to wait.

The sign he had been hoping for came one twilight evening when they sat together in the small garden high over the bay. The garden seat faced the water, surrounded by a thick grove of scented red acacia. It was the place she felt safe in, as though the naturalness calmed and reassured her. Birds were squabbling in the palms above them as a rosy, lavender sunset slowly flushed the sky. Below, the Hoklo fishermen lit the flares in the bows of their sampans and set out like fireflies to find fish.

It was the first time she had returned the pressure of his hand.

At first it was a squeeze so slight he thought he might have imagined it. It became stronger. Her small fingers began exploring the palm of his hand, measuring its span with her own, running light fingertips over his scarred knuckles and stroking in silent fascination the fine coppery hair that covered his forearm.

Ben felt sure, as he always did at times of great excitement, that she would surely hear his heartbeats as her hand cautiously transferred to the open neck of his shirt and the wiry tangle that grew to his throat. Her fingertips explored it in wonderment. Gently, he took her other hand, pressing them both hard against his chest. Drawing her to him, he kissed her, his lips light upon hers until he felt the first, faint tremor of her response.

The warmth of his lips moved against her mouth, gently at first, patiently. So much softer than she had expected, only the slight coarseness of his chin and cheek as his mouth left hers to rest lightly on her closed eyelids, her ears and throat. She smelled his clean, freshly bathed skin, the faint scent of Bay Rum, and felt the stirrings in her grow with a reckless need she had no understanding of. Boldly she found his mouth with hers, moving her lips in the way that he moved his. Hesitant at first and then with sudden wildness.

Li had known the time would come when these things would occur. The Fish had told her carefully what to expect, using her own experience with the foreign master who had once taken her roughly to his bed, in the place where his wife had slept only hours before. It did not hurt much and was soon over, the old woman had assured her.

'It is a stabbing feeling which may make you cry out and you may bleed from the wound but it is what you must do. There is no stopping it.' It was these words of the Fish that had caused Li X'ia to lie still beside her master, afraid to move, her eyes closed. Waiting for this thing to happen.

She had felt his breath so close she could smell the brandy he had taken after dinner and the licorice wood he had chewed to clean his teeth. It was not unpleasant but she dare not look at him and had pretended to sleep. Sometimes his lips had brushed her face and shoulder, light as a bird's wing. When this happened the muscles of her body had tensed with anticipation of the pain to come. She had felt her thighs tighten, squeezed together against his searching fingers. His hand had rested on her stomach and she had been unable to control her shivering. When it moved lower she had locked her legs even tighter and turned away with a violent shudder of fear. He had stopped, his hand coming away from her and then she had listened for hours to his breathing.

Now she felt his open mouth caress her lips as though to soften them, so tenderly she heard herself sigh, then crushing suddenly hard as the tip of his tongue slipped firmly into her mouth. This too, the Fish had warned her of. It was what the gwai-lo expected, for they were very strange; such things had always been whispered among the young mooi-jai. Li found that his large nose did not get in the way as she had thought it would, his strong white teeth did not bite her, as she had feared.

His tongue found hers and she returned its pressure, winding, licking, tasting him. Again, she heard her own small sound of protest as his mouth suddenly left hers. It was as though the sound came from someone else she could not control. Her disappointment was fleeting as his broad hand found her breast inside the silk of her robe. The exquisite shock that shot through her as his rough palm passed over her stiffened nipple made Li X'ia wonder if this was the pain she had been warned of.

Somewhere in the swirl of her senses she cried out again, pushing herself forward, giving her breast to him, feeling the circular movement of his hot, dry palm, roughened by the pulling of ropes, teasing the hard bud of her nipple, replaced suddenly and without warning by his mouth, his eager tongue rolling, flicking, until she thought she would cry aloud.

Then Li X'ia felt herself lifted easily as a child in his arms and borne away, down the steps of the pavilion. She opened her eyes to the glitter of the last sunlight breaking through the tall wands of umbrella bamboo, then closed them again, her arms locked around him, her face buried in the warmth of his neck.

When Ben took Li X'ia away with him aboard *Cloud Chaser*, Ah Ho was relieved. It gave her the chance to consider the situation and its effect upon her future uninterrupted. Whilst she had to admit the farm girl had made no demands of her and that all her simple requirements seemed to be easily fulfilled by the old one, that would not last. She was sure of it.

She had seen it many times before and when she brought the matter up at the mahjongg table, those around her nodded their agreement. Hadn't the famous mooi-jai, Xiao-Shi, become concubine to the rich Meng Achoi and risen to become number one in that illustrious household, above even his wives and their children? Hadn't she soon learned what power she had been given and didn't she beat those beneath her, treat them like dogs and work them like oxen? While Meng Achoi was a slave to her jade gate and did nothing to help them. This was the way it always was with the mooi-jai who pleased the master in bed. Yes, the farm girl would soon climb upon the back of the tiger, there was no doubt of it. Ah Ho vowed that it would not be allowed to happen to her.

The Villa Formosa was finished while *Cloud Chaser* was still at sea. When she returned it was to sail into the sheltered waters of Repulse Bay, not the noisy bustle of the commercial wharves in Macau. Ben had told Li nothing of the magnificent new home and all that now happened was a complete surprise to her. His arrangements had been followed in detail. As the anchor chain rumbled through the hawsepipe, it was a signal for the small steam pinnace to leave Formosa's private jetty.

He stood at the rail with his arm around her and watched the handsome little craft cut cleanly through the water, the Deverill house flag snapping from its jackstaff, its coxswain at the wheel and boatman standing in the bows. Built by the famous Hodder & Sons of Glasgow and Ben's only concession to steam, the splendid craft had been brought to Hong Kong lashed to the deck of a freighter.

His arm tightened around Li's waist as the steady chug of its engine approached swiftly, the two hand-picked crew neatly turned out in white duck uniforms.

'It is for you. To take you anywhere you wish to go. Yours to command.'

As it drew closer, its sleek twenty-five-foot length enamelled a deep royal blue, its deck scrubbed bone white, housing glossy with varnish and trimmed with bright brass, he pointed to the name on its bows. 'See, I have called it *Siu Wun*—Little Cloud.'

It was the Fish who knew first of Li X'ia's pregnancy. Li had become her reason for living. The eternity of hardship that had been the old woman's life she saw as finally rewarded through the little farm girl who had been chosen as mistress of this great and noble house. Although she could not know joy, the enchantment that sometimes showed through Li was her greatest satisfaction. Once she had worked as a midwife with the nuns among the Tanka. It had taught her every sign of a woman with child. She did not wait for Li to come to her confused and afraid that she no longer bled. There was little chance that she had learned of such things among farmhands or tending silkworms.

Each morning when Li X'ia walked the garden paths to the carved marble table and stools set in a grove of sacred black bamboo looking out to sea, the Fish would be waiting with a pot of tea, nestled in its padded wicker basket amid the bamboo containers of steamed delicacies she had placed there. The walk through the garden was one of Li's greatest delights among the many Ben had laid before her. Among the rare trees, brought from the provinces in *Cloud Chaser's* hold and transplanted almost fully grown, masses of blue periwinkles and wild Chinese violet spread freely.

Through them ran a man-made brook that emptied itself over a series of miniature falls into a lotus pond banked by carpets of deep green moss and filled with fat carp, crossed by a scarlet painted bridge. Gold and silver pheasants scratched among the trees and shrubs selected for their attraction to birds and filled with their song.

Li waited until the Fish had poured the flower tea, never sure what flavour it was, never the same two days in a row, lifting the lid to sniff the fragrance and guess—rose petal? lotus root? jasmine? chrysanthemum? The ritual had become a gentle start to each day when Ben had left, with the silver lids and saucers, Li insisting the pot was too heavy for the old woman—even with two hands she spilled it. This morning the Fish did not protest.

'You are carrying his child, mistress. We must pray and prepare for a strong and healthy son.'

The grudging acceptance Ben had enjoyed in Hong Kong's growing business and professional society quickly dried up when he brought his Chinese woman to live with him at Repulse Bay. It clearly confirmed the outspoken opinions that had always maintained the man was little better than a dockside rake, more a native than a gentleman. Clearly his oriental blood made him entirely unsuitable in civilised circles. He was asked to resign from the Hong Kong Club and was no longer welcome at the Yacht Club. It may have heightened the interest of those women who secretly admired him but it had the opposite outward appearance. Of the many invitations he had sent out for the opening of Villa Formosa only a handful were accepted.

When he took Li X'ia to the veranda of the newly built Repulse Bay Hotel for Sunday lunch, they were pointedly ignored. Although the demand for reservations in this most desirable and exclusive of Hong Kong leisure spots was always high, at least two tables near them were left vacant. Service when Ben finally demanded it, was surly, slow and deliberately inefficient. They left halfway through and never returned.

Accepting the fact of Hong Kong society's hypocrisy, although he could have named half the British businessmen and government officials on the island as keeping Chinese mistresses or of regularly attending those places set aside for such purposes, Ben quickly realised Li was safest and happiest within the high walls of Villa Formosa. He could not help observing the looks of disdain and open hostility from Chinese of all classes and his knowledge of Cantonese made the muttered insults that followed them everywhere inescapable.

Such curses, unique to the lower classes, were vile beyond belief even for a man such as Ben. They dealt mainly with speculation on the diseased genitals from which such a low-class whore must have sprung, and advised the gwai-lo who bedded her to copulate with his equally diseased mother. He would feel Li's hand grip his but otherwise she showed no real distress. Such filth was common exchange in even the pettiest of disagreements in the community from which she came.

Ben knew that retaliation of any kind could only add to her discomfort and lead to more serious confrontation. He willingly turned his back upon those expatriates whom he had at best found barely tolerable as Li turned away from those who had never really accepted and now disowned her. Instead he spent all of his time when not in the Queens Road office or at the Macau boatyard, making Villa Formosa a paradise for the woman he had come to adore beyond any concept he had ever formed of love.

The Pavilion of Joyful Moments

IN A glade of red acacia such as that she had enjoyed so much in Macau he had planted a sacred banyan tree. Already half grown it spread a canopy of large, fleshy green leaves over the glade, positioned to provide shelter from the afternoon sun and to break the winds that sometimes hustled off the South China Sea, which stretched to the far horizon as though it were an extension of Formosa's grounds.

The artisans who came to build the pavilion beneath its shade were traditional builders of pagodas brought from Hangchow by Indie da Silva as his contribution to his old friend's newfound happiness. Within a month the Pavilion of Joyful Moments was completed. Four great pillars of rare dawn redwood were surrounded by screens of aromatic sandlewood, intricately carved in designs of peach and plum blossom. Its ornate roof swept in the same skyward curves of green and gold tiles as the main house; each of its four points was mounted by an imperial lion facing the dangers borne on the four winds.

In its centre, raised above the lions, stood the golden dragon of prosperity and long life, grasping the pearl of wisdom in its protective claws. In the centre of its floor of snowy marble the open petals of a lotus flower were set in pale pink jadeite inlaid with stamens of amber, coral and blue lazurite. Advanced creepers of mimosa had been planted to cling in creamy bouquets around the pavilion's entrance. Gardenias lined the pathway of intricately patterned river pebbles that surrounded it and baskets of wild strawberry hung from its eaves.

Inside, divans of rosewood scattered with richly embroidered cushions surrounded the marble table and stools brought from the garden in Macau. Suspended from its roof-beams of polished blackbean, a simple cage of willow twigs contained a nightingale.

It was here that Ben and Li spent much of their time as he began teaching her to speak his language and she corrected his imperfect Cantonese. For company while he was away he had bought her a pair of chow puppies, balls of soft, flour-white fur with bright, black eyes, round as buttons and with tongues the colour of crushed blueberries. They had quickly become a part of Li's life at Formosa, dashing among the trees after the pheasants, trotting with her on their red leather leashes along the pathways or sleeping on the cushions of the pavilion.

To the Fish the dogs were a mystery. The quality of her peasant life had taught her that such creatures would be best served up with bamboo shoots and blackbean sauce with perhaps a dash of chilli. But the happiness they gave Li X'ia was enough for her to tolerate them. The Fish in fact was too busy taking every precaution dictated by the Chinese calendar and adding a few of her own to prepare for a boy child, to care about anything else.

Like all Chinese she had great respect for the unborn child, believing that its 'before sky' or pre-natal experience was as vital as its 'after sky' or post-natal future. Traditional Chinese precautions, always embellished by folklore, were strictly laid down. Li was permitted no soya sauce, dark soups or gravies, to ensure that the boy would not have a dark complexion and be looked upon as a peasant of low breeding. In their place she was served clear soups and whipped egg whites to guarantee that his skin would be smooth and fair, as a pale skin for a boy is a sign of future success and prosperity, not of one destined to work in the fields. She was not allowed to lift her arms above her head or do anything more strenuous than a gentle stroll through the gardens.

Most of the time Li X'ia was made to rest in bed and sip from an endless procession of herbal broths to boost her energy and strength. Teas made from red raspberry leaves and mild ginseng or clear soups of chicken and pork essence, all carefully prepared from the old recipes to 'bo', or enrich the blood, would raise the ch'i and nourish the organs, ensuring the safe birth of a healthy boy.

That the child would not be a boy was never contemplated. Every stick of joss, every prayer, every burnt offering was aimed at the certainty of a son, even to the two scallion onions left in the chamber pot for Li's use in the bedroom. When she questioned their purpose the Fish assured her solemnly that this was common practice in the village of her birth and the only reason she herself was not a man was because her simple parents had not provided two pearl onions.

Of even greater importance was the Fish's preoccupation with the peach and its powerful properties. She brewed a strong tea of peach leaves to prevent morning sickness. Petals of dried peach blossom were scattered over the bed and a slip of peachwood hidden under the pillow to guard against the hungry ghosts. For the sacred peach, the Fish persisted, was the most powerful of all fruits. Why else did the ancients use its bark to foretell the future?

The old woman's concern was so great and so protective Li could only do as she was told. Only when a fortune-teller was summoned did Li X'ia protest. She knew that her happiness was stolen, that it was not recognised by the gods and she dare not question it. The fact that she now never stepped outside the huge wrought-iron gates of Villa Formosa caused her no concern. For the long weeks that Ben was often away, she was content to sit in the Pavilion of Joyful Moments with the Fish never far away, learning the words Ben had given her to read or flying the yellow butterfly kite high over the sea.

There were many hours of stories from the Fish. Her care and attention had become deep devotion. There had been nothing in her life, now there was Li X'ia. The bond between them grew in heart and spirit. She told Li of her childhood as mooi-jai, sold at the age of five to a family of Parsees so that her parents and brothers would not starve. Li listened intently when the Fish talked of her long and painful life. Bought and sold like a piece of household furniture but of less value, that value decreasing with time and toil.

'It is not good to be worth only fifty Hong Kong dollars. It is the price of a jar of bad wine.' She sighed. 'There was a time when I was young and fresh as new rice and my feet were small as lilies. I was eleven years old when the Parsees sold me to a gwai-lo family in Hong Kong. The master was a man of great wealth. They treated me well. I was never beaten. I slept in a bed, food was plentiful and my work was not hard.'

She paused, twisting the jade bracelet on her thin wrist. 'Until he took me to his bed . . . I did not please him.' With a sudden movement she pushed it high up her forearm where it would hold. 'I have prattled enough.' From her pocket she took a small silk purse. The lines of her face set seriously.

'We must ask all gods to give the master the son he longs for or his anger will be great. I have been to the temple. These things the priest has sent you.'

She laid out the contents of the purse. There was a tiny silver lock to fasten him to life, a silver chicken's foot, so that he might scratch a good living. So that he might have no fear of dogs, a scrap of fur attached to a thread of red silk. And most potent of all, a bracelet fashioned from a copper coffin nail to give him courage in the face of ghosts and spirits.

Li, from a household of boys and a father who took no risks with demons, was familiar with all of these potent charms. She also knew the Taoist priests gave nothing away.

'These things cost money,' she protested. 'You must tell me how much.'

The Fish began to gather the teacups and the bamboo baskets. 'I have money of my own. I have saved enough.'

'Enough for what?' asked Li rising to help her.

'For my grave, of course. What else would I need money for? Please sit. Do not exert yourself. You must rest. These are my gifts to the little master.'

Li watched her stooped shoulders, still strong enough to hold the heavy tray, as she carried it slowly along the pathway to the house. The story of the old woman's sad and painful life filled her mind. When she was gone Li X'ia looked out across the misty azure of the ocean. Her heart cried out to all the gods that her child be a son. For she knew the world was no place for a daughter.

Villa Formosa was so large and its grounds so rambling that new servants had been found and the gardener who lived in his own stone house within the walls was given two boys as assistants. Ben had charged Ah Ho with the responsibility of engaging them, knowing that it gave her face and that it would be too much to ask of Li. The amah took this honoured responsibility as reassurance of the master's confidence in her.

She went about the running of the big house with an even firmer hand, supervising the cleaning of its many high-ceilinged, marble-floored rooms filled with grand furniture and rich carpets, instructing the cook in the preparation of fine food which, she confided in the kitchen, she considered wasted on the gwai-lo master and his peasant whore.

As the months went by and her pregnancy developed, Li X'ia seldom left the suite of rooms she shared with Ben—the large master bedroom with its balustraded balcony looking over the gardens, the dressing room and great study where Ben sometimes worked at night. It had become her world, and as confinement and the Fish's constant attentions kept her in bed longer each day she had no wish to leave it, except to sit in the pavilion in the late afternoons to watch for Ben's return in *Little Cloud.*

There was no contact with Ah Ho, as the Fish had been left with the full responsibility of these private rooms, as well as the serving of food from the kitchen and all of Li's other requirements. Ah Ho viewed this exclusion of her superior services as a further insult to her seniority but, as she did not recognise the farm girl as her mistress, she was satisfied to keep her distance.

The Fish did everything she could to avoid any contact between them, knowing how the amah's presence did nothing to lift the heart. She assured Li with a toothless grin that when with child a woman must not look upon the ugly, the profane or the belligerent, as it might affect the unborn.

Only once, when the old woman was resting, did Li go herself to the kitchen to ask for fresh peppermint tea to ease her nausea. The woman at the stove who turned to her was a stranger. Ah Ho appeared immediately from the courtyard at the sound of Li's voice.

'Where is the old dog bones that her illustrious mistress should soil her silken slippers in this humble kitchen?' The amah's words were filled with contempt, then suddenly bitter. 'This place is no longer for you. I am in charge here. I will send your tea when I can.'

Li heard tittering from the scullery and saw the cook smirk behind the steam of her cooking. She left the kitchen and waited for an hour. When the tea came, delivered by the mooi-jai who had taken her place in the scullery, it was cold. When she lifted the lid a large cockroach floated beneath it, heavy with the pod of its eggs.

Fear of the Sau Hai amah Ah Ho had stayed with Li X'ia. The horror of Ten Willows had not really left her, although when Ben was with her it was pushed away, replaced with happiness and sometimes laughter. When he was gone, as he was each morning after taking his coffee on the balcony, the fear returned, a slow gnawing certainty that she was still in danger.

It had begun as a small thought, remote until the strident voice of Ah Ho raised with its strange Fukienese accent came clearly from the high-walled courtyard and through the open French windows. When she opened them the Fish would scold her and close them again, insisting that no breeze must chill her.

The old woman knew of Li's fear and did everything she could to drive it from her. She believed that all misfortune was visited upon the innocent by evil spirits and had hidden her protective charms carefully throughout the room. When the master found one in Li's pillowcase, a simple slip of peachwood, he had been amused at first, and had replaced it respectfully.

When days later he found a similar slip in his shoe and the bed sheets scattered with dried petals of peach blossom he became impatient and threw the slip into the garden. He had no use for such superstitions. If he or the House of Deverill and those inside its walls needed protection it was he who would provide it. The Fish had quaked with terror. The storm she had feared was brewing, its thunder to roll. He had torn down the paper image of Chang Tien Shih, the Master of Heaven, riding a tiger and brandishing his demon-vanquishing sword, and torn it into pieces.

When he also threw out the scrap of raw ginger that hung beside it and smashed the protective mirror placed above the door to drive off the evil ones with their own hideous image, she had dropped to her knees to pray. In a loud voice the gwai-lo master threatened that unless this nonsense was stopped she would be sent back to the scullery. It was he, and the western doctor who came each week, who would see that no harm came to Li X'ia and her unborn child, not joss sticks and paper gods. When he had left, the Fish picked up the pieces of the Chang Tien Shih and burned them with her prayers and begged the Eight Immortals to spare Li X'ia from the dangers to come.

To both Li X'ia and the Fish Ben's actions invited the punishment of the gods and they had purified the room with incense and prayed for forgiveness. They must be doubly cautious now. Nothing must be allowed to invade their sanctum. When the house was asleep that night the Fish slipped silently away and walked for hours to the Taoist temple outside Stanley Village.

She passed the gate gods and entered the antechamber. There she paused to light joss to the most important of the queen's protectors—the Demon Slaying Boy, His Imperial Majesty the White Ape, Field Marshal Yin and the Unpredictable Ghost, Wu Ch'ang Kuei. Then she went into the chamber of the Taoist priest to ask for help.

Ben soon felt guilty of his intolerance and showed his deep regret for the incident by bringing home a red painted shrine to replace the paper one he had destroyed. It was made of peachwood he said, and hung it beside their door where Li could easily reach to place fresh fruit and flowers and light her joss. He was deeply ashamed, he whispered, holding her close to ask her forgiveness.

From a short voyage he returned with Indonesian sandalwood and spent many hours fashioning a cradle on the balcony, filling the room with the wood's fragrance. When it was finished Li's delight and gratitude were so great he laughed aloud. Only the Fish remained concerned. She had never before seen the image of a god destroyed and flung to the ground to be stepped upon. In her simple mind it spelled only disaster and confirmed all her long-held fears of the baby-eater.

One early morning Li was awoken by the loudness of Ah Ho's voice. She had slept badly throughout a hot and humid night and Ben had left her undisturbed, taking his coffee alone and leaving for the boathouse and his office in the central district. The Fish had opened the windows wide to the fresh breeze off the ocean. It was a clear, still morning and the servants' voices carried above the clop-clopping of wooden kegs on the stone flagging of the yard and the soft cluck of hens. First, the words of the Fish, thin and anxious, so that Li had to strain her ears to hear them: 'The mistress has slept badly. She is not well. I ask that less noise be made at this early hour so that she may rest.'

Ah Ho's reply was filled with sarcasm. 'Mistress? Mistress? What mistress is this? This house has no mistress.' The words were unmistakable. 'And who are you to order me, old dog bones? I am in charge of this house. Not the low-class whore who crawled from a basket made for pigs.'

'But Elder Sister,' The Fish's voice was almost too subdued to hear. 'She is close to her time. She must have rest.'

Ah Ho's reply brought titters from those listening. 'She is a farm girl. In her village the women drop their brats in the field and carry on planting rice. What is all the fuss about?'

Suddenly, the fear and humiliation that had followed Li X'ia for so long froze to an icy core of anger, so deep, so unexpected, it left no room for hesitation. She got out of bed and quickly bathed, putting on the most beautiful of the bedroom robes Ben had brought her from Shanghai and taking from a drawer the fan of filigree ivory chased with silver. When the Fish returned Li had dressed her own hair and sat waiting for her.

'Tell the amah Ah Ho I wish to see her.' She cut the old woman's protest short and the look on her face was one the Fish had never seen before. Quaking inside, she did as she was told.

When Ah Ho entered the room she would not look at Li's face but only above her head and through the windows to where the wide straw hat of the gardener moved among the shrubbery. She said nothing. Li spoke quietly to the Fish.

'I would like some peach tea. Please fetch some. There is no need to hurry. I wish to speak with Ah Ho.'

When the old woman hesitated, Li flicked open her fan and smiled, pointing it towards the door. 'Perhaps, instead, I will have peppermint.'

When the door had closed Li fluttered the fan close to her face, hoping it would slow the beating of her heart. 'It is hot. I am tired. I have not slept well.'

She waited, forcing her eyes to fix on Ah Ho's expressionless face. The flickering fan was the only movement between them, the sound of birds the only disturbance. No voices came from the courtyard. It seemed that the house was listening.

'I am soon to bear the master a son. I must have rest and quiet. I ask you to stop the noise in the kitchen courtyard until I have arisen.'

Ah Ho's mouth tightened but she said nothing. Li waited, then continued, encouraged by the amah's silence. 'I have heard your words before the servants. You have left me no face in this house. Why have you done this? I have given you no reason.'

Ah Ho's reply was slow in coming. 'You must be mistaken. It was not I you heard.'

Still no expression showed on the amah's face and her eyes remained fixed on the garden. Li waited, then gathering courage, continued. 'If you are not happy in this house, you are free to go.'

Ah Ho's reply was no more than a whisper. Slowly her eyes turned from the garden to meet Li X'ia's. Her mouth twisted with the effort of speech and her flaccid, powdery cheeks trembled as she searched for words. 'I have taken care of the master and his house for five years now. He does not complain.'

'And I do not complain. Only of noise when I must rest. I ask only that you give me face.' Li held the amah's hostile stare until it wavered. 'And that you do something about the cockroaches in the kitchen. They are becoming too bold and I do not wish to trouble the master with such small things.'

The door opened and the Fish came in with the wicker pot-warmer on a tray. Ah Ho's voice dropped to barely a whisper.

'I will look into these things and see what can be done.' Without lifting her eyes or waiting to be dismissed, the amah turned and hurried from the room.

Once outside the door her mutterings spewed like poison. What right had this farm hag, this spawn of a diseased goat, who should have died like a pig? What right had she to talk this way to a sister of the Sau Hai, whom she had disgraced? Ah Ho went straight to her small room off the courtyard. She sat on the narrow, hard bed to think. It was happening. Just as she knew it would.

The farm girl would soon ride the tiger. There would be no squeeze left in this house. The low-class whore would turn the master against her. She would be thrown out onto the street with nothing. Ah Ho stuck many joss sticks into the tin of sand that stood before the image of Hung Hsing, god of all poor people—'whose favours are like sunshine illuminating the world'. When their smoke was rising thinly she asked for guidance.

Late one evening a week later Ben was called to the telephone. Indie da Silva's voice could be barely heard. 'There's been trouble . . . we have a fire on our hands. Come right away.' The click of the handpiece shut off Ben's questions and he left quickly for the jetty and the boathouse where the crew of *Little Cloud* would be gambling the night away.

From the gate of the courtyard Ah Ho watched him go, then walked soft-footed along the grass verge beside the drive. Past the darkened windows of the gardener's gatehouse, keeping to the shadows, she reached the small vendors' entrance beside the main gates and silently drew the bolt. Leaving the iron door ajar she slipped into the laneway and down to the lights of the streets below.

The Fish was unable to move when she was first aroused by whispers, raising her head to listen. Only the ghostly shifting of lace curtains against the open French windows disturbed the shards of bright moonlight. A shadowy form cut through them, followed by another. They made no sound as they surrounded Li X'ia's bed. The voice when it came was coarse, hardly raised from a whisper.

'Wake up, sai paw.' The voice was harsh, the Cantonese term meaning dead hag establishing its owner as a coolie. 'You will come with us or this blade will pierce your belly and the brat it carries.' Li fought wildly as rough hands tried to drag her from the bed.

Paralysed with fright the Fish struggled upright. The cry of alarm that escaped her brought another curse.

'Silence the old one,' the coolie voice hissed. 'A sound from you and you are dead, hag. Your bones will lie here with no one to bury them.'

A punch dropped the old woman across the stretcher. Through the waves of shock and pain she heard more abuse and the cries of Li X'ia and the sound of blows.

The filthy rag forced between Li's jaws tasted and smelled of rancid sweat. The hands that grabbed for her were vicious in their haste. When she kicked out and fought them with all her strength, fists struck at her and a face thrust out of the dark, foul breath strong from its closeness. She felt the cold blade of a knife at her throat as a hand screwed at her breast.

'Do not fight me, whore.' A hand replaced the blade and squeezed her gullet. As Li X'ia felt the consciousness leaving her a terrible pain shot through her belly as though the blade had been thrust into it.

'Ayyahhh—jun hi soi,' the voice grated ferociously. 'We cannot take her. The brat is coming.'

Another voice, tense with alarm, spoke. 'We were told nothing of this. She is ready to whelp. Leave her. She is worth nothing to us dead.'

As swiftly and quietly as they had invaded the room the shadows disappeared, leaving only the blown curtains to show where they had entered. The Fish dragged herself across the room and with trembling hands closed and latched the windows, pulling the heavy drapes and lighting the gas lamp. Before its mantle had fully flared she knew it was time. The cries from the bed tore at her heart but Li X'ia was alive. The old woman drew on all her strength and came to the bedside.

No weapon had been used and the bruises were soon soothed with compresses of salt and shredded ginger. There was no time to light joss to Tien Shih whose image had been destroyed and who now took revenge. She could expect no help within this house and the servants' quarters were deadly quiet. With cool water scented with cloves she constantly bathed Li's face and arms, ready with the cup of raspberry-leaf tea whenever the pain subsided. Hours passed, and as the room began to pale with first light it was filled with the moans of agony, rising and unchecked. The Fish slid a silver chopstick between Li X'ia's teeth to bite upon and began the work she knew so well.

Li X'ia's baby came into a world bathed in a warm golden light as the first rays of sunrise touched the walls of Villa Formosa and flooded the windows. It came without trouble and the Fish's midwife's eye saw quickly that its limbs were undamaged by the violent ordeal its mother had suffered. This did not save the old woman's heart from the sudden grip of despair that caused her to cry out. 'Aaaaayyeeeaaahhh. The gods are angry. The young lord has offended them.'

She wept inside, her eyes blurred with the bitter tears of fear and sorrow. A terrible foreboding filled her. The tiny perfectly formed body was that of a girl. It seemed impossible. Never had she known the gods to be beseeched for so long or with such humble persistence, so completely, as she had beseeched them since the first day she had been sure of Li X'ia's pregnancy. Every gift had been offered, every prayer written and uttered, every precaution taken. Joss had been burned and she had begged her ancestors to grant this one great favour as the last she would ask on this earth. All had failed her. The lord of her mistress had caused them to turn their backs on all she had done. Even her many trips to the temple and the blessings of the priest had failed. She too had failed, a wretched old woman whose name had been forgotten.

She looked quickly at Li X'ia. Her eyes were tightly closed and there was none of the relief that the Fish had hoped to see upon her face; her features had not softened and were still drawn tight with pain, as though the child had not yet come. Quickly she bathed the infant in the dish of warm water and wrapped it in a soft shawl that stood ready. Seeing that the tiny form was breathing well and its colour was normal she laid it into the sandalwood cradle and turned her attentions to Li X'ia.

Still Li's face had not relaxed. It was drained of colour and her eyes were tight closed. The crease between her brows remained deep and troubled. Her breathing was fast and laboured and the Fish left her to take out the soiled things and brew a special broth to bring back strength. In the kitchen she took the clay pot of deer antler and the dried root of ginseng and she set it on the stove, stirring the flame beneath it. She turned to find Ah Ho staring at her from the doorway. The Fish had never seen such a look on the face of the amah. Her mouth was open as though to speak but no words came, her eyes stared with a burning disbelief that seemed to also show fear and anger as one.

'The young lord's child has come,' said the Fish, too anxious for her mistress to heed the intimidation Ah Ho usually fetched up in her.

'All is not good,' she continued when the amah did not answer. 'She was attacked in the night. Evil ones came and tried to take her.' The old woman's voice shook uncontrollably and was no more than a croak. She did not know that a livid bruise had discoloured the side of her face. Ah Ho stared at it as she searched for words.

'And . . . she lives?' she whispered.

'She lives. The attack caused the child to come before its time. Those who would take her have run like dogs.'

Ah Ho's hands raised to cover her face in a show of concern. 'And the child?' Her voice was thick with deceit.

'The child is unharmed,' said the Fish.

Ah Ho was silent for a moment, collecting her thoughts. 'Is the woman hurt?' she asked in a stronger voice.

'There has been great shock and she is badly bruised. I do not know what harm has been caused inside.'

The Fish poured the pale liquid into a rice bowl and returned to the bedroom with Ah Ho close behind her. The bowl was halfway to Li X'ia's lips before the Fish saw that she no longer breathed. Her wail of anguish filled the room as she backed away, the broth spilling in her hands.

No sound came from Ah Ho. Instead she stepped over to the cradle, pulling aside the cotton cover. 'The curse of all gods is on this house.' The words she uttered were without pity. 'When the master returns to find she died for a girl child his anger will be terrible to see. We must leave this house while we can.'

Ah Ho watched the effect of her words narrowly. She knew well the simple mind of such as the Fish. That fear and superstition were great in her.

'He will have no use for a girl child,' she persisted, her voice rising dramatically. 'Only a son can assure the lineage of this house and its prosperity. He will cast the child out. Return her to the place from where her mother came.'

The Fish fought hard to control her thoughts. Fear struggled with a sense of duty and concern for the child of her dead mistress. There was truth in Ah Ho's words. The rage of the mad gwai-lo would trample them like wild horses. She fought to thrust it from her mind.

'We must send for the gwai-lo doctor and the police.' She quailed, panic taking hold of her. She dropped the bowl from her trembling hands, and pointed to the telephone. 'We should tell the master in Macau. Use the electric talking machine. He must be told of this evil thing.'

Ah Ho's voice filled with accusation, as though the full meaning of what had happened was only now becoming clear to her.

'No, you must leave this place. A doctor can do nothing now. The police will blame you. They will say that it is you who let the evil ones in.'

She acted the part of one greatly afraid, waving her outstretched hands before her as though warding off the injustice that threatened.

'It will be you that they will blame,' she said coldly. 'You who were left in charge. It is you who was given responsibility for the pig-girl. You are the one they will blame.' Her eyes regained their hostile glitter as the idea took hold. 'It was my night to visit my sisters. I have only just returned.' She lifted her chin confidently. 'I was not here. You were her protector.'

The Fish backed away, the terrible fear she had felt when seeing the baby was female aroused again by Ah Ho's accusing voice. The amah's face twisted into the sneer of contempt she had shown so often when talking of Li X'ia.

'The pig-girl could not give him a son. All your prayers went unheeded. Your preparations were for nothing.'

She scooped the silver charms from where they had been laid beside the cot and threw them at the old woman's feet. 'You have failed,' she shouted. 'You were her nurse, her protector. Not I. It is you who will rot in Victoria Prison.'

A feeble cry came from the cradle, a clucking sound as the baby drew in its breath to give a piercing, juddering squeal. The amah checked herself, pointing to the crib. Her face was cruel, lips drawn thinly against her gold flecked teeth.

'The lord of this house does not need this girl brat. He took the pig-girl to his bed to provide a son, nothing more. His anger will be terrible to see. You have seen how he spits in the face of the gods. His madness will rise in him and he will kill you both with the fury of wild horses. He will trample you under his feet.' Suddenly Ah Ho became deadly calm.

'It is the revenge of Chang Tien Shih who rides his tiger upon those who destroyed his image. He will compel the mind of the young lord to turn against this girl child.'

Ah Ho could see that her words were winning over the old woman's reason. She changed her tune to one of encouragement. 'I will help you take the child from here before he returns. Gather your things while there is time. Be quick. I will make her ready. Only you can save her.'

The Fish had seen many newly born girls die at the hands of the father before their eyes had opened. In her heung hah, the village where she was born in the lake district of Tung T'ing in the Yangtze province of Hunan, she had seen them drowned like kittens, their bones no bigger than birds, half concealed in the silt when the lake went down in winter. The fears she had always carried claimed her completely.

There was no reason to doubt what Ah Ho said was true. Fear for herself was not great. Injustice was nothing new to her but the soul of her mistress's child must not be left to drift unclaimed by ancestors, unguided to its place in the western heaven. No fate seemed more terrible to the Fish.

'I must first attend to my mistress. She must not travel to the western heaven unwashed.'

Ah Ho snorted. 'Do as you must but hurry. If the master has not died in the fire, he crosses the water now from Macau.'

Working quickly with hot water and towels the Fish cleaned the body of Li X'ia then went to the storeroom for her small bundle of belongings. She returned within moments with it hooked over her arm. Ah Ho was wrapping the crying baby in a jacket of coarse black twill that had been oiled to keep the wearer dry. Its lining of red padded cotton made a comfortable refuge and the crying stopped. While the amah's back was turned the Fish took the silver-framed photograph of Ben and Li X'ia from the bedside table and slipped it into the folds of her bundle. Beneath the pillow she felt for the ivory fan that was Li's favourite possession and concealed it too in her bundle. The amah turned, thrusting the black-wrapped infant into the old woman's arms.

'Go now. Save yourself and the child.'

The Fish hesitated. 'What of the watchman?'

Ah Ho spoke impatiently. 'He too has fled the fury to come,' she hissed. 'It was he who let them pass.'

'And the others?' The Fish trembled as she spoke.

'All are gone. I will soon follow. Life is finished here. Only bad joss remains.'

When she had closed and bolted the tradesmen's gate, Ah Ho went to the kitchen and dipped a bowl of broth from the pot. It would be hours before the master could cross the water from Macau. There was time to think. Sipping the broth, she cursed those that had bungled her plans but at the same time smiled at the luck that had delivered the old woman. When she had finished the tea she let herself out of the gate and walked quickly away.

Indie da Silva was half conscious when Ben arrived at the Deverill yard. The stab wound in his lower back was not serious he said, but a blow had robbed his limbs of all movement and it was this that he cursed himself for. The fire had almost spread to stored timber, but was now well under the control of three horse-drawn fire pumps. He choked on the rum Ben held to his lips, grimacing through his pain.

'Remember what I told you. Never trust the ones you think you can. They always get you from behind.' He looked at the blood on his hand where he had pressed the wound. 'Yum Sup did this, when I disturbed him setting the fire. But it was Chang-wa who struck me down.' Indie grabbed Ben's wrist and held on through another spasm of pain. 'He's a bad one, that Chinaman. One blow left me helpless as a child.'

Ben held the rum to his lips again. 'Why? Why would Yum Sup do this?'

Indie turned away from the rum, fumbling instead for a cheroot. 'Because he is Chinese and we are not. He must have been offered much by that ape Chang-wa.' He drew up with pain and then continued. 'They left me for dead. I heard them talking. It is Chang-wa who would have burned us out but it is more than that.' He paused again to let the pain pass. 'Loafers have been sent to Villa Formosa. I'm sorry Ben. I should not have called you away.'

When the cigar was lit Ben made him comfortable in a rickshaw and took him to the Portuguese Hospital. A sudden terrible fear had closed in on Ben at the word. Loafer was the old Shanghai term for a thug. One who will do anything for a few dollars to buy opium—kill, maim or kidnap. The thought pierced Ben's heart and lodged there like hot steel. The fire had been deliberately started in the half-built hull still on the slipways and among the drums of paint and turpentine. How could it benefit Yum Sup? Kidnap. The word screamed aloud in his mind. A distraction to get him away from the house. He rushed back to the yard to call Villa Formosa, letting the phone ring and ring as his thoughts raced—it would take three hours in *Little Cloud* to return to Hong Kong. No answer came. He ran to the commercial wharf, cursing as he ran that the new motorised vehicles of the company were all in Hong Kong Ignoring the calls of rickshaw pullers who slept between their shafts, he ran until his heart felt it would burst.

The pinnace was capable of twenty knots with throttles open and Ben kept them wide all the way across Deep Bay and into the narrows of Kap Shui Mun. When the engineer came up from the hatchway of the tiny engine-room to warn him of the pressure such speed was creating Ben waved him back.

'Keep your eye on the gauges but hold your revs.'

He took the wheel himself, sending the coxswain below to make coffee. His mind fought for calm as the distant pricks of light marking the East Lamma Channel showed dimly through a thin dawn fog and the sky behind him began to lighten in the east.

The possible reasons for the fire, the false alarm that had taken him so far from the house, scattered through his mind in a whirling of fear. Whatever it was, Yum Sup had been involved. How long had he been working against them? The pirate attack on the first voyage, the opium he had found smuggled aboard *China Cloud*? It all began to fit.

'Never trust the ones you think you can.' Indie's old warning brought it all home. He gave Indie da Silva only a passing thought. A knife wound to the Macanese was nothing more than an inconvenience, just another scar to add to his collection, to make the women he stripped for widen their eyes when they bathed him.

The moment's thought for his friend was only a fleeting relief from the dread he felt for Li X'ia. It stamped the question of his mother's death like a white-hot brand in his brain. He did not need to be told that she had died cruelly and violently. He prayed that this time it was robbery. They could empty the house for all he cared. Let it be robbery. But the word would not go away— kidnap. Above the slicing swish of *Little Cloud's* bow wave, the steamy hammering of her pistons, it spoke to him, filling his mind until his heart raced with the clamour of the engine and he had to dry retch over the side.

Kidnapping was the number one form of extortion in Hong Kong, a favourite of the tongs because of its simplicity. Find a rich house, learn about those beneath its roof from an inside source and the rest was easy. Arrange to have the house unguarded, snatch the victim. A day or two later send a severed ear or a finger to the head of the family with a ransom note. It was the great fear of every well-to-do household and the reason for the security of walls, gates and gatehouses. Who could have let them in? Who could have informed them of his absence? Not Ah Ho, she was as loyal and dedicated as they came. He cursed himself for not replacing the gardener who manned the gatehouse—Ah Ho had warned him that the man was known to drink.

The sun had hauled well clear of the sea when, leaping the closing gap from the deck to the jetty, Ben bounded the steep stone steps leading up into the garden. He half hoped to find her waiting in the pavilion, keeping a lookout for his return as she so often did, the old woman ready to serve him tea. His stomach lurched when he passed it empty, its marble table bare. It was early, he told himself, as he burst through the open French doors of their bedroom calling her name. A great soaring of pure joy shot through him at the sight of her peacefully at rest, so soundly asleep he thought, that even his shouts had not roused her.

It took Ben Deverill a full moment to realise that Li X'ia was dead. Her body had been washed and put into clean nightclothes. Her hair had been tidied and the bed-linen had been changed. When he flung back the fresh sheets there was no sign of the birth of a child, only a scattering of dried peach leaves. It was as though she had never been pregnant. The joy he had felt a few seconds before turned to a bolt of unspeakable pain that burst from him in an echoing bellow of despair that filled the house. It died away and left him to drop sobbing to his knees and cover her cold face with kisses and the hot flood of his tears.

The fear that had engulfed him on the run from Macau turned without warning into rage, engulfing him. His voice found its strength, filling the empty house. 'My child. Where is my child?'

The force of his cry, so torn with grief, reached across the beautiful gardens, echoed through the trees and in the empty pavilion.

Indie da Silva left the Portuguese hospital in Macau to be at his friend's side when the Taoist priest and the feng shui man had marked the position for her burial. She had been laid to rest according to the feng shui's reading of the divine powers of nature, in exactly the right spot and facing exactly the right direction to give her spirit unhindered flight, a place that would not be disturbed by the spirits of wind and water. She would be left where the White Lion of the clouds was in harmony with the Green Dragon of the hills, in absolute peace forever.

The tomb was in a corner of the birch wood facing the sea and the sunrise, its low arched entrance sealed with rose-coloured marble. Carved in its face were the Chinese characters that spelled her name and below it the phonetic translation: 'Lee Sheeah loved by Ben Deverill 1926'. The length of the grave rose in a gently curving mound, thickly planted with wild white violets and deep blue periwinkles, to become one with the earth around it.

On Ben's insistence, the body had been dressed in the red silk and embroidered finery of a bride, with a bunch of jasmine flowers to denote she had died as a beloved wife. A large and perfect pearl was placed on her tongue to show the gods she came from a wealthy family. He had placed a cicada carved from milky jade in her closed hand, fastening the fingers with a ribbon. It was, the priest said, the greatest talisman against evil spirits in the afterworld. Great quantities of paper money, a palace of red paper and every prayer in the Taoist ritual of burial were burned to accompany Li X'ia to the afterlife. It was as though he tried to make amends to the gods he had offended, and who had punished him so terribly.

Ben had been right in assuming that the Macanese would survive and quickly overcome the knife wound. Although deep and dangerously close to the kidneys, an injury that could have killed or incapacitated a lesser man, it had done no more than inflame a fiery vengeance in Carlos da Silva. Once stitched he had left the hospital and put himself in the hands of a waterfront doctor to whom the healing of such wounds by herbal poultice was as familiar as curing a bellyache. Indie had absorbed as much as he could of Ben's terrible grief without intruding on the privacy he knew such deep sorrow must be given.

To Ben the situation had closed in upon him as a living nightmare. Not one of the servants could be traced. The British police inspector had been efficiently sympathetic but held out no encouragement towards the chances of finding the baby.

The thought that his child, boy or girl, could still be alive, tortured Ben incessantly. Was it killed or kidnapped? The bruises on Li's wrists and ankles had shown evidence of a violent struggle and Ben's western doctor said that severe shock had weakened her too greatly to withstand the birth.

Nor had the police inspector offered any hope of finding Yum Sup and Chang-wa. Such crimes occurred every day in the colony and the perpetrators were seldom seen again, disappearing into the walled city of Kowloon, outside Hong Kong's jurisdiction, or across the border into China.

When ten days had passed and no ransom demand had been

made, Indie decided it was time to speak to Ben. It was not good to sit by the telephone or alone in the pavilion day and night. He found him in the birch wood standing by the little grave.

'It is time to stop waiting now. We must find them together. Then we will discover the fate of your child.'

When Ben did not answer, he continued: 'There is always hope. They do not sell a newborn child. They must care for it, if they are to profit . . . at least till it is five years old. It is not so easy to sell a newborn child,' he repeated lamely.

It sounded a hollow possibility but Ben raised his head, reaching out a hand to his only friend.

'There is no way of finding them. The baby must have died. There would have been a demand for ransom if it had not.' He smiled at Indie's troubled face.

'I will not wait any longer. I never knew how much she meant to me. It is as though my heart has been torn out.' He looked away past the pavilion and out to sea. 'I destroyed her gods. I insulted her faith . . . Perhaps if I had not . . .'

Indie placed a hand on his shoulder. 'Do not search for blame,' he said softly. 'If there is blame then it is mine. It was I who trusted that dog-turd Yum Sup. I who brought him into your life.'

Indie dropped his hand and turned away. 'It is I who will find them and when I do . . . we shall know the truth. Then they will die.'

Before Ben could respond, Indie held up his hand. He knew that his friend was too driven with grieving, too devastated by loss to contemplate action. 'It is a thing for me to do. I will find them. I swear it.'

PART IV

The White Crane

The Crane is serene in the face of the tiger.
In its serenity there hides great power.
Its wings are a shield of great strength.
Its beak a sword of swiftest steel.
The tiger sees only the softness of a white lotus.
The Crane sees only the cunning heart of its enemy.

MASTER TO-TZE

• IMAGE FOR WHITE CRANE •

The Long Journey

THE FISH held the baby tight against her in the over-crowded cabin. The corner she had found for herself was partly concealed by an ancient armchair. Its owner, an elderly man dressed in a long blue cheong-sam, had lashed the once grand old chair to a stanchion as a precaution against foul weather. Also tied securely to it were three travel-worn suitcases surmounted by a caged bird. The Fish had chosen him as her neighbour for the long sea voyage up the South China coast and along the upper reaches of the Yangtze River to Wuchang below Hankow. There she would board a wupan, the cheap river transport of the Yangtze to Tung T'ing Lake.

The gap between the back of the chair and the cabin's bulkhead was large enough for her to crawl into and deposit her red cloth bundle. It also gave her a certain amount of protection and privacy amongst the assortment of some hundred or so people who had crammed themselves into the large, low-ceilinged cabin and claimed a sleeping space for themselves and their families.

It was a scene familiar to the Fish, part of the yearly pilgrimage of Chinese workers living in Macau and Hong Kong to the villages of their birth, where mothers and fathers, brothers and sisters, numerous aunts, uncles and countless cousins eagerly awaited their annual return from the cities of the foreign devil bringing money and gifts.

She thanked the gods that she had never told Ah Ho or the others where her village was, preferring to keep it as her secret place. Although her life there, so long ago, had been bleak it was where she could always go when she needed to and the place she would go to when she was ready to die. She needed it now. Again and again and again she had thanked all gods that no one could follow her.

The baby stirred in its cocoon of cotton padding and she screwed the top from the thermos flask she had filled with milk. She had bought it from the sampan woman who had taken her from the wharf out to the anchored junk. The milk was half gone and she prayed that the arrangements she had made with the junk captain would be kept.

Around her neck, well concealed under the layers of her clothing, hung a snakeskin pouch. In it was the money she had saved for most of her life to pay for such a journey as this, and to pay for her funeral, the money that would see her suitably buried and assure her of a safe journey to the afterlife.

No one would be waiting in her village of Yuenchow, most of her relatives had died or moved away. Only one remained, a cousin, perhaps even older than herself, who had lived alone for many years on the other side of the lake. He was a barefoot doctor, a wise and gentle man who followed the ways of the Tao and could be trusted. To her prayers for a safe journey she added one that she would find him still alive and well.

With half the remaining milk fed drop by drop and the baby asleep she wedged her bundle into the corner and allowed herself to rest upon it. Closing her eyes for the first time in over twenty-four hours, she thought back over the events since leaving Ah Ho at the gate of the great house.

It had cost only a few coins to take the cheap motor-truck transport to the junk harbour of Aberdeen. There, for another coin or two she was informed of the Fukien trading junk making ready to sail for Shanghai and had been ferried out to it by sampan. She had purchased the flask of milk and paid extra with her passage money to assure that the child would be fed on the long voyage. The junk mistress had many children of her own and for a small consideration of copper cash had promised that the baby would be well fed.

The Fish had no idea how long she had slept when a rough hand had shaken her awake. The heaving of the deck beneath her and the creak of the bulkheads told her the junk was under sail. A boy of ten stood looking down at her. When he saw she was awake he beckoned her to follow. The old man in the blue cheong-sam was comfortably dozing in his armchair. His thin white beard lifted in a nod of assurance when the Fish asked him to protect her bundle and her space.

The master's quarters were grand compared to the bare passenger cabin, its walls hung with brightly coloured paintings of Tien Hau, patron saint of seamen, presented by well-wishers to assure the safety and prosperity of the junk and its owner. High on the stern the large cabin housed his family. Watched over by his wife the junk mistress, they ranged from crawling grandchildren to robust

sons and daughters. Two huge beds took up half the space and
a table and benches where everyone ate their meals were bolted
to the deck.

A plump girl of around eighteen came from among them, a broad
smile on her simple face. A baby, a year or so old, slept soundly
in an embroidered sling upon her back. She held out her hands
for the black bundle in the Fish's arms and seating herself on
the bed, exposed her full white breast to the hungry mouth of
Ben Deverill's daughter.

The voyage of the Fukien trader was slow and tedious. It took
on cargo at Amoy and rode the heavy swell of the Formosa Strait
low in the water. At Foochow they loaded chests of tea and the
red-painted leper junks came close, to beg for food and money
to be deposited at the end of long bamboo poles.

The overcrowded deckhouse amidships reeked with the sour
smells of seasickness and the clumsy ablutions of a hundred men,
women, children and assorted livestock. The Fish had been lucky.
To avoid sending the boy back and forth when the time came
for the baby to be fed, she was allowed to bring her bundle aft
and stay in a corner of the junk master's family quarters.

For this privilege she was expected to help with the preparation
of food and the cleaning of cooking pots but the baby was fed
regularly by its robust milk-mother who began to look at it as more
than a greedy mouth tugging strongly at her nipple. The white
baby had a light fuzz of hair the colour of rosewood and when
it opened its eyes they were lustrous as new pearls.

All the way up the coast the junk master's sons manned the
four ancient, breech-loading cannons on the junk's high stern,
filled with nails, old iron and round shot. The greatest fear of
those abroad a sea-going junk such as theirs was sudden attack
by pirates. Every sail that hove into view was watched with suspicion
until it had safely passed. They cleared Pagoda Anchorage and
the sea flattened all the way to the islands of Chushan where
the narrows ran a long green swell. The Fish was able to bathe
the baby on the sunlit deck, beneath the huge spread of the mizzen
sail.

The next morning she was wakened early by the preparations
on deck as the junk approached the treaty port of Ningpo, the
last stop before Shanghai. Against the pale green of dawn the islands
stood out black and solid as carved lava stone. Channel markers
still blinked low in the water and a soundless flight of seabirds
swept past them into the mouth of the Yangtze. Moments later

as the sun rose with savage suddenness it lit the patchwork of the mountain slopes—yellow fields of mustard against blue millet and the variegated greens of rice and sugar cane.

Two weeks after sailing from Hong Kong the junk left Shanghai for the two-day journey upriver to Hankow. Here the Fish left the junk and took passage aboard the wupan that would take her through the narrow and turbulent gorges of the Yangtze. A wupan, larger than a sampan and smaller than a junk, was hastily built of condemned wood in the boatyards of Hankow to make the hazardous journey over the rapids to Tung T'ing Lake. When it reached its destination it was usually considered beyond repair and broken up for firewood. Passengers who chose to travel by wupan knew the risks involved and left the journey to the mercy of the gods, for no human hand could steer it through the raging torrents of Wind Box Gorge.

All her long life the Fish had lived by the will of the Eight Immortals who guided every step of her way. They had seldom made her way an easy one but her faith had never wavered. Even the terrible vengeance they had taken on her innocent mistress did not make her think twice about stepping aboard the wupan. The Tanka milk-mother had fashioned her a sling that held the baby safely around her neck and with her red cloth bundle hooked over her arm she had taken her place among the other passengers, confident they would be delivered safely to the quiet waters of the great lake.

Even the rapids at the mouth of the Yuan, when the wupan threatened to fall apart like a chicken crate, did not shake her faith, nor the leaking boat half filling with water, when the others talked of throwing her and the baby overboard to lighten the load. She had looked up at the rocky peaks of the gorge and, in her mind, seen the spirit of Li T'ieh-kuai, the crippled beggar who always appeared to those in distress. His iron staff and gourd of comfort would see them through the racing white water that lay ahead.

Tung T'ing Lake

I<small>T WAS</small> late on a warm summer's afternoon when the daughter of Ben Deverill sailed into the vast lake of Tung T'ing in Northern Hunan, central China. The rains were over and the waters had receded, leaving a great marsh around its foreshores, threaded with channels and backwaters. At the mouth of the lake the travellers transferred for the last time to a floating reedstack, the flat-bottomed plank-boat of Tung T'ing, piled high with the tall reeds that were both fuel and building material for the lake-dwellers.

The Fish sat on top of the reedstack, weary but contented. Waiting for the plank-boat she had stopped to burn joss to the goddess of mercy for watching over them. As they punted smoothly across the mirror surface towards the eastern shore she watched the sandmartins skim the water and the dippers diving for shrimp. The inlet wound through a thick jungle of rushes where heron and spoonbill waded the shallows. Kingfishers darted in silent spurts of colour. Above them, rustling groves of golden bamboo climbed the foothills to forests of tung and teak trees. Higher still rose the peaks of mountains, smudged blue by distance. Overhead a lark, high and alone, was swept upon by an eagle.

Like most houses of the lake people, the house of Old To was made of reed mats. Small and pitch-roofed, it faced Tung T'ing from halfway up the hillside. Windows had been cut into the thick mat with woven flaps that could be rolled up or down to let in light and air or close out wind and rain. Talismans of red paper fluttered on either side of the doorway. Beside it stood another crude building, long and narrow, its walls of grey mud brick, its roof thatched.

There was a wooden pigsty where one large sow lay on her side, a bank of squirming piglets pushing their pink snouts into her belly. Ducks and chickens picked around green rows of vegetables fenced by overlapping hoops of split bamboo cane. Nearby, a white goat was tethered in a small orchard of plum and apricot, peacefully chewing on fallen fruit.

When Old To heard voices from the woodcutters' track that

cut its way through the foothills below his house, he continued working, his brush poised vertically as its thick squirrel-hair tip flowed across the hand-made paper like the strong sweep of a blade. People seldom came to his part of the lakeside. He had chosen the spot carefully. At a good four-hour walk to the nearest village, his only neighbour was a farmer of cord tobacco on the lake's edge, so he seldom had visitors. Like the orphan boy Ah Keung, who gathered herbs for him from the distant places, they only came in desperation, when even the gods had failed to heal them.

It was well known that Old To was a sage and a healer of great skill and that he turned away no one. But there were many who were afraid to come to him for help. Rumours of his Taoist magic and sorcery were common in the lake villages. It was often said by the wood carters and goatherders, who came nearest to his hut, that he practiced alchemy and had found the secret of turning iron into gold, and the stones of the ground into jewels.

They said he kept gleaming taels of solid silver buried beneath the floor of his hut. Everyone knew there had been a time when thieves had gone to his house at night. In spite of his great age he had met them with the power and art of the White Crane warrior. His beard flying like a war banner, he had dazzled them with the speed and strength of his skill, sending them running like rabbits, their weapons left behind.

Above all, the lake people whispered, Old To had found the elixir of immortality, the potion of eternal youth, the goal of emperors. His eyes were blue as the sky in summer. This alone was the mark of great magic. In the many years since he had come to the lake district, the sage had become a legend. Reed cutters, fungi gatherers and hunters of the spotted deer and the civet cat had all added their stories in the marketplaces and in the teahouses—how he could always be seen at sunrise, teaching the dance of the White Crane to a crippled boy upon the ancient rock, a rock, it was said, the master had charged with his great ch'i. Others said they had seen him charm the wild animals to his doorstep; the panda bear, the white tiger and the snow leopard came down from the high peaks to his hut. Some swore he could bring the birds from the trees to sit upon his finger. The sound of his voice could cause the mandrake root, the priceless ginseng, to answer and tell him where it grew. Above all this, it was said, he had performed great feats of healing—made crooked backs straight and twisted limbs whole again.

In truth, Old To was a Sifu, a Grand Master in the White Crane form of empty-hand fighting and a follower in the way of the Tao. He had devoted his long life to the ethical study of Confucius, contemplation of the great book *Tao-teh-ching*, the teachings of Lao-Tzu and the Yellow Emperor's great table of herbs. He was the true barefoot doctor, a healer in the ways of nature, who knew every fibre of the human body, its every disease and ailment. Every answer to its many conditions could be found from tapping the silent pulses and correcting the flow of ch'i through its meridians, to nourish the vital organs and cleanse the blood. He had learned the art of temple-boxing within the walls of the Monastery of Ten Thousand Buddhas on Lo Shan and at the Shrine of the White Crane. His were the secrets of the universe, of darkness and light, the essential balance of the Yin and the Yang through control of the five elements—metal, wood, earth, water and fire.

Only when the light that flooded his doorway was blocked did he look up and put aside his brush. Old To did not recognise the wrinkled face of his cousin. Not until she showed him the characters of their clan, carved on the inside of the jade bangle that hung heavily from her bony wrist, did he welcome her, gently taking the baby from the sling. He showed no surprise but quickly brought chrysanthemum tea.

When she was refreshed, the Fish told her story. Old To listened carefully to every word. She had done well to bring the child, it would be safe here. He gently opened the folds of cloth that wrapped the baby girl and examined her as gently as if she were a wounded bird.

'You have brought her just in time. Her ch'i is weak. She would have died before another day.'

An hour later the liquid he had prepared stood cooling in a clay crock. When it was ready, he took a porcelain spoon and fed it patiently into the baby's mouth. 'We will call her 'Siu Sing'. Little Star. If she lives she will one day shine like one and light the sky.'

The Fish was happy to see that he was smiling. One tiny fist closed over his finger. He lifted it to test its strength. 'This one was born a month too soon. Her before-sky ch'i is weak but her spirit is strong. We must make her after-sky ch'i even stronger.'

With the last of her energy the Fish handed him the red cloth bundle. 'These things are for her when she grows. I ask you to keep them safe. I do not have long, worthy cousin.'

He took it from her, lifting the lid of a camphorwood chest. 'It will come to no harm here. Few come to this place.' He chuckled. 'They are afraid of me.'

She held out her bowl for more tea and sighed. 'I have been the cow and the donkey of others all of my life. Now my mistress is gone, I am only a turtle. There is not enough money left to bury me.'

'Rest now,' he said quietly. 'You are in the arms of all gods here.' He covered her with a quilt of padded cotton. 'Tomorrow you must go to the farm below to find a milk-mother.'

Behind him, through a narrow gap in the reed wall a human eye watched for a moment longer. When Old To returned to his work and the woman was silent, it withdrew. Ah Keung, the Forceful One, went back to his place in the herb shed to think about what he had seen and heard.

The baby was nursed through the first five years of her life by the Fish. Over the early months, a young peasant woman came each day from the tobacco farm to breastfeed the infant in exchange for medicine and herbs for her large family. Siu Sing grew quickly and strongly under the protection of 'Great-uncle To' and the loyal care of the old amah. She delighted in the beauties of the hillside that surrounded her. Flowers, insects and coloured stones from the stream were her toys; birds and animals her playmates.

Before she could stand, Old To took her on his back, roaming the hills in search of rare herbs, roots, fungus and berries. He showed her the places where small animals and strange insects hid, where fish could be pulled from the streams and where the hairy, freshwater crab could be caught. From all of this Siu Sing drew strength and understanding from everything about her. She was a mystery to those who came close to the hut. What they saw was the glimpse of a small figure, animal or human—some were never quite sure as she was seldom fully seen—no more than a movement in the thicket or the sense of eyes peering at them from the tall flax grass or the reeds close to the marshland. A figure that was never close enough to be approached, so swiftly did it turn and disappear.

There was one who reported seeing her swimming naked as a frog and claimed that her hands and feet were webbed. Another swore that he had seen her running surefooted beside a lynx across the open grassland. Those few who went to the hut when the creature was inside, or came upon her squatting at the garden plot or climbing like a squirrel in the fruit trees, saw a strange and mysterious child, of uncertain sex. Wearing nothing but a scrap of homespun cloth around its loins, with skin the even, golden tone of a summer peach. It looked at them with eyes that were not Chinese. This they knew. They had never seen one of mixed blood in the lake villages. To those who avoided sunlight by covering every inch of their bodies and protecting themselves under the widest of hats, nakedness was a sign of madness.

The child's hair was as red as flame, flying as it ran, alight as the tail of a wild pony at sunset. They returned to the village with tales of a witch's child with eyes round as stones, the colour of the wild iris, and hair of fire. Whose hands and feet were those of a toad; who ran like the leopard and climbed like the monkey. An unholy creature born of Old To's magic to protect him from the evil of his own sorcery, or to assist him in his magic. Some said she was a product of that sorcery, or of the union of woman and unicorn.

There was nothing to stop her wild freedom or the distance she kept from others she met on the hillside. Nothing to stop her from finding the traps of the hunters and releasing the animals they had caught.

She was five years old when the Fish died in her sleep. Siu Sing burst in to wake her as she always did when the morning congee was ready to serve, to find the hand outside the quilt was stiff and cold. She rubbed it between her own, but the Fish did not wake. Grand-uncle To came in with an armful of wood for the stove, dropping it quickly and taking the cold, thin wrist in his fingers. Then he covered her face with the quilt and, taking Sing outside, explained that the Fish was about to take her long-awaited journey to join her ancestors in the western heaven. She must help him, he said, to prepare her passage.

While the old woman's body was washed an uneven number of times to invite good fortune in the spirit world and confuse all demons, he set Sing to making blue and white paper flowers. Some of these he fixed to the seven-cornered lotus-flower hat he had made to put upon the Fish's head. Her face and limbs he padded with wadding from the quilt and bound tightly with strips of cotton, before dressing her in her cleanest clothes. Putting on the wooden clogs she always wore, he bound her feet together with hempen cord to prevent her leaping if disturbed by evil spirits. The blue and white paper flowers he placed at her head and feet, then covered the red talismans at his doorway with white paper strips and hung the blue and white paper lanterns he had made outside the door.

'We must give her the journey she deserves, Siu Sing. Not to be sent properly to meet her ancestors was my cousin's greatest fear.'

Sing watched as he heaped the body with armfuls of bamboo leaves. 'This is so that Lui Gung, the god of thunder, will not see her and frighten her with his great voice.'

Taking down the heavy axe, he led the way deep into the groves until they came to the biggest stand of bamboo he could find. Sitting Sing at a safe distance, he swung the axe. The great polished trunk was as thick around as his waist and so hard it struck sparks from the blade.

'I wish Ah Keung was here,' he said, spitting on his hands. 'He is in the forest seeking the tree peony and the wild ginseng.' He hefted the axe high. 'We shall have to do this alone, you and I.' The blow of the axe rang out many times before the great bamboo swayed and fell, and for hours more as he split and trimmed its thickest length into a cylindrical coffin.

The tomb of the Fish was dug from the soft, rich soil of the clearing, its low entrance raised above ground level, built up with rocks of mountain granite and facing the lake so that her spirit could leave and return as it chose to. Close by, a spring bubbled, feeding a brook of sweet, clear water that fell over large stones into a pool crowded with pale pink lotus. It was the stream where Sing collected her pebbles, and picked watercress; where she chased butterflies and where swallows shot through the clearing to take the dragonflies. 'We will call it the Place of Clear Water,' said Old To, shouldering the axe and taking Siu Sing by the hand.

When they returned to the hut, he opened the chest beside his bed and took out the red cloth bundle. 'These things are for you. You are old enough to see them.' As he spoke, untying the cloth, he set a beautiful ivory fan before her and a photograph in a silver frame. 'There is a little money too. I will keep it safe for you.'

Sing opened the fan, spreading its delicate folds of creamy ivory like the petals of a lily. Its carving unfolded a picture story of courtesans playing music beneath the trees of a palace garden. A faint perfume stirred with its opening and Sing held it to her cheek to feel its touch.

'It belonged to your mother,' he said, showing her how to use it to stay cool. Then he picked up the silver picture frame. 'This is your father and mother. Your mother rests in the afterworld of her ancestors but your father lives. One day perhaps you will find him.' He replaced the photograph in the red cloth.

'I will keep these things safe for you here in this chest until you are grown and ready to leave this place.' When he held out his hand for the fan Siu Sing clutched it to her so tightly he smiled. 'Keep it then. There is no one to steal it from you here.'

The boy Ah Keung was an orphan. Born with a twisted foot, he had been discarded by his mother and father when they found it could not be straightened. What use would he be to them in their old age? To keep him would cost them money. The crooked foot had made him defiant and a terrible fierceness was never far from him. He had flown at those who teased him, calling him an ox with one leg, and his ugliness had cost his family much face.

When they had boarded a riverboat for Wuchang they had not told him and he had returned to the rented house in the village to find it empty and locked. At the age of eight he was alone. The great anger that he felt for those around him who would never know what it was to be a one-legged ox made him begin to build a world of hatred deep within.

Ah Keung had heard of the old hermit who lived on the far side of the lake and of the healing miracles he had performed. He had waited until winter when the lake was at its lowest, and hidden under a cargo of tobacco leaf. Before he had reached the far shore the boatmen had found him and thrown him from the plank-boat. But he was halfway there and the water was shallow for miles around the lake's edge, much of it a great shelf of slimy black silt brought down by the tributaries of the Yangtze. It was the time when the lake-dwellers travelled across it in wooden tubs pushed and pulled by coolies or in sampans hauled by buffalo. He had no coins to pay to ride in a tub so Ah Keung had swum and waded through the freezing mud, his fierce gaze fixed on the distant shoreline.

Old To had found him in the shed where the herbs were stored and dried, more dead than alive. At first he had thought the scrawny boy to be a mud-caked pelican unable to fly, or a fawn that had become trapped in the marsh. He had taken him in and was amazed at the strength of the boy's ch'i, the courage he had shown in crossing the lake alone. He gave him the name Ah Keung— the Forceful One, deciding to heal him and teach him to survive through the way of the White Crane. Under the old man's skilled care, and the sheltering warmth of the little hut, the boy was soon as fit as a colt. That had been two years ago and although he was free to come and go, Ah Keung saw himself as the chosen disciple and adopted son of his master. Then the old woman had come, bringing the strange one, the jarp jung girl, and he had been made to leave his place in the master's hut to make room for them.

When he was not in the hills in search of the ginseng, he gathered and chopped wood, fed the pigs and poultry, tended the garden and made sure that he was useful. He made a home for himself in a corner of the drying shed surrounded by racks of sweet-smelling herbs and prayed that the old woman and the squawking baby no bigger than a piglet would go away. But they had stayed, and much of the attention that had been his was soon shared with the girl who grew like a weed with the passing months.

He was glad the day he returned, the basket on his back filled with precious roots, to find the old woman dead and buried. She had watched over the strange, round-eyed brat like a hundred mothers and he had always kept away from them. Ah Keung had learned two things well from this isolation. Before all else he had learned to keep his feelings hidden; to show them too soon or at the wrong time brought only trouble. This had taught him patience. It had given him a savage determination and a strange kind of confidence. These lessons made deceit come easily and the contemplation of revenge sweet and enduring.

Master To had found that the boy possessed rare strength of mind and body. His mind was as keen and alert as his limbs were strong and supple. Young muscles half formed were ready to be trained. He was like a sapling tree the tap root of which had been damaged. By all the ancient arts of temple boxing, White Crane was the one created to defend the weak against the strong. Before beginning to teach, he had told Ah Keung the legend of Adato:

Seven centuries ago the holy monk Adato had seen how his nomadic people were robbed and scattered by warlords and bandits. They had suffered greatly without the weapons to fight back. One day while meditating, Adato had seen a white crane attacked by a tiger. The slender legs and splendid plumage of the great bird seemed doomed to fall before the weight and ferocity of the tiger's powerful charge. But as he watched, the crane leapt from its path with a great beating of wings, blocking the attack and defending itself with skilful thrusts of its sword-like beak.

The legend claimed that the monk followed the crane for many days, observing its methods of survival. When it waded for fish in the shallows, the tiger, who had rested and licked its wounds, attacked again. Still the crane stood its ground, lifting from its enemy's path but never retreating. In time, the powers of fury and force were beaten by the superior skills of technique and calm. The tiger limped, torn and bleeding into the trees to die.

Ah Keung was a natural adept, so quick to learn, so fascinated by the game of combat that the master began to wonder if he was putting a deadly weapon into the wrong hand. This boy was indeed the Forceful One, but force was not the way of the Tao or of the White Crane. Ah Keung seemed to sense this hesitation. He found that long periods of meditation had taught him to anticipate the thoughts of others. He had learned the old Taoist techniques of internal breathing and these he practised in his corner of the herb shed or in the solitude of the hills, patiently building the dormant powers within him.

He was filled with a great elation, a feeling of immortality. The already powerful ch'i he had inherited from his peasant parents grew steadily within him. There was only one part of the monk's teaching that he did not understand. The way of the White Crane was the way of self-defence, never of attack. Ah Keung could not accept this. In his short life he had been shown what happened to the timid and the defenceless and he saw no value in great power unless it was used to destroy the adversary. This he fixed firmly and immovably in his mind and in his heart. Above all, when the twisted foot refused his demands of it, tripped him or hampered the speed of a movement, he commanded it to try again and again. A thousand times, if that's what it took, until the foot found a way. What Ah Keung had learned was supreme self-control.

He had nothing to do with the jarp-jung girl. When she came to the herb shed, he ignored her until she went away. An unspoken barrier stood between them and as Siu Sing grew they both accepted and understood it. But when the old woman was gone, the master had said: 'I will teach you, too, the way of the White Crane, Little Star. You will need to defend yourself in the life that lies before you now that she who brought you to me is gone.' Then Ah Keung had realised how much he despised her.

Old To had shown Siu Sing the jade amulet around his neck. 'This is the symbol of the great bird's power. One day you will wear it.' Ah Keung had been chopping wood nearby and heard the words clearly. They filled him with a fury that turned iron hard in his belly. He brought the axe down with such force it split the chopping block cleanly in two. His sacred world was about to be invaded and he would defend it. But he must wait. There was much more to be learned from the old man before the time came. Until then he would play it their way, it was all a part of the game. He had no doubt who would be the winner. His hatred of the girl grew with every day they spent together as she too was brought to the rock and began to learn the Way of the Crane.

Old To had spoken to him, sensing his resentment. It was clear to him that the boy was not of the pure clay he had hoped for. There was great trouble in his heart. He decided to test Ah Keung as all uncertain disciples must be tested.

'The Way is for all who are worthy, not just for one. You have learned much and well. Now it is the turn of Little Star, Siu Sing.' When the look of rejection on Ah Keung's face remained unmoved he put a hand on the boy's shoulder and spoke reassuringly.

'You are thirteen years old now, already a man. Sing is not yet six, two years younger than you were when you crossed the lake alone. We will still practise as before and you will continue to learn.'

Ah Keung's sullenness had still shown upon his face. The master's voice had found an edge as he withdrew his hand. 'Do not disappoint me with ingratitude and greed. Do not question my decision.'

Ah Keung realised he was going too far. 'I do not question, Sifu.' He used the honourable term 'Respected Master'. 'I will work harder and I will help all that I can.'

Old To nodded and turned away. Even his deep wisdom could not fully detect the danger he was creating.

Two years passed before Master To spoke to Ah Keung in such a way again. He had watched carefully and sensed impatience, the greatest failing of a White Crane disciple. They stood on the flat, lichen-covered rock where they trained and had been practising for three hours since dawn. The sun was well risen and the boy's powerful young body wore a light sheen of sweat. 'The time has come for you to leave this place, Ah Keung. To climb the mountain of your own choice. You must follow the way of the White Crane for three years, alone with what I have taught you. Then you must decide. If you return we shall see what you have learned.'

Ah Keung felt as though his master had delivered a blow from behind.

'Where shall I go, Sifu?' he asked, as humbly as he could. 'Which mountain am I to climb?'

'It is for you to choose. Each of us has to journey alone. Only alone can we find the path. If you do not return it is because the way is not for you to follow.'

Ah Keung was engulfed by a wave of self-pity. 'Sifu. Without you, I have no one.'

Old To's voice lost its patience. 'You have yourself. I have given you that. No one else can climb your mountain for you, or find your path. Trust yourself. It is all you will ever need. Go now.'

They exchanged the salute of respect and Ah Keung walked away, his resentment turning to the cold stone of hatred toward the worthless jarp jung who had taken his place and the fire of revenge had already struck its spark.

In Siu Sing, Master To found the perfect student. Her traumatic birth and fragile health were forgotten as time passed. Her child's limbs were flexible as the stems of flowers and her step as sure and light as a bird's. Energy gushed from her like a spring and her spirit shone as bright as the light in a raindrop. But it was her heart that Master To found extraordinary. It was open to all things and it rejoiced in the arms of nature, embracing all that surrounded her, seeking nothing more, but enquiring of everything she touched and saw and heard.

The way of the Tao answered many of her simple questions and Old To delighted in the simplicity of her happiness, the purity of her child's curiosity. He taught her the lore of Tao; the power of the earth spirit, the greatest soul of all that fed all others like a fountainhead. He showed her how to touch a tree and be one with its life-force. Above all these things, he taught her the power of the rock. It was the rock upon which they practised before the rising of the sun. An even platform of granite, a shelf that he said had once been part of a great mountain, the hardest, oldest rock of all, holding in its heart the minerals that shape the earth's crust and all of the secrets of its fiery centre. He called it the Rock of Great Strength.

'When we are in the hut or finding herbs on the hillside you may call me Great-uncle. Here, upon this rock you must call me Sifu.'

He spoke softly but there was a firmness that Siu Sing knew she must always obey. She learned the name of the lichen that patterned the edge of the rock like fine lace. And how to draw its strength through the soles of her bare feet when she stood in its centre.

'You will grow strong as a tree on this rock. Become one with it. Your legs are the trunk of the tree, your feet and toes are its roots. Send down your essence until it is linked with the essence of the rock. Nothing can move you while the ch'i is rooted in this way. You are part of the Rock of Great Strength.'

He squatted before her. His eyes, clear blue as the sky reflected in the lake, were level with hers. 'This is where you will learn the Way of the White Crane, here upon this rock. When you have learned and gone away the strength of the rock will go with you. Only you can break the link, then you will fly like the great bird and know its secrets.'

Straightening to his full height, Master To looked down at her, placing his open hand on her head. 'When you have learned this, you will never fall. To fall in the path of the tiger is to perish.'

Each day after the long hours of training were over they would come to the Place of Clear Water to sit beneath the shifting light of the bamboo on the soft bed of its papery leaves. He used to say the bamboo spoke to him, told him of the seasons and how they would be. He taught Siu Sing to listen for the whisper of the leaves and the faint creak of the slender stems against the deeper voice of the great trunks until she could also hear their message. It told her of the weather and the changes long before they came.

'The wind is in the south and it is only the fourth moon. Is it a strong wind or a little wind? Is it warm and dry or cool and heavy with the dew of the forests? Or is it in the east and hot as flame off the far deserts? Or does it bring the fresh scents of the mountains of mist from the lake?'

With him the master would bring the well-worn satchel made from the skin of a deer. It had been a barking deer that had come many times to the back of the hut, he said, and had sheltered there in winter. Then the deer had not come for many days and he had gone looking, to find it starved to death in the trap of a hunter not far from the hut.

'The deer was beautiful and it trusted me. Now it goes with me always and guards my secrets. We will be together forever.'

Unrolling the reed mat, he would take out the books and scrolls, teaching her to read the tiny characters that filled their many pages. They would study them for hours, until the lowering sun slanted through the grove and it was time to return to the hut. There they prepared the food together, taking fresh herbs and vegetables from the garden plot and picking ripe fruit from the tree.

Each morning at dawn, just as the sky showed its first breaking across the lake, and they stood together on the rock, the deep tolling of a bell came with its light. When Siu Sing asked where it came from, Old To pointed to a distant peak lost in cloud.

'It comes from the mountain of Lo Shan, one week's walk from the other side of the lake. Its voice reaches the ears of 400 villages. Each of them will take one day's supply of food each year to feed its 3000 monks. They call the bell "the Prayer of Buddha" and believe that it brings his blessing into every corner of the poorest house and the richest palace.'

Old To led the way to the hut. 'Come, we will eat before going to the Place of Clear Water.'

Their meals were fragrant and filled with nourishment, and even here there was a lesson.

'Food is nature's medicine; you must learn to use it wisely. To eat with the wisdom of the seasons you must make sure that one food is meant to be eaten with another. If you learn this, health and strength will always be yours.'

Siu Sing was eight years old when the master fetched brushes, ink and paper from the wooden chest. These were the ancient tools of any scholar, for calligraphy was the highest form of expression, from which all other arts flowed. A man who was not proficient in the forming of images with ink and brush could not claim to be scholarly or hope to compose poetry, or paint pictures and move others by his work. Nor could a Sifu of Kung Fu hope to truly master his form without first conquering the brush. Calligraphy must be his first control and its perfection his greatest goal.

The age of eight was considered the best time for a child to begin to learn. It was the number of pa-kua, the ancient trigrams that formed the centre of Taoist philosophy.

'When you can truly guide the brush you can hope to guide your own destiny and even the destiny of others,' he said softly, as he laid out a thick pile of hand-made paper and a bamboo container of brushes, 'When you control the writing of characters you can hope to control yourself.' He did not expect her to understand, but this was the beginning of all understanding.

First, he took a wad of wild cotton and cornsilk. He tossed its lightness in his hand to delight her and then rolled it into a soft round ball. Next he took down from the shelf a small inkpot made from the horn of a buffalo, showing her how it had been beautifully carved with vine leaves and a line of distant mountains. Into the pot he pushed the ball of clean cotton, pressing it down with his finger to make a pad. Then, from a hard, shiny melon gourd he poured the exact amount of jet-black ink onto it. He had made the ink himself, he said, from lampblack and the sap of acacia.

The slender shafts of the brushes came from the sacred black bamboo and their tips from the hair of the squirrel and the coat of the sable. The paper he had pressed from vegetable fibre and the pulp of the tulip tree. Soaked in rice water, it had been rolled and dried many times and hung until it was stiff and strong as old parchment, veined like the dried leaf of tobacco.

While Siu Sing watched, her eyes alight with interest, he selected a fat, pointed brush from the bamboo container and studied its finely tapered tip. Rolling it on the ink pad until it had absorbed just the right soaking of ink, he poised it upright over the untouched paper, his arm resting lightly on the surface. 'We now begin a great adventure, Siu Sing,' he said, his voice deep with the mystery of a story-teller. 'Before the tale of life can be told, first must come the making of images.'

Held perpendicular to the paper, the brush began the slightest of movements and onto the coarse, clean surface flowed the unbroken lines of his beautiful calligraphy.

'The making of images with ink on paper is also part of the Tao,' he explained, as the strong shape of the character unfolded before her. 'It is a discipline of the mind and its command of the body. It too is Kung Fu.'

His strokes were swift and certain, light as the crane in flight.

'When you can control the brush, when it gives you the image that your mind perceives as perfect, exact in every detail, when the character appears without pause or hesitation, then you have found true harmony.'

He smiled at her. 'But of course it is never truly perfect.'

When the character was finished, his brush never leaving the paper until it was complete, he set it aside and reached for a clean sheet. 'You must watch carefully, Siu Sing. And then you must copy. You must copy a thousand times and then a thousand times more, until you no longer control the brush, for the brush has found movement of its own. Then you will have discovered freedom.'

Three beautiful characters swept from his brush and when each was dry he laid a fresh piece of paper over each of them.

'See how the image can be seen through the paper so that you can follow their path? Now, I will teach you how to hold the brush.'

He closed the shaft of bamboo into her small hand, gently positioning the fingers like the holding of a flute.

Siu Sing spoke for the first time. What she had seen had so filled her with wonder no words had been necessary. 'Great-uncle To. How can I copy these images when I do not know their meaning?'

'You do not have to climb the mountain to paint its image in a picture. You will learn their meaning soon enough.' His hand closed over hers and, guided by the firmness of his fingers, she made her first hesitant mark.

If the night was clear and cool they would go to the rock and there under the moon he would teach her the paths of meditation. He said it was the greatest gift that he could give her and that once she had received it, it would never desert her. 'The lower mind,' the master carefully explained, 'is that which is concerned with the actions of the body, with breathing and circulation of the blood. It is the seat of instinct and sudden urge, the place where fear and doubt is born. The middle mind deals with the information we receive and the solving of its problems. The higher mind is the source of spiritual joy, of bliss and creativity. It is the wellspring of a deeper knowledge. To attain a clear communication with the higher mind we must first control the urge and the action. This lies in quietude. Then we are close to the gods.'

When the lessons were over for the day, they would sleep and rise early to wash in the cold water of the rain barrel. Since Ah Keung had left to climb the mountain it was Siu Sing who brewed the ginseng tea and took it to the rock to await the master. There her training was harsh and unrelenting.

'There is no gentle way to self-protection,' the master said. 'Violence heeds no other voice. This rock is hard, but so is injustice and cruelty and these are the things you must fight against.'

If Sing looked puzzled, he would speak of the beautiful white crane who wished to harm no one. 'The crane was content to live quietly in the marsh, safe in the rushes. But the tiger came seeking the crane and tried to destroy her. It will always be like this.'

When she fell and grazed her skin on the rock he would say: 'If you do not like the hardness of the rock, you must learn not to fall.'

In the early months she was shown only the stances, the precise positioning of arms and hands, legs and feet, the exact balance that allowed advance or retreat, defence or attack, block or strike. These she practised ceaselessly until every muscle cried out for rest and her mind was numbed by repetition. When she wavered the master would say: 'Violence makes no allowance for male or female, for strong or weak, big or small. Violence seeks only to destroy or possess. Upon this rock you are a warrior, nothing more, nothing less.'

The fundamentals of the stances and strengthening of muscle, bone and sinew were practised through the unbroken cycle of exercise. The skill of great stealth was learned by walking barefoot on a bed of dead bamboo without disturbing a single leaf. Patience and endurance were continually tested through total concentration. The internal organs were nourished and the blood refreshed through the control of breathing, the mind disciplined by meditation, fortifying the will and hardening the resolve to learn and achieve.

When wind, rain or blizzard turned the rock into a dangerous place almost impossible to stand upon, or the sun beat down upon it like an anvil, the practice continued.

'Violence comes in all weathers. It does not wait for comfort. It strikes from ice or fire, in the deluge or the drought. We must know all its faces, understand all its moods. You must learn to flow softly as the water in this brook. See, the stones are hard and heavy but the water moves them. If it cannot move them with its power, it wears them down with its patience.'

The many movements of the White Crane became second nature to Siu Sing. She grew much taller and stronger than a Chinese girl of her age. Years of complete freedom to run and climb where she chose, and of the continued training that had become the only focus of her life, had kept her sleek as feral cat. Rigorous as it was, the Way of the Crane did not build distorted muscle but created internal strength and perfect health.

Her constant pursuit of calligraphy and its mental disciplines had tamed her. She plaited her hair in the way of the women working in the tobacco fields. Her skin was brown as a fisherman's but with an inner glow that others did not have. The making of images and the planes of meditation had given her the ability of complete stillness, while her constant practice made her capable of sudden, devastating speed and action.

At almost ten years old, she was ready to be taught the true meaning of calligraphy: the application of each move in self-defence against an attacker. Every morning upon the rock Old To became that attacker, gradually increasing the force and intensity of his assaults to test the accuracy and strength of her resistance, varying them to assess her speed. When pain or injury resulted, its reason and its remedy were explained to her and its source treated with herbal poultice or internal medicine. Sing was taught to recognise and isolate pain and to treat it herself with acupressure, the application of the thumbs to nerve centres, blocking and releasing bloodflow to promote the circulation of ch'i. She was taught to use the healing heat of moxibustion—the burning of herbs close to the skin—and to understand the acupuncture points in their relation to the balance of Yin and Yang.

'The purpose of violence is to inflict pain.' The master told her. 'We must learn to understand it, absorb it, withstand it and defeat it. When we are hurt we must know the remedy and heal quickly, in the way of the birds and animals.'

One evening as they worked on the forming of images, Old To's fingers no longer needing to guide her brush, she asked a question: 'Great-uncle. You are my master and you have taught me many great secrets, but I am confused. If the crane is to defeat the tiger, when should it spread its wings and when should it remain hidden?'

Old To reached for a heavier brush and applied it to the inkpot. 'The crane is wiser than the tiger. It does not seek conflict, and will not reveal its powers until no choice remains. If the crane sees that the tiger is too fierce, it remains quiet or flies away. Only when violence is upon it does it rise up in the face of attack.'

Siu Sing thought about this answer for a moment and when she fully understood, she asked another question: 'For two years I have copied the images for one hour every day. Many thousands of times I have repeated them and still I do not know their meaning.'

Old To's eyes twinkled. 'You have known them all the time . . . for they mean patience . . . tolerance . . . and discipline. These are the three main teachings of the White Crane, for if its secrets are revealed in aggression, it will be overcome.'

He took a clean sheet of paper. 'You have learned them well. Now you are ready to discover others.'

A fourth character materialised under the flawless stroke of the brush. It was the symbol of Kung Fu. 'Kung Fu means only expertise. It does not signify the violence of combat but the mastery of the three images you have learned to control . . . the striving for perfection of skill.' He slid the finished character across the table.

'Learn it well, but use it when all else has failed and only in defence of your life. When you have perfected it, if that day should ever come, guard it with humility.'

The Hummingbird

WHEN SHE was ten years old, two things entered Siu Sing's world that puzzled her. The first was treachery. She was aware of cruelty. Too often she had come upon trapped animals, drawn by their cries of pain. Old To had explained the philosophy of violence as he first began to teach her the fundamental principles of the White Crane and then had spoken of treachery.

'Treachery is like the wind,' he said. 'It comes when we least expect it. On the calmest of days. There is no way of knowing from where or why. Only that it comes. You can run from it . . . or turn in its face. No life is sheltered from this wind.'

She had tried to imagine what she would do when the wind of treachery blew in her face, but she could not, for she did not understand it. Then, beside the tomb of the Fish, in the Place of Clear Water, one day she saw a hummingbird. Master To was dozing in the flickering shade. He had given her the reading lesson for the day and she was intent on the characters he had set for her to learn. The sound of the hummingbird's wings was no louder than that of a bee's; it was the brilliance of its colours that made her look up.

It hung motionless in the warm, grass-scented air, shining like a bright, blue-green jewel, more beautiful than any other bird she had seen. From flower to flower it moved in sudden spurts of light, hovering among the tall yellow spikes of water iris, its tiny needle beak buried in pollen. As she watched, enchanted, it streaked across the clearing and stopped, shivering in mid-air, as though stunned by an invisible wall.

The spider was as big as Siu Sing's hand as it bounced greedily down the silken rungs of its web. She sat in fascinated horror as it enveloped the bright jewel with its long, hairy legs, tumbling it over and over, binding the gleaming wings again and again until all colour was trapped in the sticky, fluid silver that flowed endlessly from the spider's bloated abdomen. At last the web, spun wide across the grove, stopped vibrating. The hummingbird was still and the spider began to feed. Old To's voice reached her across the clearing, his eyes still closed.

'Now you have witnessed treachery. Never forget it.'

The second thing that came into Siu Sing's life was the question of who she was, and with it came the question of God. There were no mirrors in the hut of Old To but she had seen her face each morning in the dark water of the rain butt and many times in the still surface of ponds. There had been few people to compare herself with closely, except the girl from the tobacco farm. When others came to the hut she would stare at them from a distance. She could not see that she was different to them, except that her face was not broad as theirs were, her nose not quite so flat and her eyes a little rounder. It had never concerned her. Were not all faces different? Only when she went to the village did she know that there was much more than this.

She had asked many times to be taken to the lake village and each time Great-uncle had said, No, it was not yet time. 'One day you will have to go from here and find your own way. This time will come soon enough and then you will learn. There is no reason to hurry.'

Siu Sing was never lonely. There were too many things in her world to delight and amuse her. But her curiosity was without bounds and when she saw the laden reed carts moving slowly down the hill to load the plank-boats waiting in the marsh below, she wondered where they went. And the junk sails that blew red and brown, like autumn leaves across the lake—where were they going? Her questions were endless, and finally, Old To had agreed to take her.

'It is time for you to set foot into the world outside. I will take you to the great market of Yuenchow,' he said, unfolding a simple costume. It was like that worn by the farm girls, a white wide-sleeved smock and short black trousers cut off at the knees like his own.

'I gave ginseng as large as my fingers for these clothes. I hope that you like them,' he said as he plaited her hair and told her of the Yuenchow market. 'Once each year the people come from far places to do business in the village. It is something you should see.'

He gave her strong slippers sewn from ox hide and looked at her when she was dressed. 'You have eyes the colour of pearls reflecting the dawn sky.' He chuckled. 'Do not be surprised if those in the village should stare. If they say foolish things do not heed their words.'

It took all morning to reach the village and when they did his warning could not have prepared her for what happened at the market-place where people came from mountain and plain to mix with those who never left the lake. Some had travelled from as far as the Ordos Desert with their camels, others with short mountain ponies laden with baskets of produce. Donkeys, oxen and water buffalo pulled carts of every size; pigs and goats were crammed into bamboo pens. To Siu Sing, taken for the first time from her isolation, it was a place of endless amazement.

Everywhere people jostled and jabbered to exchange coins for fruit and vegetables, basketware and cloth, clothes already made and shoes and boots of every kind. There were shiny pots and pans, bright beads and rolls of gorgeous silks the colours of the hummingbird. People everywhere shouted and danced, tumbled and played music. There were those who performed tricks of magic and told fortunes. Letter-writers squatted opposite cobblers and candlemakers and those who sold incense, miniature shrines and the images of Buddha beside the eight Taoist fairies. On a stage in the middle of the square a Chinese opera crashed and banged to the squeal of trumpets.

Very quickly Master To's words came back to Siu Sing as she clung to his hand. Why did they stare so? Why did they stop what they were doing to point and laugh or growl at her? Women braiding cured corn and hanging strips of cabbage to dry for pickling, turned and called to their children.

'She is jarp-jung, leave her. That one is cursed. Do not touch her.'

The children defied their mothers and followed after, dancing around her and shouting, 'Jarp jung, jarp jung, jarp jung.'

Old To felt Siu Sing's hand tighten in his.

'What are they saying, Uncle?' she asked when they drew away from the crowds and found a seller of sugar cane beside the village tree shrine.

'They are the foolish ones I spoke of,' he said gently, handing her a cup of cool, sweet juice and a piece of cane to chew. 'They are simple people who have not seen someone as beautiful as you.' He smiled, but his eyes were sad.

'If I am beautiful, why do they laugh and call me names?'

Old To led her to the shade of the banyan, its branches draped with a thousand paper prayers. 'They are ugly, so they do not understand beauty. It is because you are different.'

'But Uncle, I do not feel different,' pleaded Siu Sing. 'I do not wish to be different.'

She held out her hands to him and looked down at her feet. 'Do they not have ten fingers and ten toes as I have?' She touched her nose and her eyes. 'Eyes and nose and ears like mine? Inside, do they also have a heart that beats?'

Old To thought for a moment before answering. 'It is just that they have never seen eyes the colour of morning sky or a face such as yours. It frightens them, so they are silly. To them, to be different is to be feared.'

A tiny line of worry creased the smoothness between Siu Sing's eyes. *It is her first frown*, thought the old man. *It is a pity that it comes so soon.*

'What is jarp jung?' she asked suddenly, her eyes searching his. Again, Old To paused to think. He could not tell her it was the crude term for a mongrel, one tainted by the impure blood of the barbarian, for whom there is no place and no people and who holds no value.

'It means you are very special,' he replied at last. 'Like the evening star that rises before others, shines more brightly and remains apart. It too is different. Or the hummingbird. Is it not more beautiful than the sparrow?' He stood up, reaching for her hand.

'Come, we have seen enough of people. I will take you to meet one who is as you are. Will that satisfy you?'

Outside the village, on the edge of the lake where the fish-drying sheds stood, Old To led Siu Sing to a woman. She was making bricks with the mud from the lake bed. The mud was grey and sticky; her hands and arms were covered with it and it had dried upon her face and in her straggly hair. She wore the grey habit of a nun, the same colour as the mud. It was not possible to see if she was old or young. But when she looked up at Old To's greeting, Siu Sing saw that her eyes were also pale as morning sky breaking through the mist. She smiled kindly and offered them water from a stone jar.

When they had moved on, Master To spoke quietly. 'You see? There are others like you are. Far from here, across the mountains in the great world outside, there any many who look as you do.'

Seeing the woman with the light eyes had given Siu Sing great comfort. She had reached for the nun's muddy hand and held it as she said goodbye.

'Why does she make bricks?' she asked.

'She builds a church . . . a temple to her god.'

'Are there other gods than Buddha and the Eight Immortals?' asked Siu Sing in great surprise.

'There are many gods,' he answered, chuckling. 'Each of us must find our own.'

'Why does no one help her to build the church?'

'It is not their god. Those that would help are not allowed to. They are afraid they will be stoned, so they stay away. At night when she sleeps, thieves come and steal the bricks she has made. Children push down what she has built but still she builds. For many years it has been like this.'

'Why does she try, Uncle? If the people of the village do not want her, why does she continue making bricks?'

'It is called faith, Siu Sing.'

The frown returned to her face. 'Is the faith in herself or in her god?' she asked simply.

'Sometimes it is the same,' replied Master To, as they took the winding track away from the village.

SOOCHOW CREEK
1927

Two years after the death of Li X'ia, Ben Deverill stood looking down from his offices in Shanghai's Broadway Mansions. The incredible view flowed westward with the sluggish curve of Soochow Creek. It was the view he had dreamed of since Frenchy had described it to him almost twenty years earlier: 'There's no stretch of stinking brown water in the world that smells so sweet to a man of imagination. A fool smells sewage, street cooking and coolie sweat. A man of imagination smells only success.'

Squat stone bridges spanned a multitude of lighters, barges and sampans. Every cargo-carrying craft imaginable lined each side of the river, leaving a broad corridor of muddy water for the movement of goods to and from the ships anchored in the Whangpoo River. It was all exactly as Ben had pictured it. Big Ching, the customs house clock-tower, blocks of godowns, the cavernous warehouses of the great trading hongs set back from a thoroughfare teeming with handcarts, trucks, rickshaws, wheeled transport of every kind and the straw-sandaled feet of 100,000 coolies. From where he stood they poured across the bridges and over the wharves like ants following a trail of treacle. Steel drums, wooden chests and canvas bales shifted back and forth between godown and boat deck like grains of rice carried by the swarm.

Ben could have taken his place in Broadway Mansions long before this if he had wished, but he had preferred to share the small space set aside in a corner of the godown and sometimes used by the compradore until these particular rooms became available. They were the same rooms his father had occupied before the boxers of Empress Tzu Hsi and her Manchu officials had burned his house and killed his wife, a quarter of a century earlier.

Now, Shanghai was under another attack. General Chiang Kai-shek's nationalist army had taken the city and placed the Chinese section under his Kuomintang regime. Ben had watched it coming with a calm assurance. This was no butchers' rebellion. It was an organised take-over. From his capital in Nanking, Chiang had outlawed the communist party, expelled the Russians and cut off trade with the Japanese. His entry into Shanghai had been a clean and efficient one and his leaders were already talking with the hongs to form the foreign cantonments into the Greater Shanghai Municipality and an even more powerful trading block.

The Deverill Company and its fast-growing shipping arm, the Cloud Line, had been a prominent part of those negotiations, particularly those to do with the blocking of the Japanese, whose vast merchant fleet had taken a large share of the freight business in and out of Shanghai. It had left Ben Deverill in an even stronger position and with a boundless future.

When he had arrived in Shanghai in 1925 it had been perhaps the only place on earth for him to bury his grief. A place where foreign trade of any kind believed in self-government. Law and order, rules and regulations were made by the individual, and for those with the abilities and the daring to take monumental risks, there were even greater rewards. It was exactly what he needed— a city that never slept, where success was born of courage and risk.

Ben Deverill had nothing to lose. He had taken on and beaten the colossus of Shanghai business with a ruthless code of ethics and massive energy that some began to say had burned him out in the fifteen years it had taken to build one of the most successful shipping and trading companies in South-East Asia.

He had thrown himself with equal passion into the incomparable melting pot of Shanghai living. This was a place where no one ever asked another why they were there. It was taken for granted that, for whatever reason, they were seeking all that life had to offer no matter what the cost. It offered a reckless lawlessness that protected its own: American conmen, White Russian tarts, Japanese jazz players, Korean tram conductors, triad warlords, Jews fleeing from Nazis and Chinese revolutionaries fleeing from each other.

It was a place where twelve-year-old children sweated for sixteen hours a day in exchange for food. Where if a drunken foreigner ran down a Chinese it cost him $400. In the Shanghai of the twenties and thirties the extraordinary had become the ordinary, the freakish commonplace. Its hysterical vivacity was exactly what Ben Deverill had needed to help him forget.

Since turning his back on Hong Kong two years earlier, Ben thought he had closed the last door on the death of Li X'ia and the disappearance of his child, but he had not. The thought that his child might still be alive was constantly with him. Both he and Indie da Silva had exhausted every channel open to them that could bring news of Yum Sup and his accomplice Chang-wa. Together they had scoured Macau but no amount offered in the gambling dens and brothels could bring news of them.

No ransom demand had been made in the months of waiting that had almost sent Ben mad. Official investigations had been brief and shallow. He had accepted bitterly that the death of a Chinese woman living with a western man did not qualify for undue attention. Leaving Indie da Silva to manage the Macau boatyard he had closed Villa Formosa and left Hong Kong for Shanghai, while the Macanese continued the search he had vowed to pursue.

Ben had gone to his old friend Aggie Gates and she had tried to gentle his grief with prayer. She had still refused to tell him how his mother had died, but two years in the teeming, turbulent city of Shanghai had shown him its powers of destruction. He had no illusions regarding how it must have been to have ruined a man like Frenchy Deverill. Violence and hostility were as ever-present in the building of Shanghai business as the deceit of wit and cunning. It had taken endless work and relentless vigilance to make the progress Ben had made, in the way that he had made it. Inevitably it had begun to take a toll of his health and strength, something he dare not allow.

To be in any way weakened by illness or fatigue was his greatest fear. Life in Shanghai was like a crouching beast, ready to spring upon the first sign of weakness or lack of resolve and tear its victim to pieces. Failure to protect himself and what he had built became Ben's most persistent nightmare. His observation of the Kuomintang and their methods had done nothing to reduce his sense of vulnerability.

The Generalissimo's forces were made up of private soldiers whose main reason for wearing a uniform was the power it gave them to rob, rape and kill. He had seen at first-hand the routing of communists and the ferocity of the triad societies when their territory was threatened. Slow torture and open slaughter was as much a strategy of the Chinese military and the underground tongs, as it had been 1000 years before. While there remained the slightest chance that his child was alive and that the two men who might know its whereabouts could still be found, survival became his obsession.

When the English doctor he had met at the Shanghai Club became a friend, Ben had consulted him professionally. Doc Watson was in his early sixties and fifteen years of Far East medical practice, eight of them in Shanghai, had hardened him to most things. A semi-retirement, spent at the bar of every available club and hotel the city had to offer, had dulled his senses to the rest.

He had pronounced Ben fit as an athlete with the constitution of an ox when he had first examined him. A year later he had found that peak condition was becoming undermined by long hours behind a desk and an increasing intake of rum to combat the stress of ceaseless diligence.

Very much aware of the poor physical example he had allowed himself to become through the excesses of life in Shanghai, Doc Watson was genuine in his concern for such a healthy specimen as Ben Deverill. He advised something he would never have prescribed for himself, a regular routine of exercise, suggesting the swimming pool in the race-course grounds of the International Settlement or the tennis courts of the French Club.

Neither of these prospects appealed to Ben. He had never felt socially inclined and apart from a handful of hard-drinking friends he sometimes caroused with, the thought of golf or tennis did not sit well with him. He had convinced himself that it was simply a matter of time before news of Yum Sup and Chang-wa would reach him. Macau was a magnet for men like them and sooner or later they would return. When they did Indie da Silva had enough ears to the ground to find out about it. Then he must be ready to act. Ben was prepared to sacrifice everything to trace his child or avenge its death.

With this in mind he had sought out an American mercenary, an ex-sergeant of the U.S. Marine Corps. who had become a soldier of fortune available to any warlord north or south, east or west who needed a first class military advisor.

Whilst passing on the benefit of twenty years' experience of soldiering to the rabble that made up the private provincial armies of certain glorified brigands who called themselves warlords, this man had learned all they could teach him in the oriental realms of martial arts. These he had adapted to his already wide knowledge of western-style unarmed combat, combining and innovating it all into a lethal style of his own, which he sometimes taught from a well-equipped, exclusively European gymnasium on Nanking

Road. His name was Arnold Tinker. His reputation for clandestine operations and the decisive way he concluded them had once earned him the ironic title of Tinkerbell. It had often been said that Tinkerbell was more Chinese than American, preferring to spend his time on the wrong side of Chung Wha Road, well away from the Route Lafayette and the Avenue Foch. It was also well known that he was a dealer in anything from army mules to armoured cars, an arms dealer, rumoured, in spite of the poor front he put up, to be a very rich man. That he could be hired as a collector of bad debts and that protection was his sideline had never been proved. Those who did business with Arnold Tinker were not likely to talk about it.

He lived above his gym because those who came to consult him or for his instruction and paid his high fees would never have followed him into the Chinese quarter where he made his contacts. To call Tinkerbell a mercenary was to understate his abilities. He confessed to making a precarious living as an enforcer in a place where enforcement was as much part of business as gift-giving. You gave gifts to seal a bargain and used force to settle it. It was many years since he had been called by the code name Tinkerbell in the days when he had served as lieutenant to the famous Two Gun Cohen against the Bias Bay pirates. Nowadays, if he was called anything at all, it was 'the Yank' or just plain Tinker.

He had heard of Ben Deverill. In spite of being the biggest city in China, Shanghai was the smallest when it came to the activities of its captains of industry and commerce. He recognised the taipan at once when Ben first came up the stairs and into his dojo. Tinker's self-defence skills had begun with Japanese ju-jitsu and led to Okinawan karate. He was wearing the worn, black gee of an eighth Dan master when he spoke: 'I never expected to see the great Dai Fo Lo—the mad gwai-lo of Macau—in here.' He held out a hand. Tinker was half a head taller than Ben and ten or so kilograms lighter. His eyes were cold as frozen soda water. 'It must be something important. Come upstairs.'

Handing over the class he was conducting to another instructor, he led Ben up a second flight of stairs to the rooms where he lived. He spoke in perfect Mandarin to his amah, who silently left the room. Ben could not help noticing that she was young and extremely attractive, dressed in the black trousers of her calling but with a knee-length tunic of flowered silk.

'If you're wondering does he fuck his amah, the answer is, yes.

I gave up white meat a long time ago. I can't afford the White Russians and the ones I can afford would give you the black pox. Now that is clear, what can I do for you?'

The directness of his opening words told Ben there was no need to waste time and made him feel at ease. He could not help thinking that the notorious Tinker would have a lot in common with Indie da Silva.

'I need to get fit,' said Ben, equally directly.

Tinker regarded him steadily with his icy gaze. 'Is that all?'

Ben held his stare. 'I may need to kill a man. Two in fact.'

Tinker stepped over to a lacquered Korean cabinet set out as a bar. 'Whisky or gin?' was all he asked.

'Rum, if you've got it?'

He found rum and poured a generous tot. 'Since when has Ben Deverill needed someone to teach him how to do that?'

'Since he became a businessman,' said Ben drily.

Tinker looked at his own drink, a tumbler half filled with Scotch whisky. 'If I'm going to teach you to kill someone, I'll have to know something about them.'

'They are both Chinese. They were responsible for the death of my woman and the kidnapping of my child.'

Tinker drank half the whisky and thought for a moment. He did not appear surprised. 'Those are good reasons,' he said at last. 'But there are many ways of killing a man in this town without involving yourself.'

'It is something I must do personally, if the time comes.' The tone of Ben's voice was clear but it did not satisfy Tinker.

'What's wrong with a gun? You don't need to be fit to pull a trigger.'

'A gun may not be enough.'

'A gun is always enough.'

'Let's say I need the exercise. One of them is a temple boxer.'

Tinker whistled softly then drank the rest of the whisky in a single swallow. 'That, my friend, is a different story. When is this going to take place?'

'I don't know . . . but it will. I'm sure of that. I want to be ready.'

'Anything else?'

Ben had left the rum untouched, now he reached for it. 'Guns and ammunition. Any make, all you can get. I understand you can supply me.' He tipped back the rum. 'Price no object. No questions.'

Tinker put down his glass and stood up. 'That is another thing.

First we will see if you are too old or too soft to fight. Be here at six o'clock tomorrow morning. We will talk of guns when we can trust each other.'

For the next three months Ben arrived at the dojo on Nanking Road every morning at exactly six a.m. Tinker's training methods were as unique as the man himself. For the first six weeks they left the Indian clubs and barbells in the racks and the only pieces of equipment Ben was given to use were a length of greasy rope and a sawn-off broom handle. He had never been told to skip before and it didn't come easily.

According to Tinker he was ten kilos overweight. He lashed his feet with the length of heavy cord, tangling and stumbling, Tinker said, with the grace of a water buffalo. It took him back to the hated school playground where the rosy-cheeked girls skipped and hopped and he stood alone to watch them with his back to the wall. He only questioned Tinker's methods once.

'When do we begin to practise?' he gasped, sweat-soaked at the end of a session.

The American looked him in the eye without affection. 'Your wind is shot and you've got the coordination of a hippo. First we'll get your weight down and breathing back then we'll work on flexibility. No more five-course lunches at the club. No more cigars and no more booze. Maybe then we'll talk about other things.' Ben never asked him again.

The half broom handle was used to create what Tinker called dynamic tension, pitting the strength of one set of muscles against the other, making him his own opponent. When Ben could skip fast and light for fifteen minutes at a time and still catch his breath at the end of it, Tinker began to teach him breath control; how to take in oxygen long and slow, through the lungs and deep into the belly, then draw upon it as a reservoir. To this he added stretching exercises, testing muscle and sinew to its limit and then taking it further. When Ben bit on the pain of it, Tinker would say. 'If you're going to tangle with a Chinese boxer you'd better be fast as a leopard, strong as a lion, supple as a dancer and cunning as a snake. Because he's all of that and more.'

At the end of the six weeks Ben Deverill began to feel that the clock had been put back twenty years. They went running, following the miles of dirt tracks through the market gardens on the edge of Siccawei Creek. When Ben could cover ten kilometres in good time without raising a muck sweat, they started running the sleepers of the Shanghai-Nanking Railway at Paoshan. Tinker said it measured the pace and increased concentration. To Ben it was like being back on the Macau waterfront, running the sea wall, skipping the nets and crab traps, the mooring ropes of junks.

They began training with the weights and clubs between long sessions of callisthenics, to end up with a cold-water shower in the dojo and bottled water or green tea in Tinker's rooms. At the end of the three months Ben was pronounced reasonably fit. The American had never mentioned payment, or the buying and selling of weapons, or the business of killing and Ben had never asked him.

Upstairs the amah he called Lila fetched them tea and fresh fruit and left them alone.

'What about your fees? I've paid you nothing yet.'

'I've taught you nothing yet, so where's the difference?'

Before Ben could protest, Tinker said, 'All we've done is get you halfway fit. When do you fight this man?'

'I have no idea. Perhaps I never will. I just want to be ready.' Tinker waited for a better explanation.

'I cannot explain it. Something tells me the time is coming. Perhaps I am wrong but I feel it will be soon. I cannot fail. That is why I have come to you.' He paused. 'No questions. Remember?' Tinker was satisfied.

'What style is this boxer?'

'I don't know. I never saw him fight. He is known in Macau as Ironhead Chang the Fierce.'

Tinker was quiet while he peeled a mandarin orange.

'Whoever he is and whatever his form, you'll only get one chance. From here on we do a crash course in bare-handed murder— face to face. You'll forget everything you've ever learned about combat, I don't care how good you once were.' He concentrated on dissecting the fruit. 'The Chinese boxer uses his knowledge of the human body to damage and destroy. He studies for a lifetime, he never stops practising. He knows that when he does, he dies.'

Tinker sucked a section of the orange into his mouth. 'We don't have time for that. What I will teach you, you must practise until it is part of your brain. As natural to you as drawing breath.'

He pushed the fruit bowl over to Ben. He lifted his teacup in salute, sipped the hot tea noisily, then asked, 'What do you know about temple boxers?'

'That they consider fighting an art, and winning a religion,' said Ben.

Tinker nodded. 'The most dedicated and dangerous fighters you'll ever come up against, but they have a weakness. Most Chinese boxers are so caught up in some fancy form handed down for a thousand years, they forget about good old-fashioned street fighting. That's where we've got a chance. They never expect a westerner to know anything about their precious form, or to have tricks of his own. They spend upwards of thirty years perfecting a style created around some legendary monastic philosophy. All you need to learn is one or two moves. One or two strikes. So fast, so sure, so deadly they can stop a horse.'

He set down the teacup and walked to the gun case, returning with a heavy revolver. He flicked open the chamber and spun it.

'This is a Webley & Scott 455. It'll drop a rogue elephant. It speaks all languages and when it comes right down to it, it'll always have the last word.'

When Ben hesitated, Tinker left it on the table beside him.

'Think of it as insurance, just in case you're not up to killing with your bare hands.' He contemplated Ben for a few seconds as though trying to make up his mind.

'If you are determined to do this I will teach you two strikes. If you fail with one you may have time for the other. If you miss with both your life is over. My fee is high because if you succeed I have saved your skin and given you your revenge. If you fail, you will have no further use for money.' As Tinker spoke he watched Ben's eyes.

'How high?' asked Ben, meeting his gaze.

'One thousand Yankee dollars for each,' Tinker said. Leaning back he opened a drawer and took out a sheet of paper and a silver Chinese pen. 'Make out a promissory note to your accountants for ten thousand in case you die.'

Ben looked up, surprised. 'Why should I pay you so much more if what you teach me fails?'

Tinker smiled but his eyes stayed hard as ice. 'It will be you that has failed, not me. Let's say it's for wasted time. Besides,' he added, 'what will you care?'

Ben took up the pen and began to write. 'These strikes you talk of must be something very special.'

Tinker's reply was deadly flat. 'They are. No Chinese boxer would expect you to know them. That's your secret weapon.'

He pulled out a rolled chart and flipped it open. It was an old Chinese scroll showing an ancient diagram of the human anatomy, the kind used by acupuncturists and bone-crackers.

'The old masters studied every minutest detail of the human body, learning exactly where, why, when and how to strike.'

He grinned at Ben's look of confusion as he stared at the intricate drawing with its myriad tabulated points. 'Don't worry.' He laughed. 'The lesson is simple. There's only two things you need to remember about a man, any man—eyes and gonads. He's lost without either of them, so that's what we go for.'

Tinker tapped the chart like a professor. 'Eyes and gonads.'

He looked steadily at Ben for a moment without speaking. 'Or you can walk off from here and use the gymnasium at one of your fancy clubs. Forget the whole thing and carry a gun. That way you owe me nothing and you'll have a better chance of staying alive.'

Ben shook his head, as he signed the note. 'I accept your terms. You have my word this will be honoured. I'll instruct the office tomorrow.'

Tinker stood up and held out his hand. Ben rose to take it. Their hands had hardly touched when he found himself flung across the room to crash into the wall. The impact almost knocked him unconscious. He shook his head to find Tinker's hand again outstretched to help him from the floor.

'Lesson number one. When a boxer touches you it's for a purpose. He doesn't want to shake your hand or dance with you. He's got no rules and he'll incapacitate or kill you without a qualm.'

The cable Ben received from Indie da Silva six months later read: 'Have found them. One in Macau. One in Bias Bay. Can you come at once?' Ben needed no further information and booked a flight for Hong Kong that afternoon.

Indie da Silva rose slowly from his chair when Ben walked in and came from behind the littered desk with his arms outstretched. He had aged over the past three years, Ben thought as they hugged briefly. Indie wasted no time in getting straight to the reason for his cable.

'I have found the shit-eaters. The owner of an opium den on Sin Alley—it cost a lot of money.' He grinned widely in the old way. 'I knew the day would come. Rats do not leave the rubbish pile for long.'

'Where?' asked Ben quietly.

'The turd Yum Sup is here in Macau. I know exactly where he can be found.' He grinned. 'He won't be going far.'

'And Chang-wa?'

'Bias Bay. Not so easy. He now follows his true trade. He is one of the leaders in "the Nest", the pirate village of Fan Lo Kong.'

Less than an hour later Indie led the way through the narrow cobbled lane known as Sin Alley. Above them tiers of bamboo poles poked from windows hung with washing. From every doorway the smoke of opium mingled with the smells of the street and the cooking pot. There were raised voices from the fan-tan parlour as gamblers haggled over bets and every few yards an urchin waved a book of lottery tickets. From the upper windows pimps and the amahs of prostitutes called down descriptions of every sexual deviation the mind could conjure up.

The place they entered faced the waterfront of the inner harbour. It was the part that attracted boat crews, among them many of the black-skinned sailors from the Cameroons and a sprinkling of Indian shopkeepers. Lottery booths were tucked into every gap between the decaying buildings; everywhere men squatted over dice games while their women tended the racks of salted fish. Indie pushed straight through the throng of gamblers to the back of the parlour, separated from the light and the din by a flimsy partition that looked like an old junk sail.

Behind it, in the half dark, a long row of divans lined the walls. From each, the dull red spark of an opium pipe glowed and faded in an oily fug of smoke. Indie and Ben stood for a moment, allowing their eyes to become accustomed to the gloom.

'Yum Sup is one of them,' breathed Indie, moving from one to the other. 'He is here,' he said, stopping at one of the ragged figures stretched on a corner divan.

Ben looked down at what was left of Yum Sup. The laodah's deep sunken eyes stared back, empty as dead shells. He was hardly recognisable. The ravages of the drug had reduced him to a living cadaver. The telltale stretching of skin over the bones of the skull was far advanced and his prominent teeth were fully exposed. His lips, unable to close, remained in a deathly grin. Ben raised a hand to his nose and mouth at the stink that rose from the divan, so vile that even the sickly reek of pipes could not hide it.

Indie turned up the wick of the tiny oil lamp beside the divan. 'When they reach this stage they shit where they lie,' he said grimly. 'We found him just in time. Next will come the stink of death.'

A grossly fat Chinaman pushed aside the partition and stared at them. Indie said something in sharp Cantonese and the man left with a grunt of acknowledgement.

'I have paid the price of two pipes to that pig for this privilege,' Indie grumbled, looking down his large nose wrinkled with disgust. 'If we cut him to pieces that one will thank us for it.' The long tapered blade of his stiletto caught the isolated light from the lamp wick as he turned up the flame. 'Let's see just how far gone this dog turd really is.'

Indie passed the point of the blade before Yum Sup's nose. Nothing changed in the laodah's fixed grimace but his eyes followed its movement.

'You see who has come to visit you,' Indie whispered with mocking sympathy. 'You remember?'

A glimmer of change showed in the addict's eyes but no words came. His head began to rock slowly from side to side, his eyes never leaving the long double-sided blade. Indie leaned closer, the needle-sharp point against Yum Sup's cheek.

'What happened to the child?' he hissed, through clenched teeth.

Ben remained in the shadow. He knew that Indie stood a better chance of getting information than he did. Controlling the urge to grasp the scrawny stalk of the laodah's neck and throttle the truth from him, he kept silent. Indie asked the question four times patiently, carefully and close to the large leathery ear, each time a fraction louder. Still no word came from Yum Sup.

'See who is with me? It is the mad gwai-lo himself, Dai Fo Lo. He wants your life for the life of his woman and his child.'

The stiletto blade flicked once and a three-inch gash opened in the laodah's cheek. A squeal of pain, the cry of a cornered rat, caused Indie to ram his hand over Yum Sup's mouth and look sharply at the dozen or so smokers flopped around them. The smouldering pipes showed no sign of disturbance.

'We could slit this pig's offal from crutch to breastbone and they wouldn't lift a finger to help him,' Indie said, loud enough for the terrified man to hear.

Swifter than sight the knife point was transferred to the lower abdomen.

'I will take my hand from your mouth so that you can talk. Only answer my questions or I will open you like a chicken.'

Yum Sup's skull craned upward with a gurgle of fear. His jaw flew open without the strength to scream.

'You remembered something. That's good.' Indie sank the steel half an inch into the withered flesh two inches below the naval. 'What happened to the child? Speak or I'll open you up from crutch to breastbone.'

A flood of Hoklo dialect spewed from Yum Sup in a torrent too fast and too foreign for Ben to understand. Awful tears flowed from the hollow eye sockets as though the last body fluid was suddenly tapped. Indie listened intently, his ear inches from the jabbering mouth. Ben caught the names Chang-wa and Ah Ho.

'Now in English for the master Dai Fa Lo to hear. Perhaps he will spare you.'

Ben leaned down, turning aside from the odorous breath.

'I no touchee missy. I no take baby. Chang-wa, Ah Ho. They makee plan. Chang-wa send loafers, takee missy.' The words were gabbled again and again.

Only Indie's knife pressed against Yum Sup's corded throat silenced him to a snivelling whimper.

'He says your amah was the one. She arranged the kidnapping through Chang-wa.'

'Where is she?' Ben demanded close to the laodah's ear.

'Chang-wa,' babbled Yum Sup. 'Chang-wa kill her because she know he send loafers to Dai Fo Lo's house.'

'He's probably telling the truth.' The Macanese stood up and looked quickly round. 'Best to do this quietly. He can still squeal,' he said as he turned down the lamp wick. His fingers closed around Yum Sup's throat, the thumbs feeling for his windpipe cutting off all sound. The knife blade flashed.

'No.' Ben's voice was flat and definite. 'Let him die here in his own time.'

'It is too late,' said Indie, wiping the steel on Yum Sup's ragged pants.

Lai Choi San looked nothing like a queen of pirates in her richly decorated rooms above the fan-tan parlour she owned in Sin Alley. Of medium height and stature she was dressed in a full length scarlet gown with a cape of ermine tails, ornaments of apple-green jade thrust into the bun of her greying hair. Only the deeply-weathered tone of her face and hands suggested she was more than the successful madam of a well-run house. Lai Choi San had inherited her father's power as Macau's most notorious pirate chief. He had left her his formidable reputation and seven heavily armoured junks. In less than five years she had matched his ruthlessness and cruelty, adding another five captured vessels to her fleet.

Ben Deverill and Indie da Silva were the first foreigners of any

kind to be admitted to these rooms and she stood eyeing them
with caution. To one side stood the young Chinese man who had
brought them here.

'This boy tells me you are looking for Ironhead Chang the Fierce,'
she said in Cantonese with the strong accent of the water people.
Before either of them could answer, she went quickly on as though
anxious to bring their business to an end as swiftly as possible.
'I have heard of the mad gwai-lo who defied Ironhead Chang on
the mudflat and built his lorcha alone and now owns many great
ships. I respect such a man and welcome him and his friend
to my unworthy house.'

She made no attempt to sit down and left them both standing.
There was no customary offering of tea. 'Many years ago it was
Ironhead Chang who advised my father to despatch the junks
to take your vessel, *China Cloud.*' She grinned suddenly, creasing
the brown lines of her handsome face. 'You killed four of his men.'

'It was not because my ship was attacked that I wish to find
Chang-wa. Through him, my woman was killed and my only child
is lost to me.'

It was language Lai Choi understood but she folded her arms
and stared back at Ben without reply. Her face told him nothing.

'We are told he is in the village of Fan Lo Kong and that he
is protected in the Nest by the queen of pirates.'

Ben's eyes were fixed unwaveringly on hers as he continued.
'If I must, I will seek the help of the Hong Kong government and
come for him with gunboats and a hundred men. This would not
be good for your village.'

Lai Choi frowned. It was only a year since a gunboat had come
to the island, destroying a hundred homes and burning thirty junks.

'But I would prefer to find him alone,' Ben added respectfully.
'My friend also has a score to settle. We seek your permission
to enter the Nest and will pay any reasonable price.'

Lai Choi San's arms remained folded as she considered his words.
Chang was a troublemaker. He had already maimed two of her
best men and she could not trust him to take their places, he
was too hard to control.

'Chang-wa may kill you both and eat your hearts and livers.
He has been known to do this when he has defeated brave men.'
She watched Ben closely as she spoke.

'That is a risk we must take,' answered Ben, returning her gaze.
'Name your price,' he said, seeing the hesitation on her face.

'I do not need money. I have many chests of silver.' She thought a moment more. 'I offer you safe conduct on the island to do what business you will with Chang-wa. The price will be the machine-gun that killed my father's men.'

Ironhead Chang the Fierce walked naked to the end of the rickety bamboo jetty. The sun had just risen and it made his heavy frame glow with a rude, animal health. He walked with the unconscious swagger of the fighter, his short legs slightly bowed, his thick arms loose. There was little definition of muscle anywhere on his body but it was so nourished by his internal ch'i that it had developed the consistency of tyre rubber. From one hand dangled a wooden bucket on a rope which, when he reached the end of the jetty, he it dipped into the sea. Hauling hand over hand, he up-ended it over his gleaming dome, barking and spluttering like a bull seal at the sudden rush of cold water.

It was known and accepted among the lawless community of the Nest that Chang-wa liked to bathe alone early each morning and practise the exercises that gave him the strength of three men. The others of the village did not fear him—fear was something they did not accept—but they knew he was best left to himself.

Although the island village of Fan Lo Kong masqueraded as a fishing settlement, it was peopled entirely by pirates. A small granite-spiked outpost in Bias Bay, west of Macau, its large fleet of junks was heavily armed with concealed cannon and their business was not fishing but the boarding and plundering of ships and the looting of coastal villages. It was from here that sea-going piracy scoured the waters off Hong Kong and Macau, ranging the length of the China coast, spreading its net far into the shipping lanes, making the South China Sea the most infamous and dangerous stretch of ocean on the face of the earth.

When his attempt to become rich on the mad gwai-lo's money had failed so badly, there was no longer work for Chang-wa in the Chinese boatyards of Macau. Even Chang's violent reputation couldn't regain his face on the waterfront and he was not welcome in the gambling places where he had once been king. Macau was no longer a good place for him.

Eagle Beak had survived the blow that should have killed him and before she had fled across the border, the amah Ah Ho had reported that the gwai-lo's woman had died. A thousand times he had cursed the fools he had sent to take her. They should have brought her with them dead or alive, whelp or no whelp.

He did not fear the trouble they could cause but he had not forgotten the great determination of the mad gwai-lo who had stood alone on the mudflat. The three-legged dog Yum Sup had disappeared into the lost society in terror of Dai Fo Lo's revenge, while Chang would have welcomed it. He had a score to settle with those who had made him an outcast.

Lai Choi San, the queen of pirates, had welcomed Chang the Fierce to her island colony where all were brothers outside the law of any but their own. He had quickly found his place there by defeating those that challenged him and by proving his ferocity whenever it was needed. He lowered the bucket a second and third time among the fish bones and opened scallop shells that rolled with the tide beneath the jetty, then, setting it aside, he began the slow, penetrating movement of Ch'i Kung.

From behind the heavily-barred windows of stone buildings and crumbling mudbrick huts, old women muttered curses at the two foreign devils escorted through their village. The last time foreigners came, they had wiped out half the community and the old ones would have cursed more loudly, but four of Lai Choi San's top men walked beside them, two on each side. The Lewis gun had been delivered and the queen of pirates had kept her word. When *Cloud Chaser* dropped anchor in the sheltered bay just before dawn, the bodyguard had sculled a sampan out to bring them ashore. Each of the four carried long-barrelled, outdated rifles and wore nothing above their waists but bandoliers of bullets. Under wide coolie hats of plaited reeds their hair hung in long, greasy pigtails and they wore hand-made sandals of straw on their feet.

They said nothing and showed no interest in the two they had been told to escort over the mile of rocky ground to the village. It had been raining and already children played in the black mud of the roadway; mothers ran from the doorways to snatch them out of the barbarians' path. Pigs wallowed in the roadside while dogs crept warily from their approach and chickens scattered among the refuse. To Ben, the pirate village of Fan Lo Kong looked like any other fishing village on the outlying islands. Huts and houses, walled garden plots, ducks and geese patrolling the patches of rice and millet.

At first Chang-wa took no notice of the small party advancing towards him along the road from the village. No one bothered Ironhead Chang when he took his exercise. Only when they reached the jetty did he stop and squint towards them. The rattle and click of firing mechanisms being cocked carried clearly on the still air as slow recognition of Ben and Indie dawned on him. At first he thought they had been captured and the guard had brought them to him but as he moved towards them he saw the rifles were pointed at his belly. One of the bodyguards called out in raucous Cantonese. Chang-wa stopped where he was.

'You have found me, Dai Fo Lo,' he called from the middle of the jetty. 'And these dogs are here to protect you.'

'I have found you, Chang-wa,' replied Ben. 'I need no protection.'

'And Eagle Beak. You are stronger than I thought.'

Indie said nothing.

'What will you do now?' Chang asked, advancing again one slow step at a time.

'We have come to talk or to kill you,' said Ben evenly. 'It is for you to decide. Only one thing can save you.'

'What is that?' Chang snarled his contempt, as the fighter in him made instantly ready.

'Tell me what happened to the child.'

'I know nothing of a child. The amah Ah Ho was the one. Not I. It was not intended that the woman should die.'

'Those that did this thing were sent by you.' Indie spoke for the first time. 'You thought the dog Yum Sup had killed me.' He tossed something onto the jetty at the Chinaman's feet. It was a large, leathery ear.

'He has told all to the Hong Kong police. They will be here later this day. Tell us if the child is safe and where it can be found and we will defend you.' Indie slid the stiletto from its sheath. 'I will cut out your heart and feed it to the crabs unless you tell us of the child.'

Chang-wa's huge bulk seemed to fly the last few steps from the jetty in a move too fast to anticipate. Two rifle shots rang out in quick succession, both missing their mark. The men who had fired them took off like rabbits rather than try to reload, one of them dropping his weapon in his haste. Another fired, more sure of his aim, and the whack of the bullet was loud as it struck the thick pad of Chang's shoulder.

He had landed like a cat, one arm flashing out to break the man's ribs with a sickening crack. As he dropped, dark blood welled from his mouth onto the gritty sand. Chang-wa spun in a full circle, the edge of his bare foot sending the last rifle flying, as a short strike drove into the fourth man's neck with a hooking blow that left him paralysed among the litter of broken shells.

The whirlwind speed of Chang-wa's attack had been too sudden and too concentrated to involve Ben or Indie. Now he faced them in the lethal stance of his form, feet widespread, crouching as though on springs of steel.

'These dogs have the ch'i of old women. Let us see if yours is stronger, Dai Fo Lo . . . and you, Eagle Beak.' He beckoned them both to come for him, as if unaware of the blood that ran freely from the hole in his shoulder.

Ben had drawn a powerful-looking hand gun and aimed it steadily at Chang's head.

'Listen to me Chang-wa. This is a British military Webley & Scott .455 revolver, the most powerful small-arm in all Asia. It is not like the firecrackers these fools carry. It will kill a buffalo.'

Chang's mouth drew into a sneer as he spat at Ben's feet. 'The mad gwai-lo has also become a pregnant woman. His courage has deserted him, his ch'i is weak. He no longer speaks with his hands and his feet as he did on the waterfront in Macau. He can no longer defend the honour of his whore or her bastard in the way of the Empty Hand.'

The revolver remained rock steady for long seconds, the whistle of Chang's breath the only sound to break the silence. 'Finish it,' said Indie sharply. 'Finish it now or give it to me.'

Ben lowered the weapon slowly, clicking on the safety catch. 'Don't use it unless you have to,' he said as Indie took the heavy pistol from him.

The years of anguish suddenly opened up in Ben like a floodgate. All the old furies, denied for so long, screamed to be released into the leering face before him. At the same time the disciplines of common sense, the intelligence of a fighter who must not be beaten, took hold over blind hate. He said a silent prayer for the time he had spent with Tinkerbell in his gym on Nanking Road. He counted on Chang-wa being over-confident, careless in his contempt, recalling all he had been taught as the boxer flew at him. Deflecting the first exploratory strike Ben ducked the second and blocked the third.

His hooked hand drove in the sweep of the Tiger Claw to the precise spot in Chang-wa's rubbery girth. The thumb that could now pierce sandbags with ease drove deep into the flesh of his lower belly to reach the ileocecal valve at the junction of the large and small intestine. He felt the valve rupture. Tinker's relentless training had unified Ben's mind and body into one weapon, the mind always a breath ahead of the strike. He knew the Tiger Claw had found its mark and that Chang-wa would die an agonising death from peritonitis within twenty-four hours. It was not enough.

Chang-wa also knew. His eyes bulged with surprise, mad with fury at his carelessness. His huge frame shook with the impact of the blow. Before he could regain his stance Ben swung a powerhouse southpaw punch from close to the ground upward and into Chang's naked groin. In the fractional element of surprise it gave him, he repeated the punch, stepping back and slamming a snap kick into the same spot with every ounce of his weight behind it before Chang could affect a block. As the Chinaman's head was jerked forward by the triple impact Ben's open palm swung upward to smash the heel of his hand under Chang's flat nose.

The blow was driven from the straightening of his braced knee and the power of his shoulder was behind it. It was a blow that had contained every fibre of strength he could summon; driven into the exact spot and at the precise angle, it connected with hammer force. Ben felt and heard the meaty click as the nasal bone snapped. He knew without doubt that Tinkerbell's last-ditch combination had worked to perfection.

Weakening fast from loss of blood, his energy cut off by the crushing blows that had jarred the vital points of his lower body, Chang-wa sank back, thick, blackish blood drooling from his nostrils, his eyes glazing fast. He shook his head, a look of disbelief dawning as his knees gave way. He slid to a kneeling position and rocked back onto his heels as though he was about to pray. Slowly he pitched forward and lay still. The splintered prongs of bone had driven into the brain.

'I don't think we'll be needing this,' said Indie, sticking the revolver into his belt.

A sudden murmur rippled from behind them and they turned to find a group of fifty or so fetched from the village by the remaining guard. From behind them, as the ranks opened up, a figure in the glossy black tunic and trousers of a junk mistress stepped forward. Lai Choi San looked very different from the woman in scarlet silk and ermine. The thick grey skein of her hair was pinned with the carved bone ornaments of a peasant and her feet were bare.

'Your business is over now, I think. You must leave and forget this place.'

When *Cloud Chaser* had cleared the cove and was well into Bias Bay, Ben suggested a rum. He thought he detected the slightest tremor in Indie's hand as he took the glass from him.

'It's ended,' said Ben, raising his glass. 'Only destiny can tell us the answer now.'

'It's good,' agreed Indie saluting his old friend. 'If the child of Ben Deverill lives, it has its father's blood and will survive.' He drank and grinned at Ben. 'Let us hope we can clear these waters before the queen of pirates tests her new toy.' He held out his glass for Ben to refill it. 'I spiked the barrel.'

Ben looked at him over his glass. Indie nodded, eyes twinkling in his walnut brown face.

'I had a feeling she'd ask us to demonstrate.'

'You mean it's . . .?'

'Spiked,' repeated Indie. 'When the queen of pirates pulls that trigger she'll be sent to her ancestors before her time.'

The Shrine of Adato

WINTER CAME, the lake froze over, and most of the birds had flown elsewhere. Those that stayed left the tracery of their tracks in the snow outside the hut and the animals came almost daily for food. A pig had been killed in the late autumn, the meat cured with herbs and smoked into thin, nutritious sheets tied in bundles and hung from the roof beams.

The inside of the hut was warmed by embers of charcoal in clay pots and cakes of dried ox dung collected and stacked beside the woodpile. With Ah Keung gone, Siu Sing had quickly learned to cook the rice porridge for breakfast and prepare the food, gathering pine cones for the fire as fuel ran short, clearing snow from the winter vegetables and the thatch of the roof.

The winter had passed safely by for all its savage blizzards—great snows that had almost buried the hut and obscured the lake. The first brightness of spring had come, brushing Siu Sing's face as she forced open the door. Old To spoke softly from behind her, his corner cot under its bearskin still in deep shadow.

'Bring water for the tea, Siu Sing. We will not go to the rock this day. We will eat rice together and talk.'

She heard the weight of him rising from the hard bed.

'It is time for us to take a journey.'

'Yes, Great-uncle.' Sing tried to keep the excitement from her voice as she plunged the wooden dipper into the rain barrel. A brittle skin of ice broke in bright shards. Sing had never been to the other side of the lake. The groves of bamboo had been her home for all of her life and she would never have wanted more if she could not see the mountains rising across the water. They were always there, different each day, changed by the weather and the sky like the colours in a picture. She had sometimes wished she could not see them, thought that the breezy hillsides and the lake below were enough. She had no need of more. But the mountains were there with each sunrise and under each new moon and she knew one day she must cross them.

The sun climbed so brightly that she left the door open and rolled up the window mats to flood the hut with its warmth. They ate the hot conjee with the last of the salted fish and a sprinkling of chives. It seemed to Sing the most delicious meal she had ever tasted as she waited patiently to hear of the journey. Great-uncle To ate in silence; only the cry of the curlew and the distant shout of boatmen disturbed the quiet.

When he had sipped his ginseng tea and filled his cup three times, he spoke: 'You have heard the great bell that speaks from the mountains across the lake?'

'Yes, Great-uncle. It comes with the sunrise and with the full moon.'

'It is the bell of the greatest temple in all China. Three thousand monks worship there. 'It is three days' journey, on the peak of Lo Shan. It is time to take you there.'

Old To tossed the dregs from his teacup through the open door. 'Pack only small things and enough clothes and these.'

From a shelf he took down a new pair of shoes made from the skin of a musk ox, three layers thick on the soles, the tops soft and pliable. They were strongly stitched with stout strips of the same thick hide. 'Much of the journey will be on stony ground,' he said. 'I have made these for you.'

The next day Master To and Siu Sing joined a caravan of peasants on their way to the temple. Ahead of them, men and women of the village carried baskets of rice, grain and vegetables. They were happy, as the gifts they bore assured them of another year under the protection of the temple. The journey from the lake was one of great wonder to Siu Sing.

They had crossed the deep mud and shallow water in a plank-boat drawn by buffalo, with fat catfish jumping around her. As they passed through the lakeside villages and up into the hills, the people treated the old man and the strange jarp-jung child respectfully. It was now well known that this was Old To, the alchemist and sorcerer, and that the demon child was his disciple.

At the lake's edge they passed the nun still making her bricks. Almost three years had passed since Siu Sing had first seen her. Each year since that time she had come with Old To to the village for the great market. Each time the walls had been built a little higher and now as they approached she could see that the little church was finished. Perched on its beams of bamboo the nun waved to them as she thatched the roof with reeds cut from the marshes.

'You see,' said Old To. 'Everything is possible if you have faith. The people got tired of stealing her bricks and the children of pushing them down. But she did not get tired of making them. It is something you should always remember.'

The tracks they followed wound upward where the air grew colder but the effort of their climb and the energy of their ch'i kept them warm. Many wild animals crossed the track or ran from their voices; birds and monkeys called across the ceiling of trees, from gorge to gorge and over rivers. Sometimes the path had been narrowly carved from the wall of the mountain beside deep ravines, valley floors ablaze with early wildflowers.

At night they found places among rocks or the cathedral roots of a giant banyan where they could shelter and start a fire. On each awakening the sound of the bell was closer and now it lay just ahead, beneath the thin hook of moon and the last pale stars. The villagers had also travelled for several days and nights. Before the first stroke of the bell they broke their camp and went forward, their journey almost ended.

Sing watched the sky turn from luminous green to flaming orange, the night's moisture shed from the leaves in sparkling drops. She performed the breathing exercises named the Precious Set of Eight, scooping the pure air like water from a spring, and sending its torrent deep to nourish the ch'i. Old To observed her exhilaration with approval.

'It is right you should draw such strength from this place. You are close to God here.'

'Why have we come, Uncle?'

It was the first time she had asked the question. There had seemed no reason for it until now, with the end of their journey in sight.

'To pay our respects to the Lord Buddha and to visit the shrine of the White Crane. It is close by the monastery and it is there we will stay.'

For an hour they waited with the villagers outside the closed gates of the monastery.

'We must also pay our respects to the abbot and his elders. I once lived and learned within these walls. Some of my brothers still remain and we must honour them.'

The shrine of the White Crane stood within the walls of the monastery, which enclosed the entire peak of Lo Shan that reared behind the main temple and the many buildings that sheltered its monks. The shrine was small, no larger than a palace pavilion. It had no grand garden to surround it, no ornamental ponds or bridges. It stood alone beside a holy bodhi tree, the earth around it bare. Built of stone, its roof and doorway were decorated with legendary creatures.

'It is on this spot that the monk Adato taught the Way of the Crane to a nun 700 years ago.'

As Old To spoke, standing before the shrine, one hand on her shoulder, Siu Sing felt the strength of him pass into her. 'I have brought you here to also learn the deepest secret of the Crane. It is a great secret which, when you have learned it well, will give you the power of life and death over your adversary. You are my disciple now and you have proved to me that you are worthy of this gift.'

He paused to point up at the mythical creatures that lined the roof of the shrine as its guardians, crowned by a ring of stone encircling a crane in flight. Squatting beside her, he indicated the amulet he wore around his neck. It was the same as that crowning the shrine, but made of exquisite mottled jade.

'Jade deepens its colour with age when it is kept against the living skin. It absorbs the essence of the wearer—they become one. This one was worn by my master and his master before him. I am not sure how far back it goes, perhaps to Adato himself. It has been passed down from master to disciple for many generations. When I die it will be passed on to you.'

He stood, taking her hand. 'It can only go to one who can be trusted with its power and its secrets. My ch'i is strong—but

I must leave you soon. There is not time to wait until you are grown.' Master To looked down into her face.

'What you will learn here can only be used when all else fails, for its strike is more powerful than the tiger, faster than the snake, more terrible than death itself. Once it has struck its effects cannot be reversed. You are a child but I have seen your purity. I know it is safe with you. Come we must kneel before the likeness of Adato and make this pledge.'

He led her by the hand up the eight steps and into the shrine. Inside, the carved figure of the legendary monk stood life-sized above the altar. From his bag, Old To took a bundle of joss, handing some to Sing. They knelt together.

The year spent at the shrine of the White Crane passed without the counting of time. The days began with the tolling of the great bell and Sing learned the mantra of Adato, her voice and Master To's joining with it. The time had begun with fasting. Only pure mountain water was taken for the first two days. Small portions of grain porridge were slowly added. This food Old To mixed and boiled into gruel over the cooking pot left in what had once been the caretaker's annexe, a small, stone cubicle at the back of the shrine.

It was bare of all else but they had covered the floor with a mattress of thick grass which they changed each day. The sack of grain To had fetched from the monastery had been blessed by the monks, he said, letting the mixture run through his hands for her to see.

'It contains the earth's ch'i,' he explained. 'This is the grain of the fields that all men live by. Brought up the mountain from the fields below. It is mixed together in exact measure, to balance the Yin and the Yang. This, and when they are ready, the fruit of the trees, the plants and roots of the earth, is all that we will eat here. One rice bowl each day is enough.'

For many weeks they sat beneath the bodhi tree and meditated for increasing lengths of time, rising only to perform the eight stretching and breathing exercises of Pa Tuan T'sin. Sing found that in this way time had no meaning, there was only light and darkness. The rarity of the air, combined with strictness of diet, exercise and long periods of meditation, transported her into a state of euphoria. Her trance-like tranquillity was entered only by those thoughts and sounds that she permitted; the song of birds in the bo tree, the movement of leaves and the hum of insects. Her mind had become as receptive as an empty gourd waiting to be filled.

As if he knew this, Old To changed the order of things. 'You are ready to learn now. Tonight I will awaken you at the hour of three. You must meditate. Then you will see.'

Bright moonlight dusted the ancient shrine and lit the bodhi tree. It lay across the bare ground, silent and still. Into its centre, with a murmur of flight, flew a magnificent crane. Folding its wings, it stood motionless in the pool of silver and Sing saw that it cast no shadow. From the darkness another form took shape: the low-slung crouch of a tiger. Keeping to the edge of the shadows, it filled the night with its menace. Many times it circled the motionless crane, the rattle of its breath soft as a purr. When it sprang, its roar tore open the silence like a blade. It seemed to rip Sing's soul. Looking down from the roof of the shrine, from the branches of the bo tree, circling above, she watched the contest of the tiger and the crane and saw how the tiger was defeated.

When the prayer of Buddha had woken them the next day they went for the last time into the shrine of Adato. The last sticks of joss were burning when Master To spoke to Siu Sing.

'We will return to the lake now. What you have learned here is a great power. It is the gift of Adato, given to very few. Only those who are worthy are chosen, and it will remain in you for all of your life. Each day when you meditate you will again look down on the tiger and the crane. You will see 10,000 times how the crane destroys its mortal enemy. Only you will know when to use this power. Only you will know when it is time.'

Yangjingshi

MANY WEEKS had passed since they had returned to the hut. The crispness of a new season blew through the groves as Sing went to the Place of Clear Water with an armful of blossoms for the Fish's grave. As she bent over, arranging them like the fan of the peacock, there was a sound like none she had ever heard, so close it seemed to touch her. A thin, poisonous hiss of warning.

Sing raised her eyes slowly, not wanting to look, but sure she must not run. The king cobra had been coiled and asleep, its colours and patterns of earth and stone unnoticed on the small garden of river pebbles in front of the little tomb. The hood was spread wide, the flat, shiny head poised like the blade of a spear, golden beads of eyes fixed on hers as it began its gentle sway.

Sing watched the perfectly formed sections of its throat and neck, smooth as ivory and the colour of fresh bean curd. She had seen snakes before, sunning themselves coiled in sleep or winding through the cane grass. Old To had taught her each of their names, which one to fear and how to be still when she saw them and to not be afraid.

There came a sudden scything blur above her head, so close it stirred her hair. The lethal, sweeping side-kick flashed over her, delivering a knife-edged foot to the snake's head with such speed and impact that it lay stunned. A second was all it took for Ah Keung to push Sing aside and face the snake as it rose again, the long curve of it swaying back against its bunched coils, its hood strained fully open, savagely alert as Ah Keung crouched before it.

'Ah Yangjingshi,' he crooned, mimicking the sway of the cobra. 'We shall see who is faster, you and I.'

Twice the furious snake struck and each time Ah Keung evaded its venom. The third time his arm flew out to grab it beneath the gaping jaws. He rose with the length of it twisting and thrashing from his outstretched hand. He brought the gaping yellow mouth close for Sing to see.

'You see who is faster?' He grinned as with both hands he twisted one against the other, tearing the head from the body.

It had happened so quickly that by the time Sing rose to her knees, Ah Keung held the still writhing trunk high, much of it trailing the grass. He stood looking down at her, his arm still outstretched as its dying spasms rippled through the cobra's length.

'I have taught the foot well,' he said. 'It is faster and more deadly now than Yangjingshi, the king of snakes. It has saved your life, Little Star. One day I may claim my reward.' Then with a short, mocking bow, he disappeared before she could speak, taking the snake with him.

In the corner of the herb shed that night, Ah Keung carefully slit open the snake and removed its gall bladder, emptying the moss-green bile carefully into a wine cup. From his pocket he took a number of small berries, shiny and purplish-black as currants. These he crushed into the snake bile and set the cup under the stretcher he had made as a bed. At dawn the next day, in the tradition of the student returning to the master, he would present himself to his Sifu. The ritual of contest would be honoured. Ah Keung's form would be tested in full contact and assessed by the master.

Outside, the great bowl of stars emptied their reflection on the still lake and night birds silently swept the groves in search of movement. Sing watched their shadow cross the window space, listening to the crickets in the bamboo and the chorusing of frogs from the Place of Clear Water. She was unable to sleep. The one she had always feared had saved her life. At first she had not recognised him. He had grown taller and under the simple robe he wore he was now a man. The hair had been shaved from his head, but when he had walked across the clearing holding the snake she had seen the strange limp was still in his step.

Dawn broke and Sing had not slept. She heard Ah Keung leave the herb shed and then his splashing at the water butt. There was the sound of the breaking of wood across his knee to start the fire and brew the ginseng tea, just as he had always done. It was as though he had never been away. She heard him call softly outside the hut door.

'Sifu. Sifu. I have returned. It is time. The sun soon rises.'

She would not go to the rock. The ritual of contest was between master and student, it did not welcome onlookers. She had not told Old To of the snake and what had happened in the Place of Clear Water, hoping that Ah Keung would continue on his way. But the sounds outside told her he was back. Through the window space the night birds had gone and the martins skimmed the orchard in their place. The scents of spring reached her bed and somewhere on the high slopes a cuckoo called. Exhausted, she slept.

Ah Keung had learned much in the three years that had passed for him so quickly. The bitterness he had felt at being turned away had led him over many mountains to the temple of the Tiger. The monks had welcomed him when he offered his head to be shaved, and when he had demonstrated his skill in the courtyard. They had watched with amusement as the boy with the twisted foot flew like the White Crane.

Theirs was a superior skill, they said, requiring great strength and courage. He had begged them to teach him and when they tested his strength of mind over pain, he had endured it. Three small slow-burning joss sticks had been inserted into the crown of his skull. Seated in the lotus position on the steps of the shrine he had been given a mantra to focus his senses upon as the joss sticks were lit. He had not flinched when they burned lower and lower towards his bare scalp and into his flesh. He had suppressed the pain that shrieked within him until they had extinguished themselves. The triangle of small white scars that he would carry throughout his life were his badge of initiation into the fighting art of the Tiger form. For three years he had studied under the monks, his perpetual practice causing even the abbot to notice him as one who must win or die.

For many months, Ah Keung's meditation had been visited by great unrest as the time to return drew closer. One by one he had faced the senior monks, ever humble in their presence, ever watchful to learn all they had to teach, until he had taken leave of the temple to return to Tung T'ing.

It did not occur to the Forceful One that he could fail. But he knew that even his youthful strength and energy, all he had learned at the temple of the Tiger, might not defeat the great ch'i and infinite skill of his sifu.

When Master To had sluiced his face in the cold water of the rain barrel and walked to the rock, Ah Keung was waiting for him. He stopped and bowed, giving the salute of the student to the master, right fist cupped by his left palm, symbolising the coming together of the sun and the moon. He poured the cups of ginseng tea as he had always done, bringing one to the master in the ritualistic ceremony that prepared them both for combat. In a separate cup he presented the snake bile, knowing the honour he did his master. He knew it would not be refused, the bile of the snake was prized as the best of all medicines. The tonic of all tonics.

'It is from the king of all snakes, Sifu. The great Yangjingshi.'

The poison from the unripe nightshade berries would be tasteless in the bitter snake bile. He guessed it would take three minutes to act upon the nervous system. There was not enough to kill. Just enough to slow the reflexes.

The sun had risen above the hills as they began, flashing like broken mirror through the terraces of bamboo. On the lake the pelicans had already landed, spoonbills patrolled the mud and the white egrets had left the marshes in search of fish. Breeze stirred the feathery clumps of cane grass, sending bright drifts of seed swirling across the rock as the master invited the attack of his student, easily blocking and evading every familiar move. For three minutes Ah Keung continued to probe Old To's defence, showing nothing of the Tiger form, watching for the slightest signs of his slowing. He no longer thought of the one before him as his master but as an inferior opponent to be destroyed. The chance came, when, without warning, Ah Keung broke away from the pattern of boxing they were practising. Leaping high, the flashing side-kick he had practised so long slammed like an axe under Old To's heart. The master's forearm block had been a split second too late. It was enough to tell Ah Keung that the slow poison had entered the bloodstream.

The intense thrill of mastery burst like a dam in the Forceful One's mind. It splashed his ch'i like molten steel. Again and again his foot found its mark. The master had sunk his ch'i, his wide horse stance rooted to the rock as he tried to block repeated strikes, his vision blurred, his reflexes clumsy. Ah Keung's energy was a torrent that gathered with the certainty of victory, fed by the wellspring of revenge. Deliberately, he picked his marks, and steadily, carefully cut his master down. Blow by blow, the Tiger destroyed the Crane. Savagely, mercilessly, proudly.

Returning to the hut, Ah Keung quietly lifted the heavy, carved lid of the camphorwood chest. From it he took many scrolls of rolled paper and rough bound books. These he threw aside until he had lifted out the red cloth bundle. From it he took the snakeskin pouch, emptying the silver and copper cash into his hand and replacing it. A small silver picture frame surrounded the photograph of a Chinese woman seated in a flowered pavilion. Beside her stood a gwai-lo, his hand upon her shoulder. Carefully Ah Keung removed the photograph, replacing it in the red cloth with the contents of the chest and closing the lid. He rubbed the tarnished silver frame on his sleeve, slipping it into the folds of his tunic.

Sing dragged herself from the depths of sleep at the persistent shaking of her shoulder, the sound of Ah Keung's voice close and urgent.

'Siu Sing, little sister. Come Siu Sing. Sifu, I think he is dead. Siu Sing, Siu Sing.' Half dragging her from the cot he ran with her through the orchard to the rock where Old To lay, words tumbling from him.

'His heart. We were practising as always. He fell. I cannot find a pulse.'

The first part of Ah Keung's revenge was complete. The second he began exactly as he had planned. The jarp jung was easy to deceive. His show of sorrow at the death of his beloved Sifu was blended with concern for her. He would protect her now, he said. They would leave this place. There was nothing for them here. He would take her to Macau where they would find work. She must not be afraid.

When Ah Keung looked at Siu Sing, he saw she had gained the height, weight and stature of one years older. She had grown differently from a Chinese girl and more like a boy. Her shoulders were wide but round and smooth as peach skin, her legs long and slender. The hips were not wide like those of a farm girl but trim and gently curved. Only her breasts, already prominent, said she was certainly a girl.

He found that Siu Sing's eyes were still strangely disturbing when they looked his way, seeming to change colour with her moods, from the softness of an iris petal to the sudden darker depths of a disturbed pool. He did not know if she trusted him but he knew she had little choice. What he saw did not excite Ah Keung. He despised her far too greatly for physical attraction, but the sight of her washing naked at the rain barrel stirred a powerful urge to violate her, to rape and ravage her mercilessly. It fanned his hatred like a flame, making patience harder to bear, forcing it from his mind with a plan for revenge that was far sweeter to him.

She stared at him now, her eyes intent upon his throat. The jade amulet of the White Crane hung from Ah Keung's neck on its leather thong, bright as a delicate leaf against his skin.

'This amulet was promised to me, Ah Keung,' she said. 'My great-uncle and master made this pledge to me at the shrine of Adato.'

A terrible anger glimmered in Ah Keung's eyes and was quickly gone. His hand reached up to the amulet and his long fingers caressed it. A smile curved his lips.

'Then it shall be yours. But the journey we must take is long and the river is a place of thieves and the sea of pirates. I will protect it for you until we are safely in Macau.'

He saw the doubt in her eyes and swept it away. 'Come, Little Star, we must prepare our beloved sifu for his journey to the afterlife.'

They buried Old To beside the Fish in the Place of Clear Water. His few belongings of value Ah Keung placed in the herb basket together with a supply of cured pork and other dried food. While he searched the hut, Sing carefully emptied the chest of its books and scrolls, placing them in the deerhide satchel with the brushes and ink pot.

'Such things are worth nothing. They are too much to carry. Leave them.' Ah Keung's tone dismissed them as rubbish. Sing did not look at him as she continued to pack the papers carefully.

'They are his life. They cannot be left to rot and blow away or for the mice to chew. I will carry them.'

Ah Keung snatched up one small volume in its roughly stitched cover, frowning at the beautifully drawn characters on the cover. 'What does it say?' he sneered, letting his impatience flare for an instance. 'I was not taught to read as you were.' His words were heavy with resentment.

Sing held out her hand and took it from him, putting it into the satchel and fastening the bone toggle. 'It says, "Second Sunrise,"' she said, shouldering the heavy satchel. Turning her back on the reed hut, she started down the hillside towards the lake.

As they landed on the wharf at Yuenchow, Sing made off towards the net-drying shed.

'Where are you going?' Ah Keung called after her. 'We must board a junk here. It is almost the tide.'

'I must say goodbye to someone,' she called back.

'If it is the gwai-paw, you are too late.' Ah Keung laughed his unpleasant laugh. He had used the contemptuous term 'devil-hag' to describe the missionary woman. Why? Sing asked herself, as she found her way through the rows of drying nets and racks of salt fish. Why did her people treat the light-eyed nun in this way? She was kind and strong and gentle. All the things that Master To had taught Siu Sing to respect.

As she reached the end of the jetty and the patch of ground where the little church had stood, a great sadness swept over her. Only the tumble of mud bricks where the walls had fallen in confronted her. The thatched roof was nowhere to be seen and marsh birds pecked around the rubble undisturbed.

Back on the wharf, Ah Keung was bargaining with the owner of a wupan, the gaps in its clumsy planking hastily patched with strips of ox hide. He looked around as Siu Sing came up.

'The gwai-paw's god was not as strong as the east wind,' he laughed.

'What happened to her?' Siu Sing asked in a troubled voice.

'I have told you, Little Star. The east wind came and blew her temple down while she prayed inside.'

Siu Sing searched vainly for words. 'Did no one help her?' she asked at last.

Ah Keung giggled and those around him laughed at her foolish question. 'Why should they help where her god would not?'

He concluded his barter. 'Come. No more chatter, we must find a place to sit or we will be thrown out of this chicken crate into the white waters of Wind Box Gorge.'

On the long journey downriver by wupan and sampan, the other passengers stared at Siu Sing, shielding their children from her. Ah Keung looked away from her unhappiness.

'Do not blame them,' he laughed. 'You are jarp jung. You are different from us. You are different from everyone. Your ancestors do not come from the Middle Kingdom between heaven and earth as ours do.'

'Where do they come from?' she asked.

'Nobody knows the hell of the barbarian and nobody cares,' came the answer. Then he smiled and placed his arm around her, 'Except Ah Keung. I care.'

Aboard the old, five-masted Shantung trading junk they joined in Nanking, more than a hundred people crowded the decks with their livestock and goods for the journey to Macau. Sing found a corner of the cargo hold, away from them all. She preferred to go without food than to be jeered at or ignored. Ah Keung spent his time gambling with the crew as though he did not know her. When one of the junkmen found her behind the sacks of millet and maize, he stood astride her, unbuckling his belt. When she crawled away from him, he had fallen upon her.

Ah Keung heard her cries and sprang to the hatchway, causing the crewman to look up. 'Leave her,' he said. 'She is the property of a rich and powerful man. I must deliver her safely.'

The crewman was from the far region of the Ya River and understood little of Ah Keung's dialect. He ignored the warning. 'Go away boy or you will be next,' he laughed as he ripped at Sing's clothing.

Ah Keung dropped through the hatch, landing lightly on the

grain sacks. As the crewman stood to face him, the boy's foot snapped out straight from the knee, striking the man between the legs with a dull thud. His left hand whipped snake-like to grasp the throat, slowly crushing the man's windpipe. Ah Keung's voice hissed close to the purple face. Siu Sing saw the thrill of power in his eyes as he spoke.

'I said, this is the cherry girl of my uncle. No horny goat goes near her.'

The man's eyes were bulging so hideously, she had to turn away. His fingers scrabbled weakly at Ah Keung's wrist and the sounds coming from his mouth made her cover her ears. With his free hand, Ah Keung pulled her hands away and made her look.

'Why did you not defend yourself?' he asked contemptuously. 'This pig can not harm a worthy student of the White Crane. Did the old man teach you nothing? Your cowardice spits on his memory.' His fingers suddenly let go and the crewman fell heavily to his knees.

'He is yours,' Ah Keung said, stepping back. 'Avenge the name of Master To. Have you no face?'

But Sing crawled further away and hid herself deeper among the sacks of grain, pulling her town clothes around her.

'Now you see why it is I who must wear the amulet.' He spoke viciously. 'Until you are worthy.'

Three weeks later, the junk they had picked up in Nanking sailed slowly into the Macau typhoon shelter to join the maze of masts and rigging crammed inside the breakwater. Sing went on deck with the others as it threaded its way along the narrow channel through the floating village of the boat people. Again she felt as though her soul was drowning in a sea of eyes, some curious, some surprised, some amused, but all hostile. Everywhere she looked other eyes met hers but none welcomed her. When this had happened in the Yuenchow marketplace she had held the warm, strong hand of Master To. Now he was gone. She was alone.

Ah Keung found her crouched in the hold, as far from the jabber of tongues as she could get.

'What is wrong now?' he asked, unable to keep impatience from his voice. 'Where is the courage of the White Crane?'

Siu Sing looked up, hiding her tears. 'If I am not one of them, then who am I?'

'I have told you. You are jarp jung. You are no one. You belong nowhere. I am the only one who cares and can help you.' Sing tried to take comfort from his words.

'Great-uncle To said that to be jarp jung is to be beautiful,' she said, trying to put pride into her voice.

Ah Keung laughed aloud then spoke more quietly. 'Yes, it means you are a princess. A beautiful princess.' He helped her up. 'Come with me. I have a safe place for you.' He took her aft to the junk captain's wife. She was squatting over the cooking stove high on the stern, a sleeping baby on her back. Her eight children of all ages gaped as Ah Keung brought Siu Sing to her.

'This is my little sister, mother. She is from the hills of Lake Tung T'ing and has never been to such a place as Macau. She is afraid.'

He reached into his tunic and took out three copper coins. 'Will you keep her with you until I return? I go to seek work.'

The House of Fan

THE NEXT day, Ah Keung and Siu Sing stopped before a pair of huge iron gates. Rows of rivet heads studded their edges and sharp spikes ran like teeth along the top. Remnants of what must have once been paint clung to them in discoloured patches of dead skin; elsewhere across their wide expanse, rust had eaten through. They were surrounded by an even higher wall, so old that grass and weeds sprouted from it like tufts of dry hair.

The wall seemed to Sing to go on forever. Looking up she saw that ugly shards of broken glass crowned its length like the back of a dragon. She had never seen Ah Keung so excited since the time he told her of Old To's death. His voice was strangely tense as he hauled on an iron ring that hung from the teeth of a stone lion built into the brick wall. There was a grinding of chain somewhere inside and the muffled croak of a bell.

'This is the house of a mandarin. He is a very rich and very important man in Macau, a great merchant.'

Before he could say more, a slot in the middle of one of the gates slid open with a clang. Eyes peered at them through it and a voice, high-pitched and unfriendly, came from inside. Ah Keung smiled reassuringly at Siu Sing as bolts and chains began to rattle and bang. She was thankful he had returned for her early that morning, leading her through the maze of streets and alleyways before the shops had opened and most of the people were still asleep. Now she wanted to turn and run but Ah Keung held onto her arm so tightly that it burned.

'Don't worry,' he said. 'Inside is a beautiful garden where the mandarin is emperor.' He giggled suddenly. 'His name is Fan . . . Emperor Fan.'

One of the gates swung open on hinges greased with pig fat and Sing was shoved violently through, the rusty iron closing behind her with an echoing boom. The man who took her roughly by the arm was tall and thin, with the caved-in chest of the opium-eater. He carried a lead-tipped cane of bamboo, polished smooth as ivory. Bright gold showed among his large, stained teeth, so prominent that it seemed his lips could not close over them. An unpleasant sneer was fixed upon his narrow face. His ears were also large. One stuck out more than the other, flopping and flapping when he moved. Without speaking, he began to march her across the slippery cobbles of the wide yard, hissing impatiently when she tried to look back for Ah Keung. He was not there.

Fear rose up in Sing and she reacted the only way she knew. Breaking the man's grip, she ran back towards the gate. He chased after her, lashing out with the cane until it cut across her legs and back. With a sweep of her foot she toppled him, cracking his head, the cane clattering from his grasp. Other voices joined his howling as she tried to slide the heavy iron bolt. A blow from behind banged her head against it in a blinding flash of red.

As it cleared, she felt herself dragged back across the cobbles as more blows struck at her from all sides. At least a dozen coolies had run out from the long low sheds that surrounded the yard. Another clout from behind sent her sprawling. Everything within Siu Sing was poised to defend herself, but stronger than this was a calm voice that told her this was not the time.

Still stunned by the blow, she was hoisted to her feet. A soft hand lifted her chin, firmly turning and tilting her head. 'There is no need for such fuss. You are not here to be harmed.'

The words were quietly spoken in a nasal, sing-song tone. 'Open your eyes. Do not be afraid.'

The other voices had stopped their howling at the command of this high thin voice, like that of a whining woman's. As Sing obeyed, she saw before her the emperor, at the entrance of his palace. Lion dogs carved from stone stood guard on either side of its steps. His body was encased in a robe of silk, radiant as the tail of a peacock, fastened across his massive stomach with silver cords caught with toggles of ivory. To her dazed eyes he seemed seated on a throne of carved blackbean, inlaid with marble and pearl shell, the gown sweeping to almost cover two small feet encased in white cotton stockings and black slippers. The sleeve that covered his outstretched arm was very wide and as he withdrew it, Sing saw the hand that had so lightly caressed her chin was small and white as a woman's, its long curving nails shining with lacquer.

The other hand slowly stroked the cream-coloured fur of a pekinese sleeve dog; its shoe-button eyes glittered at her, black as jet. All this Sing saw before she dared look into his face. When she did, it looked back at her, white and doughy as steamed bread. Several long hairs sprang from a large brown mole on his chin and straggled down to lie on the slope of his chest. The face was so fat that its eyes were almost buried. It had the pendulous earlobes of those chosen by the gods. A pasty dewlap of flesh prevented the neck of the gown from closing. Two long, spindly moustaches drooped either side of his loose, pink, mouth. The wet tip of his tongue showed between small teeth, white as fine porcelain. High on his broad forehead he wore the close-fitting, black silk cap of a mandarin, its long crimson tassel reaching his shoulder. Behind him, half hidden in the shadows of the house, stood another man and on each side of him were two white-coated amahs. A flick of his hand sent the coolies scuttling back to the sheds as a beautiful fan spread in his hand like the gorgeous wings of a butterfly.

The fan was fluttering quickly as his eyes took in her child's body. 'Come. You belong to me now.'

As he spoke the man behind him unfolded his arms and the whole throne twisted around. For the first time, Sing realised it had wheels.

'Your brother has signed the legal papers. He has sold you to me as mooi-jai. To save your family from starvation. You are most fortunate.'

The wheels squeaked under his great weight as he spoke sharply to the amahs. 'Bring her inside and see that she is clean.'

It did not occur to Sing to run again. But she backed away from the unsmiling amahs.

'Ah Keung is not my brother. I have no family. He has deceived you, great lord. He claims you are his friend . . .' The whining voice cut her short.

'I know nothing of that. You are mooi-jai, bondservant to the house of Fan. You must do as you are told, or you will be punished.'

The theory of treachery that Siu Sing had learned had not prepared her for its reality and she knew the teachings of patience, tolerance and discipline must be fully exercised before revealing skill. On this the words of Old To had been clear: 'The crane is wiser than the tiger. It does not reveal its powers until no choice remains. If its secrets are revealed too soon, it will be overcome.'

There would be no defeating so many, no escaping the iron gate or jagged teeth of the wall. Patience must be the first weapon of defence. Clutching the deerhide bag close to her she mounted the steps and followed the emperor through the entrance of his palace.

Inside was dark and smelled of stale joss. When her eyes grew accustomed to the half light, Sing could see that it was filled with treasures. Golden screens stood in every corner, carved tables and chairs were placed so close to each other that there was hardly room to wheel his throne. Richly embroidered tapestries hung from the walls with delicate watercolour paintings of cascading waterfalls through misty gorges, and gilded temple carvings showed emperors and warlords riding into battle. Great cabinets were stacked with fine porcelain beside carved figurines and snuff bottles of jade and ivory. Huge hand-painted vases stood everywhere and beautiful carpets lay thick on the floor.

She followed the emperor's bodyguard with the amahs behind her, silent in their soft canvas slippers, only the steady squeak, squeak, squeak of the wheeled throne leading the way through a curtain of bright beads. They entered a room made entirely of glass and filled with flowers. Thick clusters of gold and orange marigolds spilled from porcelain vases painted with scenes of concubines and musicians in palace gardens, with splendid birds flashing their gorgeous tails across skies of curlicued cloud.

Bushes of gardenia and jasmine grew from the glazed dragon pots and from others a profusion of bright yellow and rust-red chrysanthemums. In a hundred small bamboo cages linnets, orioles and larks trilled and from their perches finches flitted like gems around their tiny prisons. In this wonderous place, the emperor's throne stopped and the fan opened again.

Descending the stairs that led from the floor above was a woman. Her face was thin, with eyes that seemed to burn with fever. Two meagre eyebrows arched above them as cleanly and deliberately as strokes from a calligrapher's brush. The narrow slit of her mouth was painted a dark crimson, working furiously as she stumbled towards them.

'What are you doing. Don't you know your number one wife is close to her untimely grave? Do you burn joss for me? Do you bring me peace? You do not.'

She had reached the bottom of the staircase and stood clinging to the carved post, her mouth still gasping to find breath. From her hunched shoulders hung a thick jacket of black and gold silk. A black wig, heavy with ornaments, covered her head. One long hand, made longer by curving red nails, held the jacket tight about her throat, the other dabbed a handkerchief to her lips. Her malevolent eyes found Sing. She levelled a trembling finger.

'So. I should have known. You have found another alley cat to cock her tail for you. You with the member of an infant and the weight of a buffalo.'

The pouch of flesh that hung from the emperor's dimpled chin shook as he spoke. 'She is mooi-jai, a child for the scullery. A bargain.' He held up one pudgy hand, its short fingers spread, glittering with rings. 'Only $200, my flower of flowers.'

'Wasted money, brains of a horny goat. You could not take her cherry, if she still has one, Aeeyahhh, what hopes of the tiger still spring from the mountain of bean curd. Why do you think your other cats spend each day in the gambling den?'

She collapsed again into a fit of coughing. Two bright pink spots had appeared on the emperor's cheeks as she turned away.

'See that this one does not eat too much and is kept downstairs, or she will feel the rod of Ah Kwok.'

There were ten servants to care for the Fan family and Sing was the eleventh. She learnt from Ah Sum, the scullery amah, who was also mooi-jai, a girl not much older than herself, that the man they called 'Fat Fan' behind his back was not an emperor at all but a larp cheung merchant—a killer of swine and a maker of greasy sausages, a dealer in offal. It explained the terrible sounds each morning at dawn when the pigs knew the time had come for their throats to be cut. Their squeals rent the air as keenly as the thin steel blades that silenced them. There was something else it didn't explain. At night when others slept, a dreadful moaning came and went like the undertow of a tide, rising in sudden surging waves of pain and despair.

At first she had thought it was part of a dream. But it had not been a dream. She had lain there for long hours, with her head beneath the blanket, unable to sleep. The sound would not let her rest for long. Even in the daytime over the endless rattling of iron-wheeled carts across the cobbles and the busy shovelling of coal into the boiler fires, she was sure she could hear it. When she drew water from the pump outside the scullery she would pause to listen. There it was again, somewhere separate and alone.

Ah Sum had told her all about the things that went on in the factory sheds where Fat Fan's famous larp cheung was made. He was the greatest of all sausage makers; his famous family recipe had made him the richest of all the food merchants in Macau. Twice a week the iron gates opened and a motor lorry lurched into the yard to deliver more pigs and left filled with crates of sausages, taking them down to the waterfront where they were loaded onto a junk and delivered to the eating houses and food shops he owned across the water in Hong Kong. But she did not know what it was that made the terrible sound.

She told instead of Fat Fan's family. His number one wife was seldom seen downstairs, spending her time in bed, her amahs bringing an endless procession of soups and broths to strengthen her. Ah Sum spoke of her with fear. There were two other wives, who came and went through the iron gates in sedan chairs to play fan-tan and mahjongg with other rich women. Ah Sum looked over her shoulder when she spoke of the children. There were six of them, she said, fat and white as the pigs he bred. Fortunately, she sighed, they were mostly at school. Sing asked about the man who had pulled her through the gate. He was Kwok the Rat Man, Ah Sum had whispered, watchman of the yard and its factory sheds and catcher of rats.

Kwok the Rat Man was feared by all the others. He was the favourite of number one wife, spy of all that happened in the compound. Ah Sum knew all about the men who worked in the compound. Three times a day she took them food, stacked in bamboo containers and wheeled across the cobbles from the separate cookhouse in a corner of the yard. Her stories were told in whispers as she worked beside Sing over the sink. Ah Sum had been mooi-jai to the house of Fan since she was eight years old and when she was sent to the factory sheds she was only ten. 'Do nothing to displease Fat Fan,' she whispered hurriedly, as Ah Soo the cook came in from the kitchen and told them to stop their idle chatter.

The day Sing learned what happened to those who displeased Fat Fan came soon after. At five o'clock each morning she awoke to rake the ashes and light the fires under the kitchen stoves and make tea for the amahs who rose at five-thirty. Then she threw handfuls of grain to the chickens in the walled yard outside the scullery.

There was a long stretch of garden along one high wall where the amahs grew rows of beans, white radish and yellow pumpkins. Sometimes it was visited by butterflies that danced among the melon vines then up and over the wall. But her favourite time was when she fed the birds and watered the flower pots in the Palace of Birds and Flowers and at night when she crept into the yard beneath the cold, sharp stars and through meditation returned to the hillside and the Place of Clear Water.

She was in the Palace of Birds and Flowers when Kwok the Rat Man came to fetch her. 'You are to wash immediately. Put this on.' He tossed her a folded garment of white cotton. 'Nothing else.'

The tip of his long cane snaked through the leaves of a gardenia bush to slide crudely between her legs. 'Nothing here.' He turned away. 'Then go upstairs. Be quick. The master honours you.'

When Sing climbed the wide stairs to the sleeping quarters of Fat Fan and his family, she was still shivering from the cold pump water. The smock was thin and loose about her. She had disobeyed the Rat Man and worn drawers beneath it, but still she shivered. It was almost dark, the room lit only by bright bars of daylight striking through half closed shutters. There was no one to be seen.

Was it a trick of Kwok the Rat Man? A trap to get her into trouble, to say that she was stealing? This was the day number one wife visited the town to consult the herb doctor and the fortune-teller. Sing turned to run back down the stairs but the two amahs moved from the shadow to block her way. The man who had pushed the throne also appeared before her. Without speaking he pointed to a closed door and gave her a firm shove towards it.

The door opened into a large room almost as dark as the landing except for a gas lamp of thick coloured glass that hung from the ceiling like a basket of jewels. It splashed the walls with spots of light: red, green, blue and yellow.

'Come inside and close the door.' The thin whisper of Fat Fan startled her. 'There is no need for fear. This room is a room of rare delights, a place for pleasure. Come, you will see.'

The air had a curious, sickly sweetness which made Sing's stomach uneasy. It mingled with wisps of smoke from an iron incense burner, its smouldering sparks of joss pricking a dark corner. The scene was strangely hypnotic and Sing, knowing the amahs stood outside the door, closed it softly and did as she was told.

Only when she reached the bedside did she realise the coloured splotches of light were splashed over the pallid mound of Fan's naked body, propped on its side by a pile of embroidered cushions upon a vast bed. Oily smoke rose from a thin, long-stemmed pipe he held in one delicate hand. With the other he stirred the fetid air with slow waves of a large goose-feather fan. Sing could only stare.

The planes and folds of his flesh did not seem real to her. They formed contours and shadowy clefts that she found hard to associate with a human body. As her eyes grew more accustomed to the strange light, she made out the pendulous flaps of his chest, low on the great roll of his stomach. His short, useless legs were curled beneath him and from the deep creases between his thighs, encircled by a nest of sparse black hairs, peeped what looked to Sing like a freshly peeled lychee.

Fat Fan laid the pipe aside; the tip of his tongue quivered for a second between his lips as he caressed the sacred hairs that hung from his chin, then he held out a hand to her, closing it with unexpected power around her wrist, guiding it towards the nest between his thighs. When Sing's fingers reached it, it felt damp and firm as a plum. A tremor ran over him and a tiny gasp escaped his open mouth. He pressed that part of him hard against her palm, the grip tightening on her wrist as his thrusting bulk heaved.

The plum seemed to become immediately harder and larger in her hand and her fingers could do nothing but close around it. A high, feminine cry came from Fat Fan and Sing felt her hand flooded with a warm and sticky fluid, pumping through her fingers and onto her arm. The grip on her wrist made her cry out in pain as his other hand suddenly came up hard under the smock, its fingers frantically feeling for her. The whole bulk of him convulsed and shuddered. Then, as though emptied of strength he released her and fell back with a bubbling sigh.

It seemed to Sing that all this had happened in a matter of

seconds. The iron grip relaxed on her wrist but did not release her. In her confusion Sing struck out, grasping the straggle of hairs that grew from his chin. They came away in her hand as, with a squeal, he struck her, releasing her arm. Her cry of pain seemed stuck in her throat as she wrenched open the door. The amahs were taken by surprise. One of them threw out a foot, tripping her against a carved pedestal, toppling a porcelain vase and smashing it to pieces on the tiled floor.

When the heavy wooden collar was closed on Sing's neck it felt as though a rock had been placed upon her shoulders. The dead weight of its solid wood, iron bolts and strapping forced her head downward. Kwok the Rat Man's grin of pleasure was extreme as he drove home the locking device with the heel of his hand and secured it.

The collar measured a metre across and was almost six centimetres thick. Number one wife had demanded that it be put on in the centre of the yard and that the servants assemble to watch. This was what happened to those who trespassed and destroyed property in the House of Fan.

The factory men had left their work, their grinning faces pressed to the dirty windows. The children squatted on the steps between the stone dragons and tittered as though they were watching a puppet show. The youngest clapped their hands as Ah Kwok stepped back to admire his work.

There was no sign of number one wife or Fat Fan. The Rat Man, proud of his place as official purveyor of punishment, enjoyed his position of favour by cavorting for his audience, prancing around Sing like a monkey, squatting in front of her, barking like a dog and scratching at fleas.

Using his cane from behind he prodded her forward, forcing her to circle the yard, now lined by the cheering workmen. By holding the edge of the collar in both hands and easing its weight, she could manage a barefoot shuffle over the worn, uneven cobbles. This she kept up for several circuits, even when one of the men hurled a bucket of putrid pig's blood. When the roar of laughter died, the displeasure at her resilience showing clearly on the Rat Man's face, she had not cried out, she did not beg. Her steady progress around the yard was certainly amusing and trotting behind, using his cane as though herding a stray goat, kept him in centre stage.

Siu Sing was left in the canque for a week, a week that taught her elements of physical and mental survival that would never be forgotten. All she had learned of withstanding pain and discomfort came to her aid and made endurance possible. She also learned the meaning and great power of true friendship and courage.

She had been given a willow-twig broom and an iron bucket to clean up the rubbish that was thrown at her. It had not taken long to discover that the collar was made to prevent the hands from reaching the mouth with food. It was also cunningly designed to prevent by a few centimetres the possibility of eating like an animal from the ground.

On the first night, as she listened to the howling that rose with the moon above the slaughterhouse, Ah Sum, at great risk to herself, had brought a warm cloth to clean Sing's face and feed her soup. She had also brought rice and dried fish left over from the amahs' table. But Ah Soo the cook had seen her. Ah Soo was not a cruel woman but she knew what was expected of her. If the Rat Man observed this kindness it would be reported to number one wife and it would be she who would be held responsible. So she closed her mind to any twinge of pity and acted as expected, ordering Ah Sum to empty the kitchen slops over Sing's head each morning instead of feeding it to the ducks.

No one but Sing noticed that among the vegetable peelings and cabbage leaves there were bits of bean curd, pieces of steamed bread and scraps of meat and fish. These Sing would sweep into a pile and wash in the bucket. When it was filled with water at the pump she was able to eat the food that floated on the surface. At night, when she escaped into the sanctuary of meditation, she took the kindness of Ah Sum with her and vowed that one day she would repay her courage.

Apart from five minutes of teasing from the children on their way in or out of the gate and the brief amusement of the lorry drivers, Sing was left more and more alone to wander the yard with her bucket and broom. When she could no longer stand and fell into a crouch to take the weight from her shoulders it would not be long before Ah Kwok's cane would slice viciously across her buttocks to get her moving.

When stroke after stroke failed to raise her but could not make her cry out, aware of the grinning faces from the factory sheds, he would leave her there and return grumbling to the shade of his office. The crouching figure in the grotesque collar soon became a familiar sight in the corner of the yard near the pump.

When the week was over and the canque was removed there was no attempt to dress Sing's wounds. The skin around her neck and shoulders had been completely rubbed away, and was infected. She had torn off part of the smock and stuffed it under the part where it had hurt the most and she had quickly learned at night how to try and sleep. Sitting with her back against the wall, by leaning forward so that the edge of the canque rested on the ground between her outstretched knees, she had found some sort of relief.

Ah Sum had again risked changing places with Sing by dropping a tiny pot of White Flower oil in her lap. It burned her raw flesh like fire but she knew its disinfectant qualities and used it sparingly, keeping it hidden behind the big earthen water jar by the pump. However, Siu Sing's punishment was not at an end. In the weeks following her release from the canque she almost wished for its isolation; at least she had been untouched by anything except the cane of Kwok the Rat Man.

Number one wife had forbidden her to be allowed back inside the house of Fan. 'Sell her,' she shouted from a top window when the collar was unlocked. 'Sell her to a whore-house. That is where she should be.'

The men inside the sheds whistled and cat-called. The children, wives two and three and the concubine gathered to witness her humiliation, merry behind their fans. The amahs watched silently from the kitchen steps.

'Tai tai,' Kwok's voice turned to the humble whine reserved for number one wife alone. 'She would bring little from a whore-house. Look at her.' With the tip of his cane he lifted the filthy rags Sing wore. More laughter came from the group at the entrance as he revealed her grazed and dirty shins.

'She is skinny as a bird and dirty as a stray dog. She is jarp jung. It would be a waste, Tai Tai, give her to me. There is plenty for her to do in there.' His cane pointed to the factory shed. 'She will be useful in there,' he said again.

'Do what you like with her but if she steps into this house again it will be you who will wear the collar.'

Number one wife snorted, and banged the window shut.

Kwok the Rat man was pleased with himself. He had no wish for the mooi-jai to leave this place. Outside the walls there were fools in the courts who were beginning to say that mooi-jai had rights. The same kind of fools who would say the canque was forbidden, that it was no longer allowed to be used for punishment, no matter what the crime. He did not want such idiots through these gates. What happened behind the walls of the factory compound was for him to decide. But he must not risk Tai Tai's favour. Without her support he would have no power, no protection. He must keep the jarp-jung girl in her place. Besides, she would be useful in the sheds and an amusement for the men.

The factory sheds were old. What machinery they contained was hand-operated. The long low building was separated into two main sections: the killing house, where the pigs were brought each morning to be slaughtered and the cutting room where they were butchered. Connected by sets of greasy iron rails, to take the trollies of flesh, bone and offal, above them were iron tracks of sharp steel hooks mounted on pulley wheels.

In the killing house a dozen slaughterers slit the throats and guts of the pigs driven from the styes through a ramp. Around the men's waists hung wooden sheaths containing an assortment of knives and choppers. Stripped to the waist, they worked in steam from the vats where the offal was treated and flesh rendered from bone. The floor was criss-crossed by a system of gutters and gullies to channel the blood into huge stone jars. To Sing, it was a place of unspeakable horror.

The screams of the pigs at killing time were deafening. A chorusing of terror that filled the place and the men with a kind of frenzy. Death was the only thing that could stop it. Once it was silenced, they became light-headed, like mischievous, blood-covered children, wielding their blades with exaggerated flare, slitting, slicing, chopping and mincing, chattering like monkeys, while others of superior skill mixed the right quantities of meat, lard, blood and gristle with the secret seasonings of herbs and spices that made Fat Fan's larp cheung sausages more popular than any other in Macau or on the island of Hong Kong.

Sing was set to work separating mounds of entrails from hearts, lungs, kidney and liver. She was also the water and cha carrier, hauling the iron kettle or the wooden water bucket and bamboo dipper whenever she was called. The boys who turned the big mangle-wheels of the mincing machines called her often to break the monotony of their task.

She had been given a corner in the place where those who lived inside the compound slept on rows of narrow wooden bunks. In the centre of this area was a table where they took their meals, drank cheap wine and spread the mahjongg tiles or playing cards in the light of the gas lamps.

No one touched her in the first week she slept there. Sometimes she was woken by a foot kicking her awake or the jab of Kwok's cane, urging her to bring more wine or fetch more rice from the cookhouse. When she looked up at the one who had woken her she looked into a face that was both stupid and cruel, with an expression of indecision mixed with curiosity, as though she were a trapped animal and the face was trying to decide if she was dangerous. She had been tamed but there was a look in her pale eyes that was unlike any other.

She learned to read the faces of those who found the sight of her arousing. If they came closer, the feebleness of mind she pretended turned to a savage show of madness, shrieking and snarling until they backed away. To the laughter of others, the man would spit instead and leave her, muttering his threats. It was only a matter of time before one of them became bold enough to return or they would come upon her in numbers while she slept.

Sing knew that if she were forced to display the full force of the Crane in her defence, things would change. She would no longer be looked upon as the half-devil child, the jarp-jung slut who slept on the floor like a dog, but a threat and a danger to them to be killed like a pig. The wheel-turning boys joked about what tender sausages she would make and how gladly they would turn the handles. So she protected herself in the shell of mindlessness they found untouchable, allowing the blood and muck she swilled from the flagstones to dry on her skin and matt her hair. And they left her alone. Until the night Kwok had too much wine.

She woke to the weight of him straddling her; his greasy trousers gaped open and something long and thin thrust out from them. The inflamed thing wagged and jerked as he tore at her clothing; she saw the flushed faces of the men ringed behind him.

The Rat Man had lost heavily at the table and taken more of the raw rice wine than he could hold. Someone had taunted him. One of the men, made brave by the wine jar, had recalled his humiliation when the jarp-jung had first arrived and tipped him on his head. Encouraged by the laughter of the others the man had gone further.

'Even one such as the great Kwok, whose face she has taken, is afraid to take the jarp-jung's cherry in return.'

The others roared agreement. Every man present hated the Rat Man and his bamboo cane, protected and encouraged by the rich hag. As Sing looked up at him, pinned by his weight, spittle sprayed out with the vile words he screeched at her. He would teach her respect. He was no mountain of lard like Fat Fan. He would prove who was her true master. One hand closed over her face, a finger jabbing painfully into her eye as she felt his other rammed between her thighs.

All of this happened within seconds of her awakening and her reaction came without thought. Kwok did not see where the blow came from. It struck with a shock that jerked him upright. The middle knuckle of Sing's closed fist had driven like a steel rod into the soft tissue at the base of his throat, below the epiglottis.

The strike had been so lightning fast the men could not be sure what had happened, their wits dulled by drink. In their stupor it had seemed as though Kwok the Rat Man had been seized by a sudden fit. To Sing, it had the same stunning effect, as though she were a bystander. Bent backwards, his eyes bulging and glazed, Kwok's weight still pinned her legs as he fought to find breath.

Complete silence hung for a second as, with his mouth working soundlessly, he fell backwards with a gurgling sigh. Then, howling like pack hounds, the larp cheung men fell upon her. Not one of them tried to succeed where the Rat Man had failed. This was no girl child. This was a devil. A dangerous beast. They would have killed her but they knew Fat Fan had paid money for the jarp-jung. They dared not take her life. Instead they tied her hands and feet, carrying her to the iron-bound door at the end of the slaughterhouse.

Pain was all that told Siu Sing she was conscious. Her eyes opened but she saw nothing in the blackness. A slow feeble light leaked into it and when she turned her head the opaque square of a window space floated in the dark. She did not try any other movement and lay still, watching the light, waiting for it to tell her where she was.

The crushing weight of the men's bodies, their mauling hands and driving fists still seemed to rain down and the smell of their sweat clung. Her stomach heaved, the rush of bile to her throat causing her to twist onto her side and retch violently into the filthy straw that covered the floor beneath her. The movement made her cry out. It was as though every bone had been broken and every muscle torn.

Falling back, her eyes closed as she steadied her breathing. When she opened them the light had strengthened. The window space glowed milky white with moonlight. She allowed her eyes to explore the shadows it cast, her head and neck rigid, afraid to raise a finger; row upon row of ghastly shapes, still as death, seemed to close in around her. With the effort bursting from her in a gasp of pain, Sing scrambled away from them, dragging herself backwards until her head and shoulders rammed hard against a wall. Pain was nothing to the horror that surrounded her. The familiar smell of death that filled the dark mingled with another stench more overpowering. It came in putrid waves and with it the faintest of sounds, that rose and fell, came and went, with the terrible smell. It was the buzzing of disturbed flies lifting and settling.

As her eyes became more accustomed to the light, Sing realised she was in the room where the pig carcasses were hung overnight. The place at the end of the slaughterhouse, from where those awful bellows of despair sometimes came. It was cold inside the room. The stone walls and floor trapped a clammy chill. Drained of blood, the pig corpses hung motionless, their slit throats and bellies gaping.

Something moved in the deep shadow below the window and another sound joined the spasmodic whirring of the flies. It was the rattle of chain. Sing held her breath. Her own pulse, thudding wildly in her ears, could not smother the sound. Someone or something was in the room with her. Short, laboured breaths came from the dark space beneath the window.

A cloud crossed the moon and the window dimmed, then brightened suddenly. Something dragged itself forward into the light. It was a bear. Not huge and menacing, but of medium size, like those she had seen often playing in the groves and climbing the hillside, the fur on their heavy flanks gleaming honey-coloured in the sunshine. It did not seem to see her as its black lips drew back, blunt snout lifting in a low moan. It took some moments before Sing could take in the source of the bear's terrible torment. Three of its paws had been hacked off, the stumps stuck into a bucket of tar to staunch the blood. The tar had hardened and split. The stink was the stink of gangrene.

Fat Fan sat in the Palace of Birds and Flowers, the long curve of one of his freshly lacquered fingernails absently probing the mole, large as a blowfly, on his chin. The mention of the mooi-jai caused his whole cheek to twitch. Since she had wrenched the precious hairs of good fortune and manliness from the mole, his life had become a mockery. Number one wife was turned from a crow to a dragon. Her illness, thank all gods, kept her confined to her bed but the upper house echoed ceaselessly with her ranting.

Didn't the others laugh behind his back? Had he not lost all face in his own house? Only here could he find peace among the singing of his birds and the scents of his flowers. And now this. Kwok the Rat Man's skinny hands flapped wildly as he described the madness in the jarp jung girl's unprovoked attack upon him. How her defiance and her insolence towards the simplest request of his hardworking men was no longer tolerable. The canque had taught her nothing. It had only deranged her. Such disobedience must not go unpunished.

Fat Fan disliked the cadaverous man before him, if only because number one wife favoured him so highly. He knew too, the excesses of the Rat Man's punishment. Hadn't he once tied the legs of a boy's trousers above the knees and placed rats inside, then beaten them with his cane, because he had been disobedient?

This devil-girl had brought him nothing but trouble. She was not worth her rice. She must go. He would sell her. Again, he thanked all gods that tai tai was indisposed and could not be consulted—even Kwok was not allowed to approach her bedchamber. Particularly on such a paltry matter as a bothersome mooi-jai. His damp brow creased, the smooth lids of his eyes almost closed in thought.

For a moment the movement of the fan stirred the silken strands of the scarlet tassel on his shoulder.

'No. She must not be touched,' he said finally. 'I cannot sell an injured mooi-jai. She must be unmarked, clean and strong. Where is she now?'

Kwok the Rat Man's hands flopped to his sides and he blinked his disappointment. Fat Fan's pale cheeks flushed and his voice climbed with sudden anger.

'Where is she now, dung of a donkey?'

'In the hanging room,' Kwok mumbled.

'Then take her from there and give her to the amahs. I want her to look like a princess. She must be made to shine like a jewel if I am to profit from this misfortune.'

It took the amahs of the house of Fan two weeks to heal the sores and treat the scratches and bruises that covered Siu Sing's body. She was bathed many times and rubbed regularly with sweet-smelling oils and ointments. Made to stay in the bed specially placed for her in a downstairs room, surrounded by rich and beautiful things, she was brought nourishing food and special medicines.

Ah Sum was allowed to wash and dress her hair, brushing it for hours as she talked softly to Sing. Telling her how brave she was, that there were beautiful lights in her hair. They gleamed like the tail feathers of the cockerel in the yard, she said. But nothing she could say would make Siu Sing answer her.

Fat Fan was pleased with the amah's work. The jarp-jung girl was strangely interesting when she was clean. Something else about her bothered him. In the seven days since the Rat Man had taken her from the hanging room and delivered her to the kitchen the amahs said she had not spoken a word. She seemed lost, as one who cannot hear or speak, whose eyes saw nothing. This concerned him, for if her mind had been affected she would not be easy to sell. Again, he cursed the Rat Man for his clumsiness.

Sing sat in a blackbean chair with a hard marble seat, her slim hands folded in her lap, clasping the closed fan they had given her to hold. Ah Sum had dressed her hair high, decorating it with the tiny stars of jasmine flowers. The long gown they dressed her in was the deep green of old jade. It was too big for her and its wide sleeves had been carefully rolled back, but its lush colour made her eyes of hazy wisteria even more striking. They painted her lips deep red and her brows and lashes coal black against the starch white of powder extending to her throat and the swell of her breasts.

Madam Fung's face showed nothing of the approval Fat Fan had hoped for. She stood before Sing, her head slightly tilted to one side like a teacher evaluating the painting of a promising student.

'Was I not correct?' Fat Fan could stand her silence no longer. 'Is she not rare and splendid as the phoenix? Soft as the throat of a turtle dove? White as ginger blossom and gentle as a fawn?'

Lu Wei-Fung, Madam of the Pavilion of Cascading Jewels, showed no sign of hearing him. 'Stand up,' she said, gesturing sharply with a white, well-kept hand that sparkled with jewelled rings. Sing did as she was told, rising from the uncomfortable chair.

Madam Fung's narrow eyes expertly measured her height and shape. Such a chest was not usual in the girls she chose. It could be a great asset. Stepping closer she poked an extended finger into the swell of Sing's breast.

'Did I not tell you? Am I not right?' Fan was getting increasingly nervous. He giggled. 'The size and shape of ripe paw-paw.'

'Walk,' said Madam Fung, ignoring him.

Sing rose and walked a few paces under the caged birds and among the flower pots and back to the chair.

'You are asking too much,' the madam said, turning to look at Fan for the first time. 'She is mixed blood. It is not all men that will find her pleasing. She has the hands and feet of a field worker. Her eyes are round as lychee nuts and she is not white as ginger blossom, the powder ends at her throat—she has skin the colour of a peasant.'

A large pearl of sweat escaped from beneath Fat Fan's black silk hat. He had broken the rule of number one wife by bringing his mooi-jai back into the house. It had cost him many red packets, generously filled, to buy the silence of the others. It could not last much longer. He must be rid of this jarp-jung bitch and be done with it.

Fat Fan may have been nervous but he was first of all a businessman. His fingers continued to gingerly probe the mole. 'Ah, but to an enlightened one. One who seeks the mysterious and the untouched.' His brows arched even higher and his pink mouth twitched. 'A man of taste . . . a rich man. She will be priceless as a pink finger jade.'

Madam Fung's eyes fixed unsmilingly on Fat Fan. 'Untouched? Since when have the mooi-jai of this house remained untouched?'

Fan raised his hands in protest. 'I swear by all gods I have not tampered with this exquisite jewel.'

Madam Fung's eyes remained fixed intently on his face. 'Not once?'

The pink spots that were the curse of Fat Fan appeared faintly on his cheeks. His eyes flicked away from hers to the top of the stairs and his voice fell to a whisper. 'I was most careful. On the word of my ancestors, she is pure as a lily not yet opened by the morning sun.'

Madam Fung allowed herself the slightest nod. 'We shall see.' She clapped her hands and a slight figure appeared in the doorway. The small woman who stepped forward was dressed in a plain black cheong-sam. Its high collar emphasised her long neck and fitted her slender body perfectly. She moved gracefully as a cat, her hair set in the traditional style, her face perfectly made up. She wore gold on her neck, on her wrists and on her fingers. A large black leather handbag hung from her arm. She smiled gently at Sing, offering her hand, keeping it patiently extended until Madam Fung's brittle voice snapped out. 'Go with Ah Gum. She only wishes to talk to you. She will not eat you.'

Something in the elegant woman's face, in the way her eyes also smiled as well as her lips, encouraged Sing to trust her. She took the outstretched hand.

'Show me where you sleep, Siu Sing.' Ah Gum's voice was as soft and reassuring as her smile. Behind the screen where Sing had been sleeping she sat down on the bed and patted the place beside her. 'Sit down. There is nothing to fear. I am here to help you.'

She kept hold of Sing's hand as she sat. 'You must trust me. I can take you from this place. Do you understand?'

Sing nodded slowly, tears springing to her eyes at the unexpected kindness in Ah Gum's voice.

'Does the maker of sausages tell the truth? Has he touched you?'

Sing closed her eyes and the tears dropped unchecked. Ah Gum quickly produced a silk handkerchief from the handbag, pressing it to Sing's cheek.

'He is not an honourable man. You must tell me if he lies. I am ordered to examine you. If you tell me the truth it will not be necessary.'

In her business Ah Gum had seen many girls, often younger than this one. It had taught her all the signs. There was an innocence here that she rarely found. This girl truly did not know the meaning of her words.

'Has he taken you to his bed?'

Sing took the handkerchief Ah Gum folded into her hand and shook her head. 'He has tried. But he could not. He was too fat.'

Ah Gum nodded slowly, a smile on her lips. Here was a match for that lord of all pigs.

'If Madam asks if I have examined you, you must say yes. Do you understand?'

She returned the handkerchief to the handbag and produced a small compact made of tortoiseshell, snapping it open to show its tiny mirror and powder puff. In spite of her distress, Sing's eyes widened. She had never seen such a wonderful thing. Ah Gum showed her how to use it and watched as she repaired the tear stains on her face. Again she was struck by the strange attraction of this girl. She guessed her age to be perhaps fifteen or sixteen although she was probably younger. Whatever strange blood flowed in her veins it had developed her body differently to a Chinese girl or her age. Madam Fung was right. Not all Chinese men would find her desirable but there were those who would pay an emperor's ransom for her. Ah Gum, whose name in Cantonese meant the Golden One, had been a procuress for many years and she knew of those among the rich and powerful to whom price was no object to lie with a virgin girl, especially of western blood. True, a jarp jung was not as greatly in demand, but this one was different. Madam Fung paid the Golden One for her work and her commission was generous when a beauty such as this was found. Siu Sing was indeed rare and priceless as a rose-coloured finger jade and she must be treated as one.

Ah Gum placed an arm around Sing's shoulders as they rose from the bed. 'You are leaving here now. I will take you to a place of great beauty where you will be safe and taught many things.'

She gave Sing a little squeeze. 'I will take care of you. Come, we must go now. Madam Fung is not a patient woman.'

At the door Sing hesitated.

'What is it, Siu Sing?' Ah Gum enquired.

'I must have my property. It is hidden in the scullery. I cannot leave without it.' The look on her face conveyed such great concern that Ah Gum had to laugh.

'What can you possess that cannot be replaced? Leave it. You will have new and more pleasant things to wear.'

'I cannot. It is of great importance to me. It is my duty to protect it.' Sing had become so agitated that Ah Gum paused at the door to calm her.

'If this rare treasure is of such great value I will see that it is returned to you,' she promised.

'No. I must fetch it myself. I must fetch it now.' Her words were so filled with urgency, that Ah Gum nodded.

'Fetch it then and let us leave this place.'

PART · V

Flight of the Crane

The Crane flies high
Leaving marsh and mountain far behind
The tiger watches from the cane grass
The sky is empty
The tiger waits then follows
Time and distance have no meaning.

MASTER TO-TZE

• IMAGE FOR TIGER •

Toby Hyde-Wilkins

Captain Toby Hyde-Wilkins had been with the 8th Rajputs for five years. At a little under twenty-five, he was one of the youngest commissioned officers to receive his third pip in the history of its ranks and to be awarded the Military Medal for valour. A graduate of the Royal Military College in the Berkshire village of Sandhurst he had been posted to northern India before his twentieth birthday and had quickly become subaltern to a recruitment major.

The Indian Army had fascinated Toby since he was a boy and an avid reader of Rudyard Kipling. The Indian NCOs—Subudars, Risaldars and Jemidars—were referred to by Field-Marshall Birdwood as 'God's Own Gentlemen', and Toby had found it to be so. A British subaltern newly off the boat could rely on any one of them to be always at his elbow in battle and to be trusted with his life. At Sandhurst he had learned all he could of the famous sepoy regiments—the Gurkhas from the mountains of Nepal, the Mohammedan troops of the great plains, the Jats of north-west India, Dogras from Madras, Maharattas from around Poona and the Sikhs of the Punjabi foothills. Above all of these he had chosen the Rajputs. They did not have the same religious taboos as the other tribal regiments and they drank and smoked like Englishmen.

From the first moment he marched with the major's contingent into a Rajputana village bordering the burning deserts of Rajasthan, he knew that from here came the soldiers that he would be proud to lead into battle and that these were the people he would wish to spend his life with. The old men of the village, all ex-soldiers, turned out to meet them, proudly—wearing their medals and playing the regiment's marching tune on hand-made musical instruments. The young men lined up outside the recruiting tent, their families peering anxiously from inside as the pack mule was unloaded and the table set up with the flags of the regiment and the British Empire hung behind it.

The volunteers were inspected by the medical orderly for any sign of disease or physical weakness, with particular attention to the teeth, eyes and feet. The major, with his subaltern, Second

Lieutenant Toby Hyde-Wilkins, one pace behind, would cast an expert eye over each man's physique, the set of his shoulders, development of chest, arms and legs and the steadiness of his gaze.

The old men of the village who had served their time and been retired, had already taught their sons the basics of British army drill. The young recruits would stand rigidly at attention, straining to look every inch a soldier, the beginnings of their military moustaches carefully waxed and curled, wearing their fathers' old Bombay bloomers, creased in regimental order for the occasion.

Those who were chosen lined up in the village centre, while those who would have to wait another year and try again returned forlornly to their work in the fields. To Toby Hyde-Wilkins, who came from Derbyshire where young men spent their time between the porcelain factories and pubs, the Rajput soldier was an inspiration.

For the pittance paid to their families by the British War Office, they proudly provided ten years of fanatical loyalty anywhere on earth that they were sent to defend the territory and the honour of the British Empire. Their acceptance of discipline, outstanding fighting skills and legendary courage in combat put them among the bravest fighting men on earth.

Toby was off-duty. He allowed himself a casual look across the lines, at the neat rows of married quarters where the Indian officers' wives and families were billeted, the dabs of bright colour as their saris moved against the drab khaki of the huts and their children played in the small, well-swept gardens. The Regimental Band was assembled in the centre of the parade ground for practice, white tunics spotless against highly polished black leather and silver dressing, the brass of their instruments flashing, the pipe major taking up position.

Beyond the long barracks of the Riflemen and the officers' mess, rose the hills of mainland China. To Toby, they were not as spectacular as the snow-capped peaks of Everest, nor was the stretch of rural countryside between the lines and the border as familiar as the plains of Assam. But a soldier goes where a soldier is sent and in the eighteen months since the regiment had arrived in the New Territories of Hong Kong he had adapted to his new surroundings with enthusiasm and interest.

The pipe major raised the glittering mace and the bagpipes began their drone. Toby never tired of watching the tall, dignified plainsmen swing by, straight-backed, lean and long-muscled. Proud descendants of the warrior caste of Rajasthan who claimed divine origin and had defeated the invading Moguls and Mahrattas since the seventh century, they wore dark blue turbans with high, fan-shaped cockades, scarlet sashes, with campaign ribbons bright on their chests and battle honours emblazoned on the pipe banners.

They were his people, the Corps d'Elite, just as the Regimental Officers' Mess with its legendary silver and portraits of dead heroes was his home, and its officers his family. Toby watched the bandsmen march past to the rousing tune of 'Bonny Mary McKabe', their boots polished to a glass-like finish, swinging by in perfect precision, the silver-tipped sheaths of their bayonets flat on their hips.

The Tavern
of Cascading Jewels

To siu Sing, her deliverance from the factory shed of Kwok the Rat Man truly seemed the greatest and most wonderful of all possible dreams. She stepped into the sedan chair and the softness of its cushions, the deerhide satchel safe beside her, as the iron gate clanged shut. The chair swayed, it seemed for hours, through the city streets to the old Portuguese quarter, before it stopped at a round moon-gate, set in a high wall topped with dark blue tiles. They followed Madam Fung through the gate and into a traditional Chinese garden.

The Tavern of Cascading Jewels was built in the style of a pavilion of the Summer Palace of Peking. Old stone balustrades and vermilion-painted fences faced a still moat of lily-scattered water. Small islands of ancient rock rose from its mirror surface and white swans cleaned their feathers on its banks.

The oldest and most famous of Macau's opium taverns, it had

withstood the many attempts by various lawmakers to forbid the smoking of opium. Opium was the indulgence of rich and poor alike but the poor of the waterfront dens committed crimes, suffering punishment and death in exchange for its dreams. Those who could afford to visit the Tavern of Cascading Jewels indulged themselves in the most luxurious surroundings imaginable.

Sing was taken to the room that she was to share with five other girls. They bowed politely when Ah Gum entered.

'This is Siu Sing. She is to be your sister, make room for her and treat her kindly.' She introduced each of the girls, explaining that Madam Fung named her pipe-makers after rare and precious stones.

There was Ruby—Light in the Eye of the All-Seeing Phoenix; Pearl—More Glorious than the Illustrious Dawn; Jade—Peace in the Heart of the Conquering Tiger; Emerald—Exquisite Splendour to the Eye of the Dragon; Sapphire—She Who Warms as Eternal Summer. The name chosen for Siu Sing was Topaz—Soft as Heavenly Mist on the Tallest Mountain, the name of one gone before her. It was a lucky name, they said cheerfully, for that one had become concubine to a rich and important taipan.

Sing was shown how to 'make the pipes' by the girl called Jade. A small amount of hemp and the root of the grasscloth plant were mixed with the raw opium and finely chopped with a ceremonial knife of tiger bone. The mixture was boiled in a small amount of water in a copper pan on a tripod, made specially for the purpose. Then it was dried and mixed with tobacco in the true tradition of the opium tavern-keeper and served in the water pipe.

Sing found the work easy and pleasant. Jade had become her friend and was always ready to help and advise. When the pipe had been served, all that was expected of the pipe-maker was to sit by the side of the smoker who stretched comfortably among the cushions of the divan, and to fill his cup with the strong, bitter tea of Swatow to clear his head when he had completed his journey. The men she attended expected nothing more than to gaze upon her as they drifted away on the back of the celestial dragon. For the many hours that the journey took, she learned to do as the others did—to practise the fine embroidery of silk on silk or the flowing calligraphy Great-uncle To had taught her.

The men who came regularly to the Pavilion of Cascading Jewels were mostly old or middle-aged. All were influential Chinese who were rich, or very rich, and the tavern catered for their every wish but one. It was well known that the pipe-makers were untouched.

Their virginity was considered as priceless as the jewels they were named after and they were not to be tampered with. It was also known that each girl had been brought from the rough ground of the provinces, to be shaped and polished to perfection by the skills of Ah Gum, the Golden One.

Ah Gum was no ordinary procuress. She came of high family and had herself perfected all the arts of pleasing men. When younger, she had been a favoured concubine to certain of those who could afford her exquisite services and their gratitude had made her wealthy and independent. She had also seen the fate of those girls, still children, who fell into the wrong hands and who were ill-equipped to meet the demands of their masters. Ah Gum had chosen to seek those girls of exceptional beauty, quality and promise and to turn each one into a valuable asset by teaching her the authentic techniques of early China, Japan, Korea and as far afield as Siam and India.

She had observed when very young, and from her privileged position, that common female flesh was just another commodity in Chinese society. Among the poor, it was bought and sold like any other necessity; among the rich it was acquired and possessed along with other baubles of pleasure and sometimes prized as a treasure of great value. In Macau and Hong Kong at that time a baby girl could be bought for seventy to eighty dollars and children of maturer age cost no more than $250.

Boys always brought the higher prices and the $1,000 she had approved for the purchase of Siu Sing was one of the highest she had yet known in her trade for a girl. That she had advised Madam Fung to be so generous with the odious merchant Fan was only because she expected Sing's worth to be twenty times more within the space of one year.

Ah Gum was a decent and compassionate woman. If she had ever had fleeting stabs of conscience they were quickly forgotten. If a girl was going to be abused by men she might as well learn how to use them. Far better, she knew, to sleep in silk and be fed on larks' tongues than to sleep in rags and be fed on salt fish. So, Ah Gum saw herself as a teacher. A professor of life, who took the same pride in her work as others took in the teaching the arts, commerce or history and whose scholars were just as accomplished and their place in society just as important. That she had been successful in her chosen field was clear from the abundance of gold she enjoyed and the name it had given her.

The Golden One's method of teaching came from her own experience and she had wasted none of it. Had she lived in earlier dynasties, emperors would have sent for her to train their courtesans. She would school Siu Sing in the authentic arts of seduction, the valuable skill of leading a man along the paths of pleasure and, as she put it 'causing him to yield his pearly treasure without entering the jade gate.' She called it, 'Taming the Tiger.' Through her many charts and diagrams, her exotic pictures and literature both licentious and poetic, centuries old and from a time when to displease a man of station was to suffer a cruel fate, she would unfold the secrets of men's desires and the ways in which only a woman of great skill could satisfy them.

She began by winning Sing's confidence. Not through cunning or manipulation but by an honesty and openness that soon gained the girl's trust. Sing responded to her unhurried approach and realised that she could only profit from the Golden One's great wisdom. But first she had to rid her mind of the horror that still troubled her nights. When the others slept beside her, she would listen to their soft breathing and try not to think of it. She had told Ah Gum all that had happened in the house of Fan. Only one question remained unanswered.

When finally she was able to talk of the bear and its terrible torment she asked Ah Gum the question that still echoed in her head, bringing back the image of the bear's terrible agony.

'Why?'

Ah Gum took her hand. 'Men are very stupid in such matters. They believe that there are certain things that will increase their desire, give them strength to turn the lamb into a lion.' She paused to gauge Sing's understanding, seeing nothing but confusion and pain in her eyes.

'They will eat the genitals of the tiger to give them this power. The horn of the rhinoceros, the hoof and antler of the deer and the paw of the bear.'

Sing withdrew her hand and stared at Ah Gum. 'How can this terrible thing be part of love?'

'I said nothing of love,' replied Ah Gum. 'Love is a different thing altogether.' She smiled fondly. 'Together we will discover the difference. The other is called lust. Lust is a currency. I will teach you to spend it wisely.'

Only when Sing had displayed a clear understanding of the male and female body and their vital energies, did the Golden One unveil the Prince of the Sacred Persimmon. As with all of the properties she used in her revelations, the Prince of the Sacred Persimmon was very old, extremely rare and accompanied by legend. Sing found him lying on the high couch that Ah Gum used to rest upon and to demonstrate the techniques of massage in the Place of Heavenly Rhythms, one of the many pavilions tucked away in the rambling garden.

At first Sing had thought it was her friend Jade lying under the embroidered silk of the coverlet. Jade was always willing when a live model was needed. She admired and envied the private tuition that Sing was receiving from the Golden One and, when she had conquered an uncontrollable urge to giggle, under Ah Gum's patient guidance she became a regular and favourite part of such sessions, enjoying and guiding the soft touch of Sing's exploring fingers as she was taught the arts of massage.

But when Ah Gum slid the silken sheet away Sing's eyes widened at what was revealed.

'Behold,' said the Golden One dramatically. 'The Prince of the Sacred Persimmon.' The figure on the couch was the perfect life-sized effigy of a splendidly handsome young man. He had been carved from a precious wood, its glossy hue like no other Sing had seen—in places purplish black as a ripe plum, in others the deep sheen of burnished bronze, seamed with veins of palest yellow. He lay on his back in a posture of complete relaxation, his eyes closed, his hands by his sides, as though deep in meditation. In his left hand he held the glowing orb of a succulently ripe persimmon.

'You may touch him,' said Ah Gum, her smile showing pleasure at Sing's expression of wonder.

Sing reached out to place her fingertips upon the prince's smooth chest. Its patina felt so real she withdrew her hand quickly. Ah Gum laughed.

'Don't be afraid. You will come to know every inch of him before we part.' She took Sing's hand firmly and placed it on his shapely thigh, guiding it gently downward over the contours of well-defined muscle, to his knee and back again.

'Explore him. Feel his beauty.' She chuckled mischieviously, pleased and amused by her student's caution.

'He will not awaken. But does he not cast a spell?'

She watched patiently as Sing's small hand traced the lines of the prince's noble face, gliding over more perfectly formed muscles, the planes and hollows of chest and shoulders, arms and hands, abdomen and back to thighs, calves and feet. To Sing the figure had the touch of cool marble. Ah Gum's amusement increased as Sing's eyes and fingers delicately skirted the empty socket above a scrotum modelled in minute detail.

'Our prince hides many secrets,' she smiled. 'Take his hand.' Sing did so. 'Now spread his fingers.' Each joint moved as though the hand was alive. When she looked closely, she saw that the knuckles and joints were intricately tooled by a master craftsman to move independently.

'Now bend his elbows, raise his arm.'

Delighted by Sing's exclamation of amazement she stepped across to demonstrate, lifting first one leg, then the other, then letting them fall back into a natural position. She rotated a foot on its ankle joint, splaying its toes one by one.

'Open his eyes that he may see his new mistress.'

Gingerly, Sing laid her fingertips on the prince's eyelids. At her slightest touch they rolled smoothly upward to reveal eyes so real they caused her to step back. Ah Gum laughed aloud.

'He cannot see you. His eyes are of finest onyx set in ivory. But look closely. He speaks to us.' She pointed to his finely sculpted ear.

When Sing bent closer, the tiniest of Chinese characters became apparent, meticulously inscribed all over the ear.

'And here, and here and here,' said Ah Gum, pointing with her finger.

Looking closely, Sing realised the model was covered in tiny inscriptions, so finely drawn they were almost indiscernible.

'They tell us all his innermost secrets.'

A small frown of concentration had creased Sing's brow as she tried to read them.

'They are in a tongue long buried,' said Ah Gum. 'I will teach them to you in time.'

She reached down and from beneath the couch withdrew a long flat box, its lid inlaid with characters and symbols in the same ancient hand. 'Now we will make him whole.'

Inside the box, carved from the same exquisite wood, were two rows of lifelike penises, each a different size and shape to the other, from one no larger or more significant than a raised forefinger to one so large and glorious it made Sing gasp.

'We will begin modestly.' Ah Gum surveyed the arrangement as critically as a duellist choosing a weapon. 'But not too modestly,' she concluded, selecting one of medium size and slotting it into the socket.

'See. It also moves.' The penis, its plum-shaped head gleaming, moved smoothly back and forth between Ah Gum's fingers.

Over the following weeks Sing learned all there was to know about the Prince of the Sacred Persimmon, including his fascinating legend. He had been carved, Ah Gum said, for the great general, Li-Yuan, founder of the T'ang Dynasty. His reign, she explained, was when Chinese art and sculpture were at their finest.

'Precise modelling and linear rhythms,' she sighed. 'An age of true eroticism'.

The Prince had been carved from no ordinary wood, but from the very finest ebony, taken from the heart of a sacred persimmon tree, discovered in the mountains of Shan by the emperor's son Li Shih-Min. Its fruit was said to bring hallucinations of wildest ecstasy. The Prince had never left the tree, consuming each of its many fruits and dying beneath its shade, the legend said, from terminal bliss.

General Li-Yuan had been devastated by the death of his only son, whilst acknowledging that there were far worse ways to die. He had ordered the tree cut down and commissioned the great sculptor, Sung Chow, carver of China's finest temple Buddhas, to create the exact replica of his son from its heart. The Prince of the Sacred Persimmon was one of several rare treasures looted by the Moguls from the Forbidden Palace where it had been in the care of the royal eunuchs.

Almost as precious was the Court of a Thousand Pleasures, an ivory chess set yellowed and seamed with age and handling. Each piece depicted a male and female in an act of copulation so complex it held all the mysteries of a Chinese puzzle. When she was not being taught to talk, move and dance like a courtesan, or schooled in the finer points of social etiquette, the Prince of the Sacred Persimmon and the Court of a Thousand Pleasures became Siu Sing's playthings.

J.T. Ching

J ACK TEAGARDEN Ching was an ugly man. The round flat features of Hakka heritage still showed and his skin was darker than those around him. The upper lids of his narrow eyes were as puffed as the pouches beneath them. The lower lip of his wide mouth was slack, showing discoloured bottom teeth flecked with gold; saliva gathered easily at its corners. Greed, power and cruelty were easily read in his face and his thinning black hair was flattened across his scalp with a sweet-smelling pomade.

As one of the richest and most powerful businessmen in Hong Kong, taipan Ching did not follow rules. He had started out as a clerk with the great trading hong of Butterfield & Swire. Later, as compradore, he had established interests of his own. Timber concessions in the jungles of Sarawak had led to expansion into the southern Philippines and the teak forests of Siam and Burma, to make him one of Asia's biggest timber barons. The fact that the bulk of his immense wealth had been generated through the opium trade and that at one time his fleet of opium clippers had been the largest operating in the whole of the Orient, was well known but seldom talked about.

Not that to have risen to such fame and fortune in this fashion was anything unusual. Most of Hong Kong's successful companies of any established standing had reached their current status in exactly the same way. The fact that the International Opium Convention held at the Hague in 1912 had taken the first world-wide steps to control trafficking, and that the League of Nations continued to agitate for its abolition, had only served to encourage men like J.T. Ching to make the most of things while they lasted.

As always, with those known to have been involved in the buying and selling of opium, there were plentiful rumours of treachery, mayhem and murder, piracy and double dealing. J.T. Ching was no exception. In fact, if half the colourful stories told about him were true, his exploits were legendary.

In his early sixties, J.T. enjoyed the rude health and bountiful energy that often accompany great power and immense wealth.

In a time and place where legends were commonplace and often looked upon with admiration and envy he made no attempt to discourage or deny such stories. Instead, he revelled in them, often embellishing his shady reputation, when in the right company, with tales of his own.

But as with others of his kind, his past dealings had not been entirely without their price. J.T. Ching did not consider himself addicted to opium, he preferred to tell himself that his regular indulgence was nothing more than another of the many benefits that came with success and fabulous wealth. The huge, gleaming shape of his Rolls Royce 3-V.12 motor car, the only one of its kind in Macau, was such a regular visitor at the Tavern of Cascading Jewels that it had been provided with its own garage space in the rear of the old building, well hidden and shaded by overhanging trees.

He did not admit to himself that the reason he had chosen to build a residence in Macau, when his Hong Kong mansion took up half a hillside between Repulse Bay and Stanley Village and was well known as his official residence, was because his visits to the tavern were becoming more and more frequent. And that the excellent attentions arranged by Madam Fung left very little to be desired, even for a man of his extravagant and varied tastes. Since she had introduced Topaz into his visits they had increased from once a month to once a fortnight, to once a week.

As he watched her making the pipe, deftly but unhurriedly preparing the mixture, lighting the tiny flame under the copper pan, he thought how well they had named her. J.T. knew quite a bit about jewellery—three wives and more concubines than he cared to count had made expertise a necessity. The topaz had been a favourite of kings since ancient times. Of immeasurable value, but only to the experienced and discerning eye. He prided himself that he chose his women with the same care and disregard of cost.

It was almost eight months since Topaz had first attended him and from the first moment she had appeared he knew, with the instinct of a collector, that here was a wild swan among tame ducks. Since then he had spent many of his most pleasant hours in this room, upon this divan, in her company. But there was one thing that J.T. Ching respected and embraced completely and that was the concept of tradition. Authenticity in all that he owned or aspired to came before all else.

It was why he had chosen the Tavern of Cascading Jewels as his favourite hideaway. Madam Fung's strict adherence to time-honoured custom was the closest he had ever come to doing as he was told. He felt a little discipline, like all else under the tavern roof, was good for a man used to taking any woman he found of interest, regardless of age, nationality or persuasion. Those he couldn't take he could almost certainly buy. With Topaz he would follow the rules. The girl would remain untouched until all the traditional formalities had been observed.

As chairman of several of his companies, a prominent member of the Legislative Council, and a director on the boards of many other organisations, nothing gave him greater delight than to walk away from the frustrations of a boardroom, the boredom of a committee meeting or the intrusions of a clamorous household, to board his motor yacht at the Royal Hong Kong Yacht Club and head for Macau. A drink or a rest in its luxurious saloon would see him in the Rolls, its blinds pulled down and threading its way through the Old Quarter towards another period of sublime peace, contentment and temporary obscurity.

His reverence and nostalgia for the old ways, which he feared would soon be gone from his life forever, were the only considerations he knew that could make him honour laws laid down by others. That, and the code of self-preservation born of his Hakka ancestry, had given him the brilliant craftiness that he used with such wizardry in his dealings with the British, a talent which he saw as a legitimate part of resourcefulness rather than lies and deceit.

An amah knocked discreetly and carried a tray of steaming delicacies into the room. Authentic court cuisine, prepared from the ancient recipes of the imperial palace, was yet another example of Madam Fung's resistance to change. Sing lifted the lids from the bamboo steamers and helped J.T. to such fragrant delights as miniature dumplings stuffed with pigeon and wild mushroom, swallow's nest soup, freshwater crab and crucian carp seasoned with red pepper sauce. She filled their cups from a flask of hot plum wine and took the first sip, then with a pair of silver chopsticks, which turned black at the touch of contaminated food, she tried a morsel from each dish. Even the ancient custom of food tasting was borrowed from the royal household.

'How do your lessons with Ah Gum proceed, Topaz?'

'Extremely well, sir.'

'Does she continue to treat you well?'

'Very well indeed, sir. She is a good friend to me as well as a patient teacher.'

He smiled, wondering if Sing guessed why she attended only to him and why no other man was allowed to look at her. 'What does she teach you now?'

Sing covered any twinge of embarrassment by daintily lifting a tiny dumpling to his lips. He opened his mouth to receive it but his eyes never left her face.

'The arts of pleasing a gentleman, sir. The art of butterfly hands and dragonfly wings.'

'Will you show me what you have learned when the food is gone and the pipe is ready?'

Ten minutes later, the first thick plume of smoke was drawn deep into his lungs and the familiar gateway opened upon vistas of which he never tired. Upon the naked flesh of his back the touch of butterfly hands and dragonfly wings prepared him for his exotic journey. Sing waited until his breathing was deep and even, then laid the pipe aside. Gathering up the food containers and quietly stacking the porcelain cups and bowls onto the tray, she opened the cabinet and took out brushes and ink blocks.

Four hours later, when he had opened his eyes, she was ready with small towels dampened by rosewater, cool ones for his first awakening, then warm. There would be an hour more of drowsiness and many cups, no bigger than seashells, of Iron Buddha tea, while her hands soothed him back to reality.

When he was thoroughly recovered and refreshed she called for his favourite dish of baby abalone, the tiny, mother-of-pearl ear shells, their delicate morsels steamed with lotus roots, ginger and shallots. When he had finished eating and she had bathed him in the mineral spring bath, J.T. Ching reached into the pocket of his robe and placed a small purse of blue silk before her.

'A special gift for your services,' he said, turning to the mirror and beginning to comb the hair across his scalp, watching her reflection as she opened it.

The blue topaz lay in the palm of Sing's hand so softly she hardly felt its weight, about the size of one of the pebbles she had once collected from the Place of Clear Water.

'Such a stone is very rare,' he said. 'It means I have chosen you, for you, too, are rare.'

The Yellow Dragon

THERE WAS no breath of natural air. Only the fetid blast of ventilation fans reached the bowels of the old Ho Ching Bank building. It stirred the ritual characters hastily daubed on strips of yellow paper and hung above the barred entrance to an underground chamber—the ancient credo first uttered by the secret societies of the early sixteenth century and recorded as long ago as nine AD, when the Hung society had made its name by underground rebellion against the Manchus, whose tyranny ruled all of China from 1644 to 1911.

'Overthrow the Ching and Restore the Ming.' Its motto, and still its creed in 1938, looked down on those who entered. The shifting flame of torches set in iron brackets illuminated two men, one on each side of the tall metal doors. The suck and gurgle of running water concealed somewhere in the cold concrete of their surroundings was the only sound.

Only when the murmur of voices echoed down the concrete tunnel towards them did they step inward, each grasping an iron handle that released the barring mechanism securing the entrance to the vault-like chamber. A small group appeared, led by a short, thickset man, the golden robe he wore flowing with the briskness of his step. Following him came three others—two escorting a man who walked with a strange, rising step that favoured one foot.

Subterraneous channels beneath the catwalk branched into a network of tributaries that wound beneath the streets of western Hong Kong to the Central Markets in one direction and the labyrinth of Wan Chai in the other. Still more tunnels ran as far as the Sheng Wun waterfront and inland towards the junk city of Aberdeen.

The doors swung open and for a second the clamour of many voices surged into the tunnel, swiftly silenced by the appearance of the party. Over 200 pairs of eyes watched as the group passed between them. The leader strode ahead to kneel before a decorated altar.

Upon it, in a red painted shrine, sat effigies of the legendary marshals of war, Chen Lung, the Snorter, and Ch'en Ch'i, the Blower. In lesser shrines beside and behind them stood their mortal enemies Huang Fei Hu, the Yellow Flying Tiger, and Marshal Chin Ta Sheng, the Great Golden Blade.

A thick wall of incense rose before these mythical gods of war and vengeance as the man in the golden robe knelt before them to light joss then took his place in an elevated seat carved in the shape of a winged dragon. The two senior office-bearers, wearing the traditional garb of their rank, kow-towed three times and turned to face the gathering.

The cavernous space was lit by the flames of four iron braziers marking the corners of a raised area the size of two boxing rings. Around it the ranks of the Yellow Dragon triad sat cross-legged on the floor.

The two officials were the Hung Kwan—Red Pole, the senior official of the society's Hong Kong branch; and the Pak Tse Sin— White Paper Fan, his advisor and strategist. Before them, in the centre of the square, the long, lean muscles of his bare torso lit by flickering fire, the man with the strange, feline hop stood facing the shrine.

His name was Ah Keung, one who had proved himself worthy enough in the streets and alleyways of Wan Chai and the slums of Shau Kei Wan to take the initiation ceremony into the lowest rank of Sai Lo, Younger Brother. He had drawn attention to himself by defeating three of the Yellow Dragon's senior members bringing him to the attention of the Yellow Dragon himself. The Forceful One's power did not come from the symmetry of movement and quietude of mind of authentic Kung Fu. His lightning reflexes were born of a savage and tortured determination to prevail and destroy, an iron will that had pushed his power of endurance far beyond those of other adepts.

Ah Keung's fighting form had been developed through pain, like no other known stance. His malformed foot, forced into submission by endless training, had affected his skeletal balance and from it had come his own modified style, which he called Yangjingshi—the style of the Cobra. He was before the gathering to demonstrate his martial skills before taking the initiation ceremony and the oath of the Yellow Dragon triad.

At a nod from the man in the golden robe, the two office-bearers left his side and stirred the braziers to brighter flame, then took their places on either side of the square, where they remained standing. On a signal from the Red Pole, the murmur of voices was instantly hushed as Ah Keung swept into the flowing performance of his form. All sign of the disability seen in the slight hobble of his gait disappeared in the unique fighting style he had developed as his own.

A wave of approval rippled through the assembled members when he switched faster than the eye could blink from the sweeping kicks and jabbing strikes of the Crane to the lethal short-handed grasp of the Praying Mantis. Ah Keung's agile leaps from the crouch of the Monkey to the soaring flight of the Eagle, his whirling roundhouse kicks and Tiger Claw strikes were so swift they deceived the eye of the many champions who watched him. Few had mastered all five animal forms as he had and brought them together with the speed of Yangjingshi, the king of snakes.

Whispers among the ranks of those who knew of him told how he had taken the disfigured foot and turned it into a weapon faster than the strike of the king cobra he was said to have once slain with it. He was a strange and lonely one who claimed to have been taught in the Temple of the Tiger and boasted that he had killed his master when no more than a boy, defeating all those who had taught him since.

There were many in the Yellow Dragon society who were angered by such boasting and it had reached the ears of the Red Pole. It was rumoured that in street fights the Forceful One could not be beaten even by numbers, that he fought with a ruthless efficiency that could not go unnoticed.

Ah Keung's display of Yangjingshi came to an abrupt end and with three short bows to the shrine he stood waiting, his breathing steady and even. From the front ranks between the braziers a man stood up, removing the black tunic of an adept, and stepped forward. He wore the gold sash of a triad brother of the highest level. Taking his place opposite Ah Keung, he bowed to the shrine and turned to face the initiate.

Again faint murmuring rose to a wave of excitement among the observers. This was not normally part of a recruitment ceremony. Usually the demonstration of skill was enough, followed by traditional rites of initiation. It was well known that if the Red Pole and the White Paper Fan called for a full contact tournament it could mean serious injury or death to a contestant. Such a contest was held in the old ways that recognised only the total destruction of an adversary as proof of a champion. This had been ordered by the Yellow Dragon himself, the man who sat now in the seat of judgement and watched silently as the official ceremonies were carried out.

The Golden Sash was only called upon by the White Paper Fan when it was considered that the initiate needed such tempering. Over-confidence was the seed of carelessness and there was no room in the ranks of the Yellow Dragon society for either of these. According to what had been said, the Forceful One believed himself beyond risk of defeat. He was to be taught a lesson in humility.

The Golden Sash was chosen for his superior skills in the forms of Shaolin, the ancient styles of the warrior monks that had been created centuries earlier to defeat the mounted cavalry of warlords and bandit hordes. It was for him to test the initiate's strength and stamina, to assess his style and reaction to punishment. After he had uncovered weaknesses and exposed faults in technique would come the lesson of humility, humbling him before his elder brothers. It was his reaction to such loss of face that would be judged.

But this would be no mere lesson in behaviour. Those who had seen Ah Keung fight expected much more than that. The observers muttered their opinions on the results of the contest they were about to witness. The passing of money was forbidden but bets were secretly made on the outcome, with the stakes tripled if only one remained alive. Whispering ceased as the Yellow Dragon nodded his consent to begin the contest and each fighter took his stance.

To Ah Keung there was no room for doubt. He would be the one to walk away. The man in front of him was nothing but a living mechanism of muscle, bone, nerve and sinew trained to fight. It was driven by internal organs and each one of them could be reached and neutralised through the pressure points that controlled them as directly as the circuitry of an electrical switchboard. As with the extremities, the arms and hands, legs and feet that were its weapons—immobilise the ligament and sinew that operate them and trained muscle is no longer a threat. Sinking his ch'i deep in the pit of his stomach, Ah Keung concentrated his mind on dismantling the man who faced him.

It was customary for the observers to remain silent during such a contest, for each to make his own silent assessment. This did not happen. After a moment of probing for Ah Keung's style of defence, the Golden Sash unleashed the full force of Shaolin in an exhibition of pure mastery seldom seen. But the roar that arose from the shadows was not at the great artistry and power of the Golden Sash but at his opponent's defence. It was as though every form of the five animal techniques had come together to raise an invisible wall around the Forceful One.

Quickly the Golden Sash understood that the man he faced was no novice, no ordinary street fighter whose cockiness needed a lesson in respect. Ah Keung absorbed those strikes that he did not block and counter with the indestructible shell of his ch'i and the lightning speed of the cobra. When he believed he had judged the style of his opponent correctly he set about the swift process of destruction with relentless precision.

The following morning, the Hung Kwan, who, when he was not wearing the official robes of the Red Pole looked like any other Chinese working man, sat taking his early morning rice at a street stall near the western markets. The Red Pole's real name was Jimmy Chan and it would have been impossible to guess that he was a professional killer.

Beside him on the table his songbird hopped from perch to perch in its bamboo cage. Each morning he walked it in the Botanical Gardens, like hundreds of others, hanging it from a tree while he performed his Tai Chi Tuan.

As an office bearer of a triad society, he lived two lives. A normal one with his large family and a violent one that kept them in security and comfort. It was his responsibility to control the ranks under his command in the business of extortion. The crushing defeat of the Golden Sash was still fresh in his mind. He could not remember such a contest since the days when the death of an opponent led the victor to promotion in society ranks and the esteem of the brotherhood. This contest had lasted no more than five minutes and ended with the Golden Sash defeated among the burning coals of an upturned brazier.

Ah Keung had quickly pulled him free and helped him stand, only to pierce him with Di Mak, the death touch, a blow delivered to a point of the body that triggered internal shock-waves, reversing the polarity of Yin and Yang through its lethal vibrations, resulting in paralysis and death.

Such a blow was usually dealt with a finger or knuckle strike but the blow that had ended the life of the Golden Sash had come with the force and accuracy of a lance from the lame foot of Ah Keung, the Forceful One.

There were no rules in such a contest but it was not usual, when a fight had been won, for the victor to murder the vanquished. It was a clear message in the old style and one that could not be ignored. It said that the man left standing was one of great ambition and no fear, that nothing would stand in his way.

The man in the golden robe had risen from the seat of judgement and signalled his approval. Ah Keung had been accepted into the Yellow Dragon triad in the customary way. A cockerel was beheaded and its blood, symbolising the price of disloyalty, was drained into a rice bowl to mix with wine and potent spices. A strip of yellow paper carrying the oath was then burned and its ashes added to the mixture, an oath that called down the curse of all gods upon the initiate and upon his ancestors and his lineage should he break it. Ah Keung's finger had then been cut and dipped into the bowl, to be licked clean as an end to the initiation. The Forceful One had chosen to drink the contents, draining it dry, then shattering the bowl to signify his dedication to the brotherhood, death to it's enemies and, to those elders whom he wished to impress, signalling his defiance.

There had been no room for doubt left in Jimmy Chan's mind. Ah Keung was a Sai Lo, a younger brother, to be watched carefully. Impressive though his fighting form may be, courage and skill in combat were only the grounding of a triad member, more tradition than anything else. Such abilities had their uses in confrontations with rival societies such as Wo Sing Wo, Sun Yee On, the powerful 14K and the Green Triangle but they could spell trouble if not properly controlled on the streets.

A younger brother's introduction to everyday business was to accompany his elders over the territory the triad protected. This territory covered everything from cooked food stalls, street vendors and operations as small as the delivery of noodles, to the organisation of labour markets and the running of gambling and vice establishments. It was the triad's duty to take advantage of every opportunity to profit from every activity in the Chinese community, from the cart selling fishballs through the mass labour market to the corporate structure of Hong Kong's major commercial and industrial companies.

Jimmy Chan had decided to start Ah Keung where all Sai Lo began, in the low-class bars, massage parlours and gambling dens to the higher class tea-houses and ballrooms in the red light district of Wan Chai. He reached for his tea and signalled the waiter to bring conjee. A triad member for most of his adult life, Jimmy had seen many men killed for the change in their pocket or the look on their face. Ruthlessness was the basic ingredient of extortion.

Why then, was he so unsure of the Forceful One? He had not reached the coveted position of Red Pole by hesitation or doubt.

The Brotherhood was its own protection and there were ways and means of clipping the wings of those who would fly too high too soon. This one would be shown his proper place. But still the Red Pole could not understand why this strange, fierce-eyed man with the peculiar limp and the eyes of a snake should make him feel so uneasy.

One month later Jimmy Chan stood nervously looking around the outer office of J.T. Ching. He had been summoned in his official capacity as Red Pole of the Yellow Dragon triad. Only six people knew that J.T. Ching was one of the few rich men who organised and controlled the activities of the society. It was the first time Jimmy had been called alone to the taipan's presence and it was this fact that made him so nervous. He knew very well what happened to members of the triad if they failed in their responsibilities and that rank or reputation was no protection against punishment.

The fine furnishings and fittings of the outer office were nothing compared to the private chambers of the taipan. They were on the top floor of the bank, one of the Central District's main buildings. The large room was dominated by priceless artifacts; valuable rugs and carpets covered the floor. Behind his mandarin's desk J.T. Ching sat before an exquisitely embroidered wall hanging that reached from the ceiling to the floor. It depicted a cascade of wisteria in full bloom, spilling down from a single branch. Among its blossoms cicadas could be seen and hummingbirds poised, like jewels on invisible wings, a picture of sublime peace and tranquileity. Few people had seen the opulence of J.T. Ching's private office, as the security arrangements allowed no one to pass its entry unless personally invited by the taipan himself.

J. T. Ching wore the long black gown of Chinese officialdom, his hands half hidden by its voluminous sleeves. He did not ask the Red Pole to sit, but after a moment reached for the silver lid of the delicate china cup before him. Lifting it, he sipped thoughtfully without looking at the man before him.

'This man they call the Forceful One. I have seen and heard things that do not please me.'

He replaced the cup on his desk, carefully fitting the lid.

'Is he not the farm boy from Hunan who executed the Golden Sash before the eyes of 300 men?' Ching spoke quietly, now lifting his eyes to stare at the Red Pole.

'He is the one, lord,' replied Jimmy Chan.

'I have reports that he is causing trouble in the Wan Chai district. That he calls attention to himself by beating the women of the one they call Hand-trolley Lulu and those of Three-Thumbs Poon of the Nine Dragons Ballroom.'

'It is true,' Jimmy Chan tried to show his awareness by the tone of his voice. 'He defies the orders of his elder brothers. The farm boy listens to no one. Many times he has been warned. He is a man who seeks conflict.'

J.T. withdrew his hands and folded them on the desk before him. 'Then give him conflict. Kill him and bring me proof of his death.'

'It will be done, lord,' the Red Pole said with grim assurance, saluting with the cupped fist of the black society.

When he had gone, Ching rose and looked down from the window into the bustle of Queens Road. This busy road and the adjoining flow of Pedder Street were the hub of Hong Kong business. He reflected on his decision. He had not made it lightly, as gang deaths always led to unrest in the ranks of the triad and could cause questions to be asked by the police, if they were not carried out properly. J.T. had no fear of the police but he had great concern for the strength and loyalty of those that held positions of power in the society. The Red Pole was responsible for the control of nearly a 1000 men throughout the territories of Hong Kong and Macau. He knew that the lower echelons of the brotherhood could not be stopped from abusing the authority they commanded. The gathering of payments from bars, shops and restaurants was an age-old business and a little squeeze could not be stopped. But when it threatened to call attention to bigger concerns the time had come to act.

The traditional title of Red Pole dated back to the Manchu wars when the swarming tongs of temple boxers could only be controlled by a threat greater than their own code of violence. Such a title could only be held by one who commanded total respect. When Chan had risen through the ranks to claim it, he had been wild and hungry as the one they now called the Forceful One. He had stopped at nothing to reach his position. Now he had a family and filial responsibilities. His time and loyalty were shared. It was time to replace him.

The fact that Jimmy Chan had allowed this man who called himself the Forceful One to act as he pleased suggested two things to J.T. Ching: that discipline was not as controlled as he expected and that it was necessary for his top office-bearer to prove himself capable of attending to it. Chan played an important part in an Asia-wide export business that dealt in medicinal herbs from the Chinese mainland, Formosa, Japan and Korea. The huge variety of desiccated, dried and powdered herbs was a perfect disguise for the transporting of drugs. The White Paper Fan, Henry Lu Tak, his strategic advisor, was also responsible. Ching's plans for this side of his business, which was by far the most rewarding of his many enterprises, were immense and imminent.

His connections with the Japanese Yakuza and the Mafia were impatient to step up the size and scope of the drug ring. What had become a trial shipment a few years ago had fast become a limitless demand. Chinese medicines came in an endless array so complex and incomprehensible to the western eye and mind that they were seldom inspected by the customs authority of any country. If they were, a cursory glance was normally enough. Chinese medicine was also the one export from Hong Kong that was an essential and insatiable part of any Chinese community, whether in the United States or Europe.

The potential was limitless but so were the risks unless the tight circle entrusted with the planning and execution was the very best that could be found. Profits would soon be so great that protection and security would have to meet future challenge. Already rival societies, both in Hong Kong and elsewhere, were showing signs of moving against them, infiltrating the ranks of the Yellow Dragon. Only the best of the best could occupy the position of the Red Pole.

From what he had seen of this Ah Keung he would be test enough for any man. J.T. Ching was quite certain that it was only a matter of time before the Japanese would take Hong Kong. The Yakuza he dealt with were among the most powerful and ruthless men in Japan and there was little they didn't know. He had already prepared himself for such an event and although it promised him a degree of immunity, the time had come to select a personal bodyguard. He had a feeling that the farm-boy from Hunan would prove to be his choice. If he survived the attempt at ritual execution through combat in the Walled City of Kowloon there would be no doubt of it.

Ah Keung knew of Jimmy Chan's visit to the central district and although he could not know what had been discussed he was sure of its purpose. He had created a reputation for petty intimidation and lawlessness in order to be noticed and it had worked perfectly. The street vendor he had killed and the death of the Golden Sash were only the first of a number needed to convince the Brotherhood's highest ranks of his capacity. Such worthless lives were a small but important piece of his plan. He knew perfectly well that minor offences such as the violation of street women and prostitutes, extortion through torture and the destruction of property, were expected. An appetite for street fights and the brutal immobilisation of opponents were nothing more than a nuisance to the big operators whose commercial crime syndicates worked on a scale that could influence the balance of international society.

It was there that he belonged. Down here, in the roach-ridden alleyways of Wan Chai and Shau Kei Wan, where chopper attacks were an hourly event, tyranny was a password. He was a loose cannon on the deck of a pirate junk. If he waited to rise through the ranks in the normal way he would never reach those heights to which he knew he belonged. Calling attention to himself and facing the risks were his only alternative and it had worked. Ah Keung was convinced that the time had come for him to prove himself worthy of the post of Red Pole.

Within twenty-four hours of Jimmy Chan's visit to the Central District, Ah Keung received the message he had been expecting. It came in the form of a traditional scroll. He was summoned, it said, to a meeting with the Hung Kwan in the Walled City of Ling Nam. The most lawless and dangerous place in Hong Kong territory, Ling Nam was also known by other names: the Footprint of the Giant, the Sleeping Dragon and the Caged Tiger. Although only a short distance from the airstrip of Kai Tak and in the midst of Kowloon proper, the Walled City of Ling Nam belonged to mainland China. It had been set aside in the treaty of 1898, to remain sovereign territory over which the government of Hong Kong would have no jurisdiction.

This had made the Walled City a sanctuary for any form of criminal seeking to escape the law and a breeding ground for every vice and illegal enterprise imaginable. The city occupied the side of a hill which, when first ceded, had been surrounded by market gardens and rice paddies. In 1938 it was hemmed in by the commercial, industrial and residential chaos that was fast growing up around it. Behind its thick, high walls the secret societies conducted certain of their affairs on neutral ground with absolute immunity.

Although Hong Kong's predominantly British government had

refused to accept China's claim to absolute sovereignty, the Walled City was out of their control and would forever remain in dispute. No crime, no matter how serious, could be investigated within its gates and no one would enter them uninvited. Those who did might never be seen again.

It was into this expanding crush of improvised buildings and festering alleyways that Ah Keung made his way. The very stench of it excited him with the smell of danger.

The place chosen for the meeting was in its centre, a hidden cellar sometimes used for top-secret gatherings or for interrogations— a place where a body was easily disposed of. Ah Keung moved towards it along the narrow, earthen passageways that served as streets, his every nerve conditioned for the confrontation that lay ahead, his imperfect step light with the certainty of victory. The fact that he was about to face one of the most dangerous men in Hong Kong, senior office-bearer of the triad, his station proven by a record of conflict second to none, only served to quicken Ah Keung's pace. He had learned well the vigilance and caution of the Crane and sometimes it struck harder than the claw of the Tiger. He knew exactly how he would kill Jimmy Chan. It would not be in open combat. The present Red Pole was not to be underestimated and there could be no room for the slightest possibility of defeat.

The entrance to the cellar was reached through a cluster of vice dens and was situated beneath the best known of them all—the Palace of Hong. Ah Keung had been here before and understood the procedures. He would arrive at the eating place of Sharp Chopper Lau at the appointed time. There he would wait until those that observed him were certain he had not been followed. In time he would be escorted to the cellars, searched for weapons, blindfolded and taken through a network of passages and tunnels that led to the meeting place.

The eating house specialised in dog meat, a favourite of the citizens of Ling Nam and banned outside its walls. Stripped carcasses hung beside the open kitchen, the heads left on to identify the breed of each dog and its value. He sat and ordered a bowl of noodles, selecting the chow dog meat he preferred, sipping a glass of ching cha while he waited. If they came for him before he had finished eating he would make them wait.

Opposite the noodle shop the entrance to the Palace of Hong was as decorative as a Chinese opera house. He knew it to be a centre of white slavery, a place that offered the bodies of kidnapped white women for a high price to those who sought such excesses of the flesh. He knew that they were many and that the pleasure was in the humiliation of the gwai-paw, the devil-hags who held their noses high on the outside, but who begged for mercy in this place.

He also knew that the disappearance of a white woman through the gates of Ling Nam was one of the few happenings that could bring the Hong Kong police in large numbers. Even then they hesitated, for the woman they were looking for would never be found, dead or alive. Outside the door a fat woman was attracting customers, her flesh as white as steamed bread, performing for a group of onlookers, the slithering coils of a python entwining her naked limbs.

It was a half an hour before they came for him and he passed through the sour smells of the cellar and past the vats of bean curd, along the dank, undrained passages and into the chamber. He had seen enough of triad ceremony, and enough of the man who was to be his executioner, to know he had only moments to act, but the attack would not come instantly. Although surprise was a critical element of such action, those moments would be spent to put him off guard. He also guessed the Red Pole would be alone—it was part of the creed that he should dispatch his victim without the support of others. With scarcely a movement of his fingers Ah Keung withdrew the fine needle inserted in the lining of his sleeve and palmed the small piece of cork that served as its handle.

The earthy smell receded and the blindfold was removed. His escort left him standing before Jimmy Chan. The Red Pole was not dressed in his official robe but wore the loose-fitting black sam foo of an adept. The area was wide and low ceilinged, its walls lined with the society banners and racks of traditional weaponry. Ah Keung knew that he would have only one chance to come close to the Red Pole and he had prepared the bait. Giving his salute, he immediately took from his pocket a large roll of hundred-dollar notes.

'I bring my tribute, Ah Gor,' he said, respectfully offering the money. 'Business has been good in the rat bins of Wan Chai and I have been lucky at the tables.' He spoke lightly, using the honourable term for Big Brother.

He sensed the slight hesitation of surprise on Jimmy Chan's face and took advantage of it, stepping forward with the roll outstretched in his left hand. The second the Red Pole's eyes left his in order to take the money, Ah Keung's right hand swung wide, driving the needle into the soft cartilage behind and just below Jimmy Chan's ear. Chan sank to the floor without a sound and was dead before he reached it.

The 8th Rajput Rifles

COLONEL JUSTIN Pelham lifted his arms and shrugged them into the scarlet tunic of his best mess uniform. The competent hands of his Rajput batman deftly patted and smoothed its shoulders, tugging it smartly into the position of perfection. As the C.O. of the 5th Battalion, 8th Rajput Rifles, it was Colonel Pelham's responsibility to see that when civilians, and particularly political or diplomatic wallahs, entered the regimental lines, they left entirely satisfied. That they had not only been royally entertained but, by entering the officers' mess, they had been given a glimpse of true military greatness.

His fingers reached automatically for the richly brocaded neck of the tunic and began doing up the row of gleaming buttons. He was not at all sure about tonight. To be playing host to a Chinaman who, if he was to heed any of the intelligence provided by his liaison officer, Captain Hyde-Wilkins, was little better than a confounded brigand.

With the last button secure he dropped his hands as the batman moved in with brass button plate and polishing cloth to remove any trace of fingerprints. It really was too dammed hot for full regalia but the governor had personally requested it. Colonel Pelham found the humidity of Hong Kong abominable compared with the dry heat of the Indian plains and it did nothing to improve his humour.

The batman encircled Colonel Pelham's ample waist with the gold cummerbund and fastened it securely with white gloved hands.

There was a light knock on the door and the voice of Captain Hyde-Wilkins spoke through it. 'The guard commander reports the official party is just approaching the lines, sir.'

'Come in, Toby.' Colonel Pelham had turned sideways to the mirror and was contemplating his girth, a frown on his face, made ruddy from his love of fine madeira and made even redder by the gold-encrusted rim of his collar.

'Remind me of the drill, Toby. These special requests from the governor are always a little vague.'

'The gentleman we are to entertain, sir, owns the land the regiment occupies and most of the territory around it.' Toby cleared his throat politely. 'Our request to extend the lines to take in new training ground is dependent on his decision and the governor thought an evening in the mess might convince him to release it to us, sir.'

Captain Toby Hyde-Wilkins waited while the C.O. glowered at him. 'In fact, I understand the gentleman requested it.'

'Did he indeed?' snorted Colonel Pelham.

'Yes, sir, and in particular the traditional regimental entertainment. It seems he has an interest in such things.'

'What do we call this Chinaman?' The colonel asked irritably. Toby hesitated.

'I think J.T. is his favoured identification, sir.'

'What kind of a name is that, for God's sake? What's it stand for?'

Toby paused again before replying. 'I understand it stands for, eh . . . Jack Teagarden, sir.'

Justin Pelham was no stranger to elaborate names among the nabobs, maharajahs and oriental hierarchy encountered by the Raj, but this one stunned him.

'Jack Teagarden Ching? Are you serious?'

Toby nodded, smiling. 'Apparently the gentleman is a great fan of the American jazz trombonist of the same name and jazz music in general. I believe he has extensive interests in the United States.'

When the scowl of amazement on Colonel Pelham's face had not changed, he added. 'Its quite normal, sir, for a Chinese to give himself an elaborate western Christian name.'

'Is it, by God?' He glowered at his adjutant, then shrugged. 'Orders are to see the blighter has a good time with all the trimmings. Is everything laid on for the bundobust?'

'Every kind of entertainment the mess has to offer, sir,' answered Toby.

The colonel took his cap from the batman and put it on with an air of grim determination. 'Well, we'd better get on with it, then,' he said, and strode out to receive his guest of honour.

The small pennant mounted on the front of the Rolls Royce Phantom hung limply in the heat of early evening as it crawled across the parade ground toward the officers' mess. Outside the mess entrance Colonel Pelham and Captain Hyde-Wilkins waited properly at ease, their polished mess shoes planted exactly shoulder-width apart and their gloved hands clasped behind them, as the car drew up.

The man that moved quickly from the driver's seat was too fast for the Rajput sergeant who stepped forward to open the rear door. Ah Keung slid between him and the Rolls Royce like a shadow, his hand on the door handle. The sergeant in full ceremonial uniform could only step back and salute as Ching unfurled himself from the back seat, but the insult was not lost on Justin Pelham.

'Good evening Colonel.' Ching's voice rang with a loud confidence that made the colonel wince inside.

'You must forgive Ah Keung. He has yet to learn the manners of the west.' He laughed. 'Sometimes he takes his role too seriously.'

J.T. Ching had decided that the pomp and ceremony of the occasion called for traditional dress. In place of the loud western-styled suits he usually wore, he was draped in the robes of an official mandarin. In the crook of his arm he carried the round black hat adorned with the gorgeous tail feather of a cock pheasant. Placing this squarely on his head he slid both hands into his sleeves and bowed first to the colonel and then to the captain.

'I am honoured to be a humble guest in this place of much glory.'

Justin Pelham touched the peak of his cap in salute. 'The officers' mess of the 8th Rajput Rifle Brigade is honoured by your presence.'

He stepped smartly to one side for Ching to pass. 'The sergeant will show your driver where the can take refreshment.'

Ching stopped in the doorway. 'Forgive me Colonel, but Ah Keung is rather more than my driver.' He looked directly at Toby. 'He is to me what the captain here is to you. I cannot enter without him.'

Justin Pelham's pause was hardly noticeable. 'Of course. By all means.'

'Good' said Ching, smiling widely. 'I understand there is to be entertainment. Perhaps Ah Keung will help to provide some of it.'

In the foyer adjoining the mess common room, Justin and Toby removed their caps, hanging them with those already assembled.

J.T. Ching made no attempt to take off the black hat with its metre-high feather. Noting the rising colour of the colonel's jowls, Toby stepped close, speaking quietly.

'It is a tradition, sir, to remove one's hat when entering the mess.' He held out his hand to take it.

Ching lowered his voice to match Toby's. 'You will note the button on this cap,' he said with dignity, 'is scarlet. It is the official mark of a ninth grade mandarin. It is not required to be removed even in the presence of royalty.'

'Nevertheless, sir,' said Toby firmly. 'It is the rule.'

Ching hesitated, his eyes flicking blankly to a portrait of Queen Elizabeth above the mess entrance. Slowly he removed the hat and handed it to Toby. 'I am in error. Here the rules are yours.'

Inside the common room Toby called the mess to attention as he introduced their guest. His presence acknowledged, Ching made straight for a glass case suspended above the fireplace. He stood before it in silence, staring at the magnificent curve of an Arabian dagger, its hilt intricately decorated with the fine silver wirework of the Sudan. The broad sweep of its blade was drawn from the scabbard and fixed beside it. The scabbard was also worked in silver wire, both were interlaced with a heavy gold thread, and the hilt of black rhinoceros horn was set with seed-pearls and precious stones. Toby said from behind. 'It is called "Light of the Nile", sir, awarded to the regiment at Omdurman by General Charles Gordon of Khartoum.'

Ching seemed not to hear him, appearing almost humbled in the presence of the magnificent weapon. 'It is among the most beautiful I have seen,' he breathed.

Anxious to find something of interest after the discord of the headpiece, Toby was glad to elaborate. 'It is said to have belonged to Mohammed Ahmed the Mahdi, the living god of Islam. If you look closely you will see that teachings from the Koran are engraved on its blade.'

'The Light of the Nile.' Ching repeated the name in a reverent whisper, suddenly turning to face Toby. 'I am a collector of such exalted blades. Cold steel has always been mankind's greatest leveller. Don't you agree Captain?'

'I suppose that is true, sir. Certainly the bayonet has played its part.'

Ching turned back to again admire the dagger. 'I own a bronze dagger from your country dating back to 1000 years B.C. and a collection of Swiss poniards second to none I know of, but a knife such as this was designed to pierce the armour of crusading knights. Please do not be insulted if I ask its value?'

'I have no idea, sir. It is a relic of the regiment's past and as such I suppose it is priceless.'

Around the walls of the mess were many other such trophies, including bullet-ridden pipe-banners listing the regiment's battle honours, but J.T. Ching showed little interest in these. Both Toby and Colonel Pelham were relieved when the mess sergeant announced the serving of dinner.

The mess table glittered with its famed regimental silver. Bounty of fallen maharajas gleamed in the light from three twelve-branch candelabras. Around the walls, subdued by the flicker of candle flame, the portraits of the regiment's past C.O.s, beside its Victoria Cross winners, looked down upon the high-backed chairs. At each side of the long banqueting table stood the full complement of British officers. Ching was placed facing Colonel Pelham at the head of the table, with Ah Keung to his side opposite Captain Hyde-Wilkins.

When Ching and the colonel were seated, the others sat. The meal passed with the precision of a drill order. Dishes borne on silver trays by orderlies, immaculate in full mess kit, came and went in endless parade. Toby had seen to it that a Chinese chef had been brought in to provide the best of court cuisine for the guest of honour. Throughout dinner Colonel Pelham carried on the traditional mess hospitality with stories surrounding the captured silver and the exploits of the legendary heroes that adorned the shadowy walls.

J.T. Ching ate noisily and with little concern for western etiquette, spattering the spotless tablecloth with a variety of sauces and belching loudly and regularly. Toby knew enough about Chinese eating habits to recognize this as a show of appreciation but could not help feeling that it was also an exaggerated demonstration of indifference towards his host and his surroundings. In contrast, Ah Keung sat opposite Toby eating sparingly, his eyes on the food set before him, occasionally looking up to stare about him with intense boredom.

When the port, brandy and cigars had been passed around and the pipe major had played the customary tunes of glory, Colonel Pelham rose to announce that entertainment would be staged in the regimental playing fields.

Rank upon rank of the battalion's soldiers were already assembled. Out of uniform and dressed in simple white cotton waist-cloths they stood to attention until the colonel's party was seated. At a short command from the Rajput major they sat cross-legged on the ground.

A large bonfire had been lit, its bright sparks blown into the starry night sky by the gusts of breeze from the surrounding hills. Seats had been arranged around it for the colonel's group and pitch flares blazed in a circle. Into the ring of flame leapt a troop of men in authentic Rajputani costume, performing the traditional warrior dances from the land of the princes. They were followed by the battalion's fakir, a holy man, the colonel explained, who was to the Rajput soldier what a Buddhist or Taoist priest would be to the Chinese soldier or a chaplain to a British regiment.

The fakir, his half-naked body glistening from the heat of the fire, performed a series of mystic feats, exhibiting his powers of hypnosis by conjuring the end of a rope to rise of its own accord three metres into the air and then sending a bugle boy assistant to climb it and disappear into the smoky night. This was followed by his lying on a bed of nails, the charming of snakes and swallowing of both sword and fire. When the display had concluded, J.T. Ching clapped loudly.

'Proof that the hand can deceive the eye,' he crowed 'I have heard much of the Indian rope trick, now I have seen it.' He turned to Justin Pelham. 'But do not tell me this is Hindu magic. All of these are tricks. Does not the word "faker" come from fakir, prince of tricksters?'

Before Justin could answer he went on in a quieter tone. 'I am told the Rajput soldier is one of the great warriors of India. That among their ranks are mighty wrestlers and champions of the Empty Hand.' He gestured to where Ah Keung sat impassively gazing into the fire.

'We humble Chinese also have our warriors. Ah Keung, the Forceful One, is among our best.'

Justin fought hard to contain his annoyance at the tone of Ching's voice. 'You have heard correctly. What is it you suggest?' he asked.

'That we enliven the evening's proceedings with a little wager.' Ching bit his lip in exaggerated thought. 'Shall we say the land that you require . . . against the Light of The Nile?'

'And what is the wager?' asked Captain Hyde-Wilkins after a pause, afraid that his commanding officer might choke on the answer.

'The Forceful One against any four of your best fighters.'

Colonel Pelham composed himself, as he let the effrontery of the suggestion sink in. 'And how would such a contest be decided?' His voice was an incredulous whisper.

'If Ah Keung falls once, or one of your men is left standing after three minutes, victory is yours. If each of your men falls, victory is mine.'

Both Toby and Justin were aware that several of the senior Indian officers spoke good English and had overheard the challenge. It would be an insult to their caste, their men and the honour of the regiment to refuse. With Justin's permission Toby rose and announced in Hindi the contest that was about to take place. A wave of murmuring swelled into a roar of approval from the ranks.

At a command from the Rajput major four men arose from among the seated rows of soldiers and made their way to the lighted arena, their white teeth showing their confidence. Ah Keung had taken his position in the centre of the ring as orderlies ran forward to fling logs into the settling flames, sending sparks spiralling upward, bursting into new flame. He stood calmly without attempting to remove the black jacket he wore, looking at none of his adversaries. He seemed lost in meditation.

'What rules do you suggest?' Toby asked quietly.

Ching lowered his voice in a patronising fashion, mocking the seriousness in Toby's words. 'Rules, Captain? You speak of nothing but rules. I see no need of rules. He who remains standing wins.' He waited for a reply.

'Come gentlemen, surely the odds defy rules. No magic, no tricks. A simple test of skill, courage and strength. One Chinese against four Indian champions. What could be fairer?'

As his anger at Ching's tone rose, Colonel Pelham signalled the Rajput major and the contest began. Ah Keung dropped directly into a deep Horse stance, his feet widely spaced, his knees bent as though lowered onto the broad back of a warhorse. His hands curled into fists, pulled closely into his hips. His eyes, half closed, looked straight ahead, making no attempt to seek his first opponent. It was as though, Toby thought, he was prepared to fight by instinct more than sight or sound. The air was suddenly filled with chanting from the Rajput ranks.

The first man advanced in the style of the Turk wrestler, hands held out to invite contact, to be felled from one flying kick that spun like a whirlwind. Goaded by surprise at seeing the first of their number drop like a stone, the other three moved towards Ah Keung, one from the front, one from the side and one behind. The combined voice of the Rajput soldiers fell away as they watched the Chinese fighter cut down their champions with a speed and power they had to witness to believe.

Ah Keung had hardly moved from the spot where he took his stance. He stood, sullenly defiant, searching the faces that surrounded him for more challengers. The chanting had stopped altogether and some of the men had begun to rise. Toby stood up, still shocked by the lightning savagery of what he had seen.

'The contest is at an end,' he announced in Hindi. 'The result is clear. Remain seated.'

The voices died to a hum and those that had half risen lowered themselves back to the ground.

'Dismiss the men to their quarters.' Colonel Pelham spoke quietly to the Rajput Major. 'Have the Light of the Nile taken down. Our guests are leaving.'

The Reading Book Pavilion

ONE YEAR later to the day that Ah Gum had given Siu Sing her first lesson in the beguiling of men, they took tea together as they always had in the small Reading Book Pavilion. This was a secluded spot built over the mirror stillness of an artificial lake filled with lotus and far enough from the tavern to give them privacy. The Golden One was well pleased with her accomplishment. Sing had proved a devoted student who, she had quickly discovered, already possessed a remarkable knowledge of human anatomy and its innermost workings.

She had also showed a strange kind of wisdom, an understanding of natural things, that made it very pleasurable to walk with her. When lessons were over for the day they would sometimes sit by the lakeside or explore far corners of the old garden. Sing knew the name of every tree, flower, or fresh shoot and once, with her own eyes, Ah Gum saw her coax a tiny linnet from the branches of a tulip tree to feed from the palm of her hand. On one of these walks they had discovered a small gate once used by gardeners and hidden by dense vines, set in a far corner of the garden facing the salt marsh that backed onto the far wall.

It had not taken long for them to share each other's trust and Sing had revealed the contents of the deerhide satchel that meant so much to her. She said nothing more of her life at Tung T'ing. It was as though her first twelve years in the reed hut on that peaceful hillside had been a vision that had disappeared like mist with the sunrise. A before sky experience preparing her for the horrors that had awaited her behind the walls of Fat Fan's compound. As though with the passing of the Fish and Great-uncle To, her life had ended instead of beginning.

She now viewed her future with the eyes and heart of one much older than her fourteen years. Well aware that her time at the Tavern of Cascading Jewels and the making of pipes would one day come to an end, she was content to remain hidden in its safety and comfort while she may. In that year both Ruby and Pearl had been sold as concubines and replaced by younger girls who had inherited their names. Jade would be next, content to hope that Madam Fung would find her a kindly, but above all, a rich, master.

Jade was a year older than Sing and had great ambition. She was anxious, she said simply, to test her skills in the bed of a great man. She would make herself his number one and rule over his household. She could not wait for Madam Fung to sell her cherry. Under her bed she kept a small wooden box filled with silver coins. Payment, she said, for favours bestowed upon those special gentlemen that she had pleased in special ways against the madam's strict rules.

Sing had been allowed to meet no other man but J.T. Ching and had been nowhere and seen nothing outside the walls of the Suzhou garden. Ah Gum sipped her tea and looked out over the carpet of lotus buds. It was early morning, the flowers were not yet opened, the dragonflies already hovered and butterflies fluttered over the quiet water. When she spoke she used the fond name kept for a little sister.

'I have taught you all that I can, mui mui. I will not be returning to this place. My work takes me to China.' When Sing said nothing, gazing into the pale amber of the jasmine tea in her cup, she continued softly. 'You have learned so well. I shall miss you.'

'What will happen to me, jeh jeh?' Sing responded with the fond name of big sister.

Ah Gum paused, hoping to find the right words. 'Madam Fung has paid me well to be your tutor. She will receive a high price for you.' Again, she hesitated. 'In turn, the lord Ching has paid her well to keep you for himself. It is an understanding.'

'What will he do with me?' Sing asked.

'For the present he is content to keep your services for himself alone. You are still a child, but he has given you the gift of a topaz. It means he is ready to receive you into his house.'

'Will I be his slave . . . forever?'

Ah Gum ignored the question. Instead she said, 'To be a concubine in the house of such a man is a great honour. You could become very rich and powerful in his house.'

'How many wives has he?'

'Three, I think.'

'And how many concubines?'

Ah Gum frowned, still contemplating the field of lotus where the silver and gold shadows of carp glided beneath the flat, round leaves. 'It does not matter how many. As the youngest you will be his favourite.'

'And how long will I remain the youngest?'

Ah Gum rose and threw crumbs to the fish. Ignoring the question again. 'In some things he is honourable. There are men much worse who would pay to be the first. But I must warn you. To remain his chosen one you must use everything I have taught you to please him. You must never fail him. He must value you above all others . . . or else you will be no more than a mistress to him. To be locked away and badly used. Promise me you will remember this.'

Sing stared into her teacup, wondering what the specks of leaf in her cup foretold.

'When will this happen?'

'I have told you. When you are ready. When you are a woman.'

'You have said I am already a woman.'

Ah Gum smiled at the recent memory of the day Siu Sing announced that she was dying from some dread disease. She had found her lying here in the Reading Book Pavilion, the deerhide satchel clutched to her chest, waiting patiently and without fear to bleed to death.

'Yes. Indeed you are fast becoming a woman. But Madam Fung

is in no hurry to sell you.' She laughed. 'She calls you her most precious jewel. Soon the business will be done. He has given you the topaz. It means that you are his before all others.'

'And what if he tires of me?'

'He will not. J.T. Ching is a patient man. One of the richest and most important in Hong Kong.' Ah Gum tried to keep truth in her voice as she refilled Sing's cup and then her own. 'You will have a good and fortunate life.'

'What will happen to me if I refuse?'

Ah Gum had never been asked such a question by one of her pupils before. 'You cannot refuse, mui mui. The jewel has been accepted. It is an understanding.'

'And if I run away?'

'He would seek you and find you. You would be severely punished. Do not think of it. You belong to Madam Fung, she pays richly to prepare you for your future.'

'Would they kill me?' asked Sing.

Ah Gum looked at her steadily. 'I will pretend that you have not asked me these things, but since you have I will tell you.' She took Sing's hands in hers and looked straight into her eyes. 'If you displease Madam Fung she will return you to the house of Fan and demand repayment.'

When Ah Gum had left her, Siu Sing stayed for a long time in the Reading Book Pavilion. The thought of returning to the factory compound and Kwok the Rat Man filled her with an unspeakable dread. She knew she would die before she would go back there. To be the youngest concubine in the great house of lord Ching or a secret one in the house in Macau would mean safety for a while but it could never mean freedom. Jade and the others had discussed it many times. To them freedom was insecurity. They were not afraid of the power struggles that must go on in a house of many women. They were Chinese, they relished such conflict.

Something deep inside Siu Sing told her that life would be different for her. That she would always be jarp-jung wherever she went. But she had known freedom and a place where she belonged on the hillside and in the groves around the hut of Great-uncle To. There was something else even deeper that somehow rose to overcome her fears, some part of her that replaced fear with anger, a distant voice that would not be silent. It told her there was more. That she was not born to be the slave of another. The body she had been taught to respect and understand was her own, to give of as she wished, to whoever and whenever it pleased her, it was not meant to be bartered for. Above all of this she had been shown the way of the White Crane and this set her apart from others. When she came out of her meditations the sun had set on the garden and the carp no longer flashed in its light. She had stayed all day in the Reading Book Pavilion, and now she knew what she must do.

An hour later, before the moon had risen, the deerhide satchel over her shoulder, Siu Sing made her way silently through the darkened garden to the little gate behind the tangled vines. She had taken a few silver coins from the box beneath Jade's bed and left in their place the blue topaz. As the sky brightened with the colours of dawn and the gas lamps on the wharf began to pale, she boarded the steam ferry for Hong Kong.

The Happy Butterfly

HAND-TROLLEY Lulu had been one of the first mama sans to open a bar in Wan Chai. It was well known among the prostitutes and pimps who peopled the stretch of territory on the northern outskirts of the Central District that she had earned her name the hard way and that she was fiercely proud of it. Lulu's parents had died in the plague that swept Hong Kong in 1894. She was six years old when she began foraging for food in the alleys behind the eating houses and begging on the streets. As an orphan girl you became experienced in the business of survival or you quickly perished with those who didn't.

Begging for scraps and living out of garbage bins kept you alive if you were good at it but it didn't hold much promise for the future, and the future was something Lulu was very interested in. There had to be something better than sleeping in doorways and fighting to keep the rags you wore from being pulled off your back and she had decided to find out what it was.

Before she was seven Lulu had found an old hand trolley

abandoned in the market. She had repaired it, harnessed herself
to it and gone into business running small errands for the Wan
Chai shopkeepers. As her price for despatch was cheaper than
bicycle, rickshaw, carrying pole or any other method of transport,
she soon had her string of regular customers. In no time at all
she had built a more respectable trolley with solid rubber tyres
and twice the carrying capacity, and was strong enough to push
and pull bigger and bigger loads.

Lulu's future had opened up for her when a British warship
dropped anchor in Victoria Harbour. She had found that when
the sailors flooded ashore they headed straight for the Royal Navy
Canteen on Praia East and that was where they stayed, playing
darts and billiards until drunk enough to take each other back
to the ship.

In her short life Lulu had learned that gwai-lo sailors, whether
they came off the great grey battle ships or rusty tramp steamers,
were much more generous and easy to work with than greedy
Chinese shopkeepers. Her cheerful offer to transport a sailor's
purchases back to the ship or to show him where the best bargains
might be found had seldom failed to produce a silver dollar whether
he took her up on it or not. Add to this the small commission
collected from the vendors and street stalls she took them to and
the future continued to seem brighter and brighter.

When she found the young sailor so drunk from San Miguel
beer he was unable to stand up, there seemed nothing else for
it but to offer him a ride. It was already late and the quartermaster
on watch at the gangway would soon be looking at his pocket
watch in the hope of filling the brig with stragglers. So, after parting
with what money he had left, the sailor collapsed gratefully into
Lulu's cart and was trundled safely to the wharf and put into a
wallah wallah back to his ship.

The story had soon got around. Hand-trolley Lulu was given
her name and became a celebrity on the run between the canteen,
the souvenir shops and the waterfront. She was only eighteen when
she opened her first bar, the Happy Butterfly on Lockhart Road.
It had been a small tea shop among many small tea shops and
she had saved enough to take over the lease and turn it into a
beer bar. She had learned that sailors, when they came ashore,
were looking for two things—beer and girls. Hand-trolley Lulu
couldn't see any reason why she shouldn't supply them with both.

She soon found that if you filled a sailor up with enough of
the first, it was not at all difficult to receive a handsome reward

for delivering the second, often without the sailor knowing exactly what it was he had paid for and how much it had cost. In fact, the future she had dreamed of while straining like a donkey between the shafts of her handcart had come much quicker than she expected. Decorating the walls of her small establishment with nautical souvenirs donated by satisfied customers and filling it with girls who could look a gwai-lo in the eye without vomiting, the Happy Butterfly quickly became a welcome alternative to the Royal Navy Canteen.

Another famous trade name on the Hong Kong waterfront was 'Mary's Boat Party'. Once a competitor of Hand-trolley Lulu, but without Lulu's looks and cheerful disposition, Mary had quickly found that when haggling for the attentions of any sailor it was Lulu who walked away on the sailor's arm. Built, she realised, more for hard labour than soft beds, Mary had considered the alternatives open to her if she was to share in the obvious fortunes to be made from the endless flotillas of ships that sailed in and out of Victoria Harbour. Noting the rust-streaked and weatherbeaten state of most freighters that came and went, the enterprising Mary had approached the captain of a particularly down-at-heel vessel, offering to scrub the decks, wash the paintwork, chip and paint the hull in twenty-four hours for what seemed like a ridiculously reasonable sum.

The captain had accepted the offer, firmly convinced that it was physically impossible, until Mary had descended upon his ship with an army of women carrying buckets, scrubbers, mops, brushes and drums of red lead and paint. Under Mary's supervision, the women—of every age, shape and size—completed the task to his absolute satisfaction and the reputation of Red Lead Mary's Boat Party was firmly established.

She and Lulu worked together in the business of recruitment. If a girl came to Mary for work and seemed better suited to the bars, she would be passed on to Lulu, just as a bargirl who had outlived her allure would be recommended to join the boat party. Either way, arduous as both these pursuits may have seemed as a way of life, they were both highly beneficial and amply rewarded when compared with the prospects offered by the sweatshops and factories of Kowloon.

By 1939 Wan Chai had become the girly-bar district of Hong Kong. The sidewalks of Lockhart, Hennessy and Gloucester Roads were becoming thronged with a growing number of neon signs advertising bars and massage parlours offering cold beer and hot times to lonely sailors. Hand-trolley Lulu owned six of them as well as three barber shops, a string of shoeshine stands and took commission from a dozen more and ran some 200 girls. There wasn't a move made in Wan Chai that she didn't approve or a bar opened up without her consent. Nor was there a girl on the streets that she didn't know about.

The one that stood before her now, a worn leather bag over her shoulder and dressed like someone from the past, had been brought in by Firecracker Lily, who stood back feeling very pleased with herself. This one looked like a rare find. Her commission would be plentiful. Lily, always looking out for new girls, had seen Sing walking in a daze along Lockhart Road.

'She has nowhere to go. She needs help, so I brought her to you, mama san.' Firecracker grinned her way out through the curtains that separated Hand-trolley Lulu's private domain from the stairs leading down to the noise of the bar.

In the many years since she had opened the Happy Butterfly, Hand-trolley Lulu had learned all there is to know about girls who would rather work the bars and sleep with gwai-lo sailors than work the sweat shops and sleep with cockroaches. She was a genuine whore. Not one who had been forced into it by circumstance, but one who had chosen her profession. She knew why she was a whore, how she had become a whore, and she considered whoring just as much a legitimate business as selling flowers, salting fish or making coffins. She had never forgotten her handcart days or chasing the rats from the bins outside the back doors of the chop houses to see if they'd left anything to eat.

There was a bright shrine to the gods of happy fortune in each of her bars, complete with a string of little red lights to make them feel at home, but Hand-trolley never asked the gods about her future. She hadn't forgotten that when her bones ached as she slept beneath her cart without the price of a joss stick to burn for their favour, the gods of happy fortune had been nowhere to be seen. So far as she was concerned a homeless girl's future in Hong Kong belonged and remained firmly in her own two hands or between her own two legs and that was the choice that no one else should make for her.

The green shaded light above the desk of Three-thumbs Poon was hung so low that whilst it illuminated the pile of account books and the row of soapstone chops arranged neatly beside them, it left his face partially hidden in the shadows. The only part of him that could be clearly seen was his hands, the left one displaying that strange gift bestowed upon him at birth, which had given him his well-known name. A second thumb, on his left hand, almost perfectly formed and approximately the same size as its twin, grew outward from the lower joint of his normal digit as though it had been stuck on as nature's joke.

It had the unusual effect, when it came to giving the thumbs up on a successful business deal, which he did at every opportunity, of indicating double the prospects or three times the risk of dealing with him, depending on who you were and what you wanted. Three-thumbs Poon had no doubt that his extra appendage had been presented by the ever-smiling gods to ensure his success and prosperity and he allowed nothing and nobody to interfere with their high expectations.

His hands were neatly folded in the glare of the light, his three thumbs at rest as though spotlit for inspection. He had listened patiently to Hand-trolley Lulu, all the while evaluating, from the obscurity of the shadows, the prize that she had been wise enough to bring to his famous establishment, the Nine Dragons Tea House. His voice showed none of the enthusiasm that he felt. He was a businessman and he had played this game many times before with his old friend.

'Does she speak English?' His voice when he spoke was a perfect impression of that Hollywood actor famous for devious dealings in the Orient, Peter Lorre. When he leaned forward from the depths of his huge, high-backed swivel chair the light revealed that he also bore an uncanny resemblance to that mild-mannered rogue of the silver screen. His eyes, magnified behind the thick pebble glasses, were more rounded than those of most Shanghainese and popped like a goldfish as he gazed at the tall, slender girl with the obvious attributes of western blood.

'She says no. I'm not sure. She is a mix. A Eurasian. A chi-chi.'

'You mean a jarp-jung. Do not try to change the truth.'

'She is jarp-jung. A magnificent one,' added Lulu persuasively.

'Where is she from?' The three thumbs began to twiddle around each other in slow, careful circles.

Hand-trolley Lulu removed the long cigarette holder made from pale, creamy jade. It was almost thirty centimetres long and a symbol of her status. 'You should know better than to ask such a question. I do not care where she comes from. Where she is going is my only concern.'

'What is her age?'

'She is not sure. Fourteen . . . perhaps fifteen.'

'Is she . . . she . . . do you think she . . . ?'

'A cherry girl?' Hand-trolley Lulu finished his question for him. His eyes glistened at the prospect. 'She says she is. I believe her.'

'Why do you bring her to me?' he asked, pretending uninterest. 'Is she not valuable to you?'

'I have told you. She would be wasted in the bars. She is better suited to the ballroom.'

Poon retreated again to the shadows. 'Can she dance?'

'She says she has been taught. She also says she can massage well, knows something of folk medicine and can cure a headache. She says she knows how to make a man happy and put him to sleep.'

'Does she indeed? Did she tell you how?'

'I did not ask her how. It does not matter how. What matters is that he pays. Why he pays is not my business.'

Three-thumbs Poon suddenly opened the drawer of his desk and took out a bottle of brandy and two glasses. 'Tell her to wait outside. She may be lying about her English. We will talk commission.'

The establishment of Three-thumbs Poon was the biggest and grandest of its kind in Wan Chai. Next door to a picture theatre, hemmed in by shops and restaurants, its gigantic pink and blue neon dominated the bar signs around it with nine cavorting dragons that chased each other up the side of his building in a crackling blaze of electricity. Occupying the top three floors of one of the district's tallest buildings, it was restaurant, ballroom and brothel all under one roof. The lower floor was a traditional tea house, its endless floorspace serving yum cha to anyone who cared to enter its doors. Dim sum girls with their trays and trolleys of steaming delicacies roamed among the tables calling out their wares to the families that came there for breakfast and those that just came to drink tea and talk business.

An elaborate elevator, its interior panelled with rosewood and adorned with mirrors, its brass fittings polished brightly, operated among the three floors. The next floor was a ballroom, a Chinese nightclub where from nine o'clock each evening till four in the morning men could come to drink and dance with the hostesses, while a band played Chinese versions of the latest western music and a string of female singers took turns to entertain. For those who wanted more, the elevator ran a shuttle service to the floor above where private negotiations with the hostesses could be carried out in comfort and privacy.

The top floor of the Nine Dragons Tea House was Three-thumbs Poon's proudest achievement. His business interests extended well beyond Wan Chai and although they had not taken him outside Hong Kong he was a great watcher of western movies in the theatre next door. It was here, in the many rooms and suites, that he had indulged his favourite fantasies and recreated those memorable settings that so fired his imagination. Three-thumbs prided himself there was nothing a man could ask for that could not be provided by taking the lift from the ballroom to the top floor of the Nine Dragons.

It was why, with the cooperation of Hand-trolley Lulu, his hostesses were chosen for their looks and style and for their skill in extracting the most respectable amount of money from his patrons while leaving them impatient to return for more. Like every other businessman in Wan Chai, as elsewhere in Hong Kong, Three-thumbs Poon paid regularly and handsomely for protection. It gave him the opportunity of turning away those who could not afford his superior services and seeing that his exclusive clientele could be sure of a discreet and trouble-free evening whenever they felt like it.

The Nine Dragons

IN THE first few months of the regiment's arrival in Hong Kong, Captain Toby Hyde-Wilkins had accompanied his brother officers into the downtown district of Wan Chai. Apart from joint and individual lectures from the C.O. on behaviour befitting an officer and a gentleman, followed up by fatherly warnings from the M.O. on the scourge of venereal disease, there had been fewer opportunities for sexual encounters than some of them would have liked.

It had not taken long to discover Hand-trolley Lulu's Happy

Butterfly bar, where, to titillate the imagination and ensure a full house, the 'three o'clock bath' had become a well-known attraction. To hold those who might have returned to office, ship or barracks after a long and liquid lunch, was the promise that at precisely three o'clock each afternoon the back door leading from the bar into the alley would be opened and that on the other side of the alley directly opposite, another door would open to reveal two young girls taking a bath in full view of the Happy Butterfly customers.

There would be the tin bath and, after an appropriate delay and to thunderous applause, the girls would appear fully clothed and proceed to undress and take their bath in full view of the men across the road. No law was being broken but the drinks flowed freely and when the erotic spectacle finally drew to a close, Lulu's bargirls found it much easier to entice a titillated client upstairs.

Toby Hyde-Wilkins knew that he was the only gwai-lo to frequent the Nine Dragons ballroom. Firstly, he had never seen another European under its glittering mirror ball and secondly, the little man who had been fetched to talk to him when he first stepped from the lift and sat down at a table, had told him so.

The little man had introduced himself politely as the owner of the establishment and tried to explain that the ballroom was for Chinese only. When Toby had identified himself, making it clear that Hong Kong was a British colony, adding that he had seen no notice warning gwai-los to keep out, the little man had brought him a whisky and soda on the house and left, scratching his head.

For the better part of a year now, Toby had been an occasional visitor. It was not done for a British officer to be seen in the bars of Lockhart and Hennessy Roads. Since someone had dashed across the alley and tried to join the girls in the three o'clock bath, Hand-trolley Lulu's Happy Butterfly bar had been placed out of bounds by Colonel Pelham and so had every other bar of its kind. Although he had membership to several decent clubs and the China Fleet Club was just around the corner, Toby quite often found himself in more need of some interesting female company than a game of darts or snooker.

The alternative of another evening in the mess with the interminable reminiscences of Justin Pelham had made the second floor of the Nine Dragons a welcome change, a haven he had discovered quite by accident and where his identity was reduced to that of a lone gwai-lo wearing a polo-necked shirt and the sports jacket he'd had made in Kashmir.

Toby had never been as preoccupied with sex as the officers he had served with, whether younger or older than himself, or even as a cadet at Sandhurst. While others bounced barmaids and boasted about it the next day, he had searched in vain for romance. Sex for him had always been the secret treasure only to be found after a long and difficult journey. The pot of gold waiting at the end of an extremely elusive rainbow. He had no idea why. God knows he had a healthy appetite for it, but he had always thought of it as precious. Ever since he had fallen deeply in love with Brenda Bridges.

He had been thirteen years old and she had been fifteen. Brenda always sat above the clock in the upstairs gallery of the church on Sundays, beautiful and remote. After a year of watching her and thinking of her in bed, she had seduced him in the dark shadows of the yew trees at the back of the vestry after Sunday School and regularly each Sunday after that until she became pregnant to a farm labourer and had to get married. Up till then they had made love in fields of clover, barns full of straw, haystacks, on riverbanks and once in her father's coal shed. Toby had never found anything to quite compare with it.

There had been one or two women when on leave in Bombay. Perhaps even half a dozen. They weren't the kind that you counted. Brown arms held out to him, wrists laden with glass bangles. Clinging mouths that tasted faintly of their last spicy meal and the smoke of cheap cigarettes. Over in breathless moments beneath the gaudy coverlet embroidered with sequins spelling 'Welcome Squaddy' and on the other side 'Welcome Sailor'. Uneasy weeks that followed with regular trips to the M.O. for check-ups.

Toby had not found it hard to take the well-meant advice of Justin Pelham when he raised his glass of madeira, as he often did, and said, 'The best thing to do out here is to keep it safely tucked in your trousers and your trousers always up and securely fastened.' So, it had been almost two years since Toby Hyde-Wilkins had been to bed with anything more exciting than his own thoughts and longings.

His good manners and generous tips had made him quite popular with several of the hostesses in the Nine Dragons ballroom but he had not yet taken the lift to the top floor with any of them. He was often tempted but each time, no matter how persuasive the hand upon his thigh, he had known it was for the money and not for the thrill of his embrace. Toby had faced the fact that he was incurably sentimental and that a high-class whore-house, while offering excitement and relaxation, was not the place to find what he was looking for. Then, one night, he had been contentedly sipping his scotch and soda when he saw someone whom he knew at a glance could change all that.

A girl he had never seen before was sitting a little apart from the others. The cheong-sam of orange silk fitted her like a skin. All the girls in the Nine Dragons ballroom were attractive and all of them were young—some so young they were not fully developed and if stripped of their exotic finery and scrubbed of makeup would have been found to be little more than children. This one seemed to hold herself differently to the others. When she was asked to dance she stood taller and straighter, moving with a light-footed, supple grace, holding her head with a kind of innocent dignity, as though she were unaware of the beauty she had been told to exhibit.

Toby had made a study of ballroom custom in the hours spent during his visits. He knew that the Chinese men who took the lift to the second floor, with every intention of also taking it to the top, considered tender years in a girl far more desirable than looks or style. Most of the men were middle-aged or well past it, no doubt with a tai tai—a spoiled wife—ensconced at the beauty parlour or playing mahjongg with her friends.

Such married Chinese women, he'd been assured by those who knew, considered their duty performed once they had produced children. Whatever their husbands did about sex was their own affair as long as it didn't interfere with the comfortable and uncomplicated life of the tai tai. Well able to afford the cost of a few hours' relaxation as guest of Three-thumbs Poon but not wealthy enough to keep a full time concubine, their husbands looked upon the Nine Dragons ballroom as a businessmen's club with special benefits.

It was understandable that very little notice was taken of the lone gwai-lo who dropped in from time to time, bought a drink or two for any girl bold enough to sit with him and left as quietly as he had arrived. He had never approached one of the girls himself. He was fully aware that most of them preferred their own kind. That even though they had lived under British rule all of their lives and seen the pale-skinned gwai-los wandering among their crowds, going in and out of the cinemas and shops and eating in their restaurants every day, the westerner was still and would always be the foreign devil. The barbarian that children should not look upon and whose path should be avoided.

He had observed that those who were 'westernised', which meant they spoke English and worked for a foreign company, or those that did business with the European, did so with a clever veneer of tolerance, even friendliness, that could be quite convincing. But underneath that need to earn a living, to do business, there was a gulf that could never be closed. At times, and in places like this, it made Toby feel a fleeting kind of alien loneliness.

It was why the expatriate civil service and the business community stuck together in the familiarity and compatibility of their clubs and why the British officers and their families preferred the English hometown atmosphere that had been created on Stonecutter's Island, a kilometre off the Kowloon peninsular. And it was why Toby felt so strongly attracted to the enchanting girl who sat apart, unsmiling, different, not included in the chatter and laughter of the others. She was not Chinese. She reminded him of the high-caste Anglo-Indians he had seen in Delhi and Jaipur. Not the loose living chi-chis of the bazaar but hauntingly attractive and somehow unreachable.

Toby was the first gwai-lo Siu Sing had seen up close. The Happy Butterfly bar had been full of them but it had been half dark and filled with the smoke of cigarettes. She had seen only their backs as they sat at the bar, talking loudly in a strange language, drinking beer and rolling dice. Even so, passing through them with Firecracker Lily had been like briefly entering another world. A world that the Fish had said she was a part of and that Great-uncle To had told her of.

Now that she looked up and right into the face of the one she had noticed sitting alone as though he was waiting for someone who never came, it was startling. She had not seen him approaching and the shock was so sudden she could only stare back into his eyes, as, with his hands on the back of the chair opposite, he leaned towards her.

'May I buy you a drink?'

Sing had no idea what it was he said, but in the time she had been in the ballroom she had learned to smile and nod her consent to every suggestion.

Her mind scrambled for the few words of English she had been taught by Ah Gum. Hello, goodbye, thank you, very good, yes, no. The eyes that never left her face were intensely blue. As blue, Siu Sing thought, as the sky-blue topaz of J. T. Ching, or as the eyes of Master To. She had been told by others that all foreigners looked alike, but this one had hair that was almost white, the colour of bamboo leaves when they have fallen and been bleached by the sun. His skin was not white but a pale honey-brown, which Sing realised with a strange thrill, was close to the colour of her own. And his nose. She marvelled at its shape and length. A larger version of her own. So different from others, fine and narrow compared to the flatter, broader nose of most Chinese. Suddenly remembering the right words on meeting a gwai-lo for the first time, she said with a seriousness that made Toby grin with delight.

'How do you do? May I know your name?'

For the next six weeks Toby Hyde-Wilkins visited the Nine Dragons ballroom as often as he could. If there was a duty he could avoid or bribe someone else to take over for him, he did so without hesitation. The normal training routines within the lines and any official duties elsewhere went by for Toby with one aim in mind— to take the fancy elevator up to the candlelit corner table that looked out over the electrified dazzle of Wan Chai, where Siu Sing would be waiting for him.

Toby had never been in love, had no idea how it began and had only guessed what it felt like. He only knew that since the first evening, over numerous whiskies for him and Coca Cola for her, he had been able to think of nothing but the girl of mixed blood who said her name meant Little Star. He knew very well that he was probably making an absolute arse of himself, that she was little more than a child, but it just didn't matter. To sit beside her and learn to communicate with her, knowing that each time they discovered a little more of each other, gave him more real pleasure than he had ever found making aimless conversation with the pallid daughters of senior officers on Stonecutter's Island or the desperate civil service secretaries who came to the mess dances.

To Sing it had also become a mysteriously wonderful thing. It was as though he had opened a door that had always been closed to her. With his help, the words of English she had learned parrot-like from Ah Gum began to fall into place and make sense. Each evening they spent together he would bring new words and test her on those he had left with her to study. She found that in spite of the language difficulty she had never felt happier or more comfortable with anyone since leaving Tung T'ing Lake, except perhaps in the hours spent with Ah Gum in the Reading Book Pavilion.

But there was something else when they talked together. It was not just his kindness, the gentle way he held her when they danced together or that she felt so safe with him. It was another feeling, as though she was being drawn through the door he had opened, willingly and gratefully. So that when he reached across the table to take her hand, the touch of his fingers made her heart beat faster and caused feelings of excitement inside that had never been aroused before.

Three-thumbs Poon, who made it his business to know exactly what was happening on every floor of his huge establishment, was well aware that the gwai-lo had been taking up much of Siu Sing's time. At first it hadn't bothered him; for every Coke or pot of tea he bought her and every beer or whisky he drank there was a large profit and gwai-lo money was as good as Chinese money.

If she was truly a cherry girl, and Hand-trolley Lulu had been sure that she was, he didn't want her to go upstairs with anyone or be bought out to be taken elsewhere. When the time came, and to the right client, it could be worth as much as $10,000 to take her to bed. He had already decided which room it should be: the Arabian Nights suite, with its walls and cushions of black silk and false ceiling of moon and stars. A sheikh's tent in the desert night. It was his favourite creation of romantic fantasy, based on the love nest of the famous Rudolph Valentino. So, he had not worried about the harmless gwai-lo who seemed to find her company so pleasing, until he asked to take her upstairs.

Three-thumbs Poon flatly refused. She was not for taking to bed. She was too young. Toby explained that he only wanted to be alone with her, that he would not take her to bed. Three-thumbs still refused—never had he heard such a stupid promise. Any of the other girls could be taken upstairs but not this one. Toby could buy any of the girls out and take them anywhere he chose but not this one. She was new. She was not yet ready. When Toby offered to pay double the fee, Three-thumbs remained unmoved.

'She is not ready,' he said finally, removing his glasses to polish them.

It was something the proprietor of the Nine Dragons did whenever he felt a little nervous. It gave him time to think. He had heard of the Welfare League, the organisation formed by Sir Robert Ho Tung for the protection of homeless Eurasians, and even knew its creed: 'To promote the welfare of the poor and relief of distress among the Eurasian Society of the Colony.' He replaced the thick glasses carefully and looked at Toby, his eyes swimming behind them like fish in a bowl. He did not wish this girl to be taken into gwai-lo company where questions could be asked. He was aware that to them he was breaking the law with his intentions for her.

'She is a hostess, here to dance and keep my customers company.'

'But surely she is allowed outside?'

'She is new in Hong Kong. It is not safe for her on the streets.'

Toby tried again. 'I will protect her. She will come to no harm. You have my guarantee.'

The eyes of Three-thumbs Poon grew wide with annoyance. Who was this gwai-lo to tell him how to run his business? He could not hide a flush of anger.

'Why do you come here? You do not belong in this place. She is Chinese. She is not for you.'

Toby had no wish to create a scene. The little man with the Peter Lorre eyes was right. He did not belong in the Nine Dragons ballroom. But neither did Siu Sing. He did not think it would look good on his record to be reported in heated confrontation with a Wan Chai whoremaster, so he decided not to press the issue while the little man with three thumbs seemed ready to pop with anger.

Quietly, he said, 'I come because she is here. She is not Chinese, she has western blood, and my friend, if I do not belong here, she does not belong here. See that she is treated well and think about what I have said. I will be back.'

Toby left the Nine Dragons determined to find a way to help Siu Sing. He did not know as he waited for the elevator that the way would be shown to him on his next visit.

He had decided to leave it for a month before returning to the ballroom. It gave the man with three thumbs time to calm down and would give him space to take stock of his own feelings. All he discovered, with his reasoning complete, was that he missed seeing her more than he could remember missing anything or anyone in his life.

Captain Hyde-Wilkins told no one of his rendezvous with the Wan Chai ballroom hostess he guessed was barely sixteen. When Colonel Pelham asked him where he'd been disappearing to lately or the others winked knowingly when he entered the mess, he grinned and let them think what they liked. It made no sense to him and it would make even less to them if he tried to explain it.

He knew he'd been feeling increasingly lonely for a woman and that the opportunities for meeting one were restricted to the once-a-month social function in the mess. A couple of brief affairs had ended before they began and he had faced the fact that he found the western women likely to be available to him hopelessly boring. None of this explained his obsession with the girl in the ballroom except, he supposed, the fact that he found that just looking at her excited him more than any woman he had ever seen.

Siu Sing watched the three thumbs slowly circling each other under the green-shaded desk lamp.

'It is not good that you see this foreign soldier. He will cause only trouble for you.' Hand-trolley Lulu's voice was low and filled with reproach. 'I am told you see only him. That when you are asked to dance with others you do not smile for them. Is this true?' She waited for Sing's answer. Three-thumbs Poon broke the silence angrily.

'It is true. She waits only for this gwai-lo. My clients complain that she is unfriendly. The other girls do not like her.'

The mama san's voice was filled with reproach. 'I brought you here because you would be treated well. Where you would be someone of value. Is this how you repay me, by displeasing your benefactor? By insulting my judgement?'

Sing could not find the words that would explain her feelings. Hand-trolley Lulu went on, her tone a clear warning. 'If you are sent from this place you must work in the bars where the gwai-lo is rough and crazy with drink and smells like a goat. There they will take your cherry and pay nothing for it.'

Three-thumbs Poon waved his hands under the lamp. 'Take her. Give her to the drunken sailors. Better still, give her to Mary's Boat Party. Let her work for her rice.' He dismissed Sing with a wave of his hand. 'You have brought me nothing but trouble with this one. Give her to the gwai-lo in the bars. Give her to Red Lead Mary. I have no use for this disobedient jarp jung.'

Hand-trolley Lulu knew he was bluffing. He had no intention of giving up such an investment. She took a cigarette from her handbag and fitted it into the long holder, leaning forward until it poked under the lamp for Three-thumbs Poon to light. He struck the flint of the cigarette lighter repeatedly with his double thumb.

Watching it made Sing suddenly want to laugh out loud.

'You must promise me that you will not dance with the foreign soldier again. His kind eat the flesh of Chinese babies. He is a barbarian and only pretends to be a man of honour.'

Hand-trolley Lulu leaned back, blowing smoke. 'You do not give me face by behaving this way. You must obey your benefactor and when he finds the right one to take you upstairs you must serve that gentleman willingly. He must be your lord. You must pretend great joy even if you do not feel it. Do you understand?'

Siu Sing nodded her head. 'Yes mama san.'

Hand-trolley Lulu stood up. 'I hope so. Because if you do not, things will go very badly for you.'

Since she had been taken to the office of Three-thumbs Poon, Sing had tried to please those who approached her. She had smiled when she danced with them and when they had pulled her close and fondled her she had not stopped smiling. But her eyes were always on the elevator and every time the polished brass grid slid open she hoped that Toby would step from it. He had not and it was more than three weeks since she had seen him.

Mama Lulu was right. She must forget about the foreign soldier. She must not displease the man with three thumbs again. There was good food to eat and a small room of her own. But soon, she knew, there would be another J.T. Ching. She had asked herself many times why she had run away from the safety of the Tavern of Cascading Jewels. Why she had not been pleased, as Jade would have been, to become the concubine of a rich and powerful man.

The man, dressed in black, emerged from the crowded dance floor and walked towards her. The iridescent reflections of the revolving mirror ball made it difficult to see his face but Sing never really looked at their faces. There was something in the way that he walked, a slight rising on one foot that seemed somehow familiar. It was not until he sat down in the chair opposite her that she saw it was Ah Keung.

Anger and fear rose in her as though they were live things that had been sleeping in her belly and suddenly awakened. The feeling seemed to claw its way upward until it reached her throat and there it stayed. He had changed in the two and a half years since the iron gate of Fat Fan's compound had closed between them. He had seemed nervous then. He did not seem nervous now.

'I have heard of the new jarp-jung who has been brought to

the Nine Dragons by the old whore from the Happy Butterfly. I thought I would see for myself.' His eyes were unblinking as they held hers, dropping to the swell of her breast then back again.

'They are right. She is ripe as a summer peach.' He signalled to the waiter to bring tea, his eyes fixed on Sing.

'So you are the cherry girl that Three-thumbs Poon is saving like a special cake for the Moon Festival.' An unpleasant smile shaped his mouth. 'Did not the emperor Fan take a nibble? Are you not deceiving Three-thumbs Poon and the old whore?'

The fear in Sing's throat would not move. It hurt her even to swallow.

'We have so much to talk about, you and I.' He laughed softly. 'You must tell me how to make sausages out of pigs.' Waiting while the tea was put down, he leaned back, amused at the fear that showed in Sing's face. The smile became a grin.

'You must not hate me. Did I not find you a home and work, as I said I would?' He gave a short, nasal laugh. 'Is it my fault if you did not please the emperor of swine?'

Sing had begun to master the feelings that had overcome her as she managed to find words. 'You sold me as a slave. I was not yours to sell. I trusted you.'

Ah Keung spread his hands wide, with a look of innocence. 'It was business. There was no choice. I filled your rice bowl. I had to fill my own.' His hand crept across the table to cover hers.

'It is the way of things. It is past.' Sing's words were hardly a whisper as she withdrew her hand from his grasp.

The smile faded from his face.

'I did not know that you would be badly treated. You had nowhere to go, no one to care for you. My promise was to find a place for you. This I did. Do not blame me for your failure to keep it.'

The tea remained unpoured. He leaned suddenly forward and filled her cup, then his own. 'We will drink tea and then we will go upstairs where we can talk privately. You must tell me all that has happened.'

She ignored the tea. 'I am not allowed to go upstairs. It is forbidden.'

He sipped, watching closely. 'With me it is different. The toad with three thumbs, Money-bags Poon, will do anything I ask.' The grin returned. 'He will even allow me a taste of his special mooncake if I insist.'

Siu Sing was hardly aware of her sudden movement as she flung the hot tea into Ah Keung's face. Nor did she see him stand and throw back his chair, so swift was the movement. Heads turned and the mama san of the floor pressed the button in her cubicle by the elevators. Ah Keung made no attempt to wipe the scalding tea from his face. Returning the chair to its place, he gripped the back of it till his knuckles shone white.

'So the spirit of Little Star has not dimmed. We shall see if the Crane can still fly.' The hand that shot out to grasp her wrist was swift as a lash. The other swept across her face and back in a double slap too fast to counter, jerking Sing to her feet.

At that second the lift doors opened. Three-thumbs Poon stepped quickly out followed by two others. When they saw Ah Keung, the two men he paid to take care of trouble stood back and allowed him to approach the problem alone.

He knew that the tall black-clad man was a newly appointed Red Pole of the Yellow Dragon and that the Nine Dragons ballroom was now part of his territory. He had also been warned of this man's ruthlessness and had no illusions about his power to use it as he wished.

'Please ah gor,' he used the respectful title of big brother. 'I want no trouble. Tell me what has happened to displease you?.'

Blood began to trickle from Siu Sing's lip and he tried not to notice it.

'You can teach your whores some respect,' hissed Ah Keung venomously. With a sudden pull he jerked her around the table. The instinct to resist shot through Sing's body but was balanced by an almost dormant sense of timing and the futility of defence in such circumstances. Her arm was twisted behind her by his fierce grip. With the other hand Ah Keung grasped her throat, forcing her to look into his face. 'But I will deal with this one myself.' Suddenly he released his hold and flung her backwards onto the floor.

The eyes of Three-thumbs Poon were wide with alarm. 'Please ah gor, I beg of you. She is new. She is young and inexperienced. She has not yet learned. She will be punished for her disrespect.'

Three-thumbs Poon felt the sweat pop from his forehead and run into his eyes. He blinked hard and felt like crying. Why, he beseeched himself, had the gods placed him in the path of this unspeakable one? Why had all luck deserted him? Like all those in Wan Chai who owned businesses he had heard of the Dragon's Tail, the dreadful blow that the Forceful One delivered with such consummate ease, separating the head from the spine in the time it takes to blink.

Ah Keung's fury slipped from him in the silence that closed over the floor when the band stopped playing, the singer sheathed in blood-red sequins still at the microphone. Every eye was upon him. Only the kaleidoscope of colours from the mirror ball continued its merry-go-round.

'No. Do not punish her.' He resumed his seat, indicating that Three-thumbs Poon should also sit. The singer took it as her cue to continue and the band quickly followed. Ah Keung was completely calm. He spoke as though Sing was not there. 'There is no need to punish her. You are right, she has not yet learned. I shall be the one to teach her. No one else.'

Three-thumbs Poon was close to tears. 'But ah gor. She has been promised to a man of great importance. A man of . . . ,' his voice trailed away under the threat of Ah Keung's hostile gaze.

'Now she is promised to me. Am I not important?' He turned to Siu Sing with a smile of tolerance. 'I will be back to see you soon. I hope that when I return your manners are improved.'

'It is you, my friend, who will learn some manners. I see they have not improved since we last met.' Toby stood two paces from where Ah Keung sat back, his legs spread wide. He had come from the lift without their noticing and had heard half the conversation. Ah Keung remained splayed in the chair, his face wiped clean of expression. As though Toby had not spoken he addressed himself to Three-thumbs Poon.

'What is a shit-eating gwai-lo doing in the house of Nine Dragons?' he demanded quietly, showing no sign that he recognised Toby.

Before Poon could frame his reply, Toby had closed the distance and stood over Ah Keung, who continued to ignore him, a half smile fixed on his face.

'If you get on your feet, I'll show you.' Toby's words held the light amusement of pure contempt.

Ah Keung's eyes narrowed to slits but the insolent smirk stayed on his lips. Still he did not look at Toby but held Poon's petrified stare. 'Tell this son of a pig to go from here while he can still walk. He has no place here.'

Toby was thinking fast after the first flood of anger that had made him react. He was ready if Ah Keung made a move to stand but prayed that he would stay in the chair. Sing broke the tension by springing to her feet to confront him, her face white with fury. The words she spat at him rang in the breathless silence brought a murmur of guarded titters from among the audience, as she stepped between them.

'Ah gor is right,' she hissed into Toby's face. 'You do not belong here. You belong in the gwai-lo bars with the low-class whores. Go while you can. You cause only trouble here.' With the full force of her anger behind it, Siu Sing slapped Toby's face.

The effect upon him was stunning disbelief. The situation closed in on him as the tittering broke into the roar of laughter that grew into applause. He stood motionless, struck dumb by the surprise of it. Ah Keung remained sprawled in the chair, the smirk on his face unchanged, turning his eyes finally to Toby, enjoying every second of his humiliation. Three-thumbs Poon had the grin of terror fixed on his face as Toby turned away. Even when the lift was descending he could hear the laughter, then the voice of the singer rising above it as the entertainment continued.

When he had gone Ah Keung rose and grinned his approval at Sing. She faced him, shaking with defiance.

'I am impressed, Little Star. You are Chinese after all.' His mood changed, suddenly steely cold as he turned on Three-thumbs Poon who was sweating freely, the grin of fright still fixed on his face.

'You should know better than to serve gwai-los, old money-bags. Do you want the police here?' he said icily. 'I expect you to pay for this embarrassment.'

Replacing the chair and without looking at Sing he added, 'When I return, have this one prepared for me upstairs. Let no one touch her until then.'

As he turned his back to walk away Three-thumbs Poon croaked after him. 'When will that be, ah gor?'

'When I am ready,' came the reply.

The next day Sing became ill with the thought of Ah Keung's threat to return and the certainty that Toby would not come again. Three-thumbs Poon had warned her that there was nothing he could do to help her. That her only protection would be in her obedience to the Red Pole when he demanded it and in the quality of her service to him. He allowed her to remain in her room, as the mask of fear and anger she wore would bring him no profit on the dance floor. She prayed to all the gods that Toby had understood the danger he was in and that what she had done was a warning.

Three-thumbs Poon was almost relieved when the gwai-lo was brought to his office the following day. He stayed well-hidden in the depths of his chair while his hands held the letter in the light from the desk lamp. It was written on regimental letterhead and he could not read a word of it. He could recognise the photograph of Toby's identification as Adjutant and Liaison Officer to the 8th Rajput Rifles and he listened from the shadows as Toby told him that he had come to take the Eurasian girl away.

She was believed to be the daughter of a British officer serving elsewhere. It was the reason, Toby explained, for his regular appearance at the Nine Dragons. His investigations of the girl had confirmed his suspicions and he must take her with him. Toby was correct in his assumption that Three-thumbs Poon would not risk any kind of enquiry. Sing was sent for immediately and when they had left, Poon lit an extra bundle of joss and prayed that the Forceful One would understand that he was powerless to stop them. Then, taking the brandy bottle from the drawer, he poured himself a tumbler full and cursed his abominable luck.

He would withhold the commission on the other girls supplied by Hand-trolley Lulu until the trouble caused by this jarp jung had been well compensated for. As for the Forceful One, Three-thumbs Poon removed his spectacles and polished them thoughtfully, holding them under the light and returning them to his tired eyes. He would offer him his pick of three girls and give him the tent of the Sheikh of Araby. Surely that would replace a troublesome jarp-jung.

PART · VI

The Residence of Eternal Peace

The herd boy calls across the field
his voice is lazy with the slowness of summer.
The brook hurries to feed young rice
its sound is like laughter among the stones.
The fragrance of ginger blossom fills the morning
with the scent of wild spice.
The tiger hunts far off on Lo Shan
and the smoke from the chatti fires
rises undisturbed.
There is no more peaceful place than this.

MASTER TO-TZE

• IMAGE FOR PEACE •

The Ginger Field

THE RESIDENCE of Eternal Peace was the name the Hakka farmer Po Lok had given to his home a mile outside the walled village of Pok Choy Lam, near Taipo, in the New Territories. He was an independent man and wanted his sons to be the same. Po Lok had been born inside the high walls of the village and had grown up there as his father and grandfather had, sharing his toil and his rice crop with the other families of the clan. Life in Pok Choy Lam had not changed since the walls were built in the sixteenth century against attacks by the pirate chief Koxinga and his horde of cut-throats.

When Po Lok was old enough to marry, he had taken a bride from another clan and with her came a dowry of land. Koxinga was long dead and the bandits that once scoured the surrounding hills were no more; he no longer had need of walls to protect his family. So he had moved out of the walled village and built his house on the rich piece of land that providence had provided. He and his wife had worked side by side in the fields and their farm had prospered. They had raised eight children: five sons and three daughters. The daughters had all married well and lived on surrounding farms while three of his sons still worked the acres that spread out on all sides of the Residence of Eternal Peace.

Each son had built a strong house close to the home of his father and given him many fine grandchildren. The farm produced pigs, ducks, chickens for the restaurants and its large ponds were filled with grass-eating carp. The fields grew beans, peas, cabbages, cucumber, melons and ginger. The group of four square, stone farm houses, reached by a wooden foot-bridge that spanned a fast-running stream, was screened by fruit trees. The deep well of pure sweet water that Po Lok had dug thirty years earlier stood in the centre of the courtyard.

Po Lok no longer worked the fields. He had earned the filial piety of his sons and daughters and he now enjoyed the benefits of his middle years from the vine-shaded porch he had built outside his comfortable house. As he sipped from the cup of green tea that he was seldom without, the faint pop of firearms drifted across the white field of flowering ginger. He was proud of the fact that his farm had been chosen to supply the camp of the foreign soldiers with eggs and vegetables and poultry. The familiar sounds from the firing range were always a reassuring reminder of the good business he enjoyed.

To reach the Residence of Eternal Peace you had to walk a kilometre from the main road, following a narrow track that led through the ginger field. It was just wide enough for a buffalo cart to carry produce to the market at Taipo and twice a week to the army camp at Fanling. Po Lok had no wish for more access than this to the world outside.

As a Hakka and a peasant of the soil, Po Lok was a decent and honest man but he considered it his duty to do good business. He was not ashamed that he had bargained so fiercely with the gwai-lo officer who had come to talk to him a year ago. Or that he charged twice the local price for his produce. This was the custom of the Hakka and he knew his neighbours had asked three times the true value. He squinted across the field of ginger at the two figures that were approaching, and could tell by his yellow hair that one was the British officer.

Like most Hakka peasants in the New Territories, Po Lok's was a simple existence lived according to a simple way of thinking. Unlike the city-dwelling Cantonese he did not feel bitter contempt for the gwai-lo and always made them welcome when they found reason to visit his farm. The tall one with hair the colour of ripe barley and eyes of duck-egg blue came regularly and sat with him to drink tea. This one spoke Chinese and although the dialects were different they were able to converse for hours on such things as the days of the pirates and the long history of the Hakka people.

Toby held Siu Sing's hand as they walked in the warmth of the mid-morning sun. The scent from the sea of ginger blossom that grew almost as tall as her shoulder was fresh and sweet and alive with butterflies. As they approached the house of Po Lok the dogs ran out with their usual noise, made their fuss and retreated to lie beneath the ox cart that stood beside the well. Po Lok rose stiffly from his chair to greet them, raising a hand and bowing in recognition. His wife emerged from the doorway to chase the chickens from the porch and offer them tea and refreshments.

The Residence of Eternal Peace had been well named. An air of quiet content settled over the place, beyond intrusion from outside. Even the cowherds were low-voiced, and beyond the grunting of pigs and clucking of poultry at feeding time, the chatter of running water and the tumbling of its waterwheel was the only constant sound. The Hakka people of the New Territories are known to be less excitable than the city Cantonese, except on market days when they drive their stock or cart their produce to Taipo Market, or ferry them across the harbour to the Central markets that feed Hong Kong. Then they are the loudest and most persistent hagglers of all.

Po Lok and his wife Kam-Yang welcomed Siu Sing as an honoured guest in their house. It was enough they said, that seal yeh— the young lord, had brought her there. Toby knew that the generous advance he had insisted on paying for her simple expenses had increased their approval of the idea and that they knew he had the power to take away the camp contract if they displeased him. So the smiles had been wide and the honour great. Siu Sing was welcome to stay as long as she wished.

'My only concern, young lord, is that our humble place of abode, our poor way of life and the miserable food that is set upon our table will please the siu jeh.'

Po Lok bowed in the old way as he spoke while Kam-Yang brought steamed buns stuffed with savoury pork. It was the first time Siu Sing had been called a young lady.

There was a small house of three rooms beside the brook and its waterwheel, half hidden in the grove of orange trees. It had been built for number three son but he had become restless for city life, they said, and gone across the sea to work in restaurants far away. Now he owned his own eating place, Po Lok said proudly, and lived in Kowloon. Siu Sing could use this house and would be given privacy there, he assured them, again apologising, with bowed head, for his inferior hospitality.

Siu Sing found herself instinctively drawn to these country people and their customs. She understood them better than she understood the aggressive ways of the city. In turn she bowed her head and expressed suitable embarrassment in the presence of such great generosity. She was in doubt, she murmured, only of her worthiness to receive such great kindness and to find sanctuary in such a place so obviously blessed by the gods.

With everyone's honour traditionally satisfied, the ritual of good manners properly given and received with no questions asked, Toby left Siu Sing in the Residence of Eternal Peace knowing that she would be safe there for as long as was necessary. He had known Po Lok and his family since first being taken to their farm by the quartermaster sergeant and had returned many times to share their simple hospitality and the delights of true Hakka cooking.

The farmer was typical of his kind, faithful to the traditions of his race but independent when it came to the survival and prosperity of himself and his family. He was a man to be trusted. Once or twice Toby had stayed overnight in the house by the brook and had marvelled at the tranquillity of waking up in it, to the creak of the waterwheel and the sound of chickens scratching outside the door.

Months went by and Toby visited Siu Sing whenever he could. Several times a week and on most weekends his driver dropped him off at the wooden plank that bridged an irrigation ditch skirting a field of cabbage. He would walk the kilometre through hectares of spinach, cucumbers and melons until the barking of dogs told Siu Sing he was approaching through the ginger field and she ran to meet him.

To Toby the transformation of the girl from the Nine Dragons ballroom was astounding. Kam-Yang had made her the pants and long jacket of black cotton favoured by the Hakka and she wore a wide hat of woven cane grass surrounded by a pleated valance of the same black cotton to shield her face from the sun. A healthy appetite for the plain, substantial food had filled her out and work in the fields had given her skin a fresh glow and her eyes a brightness that delighted him.

They spent much of their time together on a mat beside the brook and in the shade of the orange trees where Toby continued to teach her to read and write in English. At her shy request he had brought her English newspapers and magazines, among them the *Saturday Evening Post* and *Country Life*. When she had asked for a book to practise her reading of English he had bought her a copy of Anna Sewell's *Black Beauty*.

She had made her own ancestral shrine. The photograph stood upon a shelf, the white fan spread beneath it surrounded by flowers and fruit picked fresh from outside. A small cup stood before it which she filled each morning when she took her tea and she burned incense there three times a day. When Toby came upon her kneeling before it she was afraid that he would laugh, the gwai-lo people did not believe in such things. But he did not laugh. Instead he brought her a beautiful frame made of polished buffalo horn inlaid with ivory.

It was clear to him that this was the best of all places for her to remain while she restored herself from the traumatic experiences that had so far shaped her life. Over their many hours together Sing had told him of her past and of the treachery of Ah Keung. How the Fish had taken her to the hut of Great-uncle To and the wild freedom she had known there. She showed him the precious photograph of the western man and Chinese woman the Fish had said were her parents. She told him little of Fat Fan or Madam Fung or the Golden One, a small furrow appearing between her eyes when he asked too many questions.

It was a sign he soon learned to respect as a signal to change the subject. When the pieces of her story came together, the resourcefulness of her spirit filled him with admiration. Trust and respect between them grew and sometimes Sing tried to share with him the secrets of *The Second Sunrise*, taking out the little notebooks from the deerhide bag to spread them on the mat, explaining in words of simple charm the philosophy of nature, the way of the Tao.

In turn, Toby told her of his home in the countryside outside the famous pottery town of Derby, encouraged by the fascination on her face, the little frown of concentration as she listened intently to every word. If something he said confused her she asked him to repeat it, her eyes never leaving his lips until she understood the finest detail.

Together they explored the surrounding hills of the valley. The lower slopes were cultivated by Po Lok's sons and terraced into rice paddies. Above them was wild grassland reaching rocky plateaux sparsely covered by old trees. Pathways had been cut through the head-high grass by fuel gatherers and from halfway to the top they could look out across the valley to Taipo village and the wide blue sheet of Tolo harbour, stretching to the sea. On one of these walks they discovered a ruined temple. Half its roof had collapsed with age but its shrine was intact, the dark inner chamber still protecting the image of Kuan Yin and her disciples. On the wall behind them was hung the skin of a tiger. It was the skin, Po Lok told them later, of the last tiger to be seen in the New Territories, shot by the gwai-los on their golf course only a few months before. It had been presented to the villagers and they had offered it to the shrine of Kuan Yin.

It was at the end of the second month of Sing's sanctuary in the Residence of Eternal Peace when Toby knew he could no longer hold back his true feelings for her. Many conflicting thoughts had made him patient. He estimated her age from what she had told him at around sixteen. Although her body was that of a mature woman and they were a long way from his Church of England upbringing, it had restrained him. He realised also that if the nervous little man with three thumbs was to be believed, she was possibly still a virgin and that any sexual experience she might have had was probably forced upon her. He doubted if she had ever been kissed or embraced in the way he longed to hold her. They had walked hand in hand over miles of farmland and wild country. Her nearness, when they sat by the brook or ate together in the stone-flagged kitchen of the little house, had been enough for him until now. Now it was a day when Po Lok had taken Kam-Yang and their grandchildren to pay homage to the earth god in the walled village and to buy sweetmeats in Taipo market.

The herdsmen and duckboys were out in the fields. It was a superb day when the beautiful place was at its most peaceful, the scent of flowering citrus strong on the still, afternoon air. They had come into the cool of the house, its shutters closed against the strong, spring sunshine. Sing had removed the frilled hat and drawn cold water from the well, soaking a cloth to press against his forehead and neck.

Shyly, she went to the wooden chest where her books and the deerhide bag were kept. From it she took a tiny red box, holding it out to him in the childlike way that so captivated him.

'It is for you. A gift of thanks.'

She watched his face, the small crease of a frown appearing between her smooth brows as he opened it. Inside was a ring made from orange-peel jade, pearly white, mottled with the pale yellow and red streaks of marmalade.

'It is a finger jade,' she said, her voice as anxious as her face. 'Shaped like the brown mountain bear. It is for protection and long life.'

Toby took it from the box and slipped it on his small finger. It fitted perfectly. 'It's beautiful, Siu Sing. I have heard of orange-peel jade and the luck it brings but I have never seen it.' He looked puzzled. 'It must have cost you a lot of money.'

The frown slipped from Sing's brow in an instant and her smile was filled with delight. 'It is also for happiness,' she said, her eyes shining with pleasure. 'I was given money in the ballroom of Three-thumbs Poon. I bought it from the jade man in Taipo market. It is rare, but it was not expensive.'

Toby held out both his hands, drawing her to him and looking into her eyes. 'Are you happy, Siu Sing?' he asked gently.

For the smallest fraction of time the hint of her frown returned and then was gone. 'With you I am happy,' she said simply. 'It will not last. I do not expect the happiness to last. I expect nothing, so I am never disappointed.'

He could smell the faint aroma of her body, warm from the sun, and the sprig of orange blossom he had tucked behind her ear. As she leaned close to him he noticed her forehead and upper lip were damp with a fine dew of perspiration; wisps of curling hair clung to her temples and a single bead of sweat had tracked down her cheek, following the line of her neck to disappear between her breasts. He was so close he could detect her breath; the shoot of young barley grass she had chewed as they walked had left it clean and fresh. It seemed to him her round eyes had grown rounder as they concentrated on the fairness of his hair, her hand reaching up to touch it, feeling its texture, wonderful to her as spun silk.

The feeling that welled up like a spring inside Siu Sing made her suddenly bolder and she pushed her hand through his hair more strongly, letting the weight of it fall through her fingers again and again. The feeling did not worry her, it was always there when she was with him, like a bird fluttering to leave its cage. She felt his hands close lightly on each side of her waist and when she did not resist they held her more firmly, their warmth reaching through the thin cotton of her jacket to her skin.

Slowly Toby stepped backwards, drawing her gently but firmly with him until the back of his legs touched the bed. Carefully he lowered his body until he sat on its edge, leaving her standing before him. His hands slipped to her hips as he pulled her to him, resting his head against her breasts. Her hand pressed the damp towel to the back of his neck while she continued to gently explore his hair. He could hear the thud of her heartbeat as his hands moved cautiously over the swell of her buttocks and down her legs to the backs of her knees, feeling the smoothness of her skin sliding under the coarse weave of cotton.

He left his hands still as he felt her legs begin to tremble, afraid she would break away from him. She made no move except to draw his cheek closer to her breast. They stayed for moments unmoving except for her fingers in his hair, both afraid to make a gesture and lose this time and this place, to lose each other. When he looked up at her, her face was serious. The almost imperceptible furrow again creased the smooth space between her brows. Eyes half closed, shaded by her lowered eyelashes, she wore a look of concentration so intense he had to smile.

'You must not be afraid,' he whispered softly.

Her eyes opened wide and he could see into their smoky depths. He was always amazed by their colour, reminding him of the far pavilions, the mountain peaks of Nepal shaded by distance. The pale shade of lilac.

Standing slowly, carefully, he lifted her chin with a bent finger. 'You must never be afraid of me.' Tenderly, he touched her soft dry lips with his, brushing them lightly, then her chin, her cheeks, her temples, her eyelids. As her trembling increased he held her tighter, his arms encircling, pulling her to him as he kissed her throat.

For Siu Sing it was as though the bird had escaped, soaring unhindered into endless space, floating somewhere she had never dreamed existed. She found her mouth responding, moistened by its contact with his, returning his kisses with an even greater passion.

His lips, his cheeks, his eyes, his throat. Until he stopped her by taking her face between his hands, finding her mouth for long moments, until his hands left her face to find her breasts. The softest of sounds escaped her as his palms brushed the hard buds of her nipples. She had not realised they were aroused until he touched them and her mouth sought his with new urgency.

As though her knees had given way Sing became a weight in his arms that swung itself onto the bed, sitting where he had sat. Toby knelt before her. The cotton jacket was fastened by press-studs and one by one his fingers pulled them apart. The thinnest of vests covered her breasts beneath the jacket. So thin that he could see the dark rings around their jutting tips, strained against the damp cotton. The scents of her body were completely natural but for the hint of sandalwood soap. Deliberately Toby slid his hands over her shoulders, shedding the jacket to expose her upper arms. These he held firmly against the violence of her trembling and put his mouth gently to each breast in turn, teasing them through the skin of the material with his hardened tongue.

Siu Sing's head fell back. The thrill she felt seemed to weaken her limbs. Her knees had parted to receive him, now they closed fiercely to grip his sides. The sensation of his rolling tongue, the slight nipping of his teeth filled her mind with a great wonder. How would it feel if there was nothing between them? Anxious not to detach herself from him, Sing slid the vest upwards and over her head, crying out as she felt the tip of one breast engulfed by the eager warmth of his mouth.

When Siu Sing awoke it was almost sunset. The voices of the herdboys were approaching from the fields as they spoke lazily to the buffalo and hurried the ducks back into the ponds. The bed beside her still showed the hollow of his body in the goose-feather mattress. He had left a glass jar filled with orange blossom beside the bed. She rolled over to touch it and the smell of his hair, faint with tonic, filled her nostrils. She crushed the fleshy heads of blossom in her palm and rolling over onto her back, held them to her mouth and nose, breathing in their tangy fragrance.

A thin shroud of evening mist had formed over the surface of the fishponds and along the path through the ginger field. Toby walked it briskly, breathing in the sweet, cool air and the smoke from the chattie fires that always drifted across the hills at the close of day. There was a spring in his step that his conscience was slightly ashamed of, but only slightly. Most of Toby Hyde-Wilkins wanted to shout for joy. To fill his lungs with the scent of wild ginger and the smoke of chattie fires and roar out loud. Or curse the duty that demanded his presence at the camp.

Making love to Siu Sing had surpassed any thought or longing, any ache or flight of fantasy that had ever visited his many lonely moments. Even as he had knelt before her he had not been sure, prepared to stop at any sign of her resistance. Much as he had wanted her he would not have risked losing her by moving too quickly or too clumsily. But she had not resisted. In place of the hesitation, the innocence he had been ready for, there was instead a calm and calculated certainty of what was happening and the part she was to play in it. In fact, she had taken charge with such an air of understanding it had made him wonder where she could have gained such assurance.

She had slowed him down, steadied his eager hands and lips with whispered reminders that there was no need to hurry, no shortage of time. She had left the bed to untie the tape that held the black cotton trousers to her waist, letting them fall to her ankles. There had been none of the timid modesty he was prepared for. She showed herself proudly to him, soaking the cloth in the bucket of well water and carefully bathing while he watched. As though this was a performance for which she had rehearsed all her life.

When it had become too much to bear and he had tried to

reach for her she had pushed him gently back, removing the last of his clothes and applying the cool cloth to his healthy erection with the clinical precision of a trained nurse. Handling it with a fond familiarity that both shocked and delighted him, her fingers had brushed his scrotum lightly and fleetingly and continued down the inside of his thighs and back again.

This she continued patiently and purposefully, gauging the degree of his excitement with nothing more than a slight widening of her eyes at the size of him. Toby abandoned himself completely, quite content to die rather than have her stop. Wave after wave of indescribable pleasure had caused his leg muscles to tremble uncontrollably and as the warning of climax showed in his eyes and in his breathing, her magical fingers had moved higher to circle his naval and upward to twirl in the hair of his chest and around the excited core of his nipples. It had the effect of breaking one circuit and switching on another.

Gradually she had explored every inch of him with her eyes and fingertips, raising and calming his pulse at will. Any thought Toby may have had of teaching her the delights of sensuality such as he had learned them from the talented Brenda Bridges, or the practised efficiency of the Bombay red-light district, were forced out of his mind by peaks of ecstasy and troughs of surrender that kept his senses reeling and his imagination dazzled.

When her hands had done their work, she had bathed perspiration from the length and breadth of him, carefully and unhurriedly, missing not the smallest part of his body. She had then knelt over him and proceeded to retrace the caresses of her fingers with her warm lips and tongue, brushing his burning skin with her long lashes in the tantalising way she smilingly called 'dragonfly wings'. The fleeting embarrassment Toby had felt at his unrestrained erection when first exposed had been quickly lost under the spell of her enchanting curiosity. She had indulged herself in one brief giggle, quickly hidden behind her hand, and inspected its lines and textures as though it was a rare, exotic species; the first of its kind that she had ever captured—a wishful thought that Toby was finding increasingly hard to credit. The object of her close examination was in fact that quite familiar phenomenon likely to make itself known quite often to the younger officers of the 8th Rajput Rifles as a 'blue steel hard-on'.

Toby had almost reached the road when his thoughts of her caused his feet to leave the ground and he jumped like a boy. He calculated that her sensuous attentions had lasted for at least two hours before her tight, warm nest had enclosed him. He had spent himself twice in that time, deliriously incapable of stopping.

Each time she had orchestrated the throes of his orgasm as though he were a finely-tuned musical instrument and her expert fingers plucked its strings. Each time she had bathed him anew, coaxing him onto his stomach and massaging every muscle of his back, applying various pressures with strong thumbs and expert strokes of her palms that quickly awakened and invigorated him. When she had finally straddled him, positioning herself perfectly and taking him inch by inch with spasmodic contractions of her sphincter muscles, her own orgasm had almost instantly begun. She had leaned back, the long muscles of her widespread thighs quivering at its awakening, her head flung back as the first small exclamation of disbelief escaped her open mouth. Once, twice, three times, she had plunged down upon him, each time her cries becoming louder until they were joined by the sounds of Toby's third indescribable climax.

The Rajput driver dozing behind the wheel of the duty supply truck became instantly alert as joyful yelps reached him from the cabbage field. His bland expression was unchanged as he climbed down, adjusting his beret and opening the passenger door, smartly to attention and ready to salute. His eyes told nothing of his thoughts and he gazed above the head of the captain sahib as he bypassed the precarious balancing act of the plank and cleared the irrigation ditch in a single, flying leap. A Rajput soldier seldom observed the behaviour of a British officer off-duty but this one could not help thinking that the captain sahib had never looked quite so pleased with himself when leaving the Residence of Eternal Peace. The driver, ramrod straight, allowed himself a secret smile of approval, twisting the ends of his curled moustache as he ran round the truck to the driver's seat. He was proud of his sahib.

Siu Sing stepped outside the little farmhouse and stretched under a tree laden with dragon's-eye fruit that would soon be ripe for eating. She walked barefoot through the dewy grass beside the creek to the deep pond below the waterwheel. Wading into its depths, pushing aside rafts of flowering blue water-hyacinth, she swam to its centre and turned her face to the sun, warm against her closed lids. And silently thanked Ah Gum, the Golden One, for her tutelage, the silent Prince of the Sacred Persimmon for his patience and the Court of a Thousand Pleasures for its secrets.

Typhoon Mary

Fᴵꜰᴛʏ ᴍɪʟᴇꜱ off the Mariana Islands a turtle boat sat becalmed. In its bows, among a litter of uncleaned conch shells and hanks of rank-smelling kelp, half a dozen snapper turtles lay on their backs. Two men slouched forward from beneath the spare sail rigged as cover in the stern and stooped over them. The turtles were dying. Great tears welled from their horny eye sockets as they blinked against the sun that was slowly scorching them to death.

One of them was already dead and the men unsheathed their knives and crouched to remove its shell, cursing at its weight as they heaved the bloodied remains over the side. The younger of the two quickly rinsed his hands in a bucket of salt water and returned immediately to the shade of the sail. The older one remained standing in the bows, watching the yellow patch of the turtle's belly and pale tendrils of its flesh sink into the prisms of the Pacific. Before it had fully sunk, the grey shape of a shark moved up to meet it, and it was gone. This was the tenth turtle they had thrown over the side since the wind died. There was no market for rotten turtle meat and there had been nothing else to do but ditch them before they started to stink. The man in the bows owned the outrigger. He'd been catching turtles for most of his life and the doldrums had always been as unpredictable as the tropical storms they spawned.

He took a cigarette stub from behind his ear and lit it. It was his last and he savoured every careful drag as he urinated into the sea, the sound magnified by the eerie silence that surrounded them. He searched the horizon for signs of cloud. There were none. A school of ocean garfish patrolled the flat mirror of the surface not ten feet away. As he watched them shift with the current, following the plankton and minuscule shrimp, a ripple passed over the steel blue of their backs.

He squinted, not certain he had seen it. The slightest ruffling of the glassy surface. He was right. A patch no wider than a boat-length skittered towards them. A catspaw. Enough to tell him the wind was coming. He shouted to the boy to haul up the handlines and make sail. Lifting the bucket of seawater, he doused the turtles, grinning as the catspaw shifted this way and that, changing in shape and size, its intensity increasing as it skipped around them. The purchase block at the masthead squealed as the sail was raised, its patched belly suddenly filling and the sound they had waited for began: the movement of wood travelling over water.

The *S.S. Windsong* was two days out of French Indochina. The 5000-tonne vessel of the Deverill Cloud Line registered in Shanghai had crossed the Gulf of Tong King, passed through the narrow channel between Hainan and the Loochow peninsular into the South China Sea, headed for Victoria Harbour and the port of Hong Kong. It was almost midnight when the chief officer stood in the chart room peering closely at the barometer. The only light came from the swivel lamp over the chart table and after he had tapped the glass several times with his knuckle he switched on the main light to make sure his eyes were not deceiving him. They were not. The mercury was dropping fast towards the critical five mb that meant winds of typhoon strength were fast approaching.

He knew the pattern well. Somewhere in the southern latitudes of 7 to 15 degrees a tropical storm had started out as light airs and risen to variable winds. It had crossed the Pacific, gathering windspeed of ten to fifteen knots, and hit the southern tip of the Philippines around Mindanao. There it would have curved north on a course for Hong Kong at anything from twenty to forty-five knots. By the time it screamed into the South China Sea it could reach Force Eight gusts of 150 knots.

There had been radio warnings but there were always warnings between the north-east and south-east trade winds. Squalls were frequent in equatorial waters at this time of the year and most of the time a vessel could sail around them. This was different. The glass had dropped towards three mb and the typhoon was reported to be approaching on a 200-mile front. It was too late to turn back for the shelter of Hainan Island.

The *S.S. Windsong* could make twenty knots under full steam. If the wind speed dropped or remained steady there was a chance they could outrun it or manoeuvre away from the dangerous semi-circle within a hundred kilometres of its centre. If it gathered force, she was right in its path. The chief officer unhooked the speaking tube connected with the captain's cabin and blew hard into its copper mouthpiece.

In his Shanghai office, Ben Deverill stared at the cablegram his marine superintendent had sent over. He picked up the office phone and flipped a switch.

'How many ships do we have in the area?'

'*Windsong* and *Eastern Cloud*.' The answer came back fast. The superintendent was a Scot. Ben Deverill had bought him out of one of the biggest shipyards on the Tyne. Passage first class for him and his family, a house on fashionable Bubbling Well Road, the best schools for his kids, membership to the Shanghai Club and limited shares in the company. When the phone rang direct from Deverill's desk, Angus Cameron knew he'd better have the answers. He had checked with the Hong Kong observatory the moment the cable came through.

'Hong Kong says it looks like the biggest blow they've seen in many years. They've got eight balls up and reckon it'll be ten within the hour.'

'Keep me informed.' The click of disconnection ended the conversation.

Ben Deverill didn't need to look at his watch to know it was time to go to the club. It had become such a habit over the past few years that he was programmed to it. From the high windows of his penthouse suite in Broadway Mansions he could look down onto Soochow Creek on one side and the Woosung River from the other. He could tell from the colour of the sky and the nature of the river activity what time it was. He could also tell by the way he felt.

Doc Watson had never used the word alcoholic but he had said it didn't do to control your moods with over-proof rum or any other spirit. He'd been saying it for years along with warnings about the liver and the blood pressure and all the other problems that awaited a man in his forties who looked, acted and felt like a man of sixty.

When the Japanese had attacked Shanghai in 1937, Ben had played a prominent part in its defences and poured money into its rehabilitation. He had ordered some of his lorchas to be filled with stones and sunk to form a boom across the river at Matung to bar the invading Japanese gunboats. Nothing would ever shift him from the place he had made for himself in Shanghai except the sentence he had imposed upon himself.

Now, it was 1939. Japan and China had been waging full-scale war since the skirmish on the Marco Polo Bridge near Peking two years earlier. Severe inflation had hit Shanghai as the Chinese government, cut off from income in Japanese-occupied eastern China, began printing its own money, while the communist forces, fanning out from Yenan, had invaded most of the north. Infiltrating behind Japanese lines, they had skilfully organised the peasantry to build up the ranks of the party and the Red Army.

People were leaving Shanghai in their thousands, taking what they could of their business and belongings. For those who stayed there were still great fortunes to be made. Every hong that closed its doors meant more business for the Deverill Company and it had continued to prosper beyond even Ben's unlimited dreams. But now, the Imperial Army of Japan had taken Shanghai. They had done so with very little difficulty.

Taking his jacket from the hidden closet beside a display case of Han pottery, Ben Deverill slipped his arms into the cool comfort of its expensive silk lining and left his office. The bar of the Shanghai Club was said to be the longest in the Far East and it was where he spent his late afternoons and early evenings. Talking too much, he was well aware, of the early days, running the Hangchow Bore aboard the *Trinidad*, launching *China Cloud* and loading silk aboard *Cloud Chaser*. They were days that had gone forever and Ben found it was a fact that troubled him more than he had been prepared to admit. Recently he had stopped pretending.

When he went home to the big house on the Bund, although it was well staffed with servants and filled to capacity with books, art and treasures he had enjoyed collecting, it was empty. He had realised just how empty a week before when he had stepped out onto the balcony and raised the Zeiss binoculars. Across the water at Hongkew, Japanese marines were disembarking from the warships. Flat landing barges bristled with helmets and he could see the distinct flash of bayonet steel in the vivid sunlight. The *North China Morning Post* had been filled with protest for weeks, with the consuls of Britain, France and America sending urgent notes of appeal for restraint to Tokyo.

The Japanese would take Shanghai. Ben had been certain of it. Chinese resistance would have no chance against the attack that would come at any moment. Chiang's war was in the north. He would not defend Shanghai. Ben's guess had been right. Two days of skirmishing around the international settlements and the

Chinese quarter, had seen the 88th Division of the Chinese Army withdraw. A series of abortive air-raids by a badly commanded Chinese air force had failed to sink a single Japanese battleship. Instead it had scored direct hits on the Palace Hotel, Shanghai's finest, and the Wing On department store.

As Ben had lowered the glasses on that first day of Japanese activity he knew just how empty his home and his life had become. He had as much power and as much wealth as any man in Shanghai. When the Japanese came it would be only a matter of time and he would lose it all, just as Frenchy had done, and yet it didn't bother him at all. He had stayed for moments longer, gazing out over the brown waters, imagining again the towering masts of *Moshula*, taking in her canvas as the tug came out to meet her. Before he stepped back inside he had already decided what he would do. Sitting at his desk he took a sheet of stiff writing paper and reached for a pen.

Doctor Sun Wing-Cheu

AFTER HER first time with Toby, life for Siu Sing looked very different. She had been quite amazed by her sexual powers and the great happiness she gave him. His pleasure became her obsession and when they weren't together she would find herself planning their next time to see how she could make it different and even more erotic for him. The secrets of Ah Gum and her Court of a Thousand Pleasures were many and varied and the planning of each encounter aroused her intensely, so that by the time she saw his fair head approaching through the fields she would run to meet him, hardly able to wait to get him inside.

Passion like this was a new emotion for her and sometimes she was almost frightened by the grip of it—so strong that even when he was not there and she could only think of him it possessed and excited her so much that she explored her body with her own hands as though they were his. The wonders he aroused in her were a mystery. She had never known such feelings before.

Both Ah Gum and Jade had told her the ways to bring these sensations surging from their secret centres. 'This is the treasure of all treasures,' Ah Gum had advised Sing. 'How can you give the ultimate pleasure if you cannot receive it? Dynasties have been won and lost over this thunder and lightening and the mysteries it reveals,' she had said.

'Men consider it the greatest gift they have to give a woman. So you must learn to receive it or risk displeasure. It is the most sought-after of all possessions, the most elusive of all fantasies. Men will kill for it and women will die for it. Do not underestimate its power. Know it. Master it, control its force and you can influence the way of things.'

Sing had become adept at satisfying the senses that Ah Gum's instruction began to awaken. Sometimes it had filled the lonely space that often yawned within her. And in the arms of Jade it had brought not only pleasure but a warmth and companionship she had never known before. But these experiments were all forgotten, overwhelmed completely by the heights she reached with Toby—the hardness of him deep inside her, the discovery of his different responses building and shaping her desire. Released by wave after wave of all-consuming ecstasy, their pulses joined in the frenzy of their love-making. Her mouth clinging to his long after the joy of release.

When he was not with her she thrived on the simple life she seemed to be born for. Po Lok and Kam-Yang continued to treat her as an honoured guest while the sons and their wives and children kept to their own houses and went about their chores with a mild curiosity. When the large family came together and sat down to eat she was always invited. If they felt any of the disapproval she had come to expect, they did not show it.

Po Lok's nephew was a herbalist with a shop in Hong Kong's Causeway Bay. His name was Doctor Sun Wing-Cheu and he visited his uncle's farm regularly with his wife and three young sons. When he discovered that their guest Siu Sing had a knowledge of, and deep interest in, herbal medicine he came to the small house in the orange groves to visit her. They had become good friends and while Po Lok and Kam-Yang played with the children Sing would show him the scrolls of Master To and his many notebooks.

'There is very great knowledge and wisdom here,' he said, looking through the hand-bound volumes. 'You must guard them carefully. They are of great value.'

He had given Sing the address of his shop written on a slip of paper which she folded into one of the books.

'Visit me when you can. You will always be welcome in my home. There is much for us to talk about.'

Siu Sing's happiness was complete. She walked the countryside gathering flowers, finding the hidden places where mushrooms grew, picking fruit and working in the fields, reaping, threshing and storing rice, gathering fuel for the fires, fishing and swimming in the ponds. In the evenings she read the books Toby kept her supplied with. Under his patient schooling she had long finished with *Black Beauty* and delighted in the tales of Rupert Bear and Winnie the Poo. They made her long to see the English countryside so beautifully described and when she had finished *Wind in The Willows* she begged him to one day take her there. He held her close and promised that he would.

Each Wednesday she joined the children on the back of the ox cart and took the hour's journey into Taipo market. The village of Taipo was unique in all the territories of Hong Kong. Centred along the banks of Tolo harbour at the fork of the Lam Tsuen and Nullah rivers, it was the meeting place of two very different cultures, the Tanka boat people and the Hakka off the land. Here they joined to sell their wares in a colourful noisy crowding that delighted Siu Sing as thousands flocked from all over the colony to buy and sell, the flat-brimmed, curtained hats of the Hakka women mixing with the deep-brimmed, bellshaped hats of the boat people and the modern dress of the Hong Kong Cantonese.

For Siu Sing, her face partially hidden by the pleated valance and dressed as any other farm-girl, it was the closest she had ever come to belonging. She joined the crowds to watch the jugglers and the knife sharpeners, the puppeteers and the acrobats, the noises and colours of Chinese opera that reminded her of Yuenchow. Since she had first come to Taipo the crowds had swelled with refugees who had fled the Japanese troops now occupying Canton. Every day for months men, women and children had sailed into Tolo harbour in junks and sampans, aboard plankboats and bamboo rafts of every shape and size. Some had even swum from the mainland, or paddled their way clinging to inflated goatskins; thousands found their way across the border and many had died on the way.

They had no money and no food so they begged by the roadsides or stole from desperation. Sing wondered what terrors they had left behind if to die of starvation and sickness was preferable.

In parts of Hong Kong they were dying in the streets, people said. Cholera had broken out among them so that those few who would have shown pity could not go near them. The rat bins that were fixed to every lamp-post were overflowing, festering heaps of dead rats piling beneath them too rapidly to be taken away. The rat carts were kept too busy patrolling the back alleys and narrow ladder streets collecting human corpses. In an effort to house the refugees, the Hong Kong government had laid on a string of disused box cars on a railway siding beside the Tolo highway that ran parallel with the harbour. There they housed and fed thousands of refugees but were forced to turn as many away each week.

Along with other defence forces garrisoned in Hong Kong, the 8th Rajputs were detailed to patrol the border at Sha Tau Kok to turn back the tide of men, women and children, while police gunboats could do nothing but hail the flotillas of craft and warn them to turn back. None of it made any difference. They kept coming and nothing but bullets could have stopped them.

On the day the storm came Siu Sing was on the hillside above the rice paddies that terraced the lower slopes, cutting the tall, head-high grass for fuel. All around her on other hillsides she could see the stooping, black-clad figures of Hakka women doing the same, or on their way down with the huge bundles heaped high on their backs. The long, broad-bladed grass that covered the hills was the main fuel for cooking-stoves and the pall of its smoke hung in the air.

It was a fragrant smell, taking her back to Tung T'ing and the smoke from the fires of the rush-cutters. She looked back over the valley to the cluster of simple square houses of Po Lok and his family. Below her on the terraces one of his sons urged the muddy back of a buffalo through the flooded paddy, another sat watching the large flock of ducks dabbling along the muddy furrows.

A sudden gust of wind almost snatched away her hat, flattening the grass around her. It was welcome, as the day had begun still and oppressively humid. Po Lok had warned her that a storm was coming. She should not go far up the hillside and must return quickly if the weather changed. He didn't know that on the island of Hong Kong, a few short miles away, the observatory had hoisted ten black balls on its signal mast and that the storm shutters throughout the colony had been closed and fastened for hours. Or that all traffic had left the roads and junks and sampans were headed in from sea to take refuge in the typhoon shelters of Causeway Bay, Yau Ma Tei and Taipo village. He only needed to look at the sulphurous hue of the sky, to feel the unshifting heat and motionless air, the restlessness of his pigs and dogs to see the trees soundless and yet filled with birds.

Again the gusts came, stronger and bending the grass flat over wider areas, rippling over the hill in sudden blasts heavy with the chill of rain. Before she could shoulder the bundle of grass and begin her descent, the first deluge arrived, fat warm drops that thudded on the brim of her hat and smacked down on her shoulders. She had taken no more than a dozen steps before it was slicing horizontally across the slopes in icy blades that lanced through her clothes as though she was naked. Sing had seen such storms sweep across T'ung T'ing Lake and roar through the bamboo groves. But she could remember nothing that felt like this.

From where she stood she could see the junk village at Taipo in the distance. The grey expanse of Tolo harbour stretching to the sky, was lost in a blanket of rain driven before black storm clouds that reared like a mountain range overhead. Leaving the bundle of grass on the path, she waded into the thickest growth on hands and knees, burrowing into the protection of its densely packed root system and making a hollow for herself, crouching as low as she could. The grass where Sing dug herself a refuge was almost two metres high. Tiger grass, the locals called it. Once when tigers roamed these hills it had been their hiding place.

She wormed herself further into the dense jungle of stalks as winds slammed a hail of frozen sleet into the exposed side of the hill where she lay, lashing the grass flat. She entwined her hands and feet into its mesh of roots and clung to the earth. The noise was a ceaseless cannonade overhead. Bending before the gale, the grass formed a thick thatch, deflecting the wind before it could penetrate, absorbing the onslaught of the hail and protecting her from the full impact of the drenching rains that followed. For the moment Siu Sing was safe.

It took perhaps fifteen minutes for the rains to swamp the hillside, penetrating the tiger grass from above and beginning its steep downward run. First there was a trickle which quickly became a steady stream and then a gushing torrent. It found its way from the higher slopes through the tangled root system in a flash flood that rolled over Sing, threatening to dislodge her. When the first driving thrust of muddy water had passed over her she found that by raising her head she could keep it above the rivulets that flowed around her.

For an hour she clung on as though she too were rooted to the ground. Slowly the growth began to loosen beneath her, undermined by the runnels that scoured their way through it. The earth that she clung to for safety began to slide. The harder she held to the grass the more it weakened and threatened to come away in her hands. She tried to pull herself further into its protection but the cascade of water, mud and stones became stronger each minute.

Sing lost all concept of time. Chilled to the marrow by the constant icy deluge, she fought against the downward rush. As one handhold began to come away she grabbed another and another, slowly dragged from her hiding place by the gathering force of the mudslide that was steadily undermining the hill. Stones became larger and more frequent, splashing and slithering past her, as high, stony ground above the grass line began to crumble and shift with the downrush of yellow mud. Boulders began to come free—first the smaller ones, rolling and bouncing ahead of the landslide, striking others and somersaulting high and wide to join the avalanche as the hillside began its rapid collapse. Trees that had stood for a hundred years were torn from the peaks and flung into the valley. She saw them whirled into the thunder-black sky. As the wind roared in her ears, the earth moved and she was dragged downwards into the flooded valley.

When Siu Sing's eyelids fluttered open she was aware only of the cold. Her bones felt fleshless, exposed without protection. She could hear and see nothing. Only when she tried to raise her head did she realise that her ears had been submerged in a thick bed of silt. She tried to lift herself higher. A bolt of pain caused her to fall back with a cry, the shock so violent that she sank into the velvety mud willingly, allowing it to close again over her ears. Its freezing grip slowly replaced the searing pain as her swollen eyes strove to pierce the shadows.

The intensity of the shock caused sour vomit to fill her throat and flood her mouth, to bubble from her lips and over her chin as she expelled it. A leaden light penetrated the dark, enough to show that she was in a tomb. Grey, stone walls closed around her, weeping with moisture, the shadowy vault of the ceiling pressing down. Her attempt to rise had seared every nerve in her body, cramping her gut and loosening her bowels. It had set up a jangling inside her head that left vivid points of light dancing before her eyes.

She closed them and the bedlam in her head subsided, the spots of light began to drift away. She opened them again. A tomb. Had she been buried alive? Slowly the dots of light faded completely and in their place appeared the dim masks of faces, hideously set, eyes blazing, mouths wide with unheard threats. Siu Sing was sure she was dead. That this was her tomb and these were the demons sent to torment her. Above them, almost lost in the darkness, the colours of her rich headdress melted in shadow, the serene features of Kuan Yin, the goddess of mercy, looked down as she slipped again into unconsciousness.

Stonecutter's Island

TOBY HAD hardly slept in the twenty-four hours since the worst typhoon in Hong Kong's history had struck. He could see the roofs of the houses in the Residence of Eternal Peace from the stern of the navy cutter as he stood at the tiller. Scores of such ships' lifeboats had been supplied by the navy to search for survivors and he had commandeered one the moment he had come off-duty.

The steady chug of its diesel engine glided the boat through scenes of devastation that filled him with fear for Sing's safety. Everywhere the bodies of Hakka and Tanka peasants floated, their swollen corpses splitting the black garb to show yellowed, pulpy flesh. Some rose to the surface as the bow wave of the boat stirred the stillness of the brown waters, to swirl grotesquely and sink again when it had passed. Where the floods had begun to subside the high ground was strewn with the dead and the wailing of those who searched among them carried over the water.

The huge, grey raft of a drowned buffalo slid past, black with crows working away at its softened hide. Everywhere goats floated, blown up like round, hairy buoys; the soggy feathered clots of drowned chickens and the stark white balloons of pigs littered the water as far as he could see. The humidity that had preceded the typhoon had settled again with its passing: a dense, steamy heat that the blue sky, still patched with high remnants of cloud, did nothing to lift. It seemed to sit upon the desolation, a crushing, immovable weight, drawing a vapour of steam and creating great clouds of insects.

Toby had opened the throttle wide to cut through it but the best the heavy timber craft could do was a clumsy six knots, hardly stirring the air. Toby steadied the tiller with his knee and raised the field glasses slung around his neck. There was no sign of life on the flat roofs or in any of the trees that showed above the floodwaters. The trees, he saw through the glasses, were still filled with birds of every kind, among them the carcasses of animals caught up in the branches. In places, the unmistakable black rags of human bodies hung lifeless. The wave must have passed over the houses in its course up the valley, then quickly subsided.

He searched the floating debris of planks and lengths of broken fence. Even complete wooden outhouses drifted by and waterlogged bales of cattle fodder had formed islands for ducks and small farm animals. There was no sign or sound of survivors. The farm of Po Lok was several miles from Taipo village, where the tidal wave had rolled up the channel and followed the course of the Lam Tsuen River as far as the village of Tai Wo before it had spent its full force.

The devastation of Taipo had given Toby some idea of the storm's immensity. Hundreds of junks, sampans and vessels of every type and size had washed up as far as a couple of kilometres inland. He had seen a fishing junk high on a hill. More than 10,000 people had been reported drowned. Tolo harbour was strewn with wrecks, among them the freighter *Windsong*.

He hoped the wave would not have reached the Residence of Eternal Peace, at least not its main force, telling himself every inch of the way that he would find them waving from the flat roof of the main house, that Sing would be safely among them. He fought back the pain of despair as he scanned the deserted buildings, the silent trees still half submerged. The floodwaters had continued for another kilometre into the valley, breaking over the rice terraces before they were stopped by surrounding hills. Circling the farmhouse and the little house by the stream, he called out many times but no one answered. He swept the devastated hillsides with the powerful field glasses, hoping for a sign. They could have made for higher ground.

He leaned on the tiller and the cutter went into a wide arc, its bows headed towards the nearest dry ground.

He searched the lower slopes for an hour, calling her name, picking his way over the tides of drying mud and shale. The whole side of the valley seemed to have shifted. The clump of trees that had sheltered the shrine of Kuan Yin had disappeared, leaving only broken ground, jagged stumps and exposed roots. It was his last hope. That she might have somehow reached the high ground safely and found shelter there.

Sing was lying half submerged in the bed of silt that covered the temple floor, trapped by the courtyard walls. In the first terrible moment of finding her, he thought she must be dead. There was no sign of blood, but the mud had claimed her body like a grave, settling around her until only her face and hands showed above its smooth surface. When he found a pulse and lifted her carefully from the ooze, relief overwhelmed him. Talking softly to her unconscious weight he carried her down to the boat, his heart thudding painfully with the thought of losing her.

The military hospital on the Peak was shrouded in mist when Toby pulled up outside its emergency entrance. It swirled in eddies around him as he carried Siu Sing up its wide, tiled steps. The male orderly came from behind the reception desk, quickly producing a wooden-backed wheelchair from a number lined against the wall. When he saw that it was a woman in the mud-caked tunic and trousers of a Chinese peasant he halted abruptly.

'It's a woman, sir,' he said, stopping the chair where it stood. 'A Chinese woman. We can't admit a Chinese civilian, sir.'

Toby ignored his protest, pushing past him through the door with Emergency painted on its panel of clouded glass.

'She is not Chinese. Get me the matron,' he snapped, laying Sing gently onto the examination bench.

'But, sir.' The orderly stuttered.

'The matron. Now.' Toby's bark sent him hurrying away.

The Civil and Military Hospital on the Peak was for British and Europeans only. Sing had been admitted under an English name, a name Toby had remembered as he steered the boat through the devastation of Taipo to the landing barges that had been set up as Red Cross field hospitals. He remembered the name written on the back of the photograph . . . Deverill, and the translation of her Chinese name, Little Star. He registered her as Star Deverill.

Colonel Pelham had been against the deception, assuring Toby that she would be properly cared for in any of the Chinese hospitals that were taking in casualties. But Toby had seen the overcrowding of the wards and corridors and although they were doing all they could he had also seen the aftermath of such disasters before. It reminded him of the perennial floods on the plains of India and the hit or miss emergency first aid treatment that follows any civil defence crisis in Asia.

Margaret Pelham, the commanding officer's wife, was on the Red Cross Committee and well acquainted with members of the hospital board. She had also been married to Justin for nearly thirty years and knew that on questions of protocol he was firmly guided by the KRR—King's Rules and Regulations, the outdated bible of British military dogma that covered everything from the precise way the uniform should be worn on and off duty, to the manner in which soldiers of every rank must conduct themselves under every conceivable circumstance in peace and war.

She had never seen Captain Hyde-Wilkins, the delightful young man whom she liked immensely, so dreadfully upset. Nor had she seen a more appealing creature than the deathly pale girl on the stretcher carried by two Rajput medical orderlies. She only had to look at Toby's face, the anxiety in his eyes as he looked down at the girl, to know that he loved her deeply.

Sing remained under intensive care for eight days. She had suffered a fractured collarbone, a broken leg and head injuries. When she was transferred to the ward, Toby was waiting outside. The nurse who was taking her pulse when he came in looked up as though he were an unwelcome intruder.

'How is she?' he asked quietly.

The nurse had an Irish brogue to her voice. 'She keeps asking something about the sunrise,' she answered briskly. 'It'll be a while before she gets over that bump on her head.'

When she left the room, the starch of her uniform crackling like frost on winter grass and taking the smell of carbolic with her, Toby leaned over and kissed Sing's cheek.

Her eyelids flickered open and she tried to speak, closing them again with the effort. Toby's hand found hers and pressed it gently. 'Don't worry. Don't worry about anything. *The Second Sunrise* is safe. All your books are safe. Don't speak.'

The floodwaters had receded almost completely when he left the truck on the muddy track outside the farm the following day. The plank across the ditch had gone and some of the fields were still under water. Taking his driver with him, he started across what was left of the farm of Po Lok and Kam-Yang. The stench of decomposing animals mingled with the rank smell of drying mud and rotting vegetation. Huge, bluebottle flies swarmed everywhere. The ginger field had disappeared completely under a sea of mud and as he approached the cluster of houses there was still no sign of life. They were empty; a thick layer of mud and sand covering the floors. He was thankful to find there were no bodies in any of the rooms.

Upstairs, where Sing had slept, he salvaged the camphorwood chest, still fastened and undamaged in the litter of broken furniture. Sliding the brass pin from the lock he found its contents only slightly affected by what water had seeped under its tight-closed lid. He supposed it must have been lifted by the rising floods, floating until they had subsided. The scrolls and papers and hand-bound books in the deerhide bag were unharmed. The Rajput driver hoisted the chest onto his shoulder and followed Toby across the wasteland that had so recently been the Residence of Eternal Peace.

Toby returned to the hospital and stayed by Sing's bedside whenever he was allowed. Even the frosty nurse thawed towards him.

'You'd be Toby, I suppose,' she said, with the best she could do for a smile. He nodded.

'You'd think it'd be the only name she knows in the whole world.'

'Perhaps it is,' Toby said quietly.

Margaret Pelham had also been a regular visitor and the bedside table was crammed with fruit and flowers. Colonel Pelham had granted Toby the leave he had requested—he was entitled to it and as he had seldom taken leave in the past, it had accrued to several weeks. The colonel was well aware that he intended to spend it doing what he could to help the Eurasian girl's recovery and although it sounded a warning as clearly as a bugle call, there wasn't much he could do about it. Nor was there much that he could do when his wife informed him that the girl appeared to have nowhere to go and would be staying with her in the married quarters' bungalow on Stonecutter's Island until she was fully recovered.

Margaret 'Peggy' Pelham was an energetic woman who made herself as active in the social and charity affairs of Hong Kong as she possibly could. As the wife of the senior resident commanding officer she was first lady of the isolated military establishment of Stonecutter's Island. She had lived as an army wife wherever her husband had been posted—the Middle East, Africa or India. It made little difference to her where the regiment was stationed. It meant an existence mostly outside the normal expectations of married life and in the company of women.

It was her job to help maintain morale in the little community and to encourage as much public-spirited activity as possible among the wives of other officers and sometimes the wives and affairs of Other Ranks. She was sensibly religious, having had plenty of time for prayer when the regiment was engaged on operations, and an excellent hostess when it was not. Her only daughter had been sent back to England and boarding school when the time had come and she had learned to fill her life in such a way that left little room for loneliness or pondering the future. Peggy Pelham was ever cheerful, ever helpful and always ready to give of her best. What the Rajput soldiers thought of as a 'pukka burra memsahib'.

There was something about the Eurasian girl that seemed rather special. Peggy Pelham was all too aware of the half-caste children the British Empire was solely responsible for. Even the tightest restrictions could not reduce the numbers of fatherless babies left behind when a regiment moved on. She had seen too often the beautiful sad-eyed Anglo-Indian girls left with little alternative but to sell themselves in the slums of Bombay, Delhi and Calcutta. The girl who had obviously won Captain Hyde-Wilkins' heart certainly had British blood somewhere in her background and Peggy made up her mind to help her.

Her Red Cross commitments had kept her involved with the emergency feeding, clothing and housing of the thousands left homeless throughout the New Territories by Typhoon Mary. Now that government bodies had taken over entirely and the business of rehabilitation was well underway, she welcomed this calm and mysterious girl into her home.

Stonecutter's Island was a tiny bastion of Englishness in the hustling Chinese mass of Hong Kong. It had been ceded to the British in 1860 along with the Kowloon peninsular. No more than a few acres in any direction, it had been first inhabited by a few primitive stonecutters and impoverished fishermen. Lying about a kilometre from Kowloon, opposite the densely populated district of Mon Kok, it faced the western approaches of the harbour and over the years had seen a number of gun batteries and fortifications built to defend Hong Kong's approaches. The first powder magazine for the China Fleet had been tunnelled into its rock in 1870.

The granite quarry that gave the island its name had been used to build a prison in 1866. Later it became an isolation hospital for smallpox victims and remained an eerie reminder of the tiny island's past, one of its corner towers becoming an army chapel. Apart from this grim building, Stonecutter's had become a sanctuary of verdant woods, loud with birds. Overlooked by a high hill someone had named Wuthering Heights, winding roads and laneways led to solid old colonial bungalows, some with tennis courts, and a clubhouse with a swimming pool. Here was an élite community that was entirely cut off from the rest of Hong Kong except by authorised wallah wallahs—water taxis that operated day and night, or the official Stonecutter's ferry. Its two jetties were closely guarded around the clock by a platoon of Sikh policemen.

The Pelhams' bungalow was large and spacious, built before the turn of the century by someone who had wanted to bring something of rural England into the midst of a strange and unwelcoming place. Its rambling garden was bordered by a picket fence and a huge English oak overshadowed the five-bar gate at its entrance. In spring bluebells, crocuses, daffodils and other English wildflowers grew in profusion from bulbs planted by a succession of homesick army wives. It was the perfect place for Sing's recovery. Peggy Pelham tended her like a nurse and mother, delighting in every moment of her company.

She was surprised and pleased at the speed of the girl's improvement, even though she had refused the attentions of the regimental Medical Officer. Even with an arm and leg in plaster she seemed almost oblivious to pain and discomfort, her colour returning steadily, her eyes clear and possessed of a calm that made it a pleasure to enter her room. The bed had been moved to a window looking out onto the back lawn with its makeshift tennis court and high bank of rhododendrons. At first, the girl did not smile or talk much but listened intently when Peggy could take the time to read to her or tell her stories of India and the place she called home—the English town of Exeter in the beautiful county of Devonshire.

Sing had been asleep when Toby brought the trunk containing her treasured books and papers, but later, on seeing it safely stowed in a corner, her relief and excitement was intense. Toby had been forced to give Colonel Pelham a full account of his involvement with the Eurasian girl and while the C.O. could not approve of his conduct officially he had been secretly pleased at the pleasure his wife seemed to find in the girl's company. It had also become very clear to him that Toby was entirely smitten and having seen this sort of thing before, he could only hope it would run its course and come to a sensible and inevitable conclusion. Toby Hyde-Wilkins' military career was far too promising to be jeopardised by a passing liaison with a nameless girl.

In return for his cooperation in the matter, Justin Pelham had requested that Toby stay away from Stonecutter's until the weekends, when they would both return together. This had worked well and the six weeks of convalescence had gone by quickly and without complication. Peggy had unpacked the books from the trunk and on seeing the titles Toby had found for her, added to Sing's fascination for England by reading to her from the works of H.E. Bates.

Sing's rapt concentration on his *In Search of England* and her enjoyment of the Larkin family in *The Darling Buds of May* gave Peggy a private warmth that she had not known since being left without her daughter. She was further delighted on returning one day to find Sing bent over a page of exquisite Chinese characters, her brush seeming to create each perfect stroke as if guided by some unseen hand. When Sing offered to teach her the skill of calligraphy, Peggy was enchanted by the idea, and this became a practice between them whenever there was time.

To Sing, the time spent at the bungalow was a wonderful transition from the Residence of Eternal Peace. Each long, uneventful day when she was left to herself was spent in the airy old house with the wonderful smell of fresh-cut grass and the comforting whir and clatter of the gardener's mower as he pushed it over the lawn. The servants were well-trained and having been told that the house-guest was a member of the family, treated her with guarded tolerance. When Peggy arrived back from her social rounds there was always some small, thoughtful gift of a piece of fresh fruit or pastry or the quite wonderful thing she called chocolate. Peggy Pelham's cheerful kindness enclosed Sing in a cocoon of safety and gentleness that filled her with content.

She counted the days until each Saturday when in the late afternoon Justin Pelham and Toby came through the gate in their civilian clothes. Toby was invited to stay overnight and after dinner they would play cards or listen to the radio or visit the club to watch a movie. There was little chance to be alone until Sunday when Toby would take her for a walk around the narrow road that skirted the little island. Justin Pelham had not the slightest doubt that Toby would be into bed with the girl in a flash given the chance, but he had decided it would not be under his roof.

When he discussed the matter with his wife she merely sighed, reminding him that he had been in love once himself, and suggested that if he couldn't remember what it meant to be romantic he should at least be a little more tolerant and a little less vigilant. To which Justin replied haughtily that he .was surprised at her and that in spite of the girl's womanly appearance, it was highly likely that she was not yet sixteen.

On Sunday mornings they would attend services at St Barbara's Church, the quaint little chapel in the tower of the old prison hospital, return to the house for breakfast in the garden and some tennis lessons before lunch at the club and a swim in the afternoon. Anxious not to offend their host, Toby played along contentedly until around four o'clock when he would suggest taking Sing for a short walk to exercise her mended leg.

As the leg improved they were able to venture further and the walks became longer and longer. Toby showed her the old gun emplacements and the artillery batteries installed during the First World War. Through the labyrinth of passages, shell hoists, ammunition stores and magazines they came out to a small, rock-shaded arbour surrounding a single tree. It was a very old spruce-fir; the undisturbed carpet of dried needles and litter of cones beneath its protecting branches showed that no one came there. It became the secret, fragrant place where they could make love, unobserved and uninhibited.

The Last Cloud

INDIE DA Silva was aloft in a bosun's chair when Ben came through the fruit trees of Angel's Garden and towards the old bamboo jetty behind the Flying Angel Mission. Ben paused for a few moments before hailing him, seating himself on the old bench he and Aggie had sat upon over a quarter of a century earlier. Nothing much had changed.

The Dry-Dock was still crammed with out-of-work sailors, the tea urns and porridge pots still steamed and bubbled twenty-four hours a day and Aggie still cast off in search of souls to salvage each new day. The deep-sea skippers still called her Tugboat and everyone who crossed her bows had learned that it was good sense not to mention the question of age.

To even hint that Aggie's golden years were perhaps behind her and that twilight might be closing in, was enough to rock any boat she happened to be climbing aboard. There was no way of knowing how far into her seventies she was. If energy was anything to go by she could still stoke up a full head of steam and leave any tattooed bosun with a bowed head.

If her voice was no longer the loudest when she led the morning hymn she didn't know it, and her good eye still swept her motley congregation for signs of sacrilege. Her only concessions to the passing of the years were the spectacles she wore, a set of large, badly fitted false teeth and a stout blackbean cane which she carried more like a weapon than a walking stick.

Since 1937 there had been no more Cloud Class sailing vessels built and the Deverill boatyard in Macau had been closed down. Only the beautiful *Cloud Chaser* remained to remind them of the beginnings. Indie had lived aboard it since Ben had left for Shanghai. Staying in a house, he said, had softened him and he couldn't sleep without the sound and the shift of water beneath him. He had sailed her to Shanghai and there had been no better place for her to lay up than alongside Aggie Gates' Dry-Dock.

Ben had signed over the ship's papers to him and although his shares in the Deverill Cloud Line and all its trading companies had made him a very rich man, all Indie needed was the sun on the deck, wind in the rigging and the smell of tarred hemp. *Cloud Chaser* was all of these things to him and he spent his time keeping her in seaworthy condition, confident that the time for her to cast off her moorings would come again.

Ben watched his old friend hanging sixty feet above the water, realising that the day had almost come. Like Aggie, he guessed Indie must also be well into his seventies, but he was agile enough to climb *Cloud Chaser's* masts and hang over her side with a scraper and a paint brush, with only the cook to shout at. A pot of whitelead and tallow swung from the bosun's chair and covered Indie's arms to the elbows as he swabbed down the shrouds.

Ben could hear him singing to himself some forgotten shanty from a time long gone. More a recitation than a song, as though he was talking to himself, which he often did these days. *Cloud Chaser* was all Indie da Silva lived for and all he cared about apart from the sing song girls who sometimes sneaked aboard to keep him young.

Every inch of the boat's timbers was kept as sound as the day she had been launched. Her black hull still gleamed like ebony, gunports and the curlicued cloud of her figurehead were picked out in white. Deck planks were scoured bare and spotless, with every rope, line and halyard coiled and stowed. When Ah Poo, the cook, wasn't busy in the galley he was polishing brasswork or putting a shine to the varnished handrails. *Cloud Chaser* looked as fine and proud as any China Trade clipper that ever sailed up the Whangpoo.

This was December 1941, and it had only taken Ben a moment to make up his mind what to do when Shanghai was swept by the certainty that the Japanese would declare war on Britain and America at any moment. The choices were simple. They could get out with the rest as the International Settlements evacuated; leave everything just as Frenchy had done thirty years ago. They could stay and fight, to die on the end of a Jap bayonet or rot in some rat-infested camp. Or, there was one other choice.

For four years now, ever since the battle of Matung when they had blockaded the river with the scuttled lorcha fleet, Deverill coastal packets had been running guns to the Kuomintang. Thanks to Tinkerbell, the godown on Soochow Creek held an arsenal waiting to be smuggled to Chiang's armies still fighting in the south-west. Well hidden among crates of fine porcelain and Taiping carpets, antiques and priceless artifacts, there were enough automatic weapons, grenades and ammunition to arm 1000 men.

The thought of handing all this over to the Japanese along with his ships and everything else he had built was about as hard for Ben Deverill to swallow as boarding one of the British ships loading evacuees off the Bund, or jumping a plane for Singapore. He hadn't the slightest doubt that Indie da Silva would leap at his plan.

The old Macanese had already stated loudly to anyone that would listen that no one would shift him off *Cloud Chaser* alive, least of all some poxy Jap soldier. He regularly stripped, cleaned and oiled the Lewis and Maxim machine guns to make his point.

A loaded sampan puttered by close to the jetty; its wake rocked *Cloud Chaser* and swung Indie wide of the mast. Ben grinned at the curses hurled from the masthead upon the head of the old woman at the tiller. For just a second it reminded him again of the *Moshula* and his climb to the masthead.

The sights and sounds and smells of the busy, brown river closed around him as strongly as they had on that first day when he had stepped ashore still bruised from the Scotsman's knuckles. His love of this vast and impossible country, the place he had made for himself in it, was all that mattered to him. Nothing could take away all that it had meant for almost thirty years and nothing would ever replace it.

He thought again of the child somewhere that could be his. A young man or woman of sixteen by now, if it had lived. Ben had tried to stop wondering what might have happened. What chance a new-born infant, swallowed up by the immensity of China in the hands of a frail and demented old woman might have of survival. Especially one of mixed blood. He could only pray it had not been a female.

The will he had made held the house at Repulse Bay and his personal fortune in trust for thirty years. His Hong Kong lawyers, Pidcock and Pidcock, had instructions to investigate any reasonable claim to his estate and to honour any right of inheritance that could be judged as genuine. If no heir or heiress came forward in the specified time, Villa Formosa was to be sold and the money turned over to the Welfare League for Eurasian Homeless, along with all of the Deverill assets. When he had made that will and sent it in the despatch bag to Hong Kong two years earlier he had known this day would come and that all would be taken care of in the event of his death. It was a thought that left him with a degree of contentment.

As he sat there on the edge of the Whangpoo, the timeless magic of China all around him, Ben understood how much Frenchy had left behind to give his son a chance to live. He wondered if he would have done the same for his own child and knew that he would. A son or daughter was a reason to go on, even if you were left with nothing else as Frenchy had been. His reverie was broken as the harmonium started up in Aggie's Dry-Dock and her unmistakable voice blended with its wheezing notes, the deeper voices of the men catching up.

'Oh God our help in ages past. Our hope for years to come.'
He stood up and cupped his hands to his mouth. 'Ahoy, aloft.

Come down. We've got things to talk about, you and I.'

The following night as *Cloud Chaser* sailed on her jib in the light airs of evening she was just another masthead gliding through the mass of moored river craft on Soochow Creek. The godowns were mainly in darkness. Here and there one flooded light across the wharf to the water, its wooden doors and steel grids raised as coolies worked to unload cargoes arriving on the late tide. Oil lamps and pitch flares shone a moving light on the green-brown surface from the ports and windows of river craft tied up and anchored in the stream.

Cloud Chaser's masthead light was extinguished. To show it would have drawn attention to her size through the height of her mainmast. The Japanese were used to the constant movement of river junks, barges and sampans up and down river without lights but a sailing vessel of *Cloud Chaser's* size and class would soon draw attention.

Ben knew exactly where the Japanese maritime check-points and weigh-stations were posted and at this time of night there was little activity and even less surveillance. It was just before three a.m. when Indie jumped ashore with a bow line, his bare feet making hardly a sound as he landed on the wharf, to make the schooner fast to granite bollards.

Leaving the men below, Ben and Tinker came ashore under cover of stacked jute bales. A single guard loitered outside the Deverill godown, his rifle slung across his back in marching order. He seemed to be reading a newspaper by the poor light of a lamp pole.

'Duty picket,' breathed Tinker. 'And a slack one by the look of him.' He answered Ben's enquiring look with a nod towards the Japanese soldier.

'There's more like him all along the creek, so we mustn't make a sound.' He grinned from the deep shadow of the bales, laying a hand lightly on Ben's shoulder. 'It'll take him all of three seconds to unsling that rifle. About three times longer than you'll need.'

The distance from the cover of the bales to the guard was ten metres of open space. At Tinker's order they had taken off their shoes. The feel of the wooden quay under his bare soles, still warm from the heat of the day, was exciting to Ben. He felt light and fast, moving silently along the wall of hessian to cross the distance well away from the guard and come up behind him. The adrenalin surged as he sprinted the distance, silent as a shadow.

He smelt the acrid smoke of cheap tobacco as his right hand flashed out, fingers bent in what Tinker called the Devil's Claw.

His thumb hooked under the man's chin, the base of his fingers striking beneath the nasal bone. The ring and index fingers drove into the Japanese soldier's eyes, locking the jaw shut and forcing his head back. Ben's left hand came up with a sideways clawing strike to the adam's apple. He felt his thumb break the cricoid cartilage. Lowering the man to the quay, his palm smothered the sounds of suffocation as he waved Tinker forward.

At a quiet word from Ben a dozen men emerged from the hatchway midships and followed Indie into the godown. They left the shutters down and showed no light, bringing out the wooden boxes marked 'Chinaware' through a side door and loading them into *Cloud Chaser's* open hold. A half hour of hard silent work saw the last crate stowed and the hatch closed as the first cock crowed somewhere along the crowded river. Within minutes another and then another had joined it. The first dogs barked and children began calling to each other across the water.

They cast off as quietly as they had tied up, voices of the boat people on all sides as they slipped out into the current and headed back to the Whangpoo. By the time they had left Soochow Creek astern and were heading out into the North Channel, day was breaking in its usual riot of colour. River traffic was already busy with the sudden awakening of Shanghai; boats and lighters loaded down with goods and people headed for the ships anchored off the west bank. The declaration of war was still not official and the Japanese made no attempt to stop them. That night they had closed the airport and at any moment the gunboats on the east bank around Pudong would blockade the river.

It was not necessary to really know when this would happen. It had been the only topic of conversation, the purpose of talking for so many days now, that it was in the air they breathed. 'Getting out' was the only thing left. The employees of the great hongs, like Dents, Butterfield & Swire, Jardines and the powerful Sassoons, were clamouring for places aboard anything that could float them out of Shanghai. They cursed the taipans who had held on till the last moment, so sure that it would not come to this.

The imperial army did not want the burden of Shanghai, they had said over their drinks in the elegant clubs. The city would be safe. Left alone to do its business just as it always had. Right into the first week of December meetings had been held at the Jockey Club with the tail-coated diplomats from Tokyo. They were still bowing their assurances as the news came through on the seventh that Japan had sunk the American fleet at Pearl Harbour and was at war with Britain and the United States. The brutality and the slaughter had begun.

Indie had fitted a new AWA radio aboard *Cloud Chaser* and they heard the official declaration just as they were off Pudong. The announcement said that all British and American citizens were now prisoners of war. It instructed each person to pack one suitcase and listed the assembly points throughout the city centre where they were to await transport to the internment camps. It warned the Chinese people that any assistance given to those foreigners still trying to escape would bring the instant punishment of public execution.

Through the glasses Ben could see the activity on the quays of the east bank. The breweries, sugar refineries and factories had been under Japanese control for two years now and they had used the shipyards and dry-dock as a naval base. He could see the crews making ready aboard the fleet of gunboats, moored in a line outside the torpedo sheds.

'We're too late, my old friend,' Ben said quietly as he trained the glasses ahead to where the giant battleship *Idzuma* squatted with its attendant destroyers.

'They're making ready to blockade the channel. They'll never let a ship like this through.'

Indie was softly singing one of his Portuguese shanties as he levered the top from a case of ammunition. His brown hand tore away the oiled paper, revealing the brass and steel of heavy calibre bullets laid out bright as newly minted bullion.

'Then we'll just have to go right through them,' Indie said, straightening up with a wide grin. 'Just like in the old days, eh, Mr Deverill?'

Suddenly his arms were around Ben and they hugged, laughing like boys.

In the crew's quarters, the captain's cabin and the stateroom, beachies from Aggie's Dry-Dock filled every foot of space below decks. Ben had not bothered to count heads. Once he had Indie's approval of the plan he had burst into the mission to ask for volunteers. The hymns were not quite over and Aggie's good eye had drilled him to the spot until the last amen had died away. He had offered any able-bodied seaman who could fire a weapon and had the stomach for a fight the chance of escape. Half the men dropped their hymn books and forgot about their porridge to line up for Indie's inspection.

There must have been thirty men willing to take the risk and they had wasted no time grabbing their handful of belongings and getting aboard. Aggie Gates had refused to join them and nothing Ben or Indie could do had changed her mind. Her place was with those left behind, she had insisted. The boxers, plague, pestilence and Lucifer himself hadn't driven her out and the Japs could do their damnedest.

When one brave stoker had suggested carrying her aboard, the look she gave them caused a shuffle backwards. Instead she had made them bow their heads while she offered the seaman's prayer and told them to take all the stores they could carry from the pantry. The last they had seen of her, she was seated on the rickety bench beside the vegetable plot at the foot of Angel's Garden waving her stick.

Three top seamen had been called on deck to man *Cloud Chaser's* braces, the rest stayed below to familiarise themselves with the Russian-made light machine guns, British Lee Enfield rifles and American carbines. There was not much talk as bayonets were fixed, pockets filled with ammunition and belts of it slung over their shoulders. They were under the supervision of one man. Tinker the mercenary, the man who had fought with Two Gun Cohen, had closed the door of his gym and followed Ah Poo the cook as soon as he had read Ben's note.

The covers had been taken off the two Maxims mounted on either side just below the wheelhouse. Tinker's eyes shone with pleasure as he saw how thoroughly they had been maintained. He tested the firing mechanism, so lightly oiled it moved silky quiet. He detailed two men to feed the belts and set buckets of water to cool the barrels, then climbed the companion ladder to the wheelhouse to find the twin Lewis guns in the same excellent condition.

'They're as ready as they'll ever be below,' he reported to Ben.

Through the window Indie called his orders to the crew and they went about it barefoot, strong-armed and eager. A freshening wind had followed them up the channel and with all her sails set *Cloud Chaser's* bow cut through the wind-ruffled water like a racing cutter in a Sunday regatta on the Thames. From his place at the helm Ben felt the old thrill that he had thought gone forever. He did not need to ask if Indie da Silva felt the same. The Macanese had a grin on his face that hadn't been there since they ran the Hangchow Bore together. Tinker found their glee infectious but as a military man he held it back.

'If we can clear the river without being boarded,' he told them calmly, 'the nearest Chinese force is in the island group at Chusan. At this clip we could make it by morning.'

Ben laughed. 'Among these junks and lighters she stands out like a duchess in a Sin Alley whore-house. May I suggest a tot all round, gentlemen, to help us on our way?'

'To stoke the fire in our bellies,' agreed Indie, as he went below to the master's cabin and returned with the ship's decanter. Ben took it from him and filled three glasses with Dragon's Breath.

'This was given to me by Nate Barcoo, captain of the *Moshula*. It belonged to my father, named after his barquentine, *Windsong*.' He raised his glass. 'I give you a toast, gentlemen. To Frenchy Deverill, to the China trade and to Shanghai.'

The Japanese gunboat commander stood on the wing of its small, heavily armoured bridge, his feet spread wide against the surging movement of the deck. He muttered to himself as he held the glasses trained on the magnificent vessel off his starboard beam, then handed them to the junior officer beside him. It was not unusual to see western-rigged sailing vessels plying Chinese rivers— yawls, schooners and ketches left over from the passing age of sail. They could still trade where steam could not reach. Such craft always stood out from the latine junk sails that were part of every waterway. China's riverine system was perhaps the last place on earth where such craft still did business. But this one was different. It looked as though it had sailed straight out of the past.

The young officer lowered the glasses and handed them back to his commander, shaking his head. Both were regular visitors to the Shanghai Club and they had seen paintings of ships like this hung in the library.

'What do you think?' the captain asked.

'She is beautiful. Like those the foreigners once used to carry opium.'

'Or run guns,' said the commander, the glasses again trained on the clipper passing on his bow.

'She flies like a cloud before the wind. No Chinamen sail a ship like this.' He focussed on the small figures manning the clipper's decks.

'The crew are not dressed as Chinese dress. We will look closer at this beautiful ship.'

The junior officer stepped into the wheelhouse and snapped an order to the helmsman. Answering its rudder, the gunboat swung out in a wide curve to come up on *Cloud Chaser's* course. The engine-room telegraphs clanged for increased speed, twin propellers digging deep to lift her heavy bows, churning a white, sweeping wake.

A dash of spray reached the wing of the bridge, flung over the top of the canvas dodger into the Japanese commander's face. He tasted the salt of it, flicking drops from the binoculars before raising them again to fix on the clipper's stern. Slowly he read out the Chinese characters carved on the decorated transom, below the English name.

'Chaser of Clouds,' he murmured to himself, lowering the glasses. 'Now I am chasing you.' He called for more speed.

The gunboat he commanded had been captured from the British and had seen long service on the Yangtze and Yellow Rivers. She was a relic of gunboat diplomacy, built for cruising and bombardment more than high-speed chase. Heavy armour slowed her down; her triple-expansion steam turbine engine was designed for distance, not pursuit. Every plate in her rivetted hull trembled to the hiss and clamour of the engine-room as the pressure gauges peaked. In the tiny stokehold the furnace door stayed open as sweating coolies fed the boiler fires.

Even at the full speed of twelve knots the gunboat could not close the distance. The young officer raised a loud hailer to his mouth and called for the clipper to reduce sail and heave to. Signal flags were hoisted and a signaller sent for to flash the order by Aldis lamp. When *Cloud Chaser* showed no sign of slowing he sent two gunners forward to man the four-inch gun mounted on the foredeck. They crouched at their stations behind its shield of thick armour-plated steel. The commander gave the order and a warning shot was fired, raising a column of water ahead of *Cloud Chaser's* bows. Seconds later the clipper's jibsails collapsed as they were let go and she came up into the wind, losing way with a wild flogging of her mainsails.

The gunboat drew steadily alongside. A small party of marines poured up from the steel hatch in full battle order and formed a single rank before the bridge.

'Throw down a ladder,' the loud hailer squawked shrilly. 'We are boarding you.'

A gunport just below *Cloud Chaser's* wheelhouse gaped suddenly open and the snout of a Maxim opened up its hammering fire. Above it the wheelhouse window had dropped and a Lewis gun joined in with an explosive burst.

The two Japanese officers on the bridge flew like rag dolls against the superstructure, their blood bright on the paintwork. Before they could raise their weapons, the rank of marines was cut down with one wide sweep of the Lewis gun. The heavy Maxim struck gouts of sparks from the steel-plated shield of the deck gun. Tinker knew it was a matter of seconds before the gun would send a high explosive shell into *Cloud Chaser's* hull at point-blank range, and ignite the arsenal they had aboard. He could see the helmsman spinning the wheel to draw away to firing range.

'Get the man at the wheel,' he bawled, keeping the gunners pinned down.

Above him Indie swung the Lewis machine gun onto the gunboat's wheelhouse, shattering its small observation ports and seeing the helmsman buckle and fall. Tinker pulled the pin from a grenade, counting the dangerous seconds slowly, lobbing it neatly at the deck gun. It bounced and rolled across the deck, exploding close enough to fell the gunners.

The attack had been a savage surprise but there would be more marines below and more gunners inside the twin turrets. Tinker released his pressure on the Maxim's trigger grips and shouted up to Ben.

'Take her alongside. We've got to put her out of action.'

At an order from Tinker, the men from Aggie's Dry-Dock rushed up the companion ladder and onto the deck. Grappling irons flew out to hook onto the gunboat's rails and a cargo net unrolled over *Cloud Chaser's* side. Yelling like fiends, they swarmed down it and onto the steel deck of the gunboat.

Within seconds live grenades had been rolled down the barrels of the gun turrets and dropped into the hatches. In the tiny radio shack behind the bridge the operator transmitted the attack to the base at Pudong before Tinker killed him and destroyed the radio with a burst from a Russian P.P.D. There was no need to go below to seek out any still alive. The explosions contained within the iron hull brought blasts of fire belching from the ventilators. Her guns were out of action and a blaze had started in the engine-room. Cheering loudly, Aggie Gates' beachies leapt for the net and clambered back aboard *Cloud Chaser* without losing a man.

In the wheelhouse, Indie was leaning on the Lewis gun. He patted its stock. 'She badly needed the exercise,' he grinned.

Ben had his eyes aloft where two of the crewmen were setting the topsails to give her every inch of canvas she could carry. 'Every Jap boat from here to Ningpo will be out for us now.'

Tinker nodded. 'I blew the radio shack but the operator had time to send.'

'He need not have bothered. They'll see that from Pudong to Hongkew,' said Ben.

He pointed back at the burning gunboat; a tree of black smoke was reaching into the clear sky above her as she wallowed low in the water. The few survivors who had dragged themselves from the burning hatches staggered to the rail and threw themselves over the side. A small lifeboat had been cut from its davits and half swamped as they clawed to get aboard. Indie swung the Lewis gun to sink it but Ben put a hand on his shoulder.

'Leave it be. Let them swim, they're finished.'

Cloud Chaser was flying beneath every sail she could hold and handling her to take the best of the wind needed all Ben's strength and concentration. 'There's a case of rum in the pantry. Break it out and give the men a drink while they've a chance to taste it.' He allowed himself a wry grin. '*Cloud Chaser* never ran better. She has life again. If we can keep free and clear till dark, we'll make Chusan by daylight.'

'That depends what's waiting for us up ahead,' Tinker said. 'That radio sparks had enough time to give them the colour of our eyes.' He disappeared down the companionway to fetch the rum.

Indie reached for the *Windsong* decanter and poured two drinks. He handed one to Ben and pulled a slim box of Manila cheroots from his shirt pocket. When they were lit he hauled in a lungful of the rich, aromatic smoke and raised his glass to Ben. 'To the Battle of the Waters,' he said.

With the flying jibs re-set Ben eased the helm to bring her close-hauled into the wind and felt the leap of her response as the burning gunboat fell away astern.

The Japanese gunner raised his head behind the shield of buckled steel. His loader lay dead across his legs. With the last of his strength, he rolled the body from him and slowly rose to a kneeling position. Reaching for the brass calibration wheels, he began to turn them, first for elevation, then for traverse. His eardrums had ruptured with the shock of the grenade and blood seeped from them, sticky on his neck; the deck beneath his knees was slippery with the blood of his comrade.

He could see the crew of the clipper, bending on extra topsails and sheeting home her flying jibs. She was yawing into a new tack as her canvas took the wind. He aimed amidships of her black-painted hull with its row of square, white gunports. The high-explosive shell had already been loaded and locked into the breech before the grenade had rolled across the foredeck.

The gunner knew that at this range he could not miss, and shaking his head to clear the ringing dizziness of shock, his hand closed over the firing toggle. The range was so short that he still felt the jerk of the lanyard and the recoil of the breechblock as it spat the brass shell-case past him and *Cloud Chaser* exploded in a geyser of flame.

The St Andrew's Ball

THE MOST important event of the year on Hong Kong's social calendar was the St Andrew's ball at the Peninsula Hotel. Each November since the famous hotel had been built, the rich and powerful had attended the occasion above all others. Not to be seen at 'The Pen' on that day of all days was not to be a part of Hong Kong's successful establishment. The ball of 1941 was no exception but never before had the conversation been quite so grave as guests arrived at its grand marble entrance and spilled into the colonnaded foyer.

There had been topics of concern over earlier years. Even before its completion in 1913 the hotel's ballroom and wide balconies had been used by the British Indian regiments for instruction on the Maxim machine gun as the British Empire prepared for war with Germany. Since then, there had been typhoon, cholera, fire, pirate attack and general strikes to stimulate the conversation over pink gins, chota pegs and Singapore slings. But this was the first time that the colony had been under the imminent threat of invasion.

The Japanese were mobilising a task force assembled and ready to move towards the border between the Chinese mainland and the New Territories. British reconnaissance aircraft had reported a build-up of armour and airpower in and around Canton. Although the report that three divisions of crack Japanese infantry were preparing to move up were unconfirmed, an air of inevitability hung over the glittering assembly, already dotted with the splendid uniforms of high military rank. The Hong Kong Volunteers were on standby for call up and the Mainland Brigade, made up of British, Canadian and Indian infantry, were on full alert.

Colonel Justin Pelham escorted his wife past the gushing fountains and up the wide marble steps, followed closely by Captain Toby Hyde-Wilkins and a tall, beautifully-groomed young woman in a simple black cheong-sam, high-necked and split to the knee, with a cape of padded velvet over her shoulders. Both officers were wearing full dress uniform to perfection and Peggy Pelham was elegant in a ball gown of coffee-coloured lace beneath a stole of silver fox fur. But it was the tall girl on Toby's arm who turned heads as they entered the ballroom announced by a Sikh halvidah—an officer of the famous Lancers—superbly turned out in the scarlet tunic, white breeches and high polished boots of Frontier Cavalry.

In the two years since the devastation of Taipo and her recovery on Stonecutter's Island, Sing had blossomed under the care and kindness of Peggy Pelham. She had become as close as an adopted daughter, winning Justin's complete approval, if not his full acceptance of Toby's determination to make her his wife. With the looks and figure of an eighteen-year-old she had the style and poise of maturity to match any female in a spectacular array that represented the *crème de la crème* of Hong Kong society.

A great deal of her self-assurance was due to undreamed of events that had given some sort of meaning to the horror she had endured in the house of Fat Fan. When she was fully recovered, Peggy had begun taking her along to various charity and community welfare assemblies. Among them was that of the Welfare League and the Anti Mooi-Jai Society. Although dedicated to the protection and assistance of Eurasians, the League's mandate did not draw the line at showing similar concern for underprivileged and badly used Chinese citizens in need of help. When she had discovered this, Sing had told them of all that she had suffered behind the walls of Fat Fan's larp cheung factory at the hands of number one wife and the vicious overseer Kwok the Rat Man. Above all she had told Peggy Pelham of the little mooi-jai, Ah Sam, who had risked her own safety to help her. Within a matter of days the larp cheung factory had been visited by public health officials accompanied by members of the Anti Mooi-Jai Society.

Wu Fok Fan and his number one wife had been heavily fined for their ill-treatment of mooi-jai and the factories closed until extensive health and safety standards could be met. The canque had been discovered and confiscated, with Ah Kwok taken into custody for its illegal possession and alleged use. Most wonderful of all, Ah Sam had been taken from the house of Fan and a place had been found for her as a paid amah to a decent British family.

The joy that Sing had felt was nothing compared to her wonder at such powers. One day, she told herself, she too would have such power. She had begged to be allowed to help in any way possible and Peggy had been only too glad of her involvement. At her side, Sing had seen something of the workings of 'the Peak Set'. The dinner parties and bridge afternoons, meetings and coffee mornings in the mist-shrouded mansions and grand houses of government and civil service officials, whose wives had little to do but sit on committees that might help to justify the grandeur of their existence. Under Peggy Pelham's protective wing she had been received without too much question and had met many people from a world she slowly began to feel part of.

Her love and adoration for Toby had grown even stronger with the added emotion of a deep, abiding gratitude. Although restricted by his regimental duties and the commitment he had made to his commanding officer, she had been seen with him at certain social functions and private gatherings over past months. The pine-shaded arbour, guarded by the old gun emplacement, had remained their secret rendezvous and as many Sunday afternoons as possible had been spent in each other's arms.

Now, as he pulled out her chair at the table marked with Colonel Pelham's name and the regiment's crest, his warm hand rested reassuringly on her shoulder before he took his place beside her. Only Toby really knew how she still felt among people like this. Most would never have guessed it. Outwardly she seemed exceptionally calm, even aloof. It had become her armour.

She had quickly found that the female fraternity of colonial society was quick to investigate and take advantage of any new face, no matter how well-protected or unwelcome such attention might be. It was, for a stunningly attractive young Eurasian girl without any known background, family, name or position, a menopausal shark pool.

Sing had soon learned that to observe much, say as little as possible, but to show poise and confidence at all times was her best defence against arrogance, snobbery and intolerance. That way she remained a mystery, one that was envied for her youth and unusual beauty, and not least, the obvious devotion of the handsome Captain Hyde-Wilkins.

There was another man at the table, who rose from his seat as they approached. Sing's first impression was of how alone he looked. He was exceptionally tall, unfolding from his chair a little awkwardly, but she found the shy smile on his face pleasant and genuine. His large brown eyes were serious and deep as he took her hand and for the second their eyes met she noticed they were shadowed by long dark lashes and how pale his skin was compared to Toby's.

Colonel Pelham introduced him as Sebastian Masters, aide to the governor of Hong Kong.

'Sebastian is here to take care of a special guest at our table.' Justin nodded to the two empty chairs. 'If the gentleman decides to grace us with his presence.'

Sebastian Masters smiled his polite, serious smile as he spoke. 'He'll be here, sir. Arriving late is his way of keeping we foreigners in our place.'

He had the pleasant, even voice that comes with a good English education and the perfect manners of a diplomat. Sing felt his eyes upon her when she sat down but whenever she looked up at him, they were elsewhere. There was something about the tenseness of his bluish cheeks and jaw that made him seem uncomfortable.

With the welcome speeches over, Toby led Sing to the dance floor. She felt the stares as they passed the crowded tables. The old feeling that was always there in crowds rose in her as she knew it would. At times like this she felt little different to the seven-year-old child who had been led through the dusty streets of the lakeside village. Knowing she was stared at made her walk very straight, her head held high, looking neither right nor left. It gave her a convincing look of pride and serenity. No one but Toby would have guessed it was nothing more than sheer determination.

On the dance floor Toby held her close and whispered comfortingly as he sensed her nervousness. 'You are the most beautiful woman here.'

'But there are so many beautiful women here. Why do they stare?'

His lips brushed her ear, drinking in her perfume. 'It is called good old-fashioned jealousy, my darling.'

'It is because I am different. Not really one of them.'

He pressed her to him. 'It is because you are mine and you are wonderful. That's all that matters.'

When they returned to the table the two empty chairs had been occupied. The wide back of a man and the neat shoulders of a woman, flounced in gold tulle, were evident to them as they approached. Not until they had rounded the table did the man stand with Colonel Pelham and Sebastian Masters. The self-control that had become a part of Sing's being was almost shattered as she looked into the flushed face of J.T. Ching. The shock of recognition shot through her as though she had been violently disrobed. Justin introduced her and her heartbeat seemed to stumble then quicken as Ching slowly offered his hand.

She saw the dawning of surprise in his puffy eyes turn to complete amazement. Only her deep-rooted discipline kept Sing from crying out, stopped her from turning to run from the table, from the hotel and from the sea of eyes. Her pulse beat loudly in her ears as she fought to check her reaction.

'Miss Deverill is a great help to my wife in her work for the Urban Council and the Welfare League,' said Justin Pelham, noticing nothing.

Ching's face showed no change of expression. Only his eyes told Sing that three years and western style could not hide the truth of who she was. Their glitter of astonishment had quickly changed to faint amusement.

'It is always an honour and a great pleasure to meet those who show concern for our poor and underprivileged people.' His hot, moist hand let go of hers. 'I, too, help in my humble way.'

'Mr Ching is too modest,' Peggy Pelham broke in. 'His generosity has funded hospitals, schools and the floating boat peoples' clinic in Shatin.'

Sing sat down and Ching resumed his seat. 'Surely, we have met before?' he said, the tone of his voice communicating clearly to Sing that this was to be a game he would enjoy.

She had never told them of her time in the Tavern of Cascading Jewels as personal attendant to the man who now sat before her. There had seemed no need, with Toby's knowledge of the Nine Dragons ballroom, but now her mind raced with uncertainty. She felt her new-found confidence slipping away under Ching's unswerving gaze. With the first shock over she had quickly considered her options. There was nothing for her but to play his game and see where it led. He held all the cards but one.

To expose her he would have to admit his familiarity with opium dens and a taste for children which, considered by western standards, should be punishable by law. Her nerves quickly settled when she realised that to give her away he would have to show another side to the generous and public-spirited Jack Teagarden

Ching. She was not sure, but she did not think he would do that in this company.

For the first time her eyes switched to the woman at his side. She sat silent and still, her hands folded in her lap and her eyes downcast and Ching had made no attempt to introduce her. Her eyes lifted fleetingly to meet Sing's then flicked away. It took only seconds to realise the girl in the fussy taffeta evening dress, made up as heavily as a star of Chinese opera, was Jade. Ching turned to her for the first time.

'Don't you think we have met Miss Deverill before?'

Before she could answer, Toby interrupted, hiding his annoyance at Ching's persistence. 'I'm sure Miss Deverill would need no reminding if she had met someone as important as yourself, Mr. Ching.'

Ching ignored him. 'Deverill'. He repeated thoughtfully. 'I thought I knew every family in Hong Kong. It is a name I seem to have heard, but I cannot remember where.'

His eyebrows lifted expecting an answer. Jade's eyes were again on the table in front of her. One hand crept up to nervously touch a string of pea-green jade around her neck. Studs of the same precious stone adorned the tiny lobes of her ears. Sing felt suddenly trapped. Inside, her defences crumbled. Outwardly she showed no sign.

'I am from Shanghai, sir.'

Ching's loose mouth formed a wide ingratiating smile as he warmed to the game, recognition dawning as he spoke. 'Deverill's . . . Shanghai . . . of course . . .'

'With your permission, Captain.'

The level voice of Sebastian Masters cut in before he could say more. The diplomat had risen and stood behind Sing's chair.

'Miss Deverill, may I ask you to dance with me?'

She rose quickly, smiled at Toby, and allowed Sebastian to guide her through the tables.

'My deepest apologies, Miss Deverill,' he said as they reached the floor. 'I'm afraid I am responsible for the Chinese gentleman who seems so interested in you,' he said hesitantly. 'He has a great deal of money and rather too much influence. Therefore the governor seems to think he can do no wrong.' He laughed lightly. 'As you will have gathered, Mr Ching agrees with him.'

He took her hand and his arm rested lightly on her waist. 'I think he is something of a reprobate.' He paused as they moved to the music. 'It does not excuse his persistence and his bad manners.' He smiled down at her. 'But I cannot entirely blame him for his fascination.'

A week after the St Andrew's ball, Sing was handed a small package by the gardener. Inside, carefully wrapped in cotton, was the blue topaz that J.T. Ching had given her in the Tavern of Cascading Jewels. With it was a note written in the childlike characters she recognised as Jade's. It was important that they talked, it said, and suggested a meeting place—the Temple of the Dragon Mother on Hollywood Road.

Peggy Pelham was pleased when Sing told her she had been invited to visit an old friend on Hong Kong side. She asked no questions and was happy to accompany her across the harbour on the Star ferry and as far as the bottom of Garden Road where she had a committee meeting of her own.

Sing took the tram through the Central District and climbed the ladder streets between the rows of hawkers to the beautiful old temple. Cut off from the noise of the street by a high wall, the ornate roof of the famous Taoist shrine to Yueh Ch'eng, the mother of dragons, was all that could be seen until entering the gates.

Inside, the big main hall was in almost complete darkness. The only light came from the open door and the dull glow from great spiralling coils of joss hung from the smoke-blackened roof beams. As Sing's eyes became accustomed to the shadows, Jade moved towards her from among them. Without speaking she stood before Sing and, in the light from the doorway, Sing saw there were tears on her cheeks. Gently, they held each other for long moments.

'I come to warn you, Siu Sing. You are in great danger.'

Without speaking further, she took Sing's hand and led her past the gold-painted statue of the Dragon Mother to a narrow back door. It led to a tiny garden. Models of pagodas in glazed ceramic stood among bonsai trees and miniature fishermen sat patiently on the mossy rocks beside its pools and bridges.

'It is where I come whenever I can,' Jade said. 'It is the only place that is safe for me. And for you, now that he has found you. He will never forgive you for running away. He has lost much face,' she whispered, wiping her eyes, 'He has sworn revenge, on you and on the gwai-lo captain.'

Jade kept tight hold of Sing's hand as she told her story. Of J.T. Ching's fury when Sing had left the tavern. How he had taken her instead, promising to make her his official concubine.

'But he did not keep his promise,' she said sadly. 'Instead he made me only his mistress. I have no standing in his house. I am less than a servant. I am nothing.'

Sing remembered well how Jade had wanted only to take her place in the house of a rich and powerful man and to earn his respect and loyalty through her devotion. She squeezed Jade's hand.

'I am so sorry, Jade. If I had not left . . . if I had not made him angry.'

'It is not of your doing. I went to him many times but he wanted only you. I am to blame. I begged Madam Fung to recommend me.'

'Does he not treat you well?'

She hung her head. 'He treats me worse than a dog.'

'Does he beat you?'

'Beating is nothing to the things he does. He is a truly evil one.'

Sing felt a shudder pass through Jade.

'He will send the Forceful One to find you wherever you go. There is nowhere to hide. He will do to you what he has done to me. He blames us both.'

Sing stiffened at the name Jade had used. Her ears seemed to ring with it as though they had been slapped.

'Who is this . . . Forceful One?' she asked, hardly trusting her own voice, so frightened of the answer.

'He is Ah Keung, the chosen bodyguard, a cruel one of strange and terrible power.'

Jade began to cry and Sing held her gently, urging her to stop. She had a good friend, Sing whispered, who had great influence over such things. She would protect them both. But Jade shook her head.

'Never happen,' she said in her old way, wiping her eyes and trying to smile. 'Cannot leave. Soon he will tire of me. Then perhaps he will let me go.'

As Sing rode the tram back to Central to meet Peggy Pelham her mind was filled with thoughts of Ah Keung. Of his treachery and of his threat to one day claim the life she owed him. She was transported to the Place of Clear Water and his destruction of the snake. She recalled above all his eyes upon Toby in the Nine Dragons ballroom, eyes that would kill without hesitation. She wondered if she should speak to Peggy of Jade's warning. As a mistress Jade was entitled to nothing in the eyes of Chinese custom except that which the man who kept her chose to give. She was bound to him by fear alone. There was nothing anyone could do. A terrible premonition consumed her as the tram rattled on—a certainty that Ah Keung would always be there to bar her happiness, to take what was hers. The tiger that she must one day face had come back into her life.

PART VII

The Taking of Hong Kong

War banners are bright as flowers in the distance.
Across the ripe, yellow field drawn steel flashes
like sunlight on moving water.
The thunder of a thousand horses is louder than birds.
Soon they will see the smoke from our chimney.
The warlord is always hungry
he will head them this way.
They will take what they want and they will
burn the mustard field.
Joss will not help us then.

CANTONESE TEMPLE SCROLL

· IMAGE FOR WAR ·

The Yut Boon Jai

MAJOR-GENERAL Jiro Toshido sat in the back of the armed staff car and silently cursed the condition of China's roads. Ahead of him a column of élite assault troops of the Japanese Imperial Army marched behind their armoured vanguard. On either side of him sat a brigade major and the lieutenant who had been assigned as his general aide. They spoke across him, both leaning slightly forward to peer past his sturdy bulk as they joked about the desirability of Chinese women, and the merits of Chinese food. It was the early morning of December 6, 1941 and they were on their way to join the invasion of Hong Kong.

General Toshido did not appear to share their high spirits. He was a surly man and they made no attempt to include him in their conversation. Silently the general gritted his teeth against the jolting of the wheels over deep ruts that the half-tracked vehicles had churned up on the narrow roads. Behind his eyes, fixed so unswervingly on the column ahead, explosions of vivid colour burst in wave after wave of almost unbearable agony.

It was something he had become accustomed to hiding from his staff and his superiors. It did not befit an officer of the crack 38th Division to admit to physical weakness of any kind and certainly not an emotional one. He had learned to live with these blinding headaches for so long that he felt his jaw muscles were over-developed from biting against the pain—almost as long as he had been fighting the infestation that posturing fool Chiang Kai-shek called the Kuomintang, his so-called People's Party.

'I cannot wait to lie in a bath in this Peninsula Hotel they talk of. It should prove a comfortable billet.' Lieutenant Mashima sat back as the car gave a savage lurch, anticipation written all over his clean young soldier's face.

'Do Chinese women serve their masters as willingly and pleasingly as Japanese?' enquired Major Kojiki, absently.

'They soon will,' laughed the lieutenant, anxious to impress his superior officer with his appetite for women. They both laughed uncertainly and Major Kojiki wondered why the general beside him did not even smile. Only a knot of muscle the size of a walnut twitched at the hinge of his heavy jaw and his eyes remained closed. He did not like the young lieutenant. Only an influential father had given him the position, but in his arrogance Mashima believed it was his own superior military qualities.

Jiro Toshido was a professional soldier. His lineage dated back to Daimyo—the way of the warrior. His ancestors were feudal noblemen, knights of Bushido. His was the code of Samurai—endurance, courage, honour and, above all else, loyalty to his emperor. These were the virtues he had clung to throughout the long years of fighting inside China.

But there was a younger, more impatient element within his command. Officers who knew nothing of honour as he knew honour. It was true, the way of Samurai still played its great part in the morale of the Imperial Japanese Army but its code had been distorted to suit the ways of savagery and rapine. Hate had taken the place of honour, cruelty had overshadowed courage.

Major-General Toshido had watched the Nanking massacre in 1937, unable to do a thing against the tide of blood and the tyranny and despotism that followed in its wake. The banks of the Yangtze were clogged with the dead and dying. Entire villages surrounding the city had been systematically demolished. Every girl child physically large enough had been subjected to pack rape and when the child was no longer usable the mother was turned upon. It was General Toshido who had pressed the Japanese Government for the establishment of comfort stations in an effort to turn the troops away from mass, indiscriminate rape and the disease it was beginning to spread.

True, the comfort women, as they became officially known as, were recruited against their will, but they were controlled, medically examined daily and rewarded for their services. Toshido was fully aware that this, too, was slavery but it was preferable to the unbridled mayhem of his men let loose on a Chinese village.

Korean women were the most commonly used and the lowest paid, together with Filipina and Thai. Highest paid were the Japanese prostitutes who had come of their own accord and they were only few. He had done his best to inspect the comfort stations regularly and to maintain some kind of order in their supervision, knowing that when his back was turned Chinese schoolgirls were rounded up and that still farm-girls were brought in in truckloads to entertain the Japanese soldier free of charge.

A comfort woman averaged twenty to thirty men a day and at

times forty to fifty. Gradually they had begun to thin out, dying from such abuse, malnutrition or suicide. Finding them harder and harder to replace, the government officials again began transporting mothers and their girl children from all over China to the garrison towns and by 1940 the comfort stations were almost entirely stocked with Chinese.

When the Imperial Army had taken Canton a year later, it had all begun again and Toshido had watched the slaughter as before, had seen his troops swarm across the Haichu Bridge to the south bank of the Canton River where 100,000 Tanka lived on the water. When they had returned across the bridge at nightfall the sky was lit by burning boats; not a man had been left alive among the boat people, a woman or child untouched.

These were thoughts that crammed his mind as pain consumed him, the prattle beside him drilling like a worm into his brain. He wanted to draw the German revolver on his hip and ram it in the mouth of Lieutenant Mashima. He dare not. Already the medical officers who had examined him suspected his mental stability. His comments and endless memoranda on the conduct of the all-conquering Japanese army were well known to his superiors. To speak of such things now, even for an officer of his rank, would be seen as weakness in the face of what lay ahead— the taking of Hong Kong.

Jiro Toshido knew the private battle that raged within his conscience was slowly destroying him. At times he had filled his hand with the cherrywood grip of the Luger and almost raised the cold, blue metal to his temple. Only the fiery saturation of saki had prevented him. The code of Samurai was too deeply entrenched to allow such cowardly release. Until the emperor was victorious he would continue to prevail. And one day, perhaps, return to his family on the island of Honshu and the house from where he could see Mount Fujiyama through the maple trees.

By early December the inevitability of a Japanese attack drove all other concerns from Sing's mind. The incidents of the St Andrew's ball and Jade's warning were soon overshadowed by preparations for the defence of Hong Kong. In typical British fashion, in the face of impossible odds the 'stiff upper lip' was the order of the day. Reliable reports confirmed that an entire army corps of battle-hardened Japanese troops had been diverted from operations against Chiang Kai-shek's Kuomintang to march on Hong Kong.

Three Imperial Army divisions with air and artillery support were advancing on the twenty-two mile long border between the colony and Japanese-occupied Kwangtung.

Defending the New Territories, they would first face Colonel Justin Pelham's Queen Elizabeth's 8th Rajputs Rifles and a company of Punjabi Sepoys of Britain's Indian Army. The Mainland Brigade also mobilised a battalion of Royal Scots. Their orders were to fight a delaying action towards the first line of defence at Shatin. Fortifications of bunkers, machine-gun nests, entrenchments and hastily excavated tank traps extended east to the place called Gin Drinkers' Bay.

Captain Hyde-Wilkins had been detached from his regiment to join the staff of Defence Command Headquarters on Hong Kong Island. Sing had hardly seen him since the St Andrew's ball. When she did, he was cheerful and encouraging. Optimistic reports had been received that Generalissimo Chiang Kai-shek was withdrawing his forces in the south and massing an army to attack the invaders from the rear. Toby assured her that the disciplined British forces could take on any Japanese invasion three to one. The entire Far East British Air Force was on standby at Kai Tak airport and was well defended by Royal Artillery anti-aircraft batteries.

The reports of Chiang Kai-shek's massed relief columns proved to be false. The air attack on Hong Kong had come soon after Japanese airpower devastated the American battle fleet at anchor in Pearl Harbour. At Hong Kong Defence Headquarters signals were intercepted warning all Japanese commanders that war with Britain and the United States was imminent. At seven a.m. the following morning Peggy and Sing listened to Tokyo Home Radio, clearly received in Hong Kong, as war was declared.

General Jiro Toshido's forward formations of infantry were already moving into the New Territories at Sha Tau Kok on the eastern perimeter of Mirs Bay. He had ordered others to cross the Shumchon River and advance over the farmlands of the flat central plain towards Kowloon. Only when they were advancing down the road leading to the fishing village of Taipo did his formation encounter enemy resistance. Colonel Pelham's Rajputs were waiting for them, side by side with the Punjabis. The Japanese vanguard was cut down by rifle and machine-gun fire from every hillside. Following the assault the legendary Indian Army regiments fell back to the village, drawing the Japanese column into a second devastating ambush.

General Toshido and his staff were surprised by the unexpected action but, although losing some hundreds of men, they proceeded to drive their attackers southwards onto the Kowloon peninsular. Toshido had absolutely no doubt that they would take Hong Kong Island within the week. Overwhelming Japanese numbers and total air control made it a certainty.

Elsewhere, in darkness on that first day, squads of Japanese commandos cut through the barbed-wire entanglements and, silent in rubber-soled combat boots, got close enough to launch a surprise grenade attack backed by heavy machine-gun fire. Caught unawares, the Royal Scots were forced to withdraw. Joined by the Winnipeg Grenadiers and detachments of Sepoy reinforcements from the Island Brigade, they faced the advance as Japanese infantry poured through the Gin Drinkers' line and streamed towards Kowloon. The Hong Kong Volunteers, made up of Eurasians, held on in the streets of Kowloon as thousands scrambled for berths aboard junks, sampans and overloaded ferries to evacuate them across the harbour to Hong Kong Island.

General Toshido mounted the steps of the Peninsula Hotel he had heard so much about. Lined up outside its imposing colonial facade several squads of Sikh police were called to attention by a Japanese sergeant. They were deserters who had surrendered their arms rather than fight. He had been right, the New Territories and Kowloon had been taken in less than a week. All that remained was for him to report to his commanding general and prepare for the attack on Hong Kong Island.

Peggy Pelham stood looking around her garden. The amahs had packed as much as they could carry and the gardener was carting it to the landing stage in a wheelbarrow. Sing stood back on the bungalow's veranda waiting to leave. They had not seen Justin or Toby for almost a week and although a Rajput corporal had been sent to organise their evacuation three days earlier, Peggy had preferred to wait instead of leaving with the others. While her husband's regiment was still engaged in stemming the tide of invasion on this side of the harbour she could not bring herself to retreat to what little protection Hong Kong side had to offer. Nothing she could say or do had convinced Sing to leave her side and she had ceased trying. Air strikes against the island and artillery fire from Japanese batteries drawn up to positions along the Kowloon waterfront had already commenced and from where they stood they could hear the whistle of shells scything low over the oak tree.

As Peggy turned and began to walk back towards the bungalow Sing could see the sky-blue turbans of four Sikh policemen approaching above the hedgerow. She could hear them talking excitedly as they entered the gate and called out.

'Pelham. Memsahib. You must come with us, please.'

Peggy stopped and faced them. They must have come to collect her, she thought, the burra mem who was last to leave now that her people were assembled at the jetty. It was the way things should be. The party consisted of a sergeant, a corporal and two constables.

Sing was about to join them when something made her hesitate. The constables had grasped Peggy by each arm and, ignoring her protests, were forcing her across the grass and through the gate.

It was a matter of hours before the Japanese would land on Stonecutter's Island. The Sikh sergeant had already been informed that the entire Sikh constabulary had gone over to the Japanese invaders almost to a man. The Chinese servants of those they had taken were left to loot the houses they had worked in. In the neighbouring gardens on each side of her Sing saw the amahs filling blankets with whatever valuables they could find, tying the corners to form bundles and, with one on each end of a carrying pole, trotting off in relays.

There was no doubt in Sing's mind of what would happen to her if she was handed over to the Japanese. Quickly, she went to her room and fetched the deerhide bag. Taking food from the kitchen she made up a bundle. In the amah's room she found the black cotton sam foo of a Chinese servant and changed into it. Quietly she left by the back door and with the book bag firmly secured to her back and the bundle hooked over her arm, made her way to the hidden entrance to the old gun emplacement and its network of tunnels.

For the next fifteen days the Volunteers Fifth Field Artillery Battery and the big, entrenched coastal gun covered the eastern inlet of Lei Yue Mun Pass. Countless landing attempts were made and those that reached the shores were met with heavy resistance from crack platoons of Indian Infantry and Canadian Rifles. Junkloads of Japanese shock troops, towed by sampans, crept silently across the harbour under cover of darkness to be blasted from the water or raked with machine-gun fire before they could swarm ashore. All day and night the Japanese broadcast loud messages calling upon the island to surrender.

On Christmas Day the loudspeakers on Kowloon side continued their barrage of sound. Christmas carols blended with incessant small-arms and heavy machine-gun fire as the British made their last stand in the defence of Hong Kong. General Toshido conceded to a cup of saki with his officers and later to another in the Queen Victoria suite at the Peninsula with the imperial staff and the commanding general. Only after several jars of the hot rice wine were their spirits high. The taking of Hong Kong from what they had considered to be a handful of decadent colonialists protected by bands of inferior Indians and drunken British soldiers, had not been the Imperial Army's greatest hour. The official celebration then continued without him and Jiro Toshido drank alone well into the night.

Sing had remained hidden in the gun emplacement for three days before she was able to leave Stonecutter's island. On the third day she made her way after dark to the jetty. As she passed the Pelham bungalow, keeping to the shadows, Japanese officers could be seen through the lighted windows. Although it was four o'clock in the morning, through the incessant shrilling of crickets she could hear the gramophone playing Peggy's favourite classics under raised Japanese voices.

No sentries had been posted and in the black sam foo, keeping to the shadows, she reached the landing stage unobserved. Half a dozen sampans and wallah wallahs were strung out along the stone retaining wall leading to the jetty. Under the lightpoles that threw a pale yellow glow over the end of the jetty, two Sikh policemen leaned on its rail, talking quietly. Clouds of insects swirled like snowflakes around the lamps above them. The chorusing of the loud-speakers reached across the black waters from Kowloon with the dancing colours of reflection from the few remaining neons along Nathan Road. The smells of low tide were strong in her nostrils as she crawled inch by inch beneath the tarpaulin hatch cover of the nearest sampan. Careful not to cause movement, Sing wormed her way into the hold and waited.

Everspring

Doctor Sun Wing Cheu's herb shop, 'Everspring', was tucked away in the narrow streets at the northern boundary of Wan Chai and Causeway Bay. The shop was very old and had been built by Doctor Sun's father, whose name still remained on a painted tile above the door. A large and fading portrait of the venerable gentleman hung above the counter, looking down upon the customers from a chipped gilt frame that had turned coppery with age. It was a uniquely traditional shop. Every inch of it, inside and out, was finished in solid hornbeam, the ironwood of Foochow. The original timber was almost ninety years old and so steeped in time and rubbed with use that it had taken on the temper and sheen of polished stone.

The rows upon rows of brass-handled drawers that backed the scarred slab of the serving counter were filled with every kind of herb that could be asked for. Those that weren't stored in the drawers were ranged in cylindrical wooden bins above them, or in earthen crocks and glass jars that filled the shelves from floor to ceiling on every wall. From its high beams, where a huge old-fashioned punkah fan churned the aromatic air with the pace of a ploughing buffalo, hung the dehydrated and dedicated mysteries of the herbalist's trade. A heavily carved blackwood chair stood before the counter for the comfort of the customer, beside it a brightly coloured spittoon brightly decorated with flowers. In the middle of the counter stood a large mortar and pestle and overhead, its electrical lead looped across the ceiling, hung a magnificent silk and lacquer lantern, its once vibrant colours dimmed by dust and the smoke of constant joss.

Into this wonderful old place walked Sing, the bell above her head croaking like a frog as she entered. Doctor Sun appeared from a door in the rear under a grand old clock supported by prancing unicorns. At first he did not recognise her and only when she showed him the note in his own hand did he recall the young girl who had occupied the small house by the stream on the farm of his uncle. Sing's welcome to the shop called Everspring and into the midst of the Sun family was properly courteous and reserved.

His four young sons sat politely when they had greeted her and the doctor's wife prepared tea as Sing told her story. Inside the crowded back room, packed with heavy furniture and hung with the charts and diagrams of traditional Chinese medicine, they seemed completely cut off from the chaos that reigned outside. Although the jars on the shelves shook from time to time and the tassels on the lantern trembled, the sounds of war were deadened to a distant rumble.

Doctor Sun and his family seemed not at all frightened by the battle that raged around them. The bombardment, they said, was concentrated on the Central District, Wan Chai and the Peak. It did not care about small shopkeepers of Causeway Bay. Besides, Doctor Sun explained, Everspring was well guarded by his ancestors. One whole wall of the room was neatly arranged with ancestral tablets and the many pictures of his clan. The small shrine beneath them held a large golden Buddha with burning joss on each side and an array of gifts at its feet. He lifted his cup to Sing and the others followed. She was welcome, he said, to sit at their table and share their protection.

It had not taken very long to discover that the battle was over and that the Union Jack had been replaced by the Rising Sun. The doctor's big Marconi radio, run by accumulators, that sat in pride of place second only to the golden Buddha, kept them well informed. The Chinese citizens of Hong Kong had been liberated it announced, the morning after Sing's arrival at Everspring.

A glorious victory had been won over decadent colonial oppression. The Imperial Japanese Forces of Emperor Hirohito were the new rulers of Hong Kong, soon to be rulers of Asia, Great Britain and America. Hourly announcements continued throughout the day and into the night. The cowardly soldiers of the British king had been defeated.

The Chinese citizens, it said, had nothing to fear from their Japanese masters if they followed the new rules. The rules laid down and broadcast by a Japanese interpreter were simple enough to follow but not always understood. First and foremost came respect. Respect for every Japanese soldier, regardless of rank, would be shown by bowing low.

Failure to bow to the uniform would be seen as disrespect, a direct insult to the emperor and severely punished on the spot.

Any form of resistance, protest or questioning of the new regime would also be seen as disrespect and punished. Lifting a hand against a Japanese soldier would be punished by imprisonment or execution. Looters would be put to death by decapitation, as would anyone suspected of plotting armed resistance or sheltering British personnel who had escaped detention.

Further broadcasts told of the fate of British prisoners. Civilians, they announced, were interned in the Stanley prison camp of Shong Shi Poo and Victoria Prison. Concentration camps were being prepared to hold military prisoners of war in Kowloon and the New Territories where some would await trial and execution. Sing had no way of knowing if Toby was dead or alive. There was no way of finding out and all she could do was hope.

There was one window in the cell where Toby had lain for almost two months, unable to stand. A bayonet thrust had penetrated his groin and another had ripped through his stomach. The wounds had quickly become infected and he would have died if the Japanese major-general had not decided on an inspection of the old prison on Stonecutter's Island. It had once again been turned into a prison hospital for wounded officers.

General Toshido was a professional soldier and what little Toby had seen of him suggested he behaved like one. He had looked around the ancient stone building with its crumbling flights of stone steps and narrow passageways leading to dungeon-like cells, where they had put the seriously wounded. The walls and floor were built of huge granite blocks and the mid-winter temperature had turned them ice cold.

Toshido had ordered braziers to be brought and grass to be cut to cover the floor and had turned the old Q Stores into a hospital ward. Toby had been taken there and it had saved his life, but the space was limited and the six beds badly needed. They had returned him to the cell too weak to move but well enough to recover.

The brazier was still there but there was no fuel. The prisoners had soon used the pile of wood and burned the grass intended to cover the flagstones. They would have frozen to death if Toshido had not ordered blankets confiscated from a Kowloon warehouse to be distributed among them.

That bitter cold would come again but the administration of prisoners of war had settled into some form of order, so conditions had improved to a point where survival was possible. Those considered fit enough had been transported from Stonecutter's to the larger internment camps. Only the sick and lame were left on the island.

The window was two metres from the ground, no more than half a metre square with a single iron bar dividing its space. An old bag of cement that had turned rock hard served as a viewing platform and each of the inmates took turns to stand on it for fifteen minutes each throughout the day. Toby could not see the roof of the Pelhams' bungalow but he could see the spread of the big oak that grew at its gate.

No day had passed that he did not wonder what had happened to Sing and the others. He tried not to think of her at all. Each time a man returned from the ward or outside duty he brought another story of rape and brutality on the mainland. The bamboo telegraph ran hot with rumours of Japanese atrocities. Toby was sure that escape was possible. The guards were vicious but they were slack. They seemed to think that because Stonecutter's was an island and its inmates were infirm there was no need for vigilance. The sentries and patrol pickets were becoming bored and idle. Each time he took his turn at the window, Toby reviewed his plan of escape.

The harbour was still filled with sunken shipping, otherwise the junks and sampans seemed to have returned to normal life. But after almost a year the same scene day after day had become monotonous and he watched for birds on the slope below instead. He guessed that Peggy Pelham had been taken to Stanley camp if she had survived and he had heard that Justin Pelham had died with most of his Rajputs in the battle at Taipo.

There had been several escape attempts in the year the wounded had occupied the old fort. At first they had been allowed to exercise in the walled yard until several prisoners had disappeared into the honeycomb of passageways that networked the old building like a rabbit warren. Those who had remained hidden and reached the water were all turned over to the Japanese by the sampan crews who pulled them from the harbour.

The guard commander in charge had turned what had been an exercise yard into an execution ground and Toby had witnessed the beheading of eight British and Canadian officers. He had been too ill until now to attempt any escape of his own but he knew exactly where he would go when the opportunity came. There was a connection with the Nationalist guerrillas in the New

Territories and the way to make contact had been passed on from the main prison camp at Sham Shui Po.

A tap on the shoulder told him that his time was up and he stepped down from the cement bag to let a major of the Middlesex Regiment take his place. The window, open to the elements, gave the only light there was to illuminate the huge space and most of the makeshift bunks were arranged around it in some semblance of regimental order.

Towards the end of the winter of 1942 Major-General Toshido visited the island a second time and when Toby and others pointed out that the brazier he had authorised was useless without fuel, the general issued an order allowing parties under escort to forage for wood. Some of it had been used to fashion rough charpoys, like those used by beggars and sweepers in the streets of Bombay.

As senior ranking officer Toby had supervised their assembly and all manner of materials had been salvaged around the shoreline to use as stretchers—pieces of sailcloth, reed matting, and old tarpaulins discarded by the boat people. Chunks of driftwood, old hatch boards, flotsam of all kinds, were dragged up and turned into crude pieces of furniture. With the coming of warmer weather the privilege had stopped. It would be six months before the fuel foraging parties would begin again and when they did, he would be ready.

The Mid Autumn Festival, 1942

DOCTOR SUN and his family took Sing into their midst just as Po Lok and Kam Yang had done. Simple Hakka custom accepted that she do her share of work in the shop. As she had once cut grass, picked fruit and planted rice in the Residence of Eternal

Peace, she now learned to weigh and prepare herbal prescriptions for the patients and customers of Everspring.

The doctor was delighted by her knowledge of Chinese medicine and understanding of the human condition. In the evenings she took out the works of Master To, which they studied together, and during the day, when there were no customers, he taught her to read the five silent pulses and how to diagnose and treat the ailment with acupuncture and lighted herb sticks. She would some day make a fine barefoot doctor, he said. Already she knew more than many who claimed to be healers.

The Japanese occupation had little effect on the cloistered life of Everspring. The four sons no longer attended school. They studied hard in the back room, the large table littered with the business of Chinese medicine. When they left the shop to find necessities Sing began to go with them. Dressed in the sam foo of an amah, her hair braided into a pigtail under a wide hat of rattan, she called no attention to herself.

Japanese soldiers patrolled in pairs on every street and squads marched regularly through the heart of Wan Chai. The hatred between Chinese and Japanese was old and strong. The 'Yut Boon Jai'—Japanese boy, known as the brown monkey—had always been an enemy of China and every foot soldier who had been given the status of a ruling master made full use of this authority. Faces were slapped as a way of relieving the boredom of endless patrols. If a bow was not considered low enough it was cause for punishment. Every glance, every movement, could be seen as a mark of disrespect to the Japanese emperor. If the slap became a closed fist or a kick, what difference was there? Who would complain?

Food was scarce for the people of Hong Kong, all market produce commandeered for the army of occupation. Fresh fish and meat went straight from the markets to their depots. For the starving Chinese population collection centres were set up throughout the colony for the distribution of six catties of rice for each person per day and daily life became the finding of a dried fish, a morsel of meat or chicken. Eggs became a valuable currency.

The Japanese controlled the duck and poultry farms of the New Territories, placing guards on every property to see that nothing was hoarded. The punishment for hiding food from the supply trucks varied with the discipline of individual guards or the platoon commanders who patrolled the market garden areas from Taipo to Fanling. Many people were shot, beaten and tortured over a sackful of cabbages, a live chicken or a basket of eggs.

Shops were allowed to stay open but the price of the simplest goods was so high that only the rich and privileged could afford them. Hong Kong currency had been recalled and in its place occupation money was printed. Its highest denomination was $100 and the collecting of these notes for the purchase of black-market goods became the means of existence in the streets of Hong Kong and Kowloon. Responsibility for civil order also came under the command of Major-General Toshido and one of his first decisions was to release senior British banking staff from the Stanley prison in order to liquidate the Hong Kong and Shanghai Bank. Under heavy guard they were brought each day to help audit the wealth of the colony for transfer to Tokyo.

In spite of ever-present Japanese patrols and the random punishments they handed out, gangs of Chinese youths broke into shops and houses and held people up on the street. Burglary, shoplifting and thuggery were out of control. Those who wished to survive the threat of danger from both the Japanese and their own kind remained behind locked doors, venturing out once a day to collect the family rice ration, bowing deeply to every uniform they encountered and listening at the appointed times for the latest radio announcements of those who had broken regulations and the punishment they suffered. At all other times the switching on of radios was banned and those who were caught listening were severely beaten, their radio sets confiscated or smashed.

In spite of those daily broadcasts, acts of defiance continued to increase. General Toshido began to suspect that his orders and the consequences of disobeying them may not be getting through as clearly as he intended. He made a note to replace Lieutenant Mashima with a local Chinese broadcaster. But as he would still have no way of being certain that his exact words were relayed with the tone and authority they demanded, the idea was set aside for more pressing concerns.

He had received reports that British survivors were still in hiding and under the protection of Nationalists operating in the New Territories with the collaboration of Hakka villagers. The reports were based on rumour but claimed that whilst some of the British were being smuggled to Thailand by fishing junk, others were said to be joining the infiltrators to form a guerilla force. He issued renewed warnings through Lieutenant Mashima, stepping up activity throughout the Territories, laying on a small fleet of patrol boats to cover Mirs Bay, Tolo harbour and surrounding waters.

Doctor Sun listened intently to this announcement. His cousin

Chen Yu may be in danger, he said. As headman of Pok Choy Lam village he was responsible for the actions of those within its walls. Sing had met Chen Yu. He or his sons had visited the Everspring herb shop several times, risking danger to bring fresh eggs and vegetables. The rumours were true, they said. Certain Chinese families and people of the Hakka were hiding the gwai-lo and helping them to escape. Chen Yu and his family were among them.

Because of Chen Yu the Everspring herb shop did not go hungry, although Doctor Sun had begged his cousin not to risk the dangers of sending food across the harbour. He had sources of his own, he said. Food could be bought on the black market by those with the means. The penalties for trafficking in hoarded goods were never terrible enough to displace the Chinese god of profit and there was little the Japanese could do to stop it.

The districts of Causeway Bay, Wan Chai, Northpoint and Shau Kei Wan were impenetrable nests of high-rise buildings, ground floor shops, restaurants, godowns, garages and basements. Patrols had made token efforts to infiltrate the tens of thousands of rooms and to search the rows upon rows of warehouses and makeshift storage places but their initial zeal had been soon discouraged.

Chinese business had gone back to its own devices in these tough, downtown areas, and the administration of General Toshido had thought it best to leave things that way. The Moon Festival was approaching and the celebration of such occasions was best left alone.

A few days before the festival, Chen Yu and his sons arrived with eggs, flour and fruit for the making of mooncakes. They also brought large bundles of sugar cane, laughing because the Japanese had thought it was bamboo. It was easy to bring across the harbour by sampan and they promised to bring more. When they had left, Doctor Sun took Sing to his godown. It was a row of three converted garages buried in the back streets, far enough away from the waterfront to be off the beat of regular patrols. Each space was heavily padlocked and secured by iron shutters. Inside they were stacked to the rafters with cartons, chests and crates of Chinese medicines.

'The shop of my father is my humble business, but I have great plans for my sons,' he said, as Sing looked around the vast hoard of valuable merchandise. 'Their future lies here. The Double Elephant Trading Company. Come, Siu Sing. I will show you why I have brought you here.'

In a corner of the shadowy vault he uncovered an old sugar-cane crusher of the type she had seen in the roadside of Taipo market. It was rusty and dust-covered but the doctor pulled it into the light, reminding Sing instantly of the first time she had tasted the sweet juice of sugar cane in the market-place of Yuenchow with Master To.

'Here is a way for you to earn some money. We will clean this machine and put it at the door of my shop. We will make extra money from selling sugar-cane juice at the time of the lantern festival.'

Nine months had passed since the Japanese flag had first been raised in the grounds of Government House. Many of the mansions in the Mid-Levels and on the Peak were occupied by Japanese officers and administration staff. The bank audits had long been completed and the British bankers returned to Stanley camp. When some of them were found to have started a tunnel, they were forced to use the crude tools they had made for their escape to dig their own graves. The rest of the internees were forced to watch their execution by Samurai sword.

In the first few weeks at Everspring Sing had discovered that prisoners in Stanley were allowed no visitors, not even from loyal servants bringing them news of their property. She knew exactly where the detention centres and military prisons had been set up, and that there was no way of making enquiries about the inmates. She felt certain that Toby was still alive and went each day to Victoria Park where she tried to find out more. The park was one place the Japanese left alone, a hectare or two of public gardens shaded by banyan trees. Old and young had been coming there since the trees were planted, to take their morning exercise and sit on the seats to gossip.

It was patrolled by pairs of soldiers but unless a group became too large they were content to stroll the pathways while the old ones walked their birds and the young boxed with the shadows or performed their Tai Chi Chuan. The guards had no idea that this was where black market contacts were made and that it was developing into the centre of information on every aspect of survival under the Yut Boon Jai.

Strongest among the many rumours was the one that still claimed the Generalissimo's forces were soon to liberate Hong Kong. The great leader of the Chinese people was gathering the heroes of free China into a mighty force that would soon sweep down to liberate them. The brown monkeys would be hung from these very trees and their blood would nourish the flowers.

Sing heard talk of the many British soldiers kept in the big prison camp at the edge of Kowloon city and of those who were beheaded for trying to escape. She tried to close her mind to the talk of terrible punishments and to pray like the others for the coming of the Kuomintang.

There was another rumour that also gave her hope. If enough money was offered to the prison-camp guards it was possible to send a message to a prisoner. It was this possibility that made her work hard at the sugar-cane crusher. When Doctor Sun had suggested setting it up outside the shop of Everspring she welcomed the chance. His sons had brought the old machine from the godown and she helped them to clean and oil the parts.

Just how organised the black market in food stuffs and the endurance of Chinese custom really was, proved itself with the celebration of the mid-autumn Lantern Festival of 1942. In normal times it was the Chinese thanksgiving for an abundant harvest and a prosperous year, celebrated by the making and eating of mooncakes.

The more prestigious the family the more elaborate the ingredients of the mooncake. Lard, spices, eggs, orange peel, almonds and sugar were all a part of the rich recipe and the more salted egg yolks found in each mooncake, the more fortunate the cake and those who ate it.

Special fruits such as persimmons, starfruit, pomegranates and melons were also a part of the festive feast. The seeds of such fruit were symbolic of many sons and continued family unity. Paper lanterns were lit and those in the shape of a rabbit were towed along on wooden wheels by the children. Kites flew and firecrackers were let off, all in honour of the harvest moon and the approach to the close of another year.

Not to celebrate the mid-autumn Moon Festival was a certain invitation to bad luck in the year to come. Although the Chinese citizens of Hong Kong had very little to be thankful for in the year of 1942, and in spite of a ban on all such celebrations, it somehow went ahead under the noses of the Japanese enforcers.

The fifteenth day of the eighth moon was greeted with strings of crackers that exploded like gunfire in the streets and alleyways of the downtown districts. Kites were flown from the rooftops, and behind closed doors lanterns were lit and mooncakes of varying richness were eaten as they always had been.

Peggy Pelham had become a force to be reckoned in the women's section of Stanley Prison. She fortified the spirits of the other women when the discomforts and harsh treatment of the camp got them down. She spoke up for them when the food was impossible to eat, demanded medicine for those who fell sick and blankets for the stone beds as the weather began to turn cold. Major Kojiki was comparatively uninterested in his role as camp commandant and spent as much time attending parties or in the company of newly-acquired mistresses as he found possible.

He was more inclined to give the formidable Englishwoman what she wanted than to have a gaggle of rebellious and infirm women to contend with. He had found it quite convenient to have one voice to deal with rather than several hundred and since she had stopped asking about the whereabouts of her husband, he tolerated her demands to see him with a reasonable patience.

Peggy would not believe that Justin was dead, although there had been no word of him from Victoria Prison or the camps on Kowloon side. Information found a way of getting through and she had discovered that Toby Hyde-Wilkins, although badly wounded, had recovered and was alive on Stonecutter's Island. She had wondered about the fate of Siu Sing, but had put such thoughts aside along with hopes for Justin and turned all her strength to the business of survival and the encouragement of those around her.

In the men's section of the prison Sebastian Masters had not fared so well. Like many others he had become ill from the bad food and cramped existence. In the first months he had been active in agitating for improved conditions. As a senior government official he considered it his duty to be outspoken and called for extended exercise time, better food and living conditions. The tall, thin Englishman had become a nuisance and too outspoken. Major Kojiki had ordered him beaten and given a month of solitary confinement.

Sebastian had never quite recovered and when four of the bank men had formed an escape committee he stayed away from it. He was not strong enough, he said, and would not risk letting them down. When the four men were caught and made to dig their own graves with the other prisoners looking on, he recognised that he was afraid, weakened even further by the horror of their execution.

He was unable to rid his mind of the sound as the blade severed their necks with a single blow, the sight of the bodies rolled by the feet of the guards into the shallow graves, their heads tossed like cabbages after them. He had been among the party chosen to fill them in. Sebastian had become deeply disturbed, causing him to withdraw from those around him.

Then something had happened that concerned him even more than his hidden anxiety and waning spirit. He was aware that after lights out some of the men visited each other's beds. Long into the night their whispering reached his ears; later he saw the glow of cigarettes bought from the guards, shared in the darkness. A night came when he sensed a presence close beside him, felt the breath of another very close—not really hearing it. He did not move. There were all kinds among the hundreds that shared the dormitories. At first there had been an attempt to segregate nationalities and to organise some sort of rank system. Now, in the second year of confinement, it had soon broken down and become the way of all jails—survival of the fittest.

Only half-conscious, he allowed his breathing to continue evenly, as though he was asleep, hoping the presence would move on. A strange excitement had replaced the initial shock of fear. He found himself waiting with thudding heart. Waiting for what? There had been no real violence; apart from some petty thieving the inmates of Stanley had maintained a certain orderliness.

He did not want to speak or call out in case he was mistaken. He kept nothing worth stealing. Resisting the impulse to sit up, he waited, the blood of anticipation singing in his ears. It was a hot night and he felt suddenly vulnerable, aware of his nakedness, the tangled cotton sheet thrown aside. Sweat beaded freshly on his brow as the moments ticked by. Only the sounds of snoring came from the beds.

He had almost drifted back into sleep when the first touch came, so light he was not sure if he had imagined it. Little more than the tiny shifting of air made by a fan. Then a hand, hot against the skin of his leg, rested lightly. It lay there, briefly still, then moving with a stroking motion up his thigh. Sebastian gritted his teeth against the sensation that had gripped him in a way that sapped him of all remaining strength.

It was not fear or anger; it was not revulsion or disgust. Thoughts raced through his fevered mind—should he strike out now or should he wait? Aware of his weakened condition he wondered if he was dreaming. The fingers reached cautiously for him. The breath caught in his throat as he felt himself aroused in response to tickling fingertips. The hand, unseen in the pitch blackness, wrapped around his hardness.

With a loud cry Sebastian grabbed the wrist as it began to move him. With every ounce of his strength he squeezed, pulling the hand away as he hissed a warning. The fingers instantly relaxed and left him. A single wrench and the arm he held broke free and was gone. He stayed sitting up, flooded by a feeling of relief that he had acted and that the presence was gone. When he lay down, sleep evaded him and in its place was a feeling of crushing guilt.

He faced the truth, there in the hot night, the sweat continuing to pour from him, the ache in him unappeased, his erection jerked by each shuddering breath. Sebastian buried his face in the hard, musty pillow, knowing he had not wanted the touch to leave him. That his heart still beat wildly as he wondered if it would return. It never did.

The Moon Festival

ON THE evening of the Lantern Festival a sugar-cane grinder stood outside the herb shop of Everspring. It had been cleaned and oiled and given a fresh coat of bright yellow paint. Beside it was a long bundle of raw sugar cane. Sing turned the big handle that revolved the rollers, crushing the sweet cloudy juice into a row of glasses which she had washed in a bucket. Sugar-cane juice was a part of every festive occasion and a popular medicine for cooling the blood. She was doing good trade among the people who thronged their way to Victoria Park to claim their spot and light their candles and hang their lanterns.

The streets of Causeway Bay and all the other downtown districts of Hong Kong were alive with the crowds. At first the coloured lanterns had been few, bobbing furtively from house to house in the early dark. Then others had joined and as the festive habit of many lifetimes took over and the rice wine had its effect, the streets began to fill with lanterns, flowing like a carnival to welcome the harvest moon.

From where he stood, looking down from his private offices in the Hong Kong Club, General Toshido watched them dancing like fireflies between the tall buildings. He knew enough about ceremony of this sort to understand the force behind it. The Japanese had festivals of their own and he had seen what happened when attempts were made to suppress them. The Hong Kong Cantonese were different from the hardened mainlanders who fought for every bowl of rice. The Chinamen of Hong Kong had left such hardships behind in search of something better, they felt no allegiance to the British and if kept in order but left alone, such harmless occasions as this could cause no real trouble.

Sergeant Oshi Koda and his corporal made their way along Lockhart Road. Here and there, paper lanterns had caught alight and lay burning in the gutter. When a small boy ran by with his rabbit lantern in flames Sergeant Koda grinned but his wide face showed no real amusement. He and Corporal Yamitoshi were on duty and had been in and out of the bars that were still open in Wan Chai.

The San Miguel brewery in Kowloon was working again and although Japanese soldiers preferred their own Osaka beer or hot saki they found the Spanish brew good enough to get drunk on. In the bar called the Happy Butterfly Sergeant Koda had ordered the mama san to tear down the collection of Royal Naval capbands, photographs of British warships and the painted crests of famous vessels that covered its walls. Hand-trolley Lulu had been forced to make a pile of them in the centre of the floor and set fire to it. While it burned, they drank a toast to Emperor Hirohito. Then they locked the doors and took the bargirls upstairs.

Non-commissioned officers on town patrol were not supposed to drink but Sergeant Koda hated the Chinese and to walk among them cold sober was more than he was prepared to do. By the time they had patrolled the full length of Lockhart Road his face was flushed red from bars he had visited. Further on, as they entered the Causeway Bay area, they approached a shop with a sugar-cane machine outside.

The coolie woman who operated it bowed low as Sergeant Koda held out his hand for a glass of the soothing juice. The corporal also took one and as they stood drinking the sweet cloudy liquid they took little notice of the girl who served them.

As they drained the glasses and made to move on, Sing asked for payment. Sergeant Koda's response was to raise his hand angrily. Before it could strike Sing's face she instinctively blocked the blow. It had been a reflex action, so much a part of her that it was not a conscious act. The sergeant's thick neck bulged with anger as he struck out a second time. Again the blow was easily evaded. It was as though the coolie woman had become a shadow.

Corporal Yamitoshi was too amused to act. Too much beer had affected his better judgement. When he saw the second blow so deftly avoided he found himself laughing aloud at the look on his sergeant's face. He hardly realised that his laughter had been joined by the Chinese gathered around them. From across the street and on either side the Chinese revellers jeered the Japanese sergeant who could not defeat a coolie woman. Only when Sergeant Koda's barked command brought him to his senses did the corporal act.

Hollywood Road was the place of antique dealers. Its cramped shops opened up onto the narrow street with steel shutters and heavily barred doorways. They tunnelled back like deep rabbit warrens into the blocks of buildings laden with the treasures of early China. Jade, ivory, gilt screens, sacred temple carvings and precious woods shaped into things of exquisite beauty crammed their small dark window spaces and the basements and upper floors were stacked with more.

Normally, the little street leading down the crowded hill towards the markets was loud with the noise of vendors moving among those westerners who had arrived by ship as tourists. This was where the wealthy and famous came to find the impossible, reach out and touch the unreachable, then buy it at any price to grace the richest homes in the world.

The street was silent and almost deserted as the Japanese patrol wagon drove down the hill. The street and all its contents were now the property of Japan. Branching off from it and in direct contrast was Cat Street, the thieves' market of Hong Kong, where a crush of buyers and sellers haggled over its secondhand jumble of scrap metal, tin pots and pans, brass spittoons, broken clocks and cheap watches that packed ladder streets lined with ramshackle stalls. Cat Street had nothing the Japanese wanted. They did not know it was another black market centre.

In the back of the van, Sing lay on the metal runners of the floor at the feet of three street vendors who had not understood the rule of bowing. They had already searched Sing's unconscious body but had found nothing worth stealing. Now they sat as far from her as possible. Even her swollen face could not hide the fact that she was jarp jung. To help her would bring only more bad joss.

The patrol wagon pulled up outside the detention centre that had been set up in the Hollywood Road post office, its many small rooms used as holding cells. Sergeant Koda climbed down while Corporal Yamatoshi sprang the security bar of the rear doors. The sergeant did not wait for his corporal to pull the prisoners out and drag Sing from the back of the vehicle but walked stiffly up the steps to make his report.

The coolie woman who had raised her hand against the uniform of the emperor had proved to be of western blood. With the corporal holding her from behind, he had beaten her without mercy but still she would not tell him where she came from or what she was doing in the Chinese quarter dressed as a peasant. He had made sure that every blow he had struck was witnessed by the crowd who had dared to laugh at him.

Even then she had threatened to make a fool of him, enduring a beating that should have seen her unconscious in half the time. Sergeant Koda had taken her resilience as more deliberate defiance and it made her a special case to him. The beating had left him sweating and breathless but he could not make her cry out or beg for mercy. He would enjoy breaking this stray bitch in his own time and in his own way.

When Sing felt herself dumped on a cold hard floor of linoleum oilcloth, she lay still until a door slammed shut. Even then she only rolled over on her back and made no attempt to sit up. The heavy fists of Sergeant Koda had done their best to break her ribs but by breathing slowly and deeply she found he had not succeeded. She kept her eyes closed until she felt an arm slide gently under her neck and shoulders.

'Jeesusss . . . what did you do to get this? This is no slap in the puss.' A man's voice whispered in English with a strong American twang.

Sing tried to open her eyes but they stayed shut. The arm helped her sit, the voice was close to her ear. Other voices murmured in Cantonese and feet shuffled around her.

'Don't be scared, kid. The name is Freddy Fong. You're in the Hollywood Road hoosegow.'

Sing tried to speak but her lips would not move.

'Don't say nothin'. Your whole kisser is banged up.'

The arm that supported her was firm and tried to be gentle as Sing felt herself pulled across the floor until her back was against a wall. She tried again to force open an eye. A blurred slit revealed nothing but white and blinding light and through it the indistinct shape of a face. The light flooded her eyes with scalding tears.

'Take it easy, kid. I speak the lingo. I'll get you a doctor. They got an officer downstairs who ain't so bad.'

A hand carefully touched her face, a finger gently pulling down on her lower eyelids. 'Did you lose any teeth?'

Sing shook her head as the hand ran over her arms and legs.

Then, whispering in Cantonese, as though speaking to himself, 'Aeyah. Those Yut Boon Jai. They are sons of syphilitic bitches.' The voice spoke in English again. 'Don't say nothin'. Take it easy. You'll be okay.'

She felt something touch her bruised and bleeding lips; stinging liquid seared her mouth.

'Easy kid. Take a slug. Don't spill it. It's all I've got.'

She recognised the smell of whisky and tried to shake her head but the voice was persistent.

'This'll help, believe me.'

The whisky flooded into her throat.

'Jeeessuzzz' the voice said, as the knot of her stomach sprang loose and she was violently sick.

Cantonese voices rose in disgust. As the spasms subsided something was folded to support her head.

'You'll be okay, kid. You'll be okay.' The words repeated themselves in Sing's ear as the blackness closed in.

Freddy Fong had made a place in a corner where Sing would be left alone by the twenty or so Chinese who sat around the walls waiting to see what would happen to them. When the door opened and a bucket of cold rice with a few scraps of salt fish was left in the middle of the room, he joined the scramble and took enough for two. When he turned to find Sing had forced one of her badly bruised eyes open, he filled her cupped hands with half-cooked rice.

'Eat it slowly. Don't waste any. Getting your share in here ain't easy.'

What Sing could see of Freddy Fong was comforting. His round, moon face wore a slight grin that looked as though it had always been there, even in his sleep. She winced as the rice reached her broken lips.

'Eat it slowly. Couple of grains at a time if you have to.'

Downstairs in what had been the postmaster's office, Sergeant Koda made a special entry of the time and circumstances of Sing's arrest. The young lieutenant in charge of the centre was out of the room so he helped himself to a glass of tea. Outside in the large mailroom, now a billet for the dozen guards, Corporal Yamatoshi kept his voice down and an eye on the office door as he told of the girl who had got the better of old Pork-belly.

Sergeant Oshi Koda was not a popular man with the private soldiers and NCOs beneath him. He was a regular with many years' service, who believed he should have been commissioned. The fact that he had never got past the rank of sergeant made him a difficult and dangerous man to deal with. He was a pig to those he commanded and he took pride in his unpopularity.

The corporal's version of the sergeant's confrontation with the girl and the sugar-cane juice took on new dimensions. By the time it got around the mail room, the round-eye had flown in the air like a bird, moved like a shadow and fought like a ninja. Pork-belly had not been able to lay a hand on her until he, Corporal Yamatoshi, and three onlookers had held her down for him.

Lieutenant Mashima returned to his cubicle of an office to find Sergeant Koda drinking his tea. He didn't like the heavy-handed sergeant from Kobi. He was an untouchable from the slum where those suspected of Korean blood were allowed to live. If he hadn't become a professional soldier he would have been a shoveller of manure. The man had a knack of just stopping short of insubordination and a way of letting it be known that he had no respect for drafted officers who got their rank and privilege through family connections and not experience.

'There is one upstairs,' said the sergeant, saluting, 'that I think is with the resistance.'

'Is he British or Chinese?' asked the lieutenant.

'It is a woman. She is neither. She violently resisted arrest. Do I have permission to interrogate?'

The lieutenant had witnessed Sergeant Koda's methods of interrogation before, and it had increased his distaste for the man.

'Perhaps,' he said shortly. The telephone rang and he picked up the receiver, his eyes signalling the sergeant's dismissal.

After Koda had gone the lieutenant did his rounds and paid particular attention to the girl the sergeant had reported. Picking her out by the coppery mass of her hair loosened from its plait, he could never have told she was not Chinese from her broken face.

Freddy Fong looked up when he entered. 'This one needs a doctor bad,' he said in Japanese. 'I think she's busted up inside.' He made a gesture at the pool of vomit drying on the floor. 'She can't eat. She needs a doctor,' he repeated.

The lieutenant drew his shiny cavalry boot back a step and his nose wrinkled under his polished spectacles.

'Where did you learn to speak Japanese?' he demanded.

'Shanghai, Captain,' answered Freddy, hoping the elevation of rank would improve his chances. 'I worked for the Americans and the Japanese.'

Lieutenant Mashima knew of the Shanghainese photographer from the *South China Morning Post*. He had already decided this man would be useful.

'Captain,' Freddy put all the respect he could into the title. 'Do you know what happened to my cameras?'

'Your cameras are Japanese and German. They are too good to smash. They are safe.'

Freddy drew a long breath. He decided this was as good a time as he'd ever have. 'Captain, any time I and my cameras can serve you. Any time. I'm from Shanghai. I don't know why I'm here. I don't belong with these Cantonese . . .' He waved a hand at the other prisoners.

'You were brought here so that you may be useful to us. Do not speak until I ask you to.'

The lieutenant's eyes remained on Sing. There was no doubt that this was the work of Sergeant Koda. He smiled to himself. So this was the girl who had flown like a cat in the face of the pork belly. His eyes took in what they could of her body under the shapeless jacket and wide-legged pants. She looked strong enough in the limbs and longer than the squat Chinese. The lieutenant snapped an order, stepping aside for two guards to enter. They lifted Sing by her arms and legs and carried her out.

A faint fluttering sound seemed to come and go in the blackness behind Sing's eyes. She opened them slowly. The light was not as painful as before and past the dark humps of swelling she could see an electric fan, lengths of coloured paper flapping and streaming in the current of warm air it rotated across the room. The flesh of her face ached with the pulsing of her blood, like the slow tramping of heavy feet.

With her tongue she felt the damage inside her cheek. Her mouth was foul and dry, her nostrils clogged with blood. The metallic taste of it had given her a burning thirst. One by one she tested her joints: wrists, elbows, ankles, knees. They were stiff but nothing more. Slowly she stood up from the bed of mailbags she had been lain upon. She was alone in a small space just large enough to lie down in. A big old-fashioned weighing machine of cast iron stood in one corner.

One whole wall was of steel wire mesh which opened onto the mail room. Twelve iron beds were lined precisely along one side, an overhead cabinet and foot locker to each bed. Sing guessed she had been put in the mailroom's security lock-up. Through the metal grid of the mesh she could see four Japanese guards playing cards on the sorting bench that was now their mess table. A fifth was stretched out on one of the beds reading a magazine. Cigarette smoke and the vinegary smell of perspiration filled the air and from the open window the sound of army trucks ground up Hollywood Road towards Central, laden with market produce.

The August Moon Festival had brought an Indian summer, a last wave of dense humidity that seemed to press in through the windows where the ceiling fans just chopped it around. Sing looked about her. There was an army blanket thrown over the mailbags; a tin plate of cold food and a mug of cold tea stood on a wooden filing cabinet beside the fan. One of the guards caught sight of her movement behind the mesh.

Throwing down his cards, he came quickly to the wire and peered through. The others followed, talking in high, excited voices, as they appraised the woman who had already gained the status of a ninja. The dangerous partisan who had stolen the face of Sergeant Pork-belly. At the sound of their voices the lieutenant came from his office. They snapped to attention and quickly stood aside.

Lieutenant Mashima had the high cheekbones and long jaw of the well-bred. His skin was pale as a woman's, his black, oiled hair parted in the centre to show a chalk-white line of scalp. He had removed his jacket and loosened the buttons of his shirt in the oppressive heat. A long-barrelled German automatic was closed in a leather holster as highly buffed as his knee boots.

He spoke to Sing in Japanese. When she shook her head, asking in Cantonese if he spoke Chinese or English, he rapped another order. In moments a guard returned with Freddy Fong, the Shanghainese photographer bowing every step of the way. He glanced reassuringly at Sing before talking in Japanese with the lieutenant. After a moment he turned back to her.

'The captain here wants to know if you are all right. If you need anything.'

'I need water, teet-dah, salt and fresh ginger to make a poultice and something to wash with.'

Freddy relayed this to the lieutenant.

'He says do you need medical treatment?'

'Thank him, but tell him no. If I have these things I can treat myself.'

Freddy knew that teet-dah was the penetrating medicant applied in Chinese medicine, used externally for the drawing out of bruising and the healing of muscle injury. The Japanese officer spoke again for fully a minute. Freddy translated.

'He says he will let you have these things and then you must tell him who you are and who you are working with or he will hand you over to Sergeant Koda.'

Sing could see that the Japanese officer meant what he said. She also knew that if she had to face the sergeant again nothing would save her. To defend herself a second time would mean certain death, he would see to that. She thought quickly and calmly.

'Tell the captain that I am a barefoot healer, a herbalist, and that I practise in the shop at the place where I was arrested.'

The lieutenant engaged in another long conversation with Freddy.

'He wants to know your name and nationality. Why did you insult the emperor by attacking his sergeant? Careful how you answer, kid. The captain thinks you're some kind of spy.'

It was clear that the lieutenant also realised Sing was a woman. Dropping her eyes and using the tone of pure innocence the Golden One had taught her for such times, she spoke softly. 'How could a poor girl attack such a great warrior?' she asked humbly. 'Tell him I did not intend insult. Only to ask payment for my sugar-cane juice.'

The lieutenant listened intently while Freddy translated, then rapped an order. The guard commander was at his side in an instant.

'You're in luck, kid.' Freddy added quietly, 'he's gonna send this palooka to get your stuff.'

Jiro Toshido

THE DINING room of the Hong Kong Club was filled with Japanese officers. The cooling system had been levelled to a comfortable temperature and the smell of hot breakfast was pleasantly inviting. Silver and cut-glass vases filled with flowers had been placed on every table and Japanese music played discreetly over the sound system. General Toshido entered and was shown to the corner table he always used when staying in the suite of rooms he had commandeered as his private office.

Like the other officers of various rank who were beginning their day, he was freshly turned out in dress uniform. He did not like being ordered to entertain the Chinese taipan, whoever he was; and he didn't like to be kept waiting. Through the window he could see down into the square where a squad of soldiers was dismantling the bronze statue of Queen Victoria.

The promotion he had been promised had not yet come through although the extra responsibility was already his. Even without the full rank had come the added responsibility for military as well as civilian prisons and this had not been easy to meet. Now that order had been established, for the most part, those responsibilities took care of themselves. He had turned all his attentions to the tracing and capturing of those Britishers and Chinese Nationalists still at large or in hiding in the New Territories. Well into the second year of occupation there were still occasional break-outs from the main camp in Kowloon and now from Stonecutter's Island. He had been forced to order the execution of those who were captured and it was his leniency that had been blamed for poor security.

Repeated searches of the Hakka villages had revealed very little, and although dozens of villagers had been interrogated and some executions had been carried out as an example, there were still considered to be significant numbers of fugitives unaccounted for. Several cases of attacks upon patrols and minor acts of sabotage had been reported. Rumours that a large underground force was being armed and reinforced by mainland Nationalists continued to gain strength.

It was the reason for this early morning meeting which he would have gladly done without. The beautiful old house on Magazine Gap Road that he occupied halfway up the Peak, with its serene gardens and sweeping views of the harbour, was infinitely preferable to the clatter and chatter that surrounded him now. The debilitating headaches he suffered were becoming increasingly frequent and severe and no medical officer had been able to relieve them. He ordered plain water while he waited for his guest and swallowed several pain-killing pills.

He had been handed private despatches with regard to the man he was to meet, a Chinese who owned much of the land which the Hakkas farmed. A drug-runner strongly connected with Tokyo syndicates, the man had supplied the Japanese garrison in Canton with valuable information on Hong Kong's defences prior to the invasion and was now fully cooperating with High Command.

They believed he could be useful in the campaign against the guerilla build up threatening to break out in the New Territories. General Jiro Toshido did not like Chinamen. Nor did he like traitors and collaborators. He certainly did not trust them, but he was prepared to take any help he could get and had been ordered to do so.

J.T. Ching was fifteen minutes late. The major-general did not rise to greet him, but indicated the chair opposite, gesturing to a waiter to remove the small vase of Formosan roses that stood between them and to bring the menu. The Chinaman was wearing a perfectly cut double-breasted, pinstripe suit, flawless linen and a flamboyant silk tie. There was a red rosebud in his broad lapel. Gold cufflinks and shirt studs of jade matched a heavy ring on his small finger and the wristwatch he wore was of solid gold. He smelled strongly of Florida Water and pomade.

Ching ordered Chinese tea and asked the waiter to bring him a bowl of rice congee mixed with salted egg and dried fish. It was the staple diet of the Hakka people, he explained, and the general wondered whether it was meant to impress upon him the rich man's peasant background. He ate noisily in the vacuum style of the coolie, rice bowl held to his lips and the food shovelled into his mouth with a fast, scooping action.

Between mouthfuls he said that he had placed his most reliable man in the village of Pok Choy Lam. He would be seen as a refugee farm labourer from Canton. J.T. Ching chuckled as he wiped his chin.

'If the British are escaping through the village of Pok Choy Lam or any other village, this man will find out.' He threw down the napkin and belched loudly.

'The man I speak of is worth ten of yours,' he said, pretending not to notice the tightening of General Toshido's jaw. 'They call him The Forceful One.'

With the deerhide bag safely in her hands, Sing made a speedy recovery. The note she sent to Doctor Sun explained her predicament and asked for the necessary herbal medicines to dress her injuries and strengthen her resistance. He also sent moxa sticks and acupuncture needles.

Sing had learned to ignore the eyes upon her and the guards had lost interest in the coolie woman who burned her own skin, pierced it with needles and sat for hours in a state of trance. Lieutenant Mashima hid his fascination but noted her fast improvement. She did not seem afraid and spent her time reading from the old books she kept in the bag.

He was satisfied that she told the truth and had no intention of allowing the shit-shovelling sergeant from Kobi near her. Her face was almost healed and as the bruises began to clear he could see that she was not unattractive in her own strange way. Soon she would be well enough to be transferred to Stanley or to Victoria Prison but not until he was ready to let her go. Until then this woman would remain under his observation. He provided her with an extra blanket which she hung on half the wire to give her privacy. Her food improved and she was allowed to visit the washroom twice a day under the eye of a grinning guard.

General Toshido's headaches were well known by now to those who came under his direct authority. They had become a gauge of his moods and temper as reliable as a weathercock swung by the strength and direction of the wind predicts a storm. When they were bad, the smallest incident could bring on a rage that shook the walls with his roars. Officers he had served with for years had been stripped of rank for displeasing him and an order slow to be carried out brought instant punishment. So severe were General Toshido's headaches that word would pass ahead.

'The cage is open,' warned that the affliction was upon him. 'The cage is closed,' meant that for a time it had left him. Even when the pain was slight his personality teetered between the highly professional soldier known for fair-minded treatment of those under him, and a powder keg on a short and ever-burning fuse.

It was no secret that the brigade doctors had despaired of diagnosing and treating the major-general and their best efforts were described as the incompetent meddling of farmers' wives; or that the blinds of his private office remained drawn and several drawers of his official desk were crammed with pills and medications of every description. The man who discovered a cure or was in any way responsible for easing his suffering would be hailed as a hero by half the General Staff, with a possible promotion from the general himself.

At least, these were the thoughts that passed through Lieutenant Mashima's mind. It had been due to one of these attacks that he had lost his position as the general's aide and now found himself in charge of a post office full of beggars and idiots. He had continued to observe the girl in the lock-up at her endless reading, exercising or meditating, her mind closed to outside activity. It was a disciplined routine which she performed daily.

He demanded to know why she seemed to burn her own skin and how piercing it with needles could benefit her. She had tried to explain to him the principles of heat application and energy flow but it was her rapid improvement that had convinced him of her healing powers. It had made him reconsider his planned use of her for a far more rewarding possibility. If she succeeded, his would be the credit; if she failed, little would be lost.

Again, the chubby Shanghainese photographer had been fetched to interpret for him.

'The captain wants to know if you can cure a headache.' He winked an eye behind the thick lens of his spectacles. 'Say yes, kid. What've you got to lose?'

The Mercedes staff car, flying the imperial pennant from its front mudguard, passed through the high, iron gates of Haddon House. Set back on Magazine Gap on the Mid-Levels halfway up the Peak, it had been the home of an English government official who now claimed a narrow stone shelf in Stanley Prison, a pair of worn-out shoes and one small suitcase of clothing.

After the confinement of the mail lock-up it looked very beautiful to Sing as the car tyres crunched up the gravel drive. Tropical palms grew like slender pillars from the lawns, their trunks surrounded by well-kept flower beds and the three-storey house was white and clean.

Next to her in the back seat sat Lieutenant Mashima, his hands gripping the Samurai sword that lay across his knees. Sing had been given a clean sam foo to wear, special soap to wash with and a comb for her hair. The smell of cheap, shop-shelf newness and scented soap filled the car, blending with the smell of leather upholstery.

When Sing was shown into the room five minutes later, the only light came from the half-closed slats of a venetian blind. Major-General Toshido lay full length on a tatami sleeping mat, his head resting on a wooden block. One forearm was flung across his eyes. Freddy Fong had whispered a warning of this man's importance.

He lay rigidly still, dressed only in a plain cotton kimono. Freddy had also been ordered to translate the seriousness of his problem. In her mind, Sing repeated the words Ah Gum had assured her were best suited to every new encounter with a man on his back. 'A man without his clothes leaves his dignity in your hands.'

'Major-General Toshido. I have brought the healing woman. She is knowledgeable of folk medicine and believes she can relieve your pain.' The lieutenant's voice was little more than a cautious whisper.

'You will remain,' the general said, without lifting his arm.

Lieutenant Mashima signalled Sing to begin her treatment, stepping back into the shadow beside the doorway.

Without speaking, she first lit three sandalwood incense sticks and set them smouldering around the room. Soundlessly, she approached Toshido without thought of race or rank. His head was raised on the curved wooden sleeping block and she knelt behind it. Chafing her cool palms together to bring them to blood heat she placed the tips of her forefingers lightly between his eyes and a thumb on each of his temples. With her hands bridging his burning forehead in this way, she began a rhythmic pressure. Her fingers transferred gently to his ears and between finger and thumb she stimulated the vital acupuncture points of their fleshy lobes. Then around and under his heavy neck she gingerly felt the iron-hard tension of his neck and shoulder muscles. Methodically she began the task of unknotting them.

Within half an hour the deep furrow between his brows had smoothed and the rapid pulse had slowed and she began to feel results. By applying acupressure to certain points of the neck she had been able to put the general to sleep and the smear of opium paste under his top lip had the effect of relaxing his entire body as though it were lifeless. He did not feel the hair-fine acupuncture needle inserted in the 'heaven gate' point, the absolute centre of the cranium, or the dozen that pierced his ears.

Whilst they remained there he would stay deeply asleep. Using her regained strength and the technique Ah Gum had taught her, Sing was able to turn him over onto his stomach, removing the kimono at the same time. She estimated his weight at 200 pounds and much of it was fat.

Taking a fresh moxa stick from the bag, she held one end in the flames of the candle, turning it slowly until it glowed into a dull red coal. Moxa was the traditional cauterising method, the stick made of leaf-down from the wormwood plant rolled tightly with the pith of sunflower. When it was aglow like a burning cigar she applied its heat closely to certain points of the neck and shoulders. Lieutenant Mashima took a step towards her. She looked at him, the smoking moxa poised. He merged again with the shadows. It took an hour to use the twenty centimetre moxa stick but rigidity in the muscles had begun to disappear.

Next she took a set of round glass cups from the bag. Wiping the insides with a herbal spirit, she applied the candle until each was filled with a burst of blue flame. These she applied to trigger spots along either side of the spine. As each cup closed on his skin, the flame died, but the heated vacuum it had generated drew the flesh into the cup until it was the size of half a golf ball. These she left in place for fifteen minutes while they drew out the hidden chills from his body, rejuvenating atrophied muscles and stimulating the blood vessels.

When the cups were removed the lumps quickly subsided and Sing swabbed the back with herbal astringents and oils to penetrate the pores and release toxins. Then she began an hour of deep-tissue massage. Knowing exactly the interrelation of each small muscle and tendon, concentrating her own ch'i into her thumbs, she systematically separated and loosened the cartilage of each vertebra, at the same time revitalising the blood flow.

In the further two hours that she worked Sing had plenty of time to think. This ripe and succulent plum of opportunity that seemed to have dropped so unexpectedly into her hands could be her salvation, it must not be wasted. She knew what the watchful lieutenant had in mind for her and if she resisted him there was the alternative of Sergeant Koda.

The guards talked often of Koda's methods and the horror of it haunted her: the water torture, where the victim was held down while a hose was forced into the mouth, filling the stomach with water far beyond its capacity. When the belly was distended, tight as a balloon, Sergeant Koda would jump upon it until every organ was permanently ruptured.

Even this terrible thing could not match the abomination of the bamboo shoot. The guards had known she was listening as they described his special treatment of a woman when he had finished with her. Tied into a sitting position over a fresh shoot of bamboo, her ankles staked wide apart, the shoot would grow an inch a day. Sing had covered her ears to the rest of their description.

The threat of Sergeant Koda made any alternative worth pursuing. She had already guessed that there was nothing clinically or organically wrong with the Japanese man who breathed so evenly under her hands. It might be the pressures of his rank, years of action on the mainland or some deep emotional problem.

Whatever was causing his headaches could effectively be relieved but she had already decided he must not know this. She must become indispensable to him. A man in his position could protect her. Perhaps even lead her to Toby. All these things passed through her mind as she worked on him and before Sing removed the needles to awaken him she had made her plan.

When Jiro Toshido opened his eyes and looked around he saw the girl in the stiff new clothes of a Chinese amah kneeling by his side. She had lit fresh incense and its aromatic scent filled the room. He turned his head left and right, up and down, unable to believe how loose and relaxed he felt. The vice-like band around his head seemed to have snapped like cotton and the molten core of pain that had lanced his brain with every eye movement had melted away. In its place a euphoric state of well-being engulfed him.

'The pain is gone,' he whispered in English, blinking his eyes in amazement. 'It is a miracle. How was this done?' He picked up his wristwatch from the low rosewood table. 'Have I slept for so long?'

He climbed to his feet, lifting his heavy shoulders, marvelling at the painless movement. He turned to Sing. 'They say you speak English. Why do you not answer me?' His voice was so filled with relief that the question was gently asked.

'I am pleased my humble ability has helped the great lord.'

'But how . . . ?' General Toshido stood up and, slipping on the kimono, moved around the room, unable to believe the flexibility of his neck and upper body. He flicked the venetian blinds filling the room with bright autumn sunlight.

'Light,' he laughed. 'I can stand the light.' He turned suddenly to look at Sing. 'Am I cured? Will the pain return?'

'It may, lord.'

'Can you stop it?'

Sing stood before him and bowed. 'If I am allowed to visit the medicine shop for the things that I will need, perhaps I can.'

'Where did you learn such skill?'

'From a great master of the Tao, lord.'

'Well, he should be venerated. What do they call you?'

'My name is Siu Sing, lord.'

'Why are you in prison?'

'I do not know, lord.'

'How long will a cure take?'

'Perhaps a long time. You must be shown the ways of relaxation and follow them every day. You must be given daily massage and taught the eight precious silk-weaving exercises of Pa Tuan T'sin.'

'You will show me these ways and give me this treatment?' Toshido asked.

'It would be my great honour, lord,' Sing replied, bowing low.

General Toshido turned to Lieutenant Mashima who was still watching nervously beside the door.

'You have done well to bring this woman to me. Her skills are remarkable.'

The lieutenant bowed stiffly from the waist, one hand steadying the hilt of his sword in case it should make a noise. He could not believe his good fortune.

'She will be moved to this house immediately. Find a room for her in the servants' quarters and see that she has everything that she needs.' He turned to Sing. 'Where is this medicine shop?'

'It is called Everspring, lord. The finest of herb shops with the best of medicines. It is owned by the best of all doctors. I am only his student and assistant.'

'It is in the place they call Causeway Bay, sir,' said Lieutenant Mashima efficiently.

'Very well. Take her there. See that this shop is protected and its owner given food.' He dismissed the lieutenant.

'Go with him. You will stay here now,' he said to Sing. 'We will continue this treatment tomorrow.'

For the next six weeks Sing attended to General Toshido. The programme she set out for him began at dawn each day with meditation, stretching and breathing exercises in the grounds. With some changes to the quality and quantity of the foods he ate, an increased intake of fresh water, the benefits to his health were almost immediate. For an hour at midday and two hours each evening she repeated the treatment with variations as his mind and body continued to respond.

Every third day she was driven to Everspring under escort, for herbal prescriptions. It was an easy case of a run-down and unhealthy body aggravated by the nervous exhaustion of stress and over-work. The deep psychological disturbance that these had led to would ease with his improvement. The herbal remedies of Doctor Sun were easily and safely prescribed while under Sing's expert techniques Toshido's rejuvenation was dramatic.

As he responded, Sing was certain that the time would soon come when her ministrations would be called upon for more than the massage of his head and back muscles. Yet, to her great relief this did not happen. In fact no sign of sexual arousal came at any time. She had never known this, as the massage techniques she used, no matter how clinical, seldom failed to create this kind of result. When it did, she was skilled in satisfying it quickly and this was usually enough.

After eight weeks, the headaches had ceased altogether but he showed no sign of letting her go. She thought he was asleep as she prepared to leave him. 'Do not go,' he said. 'I have something to show you.'

Fastening the kimono, he opened the door to a pleasantly furnished bedroom, adjoining his own. 'I wish you to sleep here closer to me. I think you will be comfortable.' He did not wait for a reply but wished her goodnight and closed the door, leaving her alone.

Sing found the dressing table had been stocked with cosmetics and perfumes. The bed was soft and warm. For most of the night she lay awake waiting for the door to open and for him to come. She could not escape, the house was too heavily guarded. She would appeal to him. Beg him, if she must.

The weeks she had spent in his service had not shown him to be a cruel man or an ungrateful one. Also she had seen the photograph of a wife and grown children. She guessed his age to be around fifty-five. Perhaps Japanese men were different to Chinese. But the door did not open and he did not come. Eventually she fell asleep.

The next morning, after an hour of meditation in the garden he led her to a breakfast table set for two on the wide tiled porchway open to the grand view of Victoria Harbour.

'We will not exercise this morning. I would like you to join me.' He indicated a chair. 'There is something we should discuss.'

They ate the seasonal fruits and rice porridge in silence. When they had finished, he said, 'You have helped me greatly. You have my thanks. For the first time in many years I feel well again.' He laughed. 'Even young.'

Sing acknowledged his thanks with a slight bow of her head.

'I want you to continue this service while I am here. I do not know for how long.'

'I am honoured, my lord.' Sing kept her eyes on the large bowl of fruit.

'My officers warned against this treatment. They believed you might poison me.' He waited. 'Try to kill me. They seem to think you are dangerous.'

To avoid looking into his eyes, Sing poured more sharp green tea into his cup.

'I want you to be my . . . ' He hesitated, looking for the correct word, 'interpreter, my eh . . . advisor in dealing with things Chinese.'

He pushed back his chair and stood with his back to her looking across the grounds to the harbour still softened by mist. The air was crisp but not yet cold.

'We will continue the treatment when it is necessary. You will accompany me at certain times. Such a time as tomorrow evening when we will attend a dinner.'

Toshido was wearing a black kimono of fine twill; his greying hair was still thick and well brushed. He had lost weight and his face had gained colour. Sing could not help a twinge of surprise at the result of her own skills.

'If you wish it, lord.'

'It is all arranged. In one hour a seamstress will come and there will be others. They will take care of your needs.'

At seven o'clock the following evening Sing stood before the mirror in her own room unable to believe the transformation. The cheong-sam she wore was the deep, dark red of fine ruby wine. It fitted her body to perfection, contrasting her small waist with the sweep of her hips and curve of her breasts. The split in its tight skirt extended above her knee, exposing her leg to the thigh when she walked. The garment had been delivered with two others at five that afternoon, one a vivid emerald green, the other sapphire blue. A shoemaker had also come from Happy Valley, the place of fine, hand-made footwear. Three pairs of perfectly fitted high-heeled shoes of simple elegant style matched the dresses and from the exclusive department store of Lane Crawford a range of accessories had been fetched for her choice. She had selected an evening bag and gloves for each colour but when a black velvet box was opened to reveal a selection of jewellery she hesitated in disbelief.

The representative from the famous store was an elderly Chinese man who knelt before her, his hands shaking as he held out the box for her inspection. 'Please madam, the great lord Toshido says you must take anything that pleases you. If what I have brought disappoints you I can bring more.'

Sing reassured him that what he had brought was indeed beautiful but she took only pieces that were simple but striking—a brooch shaped as a bamboo leaf set with diamonds, a ring of square-cut rubies, one of emeralds and one of sapphires and a wristwatch of white gold. When she had chosen them the man closed the lid and placed the box beside her.

'I will leave this collection for you to consider at leisure,' he said, bowing himself out backwards.

Shortly after seven, Toshido tapped on her door and when Sing opened it he stood looking at her, quite unable to find words. She looked exquisite. The hairdresser and beautician had spent most of the afternoon attending to her. Her hair had been oiled and conditioned into a gleaming coppery rope that was coiled and pinned at her neck with a delicate ivory comb studded with seed pearls. Through the elbow-length black lace gloves her fingernails shone like perfectly shaped gems, the same blood red as her dress. The stiletto heels of black, patent leather court shoes had raised her to within an inch of his height and lent a seductive quality to her stance and movement that he could not fail to notice.

The single glittering leaf of diamonds adorned the slope of her breast just below the shoulder and the neck of the garment was cut high in the most elegantly fashionable Chinese style. Her eyes startled him with their brilliance. He had never looked into them properly before. They were the colour of amethyst, perfectly outlined, the long lashes emphasised by a touch of mascara, her brows perfectly shaped. She had allowed very little other makeup but had delighted in the spraying on of perfume.

The dinner was held at the Repulse Bay Hotel, given by the

commanding general in honour of a select party of high ranking visitors from Pacific Command Headquarters with their immediate staff. A dozen Chinese women had been provided as escorts for the high-ranking guests and the large round table seating sixteen was attended by the ten waiters and waitresses.

There was little doubt that the heavily made-up women, whilst carefully chosen, were obviously high-class prostitutes. Sing spoke only when she was spoken to, which, as most of the officers managed adequate English, and some Cantonese, was often. It was equally clear that every man at the table envied Major-General Jiro Toshido and admired his taste. Those of his own staff present were astonished by the change in him, each impatient to pass on the news that the lion appeared to have been tamed and permanently confined to his cage, its key safely in the possession of the strange woman they called Madam Ninja.

Most of the conversation was in Japanese but Sing could tell as the saki cups were emptied that Jiro Toshido was enjoying the role of squire to a girl who looked fresh and young enough to be his own child. While the Chinese women sat, their smiles set in the gaudy plaster of their makeup, Sing allowed her expression to tell them nothing. Neither confirming or denying questions behind their curious glances and inquisitive chatter.

It was two a.m. before the car returned them to the house on the Mid-Levels. Sing had noticed Toshido had filled his cup less often than others but that his face was flushed from the hot, starchy wine. She knew he was no longer a heavy drinker and the medicines she brewed from Doctor Sun's prescriptions discouraged alcohol in any form.

When his hand reached for hers in the back seat of the car she had left it cool and limp in the grip of his hot fingers. Her head was turned away from him, watching the floodlit decks of anchored battleships laid out below as the car climbed the curves of Magazine Gap, but she could feel his eyes upon her.

Inside the house, she excused herself and went to the bathroom set aside for her use. She took her time removing the eye makeup and washing herself, it would not take him long to fall asleep, she thought.

But the light that showed beneath his door remained switched on and when she was in bed it flooded her room as he entered. She pretended to be asleep as he called her name in a husky whisper. There was a moment's pause. The door closed and for moments only his breathing continued in the dark. Then his weight lowered onto the bed, carefully as though not to wake her. The thudding of her heart seemed to physically shake her as she lay there fighting to keep her breathing level and unhurried. She could hear his breath, loud in the clock-ticking silence. She felt its warmth, heavy with the smell of spirits, close to her cheek. The quilt was slowly folded back, then the sheet, to expose her naked shoulder. His hand closed upon it lightly, then gripping more firmly.

'Sing. Are you sleeping?'

She was sure that he must feel the pounding of her pulse and prayed that he would not mistake it for excitement. The hand, grown heavy as it waited for her response, slid away. She felt his breath descend as his lips grazed her cool, perfumed skin at the point of her shoulder, then draw away into her hair. There he stayed and soon his breathing became louder and stronger, until, quite suddenly, he began to snore.

Escape

THE MAIN camps for military prisoners of war were at Sham Shui Po in Kowloon, Victoria police station on the island and, through lack of space, a large section of the Stanley internment camp. Detention centres were scattered about the territory with the Hollywood Road post office serving the Western District, the Royal Observatory and the Star Ferry building in Central, and lock-ups in Causeway Bay and North Point.

General Toshido saw to it that he visited each of them at least once each week. The prison hospital on Stonecutter's Island still held sick or disabled British officers and this, due to its location, he saw only occasionally.

For reasons best known to the Japanese army medical corps stationed on Stonecutter's they had set up a serum laboratory and a snake farm. So many Japanese soldiers engaged in the South Pacific theatre were dying from snakebite that the farm had been set up to manufacture anti-snakebite serum.

The general's only interest in the operation was a report that had reached him claiming certain of the guards had taken to throwing difficult prisoners into the snake pit and that others were being used as human guinea pigs to test the antidote.

Jiro Toshido knew that he was unsuited for the post of officer commanding prison camp administration. He was a field officer, unaccustomed to desk work. He lacked the indifference to suffering that made the task a palatable one. He was a professional soldier, not a warder and his hatred for the enemy was not as blind as some.

It had been promised that this would be a temporary appointment and that his substantive promotion to full general was imminent. He would soon be returned to Japan to await his retirement. None of these things had eventuated.

The war in the Pacific Islands was not proving to be the swift and overwhelming victory the emperor's advisers had predicted and officers of calibre and experience were needed in the field. He had seen enough of war not to complain too loudly, as he had no desire to return to active duty. *It is the comfort stations of Nanking and Canton,* he thought. *They see little difference between a whore-house and a prison camp. I supervised one, now I must supervise the other.*

His life in Hong Kong, whilst busy and often boringly frustrating, was by no means unpleasant since Sing had become part of it. A new and unexpected dimension had been added with the remarkable improvement in his health and the reputation he seemed to have gained as a tiger in bed.

He was well aware that Sing's exceptional beauty and mystical charm had made him the envy of others in similar positions to his and improved his social standing considerably. Socialising had never been his strong point but now he found himself invited to every official and unofficial function that was held at any level and with Sing at his side was happy to accept them.

His main concern was to maintain the security of the occupying forces against civil unrest and, to a lesser extent, to control the detention and to some degree the welfare of enemy prisoners. Since the meeting with J.T. Ching and the placing of the Chinaman's operative in the New Territories, escape routes had almost been closed. Although the evidence of British soldiers and civilians still said to be in hiding in the villages remained a problem, the threat of action from a coordinated guerrilla force had come to no more than isolated acts of sabotage. It was clear that the Nationalist reinforcements from across the border and by sea were not to come.

Another concern, considered far less important by his superiors, was the over-zealous treatment of prisoners by elements of the military police and prison guards. Lieutenant Mashima had told him of the condition Sing had been in when brought in by a Sergeant Oshi Koda.

When he had asked her about it she had told him of the circumstances of her arrest and the methods Koda was said to have used on women he interrogated. Toshido was aware of such things and of the mixed feelings these incidents were met with higher up. Normally they were best ignored, but in the case of Sergeant Koda, demotion to private and transfer to the Pacific Task Force, which meant sweltering in some hostile tropic jungle surrounded by poisonous snakes, had given him a certain satisfaction.

As he stepped from the launch onto the jetty at Stonecutter's Island to investigate the reports of the snake pit, it was his intention to re-authorise the commencement of fuel-foraging parties as the winter drew in. Conditions in the ruins of the old fort were the most primitive in the internment system on either side of the harbour.

Many had died here in the first eighteen months of occupation and several had been executed for attempting to escape. He saw no reason why conditions should be made worse by denying the remaining prisoners warmth. Fuel was proving to be an increasing problem among the troops. The hills of the New Territories had been almost denuded of tiger grass and there were few remaining trees. The guard commander on Stonecutter's protested that what wood was left on the island should be preserved for the use of Japanese soldiers.

General Toshido roared the captain to his feet and pointed out that the thirty prisoners still occupying the dungeon of the fort were not likely to use up the island's supply of timber. Also, he ordered, with the full force of his new-found energy, there would be no more prisoners falling into snake pits, used for experiments or dying from unnecessary exposure.

It was what Toby had been waiting for. His health had slowly improved and he had maintained it with regular exercise. As the fittest senior ranking officer he volunteered to take charge of the foraging party of six men and two handcarts under armed escort.

The captain of the guard was not pleased at being forced to

carry out the general's orders against his better judgement and took a certain pleasure in organising the first party in the worst possible weather. Wind and torrential rain lashed the island from end to end, putting the escort in the mood to use their rifle butts and causing the iron wheels of the handcart to sink into the mud.

Toby had gone over the plan so many times it worked to perfection. Leading the party over the hill called Wuthering Heights to the old gun emplacement, he despatched his men in different directions. The escort's instructions were to not let a prisoner out of their sight but as the downpour made visibility difficult and there was nowhere for the foragers to go, they took cover under a tree and let them wander about picking up what wood they could find. Only when the cart was full and they started back was it discovered that the captain in charge of prisoners had disappeared into the pelting rain.

The conditions were perfect cover. Toby made his way quickly through the warren of tunnels, shell hoists and magazines with their eerie mirror-reflected lighting almost blacked out. Coming out beneath the spruce-fir and its sheltering branches he waited until a junk was headed close enough to the island's shore and swam out to meet it.

He had chosen one with boat ropes and rubber tyre fenders hanging close to the water and with its crew below or sheltering in the wheelhouse. Moving slowly under the power of its sodden sails it was easy to reach unobserved and, grasping its boat rope, he was towed away in the general direction of Tolo harbour.

In the three months since the first dinner at the Repulse Bay Hotel, Sing had accompanied General Toshido to many more. She had become more to him than a therapist by day and an adornment by night. He had found her intelligence in matters of common sense and logic to be extremely useful in dealing with problems constantly arising in the Chinese community. In addition to interpreter, translator and public relations advisor, Sing had been ordered to take over the role of daily broadcaster and her voice had become well-known as she read the bulletin of orders. She had become a companion and an invaluable social secretary, gaining the complete trust of Jiro Toshido and the grudging acceptance of those closest to him, who realised the hold she had over his temperament.

There were many personal benefits and almost complete freedom to come and go at Hadden House. A car and driver had been put at her disposal provided she reported her movements to the Magazine Gap guard post. By far her greatest satisfaction was in having unrestricted access to Doctor Sun and his family at Everspring; and in acquiring the release of Freddy Fong to act as press photographer whenever his services were needed. He had been given an old spring-wound Bell and Howell movie camera captured from the Americans. Teaching himself to use it Freddy was soon providing a newsreel service to the Japanese authorities.

The fact that her influence was able to provide a certain protection for her friends made it easier for Sing to bear the insults and abuse she attracted whenever she was unescorted. The character for traitor had been scrawled on the windshield of the vehicle she was allowed to use, stones were thrown, rotten eggs and other refuse dropped from above.

Insults and abuse were nothing new to her but she became afraid that it might be turned against the family of Doctor Sun. When Toshido threatened to send an armed escort to deal with such incidents she advised him not to. There was a certain confusion in the Chinese attitude, she explained. To the Japanese face, most were cooperative, even servile, but she was jarp jung. They resented her privileges. She had gone too far. She was the whore of the Yut Boon Jai and a collaborator whose voice dictated to them every day over the radio.

Toshido was well aware that disorder lay just below the surface and that the threat of unrest in the downtown districts was becoming a powder keg. He had no wish to set it off and reluctantly agreed when she suggested her visits to the shop should be without the car and escort. She would go alone and in the clothes she had arrived in.

It meant she had more time to sit with the doctor and to talk more openly. She learned that it was his cousin and members of his clan in the village of Pok Choy Lam and elsewhere who were hiding the British fugitives and organising their escape to Thailand on sea-going junks, known as 'snake boats'. Something had gone wrong. For months now the Japanese had been watching for them on the most carefully planned escape routes, sometimes waiting until the snake boat was well under way before boarding her.

It was as though one of their own kind was working against them from within the village, he said. But so many had come from across the border looking for work or food, no longer were the walled villages closed to outsiders and now each district had Japanese guard posts. There were roadblocks and checkpoints on all main thoroughfares throughout the Territories, the back roads were constantly patrolled and those on the border had been doubled.

Sing asked about a tall English captain named Toby Hyde-Wilkins. One with hair the colour of sun-bleached bamboo who had been a friend of his uncle, Po Lok, but the doctor said they knew of no names. Only that the network was operated by Nationalists who had come over the border ahead of the Japanese invasion and some who had followed.

He did not know their numbers but they continued to talk of Chiang Kai-shek's Kuomintang, who would soon fight alongside them, and those who cooperated would be heroes of the people. Those who did not would be marked for death when the brown monkeys were defeated.

Sing knew that even the simple Hakkas would not risk danger to help the gwai-lo unless it was turned to their advantage. Like any other Chinese, loyalty and courage belonged first to the family, then to the clan. But the Japanese were hated, sometimes even more than they were feared. The gwai-lo colonialists had left them to grow their crops and sell them in the market, but the brown monkeys took all that they grew. Not even enough was left to feed their own.

Doctor Sun would enquire about the English captain, he promised. The bamboo telephone was very reliable, he said. There were many who wished to be rewarded and exalted as heroes of the people. They drove taxis and wallah wallahs, worked in the Japanese laundries and tailor shops, served them in the restaurants and bars, delivered their supplies. If the gwai-lo captain she called Toby, the one who had been the friend of uncle Po Lok, was still alive, he would find out.

To help him in this, Sing would discover all she could of Japanese troop movements on each side of the border and the deployment of patrols. Anything that could help the escape routes to stay open. There was a large map on the wall of Toshido's study, with pins to show patrol deployment.

Also, she found the officers' tongues were easily loosened by too much rice wine, and her status as Toshido's inseparable companion caused them to overlook the fact that she was a Chinese at heart. A code was soon devised and she was able to warn of raids upon the villages in her daily broadcasts and to pass messages through the herbal prescriptions she took to Everspring. The months passed. In spite of her constant enquiry and the promises of Chen Yu, there was still no word of Toby.

The night-soil cart creaked along the rough track between duck farms and fields of winter crops. It was a dirt road like the one that had led to the Residence of Eternal Peace. A half moon, pale as a lemon slice, lit the silent fields. An early frost lay over them as even as a light snowfall, isolating farm houses where the faint glow of oil lamps prepared for the day to come. The grating of its wheels and the creak of straining traces carried on the cold air with the familiar reek of night soil, as much a part of darkness in the New Territories as the yap of foxes and the soundless swoop of owls.

The muddy track was hardened by the cold, the wooden wheels of the ox cart jolting over ruts and the deep holes left by working buffalo. The full buckets roped to its tray slopped about, stirring the incredible stench. Toby swayed with the motion of the cart. He was too tired to retch, wondering which was colder—the waters of Tolo harbour or the night air biting through the thin Hakka clothes he had been given.

The contact at Taipo market had been gruffly indifferent when he slipped into the lighted shack of the night-soil collector. It was a well-chosen rendezvous set just outside the main village. The mat shack was surrounded by a string of unhitched carts and stacks of wooden buckets. The collection and delivery of night soil had been so long a part of life for the Chinese farmer that its stink went unnoticed. To the farmer, the smell of the honey-cart was the perfume of livelihood, a sure sign that all was as it should be. While the night soil was hauled to the fields to nourish the crops, life would go on as always.

There was a strong Japanese presence in Taipo village. Several platoons of infantry were stationed in the schoolhouse and officers were billeted in the District Officer's bungalow. Batteries of artillery and entrenched machine-gun posts were dug in along the Tolo and Castle Peak roads. The soldiers did not share the Hakka peasant's enjoyment of their own excrement and gave the place as wide a berth as they would a leper colony.

The driver of the cart had neither spoken to Toby nor looked at him since they left the village. A shrivelled old man, he was content to navigate the narrow track while quietly cursing the road and encouraging the pair of oxen. Toby could not help wondering if he knew the risks he was taking.

Over the lumbering backs of the oxen the high walls and old tiled roofs of Pok Choy Lam village showed dully in the distance. The frost was beginning to rise in mist and ducks were stirring on the banks of fish ponds as the driver urged the beasts forward with the whack of a long bamboo cane.

General Toshido did not tell Sing where they were going. He seldom did. It was enough to know that she should be ready at a certain time when his tap on her door would mean the car was ready to leave. He had made no further attempt to enter her room uninvited. It was now clear to her that he was impotent and since that first occasion after the dinner at Repulse Bay he had made no further advances towards her. At first Sing had been unable to believe such fortune and had asked Doctor Sun to include an ingredient with the medicinal herbs that would subdue what little libido may have still been aroused.

The general seemed content to leave things as they were, giving the impression of a virile lover to those who wished to perceive it. Sing saw no reason to confuse this image and had become adept at playing the part of a well-satisfied mistress without saying a word. When the car passed the lights of Repulse Bay and headed towards Stanley Village she enquired where they were going.

'To the house of a Chinese man I do not trust. I would like you to observe him closely and tell me if you believe my judgement is justified.'

The huge house could be seen long before it was reached. Occupying an entire hillside, it looked more like a castle than a private home. Its spires and minarets were spotlit from the outside, illuminating the rows of tall pines that lined its boundaries. Parisian style lamp posts lit the long driveway and concealed beams shone among its landscaped shrubbery. Servants in the traditional Pekinese livery of palace eunuchs stood by at the top and bottom of a wide flight of steps leading up to a pillared entrance. General Toshido grunted his distaste as the car drew up.

They were led up the steps to a large reception area. An elaborate chandelier glittered above a sea of Italian terrazzo. Beneath it, set in Venetian mosaic, was a perfect replica of a mariner's compass in the style of the first explorers and in its centre stood J.T. Ching, waiting to greet them. Apart from brief seconds of stunned hesitation, he showed no other sign of recognising Sing. Only she could have read the same glitter of triumph in his eyes, as Toshido introduced her, as she had last seen two years earlier at the Pen ball. There was a kind of reassurance in the pressure of his fingers as he took her hand in an elaborate show of western manners.

'Welcome to my unworthy home. I compliment the general on his exquisite taste,' he said, switching suddenly to the style of a mandarin and bowing low.

Her own sickening shock at once again being suddenly face to face with him had to be quickly overcome and he made it easier by turning to usher them towards tall double doors that stood partly open.

The room they entered blazed with another bank of smaller chandeliers, illuminating gorgeous tapestries and magnificent antique furniture. He led them across a deep crimson carpet and offered comfortable chairs. A huge slab of solid rose quartz supported by crouching imperial lions provided a low table, the only item on its beautiful surface an inlaid cigarette box.

He opened it and took one, offering it to Toshido who shook his head. As always Ching was overdressed, this time in the latest American tuxedo and an evening shirt pleated and frilled with frothy lace, studded with tiny pearls.

He remained standing while a trolley was brought into the room laden with Chinese delicacies, followed by another bearing four traditional brass urns serving different flavours of tea.

'I hope I did not inconvenience you by inviting you to visit me here, General Toshido,' he said, when they had been served. 'For my organisation to be of use to you it is better I am not seen to visit your offices, or you mine. I'm sure you would agree.'

He stood with his back to an outsized marble fireplace, its mantel ranged with priceless porcelain. Noticing the Japanese general's eyes were upon a pottery figure in warlike pose he smiled with the satisfaction of a collector.

'A warrior of the great Tang general, Li-Yuan. He alone unified the Chinese Empire by the sword, much as the knights of Bushido.' He gestured lavishly at the walls around them. 'My private rooms. No one will disturb us here.' He smiled his loose-mouthed smile. 'Not even the women, unless they are invited.'

His indifference towards Sing was pointed but she was thankful for it. He obviously had no intention of letting it be known that they were well acquainted. If he had, it was not to be here and now. Instead he concentrated all his attention on General Toshido as though she was not in the room.

'Perhaps you would care to look around before we discuss the purpose of this meeting.'

Ching did not wait for an answer but proceeded to present his favourite pieces . . . Ming, Ch'ing and Yuan dynasty pottery, tapestries and dragon embroidery from palaces of the past. Figurines of priceless jade of every hue; coral and ivory.

'It is my house of treasure,' he boasted expansively.

It seemed to Toshido that the Chinaman was flaunting his opulence as though to prove his immunity, to show that he had no fear of losing a single piece.

With a flourish, Ching led them into another, slightly smaller room which contained nothing but bladed weapons. The collection covered each wall completely and others were laid out in glass cabinets. Swords, knives, dirks, daggers, sabres, scimitars, bayonets and battle axes. Every age and race was represented. He gestured grandly. 'This I call the Chamber of Righteous Steel.'

'The blade is still the most respected and feared weapon of all. Do you not agree General?'

He indicated two weapons in pride of place on a centrepiece of black velvet. One was the magnificently chased hilt of a Japanese Samurai sword, the long sweep of its scabbard encased in a sleeve of crimson velvet. It rested on a curved stand of black lacquered wood, the gold tassels of its drawstring perfectly arranged.

'The sword of daimyo, guardian of the code of Samurai.'

Beside it lay a ceremonial Gurkha kukhri, its polished grip inlaid and capped with gold, the intricate filigree of its sheath, underlain in red beige, bearing the gilt crest of the 6th Gurkha Rifles.

'And this. Is this perhaps the only blade that challenges its glory?'

'A blade is only as keen as the courage behind it. It has no glory without the hand that draws it. The challenge is in combat, not in display.' If General Toshido was offended by the comparison his tone did not show it, although Ching's alert eyes searched his face for signs.

'But here, here is perhaps the most famous blade of all.' Ching spoke of it as though to break the slight tension he had caused. The weapon he referred to lay on a silk cushion of sky blue. Its handle was carved in the shape of a springing lion set with dozens of precious stones. The blade was no more than twenty centimetres long and shaped in the wavy line of a serpent. Its black metal was seamed with strands of silver and veined with gold.

'It is the famous Lion kris of Malacca, believed by some to possess magic powers.' He lifted it in both hands and held it out to General

Toshido. 'See how the blade is fused from several different metals: steel for strength, gold and silver to appease the gods of life and death. There is no known method of forging such materials. It is said this blade is the product of alchemy.'

Next he indicated a weapon in pride of place on a centrepiece of gold cloth. 'I am sure that this will be of interest to you. My latest piece. One that, shall we say, was won from the British.' He lifted it from the cushion and offered it, hilt out, to the general.

'It is called Light of the Nile. A trophy of the 8th Rajputs. The Indian Regiment so thoroughly vanquished by your troops in the taking of Tai Po.'

When Toshido declined to take it, Ching withdrew the blade. 'They say that these minute inscriptions on its blade are chosen verses from the Koran.'

He slid the gleaming steel back into its scabbard. 'Or so I was told by the British officer who was reluctant to part with it. It is the same yellow-haired captain who we now believe is helping to orchestrate the escape bids under the noses of your patrols.'

Sing felt Ching's eyes upon her as he spoke.

The tone of the taipan's voice incensed the general, who was well aware of the toll the 8th Rajputs had taken in their ambush at Tai Po. His words held more than a polite suggestion but his host did not appear to notice it. 'Then perhaps it is time to talk.'

'First we must visit my children,' Ching said, a note of mystery in his voice, as though he had not noticed the impatience in the general's voice.

'Indulge me, General. A few moments more, please. You will not be disappointed.'

A large, high-domed conservatory led off the main room. It contained a miniature rainforest, the wide, curving fronds of fern trees spread in lacy green fans and orchids of every description dripped from full-grown trees. The atmosphere was heavy with artificial heat and moisture beaded the succulent foliage. Flights of tropical birds fluttered to life as they passed into an annexe of even more lush vegetation.

Behind stainless steel bars cleverly blended into their leafy surroundings, crouched a magnificent pair of snow leopards, their pale green eyes cold as chips of mountain ice. Surrounding them were caged monkeys of every kind.

'The ape in all its forms is worshipped in Chinese mythology. Also the leopard of the high mountains, the rarest of creatures,' Ching said, as they moved on to a man-made grotto surrounding a miniature temple, perfect in every detail and large enough to comfortably house a large dog.

He held up his hand for silence and called with a strange hooting sound. Almost immediately a beast appeared from inside the shrine. It was so frightening to look upon that Sing involuntarily turned away. Ching's voice rebuked her mildly. 'Do not turn away from a living god.'

There was something evil in his reverence.

On its haunches the creature stood almost five feet high; its enormous head bore a high tuft of black hair above the narrow slope of its brow. A ridge of bone shielded close-set, gold-ringed eyes that held a mixture of sinister intelligence and naked malevolence. It blinked lids of white skin with ape-like insolence. A long, tapering snout was hideously decorated by hairless strips of livid pink and mauve flesh, bright as a jungle orchid; its powerful jaws were bearded with a coarse growth of sulphurous yellow fur that flowed over its shoulders and down its back like a Hakka rain cape of yellow straw.

Over its head the beast wore a stout muzzle of tooled leather and silver which encased its jaws. Around its shapeless heavily-maned neck, a thick collar studded with silver and precious stones had been fixed to a solid steel chain. Sing could not repress a shiver as she noted its arms and legs were more sturdy that those of a powerful human being.

'Is he not magnificent?' Ching asked in breathless admiration. 'Mandrillus sphinx. The sacred baboon. One of the most intelligent creations of the animal world . . . and perhaps the most savage.'

As though he was speaking to himself, Ching continued with the same strange air of veneration. 'Deified by the ancient Egyptians. A favourite of the great pharaohs. Worshipped by their people. In parts of Africa he is the companion of witch doctors, the conductor of evil.' He turned to face them as though suddenly remembering a point of great importance.

'The mandrill's appetite for sexual activity is insatiable. In the wild he is known to take a harem of seven wives. Each one of them must remain totally faithful to one master.'

He was still addressing himself directly to Toshido. 'He guards them jealously from all others. If one of them so much as encourages another male . . .' His eyes slid for the first time to look directly at Sing, 'he rapes her to the point of death then gives her to the young bucks of the herd.' Ching smiled . 'Rich men of Egypt and tribal chiefs kept them to punish treacherous wives.' Suddenly he chuckled obscenely. 'It is also believed that there were passionate ladies who became quite fond of them.'

As though it understood Ching's words the creature rolled back its lips to bare yellow tusks in a brutish grin. Toshido made no attempt to hide his disgust.

'It looks to me like just another ape. I have seen enough. Let us come to the purpose of this meeting.'

Deliberately the ape turned its back, showing the violent pink of its hairless buttocks, and went back inside the temple.

'Of course, General,' said Ching apologetically. 'Let us begin.'

They returned to the large room, where Ching resumed his place against the marble fireplace and called for drinks. Toshido declined.

'Please, Mr Ching, the purpose of this meeting. It is not for the pleasure of my company.'

Ching mixed himself a drink, purposely taking his time before replying. 'It is about the village of Pok Choy Lam and the escaping Britishers. My man in the area reports of a planned escape on a larger scale than ever before. It seeks to withdraw all those who remain in hiding and take them by sea to join Chiang Kai-shek in Chung King. It is arranged by Chiang's men and if the trap is set properly it should expose those who are hiding them and end their activities permanently.'

He waited for the statement to take effect. 'We also know how they are receiving information on the movement of patrols and some of those responsible.'

The general put down his cup as Ching pressed a hidden bell beneath the mantleshelf.

'I would like to introduce the man I have asked you here to meet. He is my most able and trusted lieutenant. He is also the reason for our secrecy. I will allow him to deliver his report in person.'

Seconds later, Ah Keung entered the room. He bowed stiffly to Toshido and then to Sing. His face showed no sign of recognition and she applied all her self-control as his eyes met hers, and quickly turned away. She felt the colour drain from her face and her stomach crawled. It seemed as though she was suddenly caught up in a strange and sinister dream. Her sense of alarm was fleeting: there was no danger while she was with Toshido. The first flush of fright passed and Sing quickly collected her composure.

For an hour General Toshido listened to Ah Keung's findings and questioned him on the activities of the Nationalist underground and the hidden British. When they had finished, Ah Keung was dismissed and left as quietly as he had appeared.

'I trust your faith in this man is not misplaced,' said General Toshido, when he had left the room.

The smile slipped from Ching's face as he answered. 'Let us say he is as completely trustworthy as your beautiful companion. He is trusted with my personal safety and with the discipline of my organisation. I think if you speak to your officers in Tai Po they will reassure you of his value.'

He suddenly clapped his hands loudly. 'You have been most patient, General. Let us refresh ourselves at my humble table.'

Gesturing for them to rise and follow him, Ching led the way to a separate dining room. The long table of green jadeite was let into a sunken area surrounded by antique temple carvings. Gilt chairs lined the table and places for three were set at one end. The figure of a woman appeared and descended the steps to take her place at the opposite end of the table. Sing caught her breath as she saw it was Jade.

Three servants followed her silently down to stand one behind each chair. As soon as they were in position Jade struck a small gong and immediately the banquet began to be served. Each dish was carried down to the table and set before them for its perfect arrangement to be admired. Jade announced its origin and method of cooking, as well as its various ingredients, before the dish was divided and served.

Over the next hour courses appeared and disappeared in an endless parade, a tiny portion of each placed by Jade into delicate bowls that were replaced at each new serving. Sing controlled her apprehension by concentrating on the rich variety of food, although each mouthful felt as though it would make her physically sick. She avoided looking at Jade, who neither spoke nor was spoken to. Her eyes fixed on the procession of dishes and their perfect serving.

The conversation was kept to the progress of the war and the inevitability of Japanese dominance in Asia. Ching's comparison of the ancient strategies of the Chinese warlords to those of the knights of Bushido was not well received by Toshido and Ching relieved the tension by announcing the final dish. It was a rare delicacy, he said, forbidden by the potato-peeling British colonialists and now served in honour of his special guests.

A small round table was wheeled in and placed at his side. It was covered by a red cloth reaching to the floor and in its centre a hole the size of a rice bowl had been cut. Ceremoniously arranged around it were three silver bowls, a long-handled silver spoon and a bright steel chopper. At a word from Ching a servant knelt and reached under the table. An object resembling a small coconut appeared, forced into the hole.

As Sing looked on, the hair-like fibre of the coconut seemed to crawl and crinkle. She could not hold back a cry when the eyes of a monkey appeared among its gingery hair. The chopper flashed in Ching's hand, slicing the top from the monkey's skull as neatly as opening a boiled egg. Quickly dipping the long-handled spoon into the cranium the servant ladled the warm, living brain into the three silver bowls.

The Snake Boat

THE GREASY window of the Double Summer eating house in Tai Po village was once filled with the favourite foods of the Cantonese worker. Larp cheung sausages had hung in livid fat-filled strings, packed with chewy gristle and laced with spices. Beside the rows of roasted ducks, their crisp skins red gold with the basting of soy sauce and honey, strips of lean roast pork had dangled enticingly.

Inside the chop-up boy once wielded his chopper with confident skill as he cut up orders for the little knot of labourers who would stand watching the grease fly as the razor-sharp blade rose and fell while they waited their turn. Even now, with such food a memory, this was the place to come for a full belly at a cheap price.

The cook dispensed bowls of steaming congee and writhing dollops of noodles from wooden vats. In them there often floated scraps of pork and chicken and green vegetable. The dozen tables were crowded with men, some leaning back contentedly after a meal, others sipping tea and smoking while they waited to be served.

The Double Summer eating house was run by a thin Cantonese known as Toothpick Yap. His was the only restaurant in the village that always had food in the window and where a customer could be sure of a full rice bowl. The food was cheap, good and plentiful because the Japanese patrols had been told to leave the place alone. They knew that the small supply of ducks, pork, and fresh vegetables that ended up in the vats came from the farmers themselves and yet nothing was done to discourage it.

Ah Keung sat at the small corner table where he always took his meals. The bowls he had eaten from were still scattered on the table and the cloth was stained with spilled tea and orange patches of chilli sauce. He was dressed in the mud-stained winter clothes of a Hakka farm worker, idly picking his teeth as he watched and listened.

The little chop house was warm with steam from the vats and the big gas range, its blue flame roaring under the frying woks. Like any Cantonese restaurant it was also filled with noise, the loud pitch of chatter that never faded for a second.

He knew that this shop was left alone by the Japanese patrols because he had suggested it. This was the place where peasant farmers and their workers came to eat. It was here that they met and here where they talked freely.

Toothpick Yap would have been killed if they had known that Ah Keung came to see him every night when the eating house was closed and that Toothpick reported everything he saw and heard at his tables. And they would have chopped the tall man with the crooked step to pieces like a fat duck if they had known he was working for the Japanese.

Toothpick had been easy to convince. He had two plump wives and a host of children. The thought of losing them all one by one to Japanese bayonets had soon secured his full cooperation. So, the Double Summer chop house had become the favourite meeting place for the exchange of gossip. A safe place away from the eyes and ears of the brown monkeys.

It was here that Ah Keung got his information, here and in the fields and on the rice terraces. And it was here that he had learned of each escape plan. He had not been able to find out where the fugitives were sheltered and had advised the Japanese to cease the raids on farms and villages—they had only made them move their hiding places and tighten their security.

He was certain that the next escape bid was about to take place. Toothpick had assured him that the four men who spoke of it were Nationalist soldiers working as labourers. The rumours had been too consistent. Although the numbers changed from ten to thirty to 300 escapees preparing to leave, Ah Keung was convinced that this would be the one they had been waiting for, the last of the Britishers and more of the Chinese who had hidden enough gold to buy their way out of the colony and escape to Thailand.

When this was over the Japanese would move on the village of Pok Choy Lam, which they were now convinced was a Nationalist stronghold, and wipe it out. Ah Keung swigged the last of his tea and left the eating house to join the field party. The busy prattle did not change its pitch, no one noticed him go and no one noticed that he did not pay his bill. Only Toothpick Yap watched him move past the steamy window and climb into the truck.

Sharkfin Wong watched the chunk of meat sink slowly with the weight of the big steel hook and the heavy wire trace that shackled it to the cord line. He payed the line out as the drift of the current carried the bait away from the ship's stern. Around him hung the washing of his crew and a long string of drying shark fins were slung along the foredeck. He did not seem to notice the peeling paint of the woodwork or the scales of rust that scarred every metal part or the stink of fish gut left to putrefy on the littered decks.

The motorised fishing junk *Amoy* was named after its port of registry and listed as a cargo/passenger vessel. Like others of its kind it was a bastardised junk hull of some hundred tons authorised to carry eighty passengers below decks and in its square-built deck accommodation. That is, if they were crammed in like fish in a tin can, but the kind of passengers Sharkfin Wong took aboard the *Amoy* were never very particular.

He had landed as many as 200 at a time on the off shore islands of Hong Kong, usually mainland Chinese eager to improve their lives in the place they called the Fragrant Harbour—the place of great fortune where gold could be found and rice was always plentiful.

Illegal immigrants were a lucrative business because there were no fixed-price tickets aboard the snake boat *Amoy*—you paid what you had and if it wasn't enough you stayed on shore.

Sharkfin had made the most money when the civil war had swept through China and those who wished to escape would pay anything, including the gold in their teeth, to reach Formosa. Some he had taken to the Philippines, but pirates from the small islands of the Sulu Sea had boarded him and he had never made the trip again. He had watched while the Filipino pirates in their fast motorised outriggers had shared the women and even the children while their men looked on.

When they had finished they said the Chinese were not worth a bullet and chopped every man, woman and child to pieces with their razor-sharp bolo knives, then they fed them to the sharks. In a lifetime on the water Sharkfin Wong had never seen a feeding frenzy like that one.

He had witnessed many bad things in the flesh trade but never anything like the pirates of the Sulu Sea. He and his crew escaped the same fate by pretending to join them as they chopped off fingers to take gold rings and hands to get the jade bracelets of the women and children. He had filled the outriggers with gifts and given the pirates anything they wanted and all the brandy they could drink and finally they had left him in peace.

Sharkfin made the line fast in a barrel sling around an empty oil drum and dumped it over the side to act as a float. When the shark took the bait it would pull down on the drum and the drum would bob back and fix the hook hard, then the shark would slowly drown itself trying to cut free. He tied off the thick cord line on the ship's rail, checked the other five shark lines set around the ship and emptied several buckets of fish blood and offal over the side. Then he went below to the engineroom.

The twin Gardiner diesels had once belonged to the Hong Kong Motorbus Company. Now they were bolted down in the *Amoy's* engine-room, converted to salt-water-cooled marine engines. They were life and death to Sharkfin Wong and he kept them in the best condition he could. They had seen better days and had taken the *Amoy* many thousands of miles across the China seas for more years than he could remember. There was always the hiss of leaky valves where the cooling system had eaten through the water jacket and corroded the pipes.

He took a strip of oily rag and bound it carefully around a leak, tying it off with twine. Tapping the pressure gauges to see that the flickering needles showed a true reading, he wiped the rag lovingly over the hot pistons.

The engines had a habit of breaking down at the wrong times and he couldn't risk it tonight. This would be his last big run and he wanted nothing to go wrong. A hundred and twenty people. He did not ask who they were or why they wanted to go to Chung King. His contact in the junk city of Aberdeen had guaranteed payment in English pounds. Enough for him to join the Chinese community in Pattayah on the Gulf of Siam, build a fine house and a new fishing boat.

By the time darkness fell four sharks had been caught and gutted, their insides spilled back into the sea and carcasses iced down in the hold. It was always good to have a full hold when a patrol boat came around. Usually they took one look through the binoculars at the strings of shark fins and the general state of the *Amoy* and left it to wallow in its own bloody patch of ocean. Sharkfin Wong wasn't taking any chances; these Yut Boon Jai were different from regular coast guards.

He had to admit to feeling nervous. This was the largest number he had taken in the five trips he had made from Starling Inlet to the capital of Nationalist China.

The temple to the Spirit of the North was built against the rock cliff facing Starling Inlet at Sha Tau Kok. It had once been a popular place of worship for fishermen and any landsman that came upon it. The fishing village that it had watched over had been smashed to matchwood by the great typhoon of 1939 and the temple had slowly fallen into isolated decay.

All that remained were broken walls and roof beams that gaped open to the sky and the stone platform of its floor surrounded by a narrow parapet, reached by a flight of stone steps leading from the beach. Behind its crumbling walls a dozen British officers and men crouched against the cold wind that found its way into the ruin.

They were given some protection by the Hakka raincoats they wore, thick capes of tiger grass, woven layer over layer that enclosed the wearer like a tent. The mushroom-shaped hats of basketweave concealed their faces but their feet were bare. The miles they had trekked on foot, like any other party of labourers looking for work, had been mainly covered overnight.

A group of Chinese who had paid their way squatted closely among their bundles of belongings. They had arrived separately and kept as far from the foreign devils as they could. The escort was made up of two Hakka guides from Pok Choy Lam village and four armed Nationalists.

Toby had waited a month in the rice storage barn of Po Lok's cousin since arriving with the honey-cart. The hiding place had been dug out of the earth beneath the barn floor and had once been used to hide from Koxinga's pirates when they raided the coast and forged inland 300 years earlier.

There were hides like this in most of the walled villages that no one knew of but the head of the clan. Toby had been amply fed and meetings with the headman and his sons had taken place each evening.

The resistance movement was a ragtag group, some still half believing in the promised push of the Kuomintang armies and others who felt the Generalissimo had deserted them. Leadership was non-existent and discipline worsened every day. After each capture a number deserted, either returning over the border to take their chances by themselves or disappearing into the mass of Kowloon and Hong Kong. There was no chance of regrouping a cohesive unit under a British officer. Most of them despised the gwai-lo almost as much as they hated the Yut Boon Jai.

The Hakka farmers who had offered help under the influence of headmen like Doctor Sun's cousin, Chen Yu, were also turning away. Japanese reprisals were savage and after every capture executions had been carried out in the courtyards of their village meeting hall.

Women were taken and houses burned. There was no doubt that someone among them was informing and several suspects had been found with their throats cut. It had been decided among the British soldiers and civilians still in hiding and who had hoped to hang on, that the mainlanders were right, there would be no relief from inside China. It was time to go.

Toby had coordinated his party under the small Nationalist escort and with two of Chen Yu's sons as guide, led them across the farmlands to the ruined temple, thankful for a moonless night. Even in the dark the young Hakka boys knew every rice paddy and duck pond, every ditch and footbridge. The Japanese patrols kept to the roads and the group had seen nothing of them in the three hours it had taken to pick their way across the farmland.

Others had brought their groups in from different villages and by one a.m. there were eighty British army personnel and a sprinkling of civilians who had lived and worked around Shatin. The Chinese gathering had swelled to forty.

The big, ungainly vessel that steered into the flat waters of the inlet showed no lights, but the slow bump of its engines clearly carried to the temple. Sha Tau Kok had been selected because it was neglected by the patrols that centred their activities on Tolo harbour and Tai Po.

The snake boat was a cargo carrier/cum/trawler commonly seen on the coast, with the lines of a barge and an ugly block of superstructure aft. Only the *Amoy's* colossal sampson post and lifting derricks distinguished it from a floating farm shed. The group stayed silent as the thump of a boat being lowered and then the splash of oars was heard across the still water of the inlet.

The sudden blue-white blaze of a searchlight that knifed the darkness with one loud metallic clank of its shutter was dazzlingly brilliant. The powerful beam swept the stretch of water between the *Amoy* and the beach, easily picking out the sampan. Its sculling oar had stopped and the man steering it stood still in the stern shielding his eyes. Another crouched in its bows. A second searchlight flooded the temple, its white light sliced by the broken wall, leaving half still in total darkness. The Chinese scuttled out of the glare, treading over the British like cattle and jabbering with fear.

'Stay where you are,' a Japanese voice screeched over a loud-hailer. 'Do not move. We will show you what happens if you do not stay where you are.'

The pitch black behind the searchlight beams erupted with splintering tongues of machine-gun fire from three directions, like the guttering of electric cables chopped through. The sampan seemed to vibrate in the pool of vivid light, its occupants flying over the side as though hit by a sudden cyclonic wind.

Chunks of its hull flew after them as the sampan disintegrated and sank from sight in under thirty seconds. The battering of sound cut off as savagely as it had switched on. Only the hot engine smell of gun oil and cordite remained on the still night air.

Debris drifted in the disturbed patch of light, then the beam flicked up to bathe the rusty side of the snake boat already manoeuvering to reverse out of its position. There was the sudden thrust of its engines pumping hard until the machine-guns licked out again. Plumes of blue fire traced the length of the hull, striking the steel rails, bright as welding arcs, and the windows of the deck house were blown away before it ceased. The loudspeaker squawked again, this time in shrill Cantonese, as the light beam showed two inflatable craft, low in the water from the weight of a Japanese boarding party leaving the beach.

The unmistakable 'phattung' of a Very pistol triggered nearby. The high, graceful curve of its flare ended with a soft plop as the flowering of phosphorescence floated down. Starling Inlet lit up as bright as day. A ring of Japanese soldiers was advancing towards the granite steps that led from the sand to the temple. The Nationalist escort had flung themselves flat and opened fire over the parapet. One of them was hit almost immediately, the wide hat sent flying in a splatter of blood, his rifle clattering from his grasp.

Toby leapt for the weapon that teetered in danger of dropping from the narrow tiled ledge. Before his hand could close on it, an automatic weapon opened up directly overhead. Toby recognised the ripping burr of a Russian-made P.P.D. sub-machine gun, Moscow's answer to the British sten or the American Browning.

The prone bodies of the remaining three Nationalist soldiers were almost cut in two by the stream of fire at close range. It shut off, leaving only a ringing in the ears as someone spoke.

'Don't touch it, Captain.'

The voice from the roof above was close enough to hear above the machine-gun fire still directed in spasmodic bursts at the lumbering cargo vessel.

'Raise your hands and stand up or you join them.'

Another short rip from the P.P.D. stitched across the bodies, reducing the rain capes to a red soaked pulp. The first flare was dying and another fizzed high to take its place. The inside of the temple was lit bright as day.

The figure that dropped lightly through the broken roof was Chinese, wearing a padded, knee-length jacket. Thick peasant trousers were bound at the shins in the style of the Japanese soldier. He made no sound as he dropped like a cat and Toby saw the split-toe combat boots on his feet.

'Stand quite still, Captain,' he said calmly, signalling with the black snout of the P.P.D. for him to move away from the others.

The weapon in his hands vibrated briefly again, held so firmly that the heavy recoil of its breech action hardly moved the overheated barrel the fraction of an inch. Screams from the remaining Chinese escapees were quickly silenced. In seconds they were piled dead among their bundles.

In the electrifying silence that followed the burst of rapid fire, the man called out to those below, stepping to the parapet and holding the weapon high to show the position was secure. Then he turned back to Toby.

'Tell your men to raise their hands or they join the running dogs.' He withdrew a new magazine from the deep pocket of the jacket, shedding the used one to clatter at his feet and replacing it smartly.

'Seventy-one rounds. Enough for all of you.' The soldier grinned, stepping closer to Toby. 'Don't you remember me, gwai-lo?'

Pulling the soft Japanese cap from his head he stared straight into Toby's eyes. Toby had only ever been close to such venom once before. In the Nine Dragons ballroom. This was the man that Sing had called Ah Keung, the Forceful One.

It was daylight before they reached the village of Pok Choy Lam. Ah Keung sat by the tailgate of the army vehicle, the P.P.D. across his knees. On the floor of the truck Toby and the sons of Chen Yu lay bound hand and foot. Their bonds had been swiftly and cleverly tied. The thin grass rope encircled their necks in a running noose, then passed over the shoulder to bind the wrists as high up the back as they could be forced, then on to the heels, also trussed as high as they could go, with just the right tension to prevent asphyxiation. Only by bending the head back could they prevent themselves from being garrotted and with every jolt of the wheels over mud tracks the noose bit deeper.

Ah Keung reached down and cut the rope between their heels, making it possible for them to walk. 'You will show me where you have been hiding these gwai-los or in one hour this village will be no more.'

He spoke close to the bent-back heads of the two brothers. 'Not one will be left alive.' He jerked the noose of one, then cut him loose. 'Your ancestral shrine will be turned into a shit-house for the brown monkeys.'

The brothers led the way to the village rice store. There they shifted the heavy rice bins from a trapdoor, revealing steps cut into the clay. Prodding with the muzzle of the P.P.D., Ah Keung sent them down ahead of him, jabbing the barrel of the weapon into Toby's back.

'Now you, Captain. See that they make some light.'

The space under the rice store was six metres square, and the distance to the floor beams that formed its ceiling was just out of reach. Six stretcher beds, two benches and a wooden table were the only furnishings. Ah Keung looked around the walls of weeping clay, shored up with rotting timbers. 'Stand over there, Captain. I want you to see something.'

He cut the centre rope behind Toby's back so that his neck was released from the downward pull of his arms. 'Sit down. I will show you how I deal with those who cause me trouble.'

He laid the weapon aside, stepping up to one of the young men. His left hand whipped out almost casually and slapped the forehead, jerking the head back as his right fist drove in a piston-like uppercut to the back of the head. The youth's knees buckled but before he had hit the floor Ah Keung had stepped up to his brother and repeated the same double blow. The executions had taken less than three seconds and both men lay dead where they fell.

'They did not deserve a bullet,' he said, spitting at the jerking bodies then smiling at the look of disbelief on Toby's face.

'Do not be concerned, Captain. These dogs would not have felt a thing. It is called "Flicking the Dragon's Tail".' He demonstrated the movement in slow time. 'First the left hand slaps the head lightly backwards to tilt the base of the skull at just the right angle. Then the right hand comes up with force and . . .' He slammed the right fist into the left palm with a loud smack. 'The head is lifted neatly from its atlas, the cervical vertebra is dislocated and the spinal cord is severed. A simple trick of the Empty Hand.' He laughed again at Toby's face. 'They are fortunate. A slight change of angle and they would be only paralysed.'

'It is the trick of an uncivilised traitor and a murderer of his own people.' Toby spoke slowly, his voice rasping from the garrotte.

Ah Keung smiled patiently. 'Such skills were old when your ancestors were painting themselves blue and smashing skulls with axes of stone. Where is the difference? Which is the more primitive? Who is the uncivilised?'

He picked up the automatic weapon and turned out the lamp. 'Nothing so undignified for you, Captain. Lord Ching wishes you to die with honour and ceremony.' He smirked. 'So that the jarp-jung whore can be proud of you.'

'She is alive?' He had blurted the question before he knew it.

'Yes. She warms the bed of a Yut Boon Tai, but soon Taipan Ching will call upon her. I, too, have a score to settle there.'

Ah Keung mounted the steps. 'Meanwhile, since you find this place so comfortable and those dogs so faithful, you may stay here with them until I am ready for you.' The trapdoor closed and Toby heard the heavy bins dragged into place on top of it.

He had no idea how long he stayed in the darkness. The grass rope had been retied behind his back so tightly that any attempt to work loose threatened to choke him. The only light and air came from the cracks in the floor above. It was enough to show the two bodies crumpled where they had fallen. He guessed it was twenty-four hours before footsteps approached the trapdoor, the bins were again pulled aside and the wooden flap lifted.

'Come up, Captain. I have received my instructions.' Ah Keung's words were taunting.

'As I promised, you are to die a hero's death.'

Toby was taken out of the rice store, prodded and pushed towards the meeting place in the centre of the village. The entire population of Pok Choy Lam had been rounded up from the homes and from the fields to witness the executions. The forecourt of the old building was flanked by Japanese guards. In their centre stood six of the surviving British soldiers lined up before a table and chair with two guards behind them, their bayonets fixed. A junior officer stood at ease at one side of the table and a burly sergeant on the other.

On the table was a clipboard, a water-jug and glass. Spanning its length was a drawn Samurai sword laid beside its scabbard.

'These are the last of your brave soldiers, and yours the place of honour,' Ah Keung whispered as he shoved Toby onto the end of the line. 'In recognition of my part in this small victory, Lord Ching has granted special consideration in your case.'

The sergeant strode to the table, saluted the officer and picked up the sword with both hands. The first prisoner was forced to his knees in the middle of the courtyard. The rope that held his head back was cut, allowing it to drop forward. The junior officer stepped forward to grasp the man's hair as the sergeant spaced his feet well apart, raising the shining, graceful curve of tempered razor-sharp steel, settling himself with the concentration of a golfer. A loud exhalation of breath brought the blade flashing down. A shrill hiss escaped the sergeant's lips as the effort expelled the air from his lungs on the downward swing, blending with the singing sound of the steel's contact.

Toby had closed his eyes at the final second but the sigh of the watching crowd was not enough to deaden the sound of the blade slicing through flesh and bone or the distinct bump that followed it. He kept his eyes closed tight for the next five minutes while the sound was repeated, praying all the time that Sing would be somehow saved from this man who stood beside him.

Even in his growing fear, hers was the only face he saw. When he felt the thrust of Ah Keung's hand in his back he opened his eyes and saw only the sky, scattered with cloud and pools of bottomless blue. The rope was cut and his head dropped forward.

'Don't worry about the jarp-jung woman,' Ah Keung's voice whispered. 'I will take good care of her.'

The sergeant's face was expressionless as he handed Ah Keung the sword with a bow of ceremonial dignity. 'I have been granted the honour,' he said softly. 'I'm sure it won't take long.'

The Finger Jade

SING WAITED in the Happy Valley tea house as she had been told. The note left for her at Everspring said that if she followed instructions she would receive news of the British captain. Her heart leapt when from the envelope tumbled the mottled orange finger jade she had given Toby at the Residence of Eternal Peace. She had thanked all the gods that it came at a time when General Toshido was on a tour of the prison camps and he had left for Stanley Village straight after they had taken breakfast.

The household staff and those at the guard post had no reason to question her as she left. It was well known that the general's woman made regular trips to the herb shop in Causeway Bay and they had become accustomed to her movements. Doctor Sun had given her the note but warned her not to go. There was word of great trouble in Pok Choy Lam and he feared it may be connected. The escape had been ambushed, the snake boat taken, and many had died, including the sons of Chen Yu. She had thanked him and told him not to worry, her heart too filled with hope that Toby was alive to be cautious.

The tea house was an open pavilion in the middle of a public garden and Sing could see on all sides the strolling couples, the old ones on the benches and children chasing ducks. The man that approached her seemed familiar but she could not be sure where she had seen him.

'Where are we to go?' she asked.

The man said nothing. Turning, he walked across the park to

a waiting car and stood beside the open door, waiting for her. Sing followed him and climbed into the back seat.

Not until they had driven through Central and were headed along the Repulse Bay Road and she recognised the driver as one of his servants, did she realise she was being taken to the house of J.T. Ching. She rapped on the glass dividing panel but the driver did not turn around. Only his eyes in the rear-vision mirror told her he had heard.

J.T. Ching did not rise from the couch when she was shown into the room he called his house of treasure. He was wearing a brocaded gown of scarlet silk tied with a black sash. Before him on the low table the tripod and pan of the opium smoker stood beside two long-stemmed ivory pipes. From a radiogram came the voice of Louis Armstrong.

'At last we can speak alone. I have waited patiently and with great anticipation for this moment. The game of hide and seek was becoming tiresome.' He let her stand while he looked her up and down.

'I will not ask why you ran from the tavern of Madam Fung and left behind the token of loyalty you had accepted.' She waited while he reseated himself.

'I was too young to be the slave of any man.' Sing kept her voice level and unafraid.

Ching arched his brows in surprise. 'You were not too young for the British captain? And were you not a slave in the ballroom of Three-thumbs Poon?' You are not too young for the Yut Boon Jai.' Before she could answer, he continued: 'I treated you well. I would have protected you as I protect everything that is precious to me . . . was my company so odious that you preferred the streets of Wan Chai?'

'I was confused and afraid. I did not think I was ready for the honour you did me.'

Ching laughed drily. 'But you honour the great General Toshido?'

'I treat his health, I am his nurse. If he chooses to favour me I cannot object. I sometimes accompany him, nothing more.'

Before he could say more Sing laid the finger jade on the rose quartz table. 'Your message says you have news of the one this belonged to.'

Ching leaned back, his slack mouth closed grimly. 'Ah! Yes. This ah . . . bing-jai,' he spat the derogatory term for common soldier. 'I understand that he was the first to pluck the flower I so carefully planted and tenderly nurtured in the pleasant Garden of cascading jewels.'

He stood suddenly and walked around the room, continuing in the same sarcastically poetic way.

'Plucked before it was fully open. I have often wondered if its freshness is gone, its perfume faded.' He turned to face her, persuasive and tolerant. 'Am I to be the only one denied the secret pleasures of Ah Gum, the Golden One?' he asked, affecting a disconsolate tone. 'Come, prepare the pipes. We will chase the dragon together. Then we shall talk of the bing-jai.'

Sing shook her head. 'I will not take the drug,' she said, moving to the table. 'But I will make the pipe for you.'

'Ching's hand flashed out and grasped her wrist. 'You will do as I ask,' he hissed, pulling her violently around the table and into his lap.

The robe fell open and she could see that he was naked beneath it. Subduing the instinct to resist, Sing's mind raced. She must think first of Toby, find a way to control this situation. Anything that would gain time, to find out what Ching knew. She must pretend.

Relaxing into his lap without a struggle, Sing closed her mind to feeling as she had done so many times before. Her actions and reactions became automatic, all part of an empty process. Whatever it took, whatever she had learned of deceiving men must be at its best now, to be used to its full advantage.

His puffy eyes glittered at the slight change in her, hardly detectable, but he felt tension melt as the full weight of her body sank onto him. Felt the smooth bulk of her buttocks and thighs, thinly covered, pressed heavily against him. Sing felt his hardness straining against her. Allowed herself to move on him, just enough to tease this rod that mastered him. She heard him groan thickly with the thrill of contact.

'I have never taken a pipe. It will be my first time. You must be patient.' Her words were not submissive enough to make him suspicious. Just enough uncertainty in them to stimulate his dominance.

'Then it is fitting that you should take it with me. Was it not I who paid for your teaching in all such things?'

He reached for her, one hand roughly curling around her waist to grasp her breast, the other snaking crudely up the tight fit of her dress, forcing her legs apart.

'Is it not time I received gratitude? Am I not to be rewarded for my generosity?'

The numbness in Sing's mind and body allowed him to do as he pleased, his hasty fingers forcing aside the crotch of her cami-knickers to burrow into her. The fastenings of her cheong-sam were pulled apart by the thrust of his other hand, roughly seeking her nipple.

'Lord Ching should try to understand why my child's mind could not accept the honour of becoming his concubine. My feeling for him was such that I could not share with so many others.' Swiftly, without fuss, she disengaged herself and stood up, smoothing the tight silk over the backs of her thighs. 'You must understand I am not like others. There is western blood in my veins and it does not allow such things. It is also this that made me run from you.'

She knew that he was already too aroused to question this change in her attitude and continued to use the advantage, remembering well the effect that opium had upon him, how it soothed and reassured. Ching had always been more manageable when riding the back of the dragon.

'I will make the pipe. It will be as it once was in the tavern.'

'If you please me then perhaps we will talk of the bing-jai, but first you must smoke.' His words were husky with lust as he sat staring up at her, the smile of an idiot settled on his flushed face. Surprise and anticipation had replaced aggression. She knew that to question him now would be dangerous. Only patience and the cunning manipulation of his senses would prepare him.

His eyes followed her every movement greedily. 'In the tavern I would look upon you as a child and imagine you unclothed,' he said harshly. 'I was a fool who accepted the rules of the Dragon Woman. Now you are no longer a child and I am no longer a fool. Take off your clothes before you make the pipe.'

The order left no room for more words. He had closed the robe over his nakedness, his hands sliding back and forth, up and down his heavy thighs, over his knees, working himself up with growing expectation.

Its fastenings already broken by his clumsiness, the cheong-sam slipped effortlessly over Sing's hips. She shook her hair back into place as the garment was tossed aside. Ching licked his thick lips wetly as she bent to the opium pan.

Her underclothes of cream satin had come with boxes of others from Lane Crawford. They were flown from France, the little man said, the very latest, as were the pure silk stockings and lace suspender belt she wore.

'This too,' he breathed. 'Such a body needs no covering. Such limbs as yours are rarely seen. You have the feel of ripe summer fruit.' He gave a lascivious chuckle. 'I will drink your juice before we are done.'

'Let us not hasten our pleasure. There is reward in patience. These are the words of the Golden One.'

Sing kept her tone light, just enough firmness to convince him she was right. It took five minutes to prepare the pipes while his eyes devoured her. He had spread himself full length along the couch with no attempt to conceal his excitement. As Sing brought him the pipe she could see that he was sweating. Where the robe had fallen open the rolls of hairless flesh were damp with his heat.

Ching snatched the pipe from her, his breathing hurried as he suckled the first deep drag. 'Come. Grasp the dragon's tail,' he whispered, nodding to the second pipe as the sweet smoke began curling thinly from his nostrils.

Sing placed the ivory stem between her lips and drew on it mildly. The smoke that invaded her mouth was not unpleasant. It tasted as it smelled, cloying and seductive.

'Swallow it,' whispered Ching. 'Draw again. Harder. Take the sweet tears of the poppy deep. We will become the traders of dreams.' His hand reached out to her, already languid as he lay back from the third bubbling draught.

'Come closer. Sit by me as you once did so innocently.' His eyes sought hers, moistened by the soothing drug. 'How I longed to bury myself in you then.'

Sing expelled the smoke held in her mouth. The first signs of his musings were beginning to mould him like softening clay. She must not let him drift too far. The effects of the drug pulled at her resolve as she came within reach of him. His groping fingers found the band of satin at her waist and wrenched it downwards, reaching for her, grasping the tangle of hair, pulling at it, his fingers feeling for her impatiently.

'Closer. I will consume you.' His voice had changed in pitch to almost a whimper. Her mind closed to the obscenity of his touch, Sing seemed to yield to it, as though it was someone else he groped for.

'Yes, lord. All that you wish.' She breathed softly. 'But I cannot give willingly until I know of the Englishman. He is nothing to me, but I have reason to ask.'

Sing's heart beat fast, praying she had not gone too far, that the opium had had the effect she hoped for, that he would surrender to his need for her and tell her anything she wished to hear.

Even Sing's hesitation could not have prepared her for Ching's response. His body jack-knifed from the couch, his flat hand slapping viciously at her breasts, then punching out at her belly.

'You do not barter with me, you jarp-jung whore. You do my bidding.' He lurched to his feet, slapping her again hard across the face. The robe flapped open; his angry rod bobbed with his movement. 'There will be no bargains. I will fuck you as I please, as long as I please and as often as I please.' He thrust his face close to hers, strained red with his fury. 'Or you will not see the gwai-lo bing-jai again.'

The reaction was so violent and unexpected that Sing's instinctive reflexes took over. The arm that drove the heel of her palm into his chest was governed by the spontaneous splash of her ch'i. Although she held back its force, it sent him sprawling against the low table, grotesque in his nakedness.

When he bounded to his feet, the nose of a small nickel-plated revolver had appeared as if by magic in his hand. His face hideously contorted, flecks of saliva sprayed from his lips as he cursed her. Every foul damnation ever spawned in the gutters of China's hell-holes was choked from him. Shaking from the reaction of his outrage to the slowing effects of opium he levelled the pistol unsteadily at her belly.

As the outburst subsided, his fleshy mouth shaped a leering grin. His eyes half closed by the drug that threatened to claim him, he mouthed at her more quietly. 'The Forceful One has warned me that there is fire in your belly. That you are treacherous as a rabid bitch on heat.' His words were slurred by the opium fumes unfolding inside him. The eyes that glittered from his pouchy lids were maddened by his heightened senses.

'There was a time when one such as you, who had been chosen and went instead to another, was split in two.' He licked at the corner of his mouth. 'Bound hand and foot to a stretching frame and mounted by a stallion. Such was the public punishment for those who ran from their masters.'

Sing felt the hope of learning more of Toby slipping away. Making a desperate attempt to hold on to it, she ripped the brassiere from her breasts, letting them fall free. Ignoring the gun still trembling in his outstretched hand, she reached for the suspenders and released her stockings. Holding his flickering gaze, she rolled them from her legs, her mind filled with one resolve—the drug must be given more time.

Every moment counted. She knew that soon the virulence of his anger would drain him of energy and that peace would be all that he would crave. To escape him she must cause him to relinquish the weapon. No strike was faster than a bullet. She must be close to take it. Now she stood naked.

'You lord, can be my stallion. But first the pipe. You must rest now. Later we will arouse the tiger.'

He appeared not to hear her, staggering slightly as his arm began to tire and the pistol lowered its aim. Sing needed to take no more than a step to be close enough to strike it from him. His eyes had almost closed as he continued to mutter obscenities.

On the instant she decided to act, he suddenly backed away, raising the gun with both hands, steadying its nozzle directly at her stomach. His eyes had widened, the frenzied light in them beyond reason. 'I could split your belly and fuck you as you die,' he screamed, the pitch of his voice suddenly strident. 'But I have a better idea.' The snout of the revolver jerked towards the archway leading to the conservatory.

'We shall visit the mah-lau.' He laughed shrilly. 'You remember the mah-lau.' He used the Chinese term for ape, referring to the awful creature he kept chained in there. 'But first I will give you what you came for. You wish to know of the bing-jai,' he snarled. 'Well, you will never see him again. He is . . .'

In mid-sentence, Ching's jaws were wrenched suddenly wide. Eyes filled with surprise. Jade held the jewelled hilt of the dagger with both hands, as one would hold the shaft of an axe. She did not know how to use the knife and had swung the heavy blade sideways so that its fine pointed tip pierced his side just above the kidneys and below the bottom rib. With the added strength of her fear Jade hooked the curved, double-edged blade outward. Ching spun around with the shock, driving the steel deeper into his flesh. He screamed an oath in the instant of agony, his drug-glazed eyes seeking his attacker as Jade wrenched the knife free to swing again.

Before she could deliver a second blow, he staggered drunkenly, his free hand groped at the huge wound that had left a gaping flap of meat, he gawped with disbelief at the thick arterial blood that flooded his hand. The other swung round, the revolver still in its grasp. Then one knee buckled beneath him and he lurched sideways, pitching onto his face at Sing's feet. It had taken no more than two seconds.

Jade stood looking down at him, her feet apart, the weight of the knife still gripped like a bloody meat axe in her hands. She had come like a shadow from the Chamber of Righteous Steel and Sing recognised the Arabian dagger Ching had proudly shown Jiro Toshido.

'My curse on him and his lineage,' Jade whispered, the Light of The Nile dropping from her nerveless fingers. She stood, her face a blank, the hands that had held the weapon at her side. Before Sing could reach her she had sunk to her knees.

'A curse on him and his ancestors,' Jade whispered, staring as Ching's body twitched, his fingers clawing the carpet, trying to find words as life gurgled from him. She shook her head, covering her mouth briefly, then waving away Sing's help.

'You must go, Siu Sing. You must walk staight out as though nothing has happened. The driver will not question it. This pig never sees his women to the door. It is normal.'

Sing at last found her voice. On her knees beside Jade, she reached out to her. 'You must come with me. We must both go. I will not leave without you.'

Jade shook her head, climbing to her feet and pushing Sing away.

'No, I will follow later. No one will come here unless he calls. There will be time.'

Sing hesitated. 'But I cannot leave you here, Jade.'

'You must. I will go also but I have a plan of my own. I have often thought of this moment.' She embraced Sing.

'I knew what he would do to you.' Delayed shock had gripped Jade and she trembled violently. 'It is better to be dead.' She pulled herself together. 'His wives and concubines live in a separate part of the house. They are afraid of him. They dread his summons to these rooms. The servants hate him. They see him as a running dog who has betrayed his people and who treats them as slaves. They will see nothing and say nothing.' She smiled, hugging Sing tenderly.

'I am only his mistress, I come and go. In an hour I shall also leave. They will never find me.' They embraced again.

'Go Siu Sing. I will see you again,' Jade whispered. 'All gods watch over you.'

'And you Jade. One day I will repay you.'

SEPTEMBER 1945

THE JAPANESE occupation of Hong Kong lasted for three years and eight months. For the last two years, life in the overcrowded prison camps had become increasingly barbaric and for the Chinese and neutrals not killed or imprisoned it was a day by day battle for survival. With the coming of the Japanese everything that a hundred years of British rule had done to make Hong Kong one of the greatest trade centres of the world, replacing Shanghai as the Pearl of The Orient, had disappeared overnight.

With the rule of common law and all public amenities gone, the colony had settled into a hand to mouth existence. Conditions had become primitive in the extreme—apart from near starvation its citizens were without water, gas, electricity, food supply, currency stability, public transport or a postal service. All trade and commerce had ceased to operate and a makeshift existence of ragged desperation had taken its place.

Without other means to cook rice, available fuel supplies had soon been used up and a start was made on anything and everything that could burn. Every vacant building had been stripped of furniture, doors and window frames. Staircases and parquet flooring were torn up to burn beneath the cooking pots, together with every piece of paper that could be found. All records, books and accounts were lost forever.

Without transport of any kind and with nowhere to buy footwear, shoes were clumsily soled with pieces of tyre rubber and clothes were slowly reduced to patched and threadbare rags. In an effort to prevent Kowloon and Hong Kong becoming one immense death camp the Japanese had encouraged large numbers of its starving population to cross the border into China on the promise of improved conditions. Those who did not accept this slender hope willingly were driven across at the point of a bayonet.

The Chinese passion for gambling became the only form of amusement left behind closed doors. With the picture theatres closed or occupied by the thousands of homeless, Chinese opera and every kind of public performance banned, any game of chance was leapt upon with feverish enthusiasm.

One that had become popular was the almost forgotten sport of rat baiting. Resurrected from the slums of Canton, Shanghai and Peking where rats were as plentiful as fleas, it had become a regular pastime in the cellars and basements of downtown Hong Kong.

Without garbage or sanitary services of any kind, rats romped in the streets like rabbits in a meadow. The stink of them, the scrabbling of their claws, came from every darkened corner, from under the floors, behind the walls. They came teeming from blocked sewers up through the foundations and into the streets and buildings to invade the rotting banks of refuse. There was no shortage of rats. Pits were dug, large and deep enough to hold anything from hundreds to thousands of rats at one time. Into the pit was thrown a terrier dog and bets were taken on how many it would kill before it was pulled down and torn to pieces by the sheer weight of numbers.

With the executions and burning of Pok Choy Lam, the last escape routes had been closed, all hope of organised resistance crushed and the villages routed. What was left of a scattered Nationalist underground had simply melted into the urban shambles.

Ah Keung had realised that the death of J.T. Ching had left him without credibility or protection of any kind. He had broken away from what was left of the Yellow Dragon triad and taken refuge in the impregnable Walled City of Ling Nam. Although the Japanese had demolished its walls, even their most hardened patrols bypassed this hive of disease and hidden violence. When early patrols had failed to emerge from its depths, either disappearing completely or being dumped outside the city gates in states of mutilation that rivaled anything they had seen, the Japanese had retaliated with mortar fire and then left the Walled City alone to cannibalise itself. It was into its depths that Ah Keung disappeared.

Ling Nam was a place where force was the only law and violence was a business. The Forceful One made no secret of the fact that his services were for sale to the highest bidder. His reputation was such that few dared challenge him and those who did were soon terminated. Even among the dissipated ranks of rival triads the Forceful One was considered best left alone.

He was satisfied with the respect that soon surrounded him and it pleased him that it was born of fear. As a hired debt collector and when necessary, an exterminator, he was content to take protection money from the illicit businesses that flourished behind the crumbling facade of the Walled City. He was free to exploit those bars and brothels in Wan Chai that had once been the territory of the Yellow Dragon. None of this conflicted with the higher conquests of the societies who had sat out the war confident that the day of the brown monkey was drawing to a close. Many had disbanded, their senior officials escaping Hong Kong or lying low.

Now they began to regroup. Ah Keung was left to become a large and dangerous fish in a small and stagnant pond. The decadence and audacity of the Walled City invited him into its verminous heart and he quickly became a part of it—hated but sought out by the most powerful taipans in need of his services.

The end of Japanese occupation had been slow in coming. The series of softening-up strikes saw American fighter bombers sink all Japanese shipping in Victoria Harbour but had also levelled half of Wan Chai during the raids. Twenty Japanese warships were sunk and its air force shot down or driven from the skies. On August 30, 1945, HMS *Swiftfire* sailed into the naval dockyard in Central Victoria and Rear-Admiral C.H. Harcourt stepped ashore to accept the Japanese surrender on September 16.

The admiral's first duty had been to visit the prison camps of Sham Shui Po and Stanley Village to the feeble cheers of surviving inmates reduced to tattered skeletons, as desolate and brutalised as any liberated from the concentration camps of Nazi Germany. Among them, Peggy Pelham, grey, gaunt and suffering badly from malnutrition, searched in vain for news of her husband. With Sebastian Masters and the other inmates of Stanley she was taken to Queen Mary's Hospital before returning to what had once been their homes to see what was left.

To a devastated Chinese community the defeat of the Japanese was a signal to loot and pillage. The pre-war Chinese population had been 1,600,000. No records had been kept of those killed by Japanese shelling and bombing in the invasion, put to death, dead from hunger and disease or driven back into China, but remaining Chinese numbers were estimated at 600,000. The wealthy and positioned returned to the ruins of their businesses while the mass swept upon the homes so recently occupied by Japanese and stripped them bare before their owners could take possession.

Hours after the British had set up headquarters in the Peninsula Hotel and the British flag was once again flying over Government House and the Royal Observatory, detachments of Chiang Kai-shek's Chinese army marched across the border, and camped outside the hotel. Had they arrived there first and claimed the territory in the name of the People's Republic of China, British Hong Kong may never have risen from the ashes of Japanese occupation.

Within days of liberation, signs of life began to reappear. A fitful tram service opened up, the Star ferry began to run, shops started to open as trade faced the task of reassembly and farm produce began appearing once more in the marketplaces. A military administration took over each urban area and placed a civilian Chief Affairs Officer in charge of each sector.

While the military representatives of Winston Churchill and Theodore Roosevelt argued about who should control which area and what shape the new Hong Kong should take in the future, a body of eight capable government officials was given military or police rank and charged with the responsibility of reestablishing a semblance of civil order. One of these men, among those who had survived Stanley Prison camp, was Sebastian Masters.

On August 7, five weeks before the Japanese high command had been forced to capitulate, Sing had entered General Jiro Toshido's room to find him dead. He had changed into a ceremonial undergarment of white cotton and slit his abdomen in a cross-shaped wound which had left him slumped forward over the spreading pool of his entrails, the tip of the ritual blade protruding from his lower back. It was the day after the dropping of the atom bomb on Hiroshima. She had closed the door quietly and walking out of the grounds of Hadden House, made her way to Causeway Bay and the Everspring herb shop of Doctor Sun.

Within a week some sort of public service had been restored and the beginnings of a police force reorganised. There was no visible rejoicing in the streets of the downtown districts. A few organised parades through the streets of Central and ceremonial gatherings in Victoria Square did nothing to encourage a public-spirited response to a new freedom and the rebuilding of Hong Kong. To the remaining mass of Cantonese all their suffering had been brought about by the gwai-lo and his quarrel with the Yut Boon Jai.

They did not watch the triumphal marches and military displays—instead they set about the business of rebuilding their own lives in the only way they knew, the protection and welfare of the family group, the regaining of its place and property. Loyalty belonged only to that end.

Bitter conflicts raged in the streets and buildings as disputes over ownership and territorial rights resulted in more bloodshed. The recent years of degradation and deprivation had crushed any sense of unity or cooperation. Instead, it was replaced by the desperate scramble for gain and position.

First and foremost in this hysteria was the seeking of revenge on those who were suspected of collaborating with the enemy. There was a high degree of deception in this vicious vendetta. Few Chinese had shown open defiance of the Japanese patrols and some had been quick to gain favour wherever they could. Those who had done so were the first to point the finger of accusation and to stir up hatred of others to cover their own guilt.

It was well known that the herb shop of Doctor Sun had remained untouched and protected because it supplied medicine for the Japanese masters. And it was said that the jarp-jung woman who came to fetch it was the whore of a Japanese lord. The same low-class whore who had dared to give them orders over the radio.

When the first rock shattered the front window of Everspring, Sing was sitting with the family in the back room. It was late in the evening on the first day following the official announcement of Japanese surrender. At the head of the group that burst into the shop, smashing jars and crocks, scattering the contents of the herb drawers over the floor, were many of Doctor Sun's neighbours and those who had once been his patients. Yun Ti the tailor, Sam-Shui the metal worker, the old woman who had sold flowers on the corner, Ah Yun the laundryman and Pigfat Lee, the man who owned the butcher's shop. Doctor Sun had restrained his sons and watched the destruction of his father's beloved shop.

To resist would mean certain injury or death. Several of the mob carried meat cleavers, the favourite weapon of riots, hacking into the lovingly polished wood in mindless fury. One leapt high to smash the dragon lantern, then turned his hate upon the portrait of Everspring's founder, slashing it to shreds.

Doctor Sun had cried out but was unheard as the blackwood chair kept for customers was passed out into the street over the heads of those cramming the shop. Everything else of value began to follow and when there was nothing left to take, one of the ringleaders recognised Sing.

This woman was a jarp-jung whore, he screamed. One who had slept with the Japanese and grown fat while they starved. She had been warm while they froze. She had stepped on the faces of the Chinese people to save her own skin.

Doctor Sun tried to come to her defence. It was she, he shouted over the raised voices, who had risked her life to bring information for the honourable heroes of Pok Choy Lam. It was she who had spied on the Yut Boon Jai, informed him and his sons and those of his cousins who had helped the Kuomintang.

The crowd that had filled the back room of Everspring was in no mood for reason. The escape of a handful of gwai-lo soldiers and cowardly rich Chinese was of no importance to them. Most were too busy fighting over the Sun family's possessions to hear his words. As to the Kuomintang soldiers, they were little better than the brown monkeys. The jarp-jung whore, they cried, was a running dog and she must be punished as one.

Sing made no attempt to defend herself. She knew that if she went with them the crowd would be satisfied for the moment. It would give Doctor Sun time to leave the shop with his family, to seek protection. Or, perhaps they would be left alone. There would be new traitors to attack tomorrow.

She was led through the streets by the chanting crowd, her treachery shouted loudly to the open windows and narrow balconies. The jeering throng strengthened as it made its way through the streets of Causeway Bay. Pushing Sing ahead, the procession streamed into the airless cavern of a deserted godown. Stacks of rotting produce baskets and broken wine jars reached almost to its rafters and the stink of decay filled the gloom. The frantic babble of voices intensified as more and more fought their way in to form a ring in the centre of the floor.

A large square of reinforcing steel was lifted by a group of eager youths. A single overhead light was switched on, revealing a round pit, two metres deep and about the same in diameter. The poor light showed what at first looked to Sing like a bubbling cauldron of shifting grey mud. It seemed to ripple and seethe as though at boiling point and from it came a shrill, jittering current of sound. Forced to its edge she stared in horror. The unmistakable feral reek of rats steeped in their own urine filled her nose and throat as she was forced closer to its edge. All around her bets were changing hands.

The two pistol shots that rang out in quick succession stopped the uproar of voices as abruptly as an electric plug wrenched from its socket. Clustered at the top of the steps, a battery of bright flashlights shone down on the gaping horde. The unfamiliar khaki and silver uniform of the Hong Kong police force had appeared with wicker shields and drawn riot sticks.

Sebastian Masters stood back as his squad moved into the godown. The call had come over the vehicle's radio net as they cruised the Causeway Bay area and it had taken only moments to locate the trouble.

Sebastian had been given the Wan Chai and Causeway Bay area as his precinct. With temporary rank of police inspector he was responsible for the control of riots such as this and they had become an hourly occurrence.

He had been astonished by how little he had really known of the Chinese he had lived among for several years. The comfortable life of Government House and the long established colonial clubs had shown him nothing of the savagery of attack by meat cleaver, the mindless hatred and violence so close to the surface when survival was threatened or revenge was taken.

It took only moments to clear the area; the hundreds of people simply slipped away, while the few defiant agitators had their heads cracked or were bundled into the riot van. He looked at the girl they had pulled from the edge of the pit and wondered what she could have done to deserve such dreadful punishment. She did not seem to need the assistance of the two constables who offered to support her, walking upright away from the horror, her face without expression. As she came towards him a sergeant flashed a torch. She stopped, turning her face away, shielding her eyes from its white glare.

Even in that brief second it was clear she was not Chinese, but only when she came close to him did Sebastian realise he had seen her before. He spoke sharply to the sergeant and the torch was switched off. Behind her, paraffin was sloshed into the pit. A match was struck and thrown in. The loud 'whoof' of the explosion was followed by the squeals of burning rats.

The girl staggered at the sound and Sebastian grabbed her arm. It seemed impossible, but he had no doubt. The eyes that looked into his in that moment of despair were those of the girl he had never forgotten.

Sebastian

THE HELENA May hostel for women on Garden Road provided accommodation for expatriate women of limited means. Peggy Pelham considered herself very fortunate to have secured one of its small, self-contained flatettes almost immediately upon her release from Stanley Prison. Close to the Peak tram-cable railway, within walking distance to St John's Cathedral and the Central District, it was perfectly situated.

Certain that she would soon receive news of her husband, Peggy had returned to Stonecutter's Island to retrieve what she could of their belongings. Among them had been the chest containing Siu Sing's books and she had kept it in the hope that she would be found safe. The little island had been temporarily placed out of bounds and there was no chance of returning to live there. Peggy was also thankful for the tremendous amount of work to be done in the weeks and months following the Japanese surrender. She had thrown herself back into Red Cross duties and once again sat on the Social Welfare and Urban District Council committees while she waited to hear that Justin had been released from internment in Shanghai, Canton or Tokyo—wherever he had been sent.

It had been confirmed that some high-ranking allied officers and British government officials, including the governor himself, were transported to one of these destinations by the Japanese in the early weeks of occupation. She refused to consider that he might have been among those lost at sea when several of the Japanese ships carrying them were sunk by the US air force in early 1942. With 100,000 Chinese returning to Hong Kong each month, acute food shortages and scarcity of money, there was plenty to keep her and others like her very busy indeed. In addition to rationing of rice, flour and sugar to bona fide Hong Kong residents, some 25,000 destitute people from across the border were sustained each day by government rice kitchens.

With 60 per cent of housing damaged in varying degrees, street-sleepers' shelters had to be set up and supervised. Medical supplies and public health systems were almost non-existent, with 80 per cent of the population suffering from malnutrition and tuberculosis.

The education system had to be almost entirely rebuilt and, in addition to her many other responsibilities, Peggy Pelham took the cable tram to the Peak school each morning to teach primary classes of children fortunate enough to renew their schooling.

The only link that was left to Peggy's shattered former life was the amah, Ah Koo. The old woman had been in her service since she and Justin had first moved into the Stonecutter's bungalow. She had come with the house along with most of the rather ugly furniture, proudly shoving a well-worn sheaf of letters of recommendation into the new mistress's hand.

The letters claimed long and loyal service to a succession of British military families over a quite astounding number of years. Although, like the furniture, she had not proved to be entirely to Peggy Pelham's liking, it was quite evident that Ah Koo would be a great deal more difficult to change or get rid of. The Pelhams had learned to live with the fact that during a lifetime in the service of barbarians she had not learned a syllable of their language, satisfying herself with private mutterings in a dialect no one else could understand.

Peggy had no idea how Ah Koo had found her at the hostel, but when she appeared at the door clutching her bundle, prepared to cook and clean in exchange for a mattress on the kitchen floor, Peggy welcomed her in. In some strange way she brought with her a kind of normality and renewed hope that any day there would be another knock on the door and it would open to the tall figure of her beloved husband.

A knock did come, late one night. Softly at first, then louder, persistently. Ah Koo rose from her bed. Shoving her feet into slippers she slip-slopped across the tiled floor, grumbling her annoyance. Who would be calling at such an hour? She was old and her sight was not good, but with her eye pressed to the spy-hole she could see the man who loomed outside was a foreign devil.

Wasn't it just like a gwai-lo to wake hard-working people up in the middle of the night? She would have ignored him or told him to go away if she had not also seen the khaki uniform and silver insignia of the police force through the spy-hole. Protesting, she began unchaining the two deadlocks, releasing the bolts and opening the inner door, taking her time to spring the lock on the stout iron security grill, cursing all gwai-los under her breath. A moment later the small, neat living room seemed filled with the presence of strangers. The tall foreign police officer stood beside a strange looking coolie woman, while two Chinese policemen remained outside the door. Ah Koo continued her mutterings as her loose slippers clacked back across the tiles to waken her mistress.

A few moments later Peggy Pelham appeared from her bedroom. She blinked at the tall figure beside the chair and the dishevelled woman who sat in it.

'Sebastian, what on earth . . .'

Sebastian placed a hand under Sing's elbow to help her up. 'I have a rather pleasant surprise for you, Mrs Pelham. An old friend of yours, I believe.'

Peggy stared at the girl rising stiffly from the chair. At first the ragged sam foo, the dirt and bruising on her face, the braided pigtail, confused the older woman. Only when she looked into Sing's unmistakable eyes did she realise who it was that stood before her.

'Siu Sing. My dearest girl,' she said in amazement, opening her arms wide. 'I thought we had lost you.'

Peggy had changed. She seemed much smaller than Sing remembered her. Her fair hair was colourless, her face drawn and pale without the carefully applied make-up.

'Not quite, Auntie. And you. Thank all gods you too are safe.'

'I wanted to take her to the Ruttongee Hospital for a thorough examination,' Sebastian said, shrugging his shoulders with a grin. 'She assured me she would be all right, said she'd already put you through enough trouble with hospitals and that she can take care of herself.'

Over Sing's shoulder Sebastian could see the tears squeezed from Peggy Pelham's tight-shut eyes as they held each other close. He looked away for a long moment. When the first shock of recognition was overtaken by the joy of reunion, Ah Koo was sent to make tea and bring hot chicken soup. Sebastian stayed long enough to drink tea with them, then set down his cup, prepared to take his leave. Sing rose and offered him her hand.

'I owe you my life, sir.' She hesitated as he took it and held it gently between his warm palms.

'My name is Sebastian . . . Sebastian Masters.' He spoke softly, looking into her eyes. 'You do not remember me but I have never forgotten the evening we danced at the St Andrew's ball three years ago. I feel we are old friends.'

'I remember,' Sing smiled wearily. 'I don't know how to thank you . . . but I will never forget . . . I would not be here if you had not come when you did.' She noticed how long his fingers were, the nails well-kept, covering her hand protectively.

'You must thank the Chinese man who telephoned me. A Doctor Sun. It was he who informed us.'

He released her. 'You are in the safest of hands now.' He turned to Peggy. 'I assume she will stay here while we organise a place for her?'

'For as long as she wants to. It will be wonderful to have her with me again, quite like old times.' Peggy beamed as she saw him to the door. 'You just run along and leave her to me. We have so much to talk about.'

Sebastian paused to look back at Sing. 'Rest for a day or two, young lady. I shall see you again soon.' He turned to Peggy.

'She will need to come down to headquarters,' he said quietly, shaking her hand. 'As soon as you feel she is up to it. Don't leave it too long.'

When he had gone, Peggy had Ah Koo run a hot bath and sent the old woman off to bed. After she was bathed, her cuts and abrasions were treated and cleaned, and a bed was made up on the couch.

Sing's injuries were slight and the horror she had experienced seemed to have left no sign of serious shock. At the foot of the bed, as though it had been waiting for her arrival, stood the chest of books salvaged from the Residence of Eternal Peace. Her precious deerhide bag was still at Everspring, she hoped. Sing did not ask after the fate of Justin Pelham—there was no need. Behind Peggy's tired kind eyes the truth was evident.

'Rest now. We will talk tomorrow,' Peggy said, kissing her forehead fondly.

When she had closed the door, Sing opened the chest, taking out the copy of *Black Beauty* and holding it while she waited for sleep.

The next day Sing was well enough to telephone Doctor Sun. He and his family were safe, he said, but they would have to leave the shop. He would bring her the deerhide bag and say goodbye.

One morning, they took the Peak tram to the top of the small mountain overlooking Hong Kong and walked to the famous spot where the taipan of the Noble House had first surveyed the barrack tents and shanty town that had sprung up on the flat and featureless foreshore almost fifty years earlier. The same stretch of foreshore had become the Central District and business heart of Hong Kong.

Sing had slept deeply and undisturbed until the sharp click-clack of Ah Koo's kegs on the kitchen tiles had awakened her. They had eaten toast and boiled eggs and enjoyed the rare treat of English tea with milk and sugar. It was Peggy who had suggested the ride to the Peak. 'To blow the cobwebs away,' she said, cheerily.

Now as they stood at the observation rail, gazing out over the massed buildings piled like children's building blocks, descending precariously to the lower levels, Peggy spoke: 'Since I left that dreadful prison, I have come here each morning before attending the school to thank God for this view. It reassures me about the nature of resiliance.'

Sing knew instinctively that Peggy had something important to tell her and wondered if it was news of her missing husband. She waited for her to continue.

'I have seen many remarkable cities in my journeying with Justin for King and Country but nowhere quite as incredible as this.' She surveyed the breathtaking sight laid out before them like some gigantic tapestry, early light shining like mercury on the awakening harbour, the distant hills of China veiled in the same bright silver. This early, the Peak was usually shrouded in fog but light winds that seemed to come from all directions had blown it clear and now ruffled Peggy's hair and brought colour to her pale cheeks as she went on.

'This place will begin again. It has already started. Nothing can stop it. For all its contradictions, it will go on, as we all must. Hong Kong has indestructible faith in itself.'

She turned to Sing and took her by the hand. 'It gives me strength. I do not belong here any more than Justin did but it gives me the courage to go on. I feel its spirit.'

She paused, and Sing could see that her kind eyes were bright with the threat of tears. 'It is where I come when I face another day without him. Where I believe I shall always come.' Her hand tightened and she turned to hold Sing's eyes steadily with her own.

'Sing, my dear, dear child, I have to tell you that Toby Hyde-Wilkins is dead.'

It was well over a week before Sing went to see Sebastian at Government House. She had taken the news of Toby's death with a quiet steadiness that had worried Peggy at first, afraid that it might be the calm before the storm and that Sing would give way to terrible grief. This had not happened. Dry-eyed, Sing had asked what details there were and once she was convinced that there was no possibility that the records could be wrong, she had thanked Peggy for telling her. It was almost as though she had known. As though she had already shed her tears and buried her sadness.

'Like you, Auntie. I have known what it is to be happy, to love and be loved as you have. It is over now.'

She had not asked for further proof or the source of Peggy Pelham's information. They talked instead about the past three years and how they had survived them. When Peggy Pelham heard the story of Jiro Toshido she had arranged to have all of Sing's belongings salvaged from Hadden House and brought to the flat.

At first Sing had refused to accept them, until Peggy had pointed out that the rack of beautiful, pure silk cheong-sams were tailored to her figure, the shoes made for her feet and, as for the jewellery, it sounded as though she had earned every piece of it. It was fortunate that Peggy was well acquainted with the owners of the mansion and had stopped them just in time from giving the clothes to charity and handing the jewellery over to the police. The jewellery was put into a safety box in the Hong Kong and Shanghai Bank and Peggy had used her considerable influence to arrange a room for Sing at the hostel just across the corridor from hers.

For the visit Sing had chosen a sheath of plain dove-grey silk embroidered in the same pearly colour, with bag and shoes that matched it perfectly. A visit to Peggy's little hair-dressing salon and beauty parlour on the corner of Cotton Tree Drive had transformed her completely. The bruises and scratches that had marked her face were almost gone.

Sebastian felt the same intense pleasure at the sight of her, the same shortening of breath, that he remembered when he had held her on the dance floor of the Peninsula Hotel almost four years earlier. Somehow, the faint signs of violence that still marked her face enhanced her grace and dignity, emphasised her pride and vulnerability, but most of all her strength. Sebastian Masters knew, as she returned his grip firmly, that this was the most splendid woman he had ever seen in his life.

There was a well-used leather suite in the corner of his office, beside a tall window fringed with ivy. The office was on the ground floor and through the window, spread like a park, the grounds of Government House lay in patterns of immaculate lawns, carefully tended flowerbeds, romanesque statues and fountains.

He offered her one of the deep, old chairs and tried to disregard the whisper of her nylon stockings as she sank into it and crossed her long, shapely legs. He had tea brought and when it had been served he sat back and contemplated her, trying his hardest to retain the official manner of his position. He was wearing a light-weight, cream-coloured business suit. She noticed how well it fitted, how neat were his collar and cuffs. His dark brown tie was held with a thin gold clip. His black, wavy hair was brushed until it gleamed. His pale face was much thinner than she remembered it, but there was the same almost shy politeness in the dark brown eyes that regarded her from beneath long curling lashes.

'Where do we begin?' He was trying to keep a professional edge to his voice and seemed to be finding it harder every moment.

'From today, I hope.' Sing reached for her tea. 'I seem to have little recollection of my past.'

She felt no pang of guilt at the deliberate untruth. She remembered vividly every detail of her life but saw no use in it for the future. With the occupation at an end, everyone in Hong Kong was beginning again and she saw it as a godsent opportunity. It was as though she had flipped a switch in her mind and the past was no more. So it was not really a lie.

She sipped and lowered the cup to its saucer. 'Amnesia, perhaps,' she added, fixing him with her remarkable eyes and the faint smile he found so enchanting. 'Something like that.'

Sebastian looked mildly uncomfortable and continued hurriedly. 'It's possible, from what Peggy tells me you have been through.' He fought hard to hold her steady gaze without his open admiration shining on her like a light, choosing his words carefully. 'Perhaps we must all forget and begin again now that it is over.' He shrugged and Sing could feel his confusion. She took an envelope from her bag.

'Except for this. At least it seems that I might have a name.' She took out a photograph and laid it on the table before him.

'My parents, I have reason to believe.'

Glad of the diversion, Sebastian picked up the snapshot to study it. It was old, its sepia tones faded but still quite clear. The strong features of a young man stared back at him. He was powerfully built. Standing beside a striking Chinese girl seated on a porcelain stool, he had his hand on her shoulder and hers was reaching up to touch it. Her other hand held a large white fan. Behind them were the sweeping winged roof and carved portals of a pavilion.

He turned it over. The picture was of remarkably good quality considering the date that had been chopped on the back. Not so clear, but still visible, scrawled in pencil, were the words 'Deverill Macau, October 1925'.

Sebastian stared again at the man, the powerful set of his shoulders, his unsmiling face seeming to invite challenge. The uniform of a master mariner gave him great authority, the braided cap tucked beneath his arm.

'May I ask where you got this?' he asked, still studying it.

'It was taken from my mother's bedside on the day I was born. I was told that she died a few hours later.'

He looked up from the photograph. 'If the man in this picture is who I am almost certain it is . . .' he hesitated.

Sing felt a wave of shock pass through her. She had never known anything like it before. The two people in the photograph were as lost to her as any ancestral portrait. Faces meant to fade with the smoke of joss. This feeling had almost the keen edge of pain. She recognised it as hope. Her voice when she spoke was scarcely audible.

'You know him?' she asked, the small crease of her frown forming between her brows.

Sebastian reached for the envelope. 'I cannot be certain but I believe I do. May I keep this for a few days?'

'Of course, but . . .'

He slipped it into the inside pocket of his jacket. 'Miss Deverill. May I buy you lunch?' He looked at his watch. 'Its almost that time, and I think we may have quite a lot to talk about.'

He was the first one to call her by that name—when he had rescued her from the embarrassment of J.T. Ching and again when he had saved her life in Wan Chai. She liked the sound but did not truly feel she had the right to it.

'I have no way of knowing if that is who I am . . . no proof. Only the word of an old amah.' He raised his eyebrows. 'She died when I was five. There's no one else.'

'Would you like to tell me about it? I'd very much like to help. Perhaps I can.'

They walked to the restaurant through the public gardens, down Battery Path past the cathedral to the line of rickshaws and magazine vendors in Pedder Lane. It was a quiet place, very English in its style. Sing looked around the dark wood panelling hung with prints

of fox hunts and English seaside resorts. Horse brasses glinted
in the subdued light, a long copper hunting horn and a set of
yard-long ale glasses were featured behind the bar.

'I'm afraid I'm not very adventurous,' Sebastian said pleasantly,
as the head waiter greeted him and led them to a corner table.
Through the diamond-paned window Sing could see the bustle
of pedestrians, passing each other on the narrow pavement.

'I lunch here every day. Even at the same table. I hope you
like plain English food. This is as close as you can get to it in
Hong Kong. Jimmy's Kitchen is quite famous. It was once the pride
of Shanghai.'

'I'm afraid I'm not very hungry when I'm held in suspense. Could
we have a drink and talk about the photograph? It might improve
my appetite.'

'Unfortunately, I'm not sure that it will. That's if I'm right about
it.'

'Who was my father?' She corrected herself. 'Who do you think
the man in the photograph might be?'

'There was only one Deverill in Macau and from what I've heard
there will never be another quite like him.' He signalled the waiter,
ordered himself a gin and tonic and soda water for Sing.

'Ben Deverill was a boat-builder who went on to become one
of the most respected and powerful men in Shanghai before the
war. A legend.' He paused as the waiter set down his drink.

'You say *was* . . .' Sing spoke hesitantly, the pang rising again.
He reached across the white tablecloth to place his hand over
hers.

'I'm afraid Ben Deverill died in 1941, trying to run the Japanese
blockade of the Yangtze with a shipment of guns for the Nationalist
army.' He paused to see the affect of his words on Sing. When
she returned his stare unblinkingly, he continued.

'They say he was one of the most remarkable men in the China
trade. That he and his partner, with a handful of waterfront
reprobates, took on a Jap gunboat in a China clipper. They must
have known it was a suicide mission.'

He was silent while he sipped his drink, watching her for signs
of distress. 'The last voyage of *Cloud Chaser* made Shanghai history,'
he went on when she showed no reaction. 'The men who sailed
her were heroes.'

Sing withdrew her hand to sip from the water glass. She had
not flinched. He admired her courage. He admired everything about
her.

'Can you be sure the picture is of him?'

'When I first came out I spent a year in Shanghai. Everybody knew Ben Deverill.' Sebastian smiled. 'He was uncrowned king of the Shanghai Club.'

'You met him?'

'To speak to, only once. But I saw him several times.'

'And you're certain?'

'That picture was taken some eighteen years before I went to Shanghai. I thought I recognised him—he was no ordinary man. When I saw the name I was positive. It's true. There was only ever one Ben Deverill. I'm very sorry.'

'I never knew him,' she said quietly. 'It is no loss.'

They were silent for a moment. He did not wish to rush her. The food came. He had recommended the steak and kidney pie. Jimmy's was the only place in Hong Kong that served it, he said. She accepted a glass of lager and ate the entire meal with good appetite. It pleased him immensely—he had expected tears, or at least a show of emotion.

Over coffee, he returned to the subject of Ben Deverill cautiously. 'Do you have any other proof of identity? Anything else that might connect you with the photograph?'

'Only an ivory fan that the Fish . . .' she smiled. 'I mean the amah, said belonged to my mother. I didn't even know the old woman's real name, I can barely remember . . .' She stirred her coffee.

'Were there any other children?'

'She never spoke of any. Why do you ask?'

'Because Ben Deverill was an extremely rich man. He built a trading empire faster and bigger than anyone else had in the Orient. As I say, a legend. If this old woman was telling the truth, you are his heiress.'

The frown appeared again, a tiny furrow drawing her brows together in a way that only emphasised her perfect complexion. This look of perplexity was another thing Sebastian was finding adorable about her. How, he wondered, watching her closely, could she have remained so serene, even if half the story Peggy Pelham had told him were true? Again he reached for her hand. This time she curled her fingers around his.

'Will you let me help you, Sing? I am in a position to make all the necessary enquiries.'

She smiled and squeezed his hand. 'I'd be most grateful if you would. I already owe you so much.'

It took a matter of weeks for Sebastian to trace details of the Deverill estate. Even with the administrative chaos of the temporary military government headed by Rear-Admiral Harcourt, he and Peggy Pelham were able to pull enough strings between them.

Within a month he had made contact with the Foreign Office in Shanghai and spent hours in the offices of one of Hong Kong's most prominent law firms, lunching on two occasions with its senior partner, Alistair Pidcock. He had collected a full dossier on the Deverill Trading Company and the Cloud Line but the result was not encouraging.

Ben Deverill's will provided that his entire estate be held in trust for a period of thirty years. If no claim had been successful within that time, the entire Deverill fortune would go to the Welfare League for Homeless and Destitute Eurasians established by Sir Robert Ho Tung.

The will had been drawn up in 1939 and had at the same time transferred much of the Deverill capital from Shanghai to Hong Kong. There was also a private residence in Repulse Bay which had been boarded up since Ben Deverill left Hong Kong in 1925. It was to be sold when the conditions of the trust period ran out, these proceeds also to be given to the Welfare League.

Alistair Pidcock, the large, red-faced lawyer and chartered accountant, was vaguely known to Sebastian and had parted with more information than he normally would, due to Sebastian's government status and the quite remarkable claim he had uncovered. It being the first and only enquiry into the Deverill fortune, he had taken a strong personal interest. On meeting Sing, he had been polite, attentive and appeared to be genuinely sympathetic, promising her that, as the will dictated, everything would be done to try to corroborate her claim to be the daughter of the Shanghai taipan through thorough investigation.

At the bar of the Hong Kong Club that same evening and after a few drinks, Pidcock made it clear to Sebastian that legally there was absolutely no possibility that the evidence of the photograph could be accepted as proof of her identity. It could have been come by in any manner at all, and although comparisons with early press clippings from the *North China Morning Post* left no doubt that the man in the picture was Ben Deverill, it was the complete lack of living witnesses to Sing's true identity that made it impossible to honour. There would have to be a great deal more to go on if this girl's claim was to be given serious consideration. The lawyer raised his glass.

'Otherwise it would appear that the mystery of Ben Deverill's missing offspring sank forever with him and his partner aboard his beloved *China Cloud*.'

Repulse Bay

SING TOOK the news with the same degree of serenity Sebastian had expected she would. Thanking him for the dossier, which she would always treasure, she asked only to see Villa Formosa, the house her father had built and where she was born. The dossier also suggested that the body of her mother might have been buried in its grounds.

As Sebastian's green MG wound its way along Repulse Bay Road, Sing breathed in the fresh smell of dairy pasture. The top was down, it was a fine morning, warm with the scents of grasslands on the breeze off the ocean. She had tied her hair back with a chiffon scarf and some of it had blown loose and whipped around her face, turned away from him, looking steadily across the powder blue of the South China Sea where the butterfly shapes of junks sat on the horizon.

He tried to imagine her feelings and drove without speaking, following the lawyer's directions onto Beach Road, travelling along the edge of the shoreline, through the rich dairy pasture of Pok Fu Lam, dotted with black and white cows. On to South Bay Road to Chung Wan, then Repulse Bay, where Villa Formosa had been built.

The house was hardly visible from the road; there was a hint of its roof among thick trees behind high walls. The huge iron gates forged with the Cloud Line crest were chained shut and it took time for the key to turn in the corroded padlock. Alistair Pidcock had parted with the keys without fuss. It was the least he could do, he had said. The Deverill file was one of great personal importance to him. He liked the young Eurasian woman and would give her every chance to prove her claim.

Inside the grounds they followed the traces of an overgrown driveway, invaded from both sides by verdant growth. Sebastian picked up a large stick, using it to clear a path. He spoke over his shoulder to Sing. 'Snakes,' he warned. 'Just the spot for them.'

Through the dense growth of bamboo the house became visible— glimpses of walls faded a scrofulous pink, blotched and mottled with damp, the flash of gold and jade-green tiles where the sun struck through the high trees.

'Would you mind if I went first?' Sing's sudden request almost relieved Sebastian, the mood of the place did not uplift him.

'Of course.' He handed her the bunch of keys. 'Call if you need me . . . and please be careful.'

She went on alone to the once grand entrance then up wide steps, buried in dead leaves and almost hidden by a screen of tall grass, to high, arched double doors, hinged and bound in hammered iron. Lizards skittered from her feet as she sought the key, unlocked the doors and stepped through them. Inside was almost pitch black, airless as a tomb. There was the smell of neglect, the mossy dankness of fungus.

Sing left the door open, allowing the light to flood in. She had no wish to explore further, to investigate the shadows that began to loom like spectres as her eyes adjusted to the filtered light. It was enough to know that this was where they once lived. That this was where her life had begun and where her mother had ended hers.

Sebastian's voice came from the open door behind her. 'I shouldn't go any further, if I were you. I wasn't joking about the snakes. Exactly the kind of place they like to breed. Cobras, you know.'

Suddenly, as though his words had conjured a demon, she saw again the perfectly matched, curd-coloured sections of the cobra's underbelly, swaying in the shadows. Barring her way. She closed her eyes, driving the long dead memory from her mind.

He took the keys from her as she came out, re-locking the doors. 'I didn't mean to alarm you, but it's probably what's kept the old place from being occupied by squatters.' He pocketed the keys. 'Anywhere else would have been stripped and filled with the blighters years ago.' He tried to sound lighthearted. 'This place was too run down for even the Japs to take over. And too far from anywhere.' He laughed to lighten the sombre mood that oppressed him. 'Must have been the only place here when Ben . . . when your father built it.'

'It's not snakes that have kept them away,' Sing suggested. 'It's ghosts.'

Staring after her as she left the house, walking quickly back to the car, he gave her a moment to herself before following, trying again to consider her emotions. He had not pressed her on the full story of her past life. She would confide in him when she was ready. Meanwhile, until he had earned her complete trust, it would be hard for him to tell her that he had fallen hopelessly in love with her.

Sing took a last look at the decaying facade of the old house. The trees had grown in on it, the shrubs and succulents crowding its walls. Vines wound through the slats of its locked shutters and climbed the roof, blocking the sun, encouraging lichen.

Its sweeping eaves, thick with rotted leaves, had sprouted growth of their own. But the walls were solid stone and the tiles of its roof were timeless. From what she had learned of her father the place would have been built to last forever. It was not beyond repair, she thought, and the land it stood on was worth a great deal of money. But the place itself captivated her. Under the years of neglect she felt a calm influence that had nothing to do with time.

Neither spoke as Sebastian locked the gates and joined her at the car. She sat looking straight ahead as he climbed in.

'Are you all right, Sing?' he asked gently.

She nodded, turning her smile upon him. 'Thank you for bringing me, Sebastian. Thank you for everything.'

'Would you do something for me now?' he asked.

'If I can.'

He turned the key in the ignition and pulled out onto the deserted road. 'Stanley Village is only a few miles further on. There is a fishing community on the beach. I was able to see it from the exercise yard of the prison. Promised myself a thousand times that I'd take a walk down there if I ever got out alive.'

Half an hour later they passed the deserted walls of Stanley Prison, parked the MG and walked through the market to the narrow, stone-flagged steps that led down to the beach. Like every Chinese fishing village it presented a peaceful picture. Sampans were pulled up on the sand, their rusty anchors buried high above the tideline.

Beyond them deep-sea junks rode quietly at their moorings like cows grazing in a field. The people were Tanka, the women lacing fresh twine into broken nets strung along the sand, their men caulking and tarring the bottoms of boats. Others were cleaning and salting fish, squid and octopus, hanging them in rows outside the huts, spreading them on racks of cane in the sun. Children splashed in the shallows.

'This is the place,' Sebastian said. 'The Jap guards used to come here to eat. I always swore that one day I'd do the same.'

The seafood eating house was nothing more than a large shack, a patched tarpaulin stretched on poles from its roof to give shade. Under it stood a cluster of round tables; it was not yet midday and the chairs were empty.

They had the place to themselves and Sing took off her shoes and thrust her bare feet into the warm, coarse sand. A cheerful Tanka woman, stout and strong as a man, brought them buckets of live fish, crabs and prawns to choose from. Fifteen minutes later the crabs were served in delicious blackbean sauce, the fish steamed with ginger and shallots, prawns piled pink and hot in the centre of the table, surrounded by tiny dishes of soy, chilli and herb vinegar.

'I used to dream of this,' said Sebastian, reaching for a prawn. 'Fishermen never go hungry. Anything's available for a price.' He grinned. 'Some mornings you could smell the cooking while you ate your handful of rancid rice.'

They enjoyed the food in silence, selecting chunks of crab and cracking them with their teeth, sipping from glasses of cold Pearl River beer, listening to the shouting of children, the tumble and drag of a gentle surf.

'What did you mean about ghosts?' Sebastian asked suddenly.

'Oh, I was quite serious. Snakes would never keep away Chinese looking for a place to live, they'd catch them and eat them.' She laughed, reaching over to divide the white flesh of the fish from the bone, serving him generously.

'But they'll never go near a place where there has been violent death,' she added matter-of-factly. 'And I believe my mother met a very violent death in that house.'

Sebastian waited for her to say more. 'You didn't look for her grave,' he said at last.

'I know she's there. There is no hurry. I will find her some day.'

In the weeks they had been officially seeing each other while he traced her father's history they had lunched at Jimmy's Kitchen on Pedder Lane once or twice again but she had declined anything further. It was still not safe for her in the downtown streets and he thanked God for Peggy Pelham. Peggy had watched over her like a doting mother, guarding her privacy even from him. When he had asked her for more details of Sing's background she said that she had told him all she knew, that for anything more he must win Sing's trust. He remembered Peggy's words vividly: 'There are things in this girl's past that are best left alone. If you are to know more about them, you must hear it from her.'

Deciding there would never be a better time than this moment, he asked gently. 'What will you do now?'

Again, his heart went out to her as it always did when the tiny frown of perplexity creased the smoothness of her brow. It made her look so completely alone, yet doggedly self-sufficient. *Life has always been like this for her*, he found himself thinking. *She belongs to no place and to no one but herself.*

'I really can't say,' she answered simply.

He had the almost unbearable urge to take her in his arms and tried to keep his voice steady as after a pause, he said, 'I have to leave Hong Kong in a month or two.'

She did not look at him, as though it had come as no surprise.

'My time is up here. I've been given six months' long service leave and sickness entitlement before my next posting.' He spoke very quietly, watching for her response.

The furrow between her eyes remained as she watched the dark-skinned Tanka children playing like otters in the sea. 'I shall miss you. You have been so very good to me,' she said softly.

He watched for another breathless moment, hearing the laughter of the children coming with the splash of the waves, the hollow bumping of a wooden mallet. 'Come with me, Sing. Back to England,' he said with a sudden urgency. 'There is nothing but danger and unhappiness for you here.'

He looked out to sea as he spoke, afraid to see her reaction. For the longest seconds he had ever known his heart kept pace with the dull thud of the mallet. Then he felt her cool hand close on his. When he looked at her the frown was gone. The Tanka women turned back to cleaning fish, chuckling and muttering as the tall gwai-lo quickly left his chair and took the woman in his arms, kissing her on the mouth as only mad gwai-los do.

'Are you sure you know what you are saying?' she whispered softly into his ear as he held her. 'Quite, quite sure?'

'I've never been more certain of anything,' he whispered back holding her close.

'Make me no promises, Sebastian. I don't need promises. I will come with you and we shall see.' She buried her face in his neck.

'To be in England has been my greatest wish for so long.' She pressed her lips to the warmth of his skin, fresh with cologne, and allowed the pleasant pain of hope to rise in her again.

For much of the time in the coming weeks Sing stayed inside her room and read. She was quite content to do so, as Sebastian kept it filled with fresh cut flowers and took her out for lunch and dinner. She felt thoroughly safe with him. They went only to the little English restaurant or to his private club and stayed well away from the downtown districts. He had chosen a quiet corner of Jimmy's Kitchen to present her with a star sapphire as large as a fat pea, surrounded by diamonds. The stone was a hazy, translucent blue with an elusive four-point star that glowed in its heart.

'It reminded me of you, Sing my dearest. A bright, mysterious star lost in its own beauty.'

She accepted the ring but did not feel worthy of it. 'It does not bind you, Sebastian. You must remember that.'

She had tried to explain her feelings to him. 'I have told you that I am different, different in every way. It is not easy to be different to others.'

He took her hand and slid the gorgeous ring onto her finger. 'Unique, my darling. You are unique, just as this stone is unique . . . there is no other quite like it in the world.' Then he had given her something that thrilled her much more than any jewel. In a stiff manila envelope bearing the stamp of the Hong Kong Government, she found a British passport in the name of Sing Deverill.

She stared at it in disbelief, until he said: 'I bent the rules a little, but it's entirely official.'

Peggy Pelham was among the few who saw them off aboard the ship. Sebastian had arranged stateroom accommodation aboard a Union Castle troop ship returning military personnel from the Far East to England. Peggy came with Sing to her cabin and held onto her as the bell sounded for visitors ashore.

'Write to me, Siu Sing,' she whispered, her voice choked with emotion. 'You have become quite precious to me . . .'

'Will you stay in Hong Kong, Auntie? Now that . . .'

Peggy finished the difficult question for her. 'Now that Justin is gone? Yes Sui Sing, I will stay here, until I am sure.' She held Sing away from her and blinked away her tears. 'It may take forever.'

PART VIII

Sparrow's Green

Tie two birds together;
Though you have four wings,
They cannot fly.

MASTER TO-TZE

• IMAGE FOR DECEPTION •

Grange Estate—Kent 1946

CECILY MASTERS was pruning roses in the garden when the news of her brother's return came through on the telephone. She had heard it ring in her father's study and the sound of his voice raised in surprise and then the loud 'hah, hah, hah' of his distinctive laugh. It was the laugh they only heard on special occasions these days and it meant he was very pleased about something.

It was a glorious day in late spring, when the air was truly like a newly opened wine, its delicate bouquet spiced with may blossoms and the heady hint of young hop vines. Sunshine in England, Cecily always thought, was the loveliest there was anywhere. It was so hard-earned. For every day of uninterrupted sunshine there was at least a month of grey, watery days and chill winds. It was so much better, she thought, than having it every single day. One appreciated it so much more. It was like God smiling.

Her brother often rang from Hong Kong—usually, as now, on a Sunday morning around eleven when the papers had been read and the old house was quiet with everybody back from church. She laid another of the pale, salmon-coloured hybrid tea roses in her basket and made a note to tell Ernest the gardener there was the sign of red spider on one or two of the older bushes. Her father's loud guffaw came again and, with another deep breath of the delicious air, and a long look across the rich brown loam of the fields, the first fresh green shoots showing in the curving furrows, Cecily Masters hurried towards the house for her turn to speak to her brother.

She was mildly annoyed when, as she came up the short flight of steps to the terrace outside the study, she heard the last loud bray and some parting words, with the click of the receiver being replaced. Her father almost knocked her down as he threw open the French doors to call her.

'Wonderful news, Cecily my dear. Sebastian is home. Here. Back in England. He's coming down from London today. He'll be here in time for tea.'

His words wiped away her momentary irritation. 'How absolutely marvellous, but why didn't he tell us?'

'He says he wanted it to be a surprise. He has brought somebody with him. A young lady.'

Cecily was conscious of a distinct stab of annoyance. She loved her brother Sebastian dearly and she hadn't seen him for more than three years. She would have much preferred it if he had been alone. She quickly put the twinge aside in her excitement at the thought of seeing him.

'Where's your mother?' Duncan Masters went off through the house calling loudly. 'Connie, Connie. Connie my dear.'

As the English countryside trundled past the train window Sing realised that the wonderful warmth all about her like a sweet embrace was joy. She had often wondered what it would feel like to be in England and now, with Sebastian leaning across to point out the roofs of villages showing through spinneys of trees, she knew.

That wonderful place that she had read so much about revealed itself like the pages in her books. In the fields, waist-high with buttercup and dog daisy, lambs followed their mothers and horses and cattle lifted their heads to watch her pass.

The rattle and sway of the carriage slowed to a leisurely rumble, a bumpity bump beneath its wheels as they drew off the main track and onto a sideline, to wait with a grand hissing of steam for the signal to change.

Sebastian pulled the leather strap that let the window down and the small first class compartment was instantly filled with the distinctive smell of farmyards. He leaned out to look along the line of carriages.

'We're almost there.' His voice was boyish with pleasure. 'Look, you can just see the church.'

She joined him at the open window, following the pointing of his finger and seeing the austere grey spire poking like a warning up through the variegated green of trees in the distance.

'The house is a mile from there.'

Squeezed together in the narrow opening of the window space he pulled her back against his chest, his face in her hair.

'Welcome to the garden of England, my darling,' he breathed. His hands, firmly holding her upper arms, moved gently to her breasts and his lips brushed her neck, finding her ear. 'This is your home now.'

They were met at the tiny station of Sparrow's Green by a shortish, thickset man in a tweed jacket and cap. His face was healthily pink and the eyes that met Sing's as they were introduced were a clear grey and filled with kindness. A well-clipped ginger moustache emphasised his wide smile as he carefully took off his cap, showing thin strands of reddish hair flattened across his scalp. He took her hand in both of his.

'Welcome to Kent, my dear,' Sir Duncan said warmly, as Sebastian presented her. 'This is all a most delightful surprise.' He squeezed her hands and lightly kissed her cheek.

Past the poky booking office, through the old railway station, they guided her with the man called Ernest following with their bags on a trolley. Under the lofty tent of a horse-chestnut tree opposite the station, a pony and trap stood waiting. The last one in the district, explained Sir Duncan proudly, helping Sing up onto the little metal step and into the padded leather seat. The pony's chestnut flanks shone in the sharp light, its glossy black mane and tail well combed. Bright brass medallions gleamed on its harness.

'The only way to travel in the country,' he laughed, as her weight tilted the shafts. 'Ernest will bring the bags in the car,' he said, 'But it was such a simply marvellous day we thought you'd like to travel Kentish style.'

Lifting the reins, Sir Duncan clucked his tongue and they moved off. The ride through two miles of budding trees and high hedgerows of privet and may bush was a delight. A tartan rug tucked around her knees, the cold air colouring her cheeks and sparkling in her eyes, Sing's face mirrored her enchantment. The sight of her enthralled Sebastian.

The high tea that awaited them was a tempting assortment of fresh-baked scones and tarts, dainty wedge-shaped sandwiches and home-made jam with pots and pots of tea. Lady Constance Masters had frightened Sing a little at first—she was a rather severe woman with perfectly groomed dark hair and eyes that stared through her spectacles with none of her husband's easy generosity.

She was cordial and attentive but rather quiet, leaving the conversation to her son and his father but hanging on every word that passed between them. Even quieter was Cecily, Sebastian's older and only sister. She sat, eating very little, her eyes alert but downcast for much of the time or casting sidelong glances whenever Sing spoke to answer a question or ask one.

The conversation was guided by Sebastian, who recounted certain of his experiences in Stanley Prison, the rigours and the aftermath of the Occupation. The topic commandeered the table well after the meal had finished and they had moved to the drawing room, Sir Duncan glued to every word, the ladies suitably horrified.

Sing could feel Lady Constance's eyes upon her, her curiosity reaching out, looking for an opening. At last she said: 'And you, Miss Deverill, were you also imprisoned? It must have been simply ghastly for a woman.'

Before Sing could speak, Sebastian broke in. 'Sing had a rather torrid time of it, mother. She is still recovering and trying to forget.'

Lady Constance looked suitably chastised. 'Oh dear, how terrible. I am so sorry.'

Sebastian pushed his chair back and stood up. 'In fact, we're both rather tired from the journey. I'm for a bath.'

'That does sound rather wonderful,' Sing agreed, following his example.

'Of course, dear.' Lady Constance smiled. 'Cecily, do show Miss Deverill her room.' She stood and placed her hand lightly on Sing's arm 'I'm sure there'll be plenty of time for us to learn all about you.'

At the top of the stairs, Cecily opened the door to a large and comfortable room, golden soft in the lowering sun that streamed through the large square window.

'It was my brother's room. It has the best view of the downs.' She stood aside for Sing to enter. 'I hope you'll be comfortable. If there's anything you need . . . ' Cecily indicated a tassled bell-pull. 'Just ring for Betty.'

Sing turned away from the window. 'I'm sorry that Sebastian didn't write to tell anyone about us. I thought he had. It must be quite a surprise.'

Cecily smiled briefly as she went to leave the room. 'It is, rather. We've often wondered when it would happen. Mother was becoming quite worried.' She stepped out into the hallway, then gave a small shrug of her shoulders. 'Well, now it has. I'm sure we'll soon get used to the idea.'

She closed the door quietly.

That night Sing was too excited to sleep. Sebastian came to her door at two in the morning, silently in the light from the moon-filled window, eager and searching. He had sunk down upon her, whispering his adoration, the pillow stifling his groans as he came almost immediately.

He lay heavily on her for a few moments while his breath

quietened, then left just as silently for his room down the hallway. She did not mind that his love-making had not aroused her. It had begun aboard the ship and was always like this, hungry and impatient. She had not tried to show him the intricacies of the craft of love she had once bestowed upon Toby. He didn't seem to need it. His pleasure was all that seemed to matter and she lay bathed in moonlight too bright for sleep, not wishing to close it off with curtains, thinking of the huge moons she had shared with Sebastian over the sea, the stars that had spilled like silver lemonade into the Indian Ocean. And by day they had watched the flying fish glide on gossamer wings over the blue Mediterranean.

The five week voyage aboard the *Arundel Castle* was still fresh in her mind and her feet had hardly lost the movement of its decks. Every day of the 12,000 mile journey had been a new enchantment to her. After a day or two of slight discomfort she had lost all trace of seasickness, and been filled instead with the wonder of the sea in all its moods. Sebastian had not been so fortunate and spent much of his time in the top compartment of the little cabin in varying states of illness. There had been very little she could do for him and her days had been spent pacing the boatdeck to which the handful of female passengers had been confined.

The great ship was carrying several thousand troops back to England and their half-clad bodies lined every square inch of the decks below, whiling away the hours with their playing cards and mess tins of tea, to the comforting music of the mouth organ. There were several officers' wives accompanying their husbands home. They were typical of the women she had met through Peggy Pelham at the club on Stonecutter's Island, singing loudly in the solemn little chapel or prancing on the tennis courts. As though they knew she was not married to Captain Hyde Wilkins they had left her entirely alone throughout the voyage.

At first it had troubled her, caused a slight tug of fear, would all British women treat her this way, turning aside from any approach she made, glancing at her only to look quickly away rather than meet her eyes? She realised with an unexpected flood of anxiety how much she had come to depend on others, first Toby, then Peggy and now Sebastian. Would she ever be able to stand on her own feet, face the new and unknown world she was about to enter without depending on others? The twinge of doubt had been quickly overcome by the magnificence of the oceans she crossed. The Pacific had been rough, dark, white-combed blue one day, green or iron grey the next.

Each dawn she had watched the sunrise, breathless at its massive glory, blazing fresh apple-green from one end of the earth to the other or slashed by shelves of cloud into the riotous hues of flame. In the Gulf of Aden and entering the Red Sea the seas had flattened and the heavy, baking heat that settled over the ship seemed to intensify with every hour. The depths turned a pale luminous olive, schooled with thousands of pastel coloured jellyfish. They drifted up with the wide frilled skirts of dancers to float like fields of delicate, trailing flowers. More memorable to her than any of these were the magical nights, an immensity of stars greater even than those she recalled had showered upon Tung T'ing Lake and a moonpath that led across the world.

Sebastian had recovered from his dreadful sickness but found the crushing heat lifting from the Nubian Desert on one side and the sands of Arabia on the other was too much for him. The sun had become a huge ball of brassy yellow screened by a haze of fine sand that had driven them both below as the sky quickly darkened. When the sand storm had passed the ship entered the Suez Canal, with the high-prowed Arab dhows dropping their tall triangular sails to let the vast hull of the troopship slide past. They had watched a lone camel led along the bank under a bright sickle of moon as they glided slowly and silently through the desert, a searchlight beam sweeping the dunes ahead, and Sebastian had made love to her, there on the deck, in the shadow of a lifeboat.

He had taken her ashore in the frantic bustle of Port Said to drink gritty Egyptian coffee at the Britannia Club and bought her a handbag of camel leather. Now fully restored he had come alive again in the gentler warmth of the Mediterranian and together they had watched the porpoises ploughing in formation through the bow wave, like sleek grey torpedoes.

Then came the morning when she had gone on deck to see an escarpment of chalk white cliffs standing out starkly above the rolling green swell of the Dover Strait. Gulls wheeled like kites above them and there had been the distinct smell of land, the smell of cut pasture wet with recent rain; and as though to welcome her, a small, yellow breasted bird had fluttered out on the offshore wind to settle on the rail beside her. England. The land of Toby's birth. Sebastian's arms had folded around her from behind.

'Welcome home, my dearest,' he murmured and she felt again the shame that it was Toby she had thought of.

Through the curtains came the same damp earth scents she had breathed off Dover and the moon, bright and round as a new dubloon among its company of stars, was the same as she had seen at sea, the same as she had gloried in with Toby in the Residence of Eternal Peace.

The next morning, Sebastian looked across the breakfast table at the woman who would soon be his wife. They had risen late, at his suggestion, so that his mother and father and Cecily would have finished and they could enjoy the meal alone in the garden. He thought Sing looked calm and wonderful in the dancing patches of sunlight scattered by the leaves of golden elm.

He had known it would be another beautiful day. The sun had set so flawlessly the evening before when they had walked the mile down to the village hand in hand and he had introduced her to the local pub. The Vine was a sixteenth-century hostelry, said to have been used by Oliver Cromwell to recruit Kentishmen. Its old world charm had quickly captivated Sing.

He watched her now, biting into toast and marmalade, looking around with almost solemn concentration as she chewed. It was the way she had looked at everything since walking down the gangway of the liner *Arundel Castle* at Tilbury docks. Not exactly frowning but with an intense interest, as though if she didn't notice everything, it might all dry up and blow away, or be wiped away like the paint from a wet canvas or the pages of a book. At first he had thought she was disappointed, or a little frightened, but when he asked her, her eyes had danced and the smile that lit up her face reassured him.

'It's just that I can't believe I'm really here. I've thought about it for so long.'

She had taken his hand in her strong cool grip and pressed it reassuringly. 'I'm just so very, very happy,' she had said softly and there had been tears in her eyes.

Now, across the white tablecloth, the pretty, gleaming china-ware and silver toast-rack, he marvelled again at the strong shapeliness of her bare arms and shoulders and the healthy, pale russet flush of her skin, a colour most women could only yearn for. She caught him staring and he felt the thrill that always touched him when her eyes looked directly into his. They were, he often thought, her greatest marvel. Filled with mysteries he knew he had not fathomed, never quite the same. This morning they reflected the bluey grey of the lavender that clustered nearby, heavy with bees.

'It is all so incredibly beautiful, Sebastian. Like the stories in the books. Even more wonderful.'

He laughed, reaching across to touch her cheek. Immediately her lips found his palm and nestled there, like a warm bird.

'It's not always like this,' he laughed. 'Sunshine only comes out on very special occasions. And this is a very special occasion.' He took her hand. 'Marry me, Sing. I believe I can make you happy.'

It was the third time he had asked and each time she had answered in the same way. 'It is your happiness I must think of. The man who shares my life will have to be more than a husband, more than a lover. He must be brother, father and friend. It is a lot to ask. Too much, I think.'

'I have thought of nothing else,' he said softly. 'I believe I could be all of those.'

Her eyes searched his for a long moment before she spoke. 'Then, if you are sure, I must say yes,' she whispered.

She took his hand in both of hers and lifted it to her cheek. 'And pray to all gods that the sunshine will always stay out for us.'

It did stay out for the wedding in the little church on the edge of Sparrow's Green two weeks later. Sunshine lay over the scented Kentish landscape as though summer had made an early appearance. Gravel crunched as well-shined shoes trod the confetti-strewn pathways of the churchyard and photographs were taken before they left for the reception at the Grange. Sebastian's yellow Morgan sports car stood waiting at the curb, with the top down, as out of place beside his parents' Bentley as the cheerful urchins who had festooned its rear fender with tin cans and old horseshoes.

Sing was glad to run towards it in a final flurry of rice and confetti with Sebastian's arm around her waist. The snowy cassock of the grey-faced Reverent Tuttle had seemed strange and somehow false to her. As she had listened to the drone of prayer and the doleful singing of hymns, somewhere deep inside her there was the brassy clashing of gongs, the shrill call of reedy trumpets and the smell of joss smoke.

The bell-shaped marquee of red and white candy stripes sat on the neatly cut grass looking like a large bathing tent. Or, as one gusty female guest had remarked, 'a well sucked stick of Blackpool rock'. In spite of the superb climate and guarantees from the weather bureau, Lady Constance had left nothing to chance.

The guest list to the wedding reception had been kept to those of Sebastian's old school friends still in the district and those who could be easily contacted elsewhere. Lady Constance had asked none of the important people she and her husband had come to know over their lifetime and almost none of their close relatives. Just an ancient aunt or two, too vague to know what was happening, and Sir Duncan had insisted on one or two guests of his own whom he knew were genuinely fond of Sebastian.

He understood very well that Constance had kept the numbers down because she was not particularly proud of their only son's marriage and in this she was strongly supported by Cecily. God knows there had been enough words about it. He also knew that they felt certain it would not last. That whatever spell this oriental woman had cast upon Sebastian would eventually be broken and he would come to his senses.

It was one of the few times Duncan Masters had taken a firm stand with the women who for more years than he cared to remember had taken control of his life. He had to admit that for the most part Connie's calculations and predictions were usually well-founded. The firm hand she had always kept on things domestic and the advice in times of difficulty that had helped to guide his own career had always proved sound.

He had been grateful to her, and as they grew older, more than content to leave it that way. But he refused to share the resentment and disappointment over Sebastian's choice of a wife or the bitterness that it was bound to breed.

As far as he was concerned Sing was a damned fine girl and a sweet and intelligent one, given half a chance. He for one intended to give her all the support and encouragement he could muster, now and for the future. He had not argued over the poverty of the guest list as he had little time for most of Constance's family and his own widely scattered relatives were almost as pompous. Over the comfort of his pipe rack he had decided that for the bride's sake, the smaller the better—that was the ticket.

Even so, for Sing it was several hours of strange faces coming and going from her vision, so close she could feel their body warmth, smell their perfume and cologne. Pink faces, always jolly, with penetrating eyes and smiling teeth. She did not always understand everything they said to her. The men kissed her on the cheek and muttered their good wishes, the women extended limp hands, gushed their congratulations and turned away. No one tried to engage her in conversation and she stayed as close to Sebastian as she could.

Tables heavy with delicacies had been laid out in the marquee and two stout serving girls circulated with trays of pink champagne. Everyone seemed to be enjoying each other's company but there was no food or drink that could fill the hollowness in Sing's stomach and she was thankful when finally it was time to leave the noise of the crowd behind.

Turning back, looking over the suitcases strapped to the Morgan's luggage rack, she saw the sea of faces and waving hands grow smaller, diminishing with distance. As they turned out of the drive and onto the smooth, black bitumen of the road, the sharp stone block of Grange Manor was reduced to toy size, flickering through the long line of shimmering poplars that marked its boundary until it was gone.

Sing had tried to be happy for the first two weeks spent in the big Georgian house but had often felt uneasy. The next two months were to be the ultimate realisation of a treasured dream—as though to make up for those uncertain moments and wipe away doubt. As the nippy little sports car with its gleaming chrome horn and glove-leather seats wound through tunnels of overhanging trees, through the long twisting stretches of open country road, she realised she had only felt really free when outside the manor's thick and stifling walls.

Sebastian's father had maintained a kindly neutrality as he smoked a cherrywood from his favourite chair, watching from a comfortable distance. It had quickly become clear that Lady Constance was in as tight control of the master's household as any Cantonese tai tai. Sing had seen her physically wince at Sir Duncan's unexpected gusts of hearty laughter.

'Must you hee-haw like a village donkey, Duncan? It is most unnerving,' she would say, a mild frown of disapproval disturbing the composure of her perfectly powdered features.

It had also become increasingly clear that she did not approve of the marriage. Nor, it seemed, did his sister Cecily. They had both made Sing feel like a politely accepted guest who threatened to outstay her welcome. Both adored Sebastian in their distinctly different ways and were very clever at concealing any sign of disenchantment when he was with her. But there had been strong words about it and Sing had heard them from the grounds, even from as far as the kitchen garden behind its red brick wall.

The wife of a diplomat was his greatest asset, she heard Lady

Constance say. To marry the wrong woman was to end a career. Sebastian's smiling reassurance that this was the way all English mothers behaved, no matter who their sons married, had been enough to stop Sing from worrying. She reminded herself that if she had married a Chinese she would be treated and expected to behave as a servant in the house of her husband's family, and eventually to share him with other wives and concubines. Then a letter had arrived from Peggy Pelham and she had realised how much Peggy had meant to her, how very much she missed her. How alone and uncertain she sometimes felt. She did not say these things in her replies but Peggy's letters were soon to become her lifeline to the strange world she had known.

Now, with the wind whipping her hair and the sun on her face, watching the country unroll around her, the big house retreating further and further behind, she felt secure again. Sebastian loved her. She stole sidelong looks at him as he drove the fast little car in and out of villages and across county borders. She thought how remarkably good-looking he was in the bottle-green blazer, a silk cravat tucked into his open-necked shirt, wind ruffling his usually neat black hair and tanning his cheeks.

Often he would reach across and squeeze her knee, caressing her thigh. When he did, she obediently allowed her legs to part, making it easy for him to do as he pleased with her. Sometimes he pulled the car over and kissed her passionately, becoming so excited that he would grab a picnic blanket and find a place among the trees. Being made love to, gently at first, then urgently and fiercely, with the birds hopping among dancing leaves above and the woodland scent of bluebells crushed beneath her, was very pleasurable to Sing.

It made her happy to see how much he wanted her. How filled with desire he became, how consumed in his ecstasy. It did not matter that she seldom shared this intensity, or that even when she did it was never the same as it had been with Toby. She did not let it spoil her happiness. It was enough to be needed so desperately, to have his hands and lips and tongue so hungry for every part of her.

Only when they stopped at some homely village pub for the night, to eat a leisurely dinner and go early to the clean, fresh sheets of a comfortable bed, did she cling to him long after he was asleep, pressing hard against him, trying to satisfy the need he had aroused in her. She had tried to delay his fulfilment, extending his pleasure with her hands and mouth until he begged for relief or penetrated her with deep, final thrusts that spent him within seconds.

He came in long, shuddering spasms that seemed to fill her but left the hot core of her untouched. Once his gasps had subsided and he rolled from her, he was quickly and deeply asleep. At first she had tried awakening him, reviving him in the many ways she knew.

Sometimes, while he slept she took his hand and pressed its fingers into the still wet folds of her body, rubbing herself against them until she reached her climax. Sing blamed herself for the one-sidedness of their love-making. It was she who thought of Toby, she who compared the sleek paleness of Sebastian's skin, shadowed by its growth of fine black hair, with Toby's hard brown body, the down of his chest and forearms and shins a light sunbleached gold.

Upper Verdes

THE HOUSE that Sir Duncan gave them as a wedding present had been kept as a surprise. Part of the Grange estate, it was separated from it by Brambles' farm, no more than a mile or so from the manor. Sebastian had not wanted her to see it until their return from touring in the Morgan.

It was being painted and furnished, he said, so that everything would be perfect for them to move in. Even when the car stopped outside the picket fence that opened onto a small meadow beside the typical Kentish cottage, he did not say they were home. The name carved into the top of the five-bar gate leading into the meadow said 'Upper Verdes'.

The cottage stood beside the meadow, with a picket fence crowded with honeysuckle. It was surrounded by an acre of garden, half given over to orchard and the rest neatly planted with rockeries and flowerbeds ringed with herbaceous borders. The house was built of red brick with the upper storey sheathed in weathered shingles and a roof of Welsh slate.

Its leaded windows looked into the garden on all sides and were surrounded by tall spikes of foxglove, hollyhock and sky blue lupin. A porchway, built from rustic branchwood and covered by an extension of the shingles, formed an arbour of white rambling roses around the front door, their scent reaching beyond the fence and into the lane.

When Sebastian left the car to open the garden gate and invite her to pass through, Sing thought they must be visiting the charming home of a friend. Not until he turned the large, old-fashioned key and, kicking the door wide, lifted her lightly over its threshold, did it begin to dawn on her that this fairytale cottage was to be her own.

With joyful disbelief, she entered the little reception area with a hallway leading to the back and a polished wooden staircase. The door was opened to a sun-filled sitting room furnished with comfortable looking armchairs and settee of floral fabric in soft pastels. Dark beams were decorated with sets of shining horse brasses and the large inglenook fireplace was flanked by more bright brass and copperware.

A deep bay window, framed by a tangle of clematis, its window seat scattered with cushions, looked onto the front garden. Vases of fresh flowers had been set on every available surface and filled the lovely room with their perfume. All the rooms were equally delightful to Sing, and she fell instantly in love with everything she saw.

The cottage was intimate and small compared to the three floors of gleaming square-paned windows of Grange Manor, encased in quarried stone, the regiment of window boxes filled with scarlet and white geraniums all in perfect order. At Upper Verdes flowers spilled around the cottage in a natural profusion that stirred distant memories for Sing, like a soft breeze from a wide and distant lake. She went from window to window in breathless disbelief.

'Is it really ours, Sebastian? Our own, with no one else to share?'

He had followed her from room to room, content to watch her reaction. 'Only Mrs Monk who will come in to clean and old Sweet William who will look after the garden.'

She ran to him and held on tight, her arms locked around his waist, her cheek pressed hard against his shoulder.

'You haven't seen upstairs yet,' he laughed, delighted by her obvious enchantment. 'It has a view of the hop gardens and Brambles' farm.'

She climbed the stairs quite slowly, running her hand along the glossy polish of the cedar balustrade.

The large, airy bedroom seemed almost filled by a huge bed, its yellow and orange eiderdown already turned back. A marble stand held a large hand-painted water jug and wash bowl, and beside the open window an unruly cluster of pale larkspur, studded by pink and white carnations, had been placed on the sill. Lacy curtains moved in the billows of breeze, stirring their perfume and bringing the smell of the fields and the first flowering of hops. From the dovecote on Brambles' farm came the low murmuring of ringtails and turtle-doves and across the fields came the call of a cuckoo.

Sing ran to the bed and sank down onto its goosefeather softness, looking around at the walls patterned with faint sprigs of cowslip and primrose. A painting showed a gypsy boy lifting the shaggy white fetlock of a carthorse; in the background a gaily painted caravan camped under trees, children playing on its steps.

The picture was so large and beautiful it drew Sing to it. She stood gazing, taking in every detail. The smoke rising from the cooking fire, a dog asleep, the horse's collar and harness hanging from a low tree branch.

'It's a Constable. From father's collection. Do you like it?'

In answer Sing turned to him, holding out her arms, kissing him deeply when he came to her, unable to think of any other way to express her gratitude, so overjoyed that her feelings of happiness were beyond all words.

Instead, she led him to the bed, undressed him and then, as he watched from the pillows, took off her dress and underthings with deliberate slowness. This time she did not try to tease him with her foreplay, but brought him to erection quickly and straddled him, leaning forward so that her breasts hung full and heavy within reach of his mouth and hands.

He entered her without guiding, smoothly, easily. She ground down upon him, taking him completely. The spread of her hips moved gently at first, slippery soft in perfect coupling. Then, her knees tightly holding him, the slow circular movements quickened, her muscles tightened and gripped as she straightened upon him, his hands still seeking her stiff nipples.

She felt the coming of his orgasm, his thrusting up to meet her, his shuddering sighs becoming the calling of her name. Arching her back and plunging with his rhythm, she came with cries of disbelief at the waves of wild release that spread from the centre of her being, to flood in hot tides to every extremity of her body. Her head thrown back, her eyes closed, almost fainting from the thrill that electrified her, she saw only Toby's face smiling up from the pillows.

That first summer of her marriage to Sebastian passed in long days of contentment for Sing. They filled each one with exploration and lazy pleasure, visiting the market town of Tunbridge Wells and the house of Rudyard Kipling at neighbouring Burwash Common.

They discovered the pubs and teashops in the friendly Kentish villages of Ticehurst, Hawkhurst and Wadhurst. Rowed a skiff on lily-strewn rivers and hiked for miles over footpaths that laced the North Downs through farms and grainfields. Sometimes they put up for the weekend in cities and seaside towns like Canterbury, Maidstone and Hastings, where they ate shellfish from a barrow and swam in the cold, salt-stinging sea.

The sexual satisfaction Sing found on that first day in their new home was never repeated. It had been part of her sheer delight in the bright sunlit bedroom, the feeling that the cottage, old though it was, had been cleared of ghosts and made brand new just for the two of them. The smell of wax polish and the hint of fresh paint mixed with the air from outside, flowing with the sound of birds, the purr of a tractor through its open windows. It had all come together in a surge of happiness that had taken her breath away.

Sebastian had been there, standing back, smiling with her, so pleased at her happiness that she had wanted more than anything in the world to thank him. To love him and become part of him. But it had been Toby's name she had almost called out in the pangs of orgasm.

It filled her with a secret guilt that she had learned to hide. Sebastian must never know that she did not love him as she had loved Toby, or that his attentions in bed left her desperately needing more than he was able to give.

When Sing tried to repeat that one moment and the perfect union they had found, her dominance seemed to confuse, even repel him. She had felt him wilt inside her and it was more than a week before he had tried again. The spell had been a fleeting one and now it was broken never to be recaptured.

She learned to respond to his expectations, bringing him to

the edge of his release and pretending with her sounds that she shared his pleasure. He must never know that all she felt for him was a deep and abiding gratitude, friendship and respect. It was enough for Sing, and so much around her gave her pleasure of another kind she became resigned to a one-sided relationship that kept him satisfied and her content. His satisfaction became part of her fulfilment and things fell into a comfortable routine.

When the time came for him to return to the Foreign Office and he began commuting by the morning train, they saw less and less of each other. Breakfast would be a hurried glance at the morning paper and a peck on the cheek on the way to the car. At night he would arrive on the seven o'clock train. She asked him to teach her to drive the car so that she could take him to the station and pick him up, but he said he was concerned for her safety, especially with the icy roads of winter ahead. Perhaps next summer.

Sing found that she did not miss Sebastian during the day. It was nice to be in her house alone. She liked to go barefoot into the garden with the thick grass, still beaded with dew, wet around her ankles. She had asked Sweet William, the old man who came to do the garden, to let it grow, so that the tiny daisies and celandine could thrive amongst it.

She climbed the apple trees to pick the Cox's Orange Pippins and the big green cooking apples, tossing them down to be gathered from the grass. Those that had been spoiled by wasps she fed to the donkey that hung its head over the fence adjoining Brambles' farm. She watched a pair of white barn owls nesting in the loft of the oasthouse that stood well away from Alf Bramble's farmhouse and quite close to the fence.

Sweet William was a retired farm labourer whose long life in the fields and ditches of the Downs had seized his joints with lumbago and an hour or two of weeding was about all he could manage outside his visits to the village pub. He was a simple old man who lived alone in a tiny cottage at the end of the lane. His real name was Ted Flowers.

The nearness of soap and water to his weathered skin was something he avoided and it gave him a gamey niff that had earned him the nickname of 'Sweet William' after the fragrant bloom to be found in every cottage garden. Sing would bring him out a mug of hot tea and a thick sandwich. He took to her immediately, teaching her the name of every flower and leaf, bird and insect that abounded in and around the garden.

When Mrs Amelia Monk squeezed through the gate at ten o'clock sharp each morning, Sing would hear the tic-a-tic-a-tic of her bicycle, then the rattle of the latch and almost run to meet her. Mrs Monk was a cheerful widow, as wide around as she was tall, and every ounce of her was kindness and understanding.

She had offered to show Sing how to cook 'good plain English food' and the mornings were spent up to their elbows in flour, rolling out pastry and baking in the big black-doored oven she kept shiny as coal. She called Sing 'Ducky', telling her all there was to know about life in Sparrow's Green and how to make the most of her ration coupons.

When she had gone in the afternoons, leaving linoleum bright and woodwork gleaming, the diamond panes of the windows spotless, Sing read in the garden or, if the day was dull, worked on her translation of *The Second Sunrise*.

The eight books of Master To had been her strength and her companion through much of her life. In her darkest times they had guided and comforted her. No one had been able to separate her from them and they had always been her most treasured possession.

As she had grown older Sing realised that Old To was the closest thing to God that she had found and that his teachings had become her Bible. She had read and re-read *The Second Sunrise* many times and in many strange places until she understood its every thought and had solved its every riddle.

The decision to begin the immense task of its translation into English came to her in a dream: she was standing on the Rock of Great Strength, the beauty of the lake and the bamboo groves all around her, when she heard Master To's voice and the distant tolling of the great bell they called the Prayer of Buddha:

> Night darkens the western hedgerow.
> The colours of the peony are faded.
> The blue-cap in the bamboo is silent.
> We cannot stop this shadow.
> But in every heart there waits
> a second sunrise.

The words were so clear that they woke her and she lay watching the dawn break, comforted by them, yet aware of their warning. That morning, when Sebastian had left and the clip, clip, of Sweet William's shears came from the end of the garden, she took the thick notebooks from their special drawer and spread them before her. Mrs Monk hummed at her dusting as Sing ran her fingers over the coarse hand-made paper crammed with the tiny, perfect characters of Old To's calligraphy.

It was as though she had known all along that this moment would come and the task that she now set herself had always been waiting. It became part of every moment and in the splendour of her surrounding she saw only the beauty of the Tao.

Sometimes she walked for miles between high hedgerows of hawthorn and hazel, filling a basket with blackberries; or across open fields where majestic horse-chestnut trees flowered with waxy candles of blossom and she gathered mushrooms.

As autumn came the trees began changing colour to tawny, yellow-gold and a dozen shades of red. The fields on Brambles' farm were stripped of corn and the mutter of tractors carried over the meadows as the stubble was ploughed under.

For weeks the air sparkled crystal clear, the sky a crisp, duck-egg blue. When the winds came they were sudden and cold and the red-gold dressing of the trees was gone almost overnight, to carpet the ground and fill the ditches with what would soon become in drifts of brown rot.

The sky set grey as cement over the bare, bony fingers of woodland. One bewitching summer had ended. Sing looked back on it as though it were a wonderful story that had been read to her as Toby had once read—now it was ended and the book was closed. She opened instead the hidebound covers of Old To's notebooks.

Sing did not need to be told that her marriage to Sebastian was beginning to fail. She was content when they were alone, although the lunch each Sunday with his family had turned into a ritual that became more and more strained. Sir Duncan always greeted her warmly, coming close with his tweedy, pipe-tobacco smell and brandy breath.

Lady Constance maintained her well-mannered distance, while Cecily excused herself as soon and as often as she could. Luncheon was always preceded by church and Sing took her place in the family pew with as much belief in the Anglican god as she could find within her.

Lady Constance Masters and her daughter were very active in the church and its charitable activities and were visibly distressed when they learned that Sing had not been baptised, and positively mortified to find she belonged to no known church or accepted religion except some barbaric oriental cult she called 'the Tao'.

Sebastian only laughed when his mother voiced her concerns privately to him. He was used to her quietly overbearing sense of propriety in all things to do with the family and anything that may reflect on them. He did not even try to explain Sing's background to her.

When she asked, as she did at the earliest opportunity after their arrival, he simply said that the girl he had made his wife came from a prominent Eurasian family but had lost both parents in the war with Japan. She had also suffered enough racial and social bigotry, discrimination and cruelty to last several lifetimes, as well as untold brutality at the hands of the Japanese, from which she was still recovering.

He was sure his mother would understand, he had said. That Christian compassion would overrule the strongest curiosity and that both she and Cecily would be gentle with their questioning and considerate in their understanding.

This uneasy truce held good through the months of Sundays and on the rare occasions that Sing and Sebastian entertained them at Upper Verdes. Rare because Sebastian was well aware of Lady Constance's ability to intimidate without saying a word and of the waspish side of his sister's nature. Cecily was still unmarried at thirty and three broken engagements had resigned them all to the fact that she was not the marrying kind. This decision left her with an old-maidish intolerance of those who were married and particularly those who pretended they were happy.

She never permitted it to occur to her that she was consumed by jealousy and sexual frustration, which she took out on the broad-flanked hunters she rode to hounds all over the countryside. Cecily Masters had become what was known as a 'horsey woman'.

Like her mother, she looked upon anything pretty and feminine as frivolous and empty-headed. Her strong, life-long connections with the church conveniently branded sensuality in any form as sinful. Sing fell neatly into all of these categories and Cecily greatly resented the obvious influence this strange and alien female was holding over her brother. Even when Sing served them an excellent Chinese dinner that she had cooked and presented beautifully, Cecily said that she doubted if her delicate digestion could cope with such exotic change and poked at it as though expecting to find something alive and crawling.

The family gatherings were not a success and, in spite of Sir Duncan's attempts to show his appreciation and bring a jovial tone to the occasion, even his cheerful chortling was eventually discouraged and the evenings ended in uncomfortable silence and early departure.

It was no more successful when Sebastian's childhood friends were invited to dinner. They were all young men and women around his own age and from similarly privileged backgrounds. After an initial inquisitiveness as to Sing's nationality and pointed questioning about her home and family in Hong Kong, their interest was quickly exhausted. She was passed over in favour of discussing old times, people and events completely unknown to her.

This exclusion, intended or not, carried through to invitations extended to Sebastian, and Sing began to feel like an oddity and a liability that he was obliged to take along. It was no different at cricket matches or boating trips or visits to the theatre.

The men looked at her as though she were edible and the women as though she was vaguely amusing but hardly worth an audience. When she grabbed scarce opportunities to speak of her past life in China and Hong Kong, she began to lack the confidence to carry it through.

The fear of questions she could not answer, the guilt these thoroughbred women made her feel with their intense stares and the half hidden smirks on the faces of their men, made her hesitate. The House of Fat Fan, Ah Gum, the Golden One, Hand-trolley Lulu and Three-thumbs Poon were not topics for their dinner tables, nor were the subjects of J.T. Ching or General Toshido. Sebastian told her to wipe the past completely and she had almost managed to do so. It left her feeling blank as paper before the brush is applied.

Even her letters to Peggy Pelham became empty of news and she took longer and longer to answer those that for a while arrived each week from Hong Kong, until they came more and more rarely.

With the winds of English winter, cold and wet as the oceans they blew in from, the harmony of Sing's life began to change and darken with the shortening days.

Sweet William stayed in his corner of the pub and taxed himself with nothing more strenuous than dominoes. There were more and more days when Mrs Monk could not face the weather and in the end Sing had suggested she should not bother at all until it improved, especially when she had ridden her bicycle through knife-edged rain and spent the day coughing and sneezing in front of the inglenook over bowls of broth.

It did not bother Sing at all, she was glad to have the privacy. Sometimes the bleakness outside brought back memories of the hut above T'ung Ting Lake. She could still smell the smouldering ox dung in the terracotta stove and the incense at the feet of Kuan Yin. She remembered how the thatch would freeze white and brittle with a fringe of icicles reaching almost to the ground.

Winter at Upper Verdes was nothing like that and the house was warmed by burning beech and birch logs stored in the shed and under the eaves by the back door. It was the last thing Sweet William had done before he came for his money, rubbing his hands, knobbly with arthritis, and looking round the grey, unbroken sky.

'She'll be a cold'un this year, Missus,' nodding to the wheeling flock of starlings, spreading and converging, gathering their own, high over the rooftops. 'Birds be leavin' early, an' I don't blame 'em.'

He had gone off, the five pounds stuffed in his waistcoat pocket, bent and stiff-legged towards the pub.

Sweet William was right about the winter. It was as severe as anyone could recall. But it was not the outside cold, the hard, hoar frosts that ruined the beet crops or the chill hint of early snow that concerned her. It was the coldness that had begun to follow Sebastian into the house when the Morgan drew into the drive on those evenings when he chose to come home.

He would make some comment on the foulness of the weather and eat in silence. His increasing tiredness worried Sing. He began retiring early and was almost immediately asleep. If he came to her at all it was briefly, almost roughly, without thought of her. There were nights when he arrived on a later train, the smell of drink still strong.

Invitations to join his friends had almost stopped altogether and when he rang to make contact they were more and more often otherwise engaged. He began to blame her. She was too sensitive, too touchy, he said. It made people uncomfortable. She must try harder to fit in. She must remember, he reminded her, that she was the foreigner here. It was she who must change.

The oldest and most popular pub in Sparrow's Green was the Vine, a short walk from Upper Verdes. On weekends it became Sebastian's refuge. The local pubs were second homes to the villagers. Their cheery, low-ceilinged bars were crammed with drinkers and darts players, warmed by blazing log fires, loud with conversation, the ringing of the till and clinking of glasses. Later would be the cheery thump of the piano leading a sing-song.

On the occasions that he included her, Sing stood in the groups, a glass in her hand and tried to understand the talk and laughter that surged around her. Sebastian, absorbed by the atmosphere, tended after a drink or two to forget that she was there. He was bound to meet someone he knew and they quickly bore him off in mind and spirit. Sing's attempts to follow, to share the jokes and be part of the laughter, went almost unnoticed.

As the noise increased with the drinking and the fog of tobacco smoke thickened, her head ached and her eyes were stung red. After weeks of trying she stopped going with him and he would return after the last drink had been served. Sing did not know how to talk to him about her fears and when she tried, he turned away.

It was not his fault if she could not mix, make friends of her own or find something to do. If she did not like going with him to the Vine she should not come. He could not help it if his friends did not invite them or were hesitant to repeat those disastrous dinner parties.

Just as her dream had warned and her instinct had predicted, Sing felt the trap of her situation closing around her. The oriental blood in her veins would not allow confrontation with her husband. To turn to his parents was out of the question; it would be the greatest of insults to him. Even the kindness of Amelia Monk seemed out of reach to her.

Her attempts to strike acquaintance in the village shops were met with the polite caution shown to any stranger. Eventually, she stayed in the house entirely. Within its walls she was secure but behind even that security there was building the slow dread of losing it. There was only one place she felt wanted and useful— lost in the pages of Old To's books and the exacting task of their translation.

Snow came softly overnight, windless drifts that covered the countryside, melting the horizon into a pale nothingness that joined the sky. Black lines of leafless hedgerow sliced it into sections and the dark trees looked as though they could never again show green. The buildings of Brambles' farm sat in isolated silence, the tractor under chaff bags in the machine shed, drained of oil so it would not freeze, and the animals sheltering in barns and cowsheds with sacking on their backs. Snow was nearly a metre thick on the roof of Upper Verdes. It had buried the places where flowers had grown and the apple trees, petrified by the cold, were grey as stone.

From the kitchen window Sing saw the tracks of birds embroidering the flat, white sheet of the lawn from their search for food. They were just as she had seen them as a child, when she had forced open the hut door against the press of new snow to break the ice on the water butt and bring inside the frozen cakes of fuel. The memory, almost forgotten, was swept back with a longing for the patient wisdom of Great-uncle To.

She went outside, the snow squeaking under her footfalls, its crust hardened by frost giving way beneath her and plunging her wellington boots eighteen inches deep. Scooping snow from the frozen birdbath she scattered it with crumbs broken from the bread between her gloved hands.

From the loft of the converted oasthouse on Brambles' farm, Beatrice 'Birdie' Meadows looked down at the solitary figure of the woman who lived in Upper Verdes. She had seen her often throughout the summer, in the garden with Sweet William or drinking tea with Amelia Monk at the cast iron table on the lawn.

She had thought often of going to the fence to talk with her but had always changed her mind. Birdie Meadows knew her place and although she was renowned as the village gossip, she kept it to her own level of society, which did not include those related to Sir Duncan and Lady Constance Masters up at the Grange.

As live-in housekeeper, cook and milkmaid to Alf Bramble, the gossip did include village worthies like Amelia Monk and Sweet William, so she had asked them both what the wife of Sebastian Masters was really like. Very nice, they had said. A right good-looker but a bit on the quiet side. It was him they weren't too fond of. Sebastian high-and-mighty Masters was not their cup of tea at all. They had not been encouraging.

It was Amelia who had given her the nickname of Birdie, after 'the little bird that told me so' and the name had stuck. To tell Beatrice Meadows anything was the same as posting it on the door of the village Social Club or the church noticeboard and they felt that Sing deserved her privacy.

Sing put on her wellingtons and gloves. Sebastian's big Hebridean fisherman's jersey rolled up at the sleeves covered her in porridge-coloured wool. With a steaming kettle in her hand she opened the back door to pour boiling water on the frozen step, the way Sweet William had told her to.

A robin hopped bravely towards her, expecting bread. It was

the first she'd seen, the blood red of its breast cheery as holly berries against the glare of snow, brown head and feathers sleeked down, tail opening and closing like a tiny fan.

Squatting on the step, half closing her eyes and shutting everything but the robin from her mind, Sing held out her hand. The bird cocked a bright black eye and flew with a soft purring of wings to sit on her finger.

'Well I never,' said a voice from under the apple trees, 'I never seen the like of that in all my born days.'

It made Sing jump and the robin was gone in a blink.

'Now I've gone and scared it off,' the voice said regretfully.

From under the bare, wet branches came a figure rugged up with knitted scarves held in place by a heavy Land Army duffle coat. Thick corduroy breeches were stuck into muddy rubber boots, with woollen socks turned down at the knee.

Sing rose slowly as the figure approached.

'How . . . how did you get in here?' She managed to smile through her surprise at the pleasant, pink-cheeked, red-nosed face that peered from the folds of a tartan scarf like a Christmas elf.

'Hole in the fence. I'm from next door. Brambles' farm.' The apparition sniffed. She pulled off a brightly coloured woollen mitten as she approached, holding out a rough red hand. The eyes that twinkled at Sing were an astonishingly clear, cornflower blue, innocent and wondering as a child's, hiding nothing. Her voice was musical and friendly, her grip warm and firm.

'Birdie Meadows. I've been wanting to make your acquaintance for ever so long.'

The appearance of Birdie Meadows made the rest of the winter pass quickly. Christmas came and went almost unnoticed to Sing, except for a brief exchange of visits on Christmas Day. It was something she had never known so she did not miss the usual festivity. In no time, it seemed, the snow was almost gone, leaving lines of dirty, white slush in the plough furrows and along the gutters.

Weak sunshine began showing itself from occasional patches of watery blue. Green shoots poked through the carpets of leaves and the dark wet branches that had seemed dead forever once again began sprouting buds. The hole in the fence was two loose pickets where Birdie's pet goat had butted them out to reach the fallen apples. It was partially covered by blackberry brambles and had become Sing's private gateway to the secret world of Birdie Meadows and Brambles' farm.

'Nobody knows about this place but me,' Birdie said, slightly out of breath the first time they climbed the wooden ladder to the loft of the oasthouse.

'Now you, of course.' She heaved herself up the last few rungs and offered Sing her hand. 'And you're very welcome, I'm sure.'

Sing stood looking around in silent wonder. 'It's beautiful,' she said at last, almost under her breath, she was so taken by surprise, mesmerised by what she saw.

The wide oak boards of the floor had been scrubbed and waxed to a richly-grained finish and scattered with colourful straw mats of the kind woven by gypsies. Around the circular, whitewashed walls, even brighter cushions were scattered in comfortable piles and rickety shelves held an abundance of books. Beneath them was arranged a mattress covered with a quilt of crocheted patchwork.

Here and there the wall was pasted with printed posters of India's gods—Krishna, Vishnu, Brahma—and Tibetan prayer mandalas spun ancient patterns of mystery. An old pine table stood in the centre of this magic circle, piled high with more books and papers and a huge bowl of yellow and orange astors. A three-legged milking stool stood beneath it.

From the stout oaken beams high in the conical ceiling hung hanks of dried hops and assorted herbs, filling the space with the earthy aromas of the hedgerow. Among them long strings of hand-made wind bells tinkled.

It was none of these things that took Sing's breath away but the fact that around the room, finding every part of it, there danced and shimmered a million splinters of rainbow light.

'Crystals,' said Birdie, crossing to the big open space that looked out over farmland and beyond it to the brown fells and lees of thawing countryside. 'Pretty, aren't they? They have healing power, you know.'

She passed her hand in the air as though it held a wand. The lights shivered to life, chasing over everything in a kaleidoscope of radiance. Dozens of crystals, of every shape and size, were suspended in the light from the window by hair-fine threads of cotton.

'They're beautiful. This is a magic place,' said Sing wonderingly. 'It's like a temple.'

'It is that,' giggled Birdie. 'Though that's not what the vicar calls it. Hellfire, according to him.' She turned to a small primus

stove set on an upturned apple barrel and began pumping furiously.
'Lets have a nice cup of tea. There's lots to talk about.'

August 1947

THE THIN bleat of a hunting horn carried across the fields adjoining
the Grange estate and Brambles' farm, filtering through the thick
copse of larch and sycamore, to be replaced by the shrilling of
grasshoppers.

The red fox lifted its pointed nose; its black-tipped ears peaked
in the direction of the sound. The bleating came again, this time
with the distant yelp of hounds. The fox leapt spring-footed into
the narrow ditch and, keeping to its cover, raced along it, ears
folded flat and the white tip of its brush held low.

Cecily Masters' generous rump bumped the saddle solidly as
the tall grey hunter rounded the spinney and took another ditch.
She was an excellent rider and as usual found herself well up
among those ahead of the field. The fox had broken cover and
she could see the distant streak of its rust-red back darting over
open ground. The brown and white pack of the hounds broke
through the hedge, tumbling, howling and leaping to the scent.

The fox was making for the hop gardens on Brambles' farm.
Letting her weight rise in the stirrups, giving an inch of rein, she
leant forward over the hunter's flying mane as she gave chase.

The pickers straightened up among the ripe mustard-coloured
catkins of strong-smelling hops to cheer the fox on. Still a broad
meadow's length away it was zig-zagging through the long grass
and tall buttercups in long, loping bounds. The drag of the grass
was slowing it down while the killing frenzy of the hounds gained
ground.

Most of the pickers were gypsies, the men capped and heavily
booted, their shirtsleeves rolled up, faded kerchiefs knotted around
their throats. The brown-faced women shielded their eyes to watch
as the red and black coated riders closed behind the pack.

Sing and Birdie Meadows were among the villagers working beside the gypsies. They were close to the fence that separated the hop field from the open pasture and could see the flaming coat of the fox surging towards them like a porpoise breaking water. The first of the hounds to reach it clamped its jaws on a rear leg. The fox was down, the hounds milling around it in a flurry of yellow pollen and grass seeds.

Sing didn't recognise her sister-in-law as Cecily swung a glossy black riding boot over the breadth of the hunter's back and landed solidly in the grass. Her hair was combed back in a tight bun and covered with a stiff, black felt riding hat. Others had galloped up and the Master of Fox Hounds dismounted to call off the pack.

Bending over the still breathing animal, he deftly ended its life with a knife and, severing its brush, handed the gory prize to Cecily Masters.

'Yours, I think, m'dear,' he said and at the moment of accepting it, swishing the stump to get rid of the blood, she looked up and saw Sing staring straight at her from among the hop vines.

Lady Constance was not at all surprised to hear that her daughter had actually seen Sebastian's wife working in the fields with the gypsies from the Hollow. Since Sebastian had returned to the Colonial Office his marriage had taken the decline she had known that it would.

The Sunday luncheons had gradually dropped off during the winter and so had regular church attendance. Neither had been revived with the coming of spring and summer and contact had dwindled to occasional telephone calls. Sebastian was spending much too much of his time in the Vine or the Fox and Hounds and, from what she heard, he often stayed in London overnight, sometimes for the entire week.

She had tried to talk to her son about the situation over the telephone but he refused to discuss the matter, insisting that he and his wife were simply 'making adjustments'. Sir Duncan steadfastly refused to interfere, confident that Sebastian and Sing would work things out for themselves in their own way and without any meddling from him or, he added pointedly, from anyone else. In spite of this thinly disguised advice Lady Constance had no difficulty keeping abreast of what was happening at Upper Verdes.

Her own cook, Betty, was related to Amelia Monk who, she said, was most concerned that her mistress had taken up with the woman most of the village believed to be a simpleton or, worse, possessed by the devil. Birdie Meadows was said to worship strange and unwholesome forces from some sort of shrine on Brambles' farm.

Church circles had even begun to whisper that they believed it to be a coven. Witchcraft was said to have been practised there and the possible sacrifice of goats. Also, according to Mrs Monk, Sweet William, the gardener, who visited the Hollow regularly and knew the gypsies well, had said that they considered Sing as one of their own. Some nonsense about her knowledge of herbs and healing, a natural ability to charm wild birds and animals.

There was talk of quack medicine and strange, ritual dances and that the oasthouse had become a meeting place for the practice of heathen rites. Gypsies were seen to enter carrying strange bundles and even women from the village were known to come and go, some from miles around. Drawn there, it was whispered, by some unholy influence.

Lady Constance had no belief in witchcraft. The flights of fancy that accompanied village gossip were nothing new to her and she was thoroughly aware of the relish with which the Reverend Tuttle collected such stories as grist for God's mill. He liked to think of his church as democratically governed by its own congregation, and the presence of sinners only drew them closer together.

As a true Anglican minister he believed in the freedom and responsibility of his flock to make their own individual commitments to the Almighty and there was nothing like the threat of a little devil-worship to make them get on with it. He had spoken seriously to Lady Constance about the wisdom of Sing's baptism into the Church of England, where she would be given a Christian name and be drawn closer to the holy sacraments, the ancient creeds of undivided Christendom.

The Reverend Tuttle had absolutely no doubt that holy communion for his heathen wife was the answer to all of Sebastian Masters' problems. Lady Constance even raised the subject with Sebastian and to appease her he had asked Sing to talk to the vicar. Sing had agreed, and one summer afternoon she accepted an invitation to tea at the vicarage. When they were settled, with tea, he came straight to the point.

'Don't you want to be a Christian, my dear Mrs Masters?' he asked in a voice filled with patience. 'To be baptised into the Anglican church as your husband and his family have been? It is never too late, you know.'

'Will I then be the same as those around me? No longer different, and accepted as one of them?'

'We are all accepted equally in the eyes of God, my child. Once you are baptised, you may begin confirmation classes, making strong and certain your faith in the Lord,' he answered with infinite kindness.

'Which lord?' Sing asked the question simply.

Reverend Tuttle looked mildly shocked. 'Why, the Christian god, the Almighty Father of Jesus Christ, of course.'

'How is the Christian god different to the Lord Buddha or the Way Of The Tao?'

'But my dear young lady . . . those surely are idols . . . heathen images.' He looked visibly distressed by her questioning.

'If I am decent, if I am kind, compassionate, considerate of the sensitivities and feelings of others . . . generous in love, tolerance and kindness, am I not already a Christian?'

The patient look of understanding returned and remained fixed on the reverend's long, pitying face. 'If you have not been baptised into the church and you do not attend service, then Christ is not in you. How then can you be a true Christian?' He leaned his head on one side and regarded her as though she were a very small child.

'In the world I come from, there are many gods,' Sing said quietly. 'Nothing is done without prayer but I have seen terrible suffering and much cruelty. Once I knew a Christian who had great faith in the father of Jesus Christ.'

She told him the story of the Irish nun in the village of Yuenchow and asked him to explain why, when she had worked so hard in the name of God the Father, He had allowed her little church to bury her alive. Reverend Tuttle could not, but shook his head sadly when Sing said, 'God is a distant mountain to me. One I have seen on cloudless days. He is a mountain that I cannot climb. I sometimes feel there are too many gods and too much destruction in their name and in their service. I am not wise enough to choose but I cannot ask another to choose for me.'

She stood up in the stuffy little room, suddenly aware of the faint smell of old sweat that came from the reverend's long black frock. On the wall opposite her chair, behind his head, hung a large crucifix. Sing found herself mesmorised by the spiked hands and feet, the wracked and wretched body slumped in death, the agony of the thorned crown . . . so different from the serene smile of the Buddha. Sing knew that she did not belong here and that it would be futile to pretend.

'I do not believe I could marry into your church. It would be a great deception. Perhaps I must always remain a heathen.'

Reverend Tuttle wasted no time in passing on the hopelessness of her case to Lady Constance, who said it came as no surprise to her. More serious and immediate than the prospect of communion with God was the fact that the marriage she had known was a mistake from the beginning had become a serious threat to her son's health and happiness and was certainly affecting his diplomatic future.

She was certain that Sebastian's marriage to a woman of mixed blood and dubious background was directly responsible for the apparent hiatus in his career. This, perhaps, would not seem quite such a tragedy if his domestic life had remained anywhere near as blissful as it had first appeared.

There was no talk of children. Sebastian had insisted that to start a family would most certainly put an end to the colonial posting that he felt sure he would be offered at any time. He was hoping for Malaya, Singapore or Sarawak, perhaps even a return to Hong Kong or China, now that enough time had passed to allow them to return. He now knew, he said, that England was not the best place for them to build their future. Things would be better in the east.

The goings-on on Brambles' farm that had created so much rumour and speculation were almost childlike in their innocence. The horned symbol of evil seen entering and leaving the oasthouse on a regular basis was none other than Baba, the nanny-goat. She had surprised Birdie by producing two remarkably beautiful kids, one of which Birdie had given to Sing as a gift of their friendship.

The ritual dances were the breathing and stretching exercises that Sing had taught her new friend and which they often practised in the fresh air from the open window or the patch of turf that surrounded the old building.

Several of the older gypsy wives had a deep knowledge of Romany folklore and of the use of herbs in healing. One or two of them came with plants and roots they had gathered, to exchange thoughts and drink herb tea.

They claimed their origin was in Persia and that their people had taken generations to find their way down through Asia to the Middle East and Europe. They had never met anyone like

Sing and were fascinated by the lore of the Tao, so similar to their own rules of nature.

It hadn't taken long for those brave enough among the local women to come forward with their problems and Sing found herself giving advice on everything from backache to period pains, depression and drunken husbands. These were the things that had stirred a hornet's nest in the church hall.

Birdie had no proof of who it was that had discovered her hideaway. She suspected it was Sweet William, stooped among the alder that grew thick against the fence with a sickle in his hand.

Birdie and Sing decided that as they were doing nothing at all that could harm anyone in any way, there wasn't much to be done about Amelia Monk and Sweet William's observations except to continue to do what they were doing as openly as possible.

Whoever the intruder was, he or she must have taken one look at the cascades of light showering the portrait of Guru Ji, sniffed the lingering whiff of incense, looked upon the vividly painted faces of the Hindu deity and rushed to the shelter of the nearest Christian altar.

Birdie also supposed that the astrological charts and Tarot cards left lying around would not have helped matters. In a village like Sparrow's Green, even in the enlightened and tolerant post-war years of the late 1940s, such things were looked upon as the conjuring of demons. As were gypsy fortune tellers, dispensers of folk medicine and stargazers of any kind. In fact, all those who did not fit neatly and regularly into the square foot of church pew allotted to them.

Birdie knew that she fell into the category of the forsaken, but it hadn't been from choice. Brought up as an orphan in the Canterbury workhouse, she had lived so close to the cathedral that she could hear the choir while scrubbing the floors with sacking tied round the raw sores that were her knees. She had felt as though she was living next door to God. When the bells chimed and shook the floor she slept on she felt even closer. But no one ever took her up the grand steps and into His house with its huge doors to introduce her.

Once, she had found the courage to peep in, but the towering, cantilevered arches soared so mightily with the glorious boom of organ music it made her feel even smaller and colder and hungrier and more alone than she already was.

When she was made to thank Him for every crust of bread and dollop of cold porridge she was allowed to swallow, Birdie had done so at the top of her lungs, hoping that if He heard her, she might get something a little nicer. 'For what I am about to receive, may the Lord make me truly thankful,' she bellowed. The bread had only got harder and the porridge colder and lumpier.

When they sent her to become a milkmaid on a Kentish dairy farm at Seven Oaks she was ten years old. The porridge was warm and had a pinch of salt on it, so she thought that God must have heard her at last. Her knees were healed, but her fingers were chapped and cracked and ablaze with chilblains from milking twenty cows before dawn every morning, including Sundays.

She had kept on saying grace and kneeling in the attic to pray in some small corner of one farm after another, until she was fourteen and knew very well what it meant to have a cold and horny hand shoved up her drawers. It seemed the only kind of attention she could get from farmhand or squire. But as it often saw her better treated and better fed, she decided it must be the way God wanted her to do things.

As she grew older though, and was allowed to walk into God's house on her own two feet, the hands up her drawers had included a clergyman, a deacon and the verger. It had taken a long time but Birdie had finally decided that God only listened to those who had mothers and fathers and there wasn't much point in trying to attract His attention.

She was very sensible about it, realising that He couldn't look into every draughty corner of every mucky cowshed or attic no matter how much He might like to. Obviously girls like her were meant to find their own way to salvation without much help or guidance. Birdie Meadows was about sixteen when she came to that conclusion and decided that was exactly what she would do.

She had seen enough cruelty to know that she must be kind, enough deceit to know she must be sincere, enough treachery to know she must be honest, enough greed to know she must be generous and enough jealousy to know how to be content with her lot.

No one had told her that this added up to a decent human being, which was all God expected her to be, so she left her pew space to the behind of someone more deserving and looked elsewhere for her redemption.

Cooking, cleaning and sewing for Alfred Bramble may not have seemed a very worthwhile calling to most people but it kept a comfortable roof over her head, assured her of three square meals a day and paid enough to save up for the long journey to her true salvation.

Alf was a decent sort as clodhoppers go. He'd never found anyone to marry him because he'd been much to shy to ask and not many would put up with his farmyard manners. But he was kind and easygoing and he didn't expect much more than a bit of company.

Everyone agreed he was no oil painting but no one could say he wasn't a hard worker. Alf Bramble's place was one of the best-kept and most prosperous farms on the Downs, so if she had made his life a little easier and kept him warm a night or two, Birdie was sure wherever and whoever God was, He wouldn't mind if Alf Bramble helped out when He Himself was too busy to look after her.

It would have seemed like a pretty childish philosophy to most people lucky enough to have families and downright sacrilege to those who were on regular speaking terms with the Lord, so Birdie didn't tell anyone about it. She just let them go right on thinking she was a scarlet woman, a sinner the Lord had punished by making her 'not quite right in the head'. But it was her own concept of religion and it had taken a lot of empty bellies, cold nights and lonely tears to arrive at. So she was sticking to it until something better came along.

Then, one day, as though it was a sign that she was on the right track, she had found an advertisement in the *Tunbridge Gazette*. It said in large letters: TRUE SALVATION: DISCOVER THE ONE AND ONLY PATH TO GOD, and underneath 'The True God awaits all who tread the path of UNIVERSAL BLISS'. There were lots of other lovely words about His smiling face and open arms, enlightenment, wisdom and compassion and light. There was lots about light. Light, it seemed, was the most important thing of all. Bright, white and all-embracing.

All this had happened ten years ago and Birdie Meadows was well on her way along the path. Every Wednesday afternoon, which was her day off, and every Sunday morning since, she took the train into Tunbridge and joined the Circle of Universal Bliss in the shabby flat of God's chosen disciple, an Indian gentleman known simply as Mr Puri. They sat on the floor because material things like chairs were not necessary. It was cold and draughty in the winter and hot and stuffy in the summer, but that didn't matter because physical discomfort was a blessing.

There was never anything to eat or drink because deprivation sharpened the spiritual senses. Mr Puri proudly admitted to a galloping case of intestinal worms which he did nothing about because the body was no more than the shell in which the soul must travel.

None of this mattered because Birdie and all the other people who were on the path of Universal Bliss always brought armfuls of flowers to put in front of God's picture, which was about the only piece of furniture Mr Puri possessed.

No one in the group seemed surprised that God was decidedly dark-skinned and appeared to be much better fed than his disciple. They heaped the room with flowers as enthusiastically as Reverend Tuttle's parishioners decorated the pews of his church for the Harvest Festival.

As well as this, they provided the all-important light by hanging glass crystals in the window spaces and burning sticks of incense to purify every corner. Sitting as cross-legged as their joints would let them and chanting endless mantras, the children of Universal Bliss were transported to the burning plains of Rajisthan. It was there that God, whom Mr Puri called 'Guru Ji', had his ashram, and where ultimately, all of them would find their true salvation.

The Hollows

FOR SING, meeting Birdie Meadows was more than a turning point. It opened many new doors where all others had seemed to be closed. The hole in the fence became the gateway to another world and an escape from her loneliness and anxiety. It was a world that she seemed to belong to, far more than she belonged to the life of the Grange estate. Then she met the gypsies of the Hollow.

The Hollow was a thicket of old trees down by the green, slow-flowing river that followed the backyards of the farm labourers' cottages on the edge of the village and adjoined the bottom land of Brambles' farm. The ground between the big willow trees was well trampled by horses and wagon wheels and generations of camping.

The gypsies travelled on, Birdie told her, but came back each year as predictably as the seasons, to pick the hops and work the Kentish orchards. Birdie was the only local woman in Sparrow's Green whom the gypsies allowed to visit the Hollow, which had confirmed the church group's fear for her immortal soul. Now that the pagan wife of Sebastian Masters had also become a regular visitor she was equally doomed.

The swarthy, dark-eyed Romanies lived simply in the open, led by the strongest, bravest man among them and guided by the oldest and wisest woman. They believed in God, but worshipped Him through ancient laws of nature and needed nothing more elaborate than the moon as their altar candle and the open sky as their cathedral.

The gypsies lived by charms and talismans and were ruled by superstition. They were the 'Rom', which simply meant 'man'. No one knew where they had come from, but their Romany language was made up of many others—French, German, Greek and Persian, Syrian, Bulgarian and Hungarian. The English had decided they originally came from Egypt and had named them gypsy accordingly.

The gypsies of the Hollow needed no one but themselves. They built and maintained their own horse-drawn caravans, carved and decorated in the tradition of centuries, and cooked and ate their simple food over open fires. The men were blacksmiths and tin and copper beaters, horse traders and musicians; the women made baskets, mats and clothes pegs and told fortunes at the local fair.

They were left alone to tell their tales and practise their folklore but to God-fearing Christians they were ungodly. Children were warned to stay clear because they were dangerous and unclean and the villagers closed the door on them as quickly as they could, fearful of their curse.

To Sing they felt like family, and when Birdie had first led her across the fields to the smoke of their fires it was as though she had entered the beautiful picture on the bedroom wall and she had somehow been there before. She learned about their folk medicine, listened carefully to the legendary travels and adventures of their ancestors. They honoured her by sharing the delicacy of baked hedgehog, then played fiddle music and danced beside the fire or told stories beneath the stars.

When she worked on the translation of *The Second Sunrise* up in the glittering shrine of the oasthouse, the women would take turns to come and sit, saying little, content to watch in wonder when she took out her brushes to practise the making of images.

Another year passed in this way and Birdie Meadows became a dear and trusted friend. Sing went with her many times to the flat of Mr Puri and sat for a hundred hours on the floor chanting the psychic mantras of Guru Ji. She tried hard to feel close to Birdie's god, smiling from his nest of marigolds, white teeth and black eyes framed by a halo of frizzy black hair.

Everywhere she looked the man who claimed to be the one true god smiled down upon her, just as the Buddha smiled, or the tranquil face of Kuan Yin or the Virgin Mary looking down on her baby Jesus.

The sitting room of Mr Puri, which had nothing to sit on at all, was filled with the god's dark likeness and for a few pennies or a few shillings you could take it home in various sizes to share with it your loneliness or beg it for the release of pain. A miniature of God's face on a tin brooch or a medallion to wear around your neck cost half a pound so that you carried it always, safe in the knowledge that he was with you.

Sing could not help wondering why Guru Ji was so afraid that people might forget him or why those who came to him for help were always old, ill or frightened or troubled. All of them lonely, and lost, striving so hard to find the promise of joy and freedom from fear.

She did not detect the exaltation Birdie had spoken of, her eyes shining with trust, not a trace of the Universal Bliss that surrounded her. There seemed to be only a gnawing desperation instead of the bright light of deliverance.

But there was ash. Grey and powdery ash, fine and final and dead as that from a funeral pyre on the banks of the Ganges. It was living proof, said Mr Puri in his sing-song, Welsh-sounding voice, of God's greatness. 'It is the gift of Guru Ji. And comes to you on the wings of his love.'

He would blow a puff of it from the palm of his hand to settle on the bowed heads of his little group of followers.

The ash, he said, was the panacea of the true believer. If you believed that Guru Ji was God on earth it would cure all ills, solve each problem and answer every question. If you did not believe . . . Mr Puri would turn his palms upward and roll his eyes in a gesture of abject hopelessness, his narrow head rocking from side to side. 'Then it is nothing but dust.'

The precious ash of Guru Ji was handed out in tiny packets in exchange for the small donations that kept Mr Puri's worm-ridden body upright and enabled him to spread the teachings of Universal Bliss. It cured headaches and joint pains and all the other bitter ravages of growing old or being alone.

Sing never asked anyone if it worked because she knew they would say that it did. She had even sprinkled it finely around the rooms of Upper Verdes the way Mr Puri instructed. Tiny, undetectable pinches of it in Sebastian's shoes and inside his pillowcase, he promised, were certain to regain harmony and love and peace. She did not find this hard to believe. It was no different to the Chinese faith in peachwood, the druid's belief in mistletoe or Reverend Tuttle's trust in holy water. But it might as well have been dust for all the difference it made.

Mr Puri's head wobbled patiently, his grey, slowly dying face wearing the perpetual smile of one already at the gates of Nirvana. 'You must hand yourself over completely, my child. Do not ask why. To question why is to put your ego before the word and the power and the love of the one true God.'

She wanted so much to ask more. Surely he, as God's disciple and the truest of believers, need not suffer as he did? Alone with his worm powders and bottles of patent medicine. With his tin bath and paraffin stove, the only energy left alive in him the faith that burned in his black-ringed, sunken eyes. Were worms too great a challenge for Guru Ji?

So much had happened that was bad in Sing's life that she supposed it was just too late for her. She no more belonged on the pathway to Universal Bliss than she did in the family pew at the feet of Reverend Tuttle. She would try harder, she said to the kind little man who meant nothing but good. But she left each time enfolded in great sadness. The little group that came so regularly to the council flat, close to the railway cuttings in the little town of Tunbridge, asked for so little while they chanted endlessly and gave what they could to help supply freshwater taps to remote Indian villages they would never see.

But they had given so much more, Sing thought. The right to think for themselves, to make their own decisions, to have an opinion, the freedom to ask, have faith in themselves. Belief in their own judgements. All of these they had handed over completely in the vibrations of 1000 mantras, conducted through the wasting form of Mr Puri to nourish the plump and glowing god, bedecked with flowers on the scorching plains outside the Pink City of Jaipur.

The Rom

SEBASTIAN HAD taken himself to a corner table in the snug, a small nook with only one table leading off the saloon bar. It was the only place in the Vine where you had a good chance of remaining unnoticed. He had stopped off on his way from the station as he had been doing every evening for more than a year, this time because Cecily had telephoned and asked to see him.

It had become impossible for him to go straight home to Upper Verdes without a drink or two to raise his spirits or deaden his senses—whichever way it happened. He had lost most of his friends, his career seemed at a standstill, his family was estranged and now it appeared he was the laughing stock of the village.

'Hello Sebastian. I hope I haven't kept you waiting.'

Cecily was smartly dressed in a suit of houndstooth tweed and a brown woollen turtleneck that showed off the string of pearls on her ample bosom. She tossed her large leather handbag on the table and stood looking down at him as she drew off her kid gloves a finger at a time.

'I'm sorry for the phone call. I didn't mean to worry you but I simply had to talk.' She took off her brown felt hat and sat down in the chair opposite him. Sebastian ordered her a gin and orange and another pint of bitter for himself. They talked for half an hour before Cecily left in a flurry of indignant tears.

When she had gone he stayed on in the snug until closing time, thinking about what she had said. At first he had wondered if it was just her obvious dislike of Sing, or her protectiveness towards him that caused her such concern. He thought that perhaps she was exaggerating. There was nothing wrong with hop-picking and the gypsies from the Hollow were harmless enough.

That Sing was spending all her time next door in the old oasthouse in the company of Alf Bramble's live-in housekeeper had not surprised or alarmed him either. But Cecily's insistence that there were rumours of an unnatural relationship between Sing and the feeble-minded Birdie Meadows had made him furious.

Cecily was in tears when he had finished explaining what he thought of her jealous and malicious suspicions. He had accused her of trouble-making and called her a vicious old maid, telling her to go on home and report to mother.

After the Vine had closed and barred its doors Sebastian sat in the car till well after midnight, sipping from a quarter of gin he had bought at the bar. The news that Sing was often seen in the gypsy camp by the river and his sister's sly insinuations about goings-on in the oasthouse had given him much of his own to think about. For months now he had accepted the fact that, for the time being at least, the sexual attraction that had been so much a part of his marriage had been pushed aside. His increasing sense of failure and concern for the future had sapped him of all desire; the yearning for her touch was a need he no longer contemplated.

At first he blamed the lack of a posting. Things had not turned out at all as he had planned. The return to England to be married had been intended as a temporary move. He had expected that having a wife with Asian blood would suit him ideally for a position in the Far East and he had put himself forward for every possibility.

For almost three years now those opportunities had come and gone. The Singapore and Sarawak posts had been filled without consideration of his credentials or Sir Duncan Masters' club connections. It was almost as though they were trying to force him to resign from the service.

Doubt and anxiety seemed to have slowly emasculated him. Those things in Sing's sensuality that he had once found so captivating, he had gradually begun to think of as the professional skills and mercenary duties of the whore-house. He thought of her two years in the same house as the Japanese general. The skills that had enraptured him now filled his mind with distrust. He had been a fool. She had married him to escape Hong Kong, he was sure of it.

As their times together in bed had grown fewer and fewer her attempts to interest him had only given strength to the revulsion that was growing within him. She had never loved him. He knew enough about her background to believe she was capable of such deceit.

Didn't she claim her whole affair with the Japanese had been a calculated and patiently executed act of survival? And he had believed her. Even when Peggy Pelham had told him of Sing's deep love affair with the British officer, Hyde-Wilkins, he had dismissed it as unimportant.

How could he have been so blinded by his passion? When Peggy had told him something of the time in Macau and Wan Chai, even that had not concerned him, so complete had been his infatuation.

Now it appeared she enjoyed the company of another who used her body to keep a roof over her head. She preferred the loft of a disused barn and the caravans of gypsies to the home he had provided for her. Sebastian drained the last of the gin and tossed the flat, flask-shaped bottle into the hedge of the car park. Cecily's carefully chosen words burned into him: 'The Reverend Tuttle has good reason to believe there is something not quite as it should be between your wife and this Meadows woman.'

Sebastian switched on the ignition and let off the handbrake. The fact that he found the thought of a lesbian liaison peculiarly exciting he put down to being very drunk.

The unexpectedness of Sebastian's assault on her came as such a surprise to Sing that she resisted him for the first time, evading his clumsiness with an ease that left him dizzy and furious when she locked the door of the bedroom. To defend herself would have meant injuring him, something she could not do and when he forced his way back in she did not fight him.

This was the first time Sing had been violated in such a way. She could think of nothing else, turning her face, unable to look at him. Of all those that could have defiled her, that it should be her husband, the man she had tried so hard to care for.

When his violence failed to move her, Sebastian turned to insults, tense and burning with rage. Sing's eyes only closed the tighter, not a muscle in her body reacting. He held himself upright on his straightened arms so that he could see her face, poised above her, his head thrown back, lost in his own violent ejaculation. Then he sobbed as though in pain, his head fell forward and his hot tears splashed on her breasts.

When he had gone, naked and wordless, she washed herself thoroughly. Methodically, she did everything possible to rid herself of him. She felt no particular anguish or pain at what had happened to her, only a terrible sadness that would not bring tears and the certainty that her life with him was over.

Almost eight weeks later Sing boarded the early morning train to London. She had not seen Sebastian since that night. He had only returned to pack some clothes and fill his briefcase with papers. The letter he had written was filled with remorse. He blamed himself, he said, for everything. He had been drinking heavily. His reasons for such behaviour had been laid out in his neat handwriting one after another. The things he had said to her were unforgivable, he wrote. It would be best if he remained in town indefinitely, until his career took a turn for the better. Until she could forgive him. Until he could forgive himself.

The discovery that she was pregnant was a devastating blow to Sing. The danger and desperation of her early life had branded her with a fierce belief: that no child should be brought into the world through anything but true and abiding love. The love that binds two people in the joint purpose of protecting and guiding, nurturing and developing the child that their passion creates. The kind of love that she somehow knew Ben Deverill had shared with the woman who had given her life. A brave love, the Fish had once called it, that no one could challenge but the gods themselves. The love she had shared with Toby. When she was sure that he had died, she had decided with a calm certainty that love of a man and children could no longer be a part of her life.

Ever since the day on Stanley Beach when she had said yes to Sebastian there had been a sense of guilt in her that lodged like a cocoon waiting to hatch. At times it had pulsed with a kind of energy that threatened to break free on wings of its own. The gratitude she had felt towards him, together with the dangers of Hong Kong that had been fast closing in, had deceived her. She had never lied to him but had been forced to pretend. It was the same thing. She did not blame him.

The doctor had taken care of Sebastian from childhood and had no idea of the wall that had risen between him and his wife. Congratulating her on the excellent state of her health he remarked on what wonderful news it would be for Sir Duncan and Lady Constance.

'I happen to know that they've always hoped for a grandchild,' he chuckled as she dressed behind the screen, unable to stop her hands from shaking.

'Not much chance of expecting Cecily to give them one,' he added facetiously.

Sing had overcome the shock long enough to put on a show for him, making him promise he would say nothing to anyone, least of all a member of the family. She would tell Sebastian in her own way and then they would break the news together. On the train back from Tunbridge Wells she watched the grey damp of the fields and hedgerows passing without signs of life.

In the taxi from Victoria Station she dredged up the resolve that a sleepless night had given her, telling herself that this was the only answer. That a child would bring them together. A fresh start. She had tried through meditation to exorcise doubt from the corners of her mind but as the taxi pulled up outside the St James Club they had crowded in again.

'You all right, luv?' The taxi driver stared from beneath the peak of his cap as he took the fare. 'Want me to wait? They don't take kindly to single ladies in there.'

Sing did not reply as she went up the steps. The driver wasn't sure that she had heard him. He decided to give it a minute. She wouldn't be the first woman he'd seen looking for a bloke who wasn't there.

'Told you so,' he said to himself as in less than a moment she reappeared with a slip of paper in her gloved hand. He didn't like the looks of this young lady. Looked proper poorly, she did. He was out of his cab and had the door open for her, touching his cap as she climbed in.

'Bayswater,' he nodded, glancing at the address on the paper. 'Not far, lady.'

The elderly gentleman at the reception desk of the exclusive residential club seemed quite surprised when she asked for Sebastian.

'Mr Masters Junior has not been with us for some time. This is however, his mailing address. We do take calls for him and he's often here for lunch.'

'I am his wife. I need to contact him rather urgently.'

He scribbled an address carefully on a small square of monogrammed paper taken from a tablet used for messages, blinking behind his spectacles in a mildly quizzical way as he handed it to her.

It was a Sunday morning. By taking the first train she had arrived as early as possible to be sure of finding him with time to talk. She knew that Sir Duncan kept a room at the St James and had assumed that it was where Sebastian had been staying.

She looked out at the almost deserted streets, at people in bus queues, sitting in the windows of cafes or walking their dogs. It puzzled her that Sebastian had not mentioned he had moved. The St James had always been where he could be contacted on the rare occasions she had needed to call him. Although he had never been there, he had always called back.

Twenty minutes later Sing lifted the heavy brass knocker of a green-painted door on the ground floor in a pleasantly quiet street off Bayswater Road. Sebastian's Morgan, its cover clipped down, was parked under a tree outside. This time the cabbie had driven off and apart from a ginger cat that sidled around her feet, the road was deserted.

The distinct smell of brewed coffee came from somewhere close by. A brass bell-plate in the shape of a flower was set into the brickwork beside the door. She waited a moment before pressing it, hearing the soft purr of a buzzer echo emptily inside. She bent to pick up the Sunday newspapers left on the step.

It was a moment before muffled footfalls thumped on carpeted stairs and the pit-patting of bare feet on linoleum approached the door. It was opened by a young man, a towel tucked around his narrow hips. He was about nineteen, fair-haired and fresh skinned. She was conscious of a light sprinkling of cinnamon freckles across the bridge of his nose onto his high coloured cheeks and the tops of his shoulders. He stared at her blankly with pale hazel eyes.

'Who is it, Dennis?' Over his shoulder she saw Sebastian descending the stairs in pajamas and a dressing gown she had never seen before.

It took a long time for Sir Duncan Masters to speak when Sing had finished. She had told him everything as honestly and accurately as her state of mind would allow. The night of Sebastian's drunken assault, her confirmed pregnancy, her visit to London and her discovery of the flat off Bayswater Road. He listened without interruption, looking out of the window, his briar pipe cold in his hand.

Finally, he said in a voice thick with emotion 'My dear girl,

I am most awfully sorry to hear this most distressing news. I can only say to you that if what you tell me is true, and unhappily I am certain that it must be, you will have my every support.'

He stood, suddenly older, his energy and humour seeming to have slipped from him, as dead as the comfort of his favourite pipe. He remained standing, staring, unseeing, through the leafless garden, rubbing the polished bowl of the briar against his palm.

'Tell me what you want me to do,' he said brokenly.

'I will have his child and I will say nothing to anyone. But you must allow me to have it in my own way. In the place of my choosing and among people I trust.'

He looked deeply troubled. 'But surely . . . this is where . . . this is your home?'

'I have no home and I have no husband. I will not stay here. You must trust me as I must trust you. At all times you will know where to find me.'

Sir Duncun turned from the window to look at her, his eyes filled with sorrow and concern. 'I must do as you say. I have every faith in you.'

'When the baby is born, I must return to the only place I can ever belong . . . but I cannot . . . I will not take the child with me. This will be my only child, as Sebastian was and will always be my only husband. There will never be another.'

She held out her hand to him and he took it gratefully. 'You must not blame your son. It was I who could see the furthest, I who should have known. I should never have come here.'

Sir Duncan drew her to him and held her close to hide his anguish.

'Now,' said Sing, 'I will make tea and we will talk of the child's future. It is all that matters.'

The months of Sing's confinement were spent in the gypsy camp, beneath the willows of the Hollow. She had gone to them and they had welcomed her. Her child was born among the people she felt closest to, the Rom, worshippers of the moon, who understood the way of nature, striving for nothing but its understanding. She had ignored the entreaties of Sebastian's family. She did not need the clucking tongues and prayers from those who had ignored her. They were all powerless to persuade her and no one was allowed into the Hollow uninvited.

Sebastian made no attempt to deny the homosexual tendencies

that had haunted him since Stanley Prison and had lost any right he may have had to an opinion. Her silence about what she had discovered was honoured and in exchange his mother and sister had been forced to stay away from the Hollow and to leave her undisturbed.

She accepted with gratitude the kindness of Birdie Meadows and her friends the gypsies, their simple care and attention as her time came closer. Above all she recalled the dreadful stab of fear she had felt when the gypsy women told her she had given birth to a girl. Then she had realised through her pain that this was not China. Anxiety had been quickly calmed by the certainty of her daughter's safety, the assurance of her future.

She had not seen or touched the baby girl and had only heard its first cry. Clinging onto Birdie's hand, her eyes shut tight, she had waited until the gypsy had left the caravan, taking the bundle with her.

The agreement drawn up by Sir Duncan's lawyers was simple and direct. The child would be taken at birth as a ward of the master's estate. It laid down that Sir Duncan and Lady Constance would be the legal guardians, providing care, education, and all the rights and privileges of the family name.

On reaching the age of twenty-one the child would receive a settlement in keeping with her position as a member of the master's family. In exchange Sing had signed a rider insisted upon by Lady Constance that prohibited her from making contact with the child throughout her lifetime. The contract also stated that if she should break the covenant under any circumstances the agreement would no longer be honoured.

Sing trusted no paper, or the people who put the words on it, but she had learned to have faith in Sebastian's father. His bluff good humour had cheered her on the several occasions he had visited her during her confinement, by special invitation, filling the warm caravan with the aroma of his pipe. She had found in him a patient and enduring understanding and a sense of obligation towards her that came before the sadness and disappointment he must have felt towards his only son. In turn she had honoured her promise to say nothing of what she had discovered in the flat off Bayswater Road.

It had not been a difficult decision for Sing to make. It was a time when the Chinese blood of her mother told her clearly what to do. It was simply good business. If she signed the paper her daughter would have everything. Health, comfort, happiness, opportunity. All the protection of a titled name. If she did not, the child would have nothing. Sing had become accustomed to being torn between the emotions and contradictions of two separate worlds. It left no room for doubt.

At twenty-five she must begin her life again and could give the child nothing. The discovery of Sebastian's homosexuality had closed all doors on reconciliation. For herself she had asked the cost of a ticket to Hong Kong and sufficient money to live for one year. Duncan Masters had reluctantly agreed, insisting that she was entitled to much more.

She had asked only one other thing. That her daughter be named Nova, after the dim star that will one day light the sky. Sir Duncan had promised and, apart from a tearful farewell from Amelia Monk and Sweet William, his had been the only hand she had shaken when she left Sparrow's Green. Except at the station, when the musk-scented folds of Birdie Meadows' rose-pink sari had enfolded her with the tinkling of tiny bells. Faithful Birdie, ever filled with belief in the laws of karma, always by Sing's side in those last weeks, a symbol of lasting friendship, as she whispered. 'Om tat sat . . . God alone is. As much as I can, I will watch over her. Om soham . . . he am I, I am he. God go with you, Sing. I know we will meet again—it is our fate.'

PART · IX

Hong Kong, 1950

There is a place that I know.
The sun is warmer there.
The water sweeter to taste.
Rice grows better there.
The ox works harder
and never tires.
At the end of the day
that is where I must be.

MASTER TO-TZE

• IMAGE FOR DETERMINATION •

Alistair Pidcock

ALISTAIR PIDCOCK'S real Christian name was Albert. He had changed it to suit the profession he had chosen. Albert Pidcock had not sounded quite right for one of Hong Kong's best known and most successful lawyers. He had also added his brother's name to the polished brass plate outside the entrance to the building: Pidcock and Pidcock sounded so much grander than just Albert Pidcock. The fact that his brother Thomas had remained in Enfield, England, to continue running the family butchery did not matter. By making him a partner with the stroke of a pen and an insignificant share of the proceeds, Pidcock and Pidcock, Hong Kong Limited had opened for business in 1935. That Tommy Pidcock had never travelled further than Margate and was perfectly happy making pork pies and sausages mattered not a bit.

Alistair Pidcock was a classic Hong Kong success story. Coming out as a bank boy with the Hong Kong and Shanghai, he had quickly seen the opportunities for an enterprising young man and begun making his own way at a time when a cool head for figures was of tremendous advantage. Later he had returned to England to study law and came back with sufficient credentials to set up his practice. At almost fifty-five years of age, in 1950 he rested on the laurels of a long and successful career, looking after only a few of the firm's oldest and most valued clients and dividing the rest of his time among the bar of the Hong Kong Club, the Happy Valley race-track and the Fanling Golf Club.

He had become a large, Pickwickian man with a fleshy face of mottled pink that shone healthily in a frame of crisp white hair. He wore a pleasant expression of permanent surprise, as though he had never quite been able to come to terms with his own good fortune. His trademarks of success were well known to be a heavy gold watch chain stretched across the comfortable width of his dark-suited waistline and an ever-fresh carnation in his buttonhole.

Ben Deverill had been one of his very first clients and they had quickly become firm friends. Each had shown the same fire and determination in those early days of the Crown colony and they had soon shared each other's lasting trust. It was that trust which made him so very careful about Ben Deverill's affairs and when Sebastian Masters had first brought the young woman to see him he had been prudently cautious.

Ben had confided the nature of Li X'ia's tragic death and the disappearance of their child. Alistair observed his friend's terrible grief and vowed to take personal care of his Hong Kong business when Ben closed the Repulse Bay house and left for Shanghai. Now the young woman who claimed to be Ben Deverill's daughter was back in Hong Kong and waiting outside to see him. Alistair gave his thick, horn-rim spectacles a careful polish, adjusted his boutonniere and buzzed his secretary to send her in.

He rose as the door opened and strode around his desk to take her hand in his. 'My dear Mrs Masters, welcome back. Sir Duncan has written to me, of course. It was good of your husband to recommend us.'

'It was I who recommended you, Mr Pidcock. I am told you have taken good care of my father's affairs for a very long time. I would be most grateful if you would also manage mine.' Sing took the comfortable chair Alistair offered her as she spoke.

'I'd be more than delighted to do so, Mrs Masters.'

'May I ask you to think of me as Miss Deverill? I'd like the divorce proceedings to begin immediately.'

Alistair cleared his throat, nodding politely. 'I understand perfectly, Miss Deverill. Your father-in-law . . .' He checked himself. 'Sir Duncan has given me full instructions on your behalf and all proceedings have begun amicably.'

Sitting back, he pressed his fingertips together, contemplating her as he spoke. Alistair Pidcock had never married but he was a great admirer of beautiful women and this one was breathtaking. Whatever had gone wrong in England, he thought, it certainly hadn't done her any lasting harm. Her deep chestnut hair was styled in the latest fashion and the rest of her grooming was impeccable. When he had first met her he had detected no resemblance to the dark countenance of Ben Deverill but now he was not at all sure.

She was certainly Eurasian, with all the best of what that could mean—those quite incredible eyes and the determined, slightly square set of her jaw. In particular the air of strength about her, the superb figure that her perfectly tailored suit fitted so beautifully. Eminently feminine yet with a faintly masculine grace. Yes, he decided, this woman could very well be Ben Deverill's lost child.

'My beginnings will be small,' she was saying, suddenly making him aware that he had been staring. 'But I intend to change that.'

'I'm quite sure you will.' Alistair smiled. 'In the meantime, I assure you Sir Duncan has arranged adequate funds . . .'

Sing stopped him short. 'I wish to buy the Villa Formosa. I am aware that it is held in trust and that I have no proof of legal claim.' She lifted her eyes to his and Alistair Pidcock felt as though he was melting in front of her.

'But I ask you in the light of my claim and the right of reasonable doubt, that you give me the first option to buy when the property comes on to the market, and that you help me to open a trust account to that end. No one else must have the house my father built.'

Alistair spread his hands in a gesture of mute approval but thrust out his lower lip thoughtfully. 'Most certainly. Although I should warn you that the land alone . . . well, Repulse Bay has become Hong Kong's most salubrious address since your father . . . . since Ben Deverill built the villa.'

'I know,' replied Sing quietly, taking a folded bank cheque from her handbag and handing it to him. She followed the cheque with a weighty bag of black velvet which she emptied onto the desk in front of him. A collection of jewellery tumbled out.

'I would like to sell all of this and add the proceeds to the trust fund.'

Alistair reached across and selected a superb blue sapphire ring. 'There are some very beautiful pieces here,' he said, trying not to show his surprise.

'I know,' agreed Sing. 'I'd be most grateful if you would arrange to sell them. I'd like to hold my option with this amount and to add to it as and when I can.'

He put the cheque on the spotless blotter before him, hardly giving it a glance. 'That would be perfectly in order,' he said.

'I'm sure we can find a reputable dealer and fetch a fair price,' Alistair assured her, then added, 'Miss Deverill, I should perhaps point out that my instructions have never included management or maintenance of the property. I'm afraid it must have fallen into considerable disrepair.'

Sing stood up and offered him her hand. 'I suppose it has, Mr Pidcock. But I'm quite sure my father built it to last forever and I intend to see that it does.'

He leaned back, looking at her, then seemed to come to a decision.

'Miss Deverill, I wonder if you are aware that the Deverill estate involves a very great deal of money? A very great deal indeed.'

He watched her response closely. Sing returned his steady scrutiny without blinking. He went on. 'Several of the Cloud Line vessels were lost during the war, confiscated by the Japanese or sunk in one action or another. Three were successfully diverted to Britain where they were eventually sold by Deverill's London agent, a man named Nathaniel Barcoo. Apparently, Mr Barcoo received a directive from the Head Office in Shanghai in 1939, at the same time as I was given instruction from the same source. The directive signed over the entire European operation to him in the event of Ben Deverill's demise.'

He paused again. She looked politely interested, no more. 'With the outbreak of war and the death of Ben Deverill, Barcoo wound up Deverill's European business and retired on the proceeds. He must have been a very frugal man because he spent very little. In fact, through his astute investment and careful management of the funds he built them into a very large sum.'

'Mr Pidcock, I'm sure you are an extremely busy man and I appreciate the confidence but such details do not seem to be any of my business.' Sing spoke with the utmost respect and consideration.

'If you are able to prove to me that you are indeed who you claim to be, then it may be very much your business, dear lady.' He leaned forward to emphasise his point.

'Nathaniel Barcoo died in 1948 at the age of eighty-six and left something in the region of £1,000,000 sterling and a well situated apartment in Knightsbridge. On his death this entire amount, including the residential property, was turned over to us to be added to the Deverill trust. So you see, Ben Deverill's rightful heir stands to inherit two very substantial and completely separate fortunes.'

When he had finished, Sing responded, measuring her words carefully. 'I am grateful for your frankness, Mr Pidcock. It indicates to me that you do not entirely disbelieve my story. But as I now know that I shall never be able to present proof of my true identity in any legal sense, it is all rather irrelevant to me. All I ask and all that interests me at the moment, is the house my father built; and that I shall pay for in full, whatever its price.'

They talked for a few moments longer, then she gave him a smile so full of warmth and gratitude, a smile so utterly winning, that Alistair Pidcock suddenly felt like young Albert again.

Completely disarmed he watched her leave his office with profound regret that their meeting was over so soon. From the moment the door closed he was quite certain that she was indeed who she claimed to be.

Peggy Pelham was moved to tears of delight when Sing telephoned her from the Peninsula Hotel. When they met in the lobby, she embraced her like a long lost daughter. She asked no questions of Sebastian or why she hadn't heard for so long.

'It's so very nice to see you, my dear,' she managed, reaching for a handkerchief.

'And you, Auntie, I missed you . . . but I could not write.'

Peggy was delighted to see how marvellous Sing looked. The past four years had not aged her. Her looks were if anything even more arresting than she remembered. Peggy noticed that Sing still wore no makeup except to accentuate those extraordinary eyes. Those same smokey, unreachable depths observed her affectionately across the table.

To Sing, Peggy appeared almost unrecognisable. The thick greying hair that she had always dressed so carefully was white and thin, worn straight and cut short in the neck. She seemed slightly stooped and her intelligent eyes were magnified by a pair of steel-rimmed spectacles. She was dressed very simply and looked slightly out of place among the lofty marble pillars of the famous lobby.

Peggy was distressed to hear of the failure of Sing's marriage. It was a subject they only touched on briefly and it was obvious to her that Sing did not wish to dwell upon it. Instead, she was hungry for news of Freddy Fong and Doctor Sun, both of whom had been known to Peggy Pelham at the end of the war. They too had been branded as collaborators and she had done all that she could to clear their names. She was pleased to tell Sing that Freddy Fong had survived the post-war confusion by going to America at the invitation of someone he had known in Shanghai. Someone in the film business, Peggy thought.

He had been back in Hong Kong for two years now and had opened a film production company in Causeway Bay. Doctor Sun had also survived the mindless weeks of violence that had followed the Japanese surrender. From the moment Sing had been rescued from the godown he and his family had been protected.

Peggy had seen to it that they were acknowledged for their part in the passing of information to the village of Pok Choy Lam.

'It did no good.' She sighed. 'Even repeated reports in the Chinese and English newspapers, clearing their names along with yours and Freddy's and others who had risked their lives.' Peggy shook her head.

'It seems Chinese public opinion had made up its mind and nothing the gwai-lo could say would change it. Protesting their innocence only made things worse.'

'What happened to them?' Sing was almost afraid to ask.

Peggy quickly reassured her. 'They are fine now, so far as I know. Doctor Sun closed his shop and took the family to China. He may be back in Hong Kong by now.'

They talked for over two hours, too excited to eat. Peggy never once mentioned her husband's name and Sing did not ask about him.

She had decided to stay on, Peggy said with a tired smile. There was nothing in England for her but the empty house in Exeter and eventually the slow disintegration to an Eastbourne retirement home. She was fortunate, she added with a lift of her chin, to have been found so useful in the caretaker administration of Hong Kong.

It had not lasted though, she said. Whitehall had sent out a whole new batch of civil service bureaucrats to take over from the temporary military government and from the few civilians the military had engaged as advisers. The 'new broom' had little interest in those who had experienced the workings of Hong Kong before Christmas 1941. This was to be a new Hong Kong. A Hong Kong that depended entirely on the mass of Chinese who had crossed the border ahead of Chairman Mao and could now apply themselves to the business of making money.

It had left no room for people like her, said Peggy. She feared she was considered something of a relic, left over from a past era that was best forgotten and seldom talked about. The fact that Hong Kong had for three years and eight months been a part of the Japanese Empire, subject to great humiliation and suffering, had been placed in the category of a bad dream, which once awoken from was best ignored, as though it had never happened.

She had her pension, Peggy said, and the flat on Kennedy Road, and there were still a few people that she knew and plenty to be done for a willing volunteer in the care and education of refugees from communism.

'Not quite like the old days, my dear,' she said a little sadly, as she looked around the magnificent lobby filled with overseas visitors and those who just liked to be seen there. 'You know, I haven't been here since the ball in 1941. How much has changed.'

Sing did not know what to expect when she pulled up in the taxi outside the Everspring herb shop. She was almost afraid to look, so much had changed since she had been dragged from this place and through these streets by a screaming mob.

It was still there, as solid and immovable as it had always seemed to her. Its front windowsill was again filled with glass jars and stone crocks, displaying branches of rare deer antler, rows of desiccated sea-horses, petrified turtles and snakes preserved in liquor.

Inside, the blackwood customers' chair had been replaced, the shelves were stocked with their rows of mysterious containers. The coloured spittoon was back in position, the large abacus stood beside the mortar and pestle and the whole, cluttered scene was illuminated by a new dragon lantern, dusty but not yet as grimed with age as the other had been.

The strands of threaded bamboo parted and Doctor Sun stepped through. He stood in front of the neat lines of herb drawers that she had seen ripped open and emptied onto the floor the last time she had stood in his shop. It took him a moment to recognise her. As he did, he pressed his palms together in the old-fashioned way of greeting.

'Siu Sing. Little sister. It is you.' He came from behind the counter and took her hand in both of his. 'It is a great joy to see you here again. We did not know what had become of you. The gods have been good to us. Please come and sit. We must drink tea together.'

Three hours later and in gathering dusk Sing crossed the harbour to the Peninsula. Aboard the Star ferry, looking across the darkening water to the brightly lit streets and neons of Kowloon she could not believe that she was back. That this was the place she had left almost five years earlier, its harbour littered with sunken ships, the district of Wan Chai flattened by American bombs, the task of rebuilding just begun.

Now, Wan Chai was an electric jungle of bar signs. As the taxi passed up Lockhart Road she saw the sign of the nine blue dragons still rampant, dominating the teashop and ballroom of Three-thumbs Poon and on the corner of Hennessy Road, the Happy Butterfly still flapped its multicoloured wings. She wondered if Hand-trolley

Lulu was still the mama san and if Firecracker Lily still walked the streets in search of talent.

It was the military presence that surprised her the most. Just as she had last seen these streets peopled by Japanese patrols, they were now filled with British soldiers, who lined the footpaths waiting to cross the jam of traffic, walked in and out of the bars in pairs and groups, arm-in-arm with gaudily dressed bargirls.

Peggy Pelham had told her that the British Labour Government of 1949 had sent 30,000 troops to protect the colony against the threat of the all-conquering communist armies. They had no definite reason to suspect that Mao Tze-tung, the charismatic peasant from Hunan, was intending to take back Hong Kong in his People's Revolution, but an election was looming in Britain and to risk the tiny island would cost votes.

The tall slatted fins of a four-masted junk cut across the bows of the ferry and into her thoughts. A dark mass with hardly a light showing, engineless, it crept across their path, the junkmaster at the tiller using superb seamanship to see how close he could come to a collision. The ferry's engines shuddered into reverse, rattling the rows of seats and shaking every timber. The captain's curses were loud from the wheelhouse above as his siren blurted a warning.

Sing could not deny a feeling of admiration for the plucky junkmaster. To her he signified all that was old and new and rare and exciting about Hong Kong, standing fast in the face of odds, risking everything to improve his lot. She knew of the Tanka superstition called 'cutting the head off the ghost'. The Tanka believed that the closer a junk could sail to an oncoming vessel the better its fortunes would be—the bows of the other craft cutting off any ill fortune that may be following and neatly transferring unwanted evil spirits or bad joss to the other vessel. It was typical of the risk and reward that had built this place she had returned to and it signified her own resolution to bury the past and begin life anew.

Doctor Sun was another typical example of Chinese tenacity. At his table she had learned that since the war he and his sons had built a thriving business. Thanks to her, and the luck of the gods, he said, his godowns had been left untouched. His stock had brought great profit after the Yut Boon Jai had been defeated and he had taken his family to China to set up a profitable source of supply.

His two oldest sons would soon be ready to open shops of

their own and were already running a successful trading business in rare and expensive herbal and medicinal products. They called themselves the Double Elephant Trading Company.

'You risked all to protect us. We will never forget,' Doctor Sun had said. 'We have set aside a share for you and you will always be welcome to join us.'

The throb of the ferry's engines was like a heartbeat beneath her. This was Hong Kong, building again from disaster just as Doctor Sun and so many like him had done and just as she must do. At that moment she knew that her decision to return had been the right one.

A day later Sing went looking for Freddy Fong and found Venture Films tucked away in a crowded street close to the Causeway Bay typhoon shelter. The polished brass plate that told her she had found him looked out of place in the maze of open-fronted shops beside an entrance barred by the familiar half-open steel trellis. It was next to a restaurant specialising in Shanghai food and the smell of the shredded freshwater eels dry-frying in garlic followed her along the narrow corridor to a closed metal door and a flashing red light. A sign read, QUIET PLEASE. SHOOTING IN PROGRESS.

When the light clicked off she opened the door cautiously and peered inside. Freddy Fong was behind a mounted still camera, absorbed in directing three young Chinese girls on an improvised stage. Lights were set around it and she could make out two or three shadowy figures behind the stands. No one noticed her and she stayed outside the light to watch.

An hour later over a table in the Shanghai chophouse Freddy's moon face beamed across at Sing with deep affection. 'I can't believe it's you, kid.' His American accent was even stronger than she remembered.

'You never looked better. Where the hell have you been? I thought that sonofabitch Toshido took you with him to the land of his ancestors.'

He listened intently to her story, nodding and shaking his round head as his chopsticks picked up sliced eel and rolled it in rich, peppery sauce. 'Kid,' he said, when she paused to eat. 'You've come to the right place at the right time.'

The words tumbled from him with the old enthusiasm and energy she remembered as Freddy told her of the fortune he was well on the way to making. How a couple of advertising agencies had been chased out of Shanghai to set up in Hong Kong. He had an American buddy, he said, whom he had met in Shanghai before the war. Sam Danovich was a foreign correspondent for U.S. newswire services and Freddy had become his press photographer.

They had covered many stories together, including the Japanese attacks on Shanghai and the coming of the Kuomintang. Sam was now an independent producer in Hollywood with some great documentary credits to his name. He had paid Freddy's way out of Hong Kong just ahead of the lynch mob in 1944. They'd spent two years working together in Los Angeles and were now partners in Venture Films. Sam had put up the money to set Freddy up in Hong Kong. Sam had once been in the advertising business and knew there was money to be made there. A still photograph studio at first, to supply the ad agencies with glamour shots, then, television was on the way and theatre commercials for the movie screens. Freddy's enthusiasm was catching.

'Sam's a great guy. He's coming to Hong Kong once I'm set up.' He leaned forward, his voice confidential.

'There's a fortune to be made here in the ad business and Sam and me are first in. Then it's movies. The big time. Some rich Chinese named Run Run Shaw and his brother are set up in the New Territories but they're making sword movies. I'm talking about documentaries for the whole of Asia. A few years down the track and it's television commercials. Maybe even a feature. The sky's the limit, kid.'

He paused to fill her teacup and then his own. 'I need help, and you're just the gal for the job. What'd you say?'

Sing smiled, filled with great affection for the round little man from Shanghai.

'Freddy, I don't know the first thing about the film business.'

'You'll learn, and fast. What you've got, I need. Looks, style, class.' He lifted his cup to her.

'You get the business and I produce the goods. Between us we'll build the biggest production house in South-East Asia. You and me and Sam.'

Sing felt uncomfortable about her hesitation. Freddy Fong was one of her few old friends. One who had risked his own safety, perhaps his life, to stand up for her. Now he was offering her another chance, just when she needed one. How could she disappoint him?

'But Freddy, it will take a lot more than that for me to be of any use to you,' she said gently, raising her hands to emphasise her point. 'I can't type, I've hardly ever written a letter of any importance . . . I don't know the first thing about films. I just wouldn't know where to begin as a secretary.'

A dish of snowpeas arrived, mixed with mermaids' tresses, the dark green shredded seaweed that went so well with eels. Freddy helped her to them generously.

'Who said anything about secretary?' he enquired, his eyes brimming with excitement. 'I can get a local gal for next to nothing. No kid, I need a partner. Someone to bring in the business . . . to give the joint a little class. What'd you say, Sing? Is it a deal?'

Sing let her hands drop in a gesture of surrender, making one more attempt to make Freddy see the sense of what she said. 'Freddy,' she began firmly. 'I've spent most of the past five years locked away in an English village . . . I've hardly spoken Chinese in all that time.' She shook her head. 'I . . . I can't even drive a car.'

Freddy held up his five spread fingers and ticked them off one at a time. 'One—being in England gave you class and in this town that gives you a head start. Two—you'll be speaking Cantonese like a native in a week. Three—I'll teach you to drive this weekend. Four—you've got guts and you've been through the mill. There's nothing you can't do, kid. Five—say yes and let's get started.' He held out his hand across the table. 'Shake, partner. Welcome aboard.'

Sam Danovich, 1952

As a younger man, Sam Danovich had been a whizz in the world of big-time advertising. There were still those in the business who thought of him as a legend and others who changed colour at the sound of his name. In a few meteoric years in the beginnings of the industry he had become famous for creating some of the most brilliant and successful print campaigns ever to come out of the fledgeling Madison Avenue.

He was also remembered for three things—being fired by more

agencies than anyone else in the shortest possible time; winning more awards and making much more money than anyone else at his level; but, more than anything else, he was remembered for 'The Horse's Ass'.

It was a simple story but one that took courage and conviction far beyond that of most successful creative directors and brought tears of joy to those he had left behind. Sam had been holding down the highest paid creative spot for the biggest ad agency in the U.S.A, which meant the biggest in the world. Silberman and Gold had gone after the richest piece of business to ever come up for grabs and young Sam Danovich was their man.

It was a mid-western brewery account worth over fifty million a year to the shop that won its business. Out of the ten top agencies in New York, Sam's presentation put the right kind of smiles on the right faces at exactly the right moment. It got him a raise in salary that could see him retire at thirty-five, more power than the President and he had fun running all over the country making some great beer commercials for the cinema screen, and the new medium of screen advertising.

The trouble had come a year or so later when Sam had discovered that the red-necked beer baron he was making richer with his genius was not a very nice man. He molested secretaries and fired them if they didn't like it. His taste was in his underpants; he was a racist and a bigot.

In fact he had turned out to be a bullying, unappreciative, untrustworthy son-of-a-bitch with the creative judgement of a horse's ass.

By the time Sam was ready to present the campaign that had cost half a million to produce and taken an army of talented people six months to put together, he had decided there were better things to do in life than work for sons-of-bitches like the beer baron.

The boardroom in the glass tower of Silberman and Gold was filled to capacity with agency executives and yes-men from the beer company with the S.O.B. at the head of the table. Sam's campaign unfolded on the screen and the smiles of everyone in the room grew wider and wider, until the last beautifully-crafted scene drew to a magnificent close.

Without warning, with a suddenness that kept the smiles riveted in place, the screen was filled with the rear end of a horse, beautifully lit and in needle-sharp black and white. There was a communal intake of breath as it gently lifted its tail and galvanised the assembly with an amplified blast that shook the sound speakers. The words

'THE END' rolled up and when the lights came on Sam Danovich had left for good.

Sam had never regretted the drop in pay or the changes that one moment of glory had cost him. As a freelance journalist and documentary producer he had travelled the world and found that it suited him far more than the gloss and sham that was fast taking hold of Madison Avenue and that there was much to be seen outside the concrete canyons of New York.

As a war correspondent, the name he had made for seeing things no one else could see, doing things no one else would do and going places no one else would go, gave him a flying start when he landed in Hollywood after the war. His newsreel documentaries out of South-East Asia had won him international acclaim and it was a natural next step into feature-length motion pictures.

There were very few places Sam Danovich had not been in the years that followed the incident of the horses's ass, but Hong Kong was one of them. If all that Freddy Fong said about it was true, there was nowhere better to set up a studio and base his plans for a South-East Asia operation. As an independent he now worked out of any L.A. facility he chose and there wasn't a film lot in Hollywood where he wasn't welcome. But Sam had his eye on the Orient again. To him, there was nowhere to match its vibrance, its colour and excitement, wherever you pointed a camera.

According to Freddy, Hong Kong was picking up the pieces fast. International business, he had assured Sam, was moving back in with a vengeance and production costs were a fraction of those in Hollywood. Now was the time to move in and set up before anyone else did.

Sam owed Freddy Fong. He also counted him among his very few trusted friends. The garrulous little Shanghainese had talked them out of some very tight spots when they worked together in China and Sam had never forgotten it. He hadn't thought twice about flying Freddy out of Hong Kong when the Japs had surrendered and he'd needed help. The proposition of a film studio based in Hong Kong with a live-wire like Freddy in control made a lot of sense to Sam; especially as it would give him the chance to pursue a long-held dream.

For two years he had been developing a feature film script called *The Red Lotus*, to be shot all over Asia with its main location in Hong Kong. An impossibility out of L.A., it was a sound proposition in Hong Kong. As an independent producer and director, it would be his first feature film. The consuming fascination that the Far East had always held for him and the passion he felt for all things oriental, added up to *The Red Lotus*. The excitement and the mystery, the magnificence and the squalor, the tranquillity and the violence came together in the story.

The title came from the Buddhist belief in the legend of a lotus flower that blooms blood-red once every 1000 years for a single day. Those who look upon it, the legend claimed, would remain forever young. To Sam it signified the ultimate goal. The eternal search for immortality and the unexplained. The making of it had become an obsession.

No Hollywood studio would back him. Too big a risk, they said. Although Bogart, Lorre, Greenstreet and Bendix were making box-office success with adventure stories set in the Orient, Sam Danovich was a documentary maker. Sam had decided to finance *Red Lotus* himself. It meant putting up every cent he owned plus his reputation and his credibility as an independent. It was the kind of risk that fitted the story.

As the DC3 came in low over Kowloon to make its hair-raising descent onto the finger of landing strip poking into Victoria Harbour, Sam felt the adventure begin. Looking down he could see amahs hanging washing out on the flat, square rooftops, so close he saw the upturned face of an old man watering pots of yellow chrysanthemums on another. Rooftops were crammed so tightly together they seemed joined by the moving lines of alleyways and traffic-thronged streets.

With a banking turn the plane was over water again, and this time he fancied he could smell the dark, muddy green of the harbour. Boats of every description were ploughing its short, choppy waves, the white tails of their wakes crossing each other, perilously close. Big, wallowing junks slapped into the swell, riding under the square spread of their sails, seeming to get nowhere, yet they'd sailed 1000 miles of coastline. Among and around them was the putter-putter of sampans and wallah wallahs taking the spray, children playing and dogs barking on their wet decks. The belly of the DC3 seemed to skim their mastheads as it dropped like a hawk onto the runway.

Sing had no idea what to expect as she stood among the crowd waiting for the Pan Am flight from Guam. It was two years since she had joined Venture Films and Freddy had at last felt he was ready to show his silent partner what they had built. She had never met an American, but had heard a great deal of talk about them. Most of it from Birdie Meadows and Amelia Monk who claimed they had descended upon the English countryside like hordes of Viking raiders. Instead of horned helmets and warclubs, they had worn glamorous uniforms and used candy, chewing gum and nylon stockings to rape and pillage.

At least, that was the way Mrs Monk had put it with an indignant sniff. According to her: there hadn't been a mother or daughter safe within miles of them. 'Left the place littered with broken hearts and broken hymens, if you'll excuse the crude expression. And enough unwanted children to fill the schoolyard of every village they invaded.'

Birdie's version had been a little different. She had spoken about the Yankee soldiers and airmen with a sigh. They were real gents, she said, at least everyone she had met. Charm the pants right off a girl they could, and talk about romantic.

They were talked about by the Chinese as the 'mung-cha-cha,' the slightly crazy, whose only value was to be cheated of their pay when they visited the bars of Wan Chai. This had been confirmed by Freddy's parting words as she left for the airport. 'You can't miss him. Nuggety guy. About your height. Crazy son-of-a-gun. He's got an eye for good looking gals. I wrote him all about you. Just stand there and he'll find you.'

Sing had decided not to rely on Freddy's description and had written the American's name on a large piece of cardboard which she held in front of her. As good as his word, Freddy had long ago taught her to drive and she had driven herself to the airport in his battered TR3.

Sam Danovich was almost the last out of customs. Freddy had been right. She just couldn't miss him. The American came through the arrival gate like a well-oiled tank. He seemed twice the size of anyone around him and was made to appear even bigger by a plaid sports coat of broad patterns and loud colours. A battery of cameras was slung from his wide shoulders and he held a huge suitcase in each hand, staring about him like a lost child. Sing had made up her mind to establish the right relationship from their first meeting. She stood her ground, the sign plainly in view and waited for the heavy-set man to notice her. It only took seconds and he strode over to where she stood, dumping the cases and holding out a large, meaty hand.

'You are Sing Deverill. Right? Couldn't be anyone else.' The hand held onto hers. As he shook it he gave her a big friendly grin. 'Sam Danovich . . . a real pleasure to meet you, lady.'

'Mr Fong sends his apologies. He has a shoot he could not cancel.'

'That's Freddy. Always open for business,' he murmured, letting his eyes travel quickly over her in a fast appraisal that was not offensive.

His voice was surprisingly gentle; it didn't seem to match the rest of him. She had expected him to boom like a drum. She found it vaguely reassuring.

'You're even more outstanding than he wrote me,' he said, in the same level tone of genuine approval.

Sing withdrew her hand, holding his eyes with a look she hoped was professional. She was wearing simple work clothes and had made no attempt to put on makeup.

His clean shaven face was perspiring slightly and his easy grin showed strong, slightly uneven teeth. It faded awkwardly when she showed no response to his flattery. Fair, gingery hair had been cropped close to his head and he passed his hand over it to hide his uncertainty.

'Welcome to Hong Kong, Mr Danovich. If you'll follow me.' Sing turned and led the way to the waiting car.

He picked up the cases and followed her slim, upright figure. 'It's a pleasure to be here, ma'am,' he said, the smile still in his voice.

Sam Danovich's old love affair with Asia had begun again the moment his plane came in over Kowloon. And a new one began the moment he laid eyes on the girl called Sing Deverill. Being in love was what living was all about and Sam saw to it that he was seldom out of it. Not the life-long, heart-breaking, tragic kind of love that rules your life, but the fun-loving, 'lets have it all while it lasts' kind that puts a smile on your face and keeps it there until the next one.

He hadn't always felt that way and his alimony payments proved it. Two ex-wives were only rich because of his success but he considered half of everything he earned was fair trade for the freedom it had bought him.

He had never felt it more strongly than he did over his first three weeks in Hong Kong with Sing Deverill as his guide. To him she had taken on the identity of his dream. She *was* the Red Lotus—found once in many lifetimes, mysterious, utterly unique. Strangely untouchable.

Sam was booked into Sunning House, a small private hotel in the heart of Wan Chai. Freddy had wanted to put him in the Lee Garden, a far more respectable place for an important American visitor but Sam had insisted on somewhere 'in the middle of it all'.

'You can't learn about a place or its people from an air-conditioned hotel room,' he said over the long distance telephone. 'Find me a place downtown.'

Sunning House was perfect. Squeezed in between the restaurants, bars and massage parlours that had multiplied since the war, the small self-contained apartments were mainly occupied by Chinese, Korean or Filipino businessmen of uncertain trades and it was a favourite spot for sea captains and oil riggers on shore leave.

The fact that it was also the accepted meeting place for smugglers of illicit goods of every description made it all the more attractive. A few evenings spent in the smoke-filled atmosphere of the crowded basement bar had taught Sam more about the way business got done in Hong Kong than he could ever have learned from the Chamber of Commerce.

Each morning at eight-thirty sharp he waited outside in the hustling street for Sing to pick him up in the Triumph. There were locations to find. *The Red Lotus* was a story of intrigue and adventure set in present day Hong Kong and partly in mainland China. As permits to shoot across the border were impossible to come by, terrain, buildings and authentic settings had to be created within the colony.

Sing's knowledge of the New Territories and the Hakka and Tanka dialects got them in and out of places few foreigners had seen, but she knew that Sam's readiness with generous hand-outs had helped open the doors. He was naturally generous and genuinely, almost naively, fascinated by the people around him, even when they were ready to steal the shirt off his back. One of his first requests had been for a dozen rolls of newly minted Hong Kong dollars, straight from the bank. The pockets of his army style fatigues were weighted down with them and whenever they left the car he handed them out to beggars and children like bright, shiny pieces of candy.

At first Sing tried to advise him. 'The beggars will use it to gamble and the children will give it to their fathers to help support their opium habit,' she said, only half joking.

'What the hell,' he replied with a grin. 'It's a habit I picked up in Shanghai. Just can't help myself.'

The first six weeks went by in a succession of long, unbroken days of pre-production work and planning. Much of the film was to be shot outside the studio. Sam was determined to make the most of the variety and colour that surrounded them. For each street scene, rural setting or action sequence he looked at a score of alternatives.

With Sing at his side, clipboard in hand, there was hardly a corner of the colony they had not visited. Lunching at street stalls or noodle shops, they returned to Sunning House well after dark to review the day's events and compare notes for the following day.

Sam's generosity when it came to buying drinks had made him a celebrity in the smoky bar and a motley crew of new acquaintances made no secret of their approval of the woman he had found for himself. The more he protested and explained who she was, the more they hooted their speculations on his sex life.

Sing, who was usually dressed in the cheap Chinese clothing that made her one of the crowd, studied her notes and pretended they were talking about someone else. Sam thought she was embarrassed and suggested they go up to his room, a suggestion that was overheard and brought such a howl of approval that she suggested they stay where they were.

They ate in the little dining room next to the bar, in spite of Sam's constant offers to take her to dinner at a 'respectable' place. Her answer was always the same: it was too late for her to change and they had an early start in the morning. Desperate as he was to wine and dine her in style, Sam could not argue with the logic of the woman he had come to rely on, or disagree with her dedication to the job. Frustrated but determined to create an opportunity to be alone with her, she seemed just as determined to avoid it and the thrill he felt at the first sight of her only grew more unbearable with each day they spent together.

Sam Danovich prided himself that there had been enough women in his life to make him something of an expert on pursuit and conquest. He was too cautious in his judgement of Sing Deverill to hurry things but was certain that sooner or later they would be lovers. It was a prospect that was never far from his mind when he was with her and even when he wasn't.

On the one or two occasions when Freddy Fong stepped in, insisting that it was time for a little relaxation, and arranged banquets in the best restaurants, she seemed even more captivating. He sat across the brightly lit table unable to take his eyes off her. In high-heeled shoes, her slender neck held straight by the stiff collar of her cheong-sam, she was eye-to-eye with him on the rare occasions that they danced.

She unnerved him with her strange mixture of rare beauty and simple, unassuming charm. The strength and suppleness of her body, held close to his, moved to the music in a way that made the pulse beat in his neck. But on every occasion she had excused herself at a early hour, insisting that Freddy and Sam continue to enjoy themselves and taking a taxi back to her flat alone.

With the location surveys complete the casting of extras and stand-ins began. Set designs had been finished and construction was underway in the sound studios Freddy had leased for Sam in Diamond Hill. Sam made no moves in selecting cast, costume or props without consulting Sing. Her knowledge of Chinese culture and character and her fluent Cantonese saved much time and frustration. Her common-sense approach to the most difficult situation saw things quickly and calmly resolved with a minimum of fuss and cost.

She found that the challenges of preparing for the shooting of a feature film both fascinated and excited her. From the moment she read the script her mind began making its own observations on points of accuracy and credibility when applied to the realities and detail of life in Hong Kong and China.

She was able to contribute suggestions and improvements that the American scriptwriter could never have discovered through the most intricate and thorough research. Sam was delighted with her grasp of the story, the cool efficiency of her work, and insisted on giving her the authority and salary that went with the job of line producer.

Freddy observed them both throughout the busy weeks and was well aware of Sam's mounting frustration. As the Hong Kong pre-production period drew towards completion there was to be a two-week survey of three other Asian cities. Small second-unit scenes written for Bangkok, Singapore and Manila called for brief visits to each of these locations. Pressure would be off and if ever there was to be an opportunity for romance to have its chance, this would be it. Freddy confided his understanding to Sam over breakfast in the coffee shop of the newly built Hong Kong Hilton one Saturday morning.

'I've booked you both into the best hotels, with adjoining rooms,' Freddy said enthusiastically. 'Of course, the lady herself wanted to do it but she would have gone second rate to save budget and you'd be on different floors to avoid complications.'

Sam took several gulps at his black coffee and prepared to set about his bacon and eggs. 'I don't know, Freddy. I'm nuts about her but I don't know how to handle it. I've never known anyone like her. She runs a mile when she sees me coming unless she's got a clipboard in her hand.' He buttered a slice of toast. 'What the hell happened to her over there in England?'

'I don't know, Sam,' Freddy replied. 'But it hurt her bad. She just doesn't take chances any more.'

The Happy Butterfly

FROM THE small apartment twelve floors above the Happy Butterfly bar, Hand-trolley Lulu stepped out onto her tiny balcony. It was identical to a thousand others that looked down upon the narrow, crowded street crawling like a river below. Above the flickering rainbow of neons the apartment was dark and although it looked across at a checkerboard of other lighted windows, somehow private. The noise of the street rose like the sounds of a distant riot and, as it always did, carried the spiced and comforting aromas of street cooking.

Behind her, Three-thumbs Poon scattered the mahjongg tiles noisily onto the smooth, laminated table top and began swirling them around with both hands while Firecracker Lily, Red Lead Mary and another mama-san, known as Sally Seven Seas because of the great number of sailors she was said to have entertained, made tea and dolloped ladles of steaming fishball soup into brightly decorated bowls.

'Let's play,' called Three-thumbs. 'There's nothing to see out there. In here is where I am waiting to teach you how to play this game, and how to lose your money.' He rubbed his hands, reaching up to adjust the gooseneck light, clicking it on to flood the table.

'Keep quiet, old fool,' Hand-trolley Lulu called back without turning around. 'There is plenty of time for me to make a poor man of you. Drink your soup and be patient, fishballs are good for the brain.'

The others laughed, happily clattering the china spoons onto a tray. They were accustomed to the friendly insults the two most important people in Wan Chai exchanged so freely. This was Saturday night and it was long after midnight. They would play till the sun came up as they always did.

Hand-trolley Lulu knew exactly where each of her lucky plants were. Light from the room flowed over their broad, variegated leaves, thickly cluttered in luxuriant profusion. Each solid stem set firmly in its own brown and yellow dragon pot, they filled the small space with their healthy, dark green growth. Carefully she poured water from a plastic dipper into every pot, filling it from a bucket at her side. It was a nightly ritual that nothing could cut short.

She stood for an extra moment looking up to where, over the square roofs of the high-rise, a full moon of deep yellow hung ripe and round as a melon tree. Even with the honeycomb of lighted windows, the noise and the smells of a Hong Kong night humming like a distant swarm, these few square metres above it all were the closest thing to peace that Hand-trolley Lulu could ever wish to know.

When at last they were seated Three-thumbs again used his special flourish to mix the tiles—the bamboos and the jokers, the winds and dragons and the flowers—as each player took up his or her share of thirty-four tiles and began to stack them in a wall seventeen tiles long and two high, face-down on the table. They played the old way, the set including the four celestial seasons, and each player took the name and position of the four winds— north, east, south and west.

Their walls built and pushed together to form a square in the centre of the table. Three-thumbs Poon took the superior position of the east wind as he always did. Firecracker Lily rose to light the incense sticks before the red-lit shrine above the door.

'Joss cannot help you,' chortled Three-thumbs. 'Nor can the smile of Buddha himself save you from the luck of the celestial trinity.' He waggled his three thumbs obscenely.

The sudden rasp of the door buzzer was so unexpected it almost caused Hand-trolley Lulu to choke on her soup. 'Aeeyah . . . Dong-gwai,' . . . she spluttered, using the colloquial expression of annoyance. 'Have I bumped into a ghost? Don't they know it is Saturday night?' It was well understood in the bar far below that no one disturbed Apartment 187 after midnight on Saturday.

Outside the door Ah Keung leaned a hand on the tiled wall and wrinkled his nose at the food smells that seemed to fill the building. The slow ride in the cramped and dirty lift as it jolted to a stop on every floor had not improved his humour. He glared irritably at the remnants of red paper prayers stuck on either side of the door and the small shrine to the door god, its single rosy globe glowing at his feet. Taking a short, fierce drag on his cigarette, he flicked the butt into the shrine and jabbed the button again, leaving his finger on it. Something moved behind the peephole on the other side of the security grille as the buzzer persisted, angry as a hornet. Chains rattled and the door swung quickly open.

Even through the distortion of the peephole there had been no mistaking the black-clad form of Ah Keung. The sight of him leaning impatiently on one outstretched arm made Hand-trolley feel most uneasy. The Forceful One had never come to her door like this before. It was an understanding that all such business was carried out in the bar at street level, not in the owner's private quarters. For many years now, Ah Keung had collected from them, crawling like a snake from its nest out of the Walled City.

'Dai Gor,' she laughed, to hide her nervousness, respectfully giving him the title of Big Brother. 'Welcome. What can this worthless old woman do for someone so important at this late hour? Were the fools downstairs not expecting you? Has someone offended you? I will . . .'

Ah Keung stopped her with a raised hand. Behind her, Three-thumbs Poon and the others stayed seated, the square of tiles untouched in the centre of the round table. They all knew that Saturday night was collection night and that the money from each of the bars and from Hand-trolley's other interests would be waiting under the counter, to be handed over by the barman on duty.

The procedure never changed but they did not complain. The reputation of the Forceful One was worth paying for; not even rival gangs bothered those who came under his protection and others might have demanded more.

'Stop chattering, crazy old whore. Open this monkey cage.' He rattled the iron grid. 'Or am I to stand out here all night to die of the stink?'

Inside the small cluttered room, Ah Keung looked around him with disapproval. 'So this is the nest where the cockroaches play. With so much money I expected better.'

Hand-trolley forced another laugh. 'Business is not good, Dai

Gor. So many bills, so many payments, so many expenses. The gods have deserted me.'

Ah Keung ignored her, looking down at Three-thumbs Poon, whose features had turned bloodless at the closeness of the man he hated and feared most in the world.

'And you. The taipan of the Nine Dragons. More money than an emperor and the brains of a toad.' He gestured around the untidy room. 'Is this the best you can do for entertainment?'

Three-thumbs had taken his shirt off and sat in his singlet. The skin of his pudgy face and round shoulders glistened with sweat and his lucky hand was hidden from view.

'We are old friends here,' he said with a sickly smile. 'What is more valuable, Ah Gor?' He hurried on in case his answer might seem an insolent one. 'I hope you have not come seeking me. The money was left as it always is with Ah Kee, the senior mama san.' He half rose from his chair in a show of concern. 'I will have her liver if she has displeased the big brother.'

'Sit down, fat money-bags. It is not that. I bring news that will please you both.' Ah Keung waved away the bowl of tea Firecracker Lily offered him as he spoke.

'I am going away soon and you are both to have the honour of seeing that my farewell is a memorable one.'

Three-thumbs visibly slumped with relief at Ah Keung's words, then quickly recovered from the shock. 'Going away? We will miss you Ah Gor, will we not, big sister?'

'Yes, yes,' agreed Hand-trolley readily. 'We have been safe from the broken boys of the street gangs because of the power of your name. What will we do if you are gone?'

Ah Keung's long, pale face twisted in a mocking smile. 'You will continue to live off your whores, just as you have always done. Like ticks on the belly of a mangy dog.'

With a sudden swoop of his arm he scooped the square of tiles from the tabletop. They flew against the wall with the force of bullets, smashing the glass front of a china cabinet.

'Do not insult me with the pretence of respect. You would happily piss on my grave.'

Mary Seven Seas and Red Lead Mary sat stiffly in their chairs, the masks of makeup showing their wear under the bright glare of the gooseneck lamp.

With Ah Keung's uncharitable gaze suddenly upon her, Red Lead Mary quickly left her seat and he took her place at the table.

'Sit down, old hag,' he said more reasonably, inviting Hand-trolley with a wave of his hand. 'We will talk of my farewell celebration.'

'Anything, Ah Gor. We are greatly in your debt,' babbled Three-thumbs Poon. He spread his hands innocently. 'But what more could poor proprietors such as we are have to offer so great a brother? Have we not always paid what was asked of us?'

Hand-trolley Lulu said nothing. The Forceful One was the only man she had ever truly feared among the triad to whom she had handed a percentage for most of her life. In her trade she had seen the face of demons in many disguises but this one did not hide. This one was proud of his evil. He had taken many of her girls, left them almost dead, yet none would talk about her time with him and the light in their eyes was never quite the same. It was as though they had been shown a glimpse of the devil himself. To this one, it was more than the taking of a woman. There were rumours in the bars that he was impotent, that his sacred pouch was empty and that he could only watch the pleasure or the pain of others. Some said it was more than this. That his satisfaction came from humiliation at its most cruel; an appetite so bizarre that even the hardened professionals of Wan Chai would not speak of it. He who fornicated with ghosts. Whose desires were those of the beast.

His face was chalk white beneath the lamp, the close-cut bristles on his neck and temples blue-black, stiff and coarse as pig hair. He bent his head and they saw the triangle of white scars that crowned his skull with the mark of pain that set him apart from others.

'What do you want of us big brother?' she asked, trying not to sound quite as humble as Three-thumbs Poon. 'If it is in our power, we will provide it.'

Ah Keung placed his hands in the centre of the table, the palms together, his long fingers entwined to form a hammer fist. 'If you were a baker, old woman, I would ask for cakes.' He looked at Three-thumbs Poon. 'And if you were a tailor, you could make me a suit.' He grinned suddenly, an ugly leer of anticipation. 'But your business is whores.'

'Anything you desire, Ah Gor.' Three-thumbs turned to Hand-trolley Lulu for support. 'The best, the youngest, the most beautiful, the most passionate. Have we ever failed you?'

The club of Ah Keung's fists raised an inch and struck the table with such force the tea jumped from the cups. 'I do not talk of the dog-meat you serve up to the drunken gwai-lo. I would rather mount a cow in the field.' His hands parted and lay flat on the table. Three-thumbs removed his spectacles to wipe sweat from his eyes.

'I come to you because you are the Toad of Wan Chai. It is you, both of you, who supplied the brown monkeys with whatever they asked because you were afraid of them. It is you we do business with. You who control the market. You who buy and sell only the best.'

Three-thumbs Poon was nodding his head violently.

'Good,' said Ah Keung, dramatically. 'Now, listen to exactly what I ask.'

He leaned back and folded his arms. 'Everything that I desire must be provided exactly as I request it in finest detail. In such affairs nothing must be of inferior quality. Am I understood?' He breathed deeply, rolling back his eyes, waiting tolerantly for an answer.

Three-thumbs Poon pretended real concern. Under the cover of the table, his lucky thumb pedalled frantically with the other. 'Of course, Ah Gor. Everything must be the best, the finest . . . the most delectable.' Behind his spectacles his frightened eyes swivelled from Ah Keung to Hand-trolley Lulu, hoping for support. In his mind he sought vainly for words to express his understanding.

Ah Keung saved him further elaboration, continuing in the same exaggerated tone. 'It is seldom that I enter the garden.' He closed his eyes. 'When I do the birds must sing, the flowers must bloom, the sun must shine as it has never shone before. For me alone.'

'What garden is this, Ah Gor?' Three-thumbs Poon asked weakly in the pause that followed.

Ah Keung's eyes flew open. 'The garden of pleasure, fat money-bags. The garden of endless delights.' He leaned forward, his voice lowered. 'Now, listen to me both of you. Listen with all care.'

The next day Three-thumbs Poon took an early breakfast in his own restaurant. He sat alone at the corner table by the kitchen doors where no one else was allowed to sit. It was from here he could watch his waiters and yum-cha girls at work, read the morning papers or sort through the receipts. A telephone crouched in the middle of the table. It was from here he kept his finger on the pulse of Wan Chai, placed his Happy Valley racetrack wagers and checked his investments.

The mahjongg game in Hand-trolley Lulu's flat had not lasted through the night as it usually did. When the Forceful One had departed they had been overcome with relief but the north, east, south and west winds were no longer blowing strongly, and the game did not go on. The news of Ah Keung's departure from their lives was accompanied by demands they knew they must meet completely.

Everyone who paid protection had learned not to question the Forceful One. The stories of his fierceness were told in whispers. He was a menace from the past, they said, reviving the ancient skills of the black sorcerers. His violence when displeased shattered all in its way and mercy was unknown to him.

Even the brothers of the Yellow Dragon would not face Ah Keung, and those who had dared to plot against him had met his terrible revenge. It was as though he could enter the minds of those he suspected, anticipate their every thought. The way a serpent goes where it pleases.

All this filled Three-thumbs Poon with a heavy sense of dread. That this dung of the devil should select him and Hand-trolley Lulu to satisfy his vile wishes was a sign of their standing. As heads of the committee that ran the lucrative bar and massage parlour society of Wan Chai against the written laws of the gwai-lo government, they were held responsible to the triad enforcers.

This Ah Keung had always been a renegade. Ever since he had taken the robes of the Red Pole from Jimmy Chan he had continued in his defiance of all authority. He had smashed his way to a position of power that few could challenge. When the Yellow Dragon had disbanded he had lost some of his power to the 10K but he had never let go of the Nine Dragons and the Happy Butterfly. It was worth any price to see him go. But why was he leaving? Where was he going? Three-thumbs pushed the bamboo containers of tasty, shrimp-filled dumplings away from him. He had no appetite for food. Only for the preparations he must make.

So typical of this dung-eater to give him and Hand-trolley Lulu so little time. He sighed, removing his spectacles to knuckle his tired eyes. This would cost him dearly. But it was worth any cost, any difficulty, to please the Forceful One and to know that when it was over, he would be gone. The anxiety of Three-thumbs Poon made his paunchy gut rumble nervously as he reached for the phone.

Ah Keung arrived at the Nine Dragons Ballroom at precisely three o'clock on the following afternoon. He entered the polished brass gate of the elevator escorted by two young boys dressed in the white and gold uniforms and pillbox hats identical to those worn by pages in the Peninsula Hotel. They stood one on either side of him as the elevator rode silently up to the top floor. The well-oiled grille slid open and they escorted him to a pair of double doors with the long, gold handles of a mosque and, kneeling before him, removed his shoes. Each to a foot.

He looked down at them. Just as he had asked, they were about twelve and fourteen years old. Pretty as girls, robust and healthy. When he had entered they followed, closing the doors and sliding the long, brass bolts that prevented anyone from intruding.

Inside, Ah Keung inhaled the musky scent of jasmine incense as he looked around. This was Three-thumbs Poon's most expensive suite, reserved for taipans with chequebooks as fat as their white behinds. Walls hung with black velvet drapes and exotic tapestries gave the impression of a sheik's magnificent caravanserai. The floor was a deep mass of silken cushions, the ceiling stretching away in a nothingness of black satin, realistically spangled with stars.

Beneath it, in the very centre of the room, also covered in black satin, rising like an altar in the cunningly concealed light, was a huge circular bed, surrounded by mirrors. Beside it on a low table of jade-green marble stood the tripod and copper pan of an opium burner, beside that the bone-white stem of the pipe. Satisfied with what he saw, he sauntered to the bed and sank down on its firm surface.

The boys had been carefully chosen. They were trained in the skills of the Shanghai bathhouse, in the rejuvenating of tired men through massage and the pleasures of the bath. These two were initiates and this was the first time they had performed the extra services that were sometimes requested. On their knees before him they gave three deep kow-tows then began to silently undress each other. Ah Keung sat bolt upright on the bed, his voice husky as he told them not to hurry. When they both stood naked, their flawless bodies hairless and smooth as girls, he spoke again in the same low, sibilant hiss.

'What are your names?' he asked.

'I am Ping and this one is Pang, lord,' said the bigger of the two.

'Do not disappoint me, Ping and Pang.' Ah Keung said.

The two boys had been given exact instructions on what was expected of them. The elder of them was responsible and his nervousness showed in the eagerness to please, his air of dominance over his smaller assistant. Ah Keung stood while they took off his clothes, then lay back on the circular bed. Ping's hands were strong as a man's, developed by traditional methods, and his knowledge of anatomy was complete. The smaller boy, Ping, was less advanced, setting about the task of attending to Ah Keung's finger and toenails with the assurance of a professional.

Ping's massage technique was expert and gave Ah Keung no reason for complaint. The boy worked solidly for an hour, using the authentic Shanghainese methods usually administered by women, the kneading of his thumbs and elbows relaxing every muscle, finding every acupressure point, halting the bloodflow then releasing it to stimulate circulation. Perspiring from the effort of his labours, Ping mounted Ah Keung's back and stood upright on it.

His toes were as skilled as his fingers as he walked the back muscles, loosening the spinal vertebrae one at a time, his body-weight increasing the pressure upon trigger spots expertly sought. When this had been kept up for a further half hour he dismounted. His hot palms smoothed aromatic oils into every part of Ah Keung's body from toes to scalp, carefully skirting the genitals as he had been told.

When both boys stood back with a bow and poured him hot tea from a silver urn, Ah Keung raised himself on an elbow and sipped, languidly observing them.

'Embrace each other,' he whispered, after moments of contemplation. When they hesitated he repeated the order in a voice that jerked them awkwardly into each other's arms.

'Embrace,' he said again, the anger gone, replaced by a tone of encouragement. 'I am told you are close friends. Do not be afraid because I am here.'

The two boys touched each other lightly.

'No.' Ah Keung rapped. 'Caress like lovers. While you are here one of you is a girl. Decide which one. Hold each other. Have you not been told of this?' The sudden anger of his words brought Ping and Pang into each other's arms quickly.

His eyes narrowed. He could have been asleep but he watched closely, noting the first down of pubic hair encircling their limp stems, their neat scrotums tight with apprehension. Ah Keung studied each reaction, watching for the first thickening lift between well-shaped legs that would tell him which was the bolder of the two, which was the more sensitive.

Three-thumbs Poon had assured him they were untouched by anyone. No one had penetrated them and their pink-tipped creamy stems had not yet known a woman.

Such boys were reared especially for those who preferred them to girls, taught the same skills and when fully trained were just as sought after as any cherry girl. They exactly suited his requirements and Ah Keung could not help a nod of satisfaction; there were no bounds to the merchandise of the Toad of Wan Chai.

Ah Keung savoured the game but showed no sign of his interest. Their hands brushed each other more freely, arms enfolding as the elder boy encouraged the younger. Now fully erect, their penises probed each other's bellies, then crushed close as hesitation left them.

The hand of the one called Ping slid down to grasp the stem of the other, inhibition slipping away. Ah Keung waited for just the right number of seconds, gauging their rising excitement before ordering them harshly apart, their stiff members, risen to full hardness, flicked upward with every quickened pulse.

'Prepare me,' he ordered and they moved quickly to do his bidding, holding aside the drapes to reveal a large square bath of the same jade-coloured marble as the table. A hot sulphur spring bubbled, acid green already filling it. 'Wash me,' he demanded with the same breathy sigh.

Stepping into the bath, he remained standing. He closed his eyes for the first time as with large sponges, slick with sandlewood soap, they entered the steaming water and, kneeling, began to bathe Ah Keung's body. Encouraged by his closed eyes both boys inspected his muscular limbs, paying close attention to the coarse thatch of hair clinging to his loins as the hot, slippery sponge passed over him.

'Your hands. Use your hands,' he whispered, the words hardly audible.

Ping instantly dropped the sponge, soaping his hands and sliding them eagerly between Ah Keung's thighs, gently massaging the bulk of his scrotum with one hand, drawing the other up and down the full length of his flaccid shaft, anointing its head. It pleased Ah Keung to see their puzzled expression as he failed to respond.

'Now you,' he breathed, opening his eyes fully to look at the boy named Pang. 'See if you can do better.'

Pang had been kneeling close staring in rapt attention. Now he pushed Ping aside, eager to play his part. Deliberately, he cupped water in his hands and, lifting them several times, washed away the soap to begin again. Ah Keung listened for their quickened breathing between trickles of water, inhaling the acid scents of the sulphur spring, allowing the different feel, the more intimate fondling of Pang's inquisitive hands to fan the spark that had begun to glow inside. After a moment the hands grew even more confident, more curious, grasping strongly at the sighs of Ah Keung's arousal.

Ping suddenly joined him, afraid he would be thought uninterested. With strong agile fingers he began stroking the taut muscles of Ah Keung's thighs. Noting that both boys were still fully erect, Ah Keung stepped from the bath. Sitting on its edge he pulled Pang across his knees.

'You fail to interest me,' he snapped. 'You must be punished.' Bent over Ah Keung's soapy knees, the boy's erection slipped between them as he was roughly pushed down. Only the sound of his breath was forced from him with every flat-handed blow across his buttocks.

With each swipe Ah Keung felt the boy's hard shaft drive between his knees. He pinned it with them, judging by Pang's urgent thrusts when the boy was at his climax, then released him without warning.

Pang straightened with a small cry of frustration, jerking his hips forward, unable to hold back, as Ah Keung's mouth closed around him, sucking strongly as a calf on a tit. Feeling the warm, salty spurts upon his tongue as he drew upon the boy's fresh young essence to nourish his own.

Through this, Ping stood aside, observing intently, his cheeks flaming, a film of perspiration on his flat, button nose. His eyes wide in the throes of violent masturbation, he gasped repeatedly as Ah Keung's mouth claimed him in turn.

Ping had recovered quickly, his stem already rising again at what he witnessed. I was right about this one, Ah Keung thought. He has the instincts of a horny goat and the energy of a wild pony. He remembered himself at that age, alone in the corner of the herb shed. So healthy, his shaft was in an almost permanent state of erection, iron-hard as a sword hilt in his hand. The bottomless virility of youth. He would have more of this boy.

Without being invited Ping moved quickly to where Ah Keung still knelt beside the bath, eager to be the one to please in the same way. Before he could lower his mouth the flat of Ah Keung's hand exploded against his ear, slamming him to the floor.

'Do not touch me until I tell you to. Do not make such a mistake again.' He rose to his feet and he entered the bath.

'Go now, both of you. Prepare the pipe and order food.' He lowered his limbs under the swirling surface.

When they had gone Ah Keung lay back, spreadeagled in the generous width of the bath. He was utterly relaxed—the first twitch of erection had quickly subsided. He was in complete control. There was no hurry. He would rule here like an emperor for the next three days. When he finally spilled his ch'i it would flow like a torrent.

For ten years Ah Keung had practised the Taoist discipline of the Golden Cycle. It had taught for centuries that the semen was the most precious of bodily fluids. Sex to the Taoist master was as food and drink, a necessary nourishment of the human system, its issue the most vital of all masculine powers. Through stringent harmonising of the earthly and heavenly ch'i, endless practice of meditation, breathing and internal massage of the organs, it was possible to conquer the ancient technique of sperm retention.

Once achieved it meant the exponent could retain the full state of erection for as long as he wished. It made him capable of reaching electrifying heights of orgasm without ejaculation and of prolonging the act of penetration indefinitely. By controlling the centre of gravity in the pit of the stomach, semen could be recycled and stored, while nothing was lost from cataclysmic climax.

Evolved above the snow-line of the Himalayas by Brahman yogis in the age of the Upanishads, the Golden Cycle taught that a man's seed was the key to long life and physical superiority, that those who spilled it regularly were lesser beings, unworthy of universal wisdom and the great power that it generated. Ah Keung had mastered the Cycle completely. It meant that arousal for him was a slow and elaborate process. So disciplined were his sensual emotions that when called upon they were reborn with each new experience.

Sex was not unimportant in the rigorous physical and mental training that ruled his life, but only rarely did he exercise these hidden power spots and abandon himself to the whirlwind of the erotic senses. When he did, he drew upon every excess, every deviation the mind could conjure. He did not indulge in the feeble fantasies or taste the sexual snacks that satisfied others. Sex to the Forceful One was a banquet of the flesh, to be gorged upon without restraint.

Once each year the rule of the Golden Cycle could be broken. After 362 days without ejaculation there followed a period of three days when the discipline could be abandoned, the sea of ch'i emptied and the cycle begun again. Ah Keung saw it as a sacred ceremony, a reward for such denial of nature. To be savoured in minutest detail, and in every conceivable form.

He put all thought of what was to come from his mind and considered instead what lay ahead when he left this place. He felt no regret at turning his back on Hong Kong. He went instead to seek an opportunity dreamed of by few men who value their soul—on the island of Formosa. The place where Chiang Kai-shek and his Nationalist government had taken refuge. The place they had named Taiwan.

Things had greatly changed among secret societies. Since he defeat of the Yut Boon Jai many had returned and the triads were strengthening again. He could no longer be part of any organised gang. Too many had turned against him and were after his blood. The old code of martial honour was lost. Since the war had ended the traditions of challenge and execution by combat were threatened by influence from outside, brought back from the Chinatowns of New York and Chicago, Vancouver, Amsterdam and London. The ways of convenience were embraced too readily by the younger brothers, eager to make their mark without thought of the old creed. The bullet Ah Keung had received was sent in a silk purse, as jewellery is sent, around it the crimson ribbon of revenge. It was sufficient warning.

He knew those who threatened him. They were three Sai Lo from rival gangs. Younger brothers who were as rebellious as he had been. Anxious to gain face by challenging the Forceful One, but not in combat. The bullet spoke clearly enough, there would be no honour in his death. Ah Keung had already marked each one and planned exactly how he would kill them. They expected the gift of the bullet to drive him deeper into the vaults of Ling Nam. Instead he would go to them, one at a time, leaving a reminder for those who followed.

Guns were replacing the Empty Hand, the magazine of an automatic in place of the authentic weaponry of sword and trisectional staff, the blade of quan and the trident. A vial of acid discouraged any argument and a gun settled any score. He could no longer depend upon his reputation as a fighter to protect him. To be master of the forms was not enough. No fist or foot was faster than a bullet. No champion immune to treachery. There was only one power greater than these and he would possess it.

Since his training at the Temple of the Sacred Tiger so many years ago, he had pursued the secrets of the Black Tao: the absolute power that came with possessing the minds of others; the infiltration and control of thoughts at any distance, extra-sensory vibrations, sent to bore like a beetle into the brain of an enemy, to gnaw away until that enemy is brought crawling to your feet, ready to sell the soul rather than leap into the pit of lunacy. This was the greatest of all powers. Nothing in heaven or on earth could challenge it. The Black Tao was beyond all other concepts of human mastery. Drawn from the cosmos, faceless and unstoppable, impossible to trace, impossible to prove—it was beyond all man-made and universal laws.

But the masters of darkness were few and almost impossible to find. White Meat Hong had told him of such a master. With the burning of the books, the purging of scholars, Mao Tze-tung had banished the sifus, the grand masters of all Kung Fu, to imprisonment or exile. The Red Guard had hunted them down, driving the schools underground just as the Manchus of the Ming had done, turning the Taoist temples into bicycle sheds, pigsties and urinals.

They had outlawed all martial art except Tai Chi Chuen taught under state supervision. No other form could be practised outside the ranks of the People's Army of Liberation. Those who could escape had done so, scattering to Singapore, Thailand and the Philippines. Many had chosen the breakaway province of Taiwan across the Formosa Strait and it was here that he must go. According to White Meat Hong, Chuk Fu, the great master of the Black Tao, had left his home on the Yellow River and taken refuge on the eastern shore of Taiwan. Known as Black Oath Fu, he was said to have become one of the richest and most powerful men in China through his command of the black arts. Those few that knew of him claimed that he had found no disciple worthy of his knowledge. Ah Keung stirred his legs in the tepid water of the bath. It was he, the Forceful One who would be that disciple. Just as he had crossed the frozen mud to find the Master of the White Crane, he would cross the Formosa Strait to Taiwan. White Meat Hong had offered to pay costs and the gift to Black Oath Wu would be large. White Meat Hong was a man with many enemies and had long engaged Ah Keung to protect his interest. To further reinforce the lethal powers of the Forceful One and enhance his reputation among the tongs was worth any price.

Ah Keung stood up, flicking the drops from his skin, leaving it to dry with his body heat, reaching for a dragon robe of gold and crimson silk. Back inside the chamber the boys stood obediently apart from each other. All signs of their excitement had subsided.

On the green marble table was laid an array of food, its delicious aromas filling the room. He looked it over, carefully checking to see that what had been served was prepared exactly as he had asked, the first of many classic dishes he had ordered from Three-thumbs Poon.

Satisfied, he sat cross-legged on the cushions. Every dish and its combination had been chosen for the boosting and stimulation of sexual energy. In Taoist belief all such foods have the qualities of the aphrodisiac. He congratulated himself on his choice of rare fungi. Dish upon dish of delicate fan-shaped mushrooms in a variety of sources enriched with herbs, surrounded a large earthen crock. He lifted the lid, inhaling its spice-laden steam. With a silver ladle he stirred the contents. Money-bags had done well, this was the authentic ingredient. He chuckled when he thought of the cost—a soup so unique it was only to be enjoyed by emperors and millionaires.

Lifting one of the dumpling-sized pieces in the ladle he sniffed it appreciatively. Tiger's testicles were difficult to come by. He laughed inwardly at his own joke. The ultimate tonic, together with the stewed slices of its penis and the wild root of Korean ginseng. Few could detect such authenticity, it was easy to deceive a fool, taking payment for the tiger and serving the inferior balls of a stag. The toad with Three-thumbs had been wise not to cheat him.

When the boys had served him, Ah Keung concentrated on enjoyment of the food, not looking at either of them as they waited on him. When he had finished they poured him hot rice wine from the heated jar.

'You,' he said, pointing to Ping. 'Make the pipe.'

The boy moved quickly to the table where the opium tripod was set up. From the copper dish he took a small brown-black pellet, rolling it between his fingers while he lit the small blue flame under the pan.

'Let me see it,' Ah Keung no longer showed anger as he spoke but Ping, the side of his face still stinging, held out the pellet of opium at arm's length. Ah Keung took it, squeezing it flat between finger and thumb, sniffing gingerly.

'Again fat money-bags has not failed me. The purest patna from Bengal.' He smiled his satisfaction, handing the pellet back to watch the preparation of the pipe.

When the cord of smoke looped upward to show the bead was burning, the boy offered the pig-bone pipe with both hands.

'No,' muttered Ah Keung. 'First it is for you and your little brother.'
'Take it,' he barked when Ping hesitated. 'Do not anger me again.'
The boy lifted the long pipe to his mouth.

'Draw,' barked Ah Keung. 'Draw hard and swallow the smoke.'
Satisfied that the boy had inhaled, he nodded towards the other.
'Take it. It will calm you.'

Ah Keung watched them pass the pipe several times before he
took it. Then pulled his feet up under the robe, folding his legs
and tucking his heels into the position of the lotus. He puffed
the bead to life and inhaled deeply.

'Now we will see what fat money-bags has found to entertain
us.'

He clapped his hands sharply. Immediately three girls appeared
from behind the black satin drapes. Each wore a short happy
coat of flaming red silk. At a word from him, they shed this thin
cover and stood in perfect nakedness, stark against the night-
black surroundings. He rose and walked around them, running
an eye and then a hand over their budding breasts, their strong
shoulders. He held the pipe to the lips of each of them, murmuring
encouragement as they drew upon it.

Slowly he evaluated each in turn as a slave-master might, their
smooth backs tapering to tiny waists and plump, firm rumps. Each
yielded silently and obediently to his touch, as he slid his hand
down the length of their legs and up again to the crotch to finger
the silken tuft. Silently, he savored the quiver that passed like a
current under his palm. Was it the thrill of fear or pleasure? Ah
Keung was in no hurry to find out.

Again, he found himself nodding approval. Hand-trolley Lulu
had done well to find such quality so quickly. It could not have
been easy, even with the discerning eye of Firecracker Lily. Perhaps
White Meat Hong had been the one to provide them. Cherry girls—
fresh from Soochow, by the look of them. Prepared by the best
of teachers, perhaps for two or three years and bought for a handful
of silver coins. He guessed their ages at between thirteen to fifteen.
Yes, the old whore from the Happy Butterfly was to be congratulated.

Moving from one to the other, he let his hand rest on the mound
of each girl, moving it slightly, his fingertips skating fleetingly over
the outer lips of each jade gate. Which was slick with excitement,
which was dry with fear? He held the eyes of each girl with his
own, gauging by the return of his stare, the depth and steadiness
of her gaze, who would give the greatest pleasure, judging by how
quickly their response mounted, how long it took for their eyes

to close or drop away. Listening to their breathing, the hint of sound, balancing the scale of pleasure or pain as his sensitive fingertips moved on. Detecting innocence, testing reaction.

The last of the three was slightly older. Perhaps closer to sixteen. Her name was Peony, she said, answering him without a tremor. She returned his stare with tilted chin, her breasts jutting with pride, or perhaps defiance. Already they were crowned with nipples hard and crimped with anticipation. Her feet were placed lightly apart, as though she read his expectations.

Ah Keung took hold of a nipple, rolling it between his finger and thumb, watching for the first sign of protest as he applied the pressure. He sensed only an increasing wildness in her. With his other hand he sought her mound, feeling it thrust forward to accommodate him, the crest of fine hair thicker against his palm than the others, the slippery bud of her clitoris pressed urgently between his fingers. He moved them back and forth, slowly, steadily, feeling it enlarge with the friction of his strokes.

It took less than a minute for her eyes to show the first quickening of orgasm. He read her response expertly—the increased shivering of her thighs, the movement of her hips challenging his quickened pace. As he felt the full flood of her climax building, his fingers slipped deeper with silky ease, to be grabbed at and held by trained muscles. Her head flung back to offer the arch of her throat to his lips, she reached out with a cry to grasp his wrist, bucking hard against him.

Quickly he snatched one of the watching girls by the arm, forcing her to her knees. Peony's hands tangled frantically in the other's hair. The younger girl needed no encouragement, her tongue flicking out, driving deep. At a word from Ah Keung the third girl sprang eagerly to join them, her small eager mouth clinging like a bee to a flower, seeking first one breast, then another.

They have been taught well, thought Ah Keung, as the older girl tensed and cried out in the full throb of orgasm, then, dizzy from its intensity, embraced her sisters to repay their favours. He watched patiently as, using her hands and mouth, Peony tuned their senses like delicate instruments, from one to the other, bringing each to her finest pitch.

Peony watched Ah Keung from the corner of her eye. She felt strangely uneasy about this man. It was nothing new to stage such exhibitions and she was proud of her artistry. Give her a healthy, inexperienced farm-girl over the age of ten and she would transform innocence to shamelessness in under an hour.

Three-thumbs Poon had warned her that the Forceful One was dangerous if dissatisfied. She could not tell from his face if he found this performance pleasing. There had been no sign of his arousal. His breathing remained steady, his eyes unchanged. He sat upright as a monk at prayer.

It was why she held her little sisters back, taking them to the edge of thunder and lightening but not allowing it to strike. When their own fingers sought urgently to bring about the magic for themselves she pushed them away. This must not end too quickly, the madam of the Happy Butterfly had warned, instructing her to prolong the entertainment.

It was three years since she had been brought from the house of her father to learn the strange ways of rich men. To perform for them the acts which she and her sisters practised often, exploring, experimenting, inventing for times like this. They talked of men like this one, who sat stony-faced, impossible to arouse. Sometimes if such a man was left unsatisfied and complained, they were punished severely.

Quickly, fluidly as an acrobat, Peony flipped the length of her body to face her sister's feet positioning herself for the other's searching mouth. Seeking the familiar tight opening, she possessed it with her lips, drawing the stiffened tip of her tongue in slow, upward curling motions, probing, flicking at the lotus bud as strongly as a fingertip. The girl's legs strained tightly around her with a moan of pleasure. Peony read her sister's sighs perfectly, pressing her lips harder, nipping gently, persistently with her teeth, feeling, testing, coaxing the vibrations she created, as the first shudders began to convulse the girl's body.

As if in a trance, Ah Keung's hands floated to the sash that fastened the robe, untying it with a single jerk. Peony saw it as a signal of his readiness. Slipping her arms beneath the other's hips, lifting them to her, grinding herself down, hard against her sister's greedy mouth. They balanced each other's passion, barely controlling the current that joined them. Again, Peony stole a glimpse of Ah Keung—his hand now flew, his trunk arched backward, eyes half closed as he watched the first shivers of their climax grow and roll over them.

She could see the powerful muscles of his thighs and stomach tighten, but no sound was forced from his closed lips and there was no splashing of his ch'i. No bolts of jism shot from him. There was no pearly shower. She had failed, mistaken her timing. Still shaken by the intensity of the thunder and lightning that had again possessed her so completely, Peony crawled towards him. Hers was the task of giving satisfaction. Only she would be blamed. Fascinated by the whiteness of his rigid body, the robe open to fully reveal his reddened stem, contrasting angrily with the trace of black hair that dusted his thighs and clustered thickly at his groin, she was filled with the resolution of his fulfilment.

'Command me, lord,' she whispered, rising to her knees before him.

Before her fingers had closed around him, his hand shot out to grip her neck.

'Do not touch me until I tell you.' He forced her head back and leant over her until she could feel the heat of his breath on her face. 'Do nothing until I tell you to.'

He relaxed his grip, sliding the hand from her throat down to her breasts, squeezing and kneading them until he saw the fright in her eyes give way once more to rising excitement. His voice again took on the soft tone of reassurance as he handed her the pipe.

'Stay here and smoke, little Peony. You have done well and are chosen to be first. Now it is your turn to watch.'

He snapped his fingers. The boys had not moved throughout the exhibition. Trembling but untouched their shafts once more flicked against their bellies. At his signal, they fell upon the two other girls. Their child limbs sought each other in a frenzy of twisting, thrusting, biting, sucking. Peony began to sigh, murmuring her need, her eyes fixed on the scene before her. Presenting herself cat-like to Ah Keung with backward thrusts of her buttocks, she cried out as at last he entered her with slow measured strokes.

Silvermine Bay

SAM DANOVICH didn't feel right about following Sing. He had waited at a table in the small grocery store and teashop across the road from her block of flats since it opened at six a.m. telling himself after every gulp that this was a mistake and he'd leave after the next two minutes. An hour later she left the building, carrying a plain canvas bag slung from her shoulder, walking quickly and easily downhill towards Central. He fumbled in his pocket for change, feeling a tilt of excitement in his gut. He dropped some coins on the table and waiting till she was well ahead, sidled out into the street and started after her.

Pre-production for *The Red Lotus* was completed with a two-week break before the key people arrived from the States to commence principle photography. Sing had gently declined his offer of a holiday in Macau, or Manila or anywhere she chose. She had work of her own to do, she said, thanking him sincerely.

It had been like that throughout the survey. The door of their adjoining rooms had remained locked. Her defences, always polite, ever friendly, were always impeccably in place. Efficiency and attention to the job always a barrier to anything more.

'What the hell did the last guy do to her?' Sam had asked himself a hundred times.

Even the plotting of Freddy Fong had not helped. Their whirlwind trip through Asia had included dinners in some of the world's most romantic places—Bangkok's Oriental Hotel on the banks of the Chao Phraya; beneath the travellers' palms in the garden of Raffles in Singapore; a suite in the Manila Hotel. None of them had changed things.

When he showed signs of becoming bolder, she firmly, pleasantly, excused herself. There were notes to complete, calls to make, preparations for the following day. He still could not fault her dedication or argue with her reasoning. She was right. There was much to be done. This was not the time for relaxation, but she did not suggest that one day things might change.

Sam had never tried so hard for any woman. Never wanted one as much as he wanted her. Sing Deverill was worth waiting for. There was something about her that convinced him that one wrong move, one ill-timed, impatient gesture or word out of place, would lose her respect. If that happened, his chances of ever having her look at him as he looked at her would be lost. He was so sure of it that he had forced himself to apply the same attention to his work as she did.

During the day, travelling from one location to another in the dragging heat, sweat-soaked within minutes of leaving the hotel, it had been easy. She dressed like a man, wearing the same army disposals drab as he did, the thick mane of hair wound into a bun on her neck or crammed beneath a combat cap.

Even then it was impossible not to notice the way she moved, the unselfconscious poses that caught his eye at the most unexpected times. Climbing in and out of the four-wheel-drive, splashing her face with cool water, chasing it between her breasts with a squeezed out handkerchief. The scent of her body heat beside him.

But it was in the evenings, no matter how late, when she appeared for dinner, that he wanted to reach out and touch her. Uncluttered by jewellery, always simply but perfectly dressed, just the hint of makeup to emphasise her amazing eyes and the flush of the day's sun on her skin, she looked to him like some regal princess who had stepped from another time and place.

After a glass or two of wine he felt as though he was drowning in her presence. He had told himself that once the work was over, the planning done and documented, there would be no excuse. She would look at him differently. Come closer, talk of other things, give him a chance. It hadn't happened that way. She had other things to do. Other people to see. His frustration had finally shown.

'Suit yourself, lady,' had been all he could manage and he had left her back in the bar of Sunning House.

Now he was following her at a distance. It had to be another man. It couldn't be anything else. He must be quite a guy but Sam Danovich didn't give up that easily. He had to see what he was up against.

He was breathing hard by the time he watched her boarding the island ferry at Victoria Pier. He looked about for someone to ask where it was going. There were two wharves, four ferries, half a dozen islands. The sea of hurrying faces flowed on without a glance at one sweating gwai-lo who had lost his way. He watched her moving with the stream of people up the wide gangplank. They were carrying live poultry trussed beneath their arms, strings of crabs and clusters of salt fish, baskets of vegetables. She looked so at home among them. He felt alien and helpless without her.

The boarding platform rattled up on its chains, loops of rope lifted from the bollards and the ferry's engines began churning the litter of the harbour. As it swung slowly away, a painted sign along its boat deck read: 'Lantau Island'.

Taking a cab back to the studio he found Freddy in his office. 'Who's on Lantau Island?' he asked. 'That's where she goes. I've got to know.'

There was a brief pause while Freddy leaned back and looked

at him. 'It's her own business, Sam.' he answered kindly. 'If she wanted you to know, she would tell you where she goes and why.' He smiled. 'She's been stuck with your ugly mug for weeks now. Maybe she wants a little privacy.'

Sam put both hands on the desk and looked his friend straight in the eye. 'Freddy, I love this lady. Tell me where she's gone, I'm going to ask her to marry me.'

The grin on Freddy's face widened as he reached for a notepad. 'Why didn't you say so?' He laughed as he drew a map of Silvermine Bay. 'That's a whole new story.'

Sing watched the brown hulks of fishing junks drift by on either side, the ferry thumping leisurely away among the outlying islands. Smaller sampans sat on the water as far as the horizon. She had taken this two-hour journey many times but it never failed to interest her. The flat stretch of Hau Hoi Wan—Deep Bay—between the Chinese mainland and the New Territories, ruffled by surface fish and the flights of seabirds. Ahead, the peak of Lantau Island, the tallest in the colony, rising from the sea.

Compared to the ceaseless current of energy that charged the people and the places that make Hong Kong, Lantau was a different world. A place for fishermen and planters of rice, the fastest transport the plod of buffalo or donkey. Small villages were tucked away in coves and bays hidden from the sea by ancient battlements. It was a place of shrines and temples to gods and goddesses beside the monasteries of Buddhists and Trappists.

Silvermine Bay bit deeply into the coastline and the village of Wui Wo, closed in by rocky slopes that had once invited pirates, bronze cannons black with age still pointing out to sea.

Sing thought about Sam Danovich all the way across, wondering if she was right to refuse him even the opportunity to impress her more than he already had. She liked him much more than he knew. He made her laugh and that made her happy to be with him. It seemed an eternity since she had spent so much time in the company of a man or been so close to one. It disturbed her and when she was disturbed she withdrew.

When the feelings of need, of wanting to be more to him had come to her, Sing had closed her mind to them like turning the key in a lock. Sam was often funny, sometimes bewildered but always strong and dependable. His eagerness for life and the need to share it was inspiring to her. Everything he said and did was spiked with creativity, a dash of chilli added to a tasteless meal. She owed him much more than he knew and tried to repay it by taking away the tedium of detail, letting his creative enthusiasm explore fresh boundaries of imagination unrestricted. She dare not give him more.

Among the first to pour down the gangway onto the quay she revelled in the crush; the Hakka and Tanka people visiting their families, laden with gifts and special things for the table, the hot, dry smell of their sun-warmed clothes and the ever-present salted fish. No one stared. No vicious comment prodded her. These were the poorest of Hong Kong's people, the simplest and the happiest. Their goals were set by the rules of harvest and the schooling of fish. She was no longer jarp jung among them.

The beachside fish sales were in full cry, the Hoklo boats well up on the sand, barefoot owners displaying their catch, weighing them out on hand-held balances, threading twists of reed through the open gills. Further up was the Tanka market, tanks of running water leaping with fresh-caught prawns, the brown backs and silver bellies of fish fetched straight from the net. She bought some, taking her time to choose, bargaining the price, moving from boat to boat, stall to stall, carrying her purchases wrapped in leaves.

The summer house of Doctor Sun overlooked all of this and was a twenty minute walk through narrow lanes of green, leading upward, across running streams that fed the terraces on either side. It was a simple Hakka house, square and uninteresting from the outside, built long ago from stone taken from the hill behind it, now almost hidden by trees. A roughly paved pathway led to the concrete strip that served as a terrace and single unpainted door of weathered wood and shuttered windows, surrounded by creepers.

When Doctor Sun had first brought her here it had reminded her of the house by the pond at the Residence of Eternal Peace. Only the waterwheel was missing. He had bought it, he said, as a place to study, to rest, and to show his sons that there was another place besides the business world of Causeway Bay. He seldom used it now and had given her the key.

The rattle and clatter of the latch woke the gardener from his dozing in the shed he occupied outside the high garden wall. He rose stiffly from the cot, reaching for his wide straw hat. Taking a hoe from a corner clustered with tools, he swept the chickens from his path and entered the garden through a narrow side gate. In exchange for shelter and the privacy of the shed he kept the garden in order and an eye on the house. When Sing lifted the bamboo blinds and threw open the wide back doors opening onto the garden he was already chipping away amongst the shrubbery.

It was the garden that made the summer house a very special place, with its high stone walls, so old that clumps of fern and wallflowers sprouted from the cracks. Doctor Sun had taken advantage of every inch of earth. No more than twenty square metres, it spread out from a round court, hemmed in by shrubs and carefully planted trees. Pathways led to a single seat and pedestal table of stone set in its centre.

It was to this table that Sing took the deerhide bag and spread the books of Master To. Her translation of his eight volumes was almost complete. She felt a strange emptiness. The sheaves of hand-made paper, the scrolls and diagrams, yellowed with age and bound with hand-made twine, had been her security and comfort for so long. She had defended them before all else. Wherever she had gone, the books had gone with her. In her darkest and most dangerous hours they had been with her.

Even as a child in the house of Fat Fan she had kept them hidden beneath her bed, smelling the age of the pages as, by the light of a candle, she devoured slowly, character by character, row by row, the perfect images. They had sustained her in the Tavern of Cascading Jewels and behind the locked door in the Nine Dragons Teahouse, and had been her companion beside the waterwheel in the Residence of Eternal Peace.

Life with Toshido and the loneliness of Sparrow's Green would have been unbearable if she had not known they were close by—a separate, wise and gentle world for her to enter. To lose herself in. To learn and understand. To translate and interpret them had become her mission. It had saved her. Now the work that had taken so long was nearing its end. She lifted out the last of the notebooks. Even the singing of birds and the chip-chipping of the gardener's hoe could not distract her.

The next morning, an hour after the sun had risen over the mirror of Silvermine Bay, Sam Danovich stopped to remove his shirt. Silently he swore he would improve his physical condition as, shielding his eyes, he gazed up the steep track ahead. If this was the way she had come, the lady must be part mountain goat, he thought, throwing the shirt across his shoulder and toiling upwards.

Freddy Fong had been reluctant to tell him the location of the summer house on Lantau Island. He was the only one who knew outside the Sun family and Sing had made him promise to tell no one unless in some extreme emergency. To Sam this was as extreme as an emergency could get. He had opened the little red silk purse embroidered in gold and showed Freddy the huge, emerald-cut diamond, a flawless white.

Freddy had tossed him the keys to *Shanghai Lady*, the company boat and drawn him a simple map of Silvermine Bay, marking the spot where he would find Sing's hideaway. The boat was a converted junk fitted with two big engines and it made good time crossing Deep Bay.

He tied up at the sampan jetty and found his way up past the fish market to the square-shaped house among the trees just as Freddy had described it. His knocking brought the old man in the straw hat, armed with a hoe, hurrying loudly from the back of the house. Half a dozen silver dollars clinked into the gardener's palm bought his instant cooperation, and he led the way to the start of a steep track and pointed upwards.

Sam climbed for almost an hour up past the walls of a great red-roofed temple, the ruins of pagodas, before he saw her, a spot of colour through the thick growth that screened the path. Closer, he could see she was sitting on a flat shelf of rock, on the peak, surrounded by ancient granite spires and looking out over the sea perhaps 200 metres below.

She was wearing wide-legged trousers and a loose-sleeved tunic of orange silk. Motionless, straight-backed, her legs folded beneath her, she was so still she seemed lifeless. He knew he must not disturb her and, careful not to make a sound, he lowered himself to the ground to wait.

She looked like a goddess, he thought, worshipping the sun, facing it directly, its full strength striking the crown of her hair, the shimmering orange silk surrounding her like an aura.

As he watched she rose to begin a series of slow movements, graceful as any ballet, her body swaying, twisting, bending, flowing with the controlled motion of her limbs. After ten minutes of this, the movements became flying leaps and whirling spins that seemed to lend her wings, lifting her lightly as a feather, arms and legs sweeping the air in an intricate series of patterns.

To Sam, catching his breath in the cover at the side of the pathway, it was awe-inspiring. She made no sound, landing barefoot on the even surface of the rock like a settling bird. There was only the rush of air from her lungs as she struck out at an unseen attacker with a speed and force that astonished him. Sam knew he was witnessing something he was not supposed to see. This was no physical work-out. This was something else. A pagan right . . . a divine experience. Quietly he rose and backed away, retracing his steps down the track to the summer house.

Three hours later Sing let herself into the house. It was blessedly cool. She kicked off the thin-soled slippers and stood barefoot on the cool, flagged floor. Shedding the jacket she pulled a cord around her waist. The silk trousers slid down her legs and puddled brightly at her feet. Strips of light through closed shutters lit the spacious room, cutting across her naked body as she moved to the small, high-ceilinged bathroom and stood beneath the rush of cold water.

Another handful of silver dollars had convinced the gardener that Sam was entitled to be admitted through the side gate and into the garden. The old man's exaggerated gestures and loud exclamations had made it clear that here, at the round stone table in the middle of the garden, was where he should wait.

He had walked the garden from corner to corner. The sight of Sing, lost in a strange world beyond his reach, had sobered him. He had intended flashing the ring and taking her in his arms, regardless of everything but his need of her, his willingness to do anything for her. It had worked before with other women. Why not now with this one? Because, he told himself for the thousandth time, this was no ordinary female.

Sing turned off the water and reached for a towel. Dried, she walked back into the main room, feeling the cool air from the ceiling fan brush the skin of her back as she bent to open a camphorwood chest. From the pile of coloured silk garments she selected a fresh set of clothes identical to the one she had taken off, but in deep violet with white piping. She slipped into the trousers and tied the cord. The tunic flowed over her arms and shoulders, her bare breasts, disturbing the scent of the sweet smelling herbs and dried rose petals she kept in the chest with her clothes.

Drawing the bolts and opening the shutters she latched them back before picking up the deerhide bag and taking the path to the centre of the garden. Before she reached it the brilliant speck of scarlet in the middle of the table caught her eye. She stopped short to look quickly around, her senses immediately awakened. Whatever it was she had not put it there. She saw no one. Approaching the table cautiously she opened the purse. The diamond fell heavily into her open hand.

'It's the only way I know to tell you how I feel about you, lady.'

She spun around to see Sam standing under a tree. He kept his distance as though he was afraid to come closer. Before she could answer, he raised both hands in a gesture of surrender.

'I know I've got no right. I should never have followed you. You've never strung me along. It's just . . . ' He ran out of words, his hands dropping to his sides as he shook his head. 'Call it a gift. The biggest and best I could find.'

The total surprise, the weight of the magnificent ring in her palm, his sincere, almost apologetic tone, left Sing searching for words. Suddenly aware of her wet hair she shook it back from her shoulders, lifting her eyes to his. To Sam they seemed to light her face, the bloom of her skin to radiate energy as she held out her hand to him.

The shards of daylight penetrating the upstairs shutters had faded by the time Sam Danovich opened his eyes. He felt her heavy on his arm, smelled the closeness of her; natural body scents that had aroused him so, sweeter, more potent than any perfume. He lay still, listening to her slow, even breaths, staring into the gathering dusk, still unable to believe that she was beside him or what had happened between them. Remembering. Sifting every thought and action, afraid he would wake up to find it a dream.

Sing had said nothing. She had walked over to where he stood still half hidden in shadow, taken his hand and, opening his fingers, lifted it to her lips, leaving a kiss in his palm that seemed to shoot like quicksilver along his arm. The ring seemed clumsy and large as she placed it in the spot where she had pressed her mouth, closing his square fist around it with her unexpected strength.

'There was no need of this,' was all she had said, leading him towards the house. 'It is very beautiful, but there is no need of it, Sam.'

Sam had lost count of the women he had made love to. Some of them had been more memorable than others. Some he had thought he would never forget, others were easily and quickly lost. The hours that had passed in the cool, shady room, the soft swish and flicker of leaves outside the open window, had wiped his senses clean of any comparison. He had never been truly made love to before, never heard about, read about or imagined what it was like to be possessed entirely. His body and mind were taken over. Consumed slowly, deliberately, completely. It had begun from the moment she turned on the tepid needles of the shower, washing him with all the attention of a mother washing a child. He stood with his arms raised above his head, turning slowly with the guiding of her hands, to the endless caresses of her fingers and lips, soundlessly seeking to give him ultimate pleasure. The hot, silken gliding of her skin over his, the feel of her muscles softly relaxed under his hands, hard as an athlete's when she responded to his touch. No encounter had ever raised him to such glorious heights; she seemed to lift him, move him at will, only the language of their breathing between them. Then lying back, seeing her again, rising on wings of gleaming plumage from the rock, feeling the weight of her, the warmth of her, the length of her body pressed to his, the reassurance that she was real, reaching out he gently took her hand, watching the last of the moving light from the window on her peaceful face. He slid the diamond onto her finger, luminous as the tiny star whose name she bore.

When next he awoke, Sam blinked at the light that blazed through the shutters like molten gold. It took moments for him to accept that it was daylight; it was the first time he had enjoyed a sound night's sleep in as long as he could remember. He turned to find Sing gone, the bed no longer warm where she had been but the scents of her still lingering. He reached for her pillow, breathing them deeply, feeling like a college boy, his first fantasy come true, unable to believe that at forty-eight he could find himself so utterly, so sensationally consumed.

Climbing out of bed he threw the shutters wide to the morning. The sun flung its glittering path across the glassy bay, right up to the beach below, lighting the busy foreshore like a stage play. Shouts of the vendors and squeals of children reached him. He stretched before the open window, the warmth bathing his naked body, a grin of absolute contentment fixed on his face.

Downstairs he found her in the garden, the stone table covered with books and papers, so engrossed in what she was doing she appeared not to hear him come barefoot up the pebbled path behind her. There was a wicker tea basket. She opened the lid and lifted the teapot from its padded nest, filling a cup for him.

'Ginseng tea. It will give you strength,' she said without turning around.

'Just what I need,' he bent to kiss her neck, noticing that she did not respond.

'What are you doing?' he asked, as she turned back to the sheaves of pages filled with her handwriting.

'Something I must finish.'

'May I ask what it is?' he enquired again, not liking the feeling that he had intruded upon her or the feeling that the marvel of a few hours past must have been something he had imagined. That she hadn't really been there, or had forgotten. He felt the joy of it begin to slip away. Even the warmth of the sun seemed to suddenly cool.

After a pause he asked. 'Am I in the way?' Trying not to show the awkwardness he felt, to grow angry at the disappointment that threatened him.

Sing looked up, smiling. 'Of course not. Soon we will eat something. I have sent to the village.'

She sat back for a moment, putting down the pen, pouring more tea into her cup and taking a sip. For the first time he saw she was not wearing the ring.

'It is something I have studied and worked on for a very long time. Ever since I learned to read and write. Most of my life.'

Her eyes held his, as if gauging his reaction. 'It is a translation. Something very important to me.'

She was wearing the same silk pants and jacket, this time a pale and delicate lemon, exactly like pajamas, he thought. From a concealed pocket she took out the red purse, placing it on the table in front of him. 'I am truly honoured by your gift, but I cannot accept it.'

She placed her hand on his. 'It would mean that I belong to you and I can belong to no one. Once before I took such a beautiful gift. It did not bring happiness.'

When he went to speak, she lifted her finger to his lips. 'Please listen to me. For these two weeks I must stay here to finish my work. It is my great purpose. Since working with Freddy I have so little time to myself, coming here to be alone has become a habit. If you wish to stay you must allow me this and I will try to make you happy.'

'Sing. My wonderful . . . ' he began, reaching out for her. 'I was beginning to think last night was a dream.'

She stopped him, stepping back, and as so often before the power of her grip upon his wrist surprised him. 'But then, it must be over. There will be important things to do in the making of the film. It will be a time for much hard work. Other things must wait. Do you agree?'

'Agree? Lady, I love you. I've loved you since I saw you holding my name. I've loved you every minute since, more each day . . . until it hurts to think of you. This ring asks you to be my wife. Its the only way I know to tell you this.'

Sing released her grip and stepped closer. 'Love is hard for me to understand, Sam. I try not to do things I don't understand any more.' She dazzled him with a smile. 'But I can be happy without love.'

Before he could reply the gate in the garden wall rattled open. The gardener shuffled through, a stack of small bamboo baskets hanging from a pole over his shoulder. Sing began gathering up the books and papers, placing them carefully to one side. From the round containers she took steamed shrimps, round white rolls of hot Chinese bread stuffed with minced pork and hot rice conjee filled with chicken pieces and sprinkled with chives.

They ate at leisure and in silence. There seemed to be no reason to talk until she began to stack the empty containers, calling out to the gardener. Patiently the old man wiped the table, his wrinkled brown face expressionless under the floppy hat. When he had gone she turned to Sam.

'Each morning at sunrise, I must go up the hill. It is something else I have to do. When I return I must work here.' She began setting the books and papers out. 'Until I am ready to stop. Then we will be together.'

Sam could think of no better arrangement. He picked up the little purse and took out the ring, twisting it between his finger and thumb as it flashed like a fireball. 'I'll keep it for you. It will always belong to you.'

She watched him put it away, feeling his hurt. 'Please understand Sam. I am different. My life, everything about me is different.' She shook her head, looking away. 'It is hard to explain. I do not think I can ever love as you in the west know love. But I can make you happy as some of us in the east know happiness. And if being pleased to see someone, enjoying the sound of their laughter, wanting to be with them is enough . . . ' She hesitated

'Is it so very different?' Sam asked, holding her close.

'Yes. I was once in love,' she said, a little sadly. 'It is very different. I think I must always be alone inside. But I am content with that for I am never lonely. Contentment is close enough to happiness for me.'

She shook her head. 'Perhaps one day I will change. Until then I will make no more mistakes in the name of loneliness or misunderstanding.'

It seemed to need no further reply and Sam had none to give. Instead he picked up one of the notebooks. 'May I read some of this,' he smiled, wanting to kiss her but knowing it was not the time. 'While I wait?'

Sing nodded uncertainly, the hint of a frown appearing. 'Please do not expect too much. These are not my words but the words of a great teacher. I have tried to understand them. I do not know if others can.'

For the next two weeks they lived apart from the world of Hong Kong. Each day, after Sing had returned from the rock and finished her work for the day, they explored the green hills of Lantau. Some days they took *Shanghai Lady* out to sea, visiting neighbouring islands, swimming naked in deserted coves and from undiscovered beaches. Once Sam set a course for Macau and they stayed the night at the Bella Vista Hotel, as charming and full of welcome as the arms of a Portuguese madam.

They gambled in the casinos, among the gilded dragons of good fortune. They drank good wine on the balustraded balcony beside the harbour, the lights of crab boats working the mouth of the bay, the old Guia lighthouse sweeping the Praia Grande with its pencil-thin beam. They walked the brightly lit boulevard and looked out from the old sea wall to mud flats where Ben Deverill had built his first boat.

Then, she told him the story of her father and all she had learned of him. She no longer doubted who she was, but here in this place, the dark shapes of junks riding at anchor, the certainty of it overwhelmed her. When she spoke of Ben Deverill Sam listened intently. Ships, Macau, Shanghai . . .

When he spoke his words were measured and gentle. 'You know something lady? Ever since I first heard your name I've been trying to make a connection . . . I think I just made it.'

She looked puzzled.

'I never asked about your past . . . your family, because Freddy told me not to. I figured you'd talk about it yourself if you wanted me to know. He took her hand and looked at her, more serious then she'd ever known him.

'What is it Sam. Tell me.'

'I can't be sure about this but I think I once saw your father. In Shanghai. Before the war. He was a big man there. Its only now that I remembered his name.'

For the next half hour Sam talked about the Shanghai taipan who had been a spokesman for the International Settlement in negotiations with the Japanese authorities before war was declared with Britain and America. How he had been in the newspapers almost every day. The self-made shipping magnate who was as big and powerful in the flesh as he was in reputation.

'It's got to be your father. I had completely forgotten his name but I remember it clearly now. We covered him for a news story. Everybody had heard of Ben Deverill. There were a hundred stories about him. How he built his first boat single-handed, right here on the beach in Macau just the way you say. It has to be the same . . . how could there be two men like that?'

Sing's eyes shone with excitement. To be told this, here in the place where the legend of Ben Deverill began, by this man she had grown to care for, did not seem strange to her. It was as though some twist of fate had brought them here. For long moments she looked out at the inner harbour, breathing in the salt-sea smell of low tide across the mudflats, of drying crab pots and empty shellfish. A mango slice of orange moon was rising and the busy lights of the typhoon shelter twinkled over the granite breakwater.

'Tell me about him, Sam,' she said quietly. 'Tell me everything you can remember.'

It was late when they walked back along the boulevarde to the Bella Vista and the rest of that memorable night was spent in each other's arms. Her passion and her gentleness brought them closer than ever before.

Sam found it hard to believe that it had taken him a full and varied lifetime to find what it meant to be ecstatically happy. Each day was made all the more wonderful by what he had read of Sing's secret work. Sheet by sheet, some of fragile rice-paper, others thick and coarse, the childish handwriting of her early notes differed in tone and strength. In the centre of the first page of all, faded but distinct he read:

> *Night darkens the western Hedgerow*
> *The colours of the peony are faded*
> *The blue-cap in the bamboo is silent*
> *We cannot stop this shadow*
> *But in each heart there waits a second sunrise.*
> *To-Tze*

The promise of these opening words seemed to him enhanced by the hand of a child, each letter carefully formed, as though it were a picture. Deliberately, patiently, they filled the pages with simple thoughts, rare as old coins unearthed by time. As they flicked by with the hours upon hours of his reading, Sam realised how little he knew of this woman who had so captivated him, the bundles and sheaves unfolding, deepening her mystery. With each bundle he read, Sam began to suspect that what she had done was of unique value.

Until now, he had heard nothing of Taoism. College and university, the glass cubicles high above Madison Avenue had been far removed from ancient philosophy. Even his time in Shanghai had taught him nothing to compare with the words and images of *The Second Sunrise.*

Separate from the old books of tiny Chinese characters there were superbly drawn illustrations. Charts and anatomical diagrams on sheets of hand-pressed paper, some rolled into scrolls, some as fine and transparent as raw silk, accompanied the bundles of Sing's English translation. Each piece was adorned with masterful calligraphy, the red-waxed chop of Master To, a signature to each. There were other original drawings and pictures, their origins shrouded in myth and legend. Pale, ethereal watercolours, ink washes and bold prints, wood-cuts dyed in vibrant colours, each a priceless work of oriental art. The illustrations had been tabulated and positioned against the text, line and wash diagrams explicitly explained in the translation, ornate motifs decorating the pages like precious gems.

It took Sam a week to read through half the material. He kept his growing excitement to himself, wanting to be certain, unable to believe what each new page uncovered, each revealing a natural folklore that had become a religion. It had been buried for so long by the forces it questioned, outlawed even now, by Chairman Mao Tze-tung through fear of its simple logic.

Sing's translation had compiled enough material to fill several volumes—not historical classics suited only to the student and the academic. Her simple, unaffected style became lucid and pure when interpreting the words of the bare-foot doctor named To Tze. Lyrical couplets and poems combined with a clarity of script on paths of self-discovery and spiritual realisation. There were methods of achieving physical and mental harmony. There were the uses of preventative medicine and natural healing—acupuncture, herbalism, moxibustion, natural nutrition, the healing properties and health benefits of Ch'i Kung breathing exercises and methods of relaxation.

Sam's enthusiasm soared with each new revelation. The west coast of America was in the first stages of opening up to such beliefs. They were beginning to spread from the first ashrams of southern California to the mountains of Big Sur.

Certain medical schools of American and European universities were starting to take notice of traditional Chinese medicine. Medical teams were being sent to the newly-formed Nationalist stronghold of Taiwan where Taoist priests, barefoot doctors and Kung Fu masters, banished from the mainland, were ready to share their knowledge with the outside world.

After thousands of years there were already some enlightened fields of western medical science prepared to admit the credibility of these age-old healing and preventative techniques. He doubted if Sing had any idea that she might possess a property richer than she could have dreamed. Properly handled by the right publisher, given the right publicity and promotion, *The Second Sunrise* could be a success.

Sam knew he must be careful how he explained this possibility to Sing. The work was uniquely hers, her only real inheritance so far as he could see. It was far more than words and pictures to be shared lightly with others. She had said he was the first person to have read it and he did not underestimate the privilege. He must make her see that the contents of this old hand-sewn bag she had treasured for so long held more than a sentimental collection, and that her work on it was more than a beloved endeavour.

He approached her when he had closed the fourth manuscript. Between its covers were herbal secrets dating back to T'ien Shih, the Taoist pope of 1019 and to the Yellow Emperor, Huang Ti, scribe of the oldest known medical treatises. Here was knowledge acquired while the tribes of Europe were still living in caves dressed in the skins of animals and the subjects of China were already wearing silk.

PART · X

The Second Sunrise

He who is one with the black Tao
Stalks alone the halls of evil.
His is the voice of Satan
And his face is of ashes.
For he is lost to all but his kind.
Brother only to his own darkness.

THE CHANG T'IEN SHIH (TAOIST POPE)
A tablet found in the Dragon-Tiger
Temple 1660

• IMAGE FOR BLACK TAO •

Gabriel Saffron

GABRIEL SAFFRON poured himself another lemonade from a crystal pitcher on the bar and mopped his perspiring brow. He was always nervous before a book launching, even one as successful as he felt this one was certain to be. Astral Press had never known a failure since it released its first book from the basement of a converted fire station near Venice Beach in 1947.

It had not taken him long to become the largest publisher and distributor of his kind on the west coast and this one looked like making him even bigger.

Like anyone else who lived in or around Beverly Hills Gabe understood the value of giving the right parties for the right people at the right time. This was particularly true in the publishing business where a disgruntled critic or a bored columnist could make or break a book and its author with a few well chosen words.

Gabe Saffron simply made sure this never happened to him or his authors or their work. He did it by choosing his subjects with the care and skill of an art dealer, knowing his readers better than any marketing organisation in the country and leaving as little to chance as humanly possible.

For some reason, probably ordained by the cosmic energies that he felt sure he was a part of, southern California was beginning to hatch centres of enlightenment under its benevolent sun like rare and exotic butterflies. Although still few and far between, the self-styled sufis and shamans, gurus and swamis were gathering followers from San Diego to San Francisco. Headed by the enlightened ones who wove their own clothes, grew their own food and propagated their own dope in the foothills of the Sierras, the occult offered a welcome alternative to the disillusions of post-war American life.

Whether it was the esoteric scriptures of the cabala, the gematria of Talmud, the kami of Shinto and Zen, or the wisdom of orientalism and the promises of reincarnation—as long as it was unexplained it drew disciples in ever increasing numbers.

The day of the mystic, the spiritualist and the theosophist was well on its way and Gabriel Saffron found no difficulty tapping into the bright aura of its widening spectrum. Astral Books had pioneered an untouched field shunned by every publisher in the country and turned it into a thriving and rapidly increasing business. From poor beginnings beneath the abandoned firehouse his first thin volumes were cranked out on an old Caxton press and distributed to the sight-seers of Venice Beach at a dime a copy.

There had been no shortage of material from among the astrologers and palmists, psychic healers, diviners, poets and philosophers who were the first to congregate in that hallowed stretch of foreshore and its down-at-heel tenements. Anxious to see their work published and grateful for whatever Gabe could pay them, the contributors to Astral Press trusted him as one of their own. Gabriel Saffron was an entrepreneur but he never let them down. If a book made money, they made money. Gabe was a man you could trust.

Raised in the downtown end of Pico Boulevard he knew what it was to struggle and he understood how hungry the seekers after salvation could get. He was also a gambler and an optimist, never hesitating to expand—a more modern press, then two, then three. A string of small exclusive shop outlets for Astral Books had soon grown into full-scale distribution up and down the coast. He had bought the firehouse, converted it and it was still his main source of supply.

Protected, guided and advised by spiritualists, crystal gazers and clairvoyants, it was hard for Gabriel to make a wrong move. He had borrowed big from the banks, and moved so far up Pico that he found himself in Beverly Hills where he built Astral Abbey, looking down on the rich and famous of Hollywood.

Like the readers who had made him rich, Gabe had closed his mind to anything and everything he considered conventional. He regularly consulted several gurus of different persuasions, practiced Hatha Yoga every day without fail, managing the stressful aspects of his hectic life through Transcendental Meditation and the all-revealing travels of astral flight.

There wasn't a cult or sect he hadn't investigated, an ashram he hadn't visited or a healer he wasn't familiar with. His devouring interest in all things offering even the most bizarre alternative to what he considered the decadence of the American way had made him something of a guru figure himself.

Even his name had been chosen for him by his spiritual guide and approved by a numerologist as a combination of just the right number of letters balanced perfectly to his yogic chakras. To be given the Christian name of the divine herald, the first to announce the immaculate conception, trumpeter of the last judgement, revealer of the Koran, appealed to his strong sense of divine karma.

The stigmas of the saffron crocus were used to colour the robes of eastern mystics and he felt it suited him perfectly. Some of those who did business with him felt that for a man who had been born plain John Grey and made his first dollar selling incense and windbells on Venice beach, he sometimes took the role of archangel too literally.

Gabriel picked up the first volume of *The Second Sunrise* and admired again the look and feel of it. Production costs had been far greater than Astral usually invested in a new author but he had not hesitated. The best designers and typographers in the business had been called in to lay out its 500 pages. No expense had been spared on paper quality, printing or binding. The glossy dust jacket blazed with an ancient symbol encircled in gold light and on the back the photograph of its stunning author, Sing Deverill, gazed back at him like some oriental priestess promising to make them both a great deal of money.

From the moment he had received the first small bundle of hand-written manuscript he had known this was something very special. Sam's covering letter had outlined a profile of its author which alone had whetted his appetite. The gut instinct that seldom failed Gabriel had grown more definite with every page. He was never wrong about such things, but like everything else that could significantly affect the prosperous path his life had taken, he sought the advice of his spirit guide. His judgement had been favourably confirmed. That which had been sent to him from the east was of great antiquity, authentic in its origins, genuine in every way.

Madam Mandalay was immensely fat, propelled in a motorised reinforced wheelchair, custom built for the purpose, she glided across the white marble floors of her Bellair temple like a female Buddha caught in a stainless steel trap. Although she was billed as 'Psychic to the Stars' and was consulted by some of the most famous names in Hollywood, Gabe had often thought that her fees were as grossly inflated as her person. But they were nothing compared to the comfort he found in the confirmation of his personal deity.

The layers of flesh that garlanded her neck had so often quivered with the effort of summoning Xoomtai, the Burmese Prince from the sacred pagoda of Arakan. Xoomtai had nothing but positive things to say about *The Second Sunrise*: 'The scribe who carries this message is a chosen one endowed with mystic powers. She will bring you great rewards.'

Gabe imagined he felt the stirring of his kundalini, the serpent of sensual potency that lay coiled at the base of his spine. Madame Mandalay had convinced him of it as the message came through. The serpent was always aroused in the presence of the medium in one of her quivering trances, the piping voice of Prince Xoomtai causing her to drool. It had never occurred to Gabe that the prince always told him exactly what he wanted to hear.

From the apartment on Ocean Avenue, Sing looked down on the sweeping shores of Santa Monica. The palm-lined fringe of its beachfront was a well-watered green against wide stretches of sand reaching down to the Pacific. This was her second week in Los Angeles and she preferred the clean air off the sea to the trapped heat of Beverly Hills and the Valley.

Looking back over the first week she still found it all hard to believe. Sam had flown her from Hong Kong for the premiere of *The Red Lotus*. He had taken her shopping on Rodeo Drive and assured her she had caused a sensation on that glittering evening. She had not felt like a sensation.

The eyes upon her had not been friendly and she had sensed the falseness that surrounded her. The looks of the men were carnivorous, the compliments of the women thinly-veiled vitriol. Happy for Sam, she had shared with him the excitement of seeing the film that had taken two years to make unfold on the screen. She had stayed with him for the party that followed and celebrated the first reviews over breakfast in his favourite diner.

The diamond on her finger shot a spark against the sea-reflected light from the window. Sam had said it would be best for her to wear it while she was here in Los Angeles. It would keep the men at arm's length and the women jealous, he had grinned. She had agreed but gently declined his offer to stay in his condominium on Sunset Boulevard.

What had happened between them in the summer house at Silvermine Bay had never been repeated. The months of shooting that had followed left no time for anything but work. When he had left to begin editing at Universal Studios she had remained in Hong Kong to work on the corrections and revisions of her own work. When Sam first brought her the news of Saffron

Publishing's interest she did not fully understood what it meant. His excited congratulations were followed by a substantial advance and from that moment Sam Danovich had become her dedicated and unpaid literary agent.

'This is just the beginning,' he said, watching as she read the amount written on the bank draft. 'I know this guy Gabe Saffron. He's a nut but he can make you rich. He'll also swallow you alive if you let him.' He hugged her close. 'Just leave it all to me.'

The draft contract that arrived a month later divided the material into eight properties, each to become a separate book in the series. The Second Sunrise company which Sam formed in Hong Kong for tax purposes would contract to publish the first of them through Astral Press and to offer the remaining seven one at a time, each to be separately negotiated according to sales of previous editions.

Sam acquired the highest possible royalties for Sing on an escalating scale related to American sales, with room to manoeuvre on foreign language editions or paperback rights and retained any potential screen rights. Freddy Fong had whistled approvingly, assuring her that Sam had driven a hard bargain on her behalf and Peggy Pelham had expressed her delight by inviting them both to tea.

In the week after the premiere of *The Red Lotus* and while they waited for the launch date of her first book, Sam showed Sing all there was to see in and around Los Angeles. They attended an endless round of parties in the luxurious homes of studio executives, leading producers and directors, where Sam Danovich and his mysterious fiancée were made excessively welcome.

'They've never seen anyone quite like you. They just can't believe you're the real thing,' he chuckled. 'The genuine article. Rumour is you're some kind of witch. Gabe's crazy about you and his fruitcake friends think you're the reincarnation of some oriental goddess.'

He laughed aloud at her frown of confusion. 'Let them think what they like. In this town full of phonies it doesn't matter what they say about you as long as they say something.'

Sing viewed it all with interest. Since the crowds and flashbulbs of the premiere she had felt detached. Not entirely indifferent but strangely apart, able to appreciate and try to accept what went on around her without trying to become a part of it. It was this air of independence that seemed to have added to the perceptions of her, ranging from Asian royalty to mystic healer. As Sam advised, she simply smiled at such suggestions and gave nothing away, leaving the men to fantasise and the women to gossip.

She was happiest when driving with Sam in his gold Jaguar, speeding smoothly out to Santa Barbara to eat lobster on the pier or to Pacific Palisades where he kept his boat. The English car was Sam's great joy. He had mixed the paint himself, adding a fistful of pure gold dust and it was the only car of its exact colour in Los Angeles—in the world, for all he knew. They sailed out to Catalina Island to lie on the beach and once all the way to Mexico. They walked the breezy miles of Ocean Avenue, right outside the apartment block, following the open sea along the scenic path under the royal palms to Santa Monica pier, feeding the gulls and watching sails slowly crossing in the soft blue distance. It reminded Sing of the South China Sea seen from the heights of Repulse Bay and it made her ache to return there.

Below, on the avenue, the gold top of Sam's Jaguar glided to a halt outside the apartment block. On her way to the elevator before he had reached the security buzzer, the doors opened with a whisper and Sing saw herself in the mirror wall as she stepped inside. The dress she was wearing had been chosen by the stylist Gabe Saffron had sent and so had her hairdo. They even wanted to send a makeup artist until she protested to Sam.

'Just for today you belong to Gabe,' he explained. 'You're a hot property. He knows exactly what they want to see. Relax. You'll be a sensation.'

The dress of pale mauve silk was the colour of her eyes, styled after the cheong-sam, but with Rodeo Drive modifications; her hair was dressed to exaggerate the Asian in her. She wore no jewellery but Sam's gorgeous stone and the bamboo leaf of diamonds on her shoulder.

An hour later Gabe Saffron guided Sing Deverill through the chattering throng of his poolside guests as though she had just arrived from another galaxy. He had met them personally at the door, handing each a glass of champagne and telling Sam to run away and enjoy himself.

'For the next three hours this adorable creature is mine,' he said, taking her elbow.

'Everyone here today, my child, represents a leading magazine or newspaper,' he whispered. 'Just be your natural, charming self and answer their questions simply and briefly.'

He steered her past the display of her books in the entrance lobby, and out into a Mediterranean-style garden, its white walls lined with pencil pines and Grecian urns frothing with flowers.

The wide piazza, shaded by rose-covered trellis surrounding the long strip of a turquoise pool, was crowded with people.

Gabe stopped for brief introductions and moved on towards a gaunt woman standing alone, her hatchet face framed by ash-blonde hair under a snap-brimmed trilby hat. She wore a dark, masculine suit and casually smoked a small cigar.

'That is Kate Cortez,' said Gabe softly, as they approached. 'She is to publishing what Hedda Hopper and Louella Parsons are to movies. She's a bitch, so be nice to her.' The group separating them from the tall, thin woman fell away as Gabe called out to her.

'Kate. How wonderful you could come.' He passed Sing in front of him with the firm pressure of a father presenting his child to royalty.

'This is Sing Deverill, the lady from Hong Kong—the light in the sunrise.'

It was still dark when Sing left her apartment the following morning. The doorman on duty hardly roused himself as she sprang the security button and let herself out into the chill air. He had seen her leave at this time every morning since she arrived, so it did not surprise him. Ocean Avenue was the place for early risers. Its miles of promenade high above the beach were a mecca for runners and walkers or just those who wanted to see the sunrise.

She walked the mile to the pier and out onto its furthest point. The seafood stalls and eateries were still shuttered; the sound of the sea swished among the pilings as the homeless raised their heads from the benches to watch her pass. She had found a secluded spot, a platform reached by a set of wooden steps, almost at water level.

It was a disused landing stage, its old grey planks petrified by the salt spray and fifty years of tides. Out of sight from the first to arrive with their fishing lines, it was too small to be shared and gave her privacy. From here she could watch the gulls following the fishing boats, drink in the untouched air and, in her mind, return to the rock above Tung T'ing.

It was only here that she could think clearly, consider what was happening to her, draw in the life force and meditate. Sam had assured her that the launch at Astral Abbey had been a great success. That she had answered the searching questions of Kate Cortez and the flock of reporters in just the right way. They had loved her, he said.

Gabriel had been even more delighted. 'You were superb, child. Absolutely superb. The vultures adored you.' His moist hands and watery eyes had remained upon her for a little too long.

With the city of Santa Monica behind her and nothing but the long, wide blow of the ocean ahead, she could have been looking out at the China Sea and she felt again the longing for Hong Kong. She knew Sam was going to ask her to stay in Los Angeles. That he was already planning a series of documentaries based on the books and hoped she would leave the ring on her finger permanently, that she would marry him and become his partner.

The prospect confused her. California was a pleasant place to live, the people were friendly, once the superficial facade of Beverly Hills was separated from reality. It would be so easy to say yes.

The high-powered pressures of Hollywood that were a part of Sam's life did not intimidate her. The nervousness she felt when Toby first begun to take her out had been caused by her desire to please him, to impress his friends. The official banquets she had attended with Jiro Toshido had meant survival and the abortive expectations of Sparrow's Green had been demanded of her. Here with Sam Danovich, she felt cool and capable, indifferent to the things around her that she did not like or understand. But she knew that it could never be where she belonged.

Leaving the pier two hours later, sunshine throwing long shadows across the wet grass, she saw Sam's unmistakable golden Jaguar parked outside the Oceanview apartment block. The doorman sprang up from behind his desk as she came in, a mug of coffee in his hand. He hurriedly set it down and picked up a copy of the *Hollywood Reporter*.

'You got your picture in the paper, Miss Deverill. They said good things about your book.'

Sing returned his grin as she passed. 'Thanks Harold. That's nice to know.'

He hurried ahead of her to press the elevator button. 'And Mr Danovich is waiting upstairs. I hope it's okay. He had his own key.'

The smell of fresh brewed coffee came from behind her door as she put the key in the lock. Sam bore down on her, his arms wide, closing around her in a bear hug.

'You did it, lady. The critics loved you. All of them.' He let her go and picked up the *Los Angeles Times* from a pile of folded newspapers. 'Listen to this.'

Listening to Sam reading aloud the glowing reviews, Sing felt suddenly overwhelmed with gratitude towards him. She had always appreciated his patience, his generosity, all that they had shared together and his confidence in her. She trusted him. He was her friend, she owed him so much. How could she tell him? Taking the paper from his hands as he was still reading, she spoke very softly.

'Sam, I'm very pleased. It's wonderful and it's all thanks to you.' She kissed him lightly, her strong arms drawing him to her.

'Take me away somewhere. Away from people. Where we can be alone together. No more parties.' She smiled into his eyes. 'Away from Gabriel and people like Kate Cortez.'

His body tensed as he held her close. 'I know just the place for us,' he whispered.

The Jaguar shot along the coast road through Santa Barbara and skirted the foot of the ranges to Monterey. They had packed very little, enough for a week in the Sierra Nevada and the Yosemite Valley. Sam had a cabin there among the redwoods. He described it to her as they rested on the seawashed rocks of Monterey Bay: 'Those redwoods seem to touch the sky and the scent of them is like a drug. Its a place you will never want to leave.'

He talked of waterfalls three times higher than Niagara, Indian camps, cliffs and pinnacles as old as any in the world, lakes and rivers fed from the high Sierras. And there were the giant sequoias the Indians called totems of the gods.

The Jaguar climbed the foothills of the National Park with an hour to sunset. It was like entering a great cathedral, the vast trunks of the redwoods rising like pillars, fired crimson by the last of the day. The radiant aura of the sky struck through the canopy like a window of stained glass.

They left the car at the dude ranch closer to the road. The white-haired Indian who ran the place greeted Sam like a brother and introduced himself to Sing as Billy Yellow Bear. His tubby wife took her into the little shop and fitted her out with the things she would need, then walked ahead with a lantern as they dragged the stores through the woods by Indian sled pulled behind a pack-horse.

The log cabin was small and roughly built, but as solidly rooted into its majestic setting as the great trees that surrounded its walls. The inside was warmed by a wide hearth, the floor strewn with the skins of bear and mountain lion. It had been a trading post,

Sam said, before the valley became a park, when the Indians worshipped the sequoia in peace and no roads led to their villages.

The next two weeks were spent hiking the valley floors, marvelling at the ribbons of water that cascaded from cliff-tops almost too high to see. Billy Yellow Bear brought them a pair of mountain ponies to trek out of the valley and there were moose-hide canoes for fishing on the glassy lake.

At night, the hearth ablaze with pine-logs, Sam cooked the salmon and big-mouth bass they caught or sizzled the venison steaks Billy left in the ice-box, along with bottles of Coors beer and Californian wine. After they had eaten they made love for hours on a pile of skins before the embers of the fire.

The trails of the dude ranch led in other directions and apart from the discreet comings and goings of Billy or his wife with fresh fruit and vegetables they saw and heard no one. They slept to nightsounds and woke to the fluting of birds, to lie in each other's arms until Sam rose to spike the crisp forest air with the smell of coffee and frying bacon. It was a time Sing wished would never end.

The deep affection she felt for him was mixed with gentle caring and strange sadness. He had become the most important person in her life. But it was not love as she had once known it and she knew it never could be. Putting this from her mind, Sing had nourished his body with her own, sparing nothing of herself to give him joy, accepting in return the gift of his love.

On the last day they walked through the thick grass of the valley to the foot of Wild Horse Falls. Billy Yellow Bear said that when the storms rolled over Yosemite, lightening rode down the towering cascade in a mad stampede. They fell more than 1000 metres he said, the highest waterfall in California. It was what the tourist people had told him to say, he grinned as he left them to the beauty of the place. But he knew they came from much higher, far beyond the clouds, he called back. For this was the garden of the gods.

Where the cascade thundered into a deep pool, exploding in sparkling tumult, the air was electrified with a drifting mist. All the colours of the spectrum reflected in the diamond as Sing drew it from her finger. She reached for Sam's hand, raising it to her lips to kiss his open palm as she had done once before.

The hard feel of the ring in place of her lips as she closed his fist around it sent a physical pain through Sam Danovich. He felt the witchcraft of her in this magic place, the place he had never shared with anyone until now. It had given him renewed life to be here with her and he could not bear the thought of its ending.

'Marry me, Sing.' He did not look at her as he spoke, so humbly that she could hardly hear him over the rumble of the falls. 'Marry me.' He turned to take her by the shoulders, forcing her to look at him. 'Stay. Don't go back. You will have everything. Success, fame, all the money you'll ever need. We can come here, to this place, whenever we want to.' He paused, searching her eyes.

'I love you, lady. In a way that I have never known. You cannot leave me now. Give me a chance to make you as happy as you have made me.' His hands tightened on her shoulders and she thought he would shake her. Then there were tears in his eyes. She lowered her own, unable to watch the hurt she was causing him.

'I don't think I could live without you, Sing. Let me make you happy, it's all I ask.'

'I was not born to be happy, Sam. I was born to survive. I would not be fair to you,' she answered him softly. 'In everything I do my European side must always consult my Chinese side. It is never easy. They seldom agree.'

His fingers relaxed, sliding from her to hang helplessly at his side.

'I must go back, my dear Sam. There is something I must do alone. Something you will one day understand. Perhaps, when it is done . . . ' She did not finish the sentence, holding out her hand to him. 'I will always be your greatest friend.'

He smiled his lopsided smile. 'I guess it'll have to be enough for now, but you'll never lose me, lady. Just remember that. I'll never give you up.'

Gabe Saffron's voice was filled with concern.

'Sam tells me you're leaving. I've been trying to get you all week. Why didn't you tell me you were leaving town? Kate Cortez wants to do another story. Its all set up. The promotion is going like gangbusters. I've got three magazines bidding on a feature, talk shows, live appearances . . . ' The words flooded over the phone.

'Child, we're a smash. You can't leave now. We've simply got to talk and quickly. Translations are happening. Child, are you there?'

'I'm here, Gabriel.'

'Well get yourself over here to the house, I'll send a car. Oh, and there's some female been pestering the office all week. Says to tell you Birdie rang.' He read out an address in Venice Beach which she copied down on the phone pad.

'Be ready in an hour. I'll send the car.'

The click of the receiver cut his voice off with a steady, metallic burr before Sing had finished writing. She listened to it for seconds, staring at the address, wondering if she could have heard him correctly.

Gabriel's driver cocked an eyebrow when Sing asked to be taken to Venice Beach on the way to Beverly Hills. He parked in a lot on the ocean front and watched her disappear among the activities of the famous strip. It was a Sunday afternoon and the promenade on the edge of the sand was crowded with sightseers and street entertainers.

Fire-eaters and jugglers were side by side with fortune tellers, acrobats and musclemen. Garment stalls, hot-dog and burger stands competed with ice-cream carts and vendors selling handicrafts, sculptures and paintings.

She found the entrance beside a shop advertising Tarot readings and astral charts, and climbed the narrow stairs, her knock answered by a woman she hardly recognised as her old friend. Only the blue of her eyes made her unmistakable. Her plump body seemed to have shrunk. Her hair, once the colour of ripe corn, had lost its life.

They held onto each other, tears smudging the Indian kohl around Birdie's eyes.

'I can't believe it's really you. When I saw your picture I thought I must be dreaming.'

'Are you ill?' asked Sing anxiously.

'I have been.' Birdie blinked away her tears. 'I've never been happier to see anyone in all my life.'

'I feel the same,' smiled Sing. 'I just couldn't believe it could really be you. But I have an appointment I must keep. Come with me, Birdie. We can talk on the way and afterwards we'll move you out of here.'

Birdie sniffed and wiped her eyes. 'Not until I've given you something,' she said mysteriously. Going to the chest of drawers she began rummaging among its contents.

Sing looked around the sparsely furnished space, searching the drab walls for the illuminating smile of Guru Ji, only to find them bare.

'I've been away from Sparrow's Green for over two years,' said Birdie, bringing something from the drawer.

'From what I heard before I left, your daughter had won every heart in the village.' She placed a photograph in Sing's hand. 'This is Nova. She is safe and well.'

The photograph showed a little girl playing with a puppy. At a glance Sing recognised the gardens of Grange Manor, the big ivy-covered house in the background.

'It's her, Sing. Your daughter, Nova, taken two years ago. I only used my Box Brownie and I wasn't very close.'

Sing found it hard to speak as she blinked through her tears at the long-haired child.

'Somehow I knew I'd find you one day.' Birdie held out another snapshot. 'This one's even better. It was taken on her birthday. Amelia Monk got it from her niece who works up at the Grange.'

The photo was postcard size and in close-up. The little girl looked out with smiling eyes. The feeling that filled Sing's heart was unknown to her, a mixture of love and sadness she had never felt before. She found herself wondering what colour the child's eyes were, searching the face, so full of promise, for a sign of Asian blood and finding none. Sing sat looking at the pictures for many moments before going to Birdie and holding her close.

'How can I ever repay you? You must let me try.'

In the back of the car on the way to Astral Abbey, Sing learned something of Birdie's travels. For her, she said, the search for Universal Bliss had ended in India when she became too sick to wait for Guri Ji to look upon her and she had been put on the train to Delhi. She had followed other saviours, Birdie said with a tired smile. It had led her to a rented room and the shop she shared with a fortune teller. She had learned to read the stars, to map the lives of others through the position of the planets, but could do nothing to foresee her own future.

The photographs of the child she had made herself forget had opened a hole in Sing's heart. She had learned not to think of the little girl called Nova, with other things that were in the past. Nova had been lost to her. Now she was alive again. The knowledge that Sir Duncan had kept his word filled her with a great relief.

Over the following days, Birdie Meadows was once again at Sing's side, content to watch the success of her friend and to help her where she could. She was quite convinced that Sing's reappearance in her life was karmic destiny. The miracle that had brought them together again was no accident, no coincidence of chance.

She had to admit that the search for enlightenment, begun so long ago on the steps of Canterbury Cathedral, had left her still lost and confused. Her years in the ashram of Guru Ji had seriously affected her health. At first she had ignored the stomach troubles that plagued so many of the thousands upon thousands who flocked to the feet of the One True God. It was worth it, they said, just to be near him, to see him pass by, perhaps to have him glance their way—or if they were among the chosen ones, to be spoken to and touched.

The comfortless and unhygienic lifestyle of the ashram was a small price to pay for such reward, sleeping when you could on the hard floors of the dormitory huts, queueing for the twice-daily bowl of rice and a ladle of watery curry, searching always for a cup of drinkable water in the blistering heat. Such hardship had seemed to bring on a kind of euphoria. Through the teachings of Mr Puri, she had learned that the physical self was nothing more than a husk to temporarily house the soul and that those things seen as suffering by the unenlightened were simply steps along the path of Universal Bliss.

She had ignored the awful pains, the hours spent squatting in the rat-infested latrine, believing with all her heart that this was where she belonged. And when the believers assembled in the scant shade to endlessly chant their worship, she had felt the energy drawn from her like ectoplasm, soothed to a state of well-being by this great cosmic prayer joined with one voice to feed the radiant being before them, like bees swarming to their queen.

When the amoeba deep inside Birdie finally took root and she could not leave the hut to join the prayers, she had prayed from where she lay, hoping her voice would be heard. Guru Ji had not come to see her. One smile from his halo of golden light, one touch of his hand could have healed her, she was sure. But he had not come, sending instead two of his disciples who put her on the dust-covered bus for the hospital in Jaipur.

There she had met an American, a woman a little older than herself. They had shared a corner of the crowded ward while the dysentery was treated. The American woman said her name was Grace and she was also a disciple of the path of Universal Bliss. This was her fourth pilgrimage, she had said proudly, and she knew the hospital well.

When they were released a week later, weak and still seriously ill, she had invited Birdie to come with her back to America. She lived on Venice Beach, she said, where people understood what it was to search for God. She was a reader of the Tarot and told fortunes there. Grace had spread her pack of charmed cards upon the bed and assured Birdie that this was her karma. There was a small room above her shop and Birdie was welcome to stay there.

Birdie had no real options. She was too ill to return to the ashram of Guru Ji and there was nothing left for her in Sparrow's Green. Alf Bramble would have another housekeeper by now and she no longer belonged there. In her simple way Birdie had told herself Grace was sent by some divine power to take her further along the path, wherever it might lead.

With Sam's help, Sing had her put into the Santa Monica hospital for tests and the drugs she was given helped her greatly. The results had shown there was little to be done about the wayward cell so firmly entrenched in her intestine except strict control of diet and prescribed drugs. She had moved out of the depressing little space above the fortune-teller's shop and into Sing's Oceanview apartment. The excitement she felt at the thought of accompanying Sing on her return to Hong Kong, together with regular medication and sensible food, had already begun to rebuild her health and her faith in life.

Sing insisted it was not enough, that the drugs were not a cure and must be replaced by natural treatment as quickly as possible. Together in the limousine that Gabe Saffron had put at her disposal they visited Chinatown and went from place to place to find the right medicines. The stocks of the few herbalists were poor. There was little call for Chinese medicine, the doctors said. No one believed in the old ways except a handful of elders in the Chinese community. Sing said it was because people knew nothing of natural healing. They were suspicious of things they did not understand.

There was a doctor in Hong Kong who could cure Birdie and Sing insisted it was where they must go. She knew her time was over in Los Angeles, it was time to go and she would not leave her old friend now that she had found her.

Sam Danovich did all that he could to change Sing's mind about leaving. She should stay to oversee the compiling of her next book, he said, to keep the publicity coming, to marry him.

The decision to leave Sam and return to Hong Kong was the most difficult Sing had made since leaving England and her child. She had meditated on it for many mornings in the private place at the end of the pier. There she had seen clearly where she must go and what she must do. Her path led to the shuttered house on the bluff over Repulse Bay. And to something else she could not explain, something sinister that drew her back. Something she had always known must one day be faced.

The Walled City of Kowloon 1965

THOSE FEW Urban Council officials who had managed to penetrate the Walled City of Ling Nam reported depths of unspeakable squalor and decadence that defied the imagination of the most hardened government authority. Every conceivable vice had taken root in its labyrinth of decaying tunnels and flourished like some poisonous fungi.

So disturbing were these discoveries that efforts had been made to resettle its estimated 30,000 illegal residents and demolish the entire area—no bigger than half a dozen city blocks. Each time the bulldozers had moved in they were fought off by the sheer weight of numbers and the fanaticism of the Walled City residents. This was China, they screamed—to invade its soil was to invade China herself.

So vehement were the protests of the Anti-Resettlement Association that an already nervous British government was forced to back down, fully aware that the real number crammed into the three festering hectares of Ling Nam was closer to 50,000. Most of these were illegal immigrants from across the border, among them hardened groups of Communist agitators, with many of the rest, thieves, opium dealers, rapists and murderers. Hundreds of unlicenced shops and unregistered factories flourished under Peking's protection and the Hong Kong police force was powerless to move on one of them. Now Communist cadres recruited and trained their ranks with the same immunity.

In the heart of this mayhem, owned and operated by its most powerful gang leader, the Palace of Hong had become the centre of operations. White Meat Hong had raped and murdered a White Russian girl on the mainland. He had always been a brothel keeper and trader of flesh. His place in the old Russian concession of Harbin had been the most popular in the infamous Red Door Street of the Chinese quarter. He had specialised in the white slave trade and the flood of women and children driven from Belorussia by the Cossacks in 1938 had helped to make him rich.

The girl was not the first to die at the hand of White Meat Hong or his customers but this one was young and happened to be the favourite of a French official. Whoremonger Hong was forced to get out of Harbin in a hurry. Leaving everything behind except three balls of best Javanese opium, he had come to Hong Kong.

With the opium, he had started up again inside the Walled City of Ling Nam. There was nowhere else for him to go. He had no passport and the kind of business he liked to run was too dangerous even in the loosely policed areas of Wan Chai and Kowloon Tong, both jealously guarded triad territories. For ten years now the Palace of Hong had grown to become the stronghold of every vice the Walled City had hatched.

It was the only place where for the right price a white woman could be had against her will. There were also special performances for select and high-paying audiences from the outside. No act of sexual depravity, no bestial practice, could be imagined that was not available at the Palace of Hong. The coupling of human females and male animals had long held a bizarre fascination for some of those who peopled the Chinese underworld and if the woman happened to be white, so much the better for business.

So, White Meat Hong had prospered as the unofficial king of corruption in Ling Nam and he saw himself as its warlord. If it was women, drugs, kidnapping, extortion, false passports, the fencing of stolen property, smuggling of any kind, Hong could arrange it.

Apart from the growing opportunities of the drug traffic, women were still his main source of business. He had watched with interest as the various derivatives of opium developed and became marketable but it was an increasingly dangerous business to deal in. As head of the Hong Kong syndicate, J.T. Ching had flourished but with his mysterious death the Yellow Dragon triad had broken up and been taken over by the other societies.

While the triad fought among themselves for distribution, Hong had no wish to join the battle. Instead, he continued to buy and sell in small quantities, supplying his own modest outlets and dealing in what he knew best, the buying and selling of women of every nationality—Thai, Filipino, Korean, Indian, Japanese, even African and, whenever he could, caucasian.

A man in White Meat Hong's position was always in danger of challenge. Feared though he was by his competition and tolerated by the tongs, the more powerful and prosperous he grew, the more vulnerable he became to attack. It was for this reason he had sought Ah Keung—the Forceful One. He knew that this man had been strong enough to defy the Yellow Dragon and that he had been the chosen one of the great J.T. Ching.

White Meat Hong had eyes and ears everywhere and was one of the first to hear of the death of taipan Ching. It was he who had paid Ah Keung well to bring him the mah-lau, the strange ape that Ching had prized so. While the women of the great house had fought tooth and nail over its contents, there had been no difficulty acquiring the creature that would otherwise have been destroyed, and he had given it pride of place in his private bestiary.

It was he who had arranged Ah Keung's temporary disappearance to Taiwan to become the initiate of Black Oath Wu. With the death of J.T. Ching even Ah Keung would have eventually gone down before the revenge of those who had resented his privileged position and who accused him of the taipan's death. Like himself, the Forceful One had made many enemies through his fierce greed for power.

Wan Chai had become no longer safe for him. The Forceful One was of the old ways, a warrior whose superior skills had given him a dangerous arrogance that would have proved his downfall if he had stayed in Hong Kong. He had to be shown new ways. He had to be given powers that could not be challenged. Powers that only one such as Ah Keung could possess. The supreme power of the Black Tao. Now he was back and White Meat Hong had given him the rooms to live in on the top floor of the Palace of Hong. It was good business. With the Forceful One as his ally and so close within his house Hong had little to fear from others.

The dog boy stirred in the blackness of his space. It was not exactly an awakening, he never truly slept as others slept. His was a strange half-world where the difference between night and day, light and dark, consciousness and unconsciousness, was hard to define.

Inside the section of disused pipe he was allowed to live in he stretched out his arms to touch his ceiling and his walls. He noticed as he moved that there was hardly any pain. His small face, old and twisted into the permanent shape of suffering was incapable of smiling, but he smiled inside. Inside was where he lived, where no one else could see, a place where no one could drive him away. Where no one could laugh but the dog boy.

This was the time he liked most, when life within the walled city was quietest. Only the murmur of those who never slept and from the rooftops the first cock-crow. The flap of tarpaper that covered the entrance to the pipe was propped back with a stick to let the air in. The dog boy knew he was lucky to have this place. It was half buried in the small compound where Sharp Chopper Lau kept the dogs behind his eating house.

As the light began to grow he could see his belongings. The tin cup he sometimes used to beg with, the cracked rice bowl and chopsticks he had stolen from the noodle shop. There were other things, treasures that he kept hidden in the chicken crate behind his head so that anyone who tried to steal them would have to crawl over him. No one would do that.

The tiny pit-pat of his songbird began with the light as it hopped from perch to perch in its bamboo cage. It was the greatest of his treasures and the smile inside him grew bigger as he waited for its first shy chirrup.

There were only three dogs left in the tiny yard and they would soon be ready for eating. He would have to go up, out of Ling Nam and into the streets of Kowloon in search of more. It was at night-time he caught them. In the alleyways behind the chop houses. Wherever there was garbage. He would wait and they would come. Sooner or later they would come, sniffing to where he waited with scraps to feed them and a collar on a rope.

Some ran away but most came with him; they were not afraid of him. He knew how they felt, he could talk to them. For each stray dog Sharp Chopper Lau gave him five dollars, sometimes eight and once when the dog he found was not too skinny and already had a collar, he had paid ten.

The dog boy lay on his side, watching the strengthening light, and listening to the tiny riffling of feathers, flapping his hand at the cockroaches that had come in the night. He had never lain down any other way. The curvature of his spine made it impossible. It was why they had first started calling him dog boy, because of the way he lay down wherever he could.

Like so many of the homeless he suffered the disfigurements of bone disease that had twisted his body out of shape. Where others had died, he had found a way of surviving. Something in his mind always found a way. He didn't know it was courage. No one knew how old the dog boy was or where he had come from, so no one had told him. He did not care. It was enough to know when to come out of the pipe, when to eat and when to come back to it.

He was hungry now, as he always was when the first smells of cooking came from the kitchens. This was the part of the Walled City where all the eating houses were, in its centre, facing onto what was considered the town square, big enough for a hundred people to stand side by side. It was the largest public space in Ling Nam, where every one came to drink tea and talk or to eat at the tables and play cards or checkers.

He rolled upright and, throwing back the tarpaper flap, tumbled out of the pipe in the way he had learned, hanging the bamboo cage in its entrance. The three dogs strained on their ropes, yapping to him for food, pushing their noses into his long, crooked hands, licking his fingers as he passed. This was the day he hated most. The day of the feeding. The dogs had been in the yard for more than a week now.

Each day they had been given just enough scraps to keep them alive. Today would be different. Which one would be chosen? The yellow one, he decided—she had been here the longest and she was the biggest, high-backed and long-legged, as though somewhere in her back-street pedigree there had once been a greyhound.

He did not always make friends with the dogs he found but this one had been hard to ignore, its bony whip of a tail lashing with the pleasure of seeing him. He had heard the men talking at the tables many times about how the strange gwai-los made friends with dogs and even cats and never ate them. They laughed over their tea at the stupidity of this. So, although the dogs were his only companions, the dog boy never showed signs of pity.

Sharp Chopper Lau came to the back door with a bucket in his hand. The dog boy knew it would be almost filled with chow fan—the tasty fried rice mixed with vegetables and meat scraps, perhaps some black beans and sliced larp cheung. He waited while Sharp Chopper Lau stood on the step and looked at the three skinny dogs, from one to the other, a cigarette drooping from his mean mouth. He puffed on it, squinting past the smoke. It waggled as he spoke.

'The yellow one. Give it to the yellow one,' he said, and leaving the bucket on the step he went back inside, banging the door.

The dog boy felt the little jab of sorrow that always came when he knew which one was next, but it didn't last. With his tin mug he doled out a small pile for each of the other two and while their noses were buried he set the bucket down in front of the yellow dog. Watching for a moment while it wolfed into three quarters of the rice, he turned away and left the yard through a gap in the corrugated iron which fenced it in.

The dog boy knew what would happen next. Sharp Chopper Lau would wait until the rice had been half digested, then he would come out into the yard with a club and a length of twine. He would wind the twine around the yellow dog's jaws and tie it tight to stop it from vomiting. Then with the heavy club he would beat it to death, expertly, painstakingly pounding the carcass to tenderise the flesh and pulp the rice in its belly to a flavoursome stuffing, to be roasted and served with the meat.

The people beginning to take their places at the tables grinned as they watched the dog boy hurrying away as fast as his twisted limbs would let him, away from the terrible howling that came from the yard. One man, sitting alone at a table that was set apart for him, finished his glass of tea, left some coins among the litter of bowls and followed after him, limping in his own peculiar step. He wore no shirt and the face of a tiger was tattooed on his bare chest and on his back a striking cobra. People looked at each other, some muttered under their breath. What could Ah Keung, the Forceful One, want with such a boy that the gods had overlooked?

Sharp Chopper Lau dipped a well-worn brush into the inkpot and wrote out his special dishes for the day in crude, hasty characters. They were almost always the same but by adding this and adding that it looked as though his menu was always changing. His was the biggest eating house in Ling Nam and he had more tables to fill than the others. Thanks to the dog boy he always had dog meat cooked in different ways. It was a favourite of the residents of Ling Nam, prized for its warming qualities, and today he had prepared the meat the old Kweichow way, baked in clay. Ash fell from his cigarette onto the paper; he shook it off the still-wet ink and pinned the day's menu on the wall. In the grimy mirror he saw Ah Keung enter the door. He knew who this man was. Everybody knew him.

The Forceful One was feared in the Walled City. No one had forgotten that he had killed Jimmy Chan, the Red Pole of the Yellow Dragon society. Right here, beneath their feet in the bean-curd and noodle cellars. It was also known that three men had died violently on the day that he had disappeared, their heads lifted from their necks and spun around.

No one had heard of such deaths before or since. For two years he had not been seen. Talk around the tables had said that he too had been killed. That the Yellow Dragon had executed him. Others doubted this because no one had boasted of his death. They preferred the rumour that he had been reported in Taiwan, a disciple of Black Oath Wu. Now he was back as the protector of White Meat Hong.

Sharp Chopper Lau knew exactly how it felt to be a man feared by others. He himself was feared. Had he not chopped to death those who became his enemies? Was he not so savage with the flat steel blade, so expert in its use that none had ever compared with him? When you are such a man as this, when you run an eating house in the centre of a place without law, where only the strongest and hardest survive, you are a man who cannot afford hesitation.

He turned without looking at the Forceful One and placed the inkpot and brush on a shelf by the chopping block. His two fokis, the men who helped with the cooking and waited on tables, kept their eyes on the strips of pork and roasted ducks they were hanging on hooks in the open window space.

Behind Sharp Chopper Lau, within easy reach, the row of specially shaped cleavers rested in their wooden slots, their blades ground and honed each morning by his own hands.

'The boy who feeds the dogs. Do you own him?' Ah Keung could have been asking for a plate of noodles.

'I shelter and feed him,' answered Sharp Chopper Lau, staring straight into the Forceful One's eyes. 'I pay him well.'

'He lives like a stray dog and you pay him nothing.' Ah Keung's eyes were unblinking as he read easily the other man's thoughts, anticipated his move before it had property framed in the mind.

'I have taken him with me as my servant. Do you object?'

Before Sharp Chopper Lau could answer, Ah Keung's hand flashed out. In a movement too fast for the eye to follow, he seized the largest chopper and slashed it against the bare flesh of his own exposed chest. Again and again he struck. Red welts appeared across the snarling face of the tiger but no blood flowed. Twelve times he struck and the steel seemed to bounce from his ribs. Then, as though to show that this was no trick, he brought it whirling with such force its blade was buried to the hilt in the chopping block. Sharp Chopper Lau and his fokis could only stare, their mouths wide.

'Pull it out,' said Ah Keung in a reasonable tone. 'Pull it out and the boy remains with the dogs and in your service. Fail and he stays with me. You will have no claim on him.'

Blank faces peered from the tables through the window space as Sharp Chopper hunched over the block, both hands on the steel handle. They watched as he lifted the chopping block from the floor, applied his feet, used every ounce of his strength. Someone murmured words of admiration for the power of the Forceful One's ch'i, the protective ch'i possessed by only the greatest of masters. The ch'i of the golden bell. Soon these words were joined by jeers at the weakness of Sharp Chopper Lau.

Hong Kong 1966

No ONE but Alistair Pidcock knew that Sing had purchased Villa Formosa. Things had gone remarkably well since the success of her first book and her return to Hong Kong. The recognition she had found in L.A. had continued to grow, all the pieces falling into place, as perfectly as she could have wished. As well as quickly developing a clear and decisive head for business, she found she had also inherited her father's accurate eye for anything that could make money and return a considerable profit for a small risk.

Sam had worked closely with Gabriel Saffron to see that each year a new volume of *The Second Sunrise* was published on an international scale and that no opportunity had been missed in its promotion. Now in eleven languages, the eight volumes were in constant reprint in both hardcover and paperback. On completion of the last one, Gabriel had produced a limited-edition collector's set, superbly bound in deerskin, embossed with gold leaf and printed on hand-made paper. At $1,500 a set he had been hard pressed to keep up with demand.

Beverly Hills' most prestigious art gallery held an exhibition of the original text and artworks. They were hailed as the most valuable examples of calligraphy and authentic Chinese watercolour to have ever been displayed on Melrose Avenue. The antique and art dealers had made large offers but the works were not for sale. Once the material had played its part in the publicity machine every piece was returned to Hong Kong where Sing presented the collection to the university and the City Hall Library at a ceremony attended by both Chinese and western officials.

Through Sam's management Sing was by now an excellent businesswoman. Gabe Saffron had been right in his predictions and now, in the mid-sixties, the alternate lifestyle movement was no longer a fringe fraternity of freaks and cranks. It had swept the country. The pathways pioneered by seekers like Birdie Meadows were filled with disillusioned youth crossing South-East Asia in broken-down buses, taxi-cabs and on foot, in search of answers. Sing's books had found a whole new market.

With the devoted help of Alistair Pidcock she had invested wisely and her income from royalties more than paid for the ongoing restoration of the Villa Formosa. She had been in no hurry to begin and it was only over the past two years that she had authorised its start, becoming personally involved in its exacting process.

Sing Deverill was considered by Hong Kong society something of an enigma. She was rich, successful, talented and beautiful, yet she was never seen in the places she was expected to be seen and seldom accepted the invitations that had once come her way. In time they stopped coming and it was decided that there was something decidedly odd about her.

It suited Sing perfectly. She worked hard alongside Freddy Fong in the development of Venture Films and the company had prospered. With the recent coming of television, as Freddy had predicted, they had been without serious competition and were soon heavily involved in the production of commercial films. It had kept her fully involved and she was becoming widely respected among the international advertising agencies that were beginning to open their doors.

Sam Danovich had never given up his pursuit of her, visiting Hong Kong two or three times a year to talk business and spend some time with her. His success as an independent director had grown until he was one of the most sought-after names in Hollywood. She had taken holidays in Los Angeles and Hawaii to be with him and their relationship had grown stronger with each passing year.

Still lovers and the greatest of friends when they met, Sam had slowly come to accept the way things were for them but would not admit it was the way things would always be.

Birdie Meadows had also become an invaluable part of Sing's business and personal life. A few weeks of Doctor Sun's treatment, plus complete rest in the house on Silvermine Bay and she had completely recovered her strength and something of her old sparkle. Guided by Sing, Birdie regained some healthy weight and soon revealed a robust but decidedly womanly figure. The shine returning to her hair and the twinkle to her eyes, she had emerged a very handsome woman.

Working beside Sing as her personal assistant, Birdie became fascinated by the herbal remedies that had restored her health where western medicine could not. With Doctor Sun and his sons as her suppliers, Sing established the White Crane Medicine Company with the shares that had accrued for her in Double Elephant Trading.

She had forgotten completely about the doctor's gift of shares in 1945 and when she approached him with the idea of joint business he had reminded her. There was more than enough money to begin an export business and Sing had signed over her interest to Birdie Meadows.

The doctor's younger sons had continued their studies in America and one of them had stayed there to conduct the American end of the White Crane Medicine Company. Birdie spent her time between Hong Kong and the west coast of America as sales manager and had happily settled for a deepening understanding of Gautama Buddha and the Way of the Tao. She opened a small shop on Melrose Avenue which she called The Second Sunrise, as an outlet for the White Crane Medicine Company and a place to buy crystals, incense and astral books.

Sing was content. She found no great need of new friends but greatly cherished the ones she had known for so long. Her relationship with Sam was enough for her and their time together was all the love and romance she needed.

It was several years since Peggy Pelham had moved out of the Helena May Hostel and taken the small, well-situated flat on Kennedy Road. Its bright little sitting room looked over the harbour from the eleventh floor and led onto a tiny balcony with room enough to seat herself and one guest. From this lofty perch, reading the *South China Morning Post* and the *Hong Kong Standard* from cover to cover, she kept in touch with every aspect of life spread out below.

Justin's name had never appeared among those who were finally accounted for in the months and years after the war. The official opinion, given to her by the governor himself before he left for England at the end of his term, was that Colonel Pelham had been lost without trace in the forward defence of Tai Po village. She had received his posthumous decoration, which stood beside his photograph in a gallery of memorabilia on the sideboard, and she had applied every ounce of her strength and every whit of her intelligence to continuing life without him.

She sold the house in Exeter with no intention of ever returning to England and, with the proceeds, purchased the flat on Kennedy Road. With what little was left over, together with a war widow's pension, she was able to contemplate the future with a certain amount of independence and live in modest comfort for the rest of her life. Her only luxury was the dubious service of the ancient and irascible Ah Koo.

This morning in April 1966 she stood on the balcony, taking in the incredible view that had never ceased to fill her with renewed resolve. The long, black roofs of Victoria Barracks in their dark cluster of trees were a reminder of earlier times along with the old Supreme Court building, the Hong Kong Club and that towering concrete bunker, the Bank of China. In Victoria Park she could just make out the statue of Queen Victoria which had been discovered in a Kyoto scrapyard and returned to its proper place.

Hong Kong was changing fast. A stone's throw from the palace lion-dogs guarding the Bank of China's forbidding steps, had risen the Hong Kong Hilton. The new tower block of City Hall dwarfed the buildings around it and as far as she could see, west to Central and Kennedy Town and north to Wan Chai and Causeway Bay, cocoons of bamboo scaffolding rose like signposts to the future.

In the twenty-one years since the war, Peggy Pelham had become well known for her one-woman crusade against corruption and her untiring defence of civil rights. Against all persuasion and with the growing disapproval of Government House, she had become a champion of Hong Kong's Chinese working class. She had no idea that her stand against the exploitation of the poor by the rich, and the persecution of the masses by both the triad societies and a corrupt police force, would play a leading role in the violence and upheaval that was about to break upon the colony in a tidal wave of rebellion.

While most of her kind were enjoying the comfortable and privileged lifestyle that Hong Kong offered the well-placed and the prosperous, she was to be found in the hillside squatter camps where people lived like rats, or listening to the grievances of small business operators and witnessing for herself the appalling conditions of the resettlement areas. These were the things that Peggy Pelham saw when she looked down from her little balcony upon the breathtaking vista of Hong Kong. It was these people she thought about. The rising edifices, the foreign ships being loaded, the aeroplanes coming and going across the water were only possible because of them.

The way she saw things, it was these people that her husband had given his life to defend. Not the occupants of the luxury apartments that climbed the Mid-Levels or the colonial mansions that adorned the mist-shrouded Peak. They were too busy at the racetrack, on the golf course or playing cricket to see the unrest.

The Hong Kong she knew was changing fast. Everywhere Chinese workers were holding high the little red book containing the thoughts of Chairman Mao Tze-tung and calling for their rights. The threat of street violence hung over the colony as it watched the Cultural Revolution unfurling across the border. The screeching voice of Madame Mao broadcast reports of its glorious progress unceasingly. Her Chinese opera background gave a theatrical quality to the inflammatory tirades that blared from every radio set, in blocks of flats and salubrious apartments from the Mid-Levels to the Peak and the private residences of Kowloon Tong. In the anthills of the resettlement areas, the sampan villages of the water people and the Hakka farms of the New Territories, the Chinese worker listened.

Each day bloated corpses floated down the Pearl River from Canton, their hands tied behind their backs with wire. They were the enemies of the people, the intellectuals and scholars, those who had wasted their lives in the useless pursuit of poetry, music, letters and art. There was no place for them in the Great Leap Forward. Everywhere, amahs, factory workers, bus and taxi drivers, waiters, street-merchants and throngs of unemployed youth took up the cry, the 'little red book' always close at hand.

In a manner entirely British, the authorities continued to view these disturbances with a stiff upper lip from behind the heavily guarded walls of Government House. The news reports claiming that tens of thousands of innocent Chinese—whose crime may have been no greater than the wearing of spectacles—were being machine-gunned on the banks of the Pearl or crushed beneath the tracks of tanks in the streets of Canton, was hardly their affair.

From her tiny balcony, Peggy Pelham sipped her Earl Grey tea, the newspaper spread before her as she read the latest reports of violence. The familiar sound of chanting voices reached her from somewhere in the streets below. It was a sound that she heard every day and it had begun to haunt her. This was stronger and louder than she had ever noticed before, rising and falling with the Maoist anthem—'The East is Red'. Looking down she could see them, close packed, riverlets of little red books held aloft, marching on Government House.

There was another sound, an undercurrent that remained when the singing suddenly lulled. It had the precision of a well-oiled machine, as down Garden Road to meet them, in immaculate order behind their wicker riot shields, came the police, the studs of their polished boots striking the road like pistons.

The baton charge that took place outside the Hilton Hotel began a cat and mouse campaign in the crowded streets of Causeway Bay and Wan Chai. Gangs wielding choppers, knives and sharpened bamboo spears broke from the labyrinth of alleyways to attack police patrols and disappear with the same suddenness.

Acid was thrown from windows above and home-made steel crossbows struck without a sound. Only the platoons of Gurkhas, bland-faced and square-shouldered as they doubled through the silent streets, could keep the mobs in order. Bombs were exploded and children died.

No one saw Peggy Pelham jump from her little balcony and fall ten storeys to the road. The night-watchman thought he heard something but the Indian drivers who slept in the room adjoining the garages had heard nothing so he went back to his chair and the stirring verse of the Chairman.

The dog boy awoke, reaching out with his arms and stretching his feet as far as they could go. It seemed a long time since he had left the pipe but he still could not believe his good fortune. The one small window was heavily barred; through it he could see the sky. He felt he was on a mountaintop.

Outside was the roof of the Palace of Hong, the highest building in Ling Nam. So high it took him a long time to climb its stairs, past so many doors. The doors were never closed, the small rooms so packed with people they lived in the doorways as well, and on the landings of the stairs, using the steps as seats and a place to talk. He liked the way they moved aside for him when he made the long climb. No longer calling him names and laughing at his crab-like progress. No longer calling him 'the spider who comes out from the sewer pipe'. They were afraid of him now. Afraid that he would tell his master.

He sniffed the air, comforted by the strange, feral smell, the dung smell, like rotted straw. The stench of urine. Yawning, he rolled over and pushed himself upright in his special way. It was light enough now to see the top of the cage, the shadow of movement inside, hear the rattle of chain. At first he had been afraid of the mah-lau—he had never seen such a creature as this. Once, when he was younger he had gone far looking for stray dogs and found none he could catch. Sleeping in doorways and alleys he had gone all the way to Mon Kok and seen monkeys in the zoo but they were not like this.

He pushed open the door to let in more light. Carefully, quietly, because he knew his master would be on the roof at this time, his movements slow as drifting clouds across the thin moon that he could still see as the day came. Each morning the dog boy watched him through the crack of the door, waiting for the silent time to end, the movements suddenly so fast, so powerful, that he wanted to clap his hands, to laugh out loud and shout his approval.

The Forceful One leapt higher than he had ever seen anyone leap, twisting in the air the way a cat could, landing so lightly his bare feet made no sound, the action of his arms and legs so fast they made the swishing sound of blades, his fists and feet snapping the air with the force of steel whips.

Behind him the mah-lau yawned restlessly, ending with a low hoot, and the dog boy knew it was time to fetch fruit and to draw water. When this was done, while the creature ate in a corner, he swept out the cage and washed down the floor. Soon his master would finish his exercise and bathe from the tap on the roof, then he would go down to take his yum cha at the eating house of Sharp Chopper Lau.

While he was gone, there was a little work to do in the rooms below; the master's bed to be straightened, the floor to be swept and perhaps clothes to wash. The dog boy was proud to be the only servant of the Forceful One. It was the first time he had known the feeling of importance. He, the spider from the sewer pipe, had been chosen. Even Sharp Chopper Lau could not refuse to fill his rice bowl.

The mah-lau watched him with piss-coloured eyes. He wondered why anyone would keep such a creature, when it would be killed and eaten. The people at the tables of the eating place said it was a monster that the Forceful One worshipped and used in his magic.

Many would not talk of it at all, pretending that it was not there. That the ones who said they had seen it, eyes piercing the shadows like drops of melted gold, taken up the stairs on a thick silver chain in the dead of night, were liars and fools, like all those who slept on stairs and had bad dreams. There was one thing they all agreed upon: the dog boy had been chosen to be its keeper, to feed it and clean up its droppings as he had done for the dogs of Sharp Chopper Lau, but also he had been chosen as the Forceful One's disciple.

Down the eight steps, in the two rooms where his master lived, the dog boy went about his simple work cheerfully. It gave him pleasure to be in this room where such a great man slept. Those at the tables said he was a black sorcerer, that he spoke with the devil, but to the dog boy he was kind, saying that he too had once been twisted and lame. He knew what it was to be laughed at by the gods.

As he always did when his master was not there the dog boy peered curiously into the second room. It was the smaller of the two and the door was always closed. Inside was the blackest space he had ever seen. It was as though he stood on the edge of a moonless sky. The walls and floor and ceiling were painted endless black.

When he opened the door foul air rushed past him and he fancied he could hear the moan of spirits. It did not frighten the dog boy. There was nothing he hadn't seen or heard in his dreams and he knew the things that went on inside his head sometimes played tricks.

He opened the door wider, cautiously, as if something might escape from this bottomless well. Just enough for the light to fall upon the altar. It too was a dead, night black. Two black candles were set in brass candlesticks shaped like cobras coiled to strike. Between them lay a shallow wooden tray of grey ash and a long wand of willow wood. In front of the tray stood a bowl of white rice. On either side of that rested two golden mandarin oranges. The glint of brass, the white rice, the bright orbs of the fruit seemed suspended in the air.

Above them, hanging in a wooden frame, was a tall, oblong scroll filled with ancient and long-forgotten characters. The tablet was old and cracked, the images so faded they could hardly be seen. The dog boy stared at it for a moment but the noises he thought he could hear seemed to grow louder inside his head and he felt the hair on his neck begin to stir.

Ah Keung sipped at his ching cha, looking around the tables. There were seldom new faces, strangers were not welcome here. All the tables were crowded except his. No one ever came to share with him. He watched Sharp Chopper Lau sticking the day's menus around the walls of his eating house. He was serving dog today as well as snake. Both were very warming and good for the blood. He called out his order loudly over the chatter and Sharp Chopper Lau quickly attended to him. Ah Keung smiled to himself. How easy it was to command. He knew those around him were afraid to look his way. Even the bully Lau jumped when he opened his mouth, ever since he had taken the dog boy out of the pipe behind his shop. It had taken a hammer to loosen the chopper from the cutting block—such a simple demonstration. How ready men were to be frightened.

He was pleased with the boy. He was the perfect servant, possessing the loyalty and honesty of the lost. Unable to understand kindness but grateful not to be kicked and spat upon. One whose concept of dignity was a place to sleep and enough to eat, one easily moulded and who had already known pain and seen the blackness. He would never gossip but he listened, as familiar around the tables as a rat or a cockroach. Nothing was said of importance that did not come back with the dog boy.

A newspaper caught Ah Keung's eye. It had been left on the seat beside him. Newspapers were scarce in the Walled City and the habit was to share one among many. Those that had abandoned the table when they saw the Forceful One coming had left it behind in their haste. He picked it up and idly flicked open the first page. U.S. TELEVISION DEAL FOR VENTURE FILMS. The large headline meant nothing to him, he would have turned the page if he had not looked closer. His senses were so finely honed that he knew immediately the woman in the photograph was Siu Sing, seated at a banquet table between two men, a Chinese and a gwai-lo. He read the words beneath it: 'Hong Kong's Freddy Fong and partner Sam Danovich here from the United States, toast Sing Deverill at the Jade Lotus Room of the Hilton.'

He read on: 'The success of *The Second Sunrise* continues with a U.S. network pre-sale of Venture Films' planned documentary series to be filmed in Hong Kong and based on Sing Deverill's internationally acclaimed books on Taoist concepts of natural healing and health care. The books have brought a refreshingly simple approach to alternative methods of promoting physical fitness and mental well-being. Uncovering the ancient secrets of China's barefoot doctors, the preventative properties of herbal medicine and ancient Taoist medical practices for health and longevity, they have each been on the international best-seller lists and are now translated into twenty-two languages.'

Ah Keung read no further, folding the paper as Sharp Chopper Lau brought his food and set it down.

'Jo sun, Ah Gor. Lay ho mar. Good morning, Big Brother. How are you?' He shuffled quickly away, not waiting for his greeting to be returned. Ah Keung's mind flew back to the day he had first administered death, seeing again quite clearly the look in his master's eyes as they recognised defeat. That look had returned to him for years until he had learned to repel it: those eyes that had shown no surprise, no sign of fear of dying, no shock of pain.

Only one thing had dawned in the eyes of Old To before the poison and the savagery of the attack had closed them forever. Something that had given even greater force to Ah Keung's strikes, ignited something more than revenge and hatred in his heart. As they recognised treachery, the master's eyes had shown only pity.

The chorusing of voices that flowed around him like frogs in a pond left Ah Keung's consciousness as he saw again the deerhide bag, the notebooks, charts and scrolls he had thrown so carelessly aside. The bag that the jarp-jung had carried away. Seeing Siu Sing again, knowing where to find her, filled him with a flush of excitement. He had thought of her often during his studies with Black Oath Wu.

What he had learned in the Temple of the Sacred Tiger had been crude and clumsy compared to the arts of domination he had inherited at the feet of the Black Tao, a domination so absolute, so irreversible, so untraceable, so much more destructive than the infliction of pain and physical suffering. So much more satisfying than the finality of death—the possession of a mind.

He tasted the first morsel of dog meat, tender as chicken in his mouth. Once more part of his surroundings he savoured the food before him. The stab of anger at letting the eyes of Master To return to show him again the insult of compassion was replaced by a feeling of well-being. At last it was time for the revenge he had yet to complete. As he chewed, he thought carefully. How could he get Siu Sing to come to him?

She would be his greatest conquest in spiritual boxing. What better test of his powers? He felt the primal ch'i churn as he visualised the extent of his revenge. So absolute, so final. To bring her here, to the Palace of Hong, of her own accord. His completely. Here he would take full payment for all she had taken from him.

The Amulet

SING'S OFFICE on the second floor of Venture Films' studios looked over the Causeway Bay typhoon shelter. It was a small room with just enough space for the wide antique desk Freddy had provided and two visitors' chairs. The shelves that lined the walls were crowded with books and every surface was piled with the papers and magazines that served as her reference library.

Behind the desk, tacked to the wall above her chair, was the production schedule for the studio workload in various stages of progress. Surrounding it, pinned in clusters, were daily worksheets, production reports and other studio paraphernalia.

Just across the street from her window banks of cargo junks

and crude wooden coastal vessels sat at their berths six deep. Beyond them the bustle of water traffic plied in and out of the breakwater beside the moored yachts and motor cruisers of the rich, neatly tethered at the marina of the Royal Hong Kong Yacht Club.

It was a view Sing never tired of, always reminding her that she was part Chinese and that it was with craft like these old traders that her father had made his start, these big, grey junks that bumped alongside each other like old men, beyond change, while all around them pile-drivers thumped and jackhammers rattled.

She had spent the past two days in the summer house on Lantau with Sam and only this morning taken him to the airport after one of his flying visits. He had brought with him a contract with a major network for a series of eight one-hour documentaries based on the books of *The Second Sunrise* and Sing had accepted the roles of script consultant and executive producer. They had celebrated with Freddy Fong over a sumptuous dinner and the story had reached the newspapers.

A few days after the spread in the *South China Morning Post* had appeared there was a knock on her office door. Sing hardly looked up when her secretary announced that there was someone to see her. Before she could ask who it was, a man's voice spoke from the door.

'Forgive me, Siu Sing, for coming unannounced, but I did not think you would see me if I asked permission.'

She knew the voice of Ah Keung before she could raise her eyes to him. No one had used her childhood name since she could remember. She felt hot blood rush through her, her heart quickened with the unexpected shock of seeing him.

'You should not have come here,' she said, finding her throat suddenly dry.

'I have seen your picture everywhere. I had to be sure that this famous writer was truly the little star from Tung T'ing.'

He came into the room, closing the door and seating himself before her, seeming to fill the small space with his presence. 'You have come a long way from the maker of sausages and the ballroom of old Money-Bags Poon.' He laughed.

'What do you want of me?' Sing tried to keep her voice steady, choked by the contempt she felt for him.

'The newspaper says you enjoy great wealth and much fame from the old man's secrets.' His eyes travelled the walls as he spoke.

They lingered on the press clippings pinned to the corkboard.

'The books you hear of are my own. I have worked long and hard to complete them.'

'The words are yours, the secrets were his. We were both charged with their custody.'

Sing fought against a surge of anger. 'You dismissed them as rubbish fit only to be eaten by rats.'

Ah Keung lifted a hand to silence her. 'I was a boy. I was not given your great vision. I was not the chosen one.' He smiled, a slow, sly smile. 'Do not worry, Siu Sing. I have not come to claim my share. I wish only to return that which belongs to you.'

He took a small fold of red cloth from his pocket and carefully unwrapped it, lifting from it the jade amulet of the White Crane on a leather thong.

'You were too young to wear it then. It was my duty to protect it for you. All my life I have kept it. Knowing that one day I would find you and return it.'

'Why did you not return it in the Nine Dragons Ballroom?' she asked coldly.

'You would not let me. You have always turned away,' he answered. 'Take it. It was always meant for you.'

He held it closer up to the light from the window. The feelings that churned in her were so strong that Sing could only stare. She saw nothing but the amulet. It filled her vision, the seams of deep, grass green running like rivers through its milky translucence. The memory of it around Master To's neck was charged with a kind of warning.

Ah Keung's words seemed to come from somewhere beyond the room, to reach her from some other space. 'See? Is it not as beautiful as ever? Does it not still hold the power of the Crane? In its lustre there still lies the ch'i of the master and the blessing of Adato. Can you feel it?'

Ah Keung rose and leaned across the desk, so slowly that Sing was hardly aware of it until the amulet touched her skin, warm as a comforting finger. She started, but it was too late to stand or move away. His repellant face swam above her, his large hands outstretched. Her body stiffened with revulsion, her throat constricting. She could not speak. His voice crooned softly to her, all other sounds receding. The rattle and bang of the waterfront were replaced by his words.

'Come, Siu Sing. Allow me the honour to put it where it belongs. Is this so much to ask? Have I not returned that which the master bequeathed to you?'

His tone seemed to mesmerise Sing, as her rigid muscles gave way to a wave of uncontrollable trembling. The flash of instinct that told her to spring to her feet passed as quickly as it had shot through her. Let him do it, then he will go, a voice inside her whispered.

She felt his hands lift her hair, gently, with a long, stroking motion. Then his fingers, fastening the thong. They dropped to her shoulders and for seconds held them firmly. Sing felt his power pass through her like a current as she lifted her head, compelled to look at him. For the briefest fraction of time Sing glanced into the black eyes of Ah Keung and beyond them into the pit of evil.

A sharp knock on the door broke the spell. Ah Keung's touch left her shoulders and he moved to the window swiftly as a shadow, as Freddy Fong stuck his head around the door.

'Oh, sorry kid, I thought you were alone.'

'It's all right Freddy. We've finished our business. I'll be with you in just a moment.' Sing had to force the words from her lips. Freddy hesitated, then withdrew.

Ah Keung remained at the window looking down at the crowded causeway, his back turned while Freddy closed the door. The interruption had driven all sense of danger from the room and Sing could only look upon Ah Keung with disgust and loathing. It was as though a grip had been broken and the moments before Freddy had entered never existed. He seemed suddenly harmless. His ungainly frame appeared to have lost its menace. It slouched, all the arrogance gone.

Through the deep sense of caution Sing still felt crept an inexplicable twinge of pity at the sight of his angular face, the hair cropped close to his large skull. She had thought of him as tight-lipped and upright, now his mouth was slack, the jutting jaw less arrogant, cunning eyes downcast. No longer the Forceful One.

As though he knew what she was thinking, he spoke without looking at her. 'Is it not in your heart to forgive the mistakes of a broken boy?'

He asked so humbly that Sing could not believe she had allowed herself to fear him.

'I wish you no harm. I bear no malice. But I cannot forgive,' Sing said, her composure returning. 'We have chosen different worlds. Let them remain apart.'

'I have paid for such mistakes. While you have found fortune, I am forced to live behind the walls of Ling Nam, the Walled

City of the Damned. It is there that you can find me.'

'I will have no reason to find you, Ah Keung. There is nothing more to be said between us,' Sing said with quiet finality.

'Perhaps you are right, Little Star,' he replied simply. 'I have done what I came to do.' He walked to the door, hesitating to open it, reluctant to leave.

'I am sad that you cannot forgive. But we will meet again. I am sure of it.' The door closed and he was gone.

Outside in the blaze of sunlight Ah Keung paused to wind three gleaming hairs from Sing's head into a small curl. It glittered, bright and alive as copper in the sun as he folded it carefully into the square of red cloth that had held the amulet. He stood for a moment breathing in the hot smell of the streets, enjoying its noisy hustle. A wave of anticipation gripped him that was almost sexual in its intensity. Ah Keung smiled to himself: it was much stronger than that.

Sing sat staring through the window over the nests of junk masts. She felt completely drained of all energy and emotion. When Freddy came in moments later she had not moved, but she was thankful to hear his voice.

'What is it kid? You look like you've seen a ghost.'

'Perhaps I have,' she said, breaking her gaze to look at him.

His face was filled with concern. 'Who was that guy anyway?' he asked anxiously.

'Someone from the past,' murmured Sing, her hand reaching unconsciously to touch the amulet. 'Please don't ask me . . . it's not important.'

Freddy whistled softly. 'Hey. That's nice. Did he . . . .'

Sing cut him short as she reached to unfasten the thong. 'It is also from a time and place of long ago.'

Freddy held out his hand as she removed it. 'Can I see?'

Sing laid the jade in his palm.

'This is very old. Very special. What is it. A good luck piece?'

'It once belonged to someone who was very dear to me.' She took it from him and opened her drawer.

'Aren't you going to wear it? Its too good to keep locked away.'

'Perhaps, but leather is not really my style,' replied Sing. She smiled at him. 'Freddy, I'd like to get out for a while. Could we . . . '

He grinned, knowing exactly what she meant. He held out his hand. 'Time for tea, I think.'

They walked the couple of blocks to their favourite teashop. It was Russian, one of the few in Hong Kong that had remained open after China had become communist. Before then it had been called the 'Belorussiya'. Now its White Russian owners had renamed it 'Chanticleer', in the hope that people would think it was French.

Chanticleer had become a second office to Freddy and Sing. It sold delicious cakes and pastries at half the cost of the famous French patisseries of the Hilton and the Peninsula. Its gleaming samovars dispensed the yellow and black teas of Georgia and the red tea of the Ukraine. Upstairs were served generous bowls of goulash and borsch, stroganoff and Crimean kebabs. It was the place they went to for leisurely talk, or when they didn't want to be disturbed. Few Chinese were ever seen there and it was largely undiscovered by the expatriate community. Its customers were almost exclusively those from Shanghai who had been forced to run and start again here in Hong Kong. They felt at home in this cosy place, its walls hung with memorabilia of a time past.

When they were seated in the cubicle Freddy always occupied and he had ordered Sing's favourite cakes, he grinned across at her. 'This joint always reminds me of the place on Chapoo Road in Shanghai where Sam and me used to go before the war.'

Sing smiled back at him, touched by the warmth of his friendship, grateful for their long association, the sense of security and confidence he had always given her since the terrible days of the occupation. Suddenly, she folded her hands under her chin and said, 'Tell me again, Freddy. About you and Sam in Shanghai.'

'Tell you what?' he asked, pretending to scan the menu.

'You know perfectly well what,' she laughed. 'The time you saw my father.'

'You've heard it a hundred times already,' he teased. 'Sam says he told you that story so many times he knows it by heart.'

'I know. I want to hear it again. I want to hear you tell it.'

Freddy sat back while the White Russian waitress brought the cakes and tea, pleased to see her looking better, and anxious to keep her mind off whatever had disturbed her.

'Well, it was like I said before,' he continued when the waitress had gone. 'The Japs called this meeting of the Shanghai international ratepayers at the racecourse. It was held in the grandstand, the last of Shanghai's businessmen on one side, and a group of Jap officials in top hat and tails on the other.'

Freddy took a bite of pastry and followed it with a slurp of tea. 'There were the Americans in one group, the British in another, the French and a ragtag bunch of Italians and Scandinavians, all representing what was left of their own settlements.'

Sing licked cream from her fingers, her eyes never leaving his face, intent on every word.

'Then there was this one big son-of-a-gun sitting all by himself up in the benches. It was a cold day and he was rugged up in a big coat of Siberian fur. He looked just like a mountain bear who had crawled out of a cave after a long winter. Well, this big guy just sat there listening to the arguments flying back and forth, those little Japs piping up about more taxes and how they were the boss, then suddenly he stood up and addressed the whole group, in a voice that made sure it got heard. I can see him now, his hands shoved in his pockets and his collar turned up, a fur hat on his head. I can't remember all he said but whatever it was the Japs didn't like the sound of it.

'"What is your name?" this little Nip who was running the show, pipes up.

'"Genghis Khan," says the big man, with this voice like a bull.

'"What is your nationality?" asks the Nip.

'"Pure-bred bastard," says the big man, grinning like a wolf.

'"The Nip looks around at the rest of these little penguins, wondering what to say next.

'"What is your country?" says the Nip, trying like hell to save his face.

'"Shanghai is my country," comes the answer. "And I don't need a sawn-off, four-eyed little runt like you to tell me how to live in it."'

Freddy paused again for refreshment, pleased with the child-like look of delight on Sing's face.

'So the Nip official yaps something back and whatever it was the big man decided he didn't like the way it came out. He just jumped the rail, walked across the stretch of floor between them, picked the little guy up by his winged collar and his fancy tails and threw him out of the grandstand. Next thing we know, he's waded into the rest of them, the Japs are on the run and everyone else has joined in.'

Freddy picked up a plate of chocolate cakes and offered them to Sing. 'And that was your daddy. Big Ben Deverill.'

Sing sat back with a giggle as he refilled her cup. Freddy half expected her to clap her hands.

'He was a special kind of guy, your old man. A real old style taipan.' He topped up his own tea.

'Speaking of special guys, lady. When are you going to put the big lug Sam Danovich out of his misery? He's been carrying the torch for fifteen years now. The man really loves you. He'd marry you tomorrow if you'd have him.'

Sing picked up a napkin to brush the crumbs from her lap. 'I love you, too, Freddy, but I don't think we should get married. Do you?'

Freddy looked frustrated as he paid the bill. 'Geez, kid. Its different with you and me, we're pals. Sam's just nuts about you. I know, I've seen him with lots of . . . ' He hesitated. 'You know what I mean. He needs you. You're the only one.'

They stood up to leave. 'Let's just say I've got more important things to do than put a fence around a man like Sam. Besides,' she said, taking Freddy's arm. 'Marriage is a luxury I cannot afford. It was not meant for me. You know that.'

Freddy sighed, shaking his head as he followed her onto the street. Halfway back to the office he excused himself and ducked into a gold and jewellery store. It was one of the many around Causeway Bay, displaying clusters of gold chains glittering in rows beneath bright, white lights designed to tempt the passing trade. He came out a moment later and pressed a tiny purse of white silk into her hand.

'Just so you don't lose that lucky jade piece you got today.'

Sing unclasped the purse and a fine gold chain trickled into her hand.

Black Tao

I T BEGAN with the dream. It was always the same. From the Rock of Great Strength Sing looked out over the timeless beauty of Tung T'ing Lake. The plank-boats sailed peacefully beneath their piles of reeds, like floating haystacks, the fishing sampans sat still as grasshoppers in midsummer. In the muddy shallows the spoonbills waded in search of frogs and behind her, in the eaves of the hut, martins squabbled over the building of nests. Further up the slope the breeze through the bamboo sang to her like the harps of heaven. This place where her life had begun was the home of her soul. She stood transported by the joy of it.

Then the pale outline of the mountains would grow suddenly darker, as though a storm was coming. The tree-peonies closed their petals as if in the path of a fire and the birds in the grove stopped their song. The shadow cast itself over the lake, became a great vortex, black as oil, filling her private world.

She stood on its edge, safe at first, spellbound by its menace, unable to run as it reached for her. Her feet were bare and when she looked down at them they were the feet of a child, firmly rooted upon the rock, protected by its spirit. Her ch'i and the ch'i of the rock were one and she felt no fear.

The slime of the whirlpool devoured the patches of lichen on the edge of the rock, swallowing them as it came, burning like acid. The voice of Master To spoke to her clearly, calmly, telling her to stand her ground. To think only of the ch'i that bound her spirit to the spirit of the rock, reminding her that all things lived and were one in the Way of the Tao, that their energy was her energy. Told her to be calm. To call upon her training to withstand, to remain firm in the path of the Tiger.

At first the dreams were short and the blackness easy to repel. Inching towards her then slipping away. Every disciplined sense in her being clung to the safe, sun-warmed surface of the rock. She was immovable. As if it sensed her strength, the oily mass would withdraw, shrinking to become the glistening coils of Yangjingshi, the king cobra.

Siu Sing would see again the poisonous, toadstool yellow of its belly, pale against the shining black scales as it rose before her. Another voice would reach her. A boy's voice, almost a man's, young and confident.

'See! I have taught the foot well. Faster now than Yangjingshi, the king of snakes . . . You owe your life to me, Little Star. One day I may claim it.'

Suddenly, as though stabbed by a pin, Sing would awaken, her eyes wide and her senses sharpened by terror. Unsure if she was not still dreaming, the words of Ah Keung lingered in the dark of her room. Each time she would look at the luminous dial of the clock. It was exactly three a.m. Sometimes she would fall into troubled asleep again, often after daylight showed through the crack in the curtains and traffic sounds reached up from the streets.

The dreams came regularly, every night. Each time the same, but more powerful. More real. The black slime closing in on her, cold as death against her feet, her ankles, sucking the blood warmth from her legs until they grew numb and she could no longer feel the security of the rock.

A smudge of light would begin to appear across the room. A pale, floating shadow, the sickly pallor of moonlight shining on a deadly fungus, unmoving in the dark. Yet she was awake, heart thumping wildly in her chest, eyes wide with horror. The pain in her was real, the cold sweat, the prickling sensation that crawled over her scalp, invading every inch of her, were not part of the dream.

The pale shape, no more than a smudge at first, grew closer every time she awoke. Beside her, the loud ticking of the clock told her, without looking, that it was three. Only force of will and the switching on of the light could cut the vision's hypnotic hold, but to make the slightest move sapped her remaining strength.

Each attempt to sleep brought the apparition closer until the face of Ah Keung materialised like some virulent puffball, exact in every pore. The room seemed filled with it. His eyes drew her to him. The gold-ringed, unblinking eyes of a snake. It paralysed her with its horror.

Sing knew she was in danger of losing her mind. That to slip from the rock she clung to would whirl her into the pit that yawned before her. She could tell no one. What was there to tell. Nightmares? Where was the cure but in her own mind. She heard the words of Master To: 'Only you can break the link. You must withstand. To fall in the path of the Tiger is to perish.'

She stopped sleeping altogether, kept the lights switched on and lit many candles to surround herself with light. She called upon all she had learned, all she had practised, summoning every sane thought she had ever had to combat the creeping fear that threatened to wrap her like a shroud. Food had become unnecessary and when sense told her she must try to eat she could not force it past her throat.

Time, too, no longer mattered. It was measured only by the dread of closing her eyes. To feel again her hold of the rock slipping from beneath her, jarred by the erratic hammering of her heart and the ticking of the clock, loud and unstoppable as the hour of three a.m. came around. Then the presence of Ah Keung would again invade her room. Saying nothing now. The eye so close its black centre became the sucking heart of the whirlpool.

It was a week since she had stopped leaving the room. In the first days the daylight and the diversion of the office at Venture

Films deceived her into thinking it would pass. Freddy had stared at her with deep concern. She had lost weight and a sickly pallor had replaced the healthy bloom of her skin.

'Hey, kid. You've been working too hard. Take a break. Maybe I should call Doc Sun?'

'No,' she had assured him, she would be all right.

Nothing a few days rest wouldn't fix. She thought of Silvermine Bay but somehow knew that to move would make no difference. The influence Ah Keung was sending would follow her even across water. She told herself that if she was strong enough it would stop. She took the phone off the hook and the clock lay broken in a corner of the room.

Her body lost all trace of energy. Inside, she turned to ice but her skin burned hot. Dragging everything she could find to cover herself she lay shaking in every nerve and muscle. She could not rise, feeling the creeping warmth of her urine turn cold. With no way of knowing how long it had taken, at last she felt her link with the rock snap like a single hair and she fell, silently screaming into the maelstrom of Ah Keung's making.

The dog boy awoke whimpering. His body was stiff with cold and yet the night was sticky warm. Through the crack of the door he could see the position of the moon as it broke through silver-edged cloud, turning the rooftop white as frost. It was the same time, the same position. He did not know how to tell time but he knew it was two hours before the first cock-crow.

Beneath him, in the sealed black room, Ah Keung seemed to float before the altar. The two yellow flames from the candles were motionless, lighting nothing but the contents of the tray. Ah Keung concentrated on the revenge he had carried in his heart for much of his lifetime. More than humiliation, more than pain and destruction in the ordinary way. No matter how much she had learned or what had been revealed to her on Lo Shan, the Temple of the Tiger and the art of Black Oath Wu had shown him more.

Since his fierce determination to survive had taken him across the frozen waste of the Tung T'ing lake he had known a great destiny lay in store for him. He would have drowned in the icy mud if it were not so. He had withstood the agony of slow fire burrowing into his skull in the Temple of the Tiger and thought of nothing else. When the abbot had inserted the three burning needles of joss into his skull he had begun the lesson of endurance.

The agony had consumed his brain, drilling its way into his innermost soul and he had entered into a pact with the demons of torment—he would serve them always if they would let him withstand. The monks of the temple had looked towards the abbot to see if he would give the order to stop. None of their kind had held fast for so long. The boy's body shook uncontrolled as fire seared every nerve in its system and he screamed within, but no sound had escaped him.

He had emerged from the mantle of torture with nerves forged to iron in the crucible of pain. These he had trained and tested without relief until his ch'i was like an outer skin of armour that no blow could penetrate, no shock disturb. Since his harsh training as a child on the rock of Old To and in the mountain temple, the elimination of the White Crane master had set him on a path of preparation for this moment. He had never wavered from it. Nothing had been allowed to interfere. Yet all those things had been blown away as nothing when Black Oath Wu had opened the doors of the Black Tao to him.

In combat he could already inflict agony and injury beyond human endurance as easily as playing with a child. There were ways of striking that could permanently deplete the body of energy, shatter the nervous system and rob the organs of their function, leaving the victim to live out a half-life of recurring pain and emotional anguish. To kill was a favour compared to those things he had learned. Yet compared to the Black Tao they were as nothing. Only among the dark and faceless ranks of the spiritual boxers were all things revealed and all things possible. Only the few who dared the devil could command such ultimate forces.

By reversing the microcosmic orbit of his ch'i, the spiritual boxer also reversed the deem-mak, the death points of his body, giving immunity against even the greatest and most skilful opponent. But these were mere protective devices. The real force of the Black Tao turned night into day, light into darkness. It could capture and possess a human soul.

Ah Keung's lips moved soundlessly as he recited words from the suspended tablet only he could read and understand. He was naked in the closed and airless room. The candle flame illuminated the intricate tattoo of the striking cobra that climbed the length of his spine, at its head the symbol of Yin and Yang was turned upside down. On his chest, executed with the detail and perfection of Yakuza ninja, covering his flesh from shoulder to shoulder, was the snarling face of a charging tiger.

He had lost all sense of weight, transported in a state of mental levitation. Before him in the tray of ash a single character had been drawn. It spelled Sing's name. Stretched across it, gleaming in the yellow buds of light, lay the three strands of her hair. His body shook as they suddenly flared to flame then curled to nothing. From the surrounding blackness a gust came, whirling the ash, disfiguring Sing's name, settling to nothing.

When Freddy Fong had called Sing's flat five times without an answer, he knew something was wrong. He wished Sam was here. Sam would know what to do. Sing was not the type you worried about, she was the type you went to when you had worries of your own. She had said she was okay and that she could soon fix it and that should be enough. It had been a week, and now the phone was dead and she could not be reached.

He rang the Everspring herb shop and spoke to Doctor Sun. 'It's Sing, Doc. I can't raise her. Its been a week. I'm worried. Then I thought maybe she's over on the island.'

Doctor Sun's voice was always calm and reassuring but Freddy thought even he sounded cautious. 'She never goes to the summer house without telling me. This is not like her,' the doctor said after a pause. 'She is her own best healer, but if you have not heard . . .'

Freddy made up his mind and jumped in. 'Doc. I'm going over there, can you come?'

'I'll leave in five minutes,' came the reply.

It had taken Freddy's raised voice, followed by a hundred-dollar note, to convince the Sikh watchman that he should open Sing's door. Doctor Sun had arrived only minutes later. He did not need to take her pulse before speaking in a way Freddy had never heard him use before. His voice was strangely tight with anxiety. To him the condition of a patient was obvious at first glance. Facial diagnosis was the basis of Chinese medicine and he was shocked by the blackness that showed beneath the deadly pallor of her skin, a blackness only he could detect.

'Our little sister is in very great danger,' he said taking her wrist, his four fingertips playing lightly on the faint rhythms of the silent pulses.

'Her organs have been drained of energy. The flow of her ch'i is blocked.' His voice was shaken. 'We must get her away from here.'

'What is it, Doc? What the hell is it?' Freddy whispered, sounding as though he was going to weep as he looked around the untidy room. 'She must've been like this for days.'

He strode to the windows, jerking back the curtains and opening the glass doors.

'It is a sickness of someone else that attacks her. A terrible sickness.' Said the doctor grimly.

Freddy's round face was white with concern. 'We've got to get her to a hospital, fast.'

Doctor Sun shook his head. 'No hospital can help her,' he said, stripping back the bedclothes.

'What d'you mean, Doc? You telling me she's going to die and we can't take her to a hospital?' Freddy demanded.

'I cannot explain now. Come you must help me. There is only one place for her. We must hurry.'

The Pearl Pagoda

N O ROAD led to Po Lin, the Temple of the Precious Lotus. Built long ago on the highest point of Lantau Island, it was among the largest Buddhist temples in Asia. Its grandeur had been added to over the centuries, changing it from a humble mountain shrine and burial ground to a monastery housing over a thousand monks. Rich families donated large sums to its improvement and upkeep in the hope of a privileged place in the afterlife, and often to conceal the methods they had used to collect their earthly wealth. It was a matter of good business and had nothing to do with conscience.

Such generosity sometimes saw their names included in the prayers that rose above the towering scarlet eaves of the main temple, soaring like eagles' wings towards heaven. To be mentioned in the prayers of Po Lin was only for those who excelled all others with their generosity but as the great Lord Buddha was beseeched to bring them even greater fortune, those that could afford to buy their way to immortality had continued to better each other in the number of their yearly visits and the size of their offerings. The abbot had become well schooled in the greed and fear of ordinary men.

Doctor Sun was always welcome there. He had not donated huge amounts of money since building the summer house at Silvermine Bay, but he had supplied the monastery with herbs and medicines needed among the monks and novice nuns who lived within the temple walls, and he had always come when his skills were called upon. On more than one occasion he had been able to treat and heal an illness that would have otherwise brought death to Po Lin. The abbot had not forgotten the lives that had been saved. Now the doctor had brought a stricken one to him, one he said was beyond the help of ordinary medicine, whose malady was spiritual not physical. It was not the first time the abbot of Po Lin had seen a victim of Black Tao; not the first time he had agreed to use the powers of light in an effort to repel the horror that assailed them.

It had taken under two hours to bring Sing's unconscious body across the water in *Shanghai Lady*. Freddy, Doctor Sun and two of his sons had carried her on a stretcher from the tortuous dirt road, along the two kilometres of track worn by the feet of monks on their way to beg for alms in the villages below. Even for Doctor Sun, the abbot could not allow a female to be brought into the main temple. It would have been an act of desecration.

Instead she was taken higher, to a rocky point that looked down on the temple roofs. It was the highest pinnacle on the island, the abbot said, and this made it the highest point in Hong Kong and all of its neighbouring islands. On it stood an old pagoda, the oldest of all those that surrounded the temple like silent sentinels, seldom visited and in various stages of disrepair.

The abbot did not know when the Pagoda of the White Pearl had been built, only that it had stood for many centuries, and that it was the chosen domain to do battle with the powers of darkness. He watched as the four men carried Sing into its first chamber.

'We must take her up the stairs to the highest place. It is where I come to meditate and study. It is important that she lies in a holy place.'

The stone steps were narrow and it took the two youngest men to carry her up the eight tiers to the top. The eight chambers of the Pearl Pagoda grew smaller with each stage of the ascent, until Sing was laid on a rough bed in the centre of the topmost chamber. It was almost sunset and a burnt orange glow lit the six-sided room through a small, pointed window space set in each wall.

Prayer cloths hung like flags from the high, conical ceiling. Religious mandalas surrounded a heavily carved reading lectern and a Tibetan prayer wheel. From a corner, lit bright as bronze by the fading sky, a statue of the Buddha in meditation looked down on the bed where Sing lay. On the small altar table before it, an iron incense burner in the shape of a lion-dog bristled with the sticks of burned-out joss. Without speaking the abbot replaced them with eight fresh sticks and lit each in turn. Taking handfuls of thick candles from a chest beneath the altar he passed them around.

'She must be surrounded by light at all times, the flames lit with the prayers of her family. It is in darkness that the evil lives.'

'We are her family,' whispered Doctor Sun.

From the chest the abbot took a thick mein toi, the padded quilt valued for its lightness and warmth. They did not need to be told to remain silent as he began to pass his hands over Sing's shivering body inches above the quilt, his open palms searching the magnetic field for a sign of the source. Through his half-closed eyes he conjured her aura: its colours were dimmed, oppressed by a blackness that pressed in upon her, a malignant shadow that had penetrated its ambience and was slowly swallowing her life force.

'This one has been cursed by the darkest of powers. It is filled with a great hatred. A powerful evil.' His hands stopped above her forehead and they could see that his fingers began to tremble. 'She has great strength but her enemy might be greater.'

His low voice seemed to fill the hexagon shape of the chamber with faint echoes, his saffron robe to blaze in the last of the daylight. One hand, still trembling with the force of the vibrations it had detected, moved to her throat, reaching to touch the jade amulet around her neck. The abbot's fingers closed around it until his fist shook violently and he let it go as though burned. Carefully, he unfastened the chain and held it dangling for them to see.

'The evil began here. It is this that has been used as a key to the doorway of her soul.' He took it to the altar and laid it at the feet of the Buddha.

Doctor Sun spoke for the first time. 'Are we too late, lord?' he whispered.

The abbot thought before he answered. 'There is great spirit in her and great goodness. If there were not, her mind would be lost by this time and soon her body would follow.'

He allowed his voice to soften with a lilt of encouragement. 'I think you have brought her here in time but it will not be quick. She will be here for many weeks. Go now. Leave her with me. There is much to be done before she is restored to you.'

Doctor Sun led the way down the steps, their feet echoing on the worn stone. Freddy spoke in a whisper but his voice seemed to fill the chambers of the pagoda as they descended.

'What the hell is going on, Doc? This joint is like a tomb.'

'She will be safe here. We will light joss at the temple.'

'Then what'll we do?'

'Then we must stay close and wait.'

'What if that's not enough, Doc?' Freddy pleaded, shaking his head in disbelief. 'That kid is a sister to me. I need to know more. I don't believe in this black magic hocus pocus. This is 1968.'

'I wish you were right,' Doctor Sun answered patiently. 'But the Black Tao is very real, more dangerous than any blow or any weapon, more deadly than any known disease.'

They reached the bottom chamber of the pagoda. A young female novice was waiting with a lighted torch to lead them back to the temple.

'You mean . . . this, this stinking black creepy shit could still kill her . . . she could die?'

Doctor Sun kept quiet for a moment as they picked their way down towards the dim lights of the monastery. When he answered his tone was firm and determined. 'Siu Sing is very strong. She is different from others and has learned many mysterious skills in her lifetime. The abbot has great strength, also. Together with our thoughts and prayers they will defeat the one who seeks to destroy her.'

Freddy hesitated. 'What if they don't?'

'Then our little sister will die and her soul will be lost in a terrible place.' He shook his head. 'There will be no rest for her spirit.'

They came through the kitchen gardens at the back of the temple. Doctor Sun spoke softly to the novice and she left them.

'We must light joss and stay here tonight. She needs our prayers and our thoughts to be close.'

At the foot of the steps leading up to the temple stood an iron brazier, half filled with hot ash. They took red paper prayers from the old monk attending it, watching them flame and crumple, lifting in a flowering of sparks into the darkening sky.

The great temple was lit by row upon row of candles. A standing Buddha towered six metres above the altar, surrounded by consorts, encased in a burnished sheath of gold. Spirals of slow-burning incense hung from the ceiling, so high it was lost in shadow. Doctor Sun produced a small packet, handing Freddy several sheets of gold leaf, no larger than postage stamps. Together they approached the altar and, holding the gleaming fragments over candle flame to warm, stuck them onto the huge wooden feet of the Buddha where thousands of others had formed a gleaming skin.

Morning for the monks of Po Lin began with the striking of the temple bell. Wavering currents of sound followed its boom far across the island and out to sea as sixteen tonnes of bronze was struck by a suspended mahogany log. Deep in the black, airless pit, Sing felt its vibration. Heard its great voice and the thousand others that joined it, continuing its note in an endless mantra.

The serpent that watched over her seemed to stiffen, the studs of its eyes to lose their concentration. The chanting penetrated the blackness, seeking her. She breathed it in like life-giving air and held it deep inside her. The abbot remained in motionless meditation. Outside the pagoda, 1000 monks had formed a circle around the ancient tower, their minds directed to the eighth chamber of the Pearl Pagoda to add their strength to the one he protected.

Sam Danovich was in the dubbing studios at Universal when the call came through. He had told the panel operator to take a message but went quickly to the phone when he was told the call was from Hong Kong. Sam had never known Freddy Fong to sound so worried and when he heard why, his fist tightened on the receiver.

'How bad is she? . . . What do you mean you don't know what's wrong with her? Goddammit, Freddy.'

He paused, listening. 'Slow down . . . which hospital is she in? Can I talk to her?' His face turned clammy cold then hot as Freddy's words crackled over the line.

'What'd you mean, she is not in a hospital? You're goddam right I don't understand.' His voice was rising, the engineer on the sound mixing panel looked at him sideways.

'Freddy, you hear me? You get Doc Sun and you get her to the best hospital in Hong Kong. You hear me, Freddy. I'll be on the first plane out over there.'

Birdie Meadows felt none of the pleasures of home-coming as the taxi took her through the village of Sparrow's Green. As they drove past the Fox and Hounds, she wondered idly if Sweet William still stacked his dominoes and supped his pint in the Four Ale Bar. And, as the church came into view, if Reverend Tuttle still baptised babies at the marble font, and buried the dead in the dense shade of the yew trees. The road to the Grange had not changed, the high hedges of blackberry and banks of cow-parsley still hemming it in. Behind them stretched the hop gardens and ploughed fields of Brambles' farm.

She had stopped only long enough to drink a cup of tea with Amelia Monk, whose arthritis kept her in her cottage these days but who still knew more about what went on around the village than anyone else. Yes, Sir Duncan Masters was still alive, she said, cutting a wedge of seedcake for Birdie. Lady Constance had passed away and Cecily ran a riding school outside Tunbridge Wells. As for Sebastian, he had been posted to somewhere called Borneo, she said, and was sick with malaria the last she heard. Nova had been at boarding school since she was eight, and now attended some posh college. A fine, strong girl with the look of her mother, according to Mrs Monk.

As the square block of the Grange showed through the flickering poplars, Birdie took a deep breath. From the moment she had taken the call from Sam in Los Angeles she had wasted no time in getting to England. Sing was seriously ill, he said. From what Freddy Fong had told him she could die. There was no time to lose.

Birdie Meadows had taken it upon herself to decide what should be done. Ever since she had stayed by Sing's side in the gypsy caravan under the willows of the Hollow and seen the baby born, she had known this day would come. She had never been able to come to terms with the heartless bargain Sing had been forced to make with the Masters family. She remembered also Sir Duncan's concern for Sing's welfare and guessed the harshness of the contract was the work of Lady Constance and her daughter. Now she shivered in the sharp chill that cut across the estate, whipping the ivy-covered walls, as she climbed from the taxi.

Sir Duncan Masters could not have been more attentive. Over tea, served in the library, he listened with great concern to Birdie's story. The eight collector's volumes of *The Second Sunrise* in their special carrying case lay open on the table before him. He was becoming frail with age, his hands trembling as he lifted the first volume and opened its covers. Tears clouded his vision as he brushed the fine paper with his fingertips, as Birdie told what she knew of Siu Sing's life and the loneliness she had known, the strength she had found to fill the emptiness in her heart, to bury the memory of her only child. But how she, Birdie Meadows, had opened up the wound by showing her the photographs, and how desperately important it was for Sing to see her daughter Nova before it was too late.

When she had finished the old man sat quietly for a moment, the open book on his knees. 'Nova is at school. I will send for her at once,' he said. 'I will make all the arrangements for her to travel with you to Hong Kong on the condition that I accompany you.'

Birdie must have shown her surprise. He smiled at her, some of his old sparkle returning. 'The only thing that makes one grow old is staying locked up. A trip to the Orient should be just the ticket.'

The Hookmaker

THE NUN left the Pearl Pagoda and made her way past the temple, down the steep slope towards the narrow valley with long, swinging strides. Her spread, flat feet had never known anything but the hand-made sandals she wore. Surefooted over the loose gravel of the path, she followed its winding to the place where the bright green of young rice sprouted on the terraced sides of a fast-running stream. The water fell in a series of gentle cascades and far below the paddies shone like fragments of glass. Beyond them were the jumbled roofs and junk masts of Tung Chung fishing village.

She did not relish this errand for she was deeply afraid of the Hookmaker. It was whispered among the other novices that even with a glance of his eyes he could turn a human being into a three-legged toad. Birds fell from the sky, they said fearfully, flowers withered with his passing, if he was displeased, so great was his power. To leave the monastery and go to the village at Silvermine Bay for supplies was a rare pleasure and it was an honour to be chosen. But this was an honour she would have gladly given to someone else. The nun decided to slow her pace and delay the journey. The sun struck pleasantly warm on her shaven head and through the thin cotton folds of her ash-grey robe.

The track wound down beside the shallow steam, its banks thick with ragweed and aniseed as tall as her shoulder. Halfway down she stopped to drink, cupping her hands in the clear sweet water and watching the blue-bodied dragonflies skimming the reeds. Soon enough she would reach the bottom and the dogs would come barking from the village, splashing through the rice fields to warn her to stay away. They were lean and hungry but they did not scare her the way the Hookmaker did. She had already decided what she would do. When she arrived at the hut of the Hookmaker she would cover her eyes, deliver her message outside his door and run back across the paddy before his eyes could follow.

The Hookmaker had lived on Lantau Island longer than anyone else. Tung Chung was its oldest village and the fishermen said he was there before the first house had been built. When the junks called in for water to repair their nets he had been there to exchange his fishhooks for food. He made them from the claws of animals, barbs of seashell and the beaks of birds bound into slivers of bone, carved with ancient characters that no one else but he could read.

It was believed that his hooks were charmed, for they always caught the finest fish. If a man who possessed such a hook fished beside a man who did not, his catch was certain to be the greater. And when a storm swept the islands, the sampan with his hooks aboard was sure to reach land safely. This was firmly believed by the fishermen of Lantau.

So great was his magic that some had begun wearing his hooks around their necks as talismans to attract good fortune and keep away demons. People had gone to him for help and there were many stories of his spells and the sorcery he made. This had been so for as long as the water people could remember, but no one could say how many years he had lived. Still, the Hookmaker charged nothing for his work, only accepting fish and other food as payment. The water people kept his small hut in good repair and the racks of bamboo cane outside well-stocked with dried fish, sea slug and shark's fin. Looked upon as a wizard, his advice was sought on every problem and his blessing on every birth, marriage or death. But it was in the destruction of evil spirits, the chasing of demons, that the Hookmaker had his greatest power. So great that even the abbot of Po Lin at the top of the valley sometimes sent for him to come to the temple.

From the doorway of his hut the Hookmaker sensed the approach of the nun long before she had reached him. He watched her come slowly along the edge of the sea, then lowered his eyes. Listening for the slap of her sandals on the stony path that led from the beach, he stayed bent to his work as she approached. He had no wish to frighten her. The wide hat he wore shielded his wrinkled face as she spoke.

'Sifu,' she began, standing well back. 'Great master. I come from the temple of Po Lin. The holy abbot asks that you come to the Pearl Pagoda. There is one who does battle with a demon. He fears she will be overcome without your presence.'

The nun stood ready to turn and run if the Hookmaker should raise his head to look at her. He knew the story of his deadly gaze and kept his eyes lowered.

'Tell him I will be at her side before another tide has risen. But first he must send four strong men and a chair to carry me. Go, before I raise my eyes to you.'

Under the wicker hat his toothless gums showed in a chuckle as he listened to the sound of her fast-running feet.

Sing remained in the eighth chamber of the Pearl Pagoda for thirty days and nights before she became conscious of her surroundings. It seemed to her that she had never known anything else but the blackness of the pit, felt anything but its slimy walls or seen anything but the eyes of the cobra. The darkness had echoed only with her cries and the taunting laughter of Ah Keung. Then, slowly, it seemed that the tarry blackness and the chaos began to fade and the eyes of the snake grew less consuming.

A pinprick of blue light appeared above her and very slowly grew in size. It seemed to take an eternity, days, weeks, months, she had no way of knowing, until gradually it claimed her, surrounding her like a bright bubble. She could feel its warmth against her skin, feel it dry the chill damp of her sweat. Slowly the night receded and the towering threat of the serpent diminished with it, until both were gone.

The patch of bright blue became framed by a dome-shaped window space. A single puff of white cloud floated in it, light and soft as a blown feather. Sing felt the hot flow of tears and lay for a long time looking only at the little cloud. As she watched, it seemed to gradually grow in size, to have movement of its own, coming closer and closer until she saw it was a great white bird. Its wings rose and fell with a majestic, dreamlike slowness, tilting and gliding in the air currents, controlling the winds. It soared and dived through the blue prisms of the sky with splendid grace and dignity. She heard the voice of Master To calling to her and tried to rise. To her joy she found that she could move lightly as air. The pain that had come with the darkness was gone. She seemed part of the light, part of the sky, felt the cool stone of the window ledge rough against the soles of her feet as she sprang from it to join the crane in its flight.

The nun who sat beside her, spooning the thick brown mixture patiently into her mouth saw the eyelids flutter and open. Sing looked up into the sombre, ageless female face, unlined and yellow, shaven skull as grey as the robe she wore. The taste of the herbal medicine was rank in Sing's mouth and nostrils. The nun wiped it from her chin and set the bowl aside. Even the slight rustle of her robe as she arose was comforting after the bedlam of the pit. The bright orange garb of the abbot took the nun's place, his brown arms and shoulders bare as he leaned over to look into Sing's open eyes and spoke to her quietly.

'The worst of the battle is over, Siu Sing. You are strong enough now to defend yourself. This is the one who will show you how.'

The abbot stepped aside to make way for a very old man. The face that was lowered close to hers was so masked in wrinkles that only the brightness of his eyes showed life. A thin cluster of snow-white hairs straggled from his chin and sprang from his scalp in wisps as fine as cobweb. His weathered cheeks had sunk in and when he spoke she could see that this shrunken gums were toothless.

'I am the Hookmaker,' he said in a thin whisper. 'I am the one who will teach you how to fight with your mind.'

Sam Danovich paced the garden paths of the summer house while

Doctor Sun sat at the stone table diligently reading a book. The beautifully decorated teacup at his elbow was covered with a silver lid and another stood beside the padded basket that held the teapot, the same set that Sam had drunk from so many times with Sing.

'Doc. I just don't get it. Why can't we go up there and fetch her?'

Doctor Sun turned a page without looking up. 'Because the abbot said he would send her to us when she is ready to come.'

'And he said it would be today, right? Hell, Doc, I've been cooling my heels for more than a month now. I don't even know what they're doing to her up there on that spooky mountain. It's driving me crazy.'

The doctor sighed, removing his spectacles and closing the book. 'I have told you a hundred times, Mr Danovich. This is no ordinary illness, it responds to no ordinary treatment. There is no ordinary cure. You must trust me. She is in the only hands that can help her.'

He opened the basket and withdrew the pot. 'It is better that you sit and take tea. The others will be here soon.'

'I'm sorry Doc. Its all so hard for me to understand. I just can't believe that this is happening. I feel so helpless.' Sam sat down on the other stool and obediently accepted the hot tea.

'It is a very special tea, made from the dried shells of the cicada, it will calm your nerves.'

Sam did not seem to hear him, sipping morosely, staring towards the end of the garden to where the gardener idly chipped away with his broad-bladed hoe.

Doctor Sun glanced at Sam hunched on the little stool like an agitated schoolboy. Soon he will be chewing his fingernails, he thought. He liked this gwai-lo. Freddy Fong had told him how much Sing meant to the American and of his love for her. Doctor Sun had come to look upon Sing as his own daughter. He was an enlightened Chinese and had recognised her great worthiness from the moment he first met her in the Residence of Eternal Peace. He knew of her special strength and brave spirit and how they had endured. He and his family owed her more than he could ever repay.

'Will she be cured?' Sam asked again, past caring how often he had repeated the question. 'Can I take her away? Will she be able to . . . ?'

Doctor Sun lifted a patient hand to stop him. 'She will be out of danger. The protection of the temple, the powers of the abbot and the prayers of the monks have weakened this evil thing but it still reaches out for her. The Black Tao is very strong, it will pursue her again, will not rest until it has poisoned her mind. It seeks to possess her or destroy her.'

Sam jumped to his feet, flinging the contents of the cup into the bushes. 'Why? Who can be doing this. Who could hate her so much? What do they want?'

'Only Siu Sing can tell us that,' said the doctor, subdued by Sam's anguish. 'It is something only she knows. Something only she can face.'

'I'll take her away. Back to the States, the best hospital, the best doctors in the country.'

'It is too late, Mr Danovich. The seed has already been planted in her mind. It has taken root and begun to grow. The abbot has only slowed its flowering. Wherever she goes, it goes with her. Only she can cause it to wither and die or tear it out by the roots. She must face it here, where it lives and breeds. She will not go with you until this is done.'

The doctor's words twisted Sam's gut. 'What will happen next?' he asked huskily.

'Do not be afraid. She has strength and courage beyond our understanding.'

'Then why is she so sick? Why do you say she is still in danger?'

'Sit down. I will try to tell you. But you must listen carefully if you wish to help her. Do not think with your heart.' It was Doctor Sun's turn to leave his seat and stand for a moment admiring quiet beauty of the garden, his hands clasped behind him.

'The abbot is a Buddhist holy man. The sanctuary of the temple is a holy place. The Buddhist faith can only protect, it cannot attack. It can reject, but it cannot destroy. The abbot has blocked the black forces and returned them to their source. This reflects the evil upon the sender. It will weaken him but it will not stop him. The abbot will not destroy the evil one as the death would then be upon his karma. He has protected Siu Sing as far as his godliness will allow. He will not step beyond that.'

Sam stared, helplessly searching for words. 'Well, what will stop the son of a bitch? A bullet?'

'To kill him will not release her. If he dies, the spell remains. Also, there is no way of finding her attacker. Only she knows where he is. She will not tell. Siu Sing understands the ways of the Black Tao. As I have told you, she and she alone can face her tormentor.'

'If the abbot can't do any more to help her, who can?' Sam begged, anxiety and frustration showing heavy in his voice and pain in his eyes.

'He will send for the Hookmaker.'

Sam stared at Doctor Sun, his face a blank. Before he could open his mouth, the doctor continued.

'The Hookmaker is a Taoist holy man of great and ancient wisdom. He is the maker of charms, a spiritual warrior with no fear of karma. He will teach our little sister to fight back if the attack is renewed. He is what is known in the west as a white witch, a wizard or sorcerer.'

Doctor Sun came over to where Sam sat and put a hand on his shoulder. 'I have told you, Sam Danovich, that this is no ordinary malady . . . but our beloved Siu Sing is no ordinary human woman.'

Sam tried to grin through his fear. 'You can say that again, Doc,' he said softly. 'But there must be something we can do to help get her through this. Some way of stopping it. The police? Surely they . . .'

The doctor cut him short with a shake of his head. 'The police would think that she is mad. That we are all mad. They would laugh at her. Take her to hospital, put her into a box and lock her up.'

Doctor Sun seemed sobered by what he had said and Sam could see the flash of anger mixed with the worry in his eyes. 'Those who have chosen the path of Black Tao know this. They are beyond any law, any normal concept of human behaviour. It is why they are so dangerous, so untouchable.'

Everything that Sam had ever learned in his life rebelled against the hopelessness of the doctor's words. 'I'll make her tell me where he is. I'll find the son-of-a-bitch and kill him with my bare hands.'

Doctor Sun again shook his head firmly. 'No, Sam. You and ten more like you would be helpless as children against this man. We can only surround her with our love and the protection of our thoughts and prayers. Siu Sing will do the rest. Have faith in her, she has strengths even we have not yet seen.'

Freddy Fong took the wheel of *Shanghai Lady* from the boatboy as she nosed into Silvermine Bay. In the comfortable cabin below, Birdie Meadows held the hand of the tall young woman she said was Sing's daughter. It had taken Freddy a long time to accept the idea that the woman he had known for so long had a child of her own. He thought he knew everything there was to know about her, that ever since he dragged her, bruised and bleeding, across the floor of the Hollywood Road post office, she had told him everything.

There was no mistaking the girl was hers. Although her hair was blue-black, without streaks of copper, the reddish sheen of her mother's, and her eyes were a deep ink blue, there was something about her that left no doubt. Her perfect skin was paler, her body almost fully formed and she possessed the same thoughtful calm as her mother.

From the shelf of rock above the temple of Po Lin, Sing stood with her face lifted to the sun, absorbing its light and its warmth, using the power of her mind to surround herself with a golden light. Behind closed eyelids she concentrated on breathing deeply the rarified air off the sea, noting with satisfaction the unhindered ebb and flow of its circulation through her body. Lost to everything but the slight sounds of wind stirring the grass, faint as the rustle of insect wings, she willed the oxygen through her lungs, following the upright line of her spine and into her lower belly, then back again to complete the cycle in gradual silent exhalation.

She had meditated there since dawn, as she had each day for a further month since climbing from the pit. This had been followed by the gentle movements of Pa T'uan T'sin, the Precious Set of Eight Silk-Weaving Exercises. These quickly restored flexibility of her limbs, nourished the solid and hollow organs of her body, returning new strength to every muscle and cleaning and refreshing her bloodstream. Each day she had become stronger, and at night, if thoughts of Ah Keung were transmitted she would surround his face with the ring of fire as the Hookmaker had shown her. She would watch his image consumed by the flames of its own hate.

When Sing was brought down from the Pearl Pagoda to the summer house, she came in the same sedan chair that had carried the Hookmaker. It had once transported rich mandarins to and from the temple but now was only used for those who could not climb the peak without help. She had tried to refuse it but the abbot had insisted.

'It is fitting that you should go from here as an empress.'

'But I am no empress, Father. I am in need of exercise,' she had laughed.

'Your friends await you. Go to them as a conqueror returning from war.' He had bowed to her and she could not refuse.

Sam was the first to see it coming, a dark red speck escorted by spots of saffron yellow, moving steadily downward through the trees.

'I see her,' he shouted. 'She's on her way.' Hurrying outside, the group stood staring up the steep track behind the summer house as the procession wound steadily downward towards them.

They were waiting for her at the top of the steps that led from the track and onto the stone patio, silently, among the potted bougainvillea, watching her approach. No one spoke as the closed canopy of the sedan swayed towards them over the last stretch and then was lowered to the ground.

Only when Sing climbed from it and stood smiling down at them did Doctor Sun begin to gently clap his hands. It was the Chinese way of showing great satisfaction and approval of courage and good fortune, of the performance of the gods and the universe in general. The others joined in, first Freddy, then Sam and tearful Birdie. Sing stood looking down at them. She was dressed in the faded simple robe of a novice.

Even at a distance they could see the marks of her ordeal. Her face was thinner, the bones prominent above her drawn cheeks and dark patches showed beneath the hollows of her eyes. Her hair, drawn back into a pigtail, seemed to have lost its lustre. But her eyes were serene and the smile she wore was the smile they knew and had missed so much. The monks picked up the shafts of the chair and started back up the track as she walked towards her friends.

Sam was the first to move. He strode forward a few paces and stood waiting. As he watched her cover the last few steps between them, noting the sandals, too large for her feet, and seeing close the ravages of her suffering, he was shaken by the true depth of his feeling for her. The emotions that welled in him were almost frightening in their intensity, a mixture of the joy of seeing her and anger and hate at what had been done to her.

When Sing reached him Sam was almost afraid to touch her, she seemed so frail in the folds of the robe. It was her eyes that reassured him, washed clean, it seemed, by two large tears that sparkled briefly, then fell heavily from her lashes. Those remarkable eyes that had always intoxicated him were unchanged. He wanted to crush her to him, instead he held out a hand and felt the firmness of her grip as he led her down to the others.

Doctor Sun bowed low three times, Freddy hugged her close and Birdie sniffed hard for control as Sing embraced her. Each of them contained the great excitement they felt for what was now to come and as they had arranged, Dr Sun, spoke first.

'Someone else awaits you, Siu Sing.'

Without the need for more words, Birdie took Sing's hand, leading her into the house and drew her to the glass doors that opened onto the garden, urging her gently through and closing them after her.

The girl at the stone table sat looking towards her as Sing stepped from the shadow of the arbour into the sunlight. Then she rose and they walked slowly, uncertainly, towards each other. There had been no need for Birdie or anyone else to tell Sing that this was her daughter. The girl stood straight, her long, dark hair framing her face and falling heavily over her shoulders. The slightly squarish set to her jaw, that Sing recognised startlingly as her own, was softened by a complexion of the same English paleness as Sebastian's. The eyes that looked so searchingly into hers were damson blue, almost violet in their depth, and round as penny pieces.

'Mother,' she said in a gentle voice. 'I hope you are feeling better now. Aunt Birdie has told me all about you. I've come to help you get well again.'

The day after their reunion Sing crossed to Hong Kong with Freddy Fong in *Shanghai Lady*. In the Jade Lotus Room of the Hilton she lunched with Sir Duncan Masters. He rose to greet her with his old warmth and it was as though the years fell away and they were once again on the platform of the little railway station of Wadhurst, outside Sparrow's Green. Ageing had not stolen his charm or dinted his generous good humour.

The unspoken bond that had formed between them then seemed to have grown over time and distance, undiminished, as though the unhappy circumstances that caused their lives to cross had strengthened instead of weakening its links. He praised the books that now took pride of place in his extensive library back at the Grange, unstinting in his frank admiration for what she had achieved.

The lunch lasted throughout the afternoon and nothing was left undiscussed: Nova's progress at school and now in college; her leaning towards the aesthetic, showing excellence in design and the visual arts; her sweetness and her mischief as a small child; the life they had shared with her at Grange Estate.

He did not speak about the passing of Lady Constance except to say it had happened peacefully five years earlier. There was no mention of Cecily and when Sing enquired after Sebastian the answer was brief.

'My son never seemed the same since Hong Kong,' Sir Duncan mused. 'Something happened to him in that cursed prison that he never quite got over.'

Sebastian had not returned to England, even for his mother's funeral, he continued, scarcely hiding his disappointment. Still and all, he had done well for himself, all things considered, a senior ambassadorial post in Singapore no less.

'Seems perfectly content to stay where he is . . . hardly seen the child . . . she scarcely knows him.' Sir Duncan paused to reach for his briar, then stopped himself. 'Don't suppose it's allowed in here,' he chuckled. 'The good thing about home is that you can do what you like in it. Can we go upstairs?'

Sing went with him to his room and he asked her in for a moment, there was something important he must say. He was aware of his years, he said between puffs as he lit the pipe, and it had worried him. Now that Nova knew of her mother he would like the relationship to grow, to somehow make up for lost time. He suggested Nova stay for a while, as long as she liked within reason—there was no harm missing a term and he would personally speak to Nova's principal.

'It's not every day a girl of eighteen discovers she has a beautiful and accomplished mother. The girl belongs here with you, for a while. God knows you deserve each other.' Nova would turn twenty-one in three years, he went on, and as the agreement had stated she would come into an adequate allowance and, of course, a proper share of the Grange Estate in the event of his death. With the room filled with the pleasant aroma of pipe tobacco, he took Sing's hand in his.

'Seeing you again and all it can mean to Nova's future is all I could ask. It has made me very happy,' he said. 'Now go and spend some time with her. I'm perfectly comfortable here for a day or two.'

Having Nova by her side, learning all about her, quickly restored the rest of Sing's physical and mental strength and gave her life new meaning. Sir Duncan had spent several delightful days sightseeing with them and with Freddy's help and Sam's company she had made sure it was a memorable time.

For several joyous weeks after he had gone Sing and Nova roamed the island of Lantau. They gathered wild flowers among the hills and swam from the end of the beach at Silvermine Bay. Each morning they watched the fishing sampans pulled up on the sand and helped to untangle starfish and spider conch from the nets. Doctor Sun had returned to Everspring to run his business and Freddy was back at work in the studio. Sure that Sing was now safe, Sam had returned to Los Angeles or urgent business.

Birdie had dispensed with the services of the cook and two amahs that Doctor Sun had provided to attend to Sing's needs. It would be much better, she said, if she took care of her the way Sing had once cared for her, and the good doctor had bowed to her firm suggestion.

Every dawn, before Nova was awake, Birdie heard Sing leave the house to climb the track to the place she called the Rock of Great Strength. Sam had told them both that the first two hours of daylight belonged to Sing alone and that this was the time when she healed herself.

When Sing returned from the peak to take a shower bath, breakfast would be waiting before they left for the village or to find new tracks across the island, around the coast or through the hills. On the weekends Freddy arrived in *Shanghai Lady* to take them cruising the outlying islands, to picnic on the hidden beaches, to Hong Kong for dinner at the Yacht Club or a banquet in the Great Shanghai restaurant in Kowloon. Sing did not stay away from Lantau for long. The abbot had warned her that although the psychic attack had been stopped it could prove to be like the eye of a storm. It would not take her enemy long to marshall his powers afresh and change his strategy. He could renew his assault at any time. She should remain on the island, close to the temple and to the white magic of the Hookmaker, until it was clear that the Forceful One was finally defeated.

With each day Sing felt her own strength developing to a level she had never known. The delight of being with the daughter she had never hoped to see had driven the deep depression and sudden bouts of unexplained anxiety from her mind. The great unhappiness and physical exhaustion that had enclosed her like a fog and followed her every waking step had withered, shed and left behind like the discarded skin of a snake.

The salt-fish smell from the Hookmaker's hut was strong on the off-shore breeze as Sing ran along the sand towards it. She had made the journey down the valley without stopping and had run through the village with the dogs barking at her heels. Arriving at the hut, she stood catching her breath, watching the old man's crooked fingers fashion the delicate detail of a charm. He sat on the log of driftwood, its grey texture as seamed and weathered as his wrinkled hands.

'I see you are strong again, Little Sister. Yet you have come to see me. Is our work not done?'

He squinted up at her, the wicker hat shading his face and protecting his bony shoulders from the sun.

'I fear that it is not, Sifu.' She spoke very quietly, seating herself on the log beside him. 'The dream came again last night. No longer in the form of Yangjingshi but as Lou Fu, the tiger.'

She watched in silence the comforting gentleness of his old hands, the infinite patience of his miniature carving. 'I know the one who does this thing. He will not be so easily defeated.'

'This is possible,' the Hookmaker said at last. 'I have come to know the heart of this Forceful One. He bears the venom of the cobra and the teeth of the tiger. Such a one knows only victory or death. It is his creed.'

'I fear for those close to me. If he tests my strength and fails again he may turn his venom on them, to bring me to him.'

He nodded, setting aside his work and looking at her closely. 'It may be so,' he said, his eyes searching her face. 'You are strong again but so is he.'

'I must face him, Sifu. I have always known this.'

'This is his intention. What he cannot possess with the mind he will destroy with the body.'

Sing withdrew a slip of red paper, unfolding it and laying it before him. 'I have written this message in the old style. I ask you to lay your hands upon it. To bring him to me. There can be no peace for me until this is done.'

He picked up the red paper filled with flowing calligraphy, reading it carefully. 'You are indeed a maker of fine images. How can such a challenge be ignored? It is written in the way of tradition, from one student to another of the same master.' He turned to her.

'He will not refuse?'

The Hookmaker folded the paper and held it between his palms for silent moments, his eyes closed. When he spoke, it was in a whisper. 'He has the cunning and the speed of the king of snakes . . . The courage and the power of the tiger, lord of the earth.'

'I know this is so, Sifu. I come to you for the blessing of your protection and for the amulet.'

'It is ready, Little Sister. Come inside.'

After blazing sun and the glare of the sand the inside of the hut was cool and almost dark. Sing was aware of a great sense of mystery as she stood in the doorway and peered into shadowy corners. The Hookmaker crossed to a recess in the wall where the sparks of joss illuminated the shadowy figure of Kuan Yin. The goddess of mercy wore the same serene smile that had watched over Sing in the hillside temple when she lay broken at the foot of her shrine.

From Kuan Yin's neck, the Hookmaker removed the amulet of the White Crane. With it held between his palms, he bowed three times then turned and brought it to the light from the doorway.

'It is purged of the evil one's essence. Cleansed by the blessings of Kuan Yin and imbued with the warrior spirit of Kuan Kung, the God of War. I have called upon all my powers to sanctify it.'

He held the amulet high so that a shard of sunlight struck through it. For a fraction of a second it seemed to radiate pure light; the rivulets of moss jade flared with a green flame that surrounded the symbol of the Crane in its protective circle.

'The substance of the Snake and the Tiger absorbed for so long from the evil one's being is no more,' he muttered. 'Only the enduring spirit of the Crane remains and the ch'i of its master.'

He fastened it around Sing's neck. 'Remember only one more thing. To the black one all things are reversed. Night is day. Darkness is light. Evil is good. The laws of the universe are turned upside down. Only chaos reigns. Do not forget this. Reverse the eight trigrams and you will triumph. Let the Yin become the Yang. Black become white.' He handed back the folded red paper.

'Send your message. It will find him and he will come to the appointed place at the appointed time.'

The Crane and
the Tiger

BEHIND SING'S closed eyes the images locked for so long in her subconscious mind burned bright. She did not feel the cold chill before the dawn and there was no discomfort in the stillness of her limbs. For three hours she had sat in the position of the Lotus, the relaxed palms of her hands pressed lightly upon her abdomen, the thumbs hooked to connect the circuit of her ch'i. Her spine erect, she drew strength from the Yin of a white moon, aware only of the slow, deep rhythm of her breath in its unbroken cycle. From the jade around her neck, heat seemed to pulse, penetrating the centre of gravity behind the umbilicus.

There was no doubt in her mind that Ah Keung would come. Doctor Sun had sent a reliable man into the Walled City to deliver her challenge. The Forceful One had not been hard to find at the Palace of Hong. She did not tell the doctor of the note's contents or of her intentions, and he did not ask. She had told no one but the Hookmaker. No meeting had ever been more isolated, more secret than this.

When she opened her eyes the first faint flush of sunrise was turning the low moon pale and transparent as ricepaper. Half an hour more and Ah Keung would face her here. The Hookmaker had said it would be so. The message received within the Walled City would not be ignored. The Hookmaker's words were clear and certain: 'Where the serpent has failed the tiger must triumph. Only this will satisfy him. He will come and you must be ready.'

As the sky lightened, she sensed his unseen presence. Knowing she was watched, Sing walked to the centre of the rock and called Ah Keung's name. 'I am here, Ah Keung. The sun is rising. Soon there will be no more darkness. I am ready to meet Ah Keung, the Forceful One, face to face in its pure light.'

The challenge echoed among the rocks. No answer came but she could feel his presence.

'I am here, Ah Keung. We are as we were at the beginning. Only the rock between us,' she called. She faced each direction, watching for his shadow.

'I could think of no better place to meet,' his voice replied. 'There is no one to know what happens here.' His laughter was short, echoing among the spires, seeming to surround her.

'Only the old man is no longer here with us.' His tone mocked her as he stepped into the growing light.

'He is here, Ah Keung. Master To lives through me. The amulet is restored. I shall revenge his death.'

'You know, then.'

'That you tricked him? I have always known of your betrayal. You would never have defeated him without treachery.'

He was wearing the loose black garb of the Kung Fu fighter, trimmed and cuffed with white. One by one he undid the corded loops that fastened the jacket across his chest and flung it aside, kicking the canvas slippers from his feet to pad catlike around her, the wide-legged pants held around his waist by a crimson sash. On his chest was the charging tiger, on his back the cobra poised to strike. She turned with him as he stalked in a wide circle, keeping his distance, never taking her eyes from his.

'All great masters must one day fall. It has been the Way of the Empty Hand for a thousand years.' His words held the lilt of amusement.

'It was not so.' Sing's voice was filled with contempt. 'You deceived him. Betrayed his trust. You are a coward, Ah Keung.'

The reply was edged with menace, all lightness gone in a flash. 'It was I who was betrayed. I who lived with pain. I who endured.'

He snapped out his foot in a high frontal kick, flaying the empty air like a whiplash. His voice became pitched with bitterness. 'And I alone who defied the gods and dragged their curse high into the mountains in search of the man-root. I, Ah Keung, who respected and honoured my master above all others.' He checked his growing fury, his voice dropping to a growl.

'My reward was the cold and loneliness of a shed beside the beasts, rejected and unworthy. You were the chosen one. He held nothing back from you, even the secret of Lo Shan.'

'I was a small child. I could not be blamed, yet you took your revenge when you sold me to the house of Fan as a slave,' said Sing evenly.

'I found you a home,' he barked. 'A place where you would be given work, food and shelter.'

'You made me a slave in a cruel place.'

Sing worked upon his anger. It was a warrior's greatest enemy. Speaking more softly, she continued to probe him. 'We were even, you and I. But it was not enough. You killed the one I loved and for that you will never be forgiven.'

He sneered. 'It was the brown monkeys who killed the gwai-lo soldier. Not I, though I held the blade.'

'It was you who guided them, I know it. You who was the traitor.'

Her scorn was aimed to infuriate him. 'You are a failure, Ah Keung. While I have made something of my life, you have lived with only darkness. You are no longer a man. There is nothing you can do to me.'

As she spoke, Sing began unhooking the fastenings of her jacket.

'Why are demons your only messengers, Ah Keung? Is it because you could not face me in the light? Is the cunning of the snake and the power of the tiger only great in dreams?' She stripped off the jacket and threw it from her.

'I am here now. Where no one can help me. I was not afraid to come. I am no longer the frightened child, but you are still the boy with a twisted foot. All gods spit upon you.'

Ah Keung spun around, dropping into the crouching stance of the Tiger form, taking three fast steps towards her then stopping, spitting his contempt. 'Oh no, Little Star. It will not be so fast. I have often wondered what it was the old man showed you on Lo Shan and at the sacred shrine of Adato. Did you learn? Have you remembered? Do you practise? I hope so. I do not want to see you die too quickly or too easily.'

As he closed his fists, the muscles of his chest and abdomen twitched and the snarling face of the tiger seemed to spring to life. She stood perfectly still, silhouetted against the vivid sky, framed by the molten lip of the new sun. Her arms rose like wings, loosely erect. The giant shadow of the Crane was flung towards him across the face of the rock in the sudden burst of full sunrise.

His spring triggered in her the mechanism that had been set and coiled for so long, spilling the white-hot crucible of her ch'i, splashing like quicksilver to race into her veins. She felt the spirit of the great bird enter her, lifting her on its wings. Surer, lighter and higher than ever before, she evaded the rush. He was blinded by the sudden ferocity of the sun that her movement had revealed and in that fragment of time her arms, arched high, dropped with the weight and hardness of stone. The right blocked his clawing strike to her throat, absorbing the full shock of its power upon her forearm. Willing her ch'i into the very marrow of the slender bone, turning it for that fraction of an instant to steel, the fingers hooked into an iron claw, striking his dazzled eyes.

As her blow drove deep, Ah Keung's mouth flew open, his curse of surprise beaten by the speed of Sing's left hand. Her left arm flew in a wide arc, supple as the neck of the crane, its fingers bunched and rigid as the lethal beak, under Ah Keung's attacking arm, driving home with the force of a spear-head, upwards to a spot slightly below the armpit. Allowing for the shifting of the pressure points. Letting her senses guide her. Every last grain of Sing's ch'i, every ounce of her will-power and every second of her training went into the lethal strike of deem mak, the death touch.

She felt it impact the soft, vulnerable flesh between the muscles, penetrating tissue between corded cartilage, piercing through taut sinew to reach the nerve juncture. She was so finely tuned to his savage vibrations she felt the contact, felt the electric spasm run up her arm, but drove further with the full momentum of the blow swung with the force of a battle axe. No sound escaped Ah Keung's gaping jaws; his sightless eyes stared blindly at the full force of the sun.

Every muscle seemed to quiver and jerk at once. His hands flapped helplessly, fingers trembling and out of control. One violent convulsion bucked him like a high voltage shock and blood flowed from his mouth where he had bitten through his tongue. Sing stepped back as he dropped suddenly and awkwardly to his knees, to pitch forward and lie twitching at her feet.

The madhouse overlooked the ladder streets leading down to the central markets. Steep flights of narrow granite steps were crowded with the stalls of street hawkers selling farm produce, cheap jade, haberdashery, live fish, ducks and chickens. It was here the amahs came with the children in their care to fill their baskets, to eat soup and rice noodles from the food carts at the bottom of the steps.

While they ate and gossiped the children chewed coloured sugar sweets and watched the puppet man or the noisy opera. Across the street in the markets, under the wide roaming, steel-braced roof, pigs and cows were cut up with surgeons' skill, the razor-edged steel moving so fast it was hardly seen at work. Hoses washed down fishheads and iron-wheeled trolleys trundled quivering piles of offal across the greasy floors.

This was the scene that would soon greet Doctor 'Crackhead' Woo as he looked out from the barred window of his office on the top floor of the madhouse—a vast old building of grimy stone, its few mean windows heavily barred and behind the bars a screen of dirty gauze to keep out the daylight. Behind that the howls and shrieks of the mad were well known to the hawkers of the ladder street and would soon compete with the noise outside.

This was very early and the noises inside and out had not begun yet. Just the trucks coming and going from the market, the stalls still shuttered and the vendors sleeping, chained to their wares. The only time when things were quiet, this hour or so before the first rice of the day, thought Crackhead Woo as he drank his bowl of tea. His name came from the stick he always used to clear a path through those who were slow to move out of his way.

As though to prove him wrong about the quietness a discordant shriek pierced the corridor to his quarters as though seeking him out. He stopped to listen. Doctor Crackhead could usually put a name or a face to the hideous noises that rose and fell within the dormitories. This one came again in a prolonged howling that ended with loud shouts from those it had disturbed. Soon the others would be aroused and the cacophony of the day would begin. He recognised the cry of the man in the detention cell on the floor below and made a mental note to visit him on his morning rounds.

First, he would take his walk around the walled area. He would pace briskly around it and back for his early rice before they opened the dormitories. Then what little quiet there was would be gone and the exercise yard would be crowded with the lost ones. He preferred to think of them as the lost instead of the mad. He was not a heartless man but, like most Chinese, quite insensitive to the condition of insanity and had come to view their suffering with a certain indifference.

Serious concern for those committed to his care was non-existent in the colony of Hong Kong. Partly because they were all Chinese, so the gwai-lo medical authorities hardly knew of the Institute's existence, but mainly because madness was seen by the local population as an affliction of the damned. A curse upon the soul called down by righteous gods upon those who deserved it. Far from being pitied, the demented were looked upon with the same amount of intolerance as the cripple, the leper or the carrier of plague but with the added dimension of amusement.

Those who passed the walls would always stop to hoot and growl along with those on the other side. It was the thing to do. By afternoon there would be the usual number of amahs and children. They would scream and groan, pull faces and jump up and down outside the great barred gate to make the children laugh and mimic the ones inside who called back at them. It was important that the young ones learned to laugh with them, so that the evil spirits that tormented the lost ones would not turn their blazing eyes upon them.

Doctor Crackhead Woo had been director of the Bonham Road Institute for almost fifteen years and had become accustomed to its primitive conditions. He was not paid very much and he never requested improvements because he knew it would do no good. The fact that the old stone building and its rambling outhouses were overcrowded far beyond their original capacity; that half the inmates slept on unswept floors; that it froze like a meatworks in winter and was a baker's oven in summer, was something he could do nothing about. That his staff were mainly drawn from among its more docile patients, food and medicine were in short supply and of the poorest possible quality, was accepted without complaint.

The consequence of this was that every misfit, freak and monster to rear its head in society was immediately and without consideration bundled through the gates of Doctor Crackhead's madhouse. There they joined the hideously deformed, the inbred, the mentally deranged and the criminally insane in a bedlam of darkness which he had convinced himself was the purgatory they no doubt deserved. It was this attitude that enabled him to keep his job and occupy the office on its top floor.

The squeeze was not usually good for Doctor Crackhead but occasionally there were those who paid to admit one of their own they could no longer control. Then he sent the two burly mainlanders from Fukien in the lock-up van. They were not qualified in any nursing skill except that of restraint and seldom needed to use the canvas and leather straight-jackets they carried.

There had been such a piece of good fortune only a week or two ago—the victim of a mysterious attack who had been brought across on the ferry from Lantau Island. This one had been blinded and crippled, left mindless as a child. With him came a strange creature, boy or man was hard to tell, who moved in the way of an animal. He said he was the servant of the mindless one and would not leave him. He had been fetched from the Walled City by the one who had paid well to admit them both.

Doctor Woo never enquired too deeply into who it was that signed the admission certificate. The police were seldom interested and experience had told him that they always used a false name, just as the names of those he took in were invented. The payment in this case had been anonymous but by far the most substantial he had ever received. Enough to cover the medical and living expenses for both of them indefinitely. It had included the contract of a foreign solicitor's office in the Central District named Pidcock and Pidcock, which guaranteed their upkeep for life.

It wasn't often an opportunity for handsome squeeze came along as this one had, still allowing ample for the best of treatment and accommodation available, and the director had quickly seen to it. The paper said these two were known as Ah Keung and the dog boy. A brief examination had convinced him that neither of them was potentially dangerous and, on release from the hospital ward, he had arranged for them to occupy one of the small private rooms reserved for those who could afford them.

It was little more than a cell but greatly preferable to the sprawling dormitories and the havoc of the common area. He had even supplied a wooden wheelchair, something that delighted the dog boy as he pushed his silent, sightless master around and around the special area set aside for those who were considered totally harmless.

Taking a stout walking stick from the collection kept in a large porcelain vase by the door, Doctor Crackhead weighed its balance with the care of a champion golfer selecting a club and left the room for his early morning rounds.

A few days before Nova was to leave Hong Kong and return to England and her last semester before entering university, Sing took her one last time to the market in Silvermine Bay. There they chose the very choicest fruits to fill a basket. It was very early and the farm women were still setting up their stalls. The ox and donkey carts were arriving, loaded with local produce.

'Who are they for?' Nova asked, as they stopped before a pile of golden persimmon.

'For someone very important. Very special,' smiled Sing feeling the fat, shining orbs for just the right one. 'Someone we must pay our respects to before we say goodbye.'

With the basket full of starfruit, pummelo, lychees, persimmon and plum they walked down to the beach where the Hoklos were unloading their sampans and bought a fresh fish. Carrying the basket between them they followed the valley path beside the waterfalls, where kingfishers shot through the rushes.

Two hours later the villagers of Tung Chung watched them pass along the narrow road to the sea, between the stilted houses and upturned boats. Keeping a respectful distance, some smiled and murmured a greeting. Even the dogs were stopped from barking. It was well known that this was the jarp-jung woman who was blessed by the abbot of Po Lin and protected by the magic of the Hookmaker.

At the beach, they took off their sandals, the sand warm under their feet, as they walked along the edge of the sea.

'Jo sun, Sifu—good morning, Master.' Sing called as they climbed the worn stone steps to the Hookmaker's hut. The old man was seated as he always was on the log of driftwood.

'Jo sun, Siu Sing. You have brought another,' he said, without raising his head. 'Is she afraid of me? May I look upon her?'

Sing laughed. 'She is not afraid of being turned into a three-legged toad. I have brought my daughter for your blessing, Sifu.' She placed the basket of fruit at his side. 'We bring a gift of fruit with our deep respect and our endless thanks.'

The Hookmaker lifted his eyes to look at Nova. The brightness of them startled her. They were like the eyes of a mischievous child in a face of great age. She smiled at him uncertainly.

'She is a worthy daughter,' he said and stood up with surprising agility. 'You must both sit and drink tea with me.' He rolled up the window flap to let in the light.

Inside the little hut joss burned in the corners and the walls were hung with the treasures of many tides—the bones of cuttlefish, shells of every shape and colour, the twisted sculpture of driftwood, dried starfish and the jaws of sharks. Every piece had been finely carved or painted with beautiful scenes of ancient China, and among them, hand-made fish hooks of every size and type were displayed.

His table was the hatchboard of a junk, swept ashore after some violent storm. Everything around them, he said, came to him from the sea. He made them bitter black tea and asked nothing about Ah Keung or Sing's ordeal. It was as though it had never taken place. He talked instead of Koxinga the pirate and the time when his five-masted war junks anchored in this very bay. When the old iron cannon on the sea wall belched with fire.

He talked of many things for an hour and when it was time for them to leave, he went to the bench that held his tools and brushes. 'I have made this for you,' he said, as he handed something to Nova. 'I knew you would come.'

It was the tip of a whale's tooth, he said, bound into a section from the wingbone of a sea-eagle and intricately decorated with mystic symbols.

'It is very beautiful,' breathed Nova. 'I will keep it always.'

'Once, when I was a young man,' chuckled the Hookmaker, 'I could paint an emperor's garden upon a grain of rice. Now my eyes are old and the art is lost to me, but I can show you the garden of my memory.'

Suddenly he stretched out his hand and held it inches above Nova's head. It seemed to her she sensed its heat, felt her hair lift under its power.

'Close your eyes,' he said. 'And tell me what you see.'

Nova's mind looked upon the garden as though a gate had been flung open. A beautiful pavilion, its swooping roof as green as an emerald, sat among arched bridges and sparkling cascades. Crystal clear water flowed into pools crowded with lilies and sunlight flashed on the bright gold backs of carp. Birds called in the clumps of black-stemmed bamboo and beyond the garden, through a screen of red acacia, she could see the ocean, shining like glass under a new sun. When he took his hand away it was gone.

'Remember this place,' he said softly. 'Take it with you wherever you go. When darkness comes, hold this charm and the gate will open. Walk among its flowers for there is no garden more fragrant and peaceful than the garden of the mind.'

In the years that followed, Nova's letters always mentioned the magic charm of the Hookmaker, quite sure that it had a lot to do with her success and happiness and her radiant good health. Sir Duncan Masters had passed away, leaving her a generous inheritance. Content in the knowledge that her daughter was making progress towards her own goals and independence, Sing had thrown all her own energies into her work with Freddy Fong, as well as keeping an eye on the White Crane Medicine Company and The Second Sunrise company.

Venture Films (HK) Ltd, had expanded its studio space, with three full production units supplying commercial facilities, crew and equipment for Asia's growing advertising industry. Sam sent a keen young American director and Freddy trained an efficient team of local cameramen, film editors, lighting technicians and production assistants.

Sing still acted as consultant on styling, and creative matters and the series of documentaries on the history of Chinese medicine and its application in the western world had been well received and fascinating to work on.

Sing's share of the royalties from network syndication went to her proudest undertaking—the Margaret Pelham Foundation—a string of public shelters and welfare centres across Hong Kong and the New Territories. The largest of these was the Justin Pelham Memorial School for Hakka children in Taipo village. With Alistair Pidcock's careful handling, the Margaret Pelham Trust Fund had grown steadily. That the money could be channeled into such things as these, that she had been asked to sit on the committee of the Welfare League and to head up an action group for destitute Eurasian children, was the undreamed-of pinnacle of success to her.

All of this Sing reflected upon as she stood alone in the beautiful gardens of the Villa Formosa. She had spared no expense in its restoration and was at last satisfied that this was as close as she could hope to get to its original splendour. It had been her personal and very private obsession for the past several years and the quiet pride she felt as she surveyed its completion was a very private joy.

She had told no one of successfully negotiating ownership with Alistair Pidcock. He had come to value Sing Deverill as a client and liked her immensely as a person. He had also come to believe her story completely and was now convinced beyond the slightest doubt that she was indeed the taipan's only living offspring and the rightful heir to the Repulse Bay property. As much as anywhere this was where she belonged and she asked for nothing more; insisting that the remainder of the Deverill fortune be put into trust for the Welfare League of which she had become a director. To keep things entirely legal Alistair had sold the Villa Formosa to her for the sum of one Hong Kong dollar, suggesting that the monies she had so diligently saved against its purchase could now be put to the formidable undertaking of its restoration.

Sing had used the money gradually and intelligently. Instead of lavishing such an unexpected windfall on a flurry of activity from teams of tradesmen, she had continued to seek out exactly the right craftsmen for exactly the right job, setting each task to her strict specifications. Slowly, piece by piece, under her careful supervision the original materials were repaired or replaced.

As she had hoped, the foundations and walls had proved solid as a fort. The heavy glazed tiles, fit for the roof of the grandest palace, were in perfect condition beneath the carpet of mould, and now gleamed green and gold as a spring meadow. As she stood, shaded by a copse of mature silver birch trees, looking back at the splendid old house, she was sure her father would have approved. She was certain that this was how he had gone about the creation of this lovely place for her mother—with patience and love that would last for many generations to come.

Inside, the broad-planked mahogany floors, the chestnut and teakwood panelling and staircase were solid as ever and had bloomed anew under the polisher's hand. When the splendid filigree of lofty ceilings had been exposed, cleaned and whitewashed, their elaborate cornices and central mouldings were once again picked out in rich enamels with delicate friezes of gold leaf.

Alistair Pidcock took her to the Jockey Club on the day Sing announced to him that Villa Formosa was completely reborn. Over coffee, after a sumptuous lunch, he handed her a set of three iron keys.

'These are the keys to your father's godown. I've been keeping them for this day, although I never thought I'd see it,' he said, beaming his heartfelt goodwill.

'No idea what's in it but I should imagine it's his bits and pieces. Which of course, go with the house.'

Leaving him to enjoy his port and cigar, Sing drove, consumed with excitement, to the address stamped on the metal disc attached to the keys. The godown was located in an old waterfront block on West Connaught Road opposite the Hong Kong-China Ferry Terminal. The three big brass locks opened with surprising ease and she stepped through the small door set in the iron shutters into its musty shadows. High above, light came from barred windows and a sloping skylight, to fall upon piles of crates and tea-chests. Aside from these, carefully arranged, covered with dust sheets and draped with cobwebs, was a wide array of beautiful blackbean and rosewood furniture and a treasury of priceless antiques. Heavily framed oil paintings stood beside delicate watercolour scrolls, gilded wall-carvings and tapestries. Rolls of splendid rugs and carpets were stitched into waterproof canvas and from the rafters, shrouded in dusty hessian, hung splendid chandeliers.

Sing spent the whole of the afternoon uncovering her heritage, knowing that every piece had been chosen by Ben Deverill's own hand. Last had come the most thrilling discovery of all. Uncovering two huge oil paintings under a sheet of sailcloth, Sing stood face-to-face with a life-sized portrait of her father and mother. There was not an instant's doubt that this was who they were.

As in the precious photograph, Ben Deverill was severely dressed in the square-rig serge of a ship's captain, cap beneath his arm, one large hand resting protectively on the shoulder of a handsome Chinese woman in a dress of yellow silk. The second canvas showed a tall ship under full sail, racing through a lively, blue-green sea, spray flung high over her prancing bow, her tiers of billowing canvas lost in flying cloud.

Only one question remained unresolved now that her own future was established. It was one that had stayed in the back of her mind since the terrible day that J.T. Ching had died at her feet, clawing to reach her with his last breath. Time had all but erased the memory, but now as she contemplated the completion of her long-held dream, it returned with compelling clarity. Sing had always been quite certain that Jade had saved her life. There could be no true fulfilment until she was found and some how repaid. Casting her mind back to the loneliness and fear she had felt on escaping the tavern of Madame Fung, the emptiness she had known on the busiest street, in the midst of the biggest crowd, she knew exactly where she would begin.

The Mikado

THE MAN who located Hand-trolley Lulu for Sing was the same man that Doctor Sun had used to take her message into the Walled City and who had so easily found Ah Keung. He was a man to be trusted, the doctor laughed, so long as he was paid to be. For a reasonable fee depending on the amount of travelling involved, Shoeshine Lee would find out anything you wanted to know or track down anyone you wanted to find.

It was Shoeshine Lee who had told them of the dog boy and who had again entered Ling Nam to fetch him to Lantau and he who had delivered them both to the madhouse of Crackhead Woo. He could be relied upon to go anywhere with his portable shoeshine stand on his back; there was very little he did not know about the streets of downtown Hong Kong and what he didn't know, he would soon find out.

He had immediately known of Hand-trolley Lulu and Three-thumbs Poon. Weren't they the taipans of Wan Chai, the most famous and respected names in the bar trade? Who did not know them? Shoeshine knew where they lived, where they ate and played mahjjong; he knew every bar, eating house, massage parlour and whore-house they owned between them and exactly where to find them at any hour of the day or night.

Asked about the girl called Jade, though, he shook his head, showing the one large gold tooth that gleamed like a lucky nugget when he drew his thin lips back to contemplate a problem. There were a thousand times a thousand Jades in the bars of Wan Chai and all of them used some other name. It was the fashion, he grinned, to use a famous foreign name to attract business. They would have to ask Hand-trolley Lulu or her head mama san, Firecracker Lily. They knew every girl on the streets, young or old, fat or thin, ugly or beautiful. He had sloped off, his heavy box of brushes, rags and shoe polish slung from a leather strap on his bent little back, pleased to have earned such an easy twenty dollars.

Hand-trolley Lulu was almost eighty years old and now seldom left her flat high above the busy traffic of Lockhart Road. It had taken fifteen minutes to get her to open the door. Only when Sing spoke of Three-thumbs Poon and the Nine Dragons and Ah Keung, the Forceful One, who was no more, did she grudgingly take the chains from her door. No, she did not remember a girl named Topaz whom she had once taken to work in the Nine Dragons Ballroom of Three-thumbs Poon. And she certainly didn't recognise the well-dressed jarp-jung woman who stood before her asking foolish questions. She was just an old woman causing no trouble and minding her own business.

'I do not come to cause you trouble, ah paw. I come only in

search of my friend and hope that you will help me to find her.'

'How can a poor old woman help such a fine lady? Do you not see I am blind and deaf?'

'I think you see and hear very well, ah paw.' Sing used the respectful term for old lady in a soft but firm voice. 'And I do not think you are so poor. Did you not grow fat on the American soldiers from Korea and Vietnam? Did the money spent by them in your establishments not make you rich? Is it not you and Three-thumbs Poon who have now built the Mikado Nightclub on Devoux Road, to empty the pockets of the Japanese? I do not think the gwai-lo police chief knows exactly what entertainment you provide them.

Behind her spectacles and in the frantic graspings of her still nimble mind, Hand-trolley Lulu realised this one was who she said she was and she was no fool. How could she know of the Mikado and of her partnership with that donkey-headed Three-thumbs Poon? Had the pig-brains been talking too much?

She straightened up and waddled to the small untidy kitchen, returning with a large thermos flask of hot water from which she poured two cups of green tea.

'Sit down, siu jeh,' she used the term for young lady, and the acting had gone out of her voice. 'We will drink tea while you tell me about your friend.'

Secretly, Sing smiled inside. The twenty dollars she had paid Shoeshine Lee was well spent and the hint of blackmail had worked just as she hoped it would.

The Mikado was Wan Chai's newest and grandest nightclub. Situated only a few blocks from the Nine Dragons, its imposing neon sign rose high above the flickering jumble of lesser signs. It took the form of a huge peony flower, its petals wide open to the night with multi-coloured electric stamens shooting from its heart, announcing across the length and breadth of Devonx Road that this was the Mikado. It stretched across the street like a dazzling bridge of changing colour. Perched on one corner of its gigantic 'M' was a large butterfly, happily flapping its tireless wings from pink to blue to green to yellow and back to pink.

The vivid strobing of its rainbow hues washed over Jade's skin as she prepared for her next act. She was tired. Her limbs ached from dancing seven nights a week. Now it was almost midnight and hers was the act that opened the show. The pain in her head came from lack of sleep, her mouth was sour from stale alcohol and her eyes were stung red with tobacco smoke from hours of hustling drinks at the tables. She looked at herself in the glare of the makeup mirror, repairing the starch-white powder and bright puce of her cheeks, the coal-black brows and lashes. There was nothing such a mask could not hide, even her age.

From the box of gaudy trinkets on the dressing room table, she chose two small cups no bigger than a dollar piece, each hung with a shower of sequins. Lifting her breasts one at a time, she cleaned the nipple with vaseline, flicking it to life with a long silver fingernail, and then applied vegetable gum. To each aroused nub, she fitted one of the little silver cups so that glittering strands of sequin seemed to flow from her flesh. Then, with a final check of her face and a test swing of each large breast that sent the sequins whirling, she sank down on the littered couch.

It was ten minutes before the first act and she lay back, grateful of the rest. Work at the Mikado was harder than the bars but now she didn't have to lie with the American soldiers unless she wanted to. Her tired mind went back to the plastic flower factory in Kowloon where she had hidden herself for the first five years after driving the knife into the back of J.T. Ching. There she had been one among hundreds who worked sixteen hours a day in the beehive of the Sincere Flower Company.

It was a place where only the desperate came to work because the pay was small and the hours long. Where you could sleep on the floor beside your work bench for a few cents a night and the rice was brought around to you so that you did not stop work. It had been a good place to hide until the bad air affected her lungs and the fine work had almost ruined her eyesight.

Talk among the girls had been of the bars in Wan Chai where the American soldiers and sailors from the war in Korea were coming to spend their money like water. Rumours said that a girl who was not afraid to lie beneath a gwai-lo could become rich and receive a fortune in gifts. The one who spread these rumours was called Firecracker Lily, and she came from the Happy Butterfly Bar owned by the famous Hand-trolley Lulu.

Each month she would come in her fancy clothes and high-heeled shoes to walk among the work rooms and look for pretty girls. Many times she had offered Jade the $500 that she used as bait. It was an advance, she said, and that she could earn this much in one night as a bargirl. Jade would have gone with her, but she was afraid she would be caught and sent to prison. Then, when enough time had passed, she had said yes and gone with Firecracker Lily.

For years she worked in Hand-trolley Lulu's bars, helping the Americans spend their money. It had not been hard. She earned a small commission on every glass of cold tea she made them buy her, and if they paid her bar fine, she kept part of the money for going upstairs. She used the things she had learned from the Golden One and soon became a great favourite. Hand-trolley Lulu was so proud of her that she had been sent with certain other chosen ones to have the Operation.

The operation was the dreamed-of goal of every bargirl—to have the large breasts and round eyes of a Western movie star. Until this was possible, the girls had padded their bras and taped the upper lids of their eyes with transparent sticky tape before applying makeup to make them look wider.

The operation was expensive, performed by only one or two special doctors and reserved for the stars and starlets of Run Run Shaw, the high-flying callgirls of the Hilton, or the mistresses of rich men.

Hand-trolley Lulu had paid for the chosen ones and taken the cost from their commission. It was good for business, she said, the gwai-lo did not like a flat chest and would pay extra for a girl who was big in front. She had been right and business for Jade had never been better. While she was at it, Jade had paid her own money for the eyelid operation. The simple stroke of a scalpel that changed the narrow eye of the bar girl into the glamorous eye of the film star.

The nightlife of Wan Chai had gone well for her since that day. She had changed her name to Sabrina, after the English star who Hand-trolley Lulu insisted had the biggest tits in all the world and who all the gwai-los dreamed of sleeping with. She had dyed her hair blonde and Sabrina Wong had become the most sought-after prostitute on Lockhart Road, so well known that she had been able to put her price up to more than double and only take upstairs those that she chose to. In the Vietnam war of the sixties, her commission had been better than ever. With Hong Kong declared a number one centre for Rest and Recreation, the bar business had boomed overnight.

Jade rested a weary arm across her eyes as she glanced at the clock on the dresser, glad to see she still had five minutes. She wished often that she had saved her money instead of gambling. Some she knew had retired when the war was over and opened a beauty parlour or a bar of their own. She had not, and it was why she now worked as a stripteaser in Hand-trolley Lulu's new nightclub.

They both knew she was becoming too old for the bars; and although she had always been careful and the rules were strict, she had not been without her share of disease. It had dulled her enthusiasm. But her ch'i was good and her skin had stayed smooth, she had looked after her body as best she could, and with lighting and makeup, could still bring applause from the brown monkeys.

The Japanese tourists had replaced the American soldier in the glittering caves of Wan Chai. They did not drink cheap beer in pokey bars the way that the gwai-lo soldiers still did. They demanded luxury and entertainment which they paid for handsomely. The string of nightclubs that had sprung up along Devoux Road did a roaring trade in the darkened dens of candle-lit tables and spot-lit stage. The cover charge was high and they expected much for their money.

Jade climbed off the couch and fitted the high multi-tiered crown of silver sequins onto her head, then reached for the sequinned cloak and fan of white ostrich feathers. She knew it was only the size of her breasts that the audience clapped and shouted for and that they were impatient to see her finish. Hers was the only clean performance of the Mikado's sex show. She was supposed to put them in the right mood for the other acts—a couple from Europe, the man and the woman who made love in centre stage with the energy and ingenuity of circus acrobats; the lesbian exhibition with the outsized dildos and the Korean contortionist who could smoke a cigar between her legs, cut a banana in half or shoot a hard-boiling egg across the stage.

Jade had refused to take part in such displays and did not wish to strip naked. Firecracker Lily had agreed to the spangled G-string and the tassels on her nipples. Her time was drawing short. Perhaps another six months, another year and Sabrina Wong, exotic dancer, would have no place left to go. She sprung the little drawer in her trinket box and saw that the small cellophane packet of white powder was still safely in its place. This was the real reason why there was no money to buy a bar or a beauty shop, and why her limbs ached and her mouth was dry as paper and her head filled with pain. It was why she had gambled, to buy more.

For more than three years, she had hidden her heroin habit from Hand-trolley Lulu and Firecracker Lily. She always looked to reassure herself that it was there before she went on stage, to know that when she came off, it would be waiting.

From the darkness of the back tables reserved for VIPs Sing and Freddy Fong watched as the coloured spotlights shone on Sabrina Wong and the band played her entrance. Sing's hopes were immediately doused by a flood of doubts. Surely the old woman had been mistaken, or had lied to her. This was not Jade. In the cunning lights that flipped over her body ablaze with glitz, the small figure on centre stage began its sensuous routine.

When Jade returned to her room, Sing and Freddy were waiting for her. Hand-trolley Lulu had cooperated all the way and Fire-cracker Lily had taken them there without hesitation. Sing felt she had to be certain.

Jade's mouth opened and closed as she stared at the woman before her. When she spoke, Sing recognised the small voice even time couldn't disguise.

'Siu Sing,' she whispered, weeping through the mask of her make-up. Then she smiled. 'Do you think Ah Gum would approve?'

As Sing took a step towards her, Jade's knees buckled and she fell to the floor before Freddy or Sing could reach her.

The Liuyuan Garden

KUK-FAI was from the province of Chekiang in South-Eastern China. He had been a gardener all of his life, beginning at the age of ten as assistant to Chiang Ye-Shi, Attendant of the Celestial Sanctuary. Chiang was renowned for transforming barren and neglected ground into paradise and had worked in the gardens of many palaces. For more than thirty years Kuk-Fai had toiled beside his revered master until the old man failed to rise one day from beneath the plum tree he had planted as a boy.

In those thirty years they had planned and created many splendid gardens for the rich and privileged throughout China. When his great teacher had passed on to the rewards of the afterlife, Kuk-Fai had been called to Soochow to supervise the famous Liuyuan garden and there he had remained for many years among its lotus pools, bridges and pavilions, until the Communists had come and he had been forced to work as a street sweeper while the glorious garden, once described in the famous poem *The Dream of The Red Chamber*, withered and died. Its ponds and ornamental lakes became choked with the refuse of Red Guard soldiers, its pavilions crammed with their bicycles and reeking of their urine.

Kuk-Fai had escaped from China with the thousands who crossed the stretch of water clinging to inflated pig bladders, to brave the barbed wire and machine-guns of guard posts on the Hong Kong border. He had found no work in the British colony for a gardener. This was a place of concrete piled to the sky, where shrubs and flowers were planted on rooftops and grew in pots. He lived in a hut made from scraps of wood and tin that he carried up the steep hill at Northpoint, one among 10,000 squatters. He had come after many others and was forced to build his hut high on the slope where it would be first to wash down when the big rains came, and where the tracks were too steep to climb. So he had stayed in the hut and dreamed of the Liuyuan garden.

Kuk-Fai did not know how the jarp-jung woman had found him, but one day she had come, climbing the path through the squatters' huts to his door. There was work for him, she said, and a stone house to live in. This had been five years ago and now he looked out with great pride at the garden he had made. It would be his last and everything he had ever held in his heart had been put into its creation. The making of the Liuyuan garden of the Villa Formosa had saved his life and given him a home set in a small plot of its own, hedged by bamboo. The jarp-jung woman paid him well and treated him honourably, so he returned her respect.

Each morning Kuk-Fai looked out from the door of the neat stone house while the mist still lay over the surface of the ponds and knew this was the most beautiful garden he had ever created. A paradise worthy of Chiang Ye-Shi the Attendant of Celestial Sanctuary. Under his eye, the coolies had worked tirelessly and whatever was needed had been provided. Now he breathed in the sweet scent of flowering red acacia and began his slow walk along the paths and over the bridges to feed the fat golden carp that stocked the ponds.

The day before the opening of the Villa Formosa and her forty-fifth birthday, Sing walked the pathway to the birch wood, stooping to add a long-stemmed periwinkle to the blue cluster in her hand. The glossy green cover of crowded leaves spread thickly through the trees on either side of the pebbled path. She followed it to her mother's tomb, its pink marble face surrounded by a deep bed of white stones, and placed the bouquet in one of the small urns that stood before it.

Remaining there for a few more moments, she let her eyes follow the path on through the trunks of dull silver to the pool surrounded by blue and yellow spikes of flowering iris, and on again to the pavilion. China was full of pavilions and she had seen many in her early travels with Old To. They were the most beautiful expression of China's oldest heart. The place of rest and reflection, where only the rewards of quietude were sought. She was quite sure this was the most beautiful of them all, its curving eaves shaded by the thick canopy of the banyan, rising like a memorial to love.

The tranquillity of the garden engulfed her. Its chuckling streams brought back thoughts of the Place of Clear Water and, as though to add to the memory, a bluecap began calling. She drew in the perfumed air, watching the gardener scattering food to the fish as he crossed each bridge, remembering fondly the day she had asked Alistair Pidcock for permission to develop the grounds.

'Why not?' he had said, his surprised eyes wide behind his polished horn rims. 'Who could object? It is your money and one day it will be your property.'

Now all was finished. Today Nova would arrive from Paris where she had been studying art, and Sam Danovich and Birdie Meadows would fly in from Los Angeles. Tomorrow they and all her closest friends would attend the first dinner to be held in the Villa Formosa since Ben Deverill had locked it up and left Hong Kong for Shanghai.

She had chosen the servants carefully and they moved about the big house silently and efficiently, preparing to receive her guests. The cook had once run the kitchens of the Grand Hotel in Shanghai and the menu he had prepared for the banquet to be held on the following day read like imperial court cuisine. Reluctantly she turned her back on the peaceful garden and, filled with excitement at the thought of seeing her daughter again, prepared to drive to Kai Tak in her white Mercedes.

Epilogue

Iᴛ ᴡᴀs the most perfect of days. A warm mantle of sunshine had settled over the gardens, bees rummaged among the flowers and butterflies skipped in and out as Sing led Nova along the sunny walkways. They stood for a moment at the shaded graveside of Li X'ia, and drank tea together in the pavilion, talking through the splendid morning. Nova had slept soundly in the lovely room Sing had made ready for her and after her long and tiring journey had rested until late. When she first looked out onto the garden with Sing at her side. Nova reached for her mother's hand.

'It is the garden,' she whispered softly. 'Oh, mother. It is the garden of the Hookmaker.'

They walked through it together, talking for hours of each other's lives. Talking and listening, asking and answering. Sing told of her work with the Welfare League and the Peggy Pelham Foundation; of the success of her other businesses and her plans for a line of health-care products and perhaps cosmetics. Even Birdie's dream of health farms, designed on the principle of the ashram but with health and hygiene, comfort and nutrition an essential part of spiritual development. There were no limits to the prospects and possibilities under the name of the Second Sunrise.

Nova was captivated by her mother's vision of the future. Her own education had given her a Bachelor's degree in marketing and business management and a Masters in Fine Arts and Design. All the ingredients, she laughed, necessary to represent her mother in London and to open the first Second Sunrise salon. Filled with the newest ideas in creative direction and modern merchandising, Nova brimmed with a plausible enthusiasm that Sing found both infectious and impossible to deny. With an agreement to meet in the Causeway Bay office and discuss the prospects in detail, they returned to the house to receive the guests.

Sam Danovich was the first of the others to arrive, still driving Freddy Fong's old TR3.

'It reminds me of you. It was in this little buggy that I first fell in love with you lady,' he said, as he climbed out, folding Sing firmly in his arms, holding her close.

Taking her hand, he kissed its palm and slid the emerald-cut diamond onto her finger. 'Happy birthday, lady.'

'This is beginning to become a habit,' she whispered. When she went to say more he closed his hand warmly and strongly around hers and stopped her with the light touch of his lips on her mouth.

'Nobody gives back a birthday present,' he said softly. For long moments, alone together on the steps of the wonderful old house, Sing held him close and they kissed as never before.

'Welcome to my father's house, Sam,' she said finally, stepping back and taking both his hands to lead him inside.

By five o'clock everyone had arrived. Sing took a moment to herself, watching from the terrace as these people who meant so much to her explored the delights of her Linyuan garden. Sam walked with Nova, talking quietly as they stopped to watch the peacock showing its plumage, trembling its gorgeous fan like a shimmering tambourine. She heard Nova's musical laughter and Sam's deep voice coming to her on the late afternoon air, filling her with love and satisfaction beyond all her past imaginings. Dear, dependable Sam, a little wider, a little older, but youthful as ever and just as full of life and plans for the future.

Doctor Sun, quite old now, but content with quiet wisdom, arrived followed by his married sons and their wives. The White Crane Medicine Company was flourishing, thanks to his guidance and the tireless enthusiasm of its marketing director,Birdie Meadows, and their obedient energy. As though on cue, she heard Birdie's chatter now, and saw her, a vision in a sari of filmy white trimmed with gold, a small diamond glittering in the side of her nose. Freddy Fong walked beside her, corpulent and successful.

Alistair Pidcock appeared last of all, his gold watch chain replaced by a crimson cummerbund and a matching carnation pinned to the lapel of his dinner jacket. He left his silver Rolls well up the drive and stood looking at the house until a servant told Sing that he was there. She walked up the driveway to greet him. His usual hearty goodwill was quietly subdued as he took her hand. Sing thought she detected a slight tremor in his voice as he said softly, 'My dear Miss Deverill. Words cannot describe my feelings at this extraordinary moment.'

Removing his spectacles, he took out a large white handkerchief and dabbed briefly at his eyes. 'I never dared dream that I would see this day.'

He withdrew a long stiff envelope from his breast pocket. 'Your father's last instruction to me was to hand this to the person who laid claim to the Villa Formosa, at my own discretion.' He thrust it into her hand. 'I was to give it to the person I considered to be his rightful heir, if such a person were ever to come forward and whose validity was, in my opinion, beyond all possible doubt.' He bowed his head. 'I regret withholding it for so long but I had to be utterly certain. This seems to be the perfect moment. I'm sure you agree.'

Sing pressed his hand. 'My father was very fortunate to have a friend such as you,' she said gently. 'And because of you I am also greatly blessed.'

They stood for a moment more looking back at the house framed in the pale purple of twilight.

'This is breathtaking,' he said, the words catching in his throat. 'Simply breathtaking.'

Later, with everyone enjoying cocktails in the great room or on the terrace to watch the last of a searing sunset, Sing slipped away to the pavilion and, in the soft light remaining, she broke the wax seal on the envelope bearing the Cloud Line crest. Inside were the original deeds to Villa Formosa and an attached letter. The letter was written in a bold, flowing hand, even, straight lines that filled both sides of the thick sheet of paper:

'My most precious child. I pray to all the gods of both East and Western heavens that you will one day read these words. Know above all that I was a decent man who loved your mother as deeply as one human being can love another. We cared nothing of race or time or place. We breathed the same air, were warmed by the same sun and cooled by the same breezes, together, under one moon and the same bright stars. This was enough for us.

I can only hope with all my heart that life has not been too cruel and that you too may find such love. It is good to share both happiness and grief. Life is lonely without it. I know now that bitterness destroys but you must be told that the death of your sweet mother was avenged.

That you are reading this letter means my good friend Alistair Pidcock has carried out my wishes. This house was a dream of mine. It was meant to shield my loved ones from eyes and tongues that could not see true beauty. That the dear one who was your mother should have this taken from her so cruelly and unjustly has left me with nothing but despair.

May the Villa Formosa give you shelter and make some small recompense for any indignities you may have suffered in a world so violently thrust upon you.'

The letter was signed—'Your loving and devoted father Benjamin Deverill.'

The dining room of the Villa Formosa opened onto the wide terrace. Beyond it, past the silhouette of the pavilion and the dark tracery of the banyan, the moon sailed high above the sea, stars spilling in wild profusion into velvet depths. Air pleasantly cool, heavy with the perfume of night-scented flowers, teased the flames of gleaming candelabras set along the centre of the table.

It had been a truly sumptuous meal of many superbly presented courses, perfectly served. It began with steamed lobster and scallops with melon and sesame seeds, followed by double-boiled superior shark's fin with Yunnan ham; steamed bamboo pith filled with supreme bird's nest; smoked minced pigeon served with star fruit; scrambled fresh milk with spicy crab claws; steamed twin peak garoupa; fried rice 'man wah' style and a seasonal fruit platter.

Candlelight reflected warmly on the deep blush of rosewood and crystal glassware as Sam Danovich rose to propose a toast to their gracious hostess and dearest friend, Sing Deverill, mistress of Villa Formosa.

The company stood to raise their glasses. Sam had changed into a stylish tuxedo. Sing could not help thinking of the awkward man in the loud check sports coat she had first met. The years had been good to him—his hair, still thick, showed attractive streaks of silver, and his waistline was almost the width of his broad shoulders. He looked handsome, solid and dependable as always. When the toast was drunk and the others were seated Sam remained on his feet.

He looked at Sing silently for a moment, as though seeking the exact words. She was wearing a fitted cheong-sam of the same pale yellow as the dress worn by Li X'ia in the portrait behind her, emphasising the startling resemblance in their features. At her throat she wore an exquisite pendant of marbled jade set in gold, creamy white seamed with grass green. Only Doctor Sun and

Freddy Fong knew its true significance—that for her to wear the sacred amulet of the White Crane had put the blackness of the past behind forever.

Seated at the head of the table, her striking face aglow in the friendly light, she took Sam's breath away.

'Folks, I've got a little something to add to that toast,' he managed at last. 'Something, I've been waiting to say for a long time now. Years, in fact.'

He raised his glass high. 'I'm going to marry this incredible lady. I don't know when, I don't know where, but that's what I'm going to do and I call upon her now to deny it in the face of this company.'

When the chorus of approval had frittered away, it was Sing's turn to reply. Behind her on the panelled wall the portrait of Ben Deverill and Li X'ia looked down upon the company.

'This is the happiest occasion of my life and every one of you helped to make it possible.'

She turned to smile at Nova. 'It is made all the more wonderful by having my wonderful daughter here among my greatest friends. As to denying the intentions of Sam Danovich,' she held up the flashing diamond. 'I can only say he usually does what he says he will do.'

She raised her voice above the laughter and reached for her glass. 'In that regard he reminds me of another bull-headed man of great importance in my life.' Sing turned to face the portrait.

'I ask you all to drink to Captain Ben Deverill and those like him. The men who shaped the destiny of Hong Kong and the wonderful women who were brave enough or foolish enough to love them. To my mother, Li X'ia.'

With the solemn toast drunk and when Sing had again taken her seat, Nova rose a little shyly. She was greeted by immediate silence. Like Sing, she thought about what she had to say, twisting the stem of her champagne flute and looking gravely from face to face. Her eyes, dark in the subdued light, came to rest on her mother. When she spoke in the hush, her voice was careful and clear.

'Until a few short years ago I did not know I had a mother. To discover that this was wrong gave me the greatest thrill of my life. Since that unforgettable day every moment has been richer because of her. To be able to share the love and friendship, the loyalty that fills this marvellous place is a privilege and a joy I shall remember for the rest of my life.'

Nova looked only at Sing as she went on, 'To see the picture of my grandparents standing behind you only adds to the wonder of this moment. I believe I am the luckiest of people to have your brave and adventurous blood in my veins. I pledge to use all that it has given me to further the Deverill name and its cause. To make what I can of my grandfather's skill in business with the creative courage of my remarkable mother and to help her continue to build what was started so long ago.'

She raised her glass. 'To you, my dearest mother . . . and to the Deverill name.'

At dawn the next morning, Kuk-Fai the gardener stepped from his house and looked up at the breaking sky. It reflected the silvery pinks and pale purples of newly opened pearlshell, delicate shades that grew warmer each moment with the approach of daylight. He went to his toolshed and filled a small basket from the sack of fishmeal. The handwoven cane grass sandals made no sound as he crossed the first bridge. With the growing light the lotus flowers were opening and dragonflies still slept on their leaves. A movement caught his eye and he saw that the jarp-jung woman was standing in the pavilion looking out to sea. As he watched, she began to move. Her arms rose in a graceful arc as she bent this way and that, as a reed bends in the breeze, the motions flowing like water from a mountain spring. Drifting, it seemed, lightly as a bird.

Heavenly ch'i flowed through Siu Sing's body as the first blaze of sunrise exploded above the China Sea. She felt the presence of Li X'ia and her old servant, the Fish. Across the glittering path where splinters of pure light danced and dazzled, she thought she saw the topmasts of a fast-raked schooner, chasing pink tufted clouds across the flaming sky.

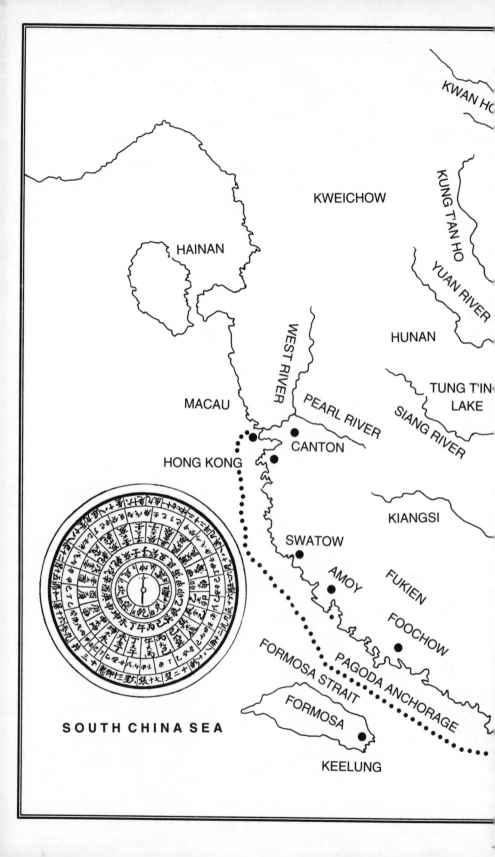